DUNGEONS & DRAGONS®

FELL'S FIVE

Dungeons & Dragons®
Fell's Five

Credits

Written by	**John Rogers**
Art by	**Andrea Di Vito**
Additional Art by	**Denis Medri**
Horacio Domingues	**JUANAN**
Guido Guidi	**Vicente Alcazar**
Nacho Arranz	**Andres Ponce**
Colors by	**Aburtov and Graphikslava**
Additional Colors by	**Andrew Dalhouse**
Lettering by	**Chris Mowry**
Shawn Lee	**Neil Uyetake**
Series Edits by	**Denton J. Tipton** **John Barber**
Collection Edits by	**Alonzo Simon** **Zac Boone**
Collection Design by	**Neil Uyetake**
Collection Cover by	**Wayne Reynolds**

Special thanks to the D&D team at Wizards of the Coast.

For international rights, contact **licensing@idwpublishing.com**

ISBN: 978-1-68405-804-4

24 23 22 21 1 2 3 4

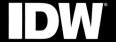

Licensed By:

Nachie Marsham, Publisher • **Rebekah Cahalin**, EVP of Operations • **Blake Kobashigawa**, VP of Sales • **John Barber**, Editor-in-Chief • **Justin Eisinger**, Editorial Director, Graphic Novels and Collections • **Scott Dunbier**, Director, Special Projects • **Anna Morrow**, Sr. Marketing Director • **Tara McCrillis**, Director of Design & Production • **Shauna Monteforte**, Sr. Director of Manufacturing Operations

Ted Adams and Robbie Robbins, IDW Founders

www.IDWPUBLISHING.com

Facebook: **facebook.com/idwpublishing** • Twitter: **@idwpublishing**
YouTube: **youtube.com/idwpublishing** • Instagram: **@idwpublishing**

Originally published as DUNGEONS & DRAGONS issues #0–15.

Introduction

When IDW was nice enough to offer me one of the *Dungeons & Dragons* comics they were launching, while on the phone for the very first conversation I scribbled "working class heroes" on a pad. And so Fell's Five were born…

"Working…"

I'm fascinated by systems. Your proto-*Dungeons & Dragons* group travels the world, kills monsters, and takes their stuff. I'm not the inventor of the term "murder hobos," but it certainly seems appropriate. But what kind of world, exactly, requires traveling bands of skilled mercenaries? What kind of world has dungeon ruins reeking of magic and death scattered across the landscape like deadly reality-bending Easter eggs? And perhaps most importantly, what kind of towns spring up *in between* those cursed places? What's the economy like? Even subsistence agriculture requires a thriving trade system (axe heads don't grow on trees, kids), never mind the sprawling stone metropolises that support wizard towers and griffin stables.

Fell's Five work for a living. They're not speculative spelunkers in exotic ecosystems, slaughtering native life forms in order to collect the gold coins left behind by previous, less-talented adventurers. They act as security, investigators, trouble-shooters, bounty hunters. Their world has a frontier vibe, a mix of the Old West and the Caribbean during the time of high piracy. Just because people in a world of dragons live surrounded by violence doesn't mean they want to live in chaos. A stable adventuring party would only be allowed to exist because they reliably solve more problems than they cause. Because they work for a living.

This is why these comics detoured into questions of infrastructure: why are there so many narrow-corridor dungeons (because corridors that can only fit humans are dragon-proof)? How does air move around in an underground complex? How do you move furniture up into those high-topped wizard towers? What are the terms of an adventuring party's contract? Adric Fell is never presented as a tactical genius. He's just the guy with the plan. It's often a bad plan, but at least it's a plan. He's a working-man with a sword, not the inspired leader of armies.

"Class…"

"Farm boy who's secretly the heir to the throne" fantasy fiction is very nice to read when you're a misfit 14-year-old and can think, "Ah, I'm not socially awkward, I just haven't found my magic sword yet." But with age should come the awareness that predestined greatness due to magical bloodlines is the sort of claptrap real world empires were built on. The sort of empires that could only function by making sure that clever, resourceful yet non-special people didn't rise high enough to threaten the positions of the random yobs who won the genetic lottery.

No, give me the working class. Lieber's Fafhrd and the Gray Mouser—half-drunk and constantly in the wrong place at the right time. Joe Abercrombie's Nine-Fingered Logen, the barbarian too smart for his own good. Glenn Cook's Black Company, and Erickson's Bridgeburners, "First in, last out." A hero who pulls off the impossible with sweat and smarts and blood, not Daddy's magic heirloom. In short, Destiny can go suck an egg.

Adric Fell is a war veteran running on charm and a precise understanding of his capacity for violence. Khal Khalandurrin's a poet serving a God for faith and true love. Varis the elf is a bowman for hire, and Tisha Swornheart is daughter of librarians. And Bree—delightful, murderous, street-thug Bree. Not a single one of them has a relative worth two copper pieces, not a single one with a drop of royal blood in their veins.

Fells' Five are scrappers. That means they talk like scrappers. No "thees" and "thous" for our group. No epic poetry tripping off the tongue. Our role-playing adventure parties, in the end, are run by everyday friends who sound just like we do. Why should our proxies in the fantasy world sound like weekend theater productions of *Camelot*?

"…Heroes."

Anti-heroes are all the rage. But personally, I want my role-playing game to be where I can fulfill my fantasy, and let's face it, in modern society, one of the most pervasive fantasies… is *justice*. Our world is unwieldy, a place where change comes slowly if at all. So why not let our fantasies be fantasies of sacrifice and kindness? Granted, Bree will slit your throat for a hot coffee and a cold coin—but she's a necessary evil in an evil world, not the ringleader. Adric Fell and most of his friends are inherently decent folk. They're not saints. But you'd be damn glad they lived on your block, in a pinch.

Once we established our world of working class heroes, the truly great insight IDW brought to the table was in pairing Andrea Di Vito with this approach to fantasy. Andrea's got a classic look, a perfect complement to the meta-nature of the Fell's Five books. Andrea's clean art made me believe in Adric's world. I believed they existed, they smelled earthy, their clothes were handmade. I believed, thanks to Andrea, in a real world that just happened to have magic in it. And he can land a joke, which is crucial. *Dungeons & Dragons*, after all, is an intensely social game. It's used to tell a wide range of stories over a wide range of world-types, but if you play in a bunch of groups you find the one common denominator is *laughter*. D&D players love to have a good time. Andrea, IDW, and I really wanted the book to be like the fun adventures of characters that you'd like to game with every week. We're a pulp book. Pick us up, enjoy the great fight art, laugh at the banter, and steal tons of ideas for your own campaign.

Or, hell, if you really like it, maybe you'll try playing the game if you're not already a player. That would be cool.

John Rogers
November, 2013

Art by Wayne Reynolds

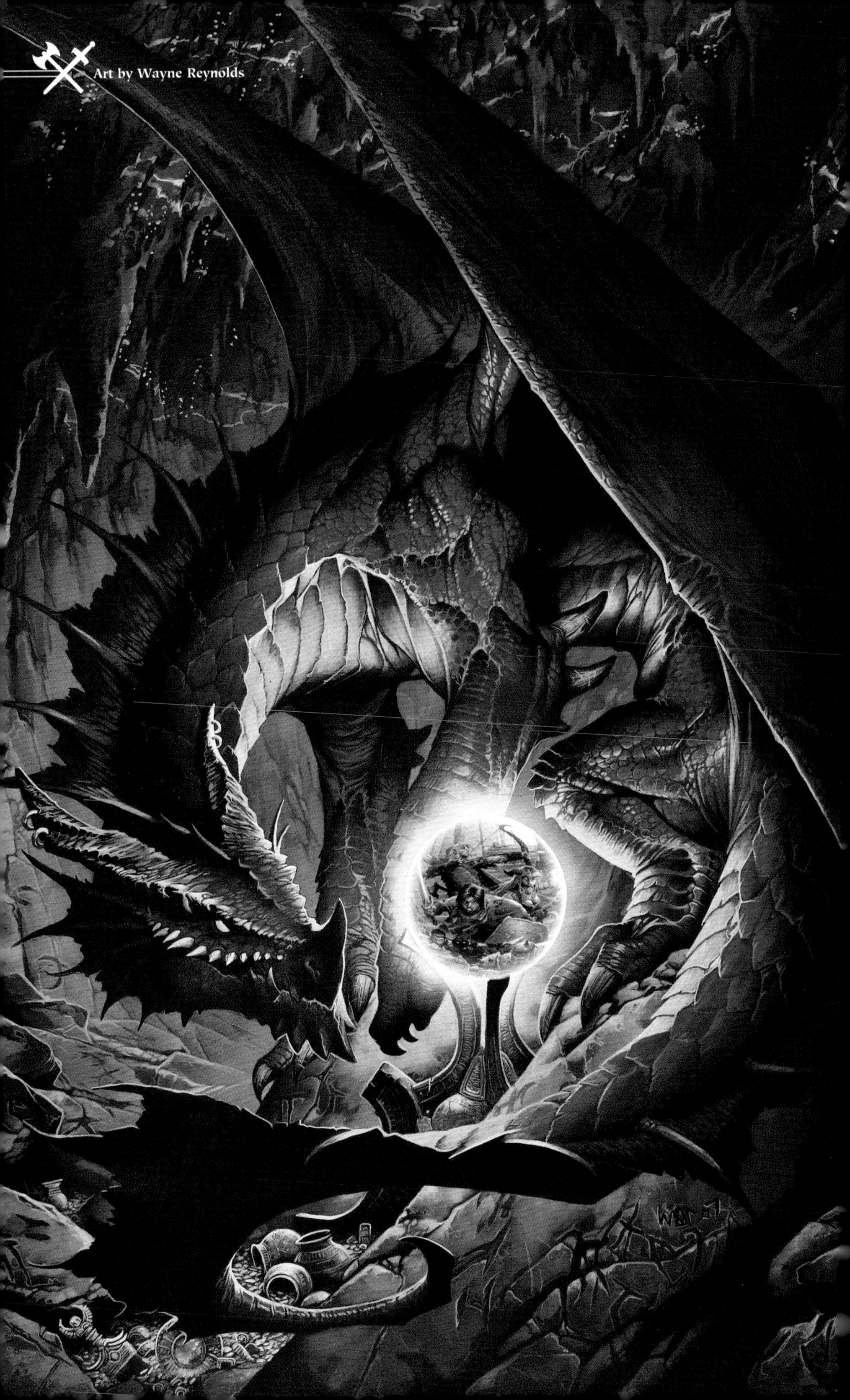

CHAPTER 1

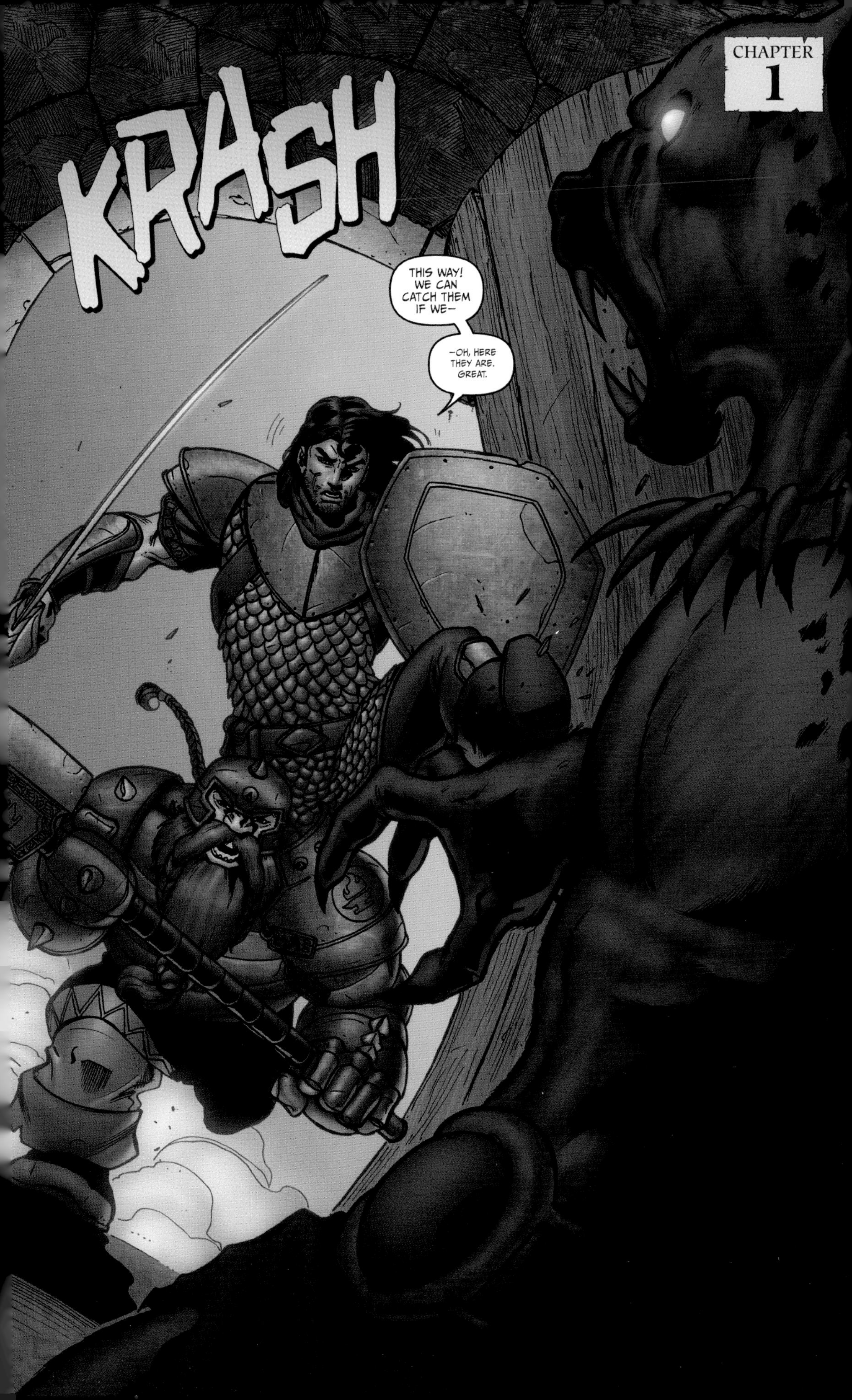
KRASH
THIS WAY! WE CAN CATCH THEM IF WE—
—OH, HERE THEY ARE. GREAT.

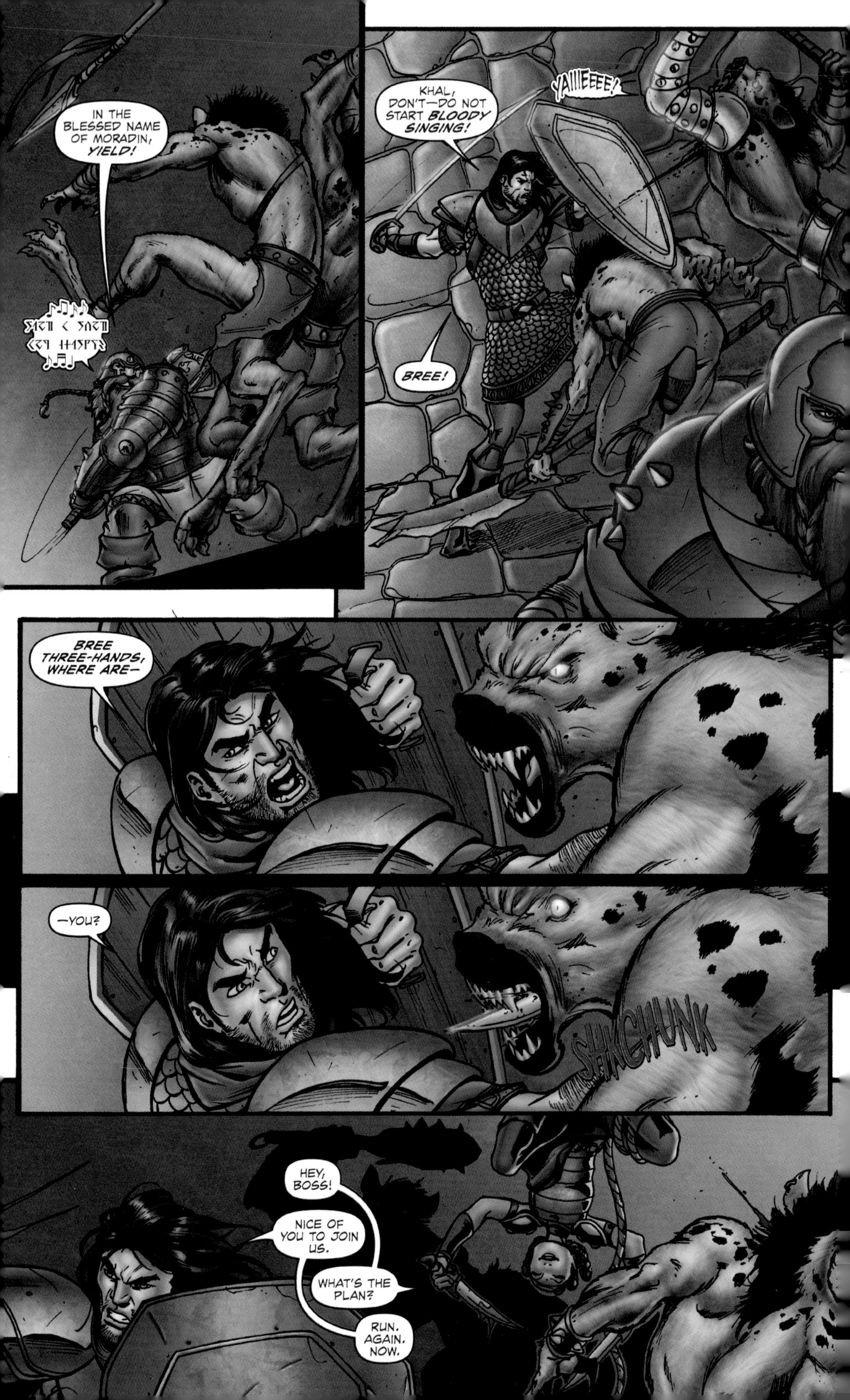
IN THE BLESSED NAME OF MORADIN, *YIELD!*
KHAL, DON'T—DO NOT START *BLOODY SINGING!*
YAIIIEEEE!
KRAACK
BREE!
BREE THREE-HANDS, WHERE ARE—
—YOU?
SHHCHUNK
HEY, BOSS!
NICE OF YOU TO JOIN US.
WHAT'S THE PLAN?
RUN. AGAIN. NOW.

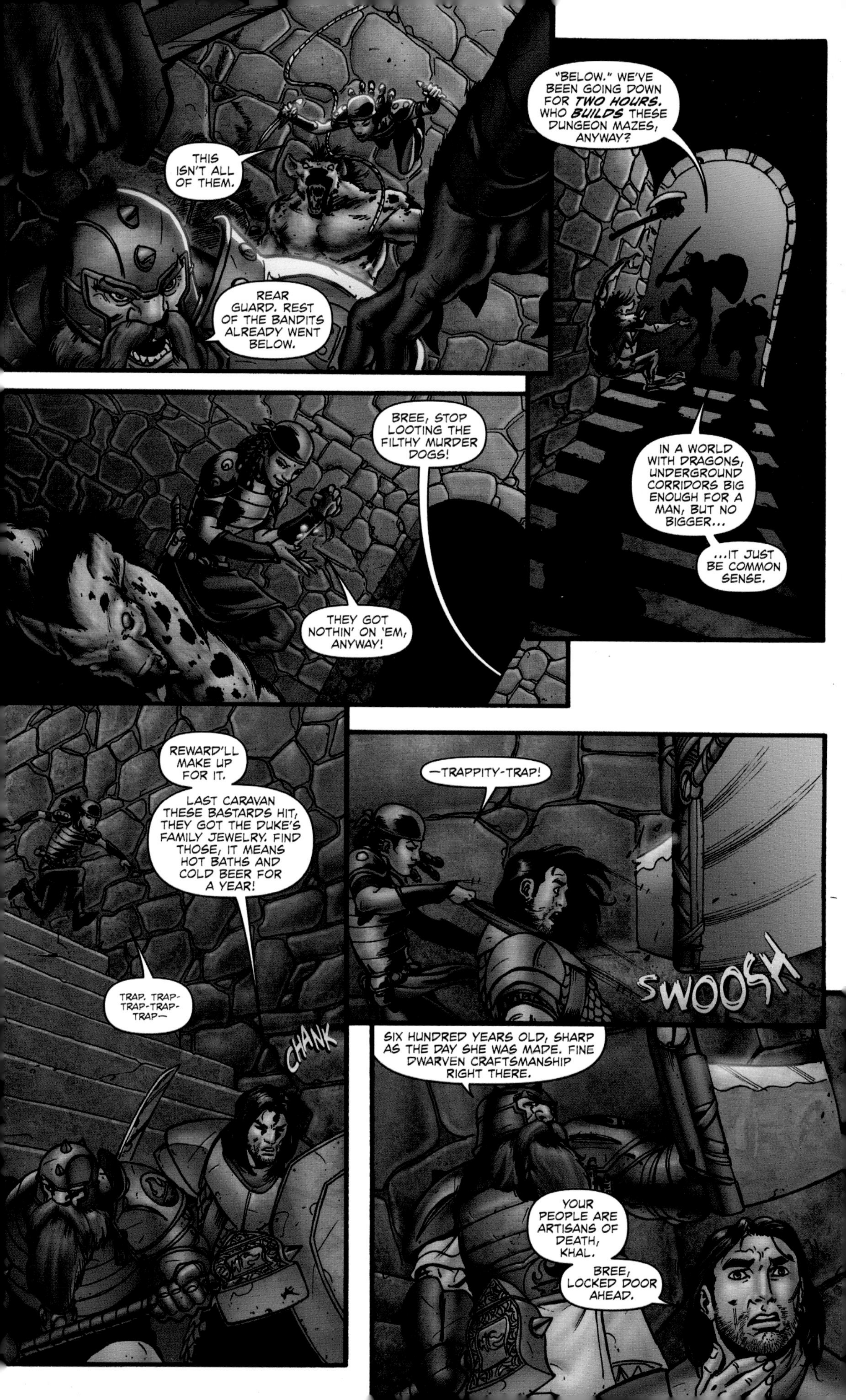
THIS ISN'T ALL OF THEM.
REAR GUARD. REST OF THE BANDITS ALREADY WENT BELOW.
"BELOW." WE'VE BEEN GOING DOWN FOR TWO HOURS. WHO BUILDS THESE DUNGEON MAZES, ANYWAY?
IN A WORLD WITH DRAGONS, UNDERGROUND CORRIDORS BIG ENOUGH FOR A MAN, BUT NO BIGGER...
...IT JUST BE COMMON SENSE.
BREE, STOP LOOTING THE FILTHY MURDER DOGS!
THEY GOT NOTHIN' ON 'EM, ANYWAY!
REWARD'LL MAKE UP FOR IT.
LAST CARAVAN THESE BASTARDS HIT, THEY GOT THE DUKE'S FAMILY JEWELRY. FIND THOSE, IT MEANS HOT BATHS AND COLD BEER FOR A YEAR!
TRAP. TRAP-TRAP-TRAP-TRAP—
CHANK
—TRAPPITY-TRAP!
SWOOSH
SIX HUNDRED YEARS OLD, SHARP AS THE DAY SHE WAS MADE. FINE DWARVEN CRAFTSMANSHIP RIGHT THERE.
YOUR PEOPLE ARE ARTISANS OF DEATH, KHAL.
BREE, LOCKED DOOR AHEAD.

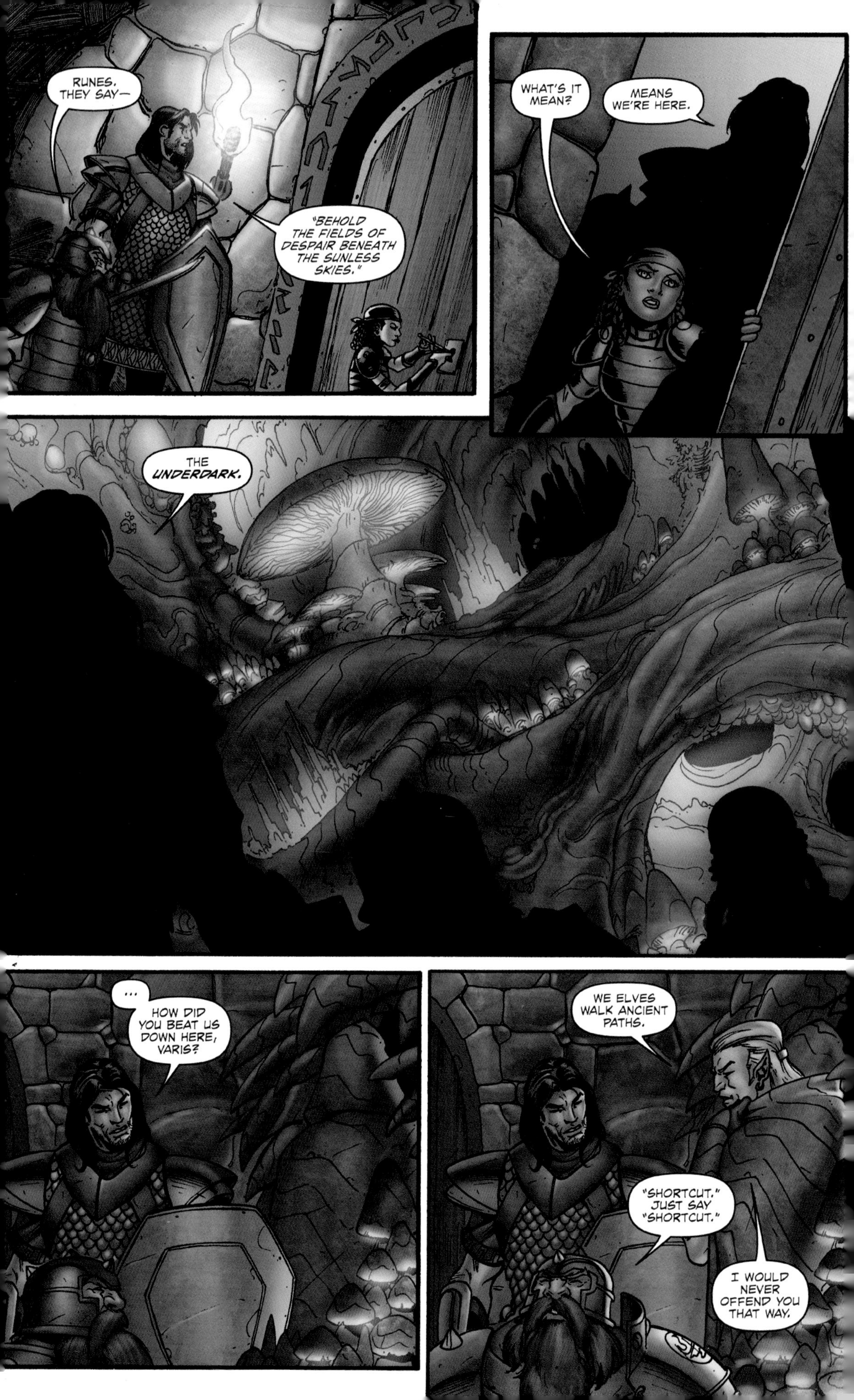
RUNES. THEY SAY—
"BEHOLD THE FIELDS OF DESPAIR BENEATH THE SUNLESS SKIES."
WHAT'S IT MEAN?
MEANS WE'RE HERE.
THE UNDERDARK.
...
HOW DID YOU BEAT US DOWN HERE, VARIS?
WE ELVES WALK ANCIENT PATHS.
"SHORTCUT." JUST SAY "SHORTCUT."
I WOULD NEVER OFFEND YOU THAT WAY.

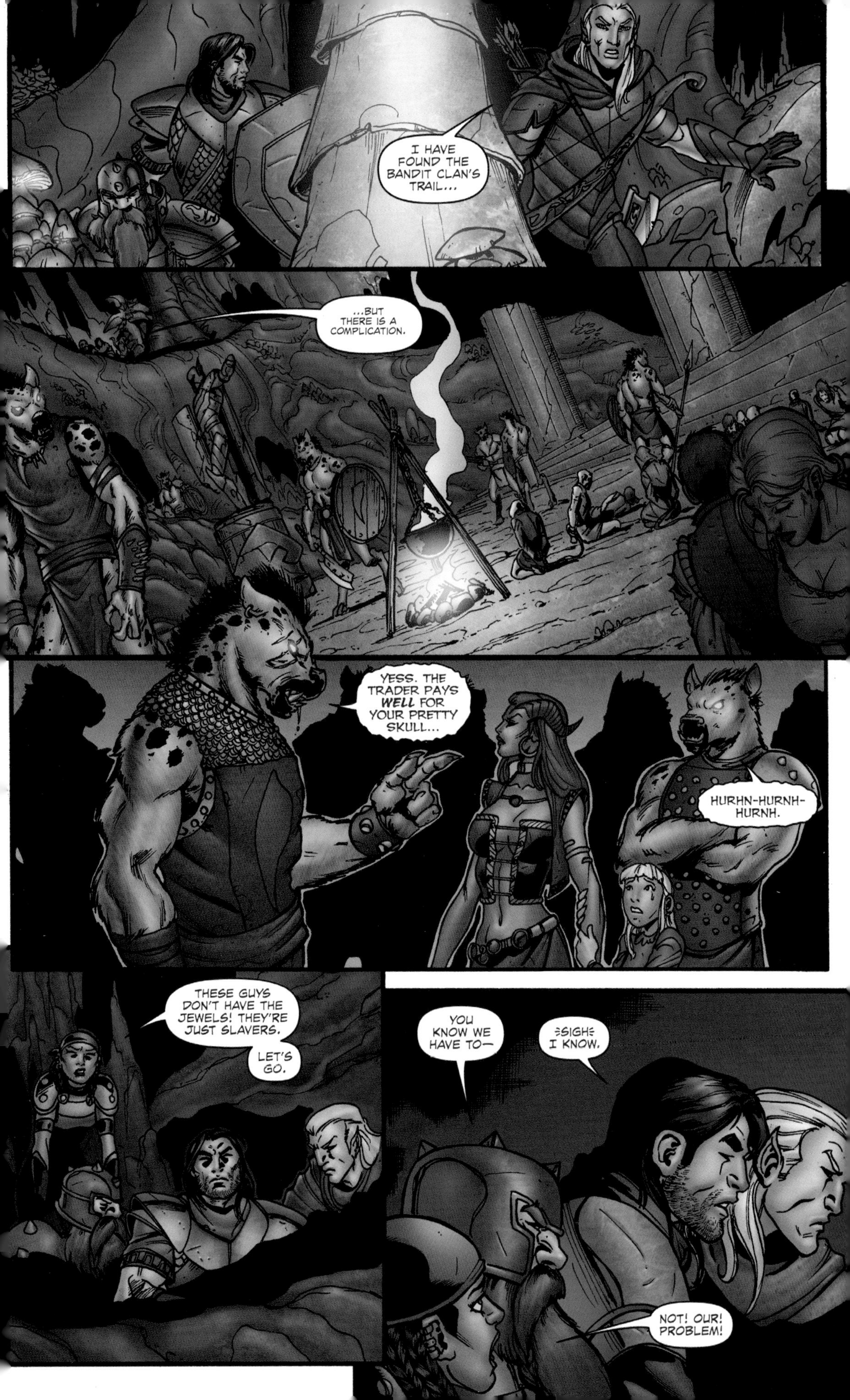
I HAVE FOUND THE BANDIT CLAN'S TRAIL...
...BUT THERE IS A COMPLICATION.
YESS. THE TRADER PAYS **WELL** FOR YOUR PRETTY SKULL...
HURHN-HURNH-HURNH.
THESE GUYS DON'T HAVE THE JEWELS! THEY'RE JUST SLAVERS.
LET'S GO.
YOU KNOW WE HAVE TO—
=SIGH= I KNOW.
NOT! OUR! PROBLEM!

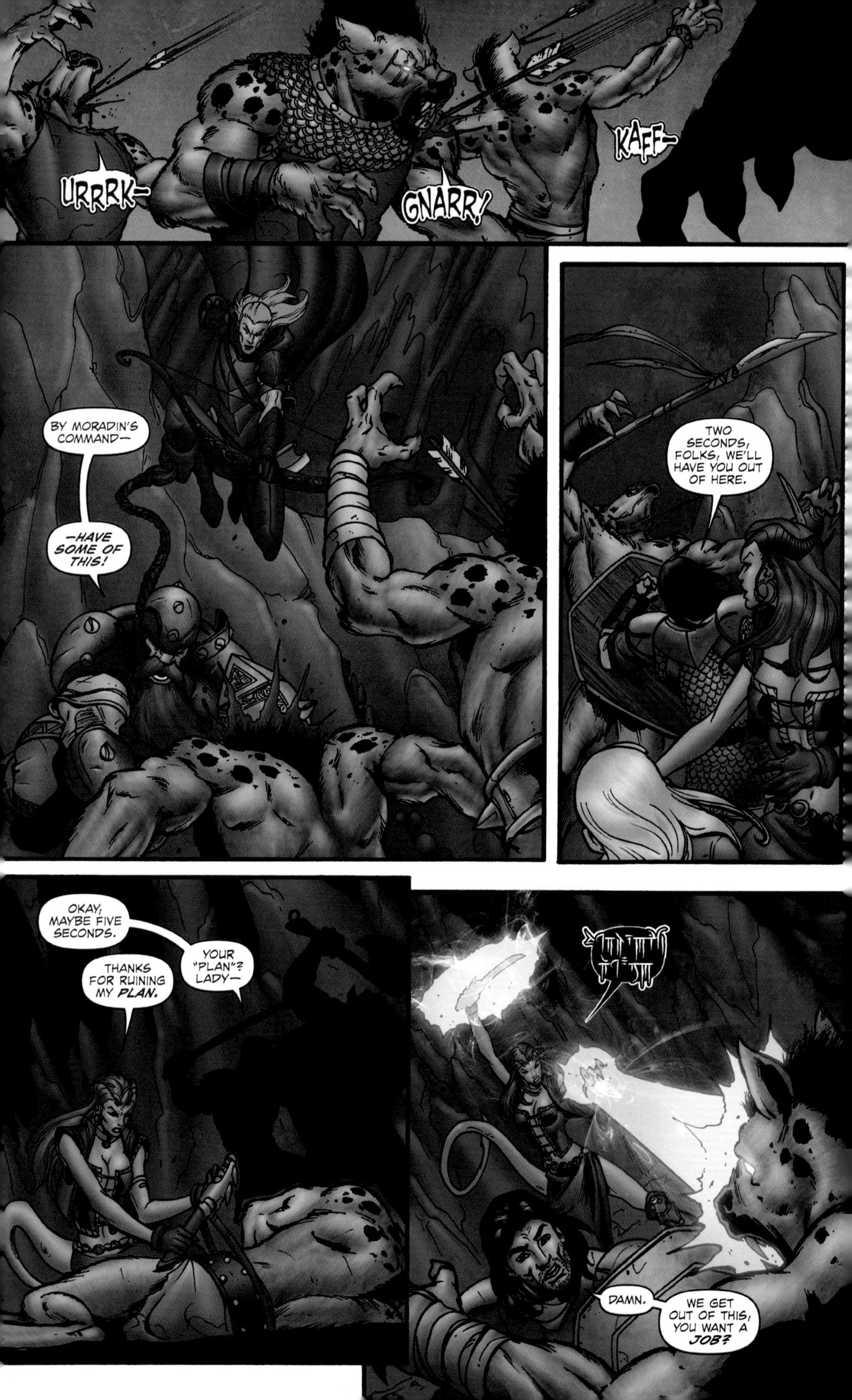
URRRK—
GNARR!
KAFF—
BY MORADIN'S COMMAND—
—HAVE SOME OF THIS!
TWO SECONDS, FOLKS, WE'LL HAVE YOU OUT OF HERE.
OKAY, MAYBE FIVE SECONDS.
THANKS FOR RUINING MY *PLAN.*
YOUR "PLAN"? LADY—
DAMN.
WE GET OUT OF THIS, YOU WANT A *JOB?*

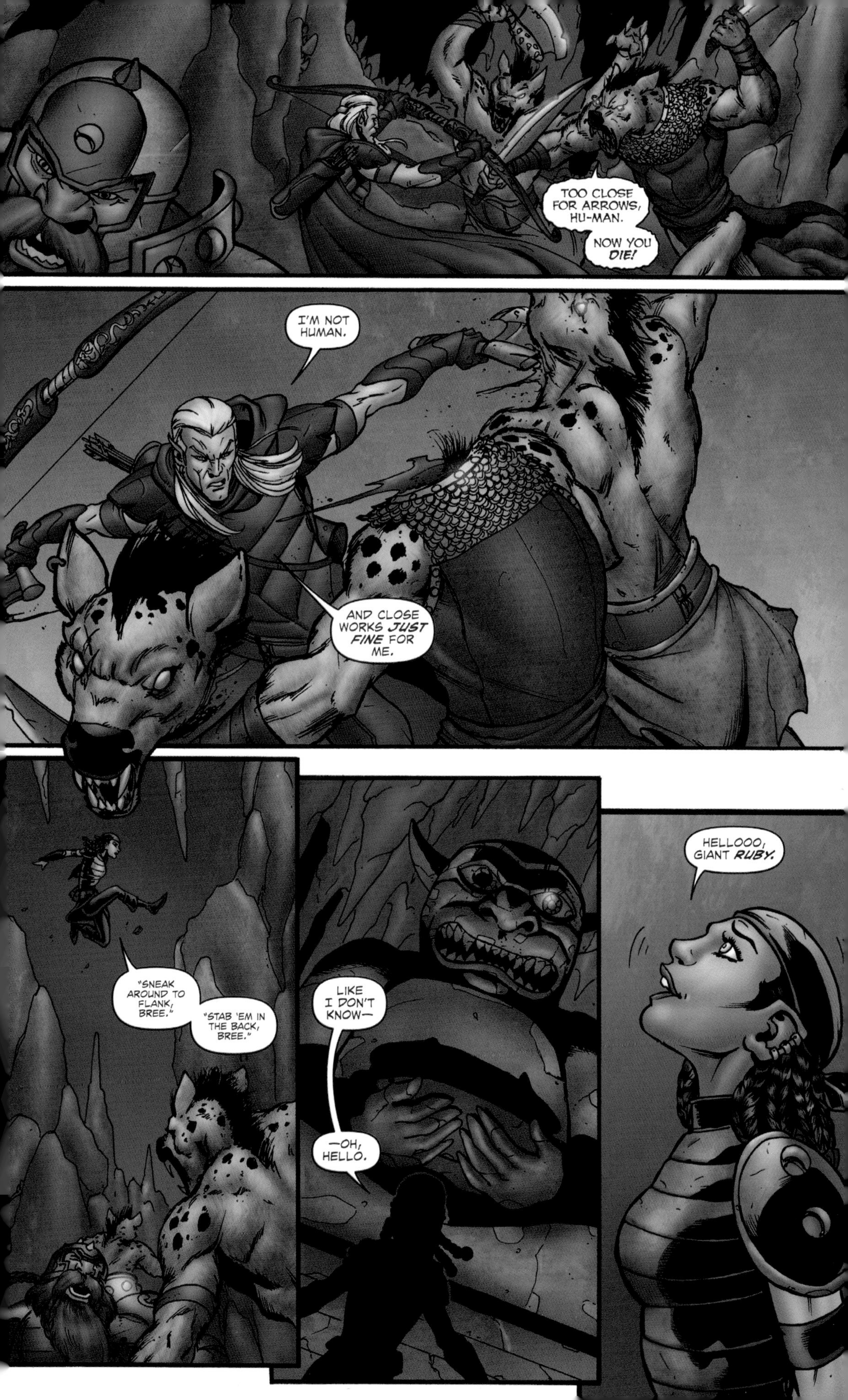
TOO CLOSE FOR ARROWS, HU-MAN.
NOW YOU *DIE!*
I'M NOT HUMAN.
AND CLOSE WORKS *JUST FINE* FOR ME.
"SNEAK AROUND TO FLANK, BREE."
"STAB 'EM IN THE BACK, BREE."
LIKE I DON'T KNOW—
—OH, HELLO.
HELLOOO, GIANT *RUBY.*

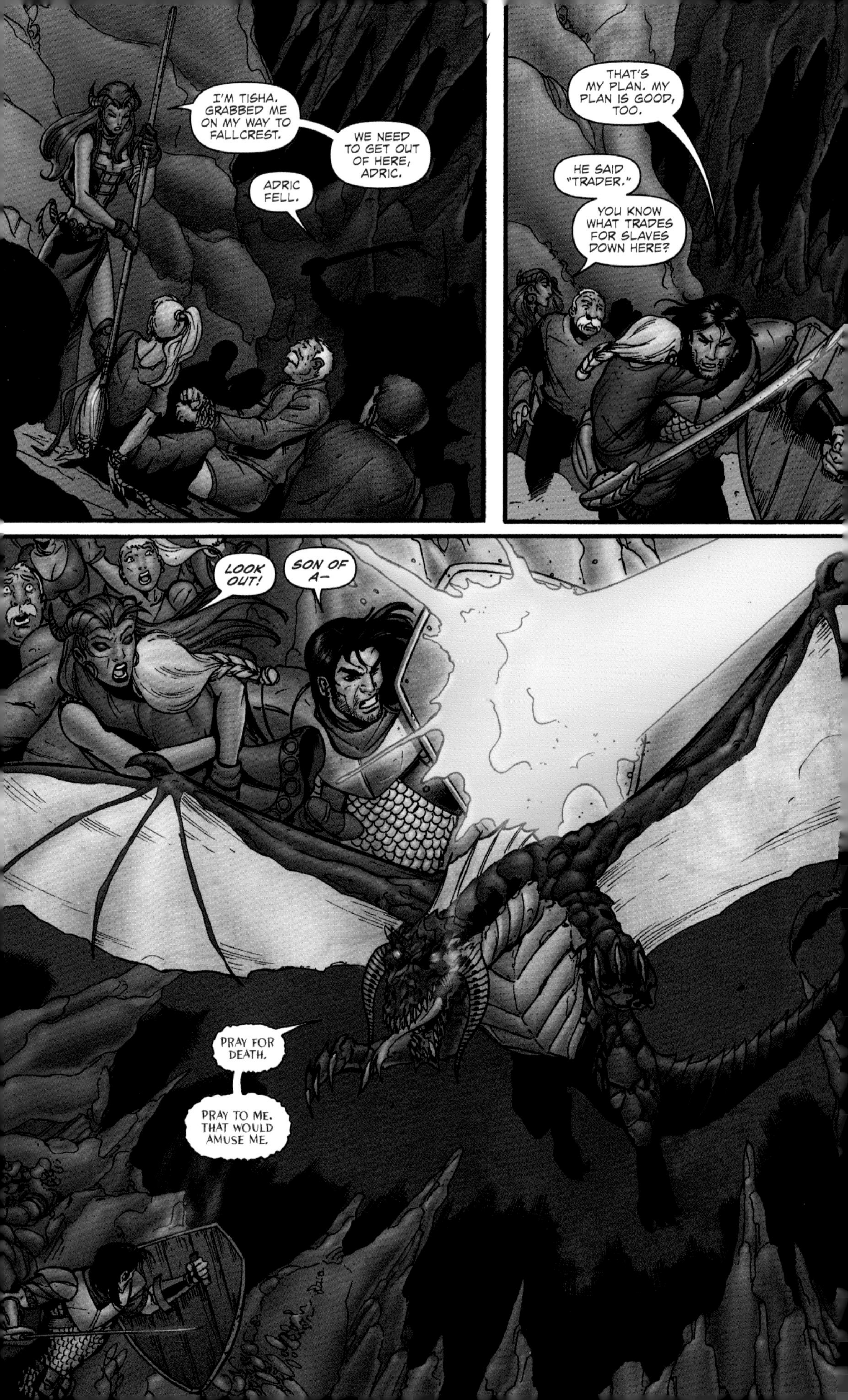
I'M TISHA. GRABBED ME ON MY WAY TO FALLCREST.
WE NEED TO GET OUT OF HERE, ADRIC.
ADRIC FELL.
THAT'S MY PLAN. MY PLAN IS GOOD, TOO.
HE SAID "TRADER."
YOU KNOW WHAT TRADES FOR SLAVES DOWN HERE?
LOOK OUT!
SON OF A—
PRAY FOR DEATH.
PRAY TO ME. THAT WOULD AMUSE ME.

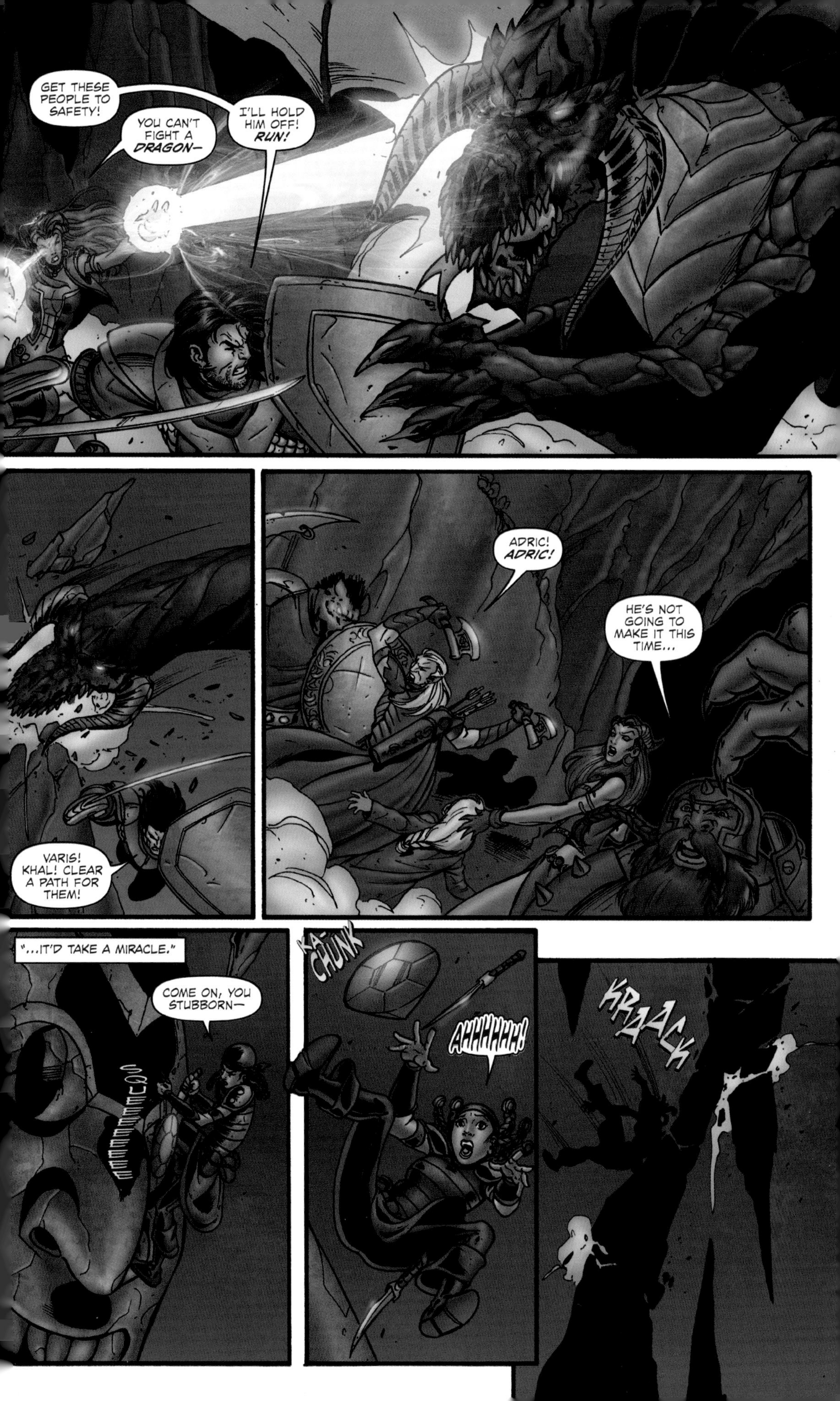
GET THESE PEOPLE TO SAFETY!
YOU CAN'T FIGHT A DRAGON—
I'LL HOLD HIM OFF! RUN!
VARIS! KHAL! CLEAR A PATH FOR THEM!
ADRIC! ADRIC!
HE'S NOT GOING TO MAKE IT THIS TIME...
"...IT'D TAKE A MIRACLE."
COME ON, YOU STUBBORN—
SQUEEEEEEEE
KA-CHUNK
AHHHHHH!
KRAACK

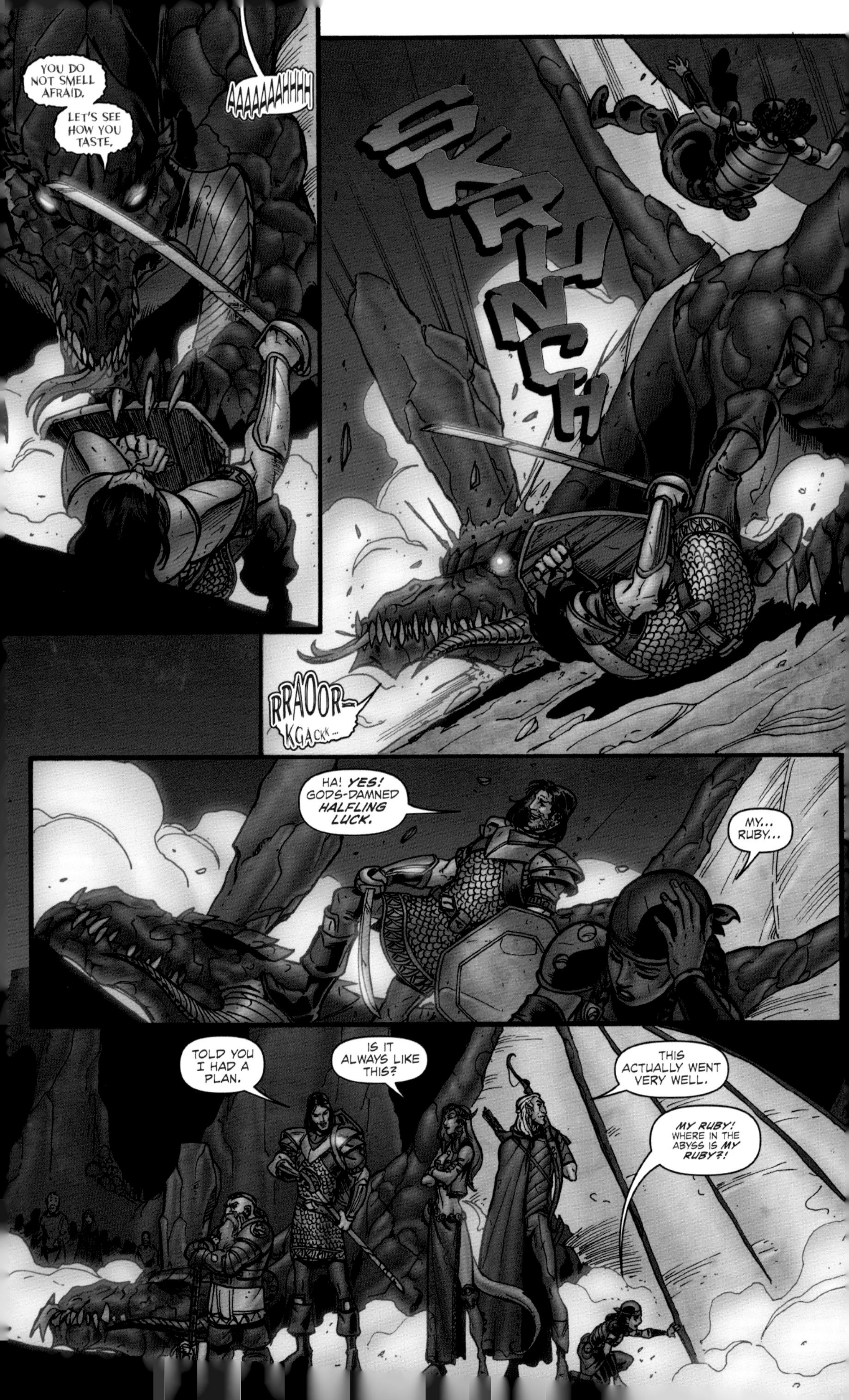

YOU DO NOT SMELL AFRAID.
LET'S SEE HOW YOU TASTE.
AAAAAAAHHHH
SKRUNCH
RRAOOR-KGACKK...
HA! YES! GODS-DAMNED HALFLING LUCK.
MY... RUBY...
TOLD YOU I HAD A PLAN.
IS IT ALWAYS LIKE THIS?
THIS ACTUALLY WENT VERY WELL.
MY RUBY! WHERE IN THE ABYSS IS MY RUBY?!

Art by Tyler Walpole

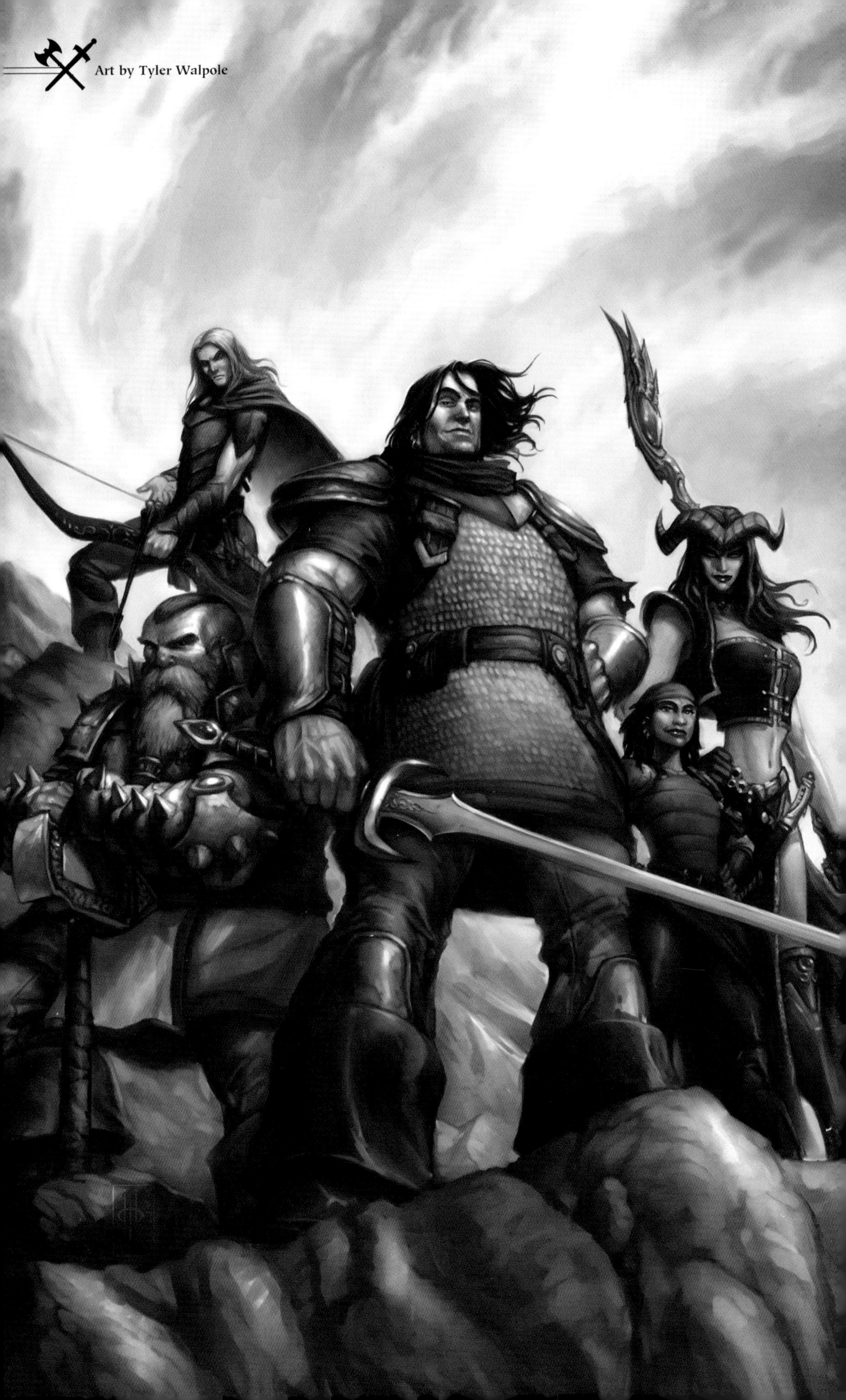

CHAPTER 2

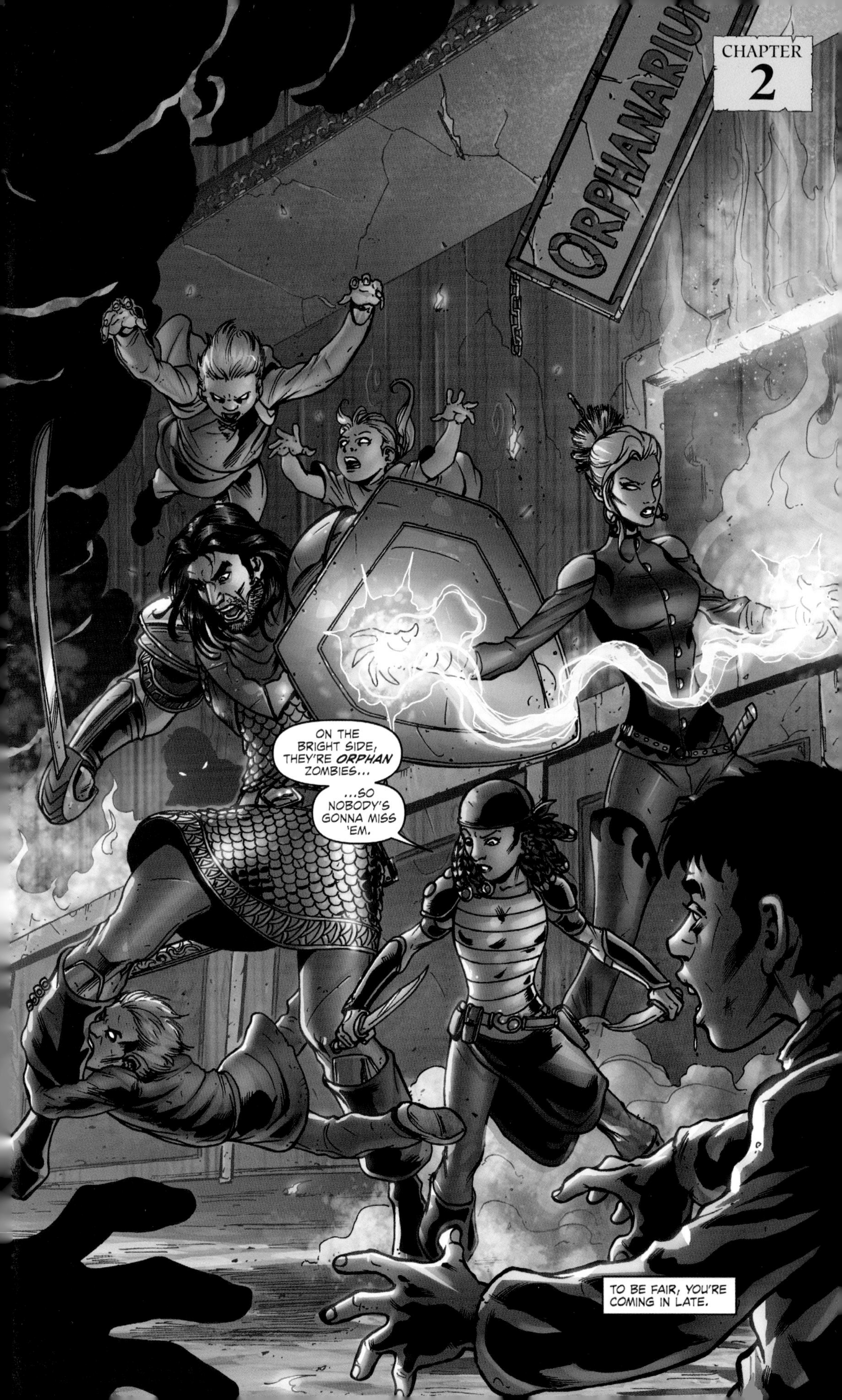
ORPHANARIU
ON THE BRIGHT SIDE, THEY'RE *ORPHAN* ZOMBIES...
...SO NOBODY'S GONNA MISS 'EM.
TO BE FAIR, YOU'RE COMING IN LATE.

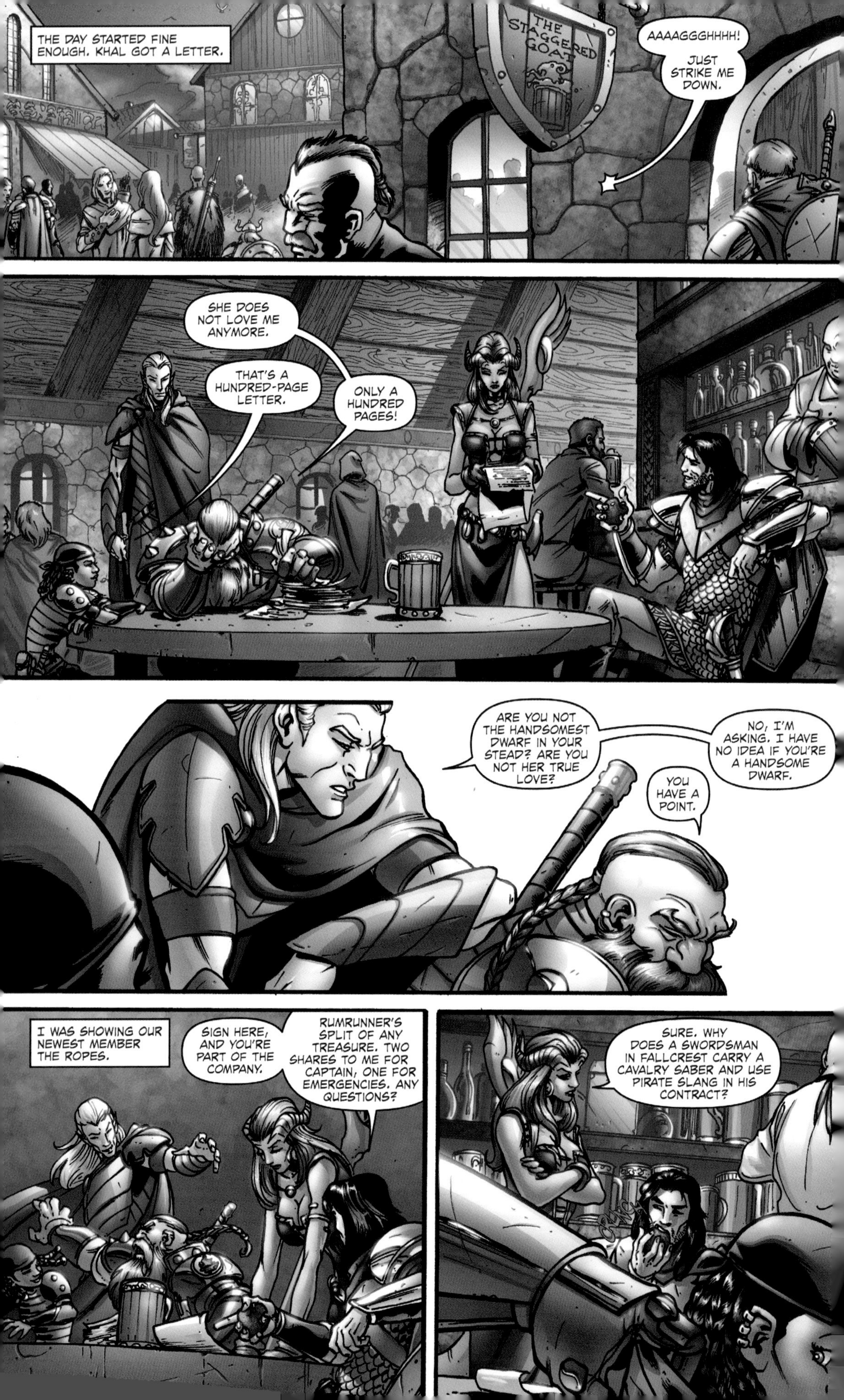
THE DAY STARTED FINE ENOUGH. KHAL GOT A LETTER.
THE STAGGERED GOAT
AAAAGGGHHHH!
JUST STRIKE ME DOWN.
SHE DOES NOT LOVE ME ANYMORE.
THAT'S A HUNDRED-PAGE LETTER.
ONLY A HUNDRED PAGES!
ARE YOU NOT THE HANDSOMEST DWARF IN YOUR STEAD? ARE YOU NOT HER TRUE LOVE?
NO, I'M ASKING. I HAVE NO IDEA IF YOU'RE A HANDSOME DWARF.
YOU HAVE A POINT.
I WAS SHOWING OUR NEWEST MEMBER THE ROPES.
SIGN HERE, AND YOU'RE PART OF THE COMPANY.
RUMRUNNER'S SPLIT OF ANY TREASURE. TWO SHARES TO ME FOR CAPTAIN, ONE FOR EMERGENCIES. ANY QUESTIONS?
SURE. WHY DOES A SWORDSMAN IN FALLCREST CARRY A CAVALRY SABER AND USE PIRATE SLANG IN HIS CONTRACT?

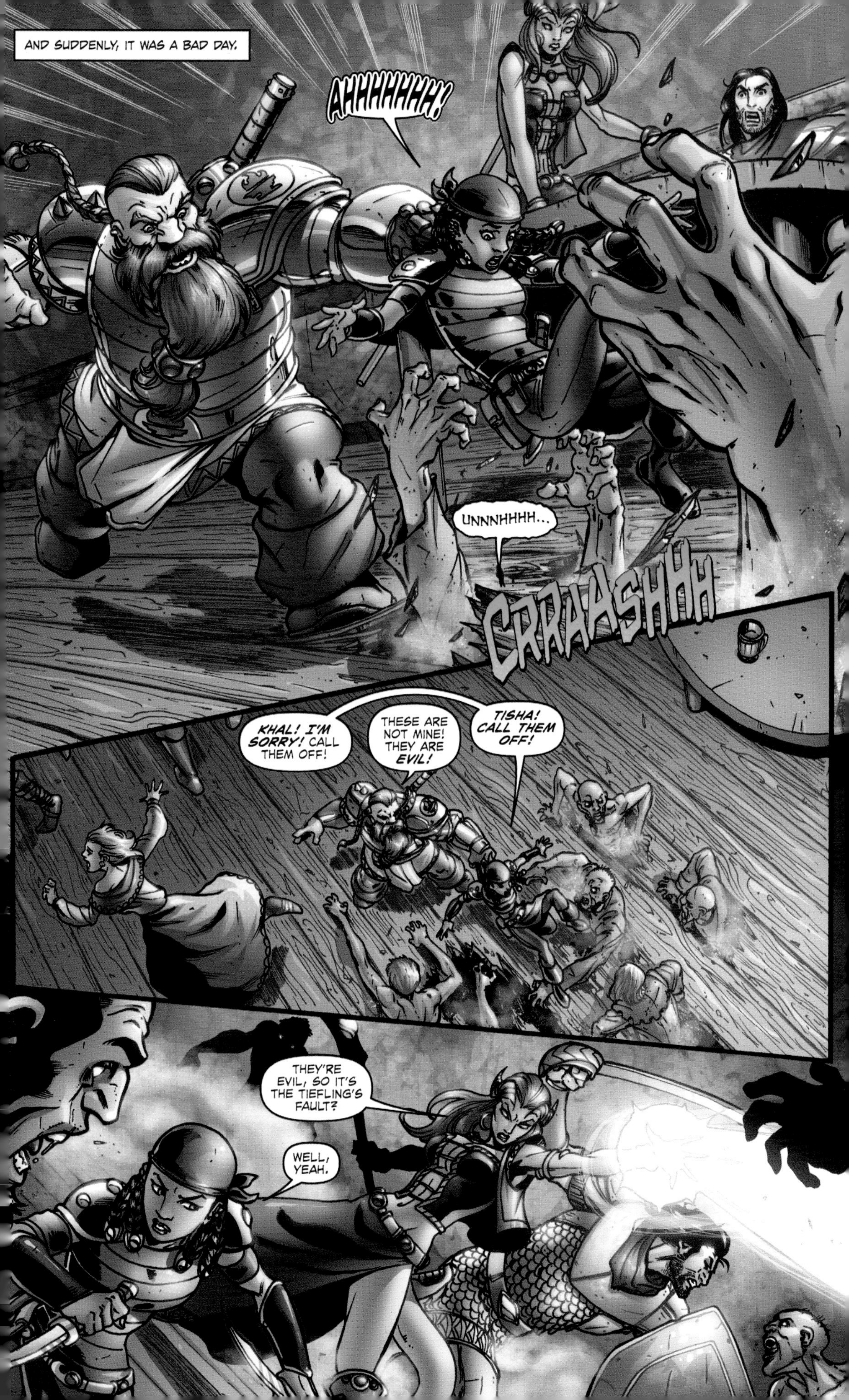
AND SUDDENLY, IT WAS A BAD DAY.
AHHHHHHH!
UNNNHHHH...
CRRAASHHH
KHAL! I'M SORRY! CALL THEM OFF!
THESE ARE NOT MINE! THEY ARE EVIL!
TISHA! CALL THEM OFF!
THEY'RE EVIL, SO IT'S THE TIEFLING'S FAULT?
WELL, YEAH.

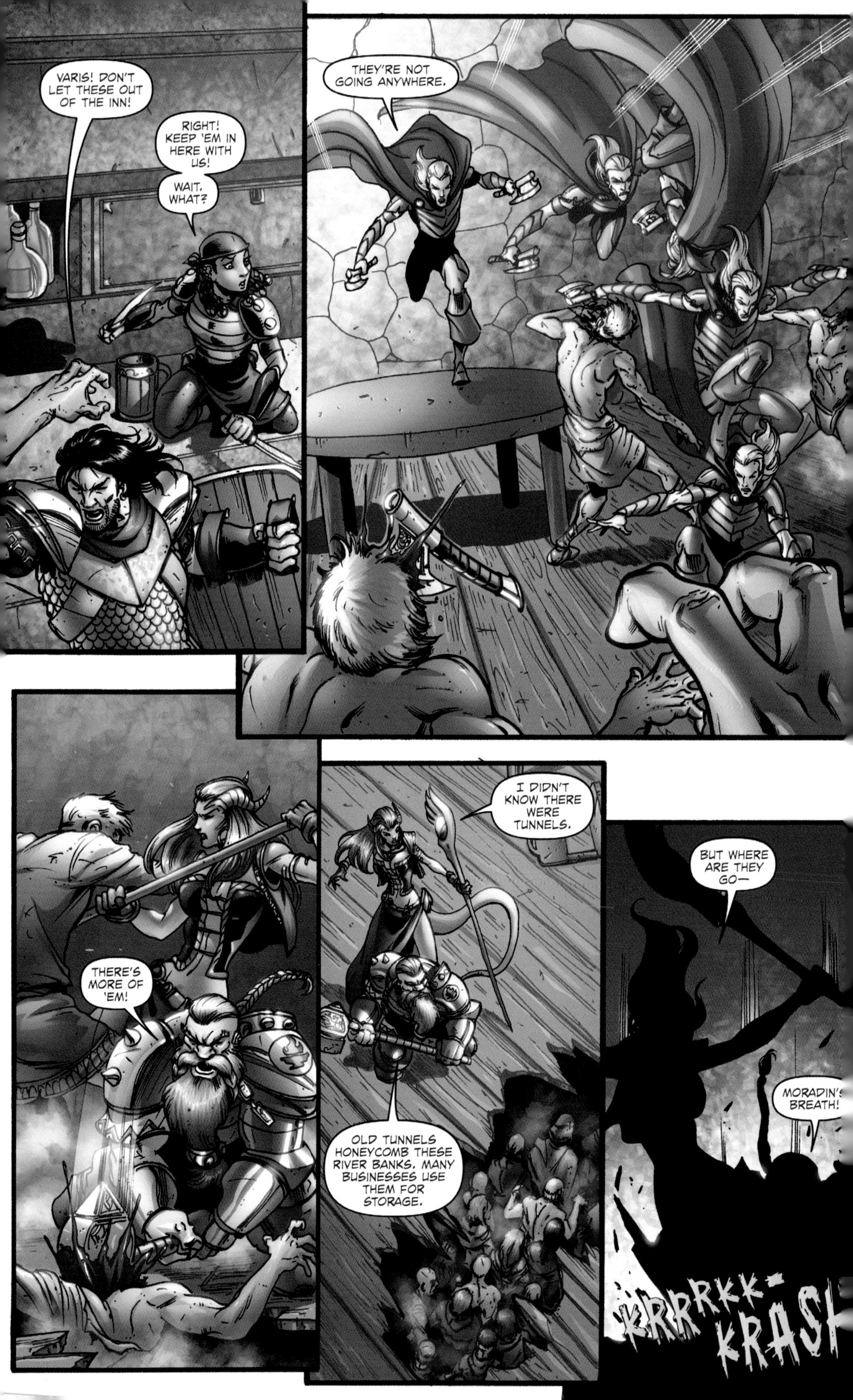
VARIS! DON'T LET THESE OUT OF THE INN!
RIGHT! KEEP 'EM IN HERE WITH US!
WAIT. WHAT?
THEY'RE NOT GOING ANYWHERE.
THERE'S MORE OF 'EM!
I DIDN'T KNOW THERE WERE TUNNELS.
OLD TUNNELS HONEYCOMB THESE RIVER BANKS. MANY BUSINESSES USE THEM FOR STORAGE.
BUT WHERE ARE THEY GO—
MORADIN'S BREATH!
KRRRKK-KRASH

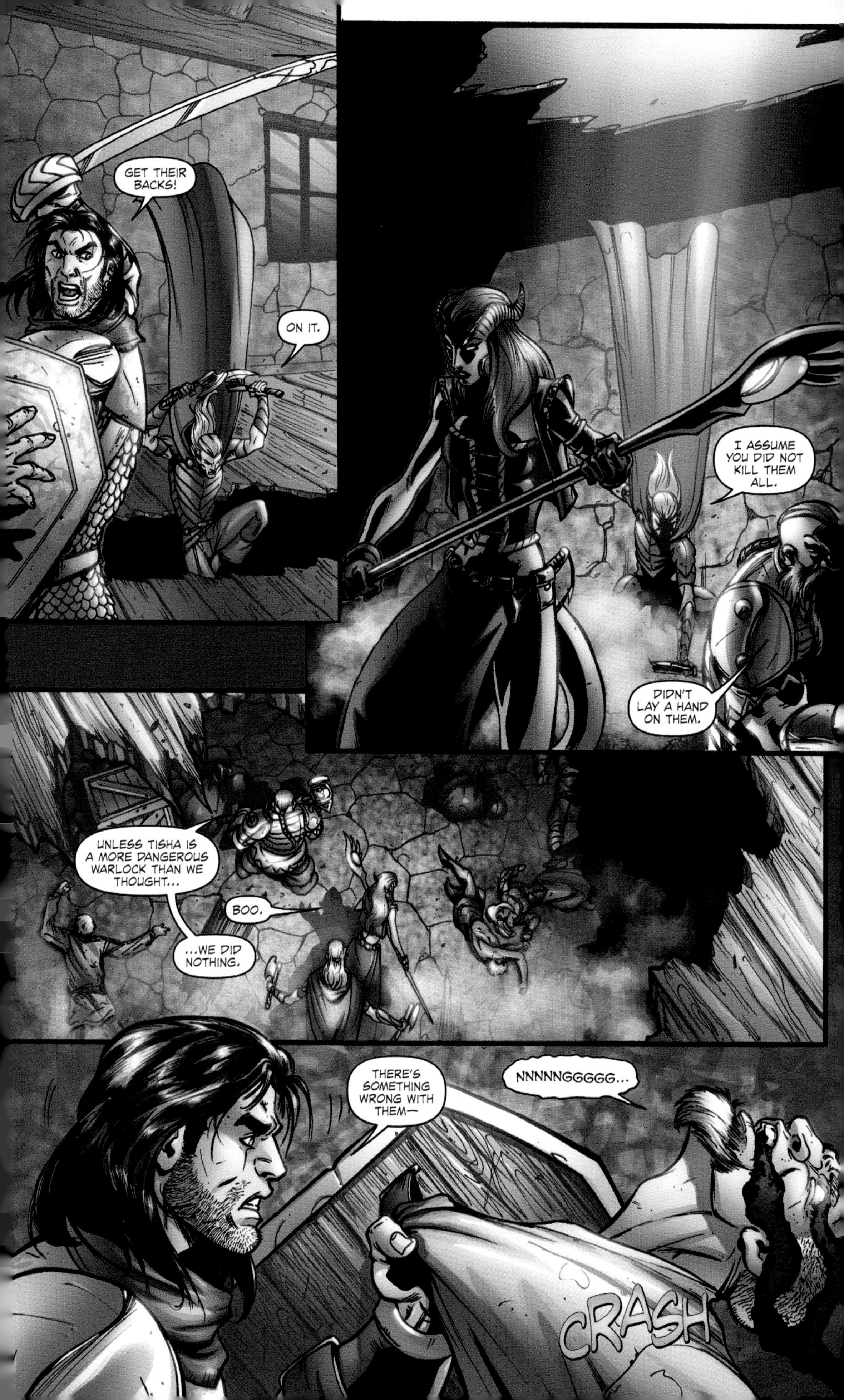
GET THEIR BACKS!
ON IT.
I ASSUME YOU DID NOT KILL THEM ALL.
DIDN'T LAY A HAND ON THEM.
UNLESS TISHA IS A MORE DANGEROUS WARLOCK THAN WE THOUGHT...
BOO.
...WE DID NOTHING.
THERE'S SOMETHING WRONG WITH THEM—
NNNNNGGGGG...
CRASH

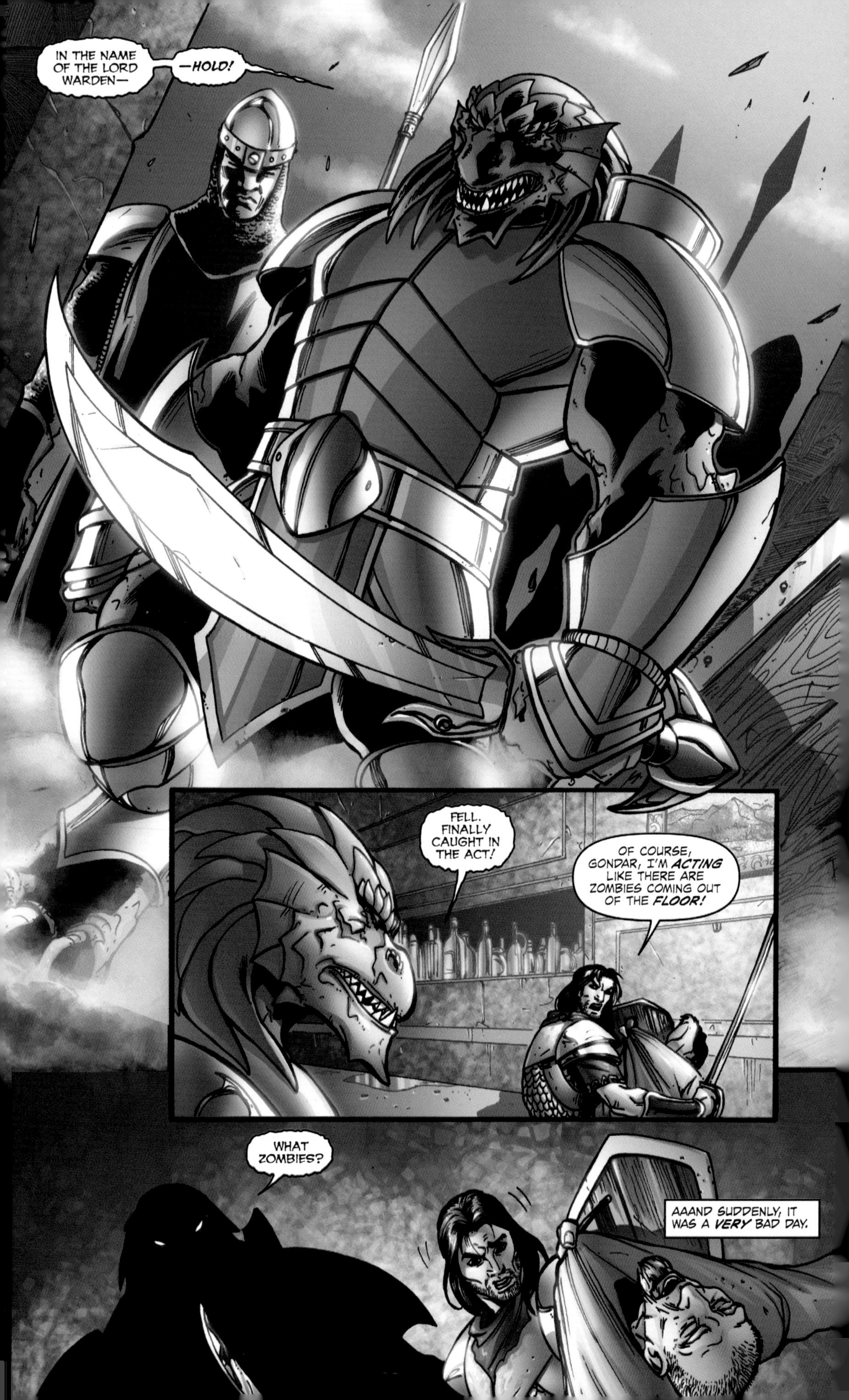
IN THE NAME OF THE LORD WARDEN—
—HOLD!
FELL. FINALLY CAUGHT IN THE ACT!
OF COURSE, GONDAR, I'M ACTING LIKE THERE ARE ZOMBIES COMING OUT OF THE FLOOR!
WHAT ZOMBIES?
AAAND SUDDENLY, IT WAS A VERY BAD DAY.

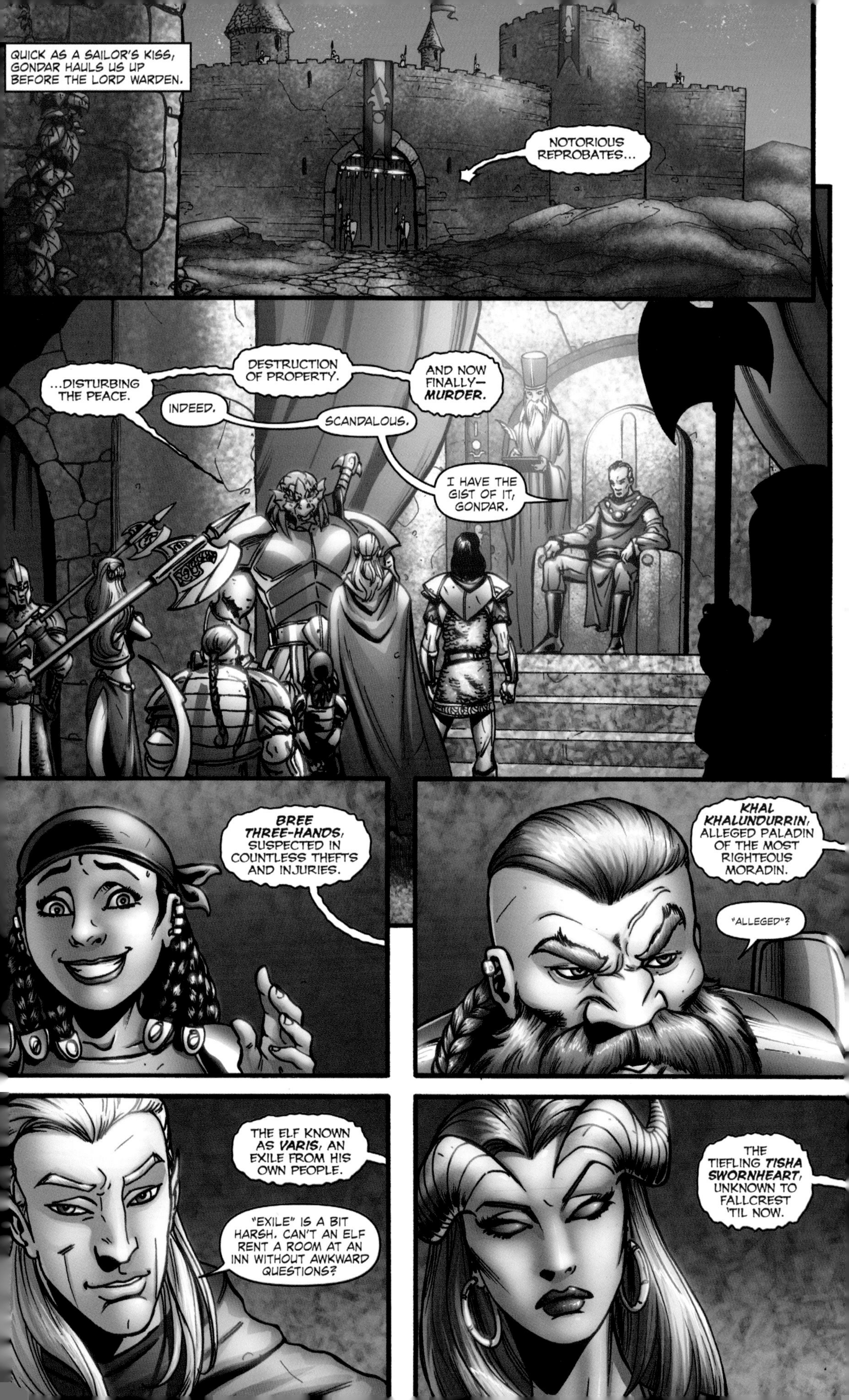

QUICK AS A SAILOR'S KISS, GONDAR HAULS US UP BEFORE THE LORD WARDEN.
NOTORIOUS REPROBATES...
...DISTURBING THE PEACE.
DESTRUCTION OF PROPERTY.
AND NOW FINALLY— ***MURDER.***
INDEED.
SCANDALOUS.
I HAVE THE GIST OF IT, GONDAR.
BREE THREE-HANDS, SUSPECTED IN COUNTLESS THEFTS AND INJURIES.
KHAL KHALUNDURRIN, ALLEGED PALADIN OF THE MOST RIGHTEOUS MORADIN.
"ALLEGED"?
THE ELF KNOWN AS ***VARIS***, AN EXILE FROM HIS OWN PEOPLE.
"EXILE" IS A BIT HARSH. CAN'T AN ELF RENT A ROOM AT AN INN WITHOUT AWKWARD QUESTIONS?
THE TIEFLING ***TISHA SWORNHEART***, UNKNOWN TO FALLCREST 'TIL NOW.

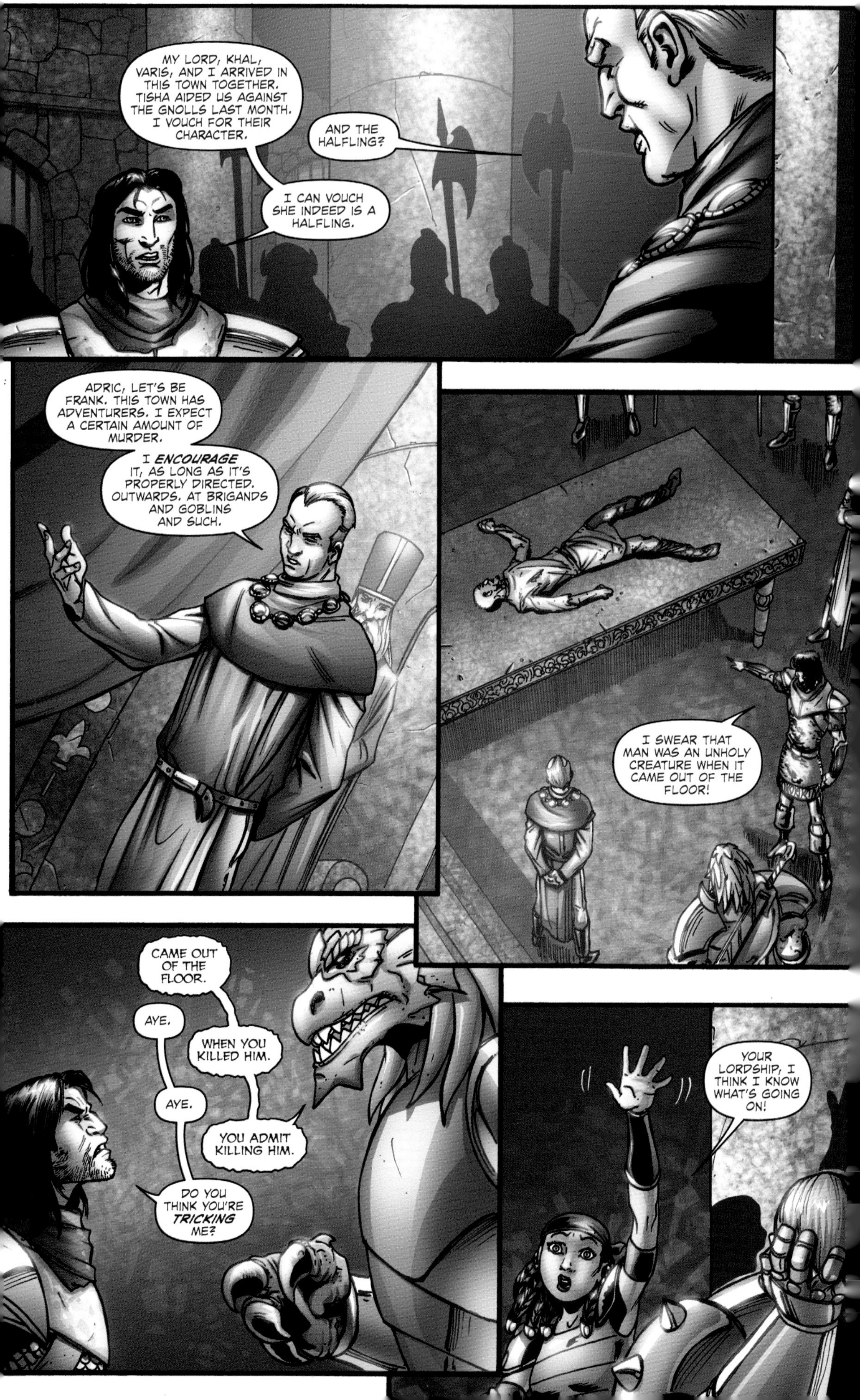
MY LORD, KHAL, VARIS, AND I ARRIVED IN THIS TOWN TOGETHER. TISHA AIDED US AGAINST THE GNOLLS LAST MONTH. I VOUCH FOR THEIR CHARACTER.
AND THE HALFLING?
I CAN VOUCH SHE INDEED IS A HALFLING.
ADRIC, LET'S BE FRANK. THIS TOWN HAS ADVENTURERS. I EXPECT A CERTAIN AMOUNT OF MURDER.
I *ENCOURAGE* IT, AS LONG AS IT'S PROPERLY DIRECTED. OUTWARDS, AT BRIGANDS AND GOBLINS AND SUCH.
I SWEAR THAT MAN WAS AN UNHOLY CREATURE WHEN IT CAME OUT OF THE FLOOR!
CAME OUT OF THE FLOOR.
AYE.
WHEN YOU KILLED HIM.
AYE.
YOU ADMIT KILLING HIM.
DO YOU THINK YOU'RE *TRICKING* ME?
YOUR LORDSHIP, I THINK I KNOW WHAT'S GOING ON!

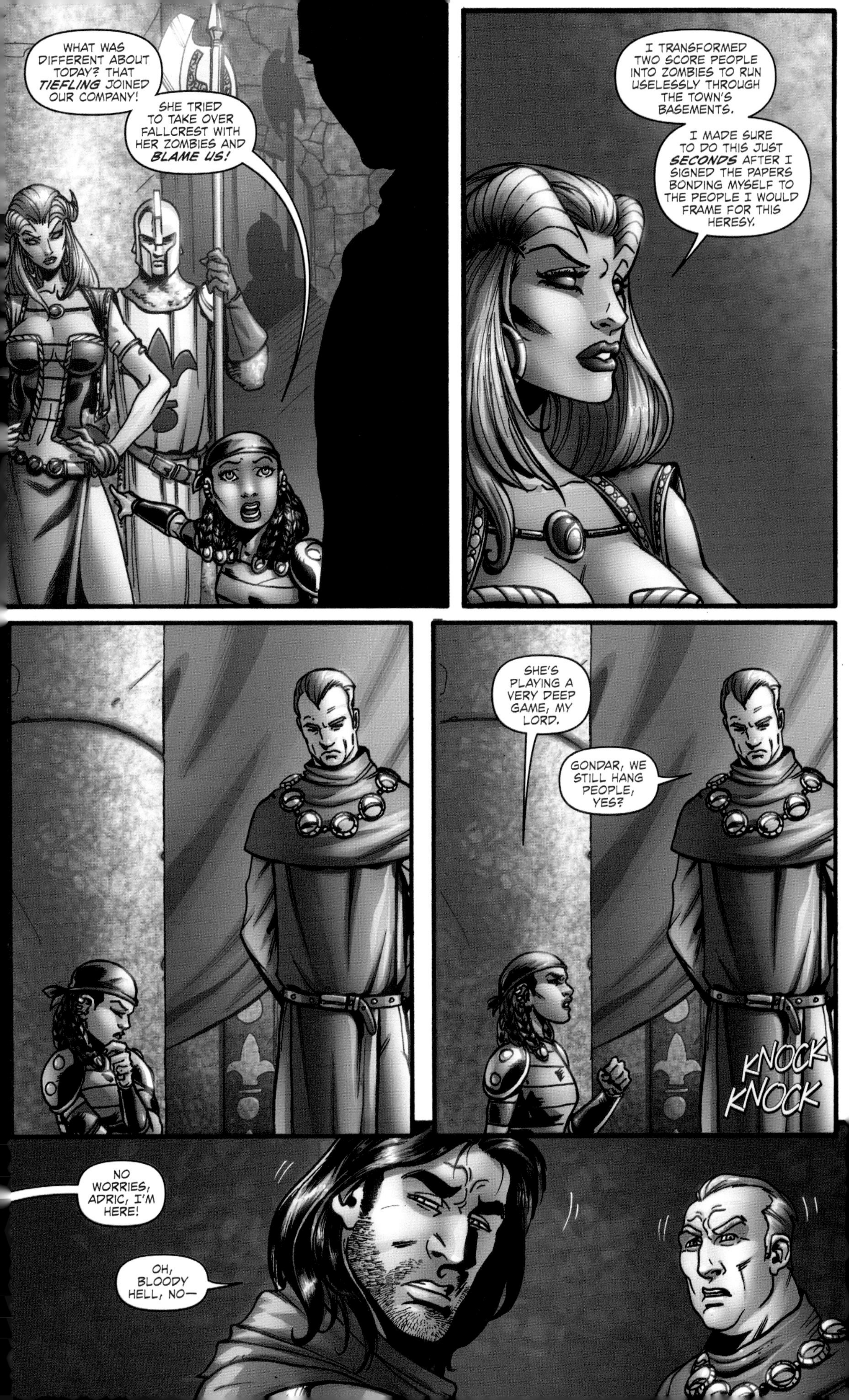
WHAT WAS DIFFERENT ABOUT TODAY? THAT TIEFLING JOINED OUR COMPANY!
SHE TRIED TO TAKE OVER FALLCREST WITH HER ZOMBIES AND BLAME US!
I TRANSFORMED TWO SCORE PEOPLE INTO ZOMBIES TO RUN USELESSLY THROUGH THE TOWN'S BASEMENTS.
I MADE SURE TO DO THIS JUST SECONDS AFTER I SIGNED THE PAPERS BONDING MYSELF TO THE PEOPLE I WOULD FRAME FOR THIS HERESY.
SHE'S PLAYING A VERY DEEP GAME, MY LORD.
GONDAR, WE STILL HANG PEOPLE, YES?
KNOCK KNOCK
NO WORRIES, ADRIC, I'M HERE!
OH, BLOODY HELL, NO—

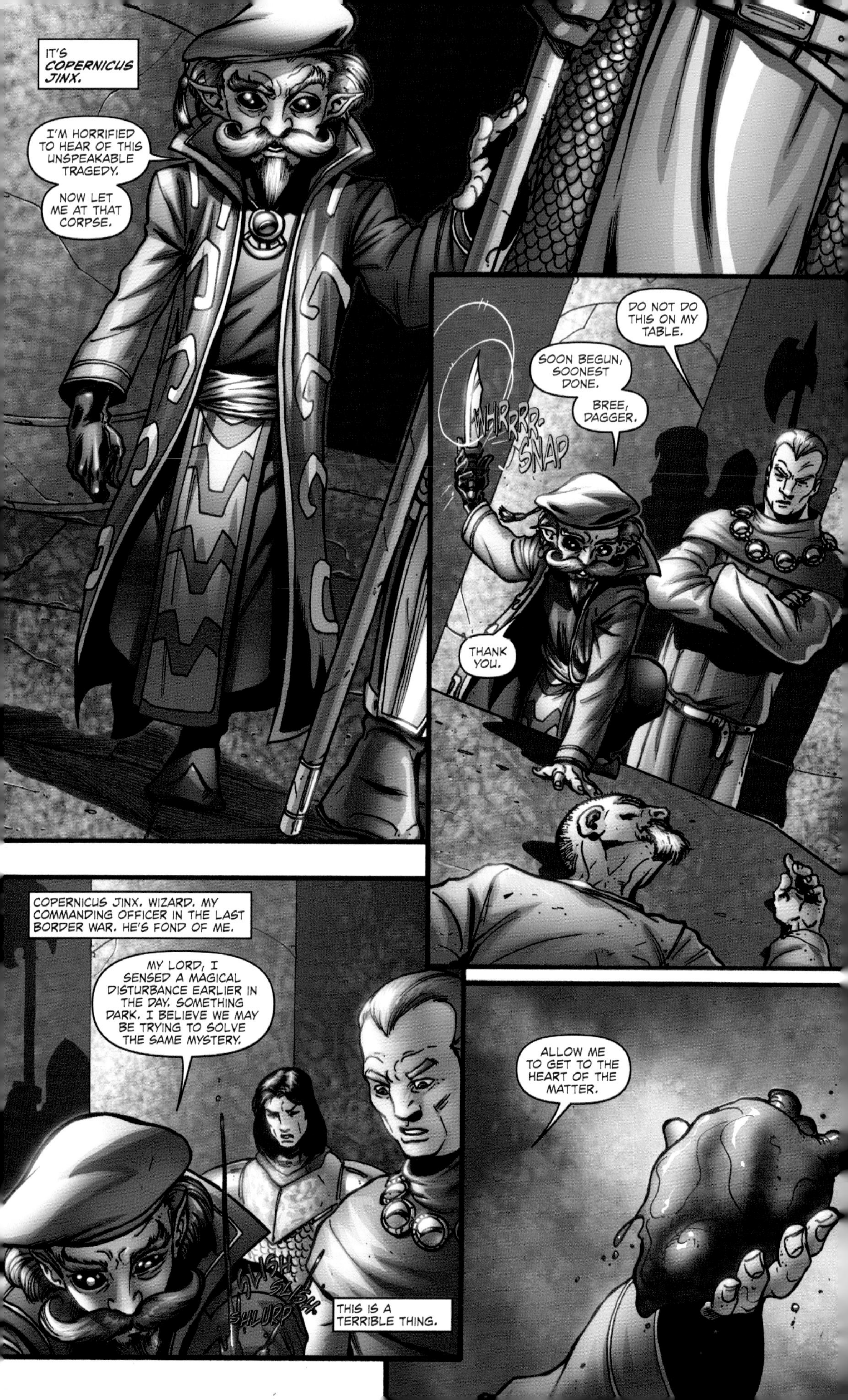
IT'S *COPERNICUS JINX.*
I'M HORRIFIED TO HEAR OF THIS UNSPEAKABLE TRAGEDY.
NOW LET ME AT THAT CORPSE.
DO NOT DO THIS ON MY TABLE.
SOON BEGUN, SOONEST DONE.
BREE, DAGGER.
WHIRRRR-SNAP
THANK YOU.
COPERNICUS JINX. WIZARD. MY COMMANDING OFFICER IN THE LAST BORDER WAR. HE'S FOND OF ME.
MY LORD, I SENSED A MAGICAL DISTURBANCE EARLIER IN THE DAY. SOMETHING DARK. I BELIEVE WE MAY BE TRYING TO SOLVE THE SAME MYSTERY.
SHLISH SHLISH SHLURP
THIS IS A TERRIBLE THING.
ALLOW ME TO GET TO THE HEART OF THE MATTER.

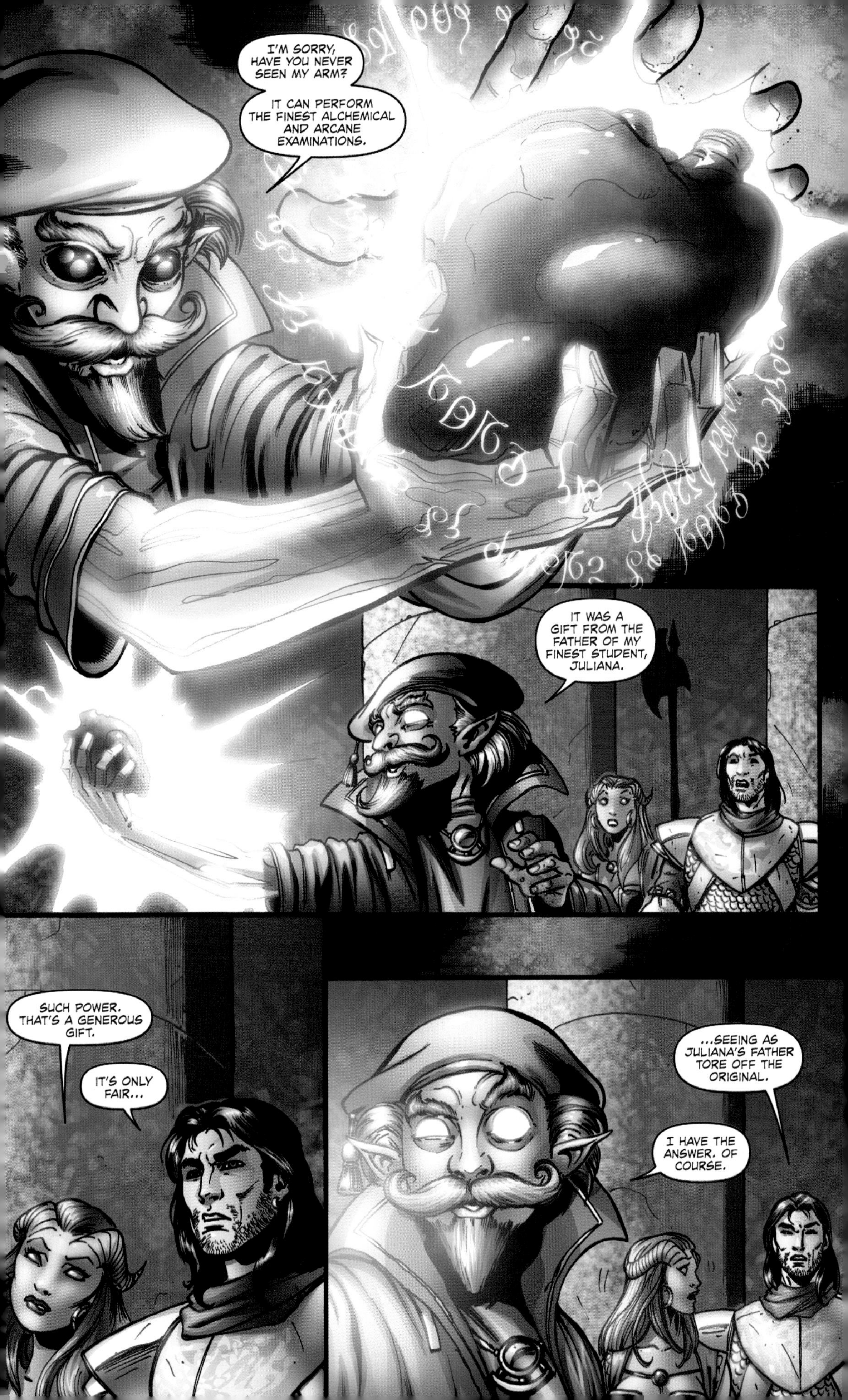
I'M SORRY, HAVE YOU NEVER SEEN MY ARM?
IT CAN PERFORM THE FINEST ALCHEMICAL AND ARCANE EXAMINATIONS.
IT WAS A GIFT FROM THE FATHER OF MY FINEST STUDENT, JULIANA.
SUCH POWER. THAT'S A GENEROUS GIFT.
IT'S ONLY FAIR...
...SEEING AS JULIANA'S FATHER TORE OFF THE ORIGINAL.
I HAVE THE ANSWER, OF COURSE.

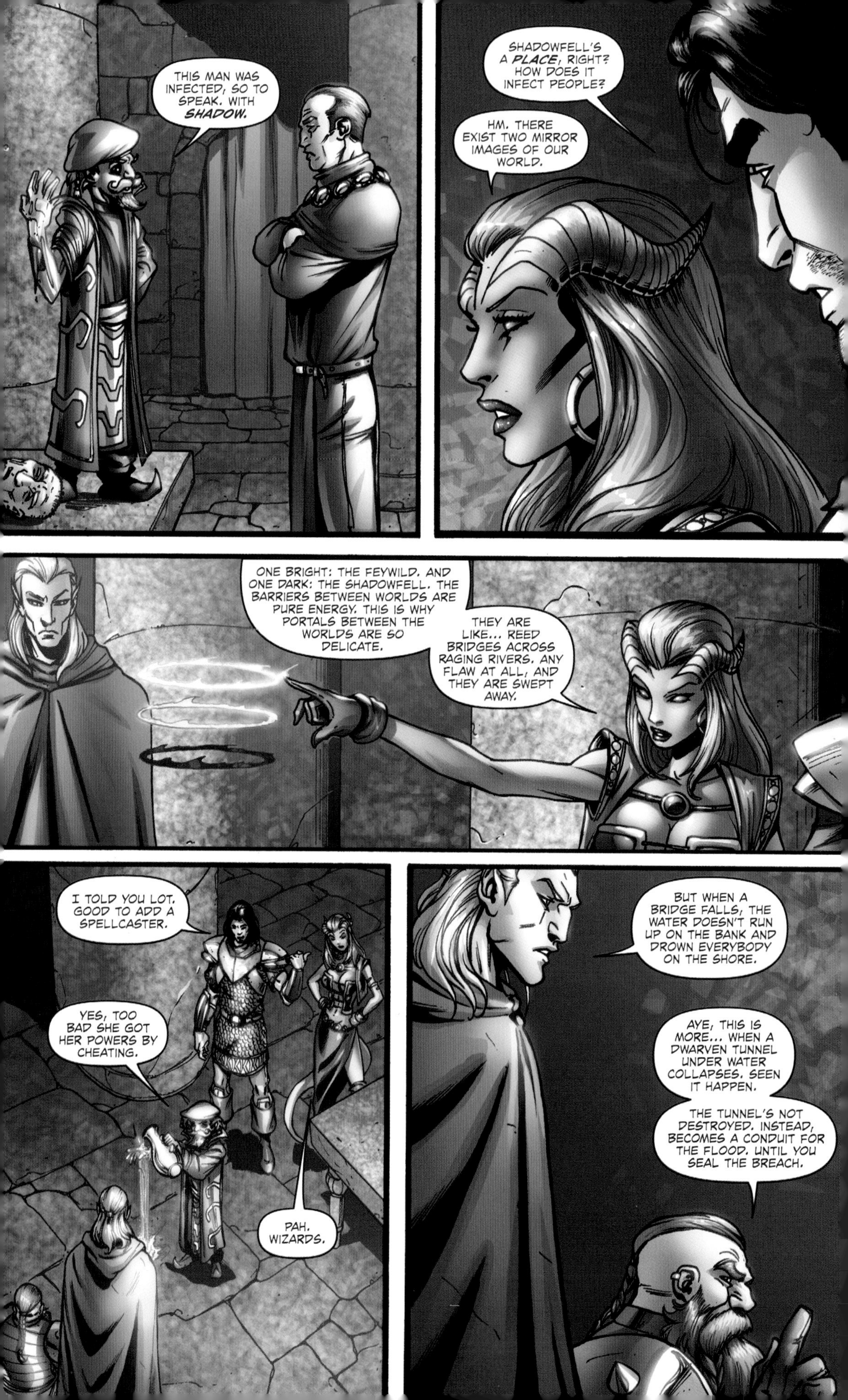
THIS MAN WAS INFECTED, SO TO SPEAK. WITH SHADOW.
SHADOWFELL'S A PLACE, RIGHT? HOW DOES IT INFECT PEOPLE?
HM. THERE EXIST TWO MIRROR IMAGES OF OUR WORLD.
ONE BRIGHT: THE FEYWILD. AND ONE DARK: THE SHADOWFELL. THE BARRIERS BETWEEN WORLDS ARE PURE ENERGY. THIS IS WHY PORTALS BETWEEN THE WORLDS ARE SO DELICATE.
THEY ARE LIKE... REED BRIDGES ACROSS RAGING RIVERS. ANY FLAW AT ALL, AND THEY ARE SWEPT AWAY.
I TOLD YOU LOT. GOOD TO ADD A SPELLCASTER.
YES, TOO BAD SHE GOT HER POWERS BY CHEATING.
PAH. WIZARDS.
BUT WHEN A BRIDGE FALLS, THE WATER DOESN'T RUN UP ON THE BANK AND DROWN EVERYBODY ON THE SHORE.
AYE, THIS IS MORE... WHEN A DWARVEN TUNNEL UNDER WATER COLLAPSES. SEEN IT HAPPEN.
THE TUNNEL'S NOT DESTROYED. INSTEAD, BECOMES A CONDUIT FOR THE FLOOD. UNTIL YOU SEAL THE BREACH.

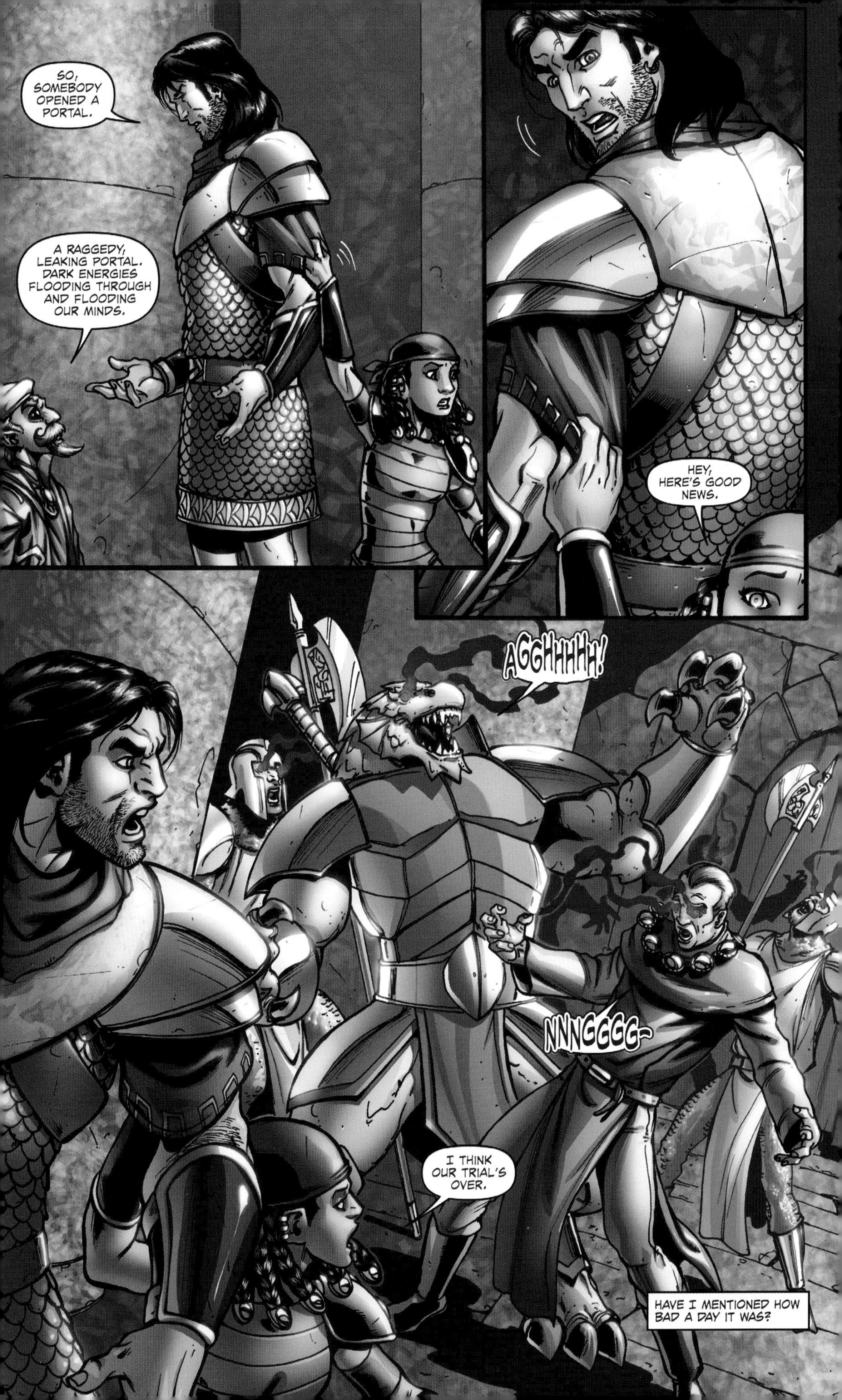
SO, SOMEBODY OPENED A PORTAL.
A RAGGEDY, LEAKING PORTAL. DARK ENERGIES FLOODING THROUGH AND FLOODING OUR MINDS.
HEY, HERE'S GOOD NEWS.
AGGHHHHH!
NNNGGGG-
I THINK OUR TRIAL'S OVER.
HAVE I MENTIONED HOW BAD A DAY IT WAS?

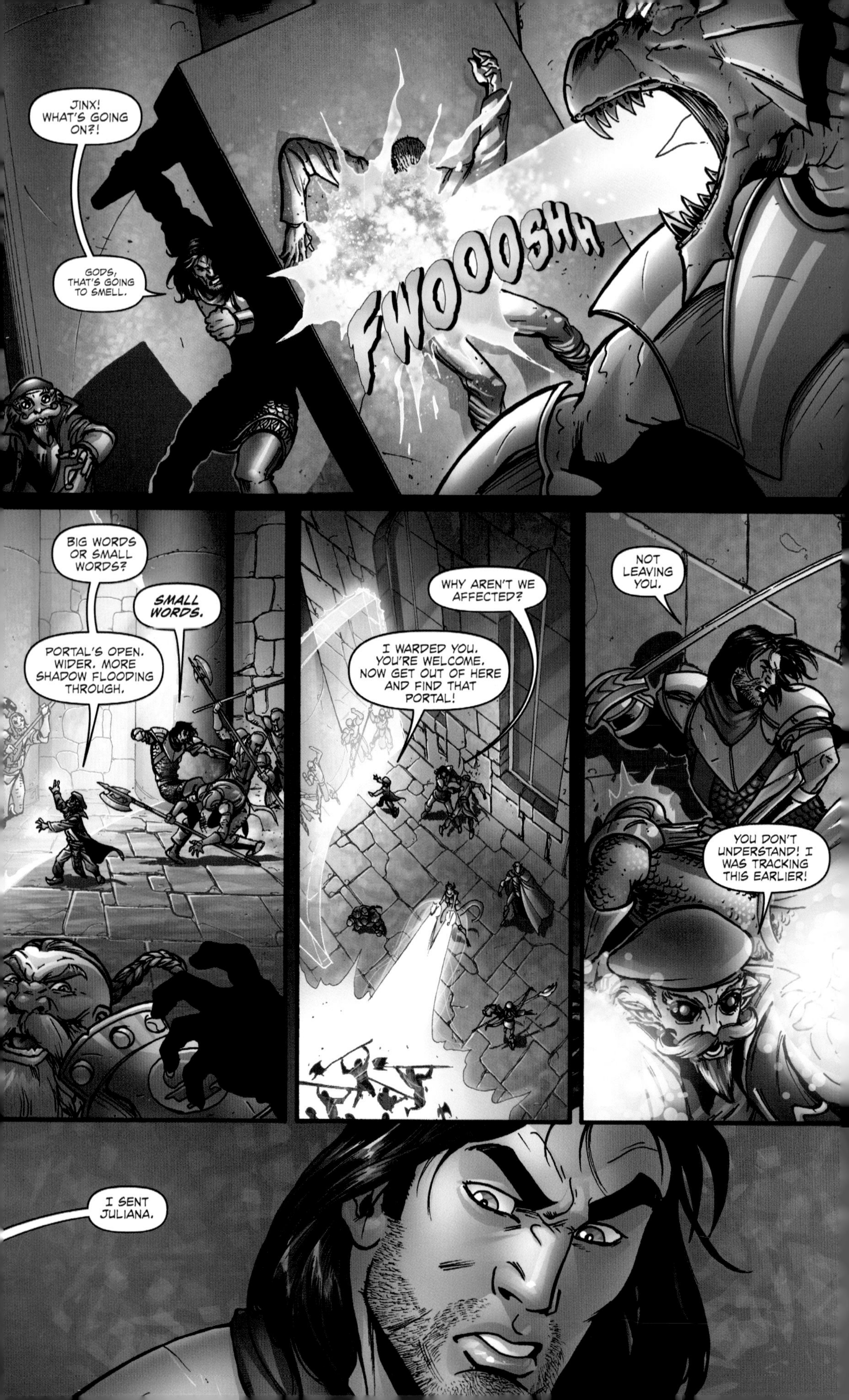
JINX! WHAT'S GOING ON?!
GODS, THAT'S GOING TO SMELL.
FWOOOSHH
BIG WORDS OR SMALL WORDS?
SMALL WORDS.
PORTAL'S OPEN. WIDER. MORE SHADOW FLOODING THROUGH.
WHY AREN'T WE AFFECTED?
I WARDED YOU. YOU'RE WELCOME. NOW GET OUT OF HERE AND FIND THAT PORTAL!
NOT LEAVING YOU.
YOU DON'T UNDERSTAND! I WAS TRACKING THIS EARLIER!
I SENT JULIANA.

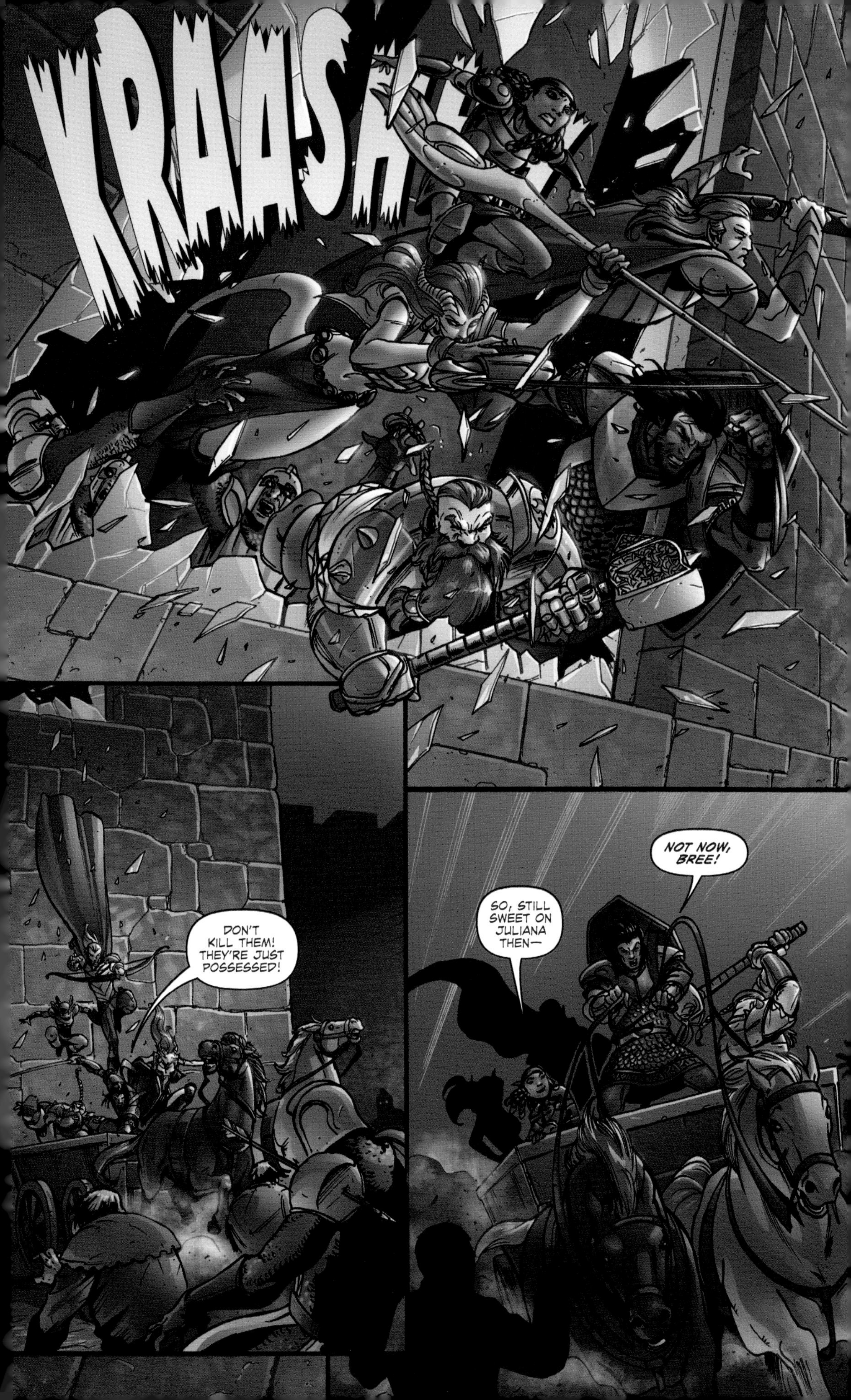
KRAASH
DON'T KILL THEM! THEY'RE JUST POSSESSED!
SO, STILL SWEET ON JULIANA THEN—
NOT NOW, BREE!

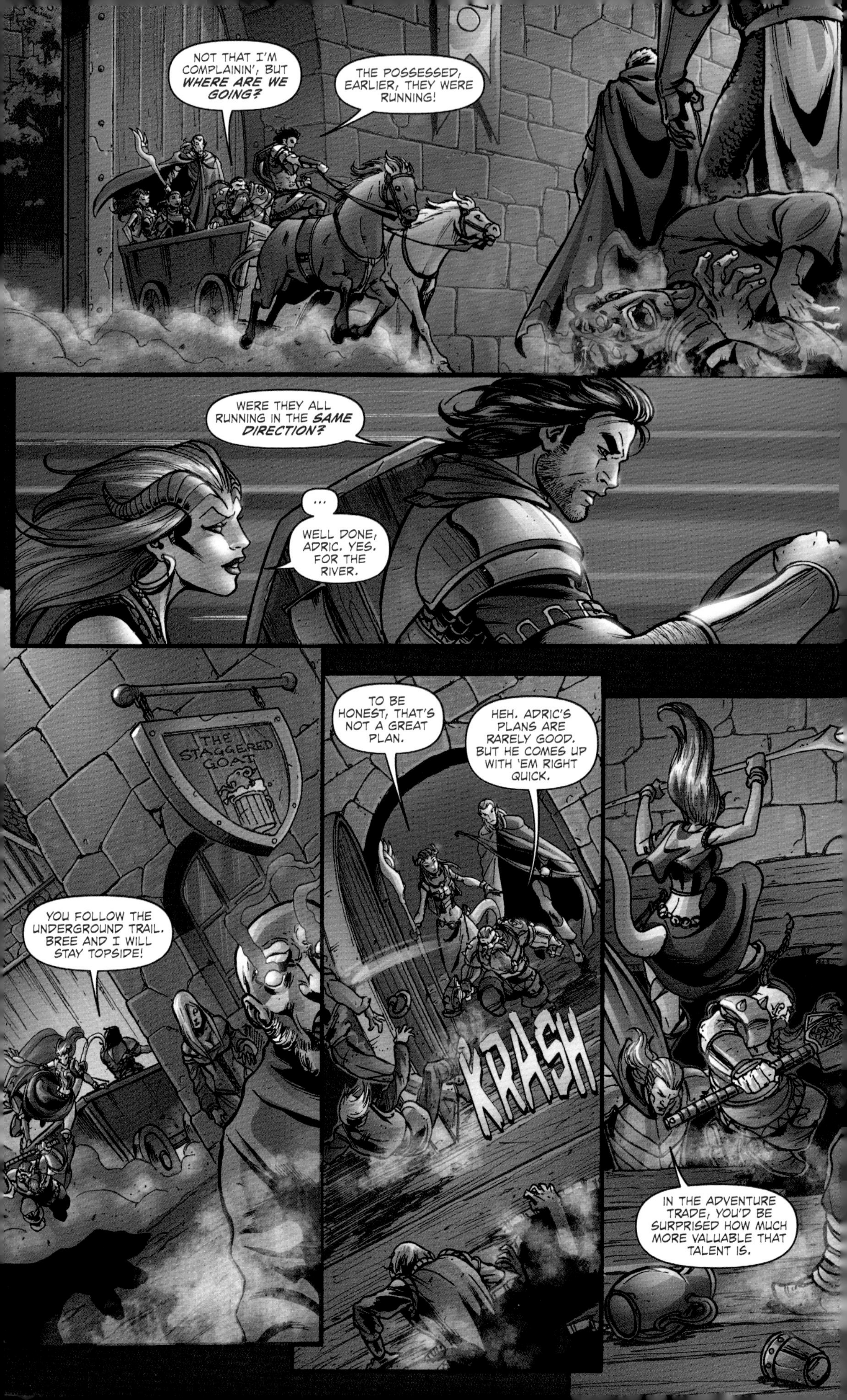
NOT THAT I'M COMPLAININ', BUT *WHERE ARE WE GOING?*
THE POSSESSED, EARLIER, THEY WERE RUNNING!
WERE THEY ALL RUNNING IN THE *SAME DIRECTION?*
...
WELL DONE, ADRIC. YES. FOR THE RIVER.
THE STAGGERED GOAT
YOU FOLLOW THE UNDERGROUND TRAIL. BREE AND I WILL STAY TOPSIDE!
TO BE HONEST, THAT'S NOT A GREAT PLAN.
HEH. ADRIC'S PLANS ARE RARELY GOOD. BUT HE COMES UP WITH 'EM RIGHT QUICK.
KRASH
IN THE ADVENTURE TRADE, YOU'D BE SURPRISED HOW MUCH MORE VALUABLE THAT TALENT IS.

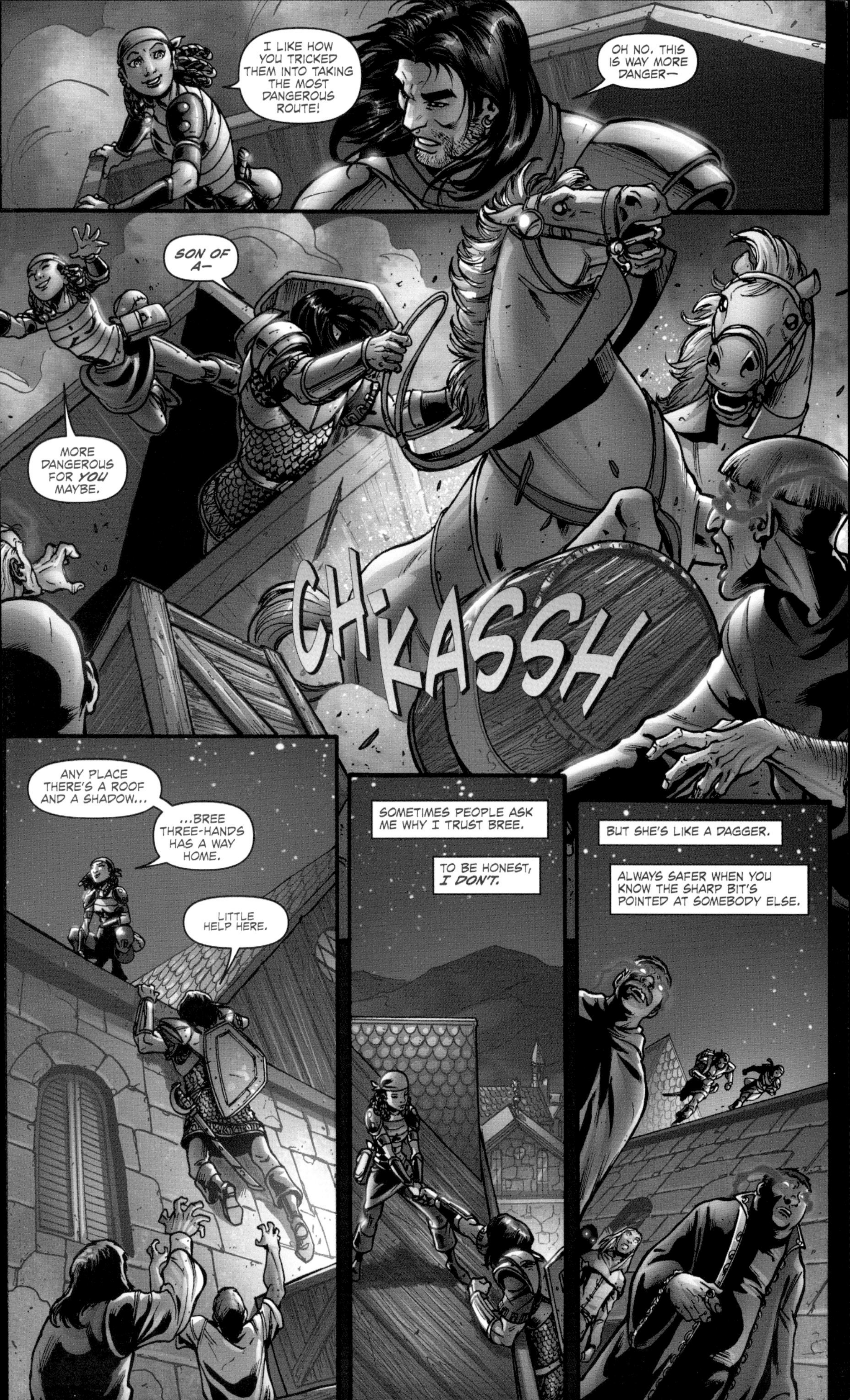

I LIKE HOW YOU TRICKED THEM INTO TAKING THE MOST DANGEROUS ROUTE!
OH NO, THIS IS WAY MORE DANGER—
SON OF A—
MORE DANGEROUS FOR *YOU* MAYBE.
CH-KASSH
ANY PLACE THERE'S A ROOF AND A SHADOW...
...BREE THREE-HANDS HAS A WAY HOME.
LITTLE HELP HERE.
SOMETIMES PEOPLE ASK ME WHY I TRUST BREE.
TO BE HONEST, *I DON'T.*
BUT SHE'S LIKE A DAGGER.
ALWAYS SAFER WHEN YOU KNOW THE SHARP BIT'S POINTED AT SOMEBODY ELSE.

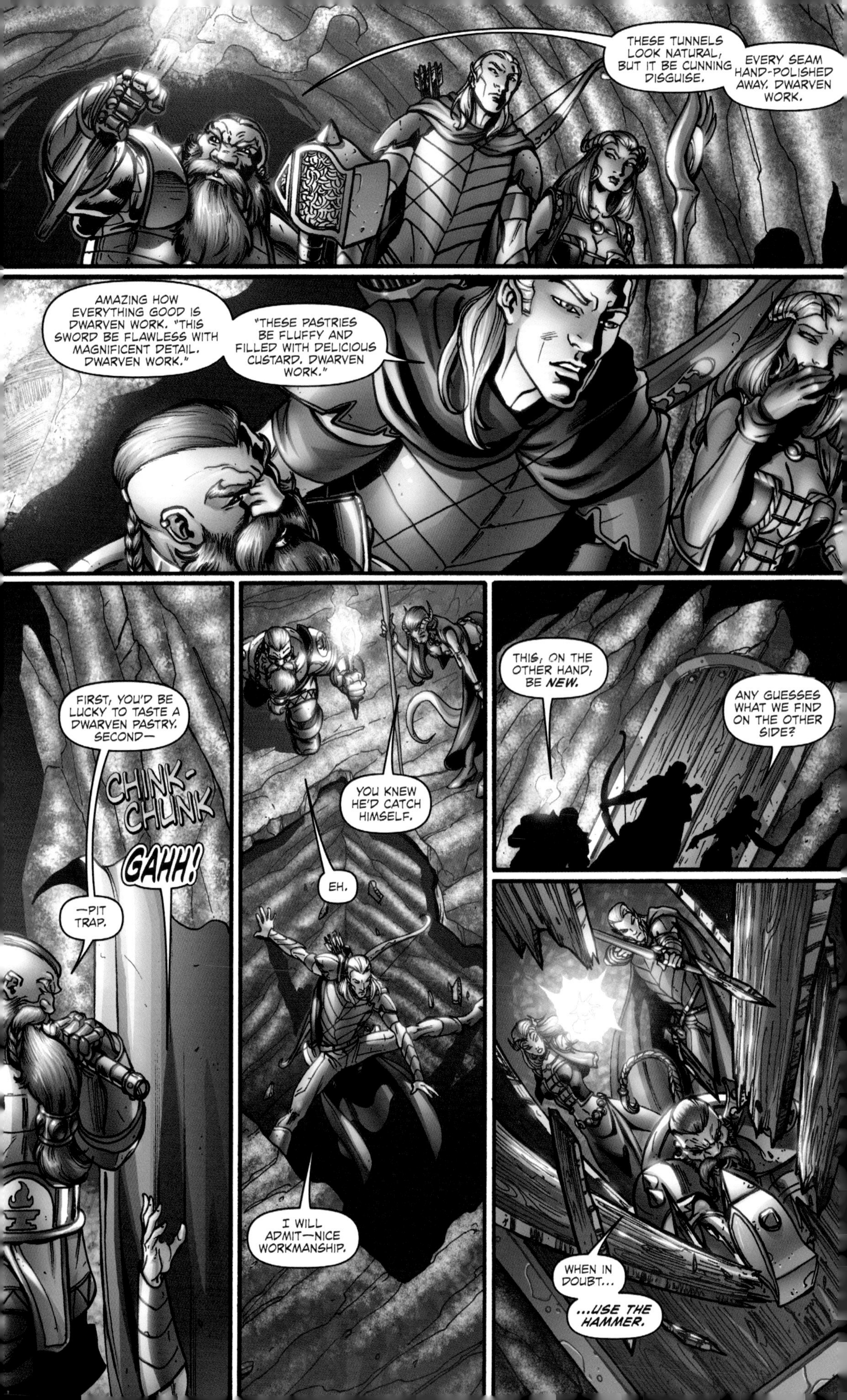
THESE TUNNELS LOOK NATURAL, BUT IT BE CUNNING DISGUISE.
EVERY SEAM HAND-POLISHED AWAY. DWARVEN WORK.
AMAZING HOW EVERYTHING GOOD IS DWARVEN WORK. "THIS SWORD BE FLAWLESS WITH MAGNIFICENT DETAIL. DWARVEN WORK."
"THESE PASTRIES BE FLUFFY AND FILLED WITH DELICIOUS CUSTARD. DWARVEN WORK."
FIRST, YOU'D BE LUCKY TO TASTE A DWARVEN PASTRY. SECOND—
CHINK-CHUNK
GAHH!
—PIT TRAP.
YOU KNEW HE'D CATCH HIMSELF.
EH.
I WILL ADMIT—NICE WORKMANSHIP.
THIS, ON THE OTHER HAND, BE *NEW.*
ANY GUESSES WHAT WE FIND ON THE OTHER SIDE?
WHEN IN DOUBT...
...USE THE HAMMER.

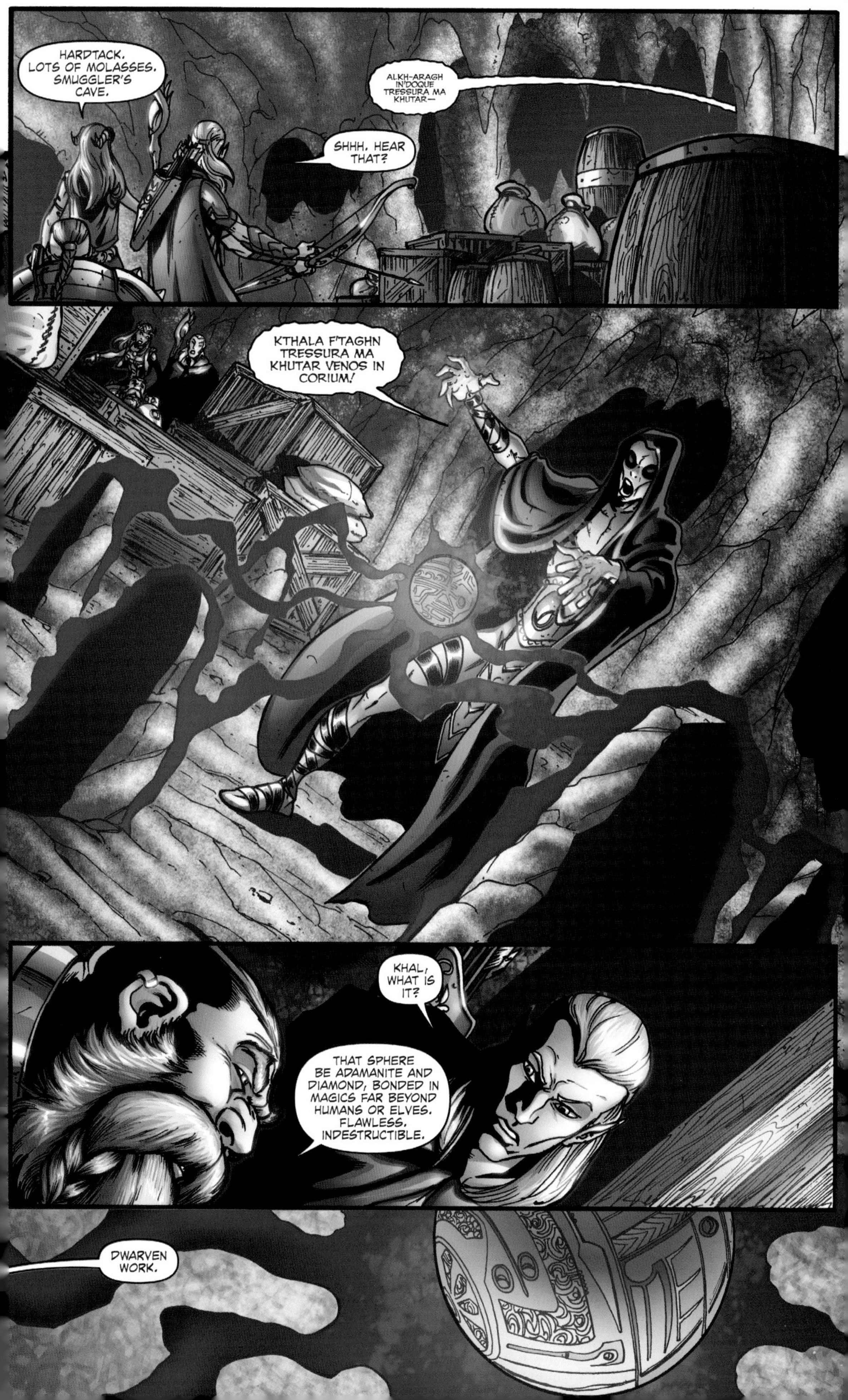
HARDTACK. LOTS OF MOLASSES. SMUGGLER'S CAVE.
ALKH-ARAGH IN'DOQUE TRESSURA MA KHUTAR—
SHHH. HEAR THAT?
KTHALA F'TAGHN TRESSURA MA KHUTAR VENOS IN CORIUM!
KHAL, WHAT IS IT?
THAT SPHERE BE ADAMANITE AND DIAMOND, BONDED IN MAGICS FAR BEYOND HUMANS OR ELVES. FLAWLESS. INDESTRUCTIBLE.
DWARVEN WORK.

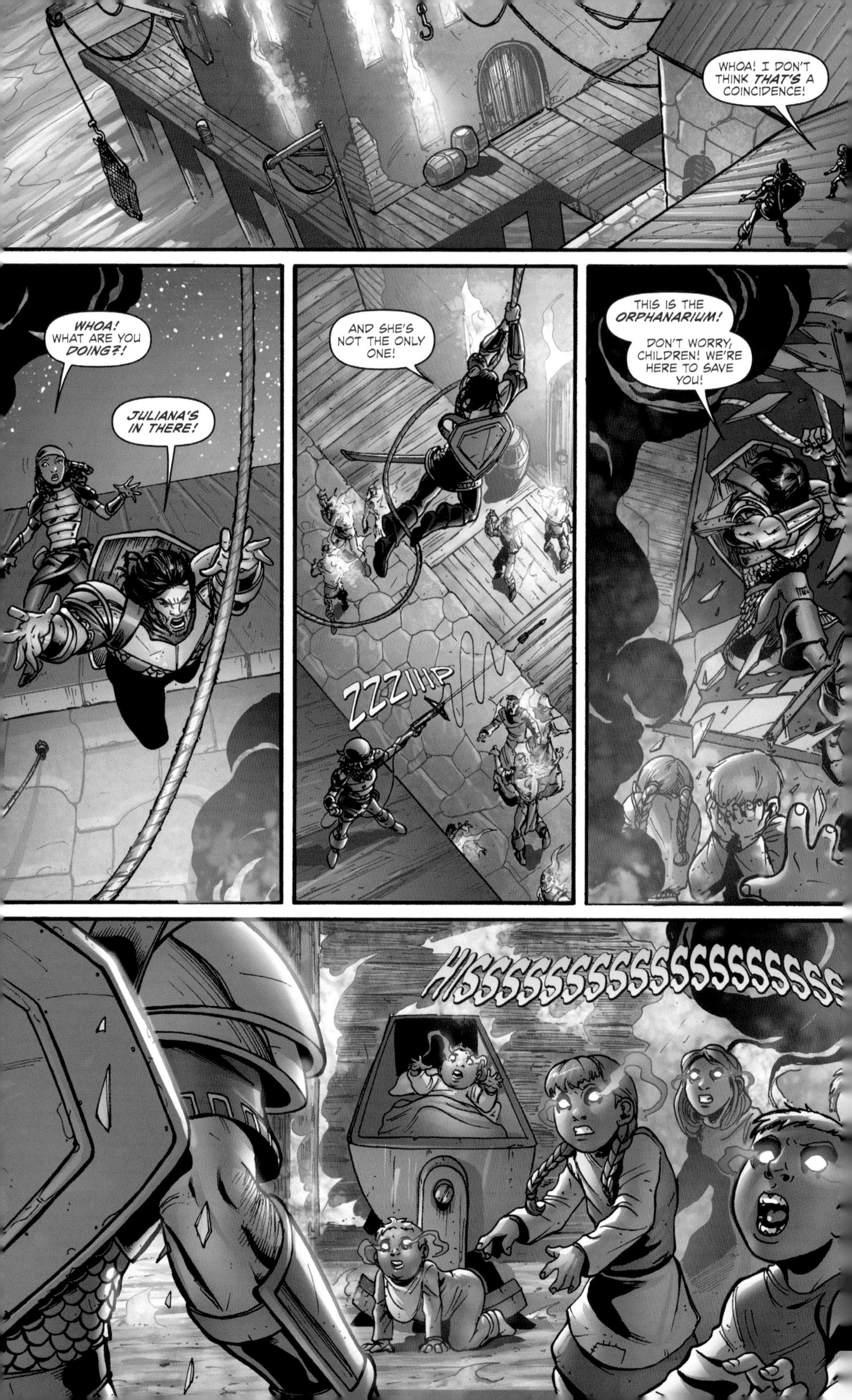
WHOA! I DON'T THINK *THAT'S* A COINCIDENCE!
WHOA! WHAT ARE YOU *DOING?!*
JULIANA'S IN THERE!
AND SHE'S NOT THE ONLY ONE!
ZZZIIIP
THIS IS THE *ORPHANARIUM!*
DON'T WORRY, CHILDREN! WE'RE HERE TO SAVE YOU!
HISSSSSSSSSSSSSSSSSSS

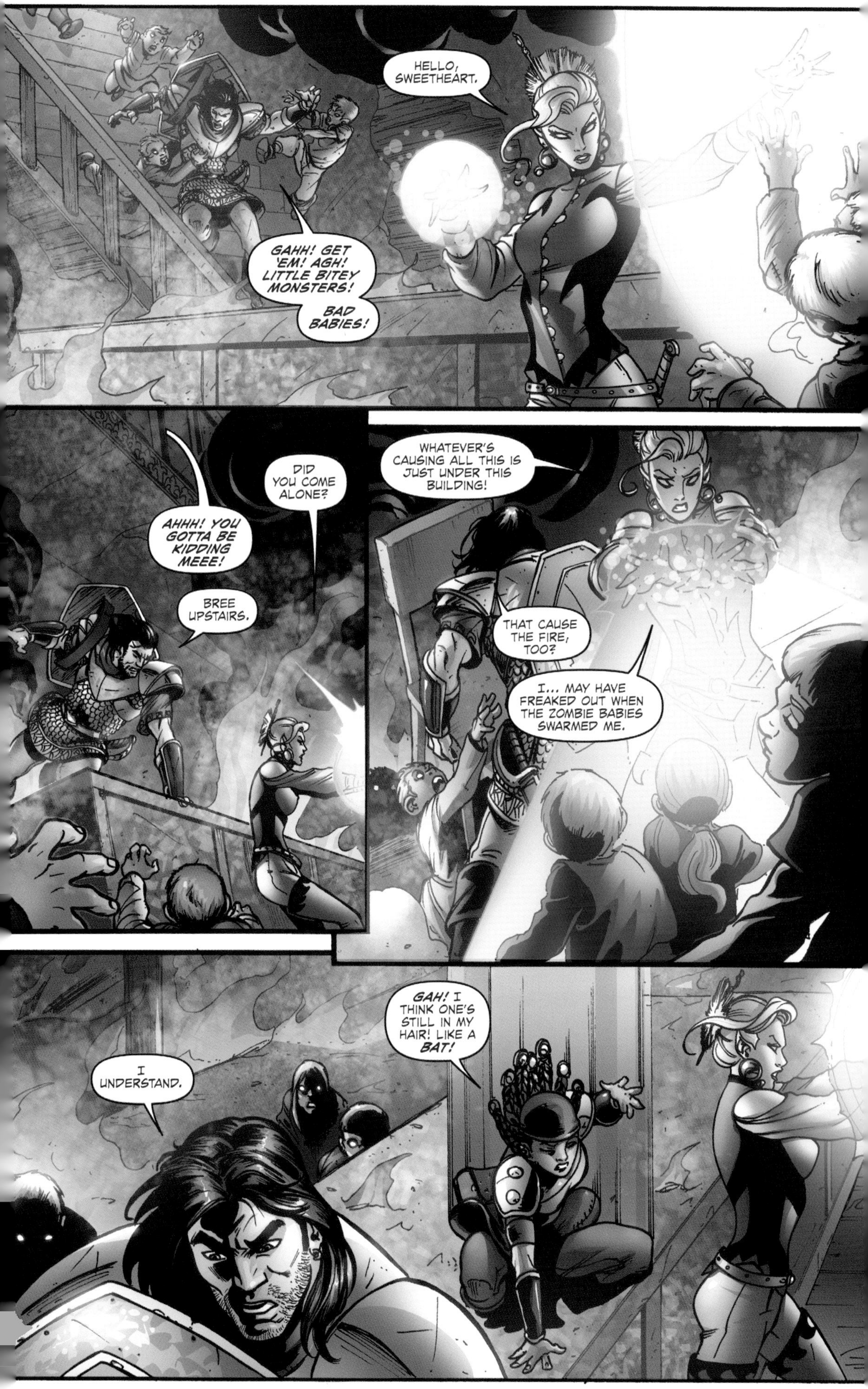
HELLO, SWEETHEART.
GAHH! GET 'EM! AGH! LITTLE BITEY MONSTERS!
BAD BABIES!
DID YOU COME ALONE?
AHHH! YOU GOTTA BE KIDDING MEEE!
BREE UPSTAIRS.
WHATEVER'S CAUSING ALL THIS IS JUST UNDER THIS BUILDING!
THAT CAUSE THE FIRE, TOO?
I... MAY HAVE FREAKED OUT WHEN THE ZOMBIE BABIES SWARMED ME.
I UNDERSTAND.
GAH! I THINK ONE'S STILL IN MY HAIR! LIKE A BAT!

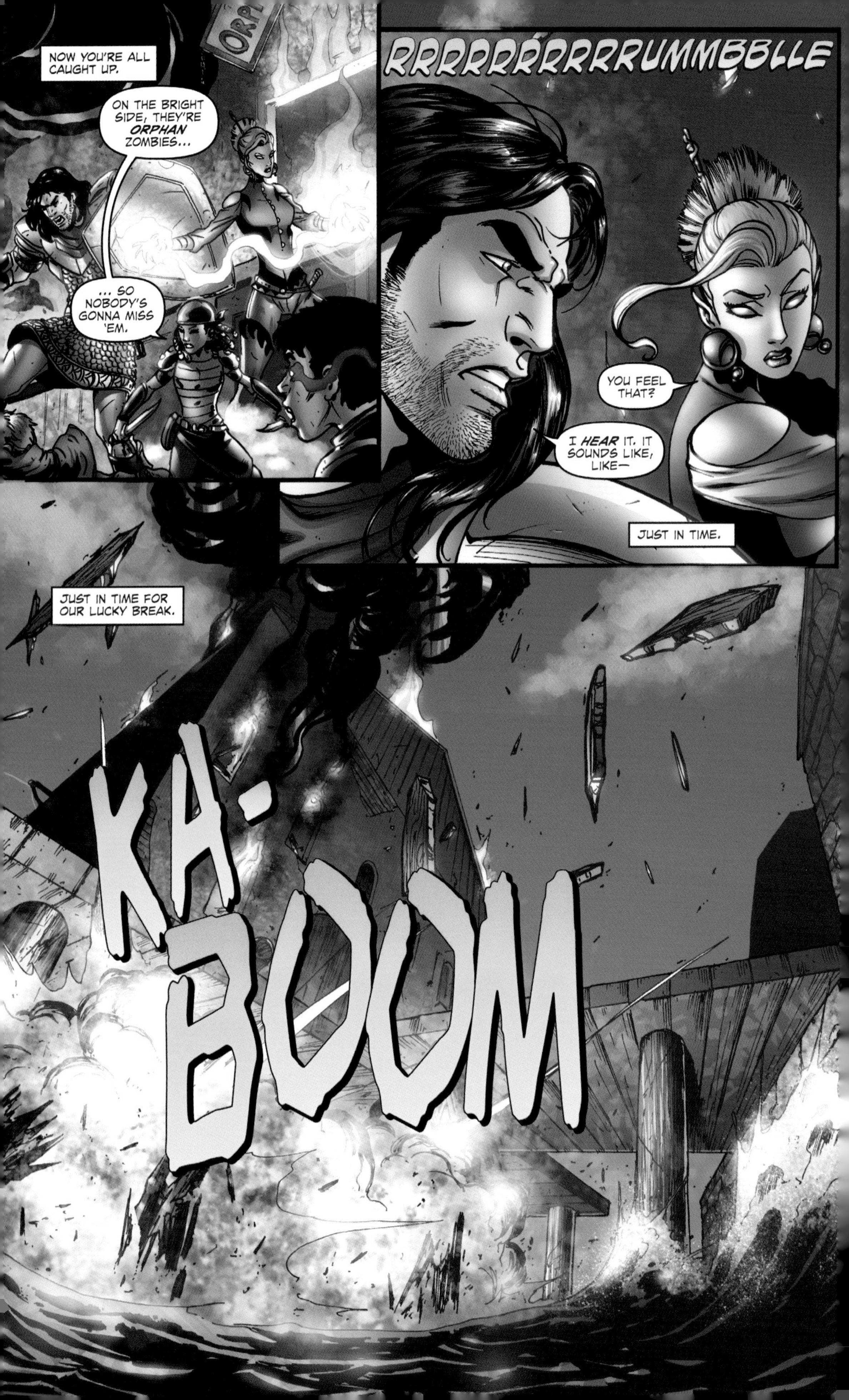
NOW YOU'RE ALL CAUGHT UP.
ON THE BRIGHT SIDE, THEY'RE ORPHAN ZOMBIES...
... SO NOBODY'S GONNA MISS 'EM.
RRRRRRRRRRRUMMBBLLE
YOU FEEL THAT?
I HEAR IT. IT SOUNDS LIKE, LIKE—
JUST IN TIME.
JUST IN TIME FOR OUR LUCKY BREAK.
KA-BOOM

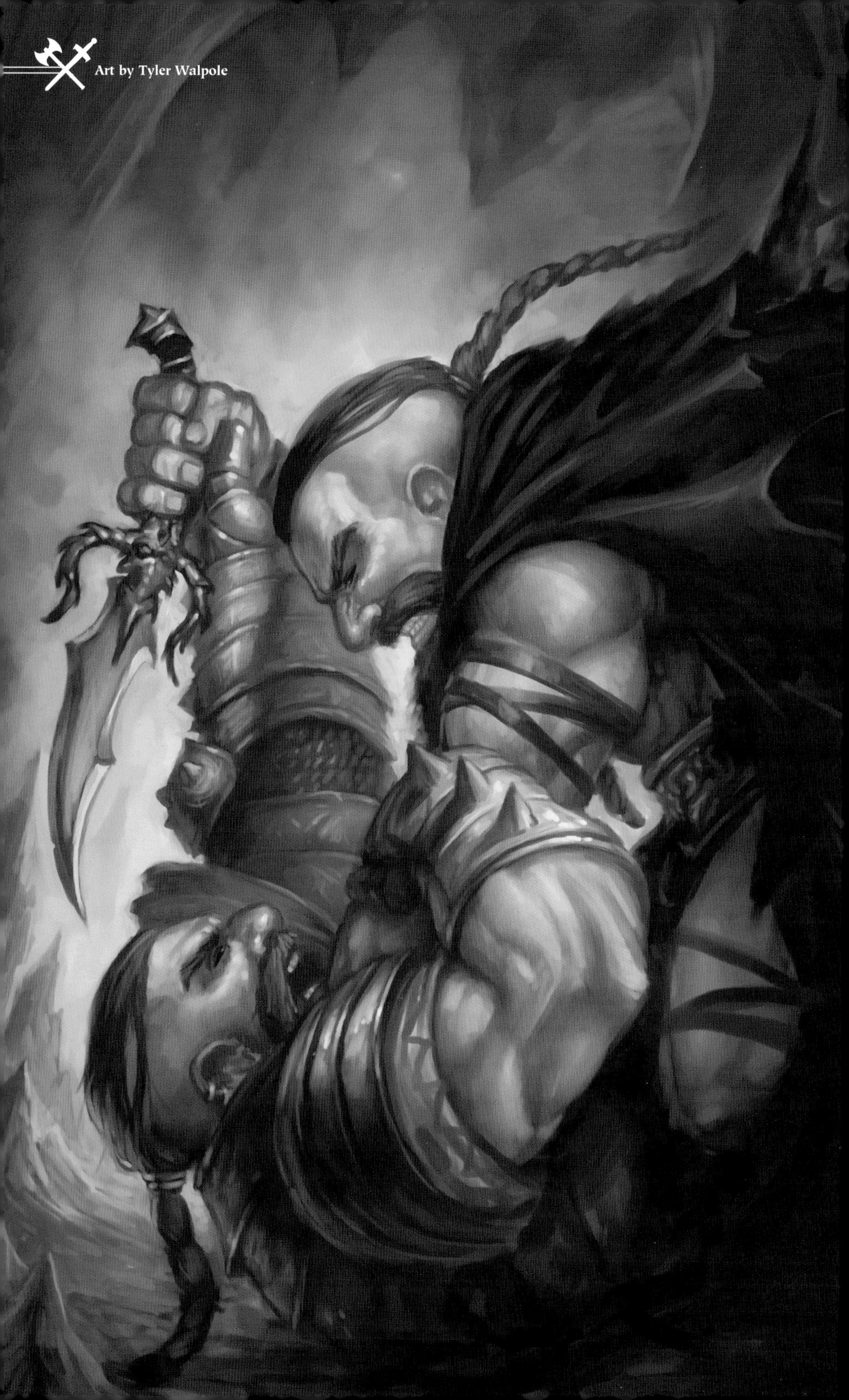

Art by Tyler Walpole

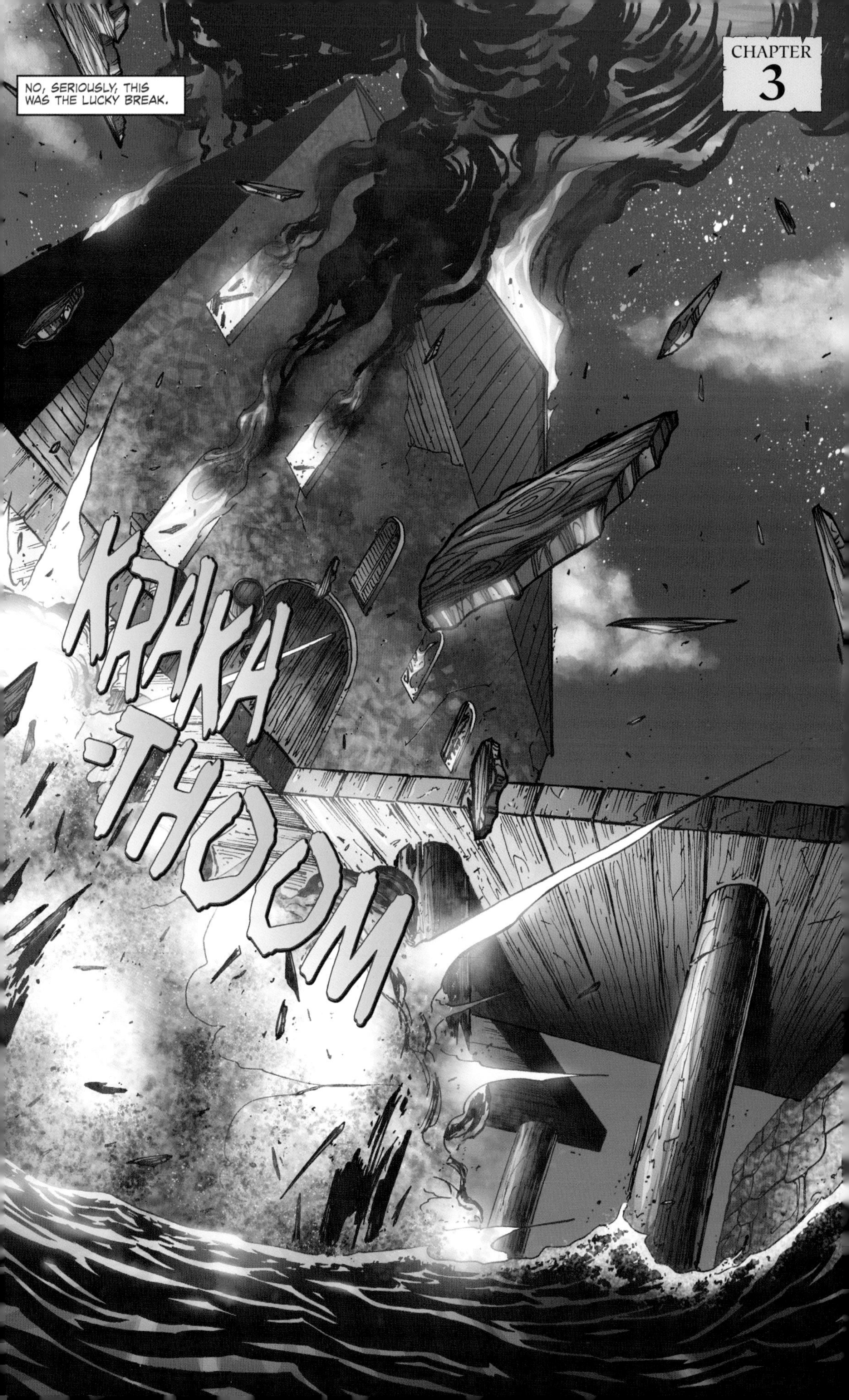
CHAPTER 3
NO, SERIOUSLY, THIS WAS THE LUCKY BREAK.
KRAKA-THOOM

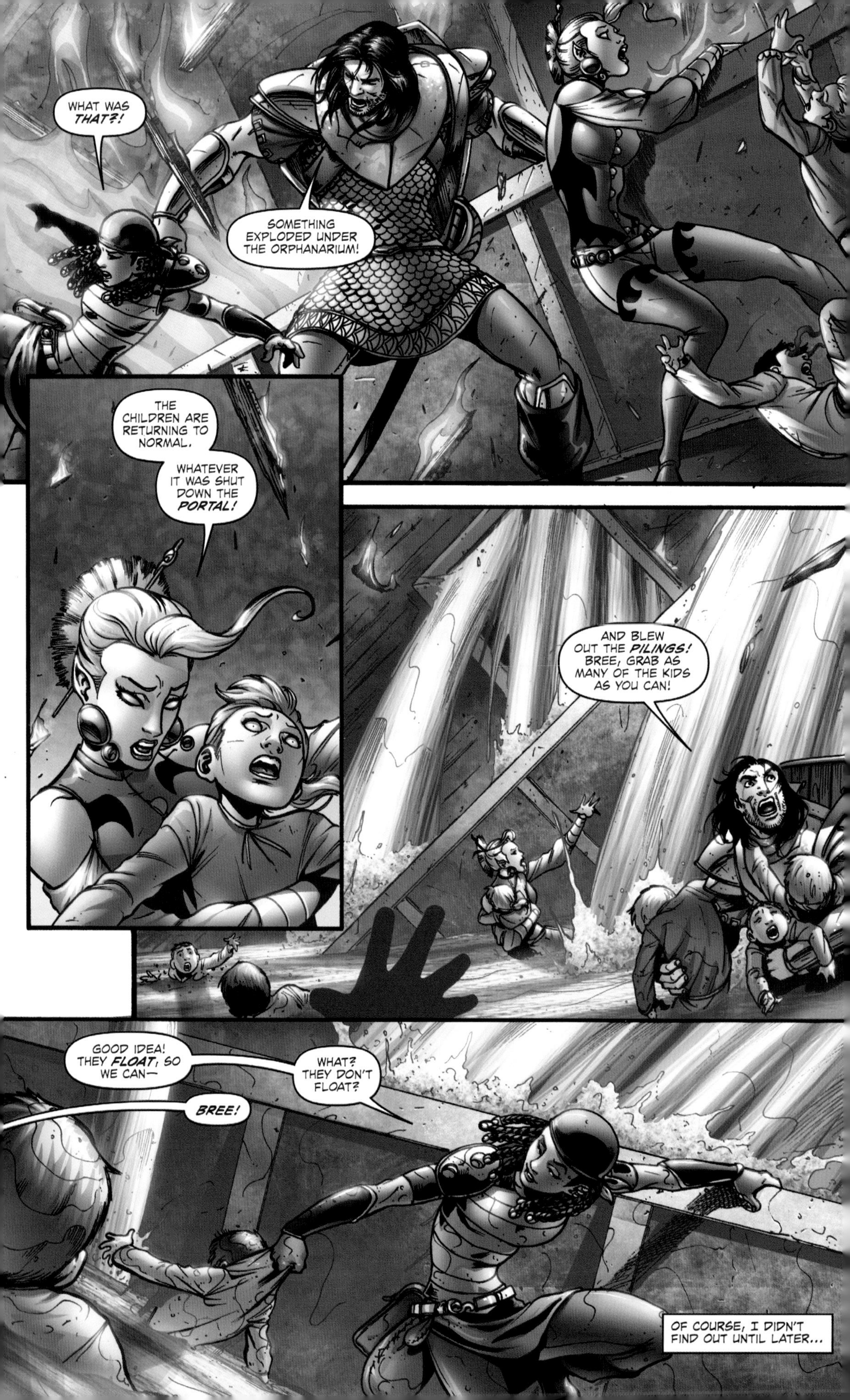
WHAT WAS THAT?!
SOMETHING EXPLODED UNDER THE ORPHANARIUM!
THE CHILDREN ARE RETURNING TO NORMAL.
WHATEVER IT WAS SHUT DOWN THE PORTAL!
AND BLEW OUT THE PILINGS! BREE, GRAB AS MANY OF THE KIDS AS YOU CAN!
GOOD IDEA! THEY FLOAT; SO WE CAN—
WHAT? THEY DON'T FLOAT?
BREE!
OF COURSE, I DIDN'T FIND OUT UNTIL LATER...

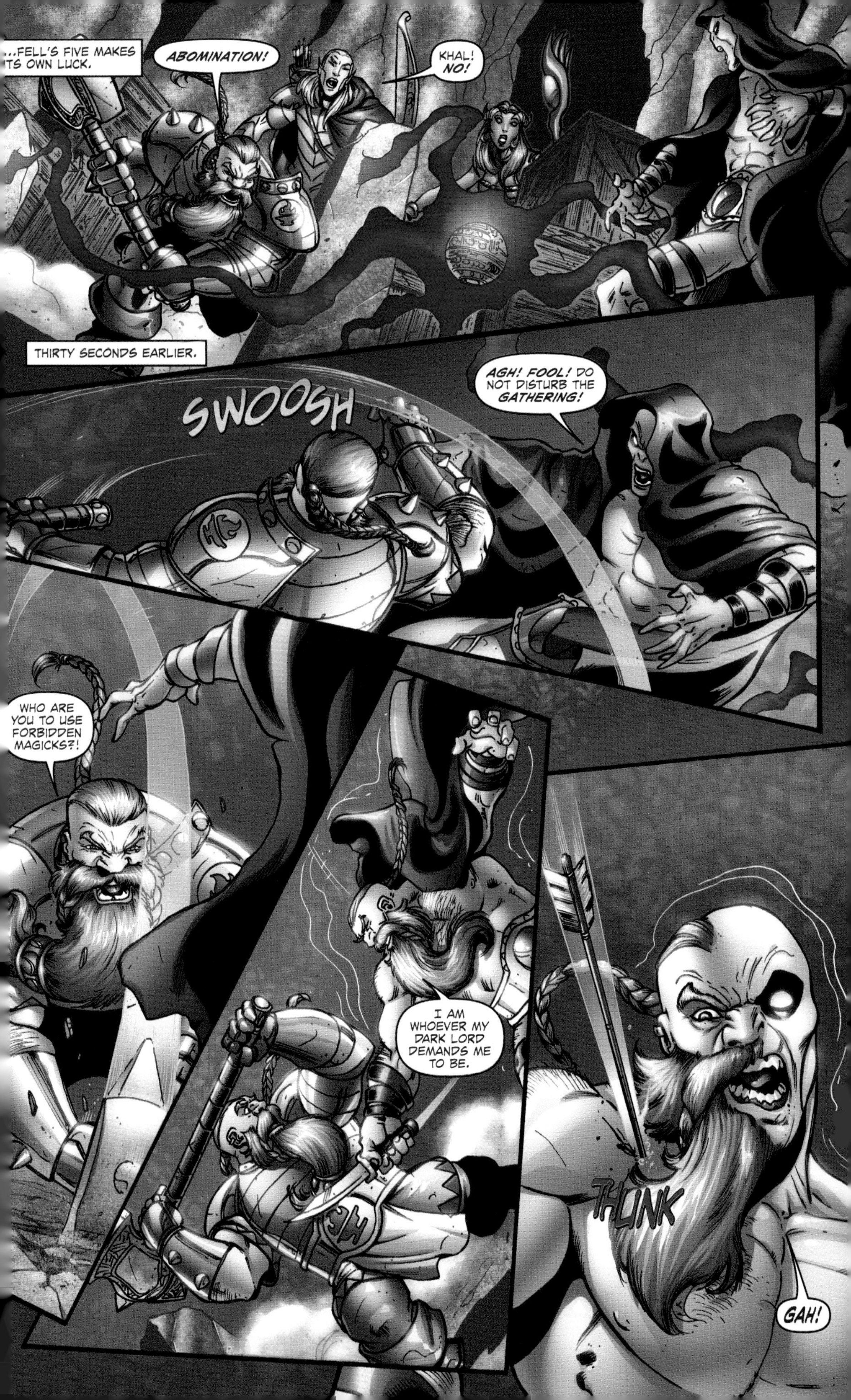
...FELL'S FIVE MAKES
ITS OWN LUCK.
ABOMINATION!
KHAL! NO!
THIRTY SECONDS EARLIER.
SWOOSH
AGH! FOOL! DO NOT DISTURB THE GATHERING!
WHO ARE YOU TO USE FORBIDDEN MAGICKS?!
I AM WHOEVER MY DARK LORD DEMANDS ME TO BE.
THUNK
GAH!

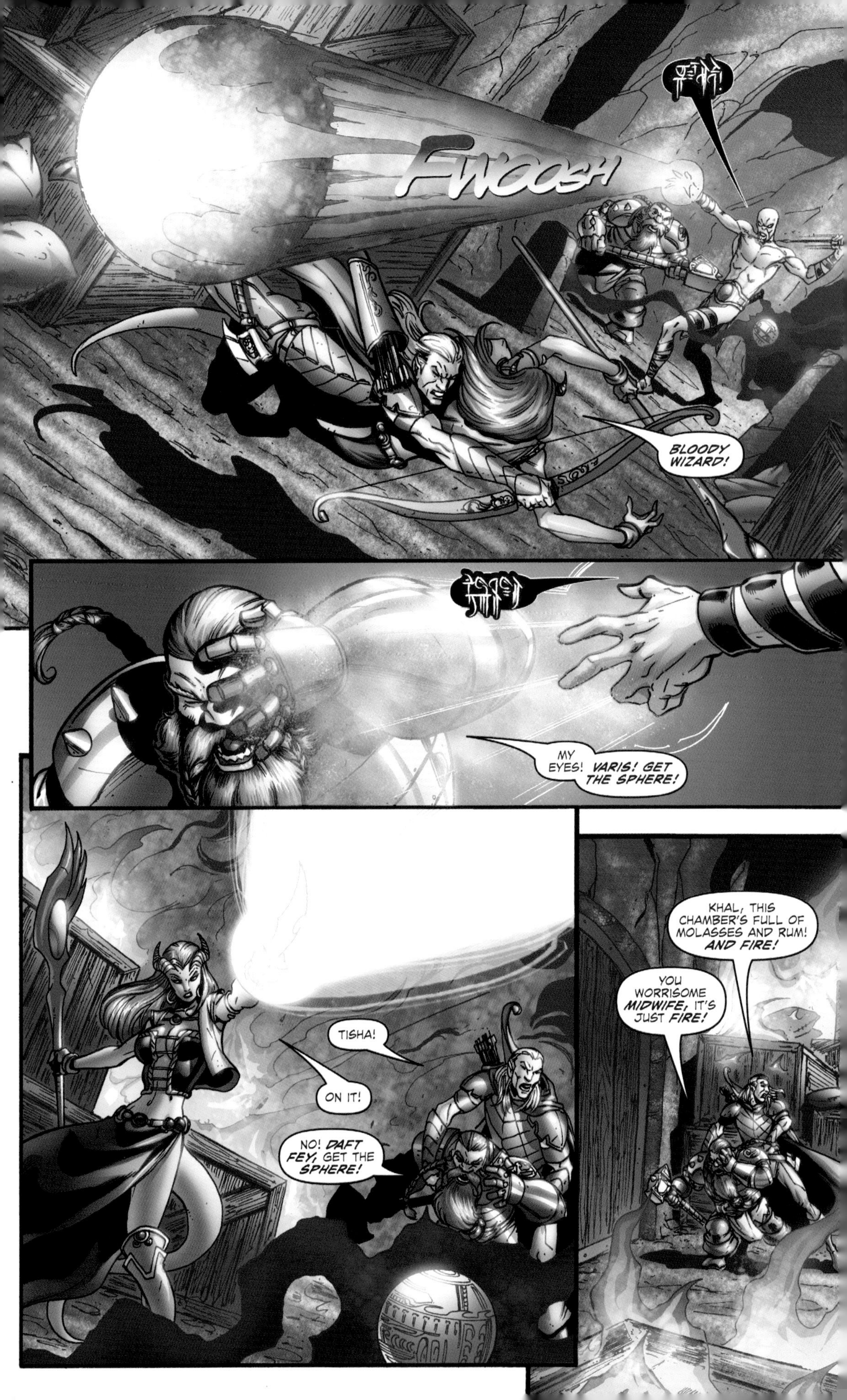
FWOOSH
BLOODY WIZARD!
MY EYES! VARIS! GET THE SPHERE!
TISHA!
ON IT!
NO! DAFT FEY; GET THE SPHERE!
KHAL, THIS CHAMBER'S FULL OF MOLASSES AND RUM! AND FIRE!
YOU WORRISOME MIDWIFE, IT'S JUST FIRE!

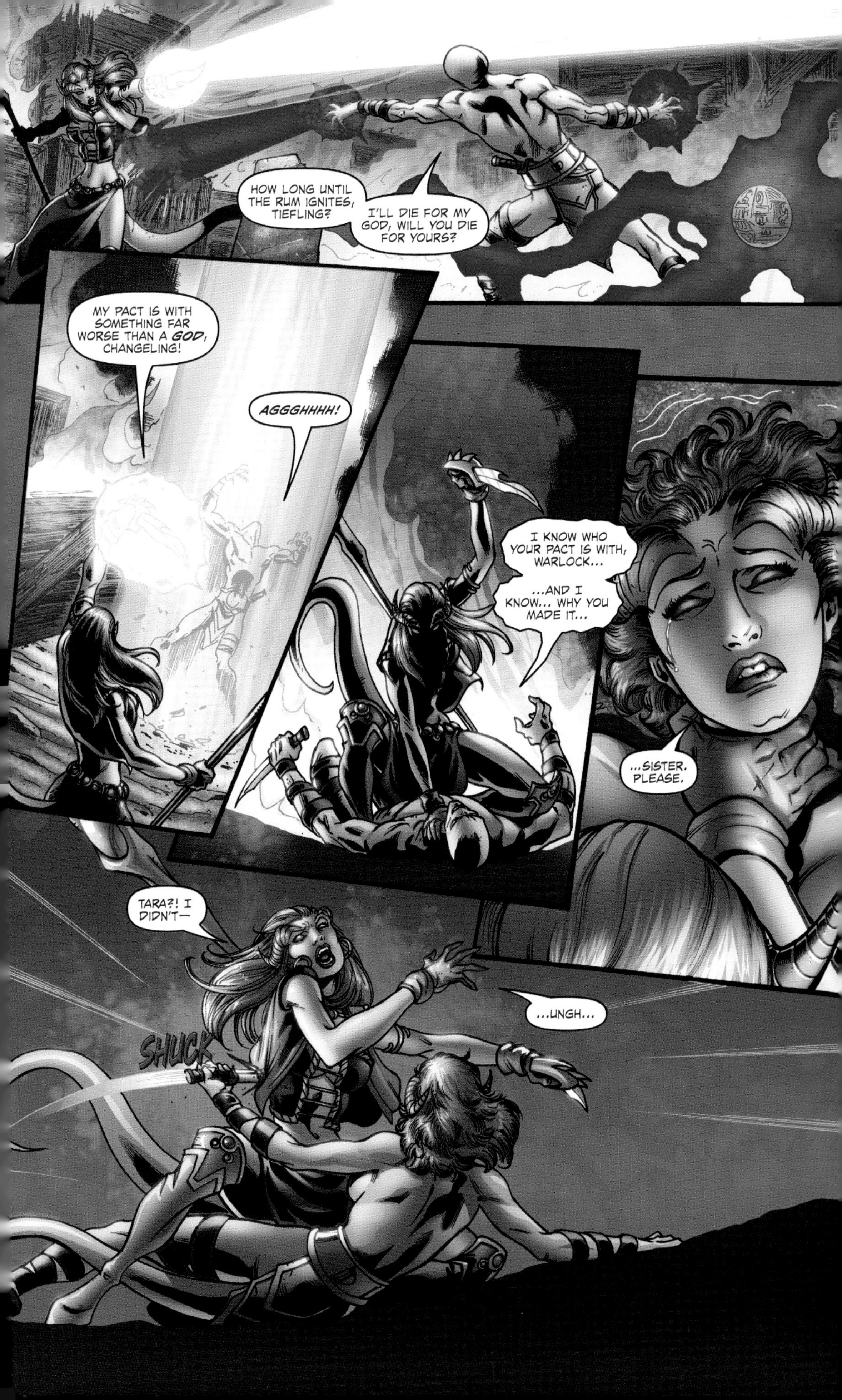

HOW LONG UNTIL THE RUM IGNITES, TIEFLING?
I'LL DIE FOR MY GOD, WILL YOU DIE FOR YOURS?
MY PACT IS WITH SOMETHING FAR WORSE THAN A *GOD*, CHANGELING!
AGGGHHHH!
I KNOW WHO YOUR PACT IS WITH, WARLOCK...
...AND I KNOW... WHY YOU MADE IT...
...SISTER. PLEASE.
TARA?! I DIDN'T—
...UNGH...
SHUCK

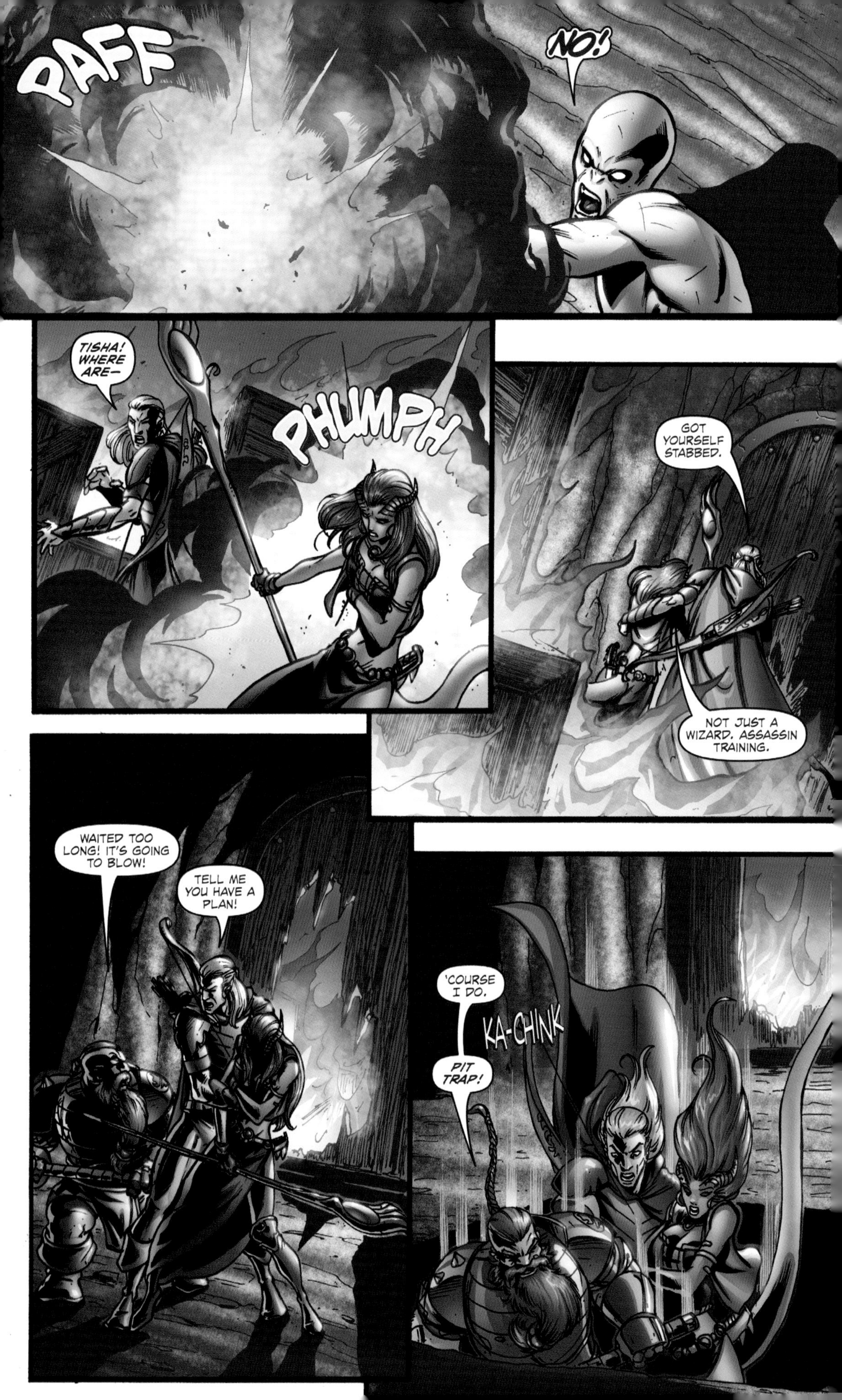
PAFF
NO!
TISHA! WHERE ARE—
PHUMPH
GOT YOURSELF STABBED.
NOT JUST A WIZARD. ASSASSIN TRAINING.
WAITED TOO LONG! IT'S GOING TO BLOW!
TELL ME YOU HAVE A PLAN!
'COURSE I DO.
KA-CHINK
PIT TRAP!

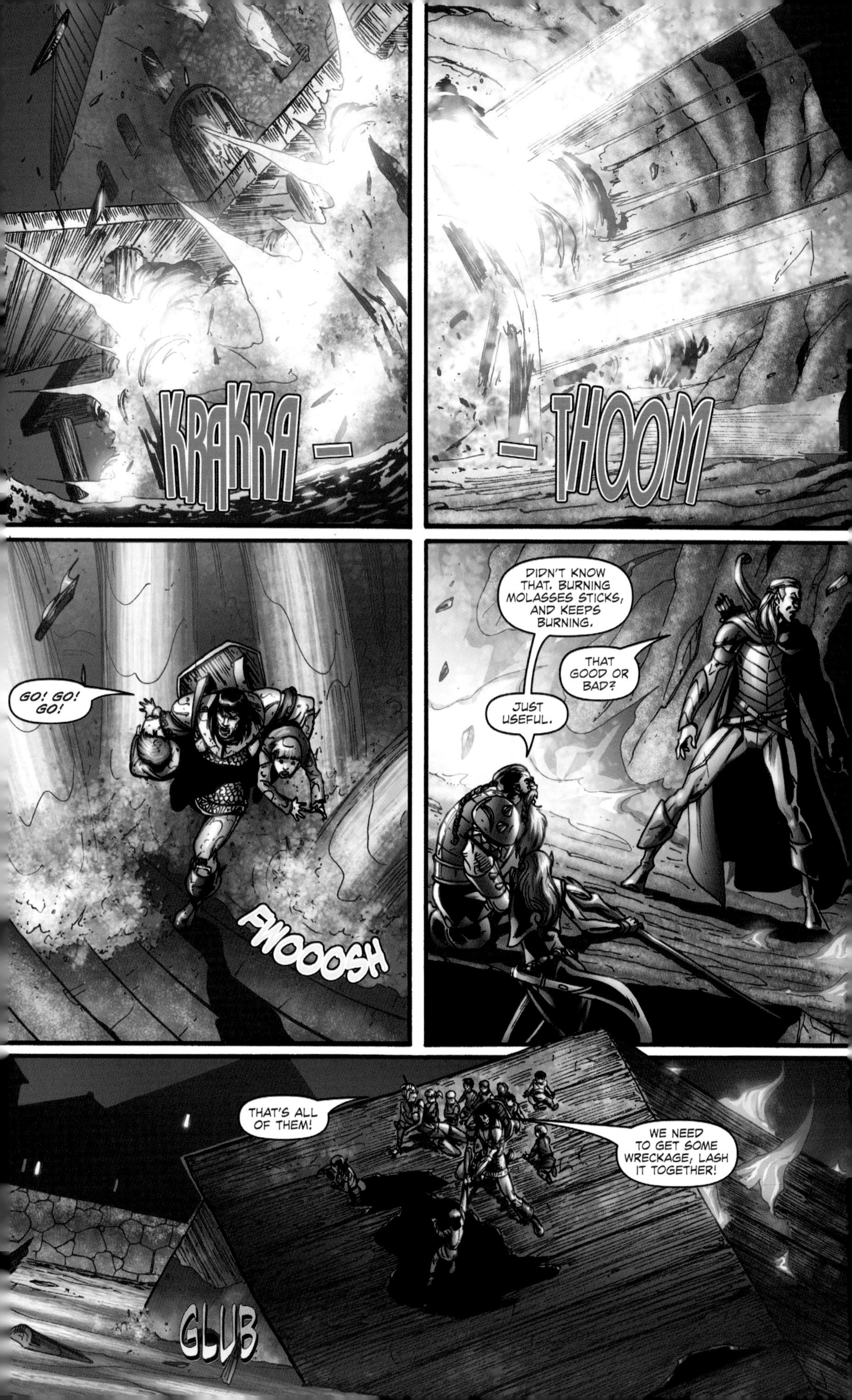
KRAKKA –
– THOOM
GO! GO! GO!
FWOOOSH
DIDN'T KNOW THAT. BURNING MOLASSES STICKS, AND KEEPS BURNING.
THAT GOOD OR BAD?
JUST USEFUL.
THAT'S ALL OF THEM!
WE NEED TO GET SOME WRECKAGE, LASH IT TOGETHER!
GLUB

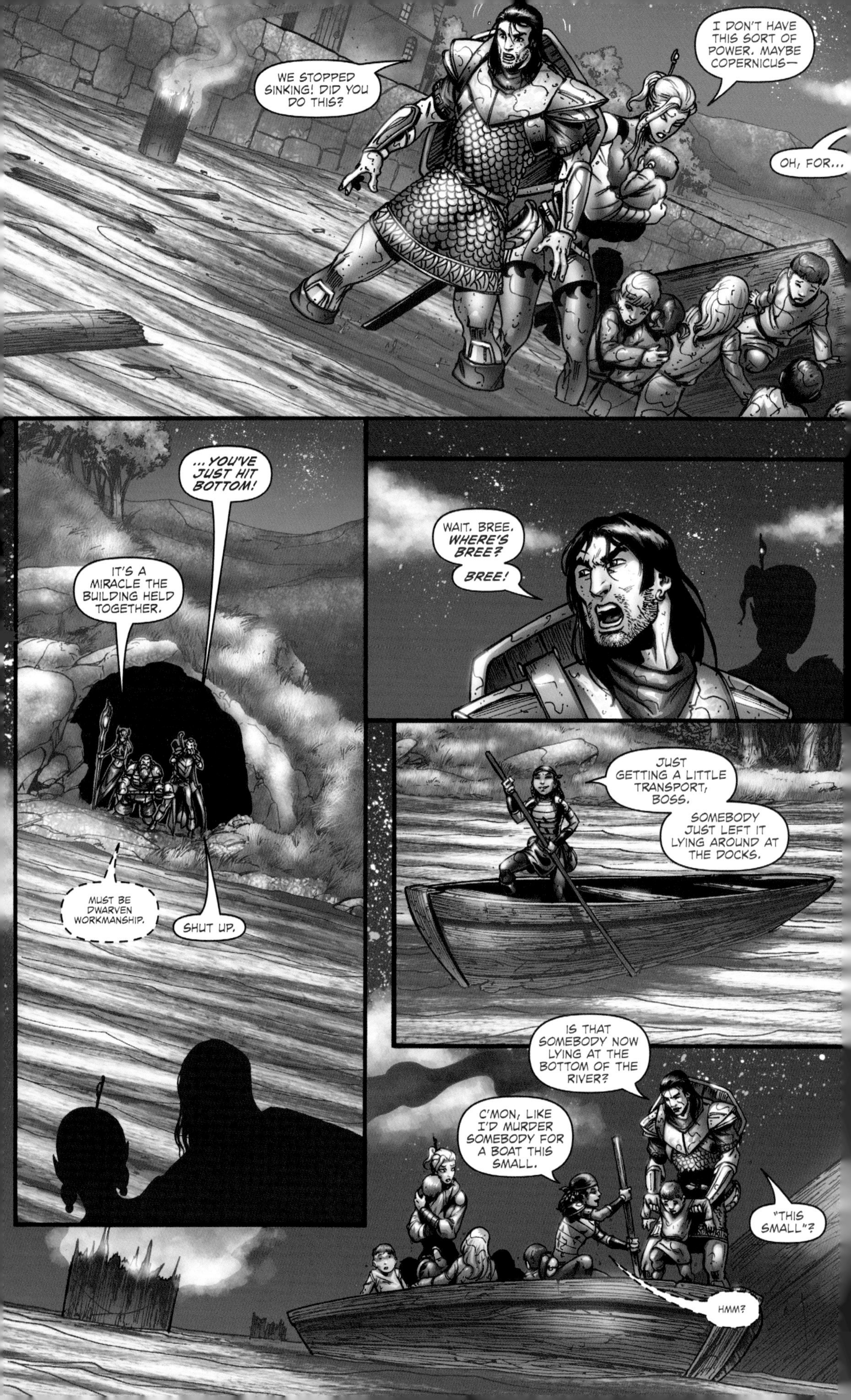
WE STOPPED SINKING! DID YOU DO THIS?
I DON'T HAVE THIS SORT OF POWER. MAYBE COPERNICUS—
OH, FOR...
...YOU'VE JUST HIT BOTTOM!
IT'S A MIRACLE THE BUILDING HELD TOGETHER.
MUST BE DWARVEN WORKMANSHIP.
SHUT UP.
WAIT. BREE. WHERE'S BREE?
BREE!
JUST GETTING A LITTLE TRANSPORT, BOSS.
SOMEBODY JUST LEFT IT LYING AROUND AT THE DOCKS.
IS THAT SOMEBODY NOW LYING AT THE BOTTOM OF THE RIVER?
C'MON, LIKE I'D MURDER SOMEBODY FOR A BOAT THIS SMALL.
"THIS SMALL"?
HMM?

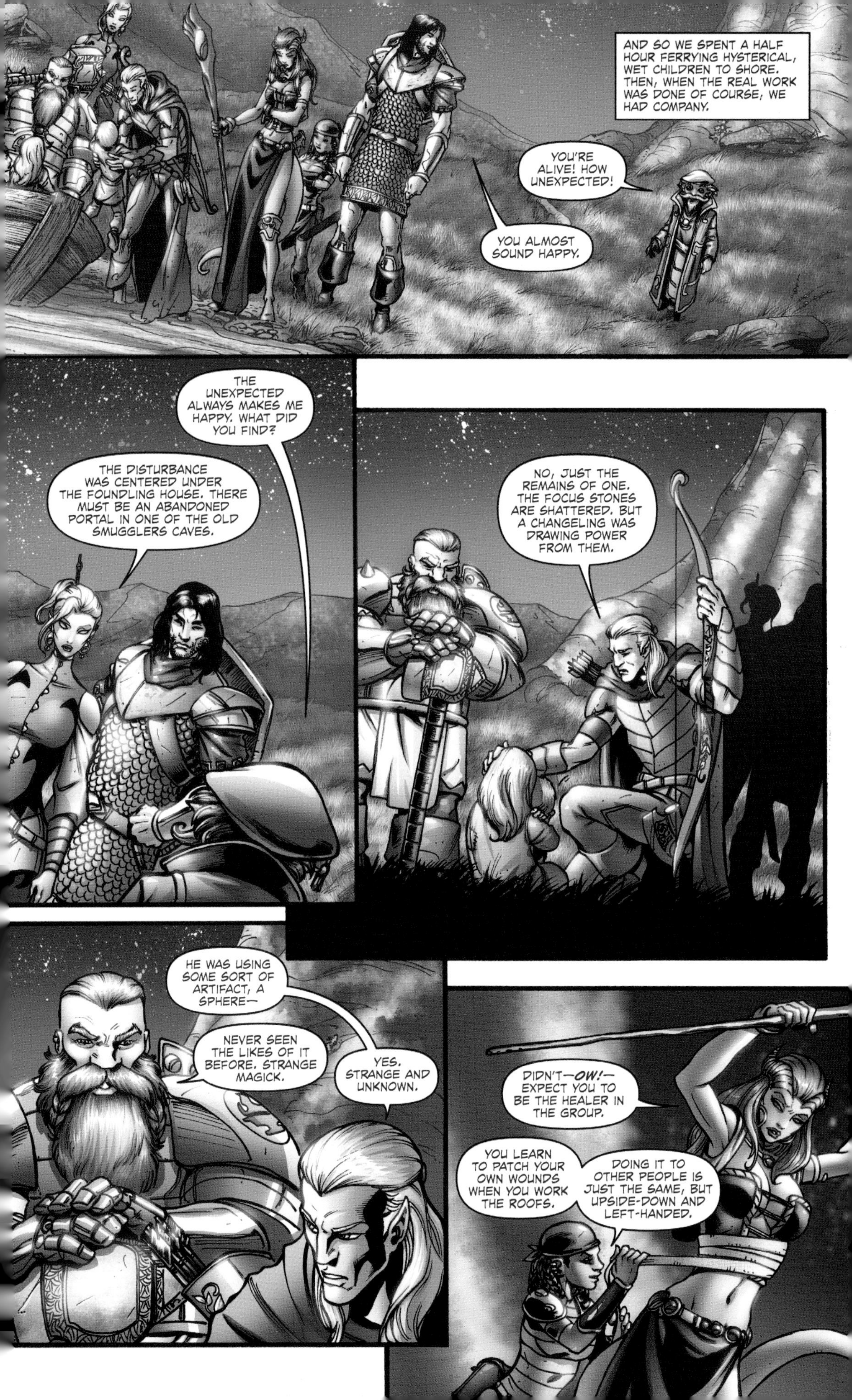
AND SO WE SPENT A HALF HOUR FERRYING HYSTERICAL, WET CHILDREN TO SHORE. THEN, WHEN THE REAL WORK WAS DONE OF COURSE, WE HAD COMPANY.
YOU'RE ALIVE! HOW UNEXPECTED!
YOU ALMOST SOUND HAPPY.
THE UNEXPECTED ALWAYS MAKES ME HAPPY. WHAT DID YOU FIND?
THE DISTURBANCE WAS CENTERED UNDER THE FOUNDLING HOUSE. THERE MUST BE AN ABANDONED PORTAL IN ONE OF THE OLD SMUGGLERS CAVES.
NO, JUST THE REMAINS OF ONE. THE FOCUS STONES ARE SHATTERED. BUT A CHANGELING WAS DRAWING POWER FROM THEM.
HE WAS USING SOME SORT OF ARTIFACT, A SPHERE—
NEVER SEEN THE LIKES OF IT BEFORE. STRANGE MAGICK.
YES. STRANGE AND UNKNOWN.
DIDN'T—OW!— EXPECT YOU TO BE THE HEALER IN THE GROUP.
YOU LEARN TO PATCH YOUR OWN WOUNDS WHEN YOU WORK THE ROOFS.
DOING IT TO OTHER PEOPLE IS JUST THE SAME, BUT UPSIDE-DOWN AND LEFT-HANDED.

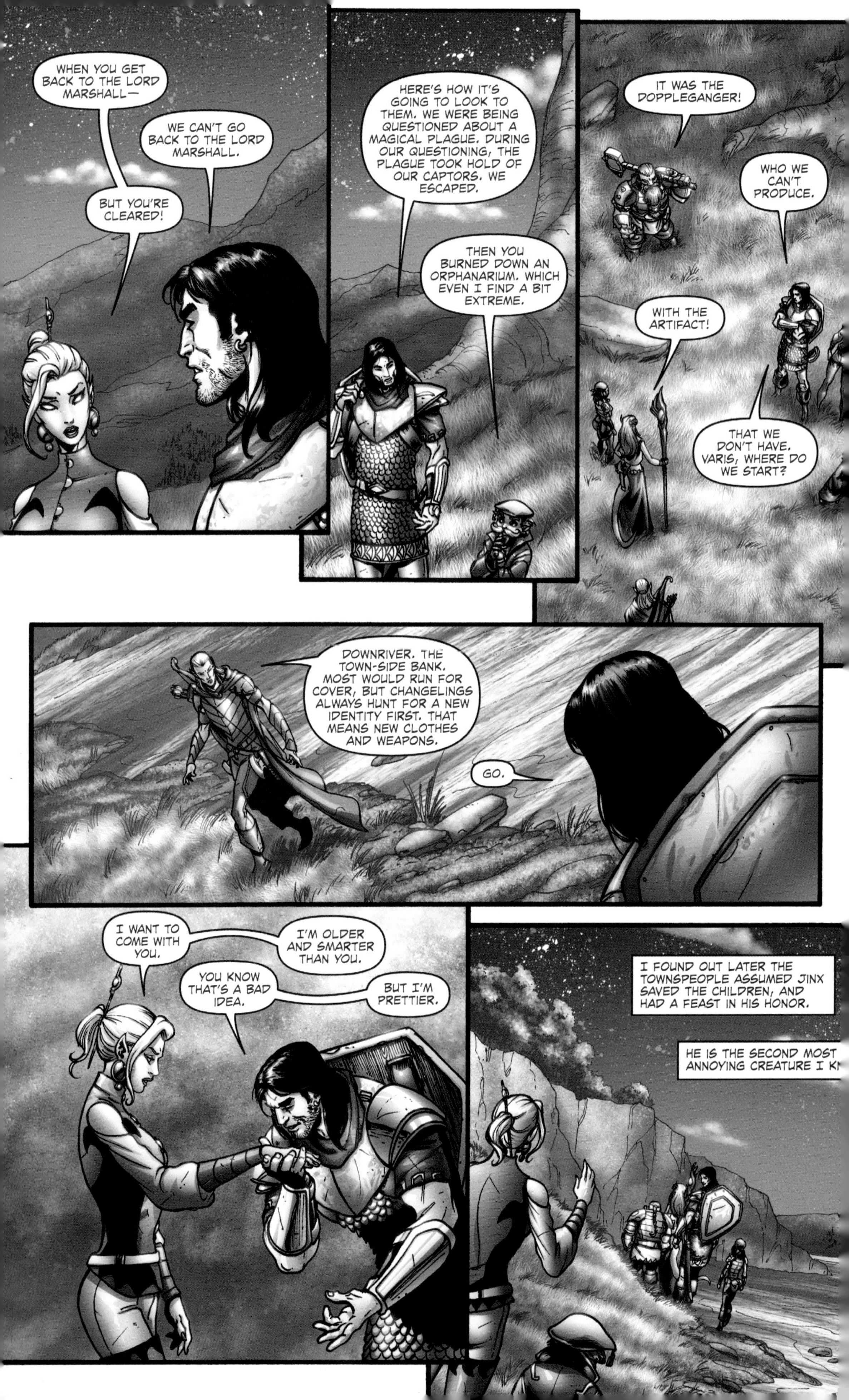
WHEN YOU GET BACK TO THE LORD MARSHALL—
WE CAN'T GO BACK TO THE LORD MARSHALL.
BUT YOU'RE CLEARED!
HERE'S HOW IT'S GOING TO LOOK TO THEM. WE WERE BEING QUESTIONED ABOUT A MAGICAL PLAGUE. DURING OUR QUESTIONING, THE PLAGUE TOOK HOLD OF OUR CAPTORS. WE ESCAPED.
THEN YOU BURNED DOWN AN ORPHANARIUM. WHICH EVEN I FIND A BIT EXTREME.
IT WAS THE DOPPLEGANGER!
WHO WE CAN'T PRODUCE.
WITH THE ARTIFACT!
THAT WE DON'T HAVE. VARIS, WHERE DO WE START?
DOWNRIVER. THE TOWN-SIDE BANK. MOST WOULD RUN FOR COVER, BUT CHANGELINGS ALWAYS HUNT FOR A NEW IDENTITY FIRST. THAT MEANS NEW CLOTHES AND WEAPONS.
GO.
I WANT TO COME WITH YOU.
I'M OLDER AND SMARTER THAN YOU.
YOU KNOW THAT'S A BAD IDEA.
BUT I'M PRETTIER.
I FOUND OUT LATER THE TOWNSPEOPLE ASSUMED JINX SAVED THE CHILDREN, AND HAD A FEAST IN HIS HONOR.
HE IS THE SECOND MOST ANNOYING CREATURE I K

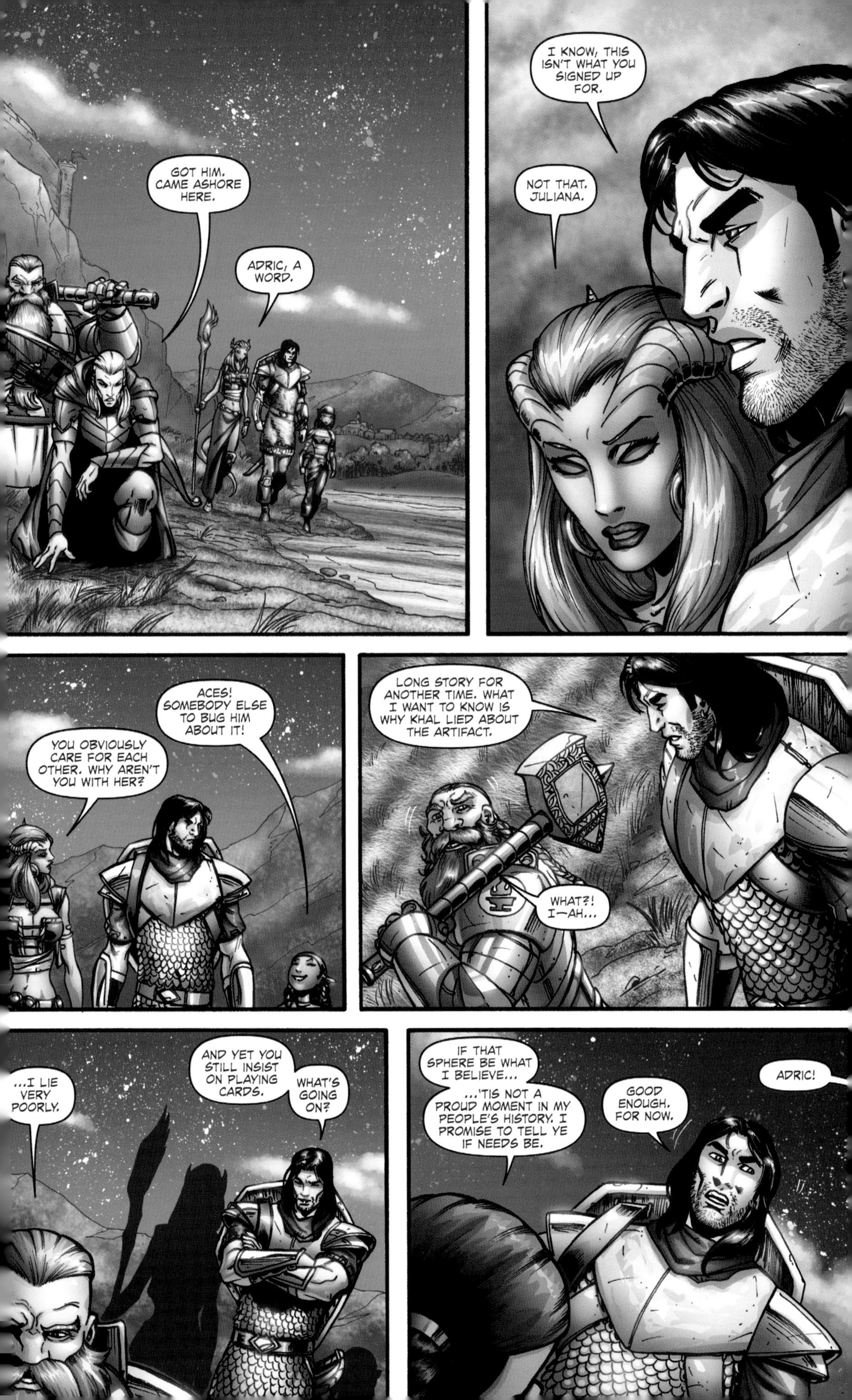
GOT HIM. CAME ASHORE HERE.
ADRIC, A WORD.
I KNOW; THIS ISN'T WHAT YOU SIGNED UP FOR.
NOT THAT. JULIANA.
YOU OBVIOUSLY CARE FOR EACH OTHER. WHY AREN'T YOU WITH HER?
ACES! SOMEBODY ELSE TO BUG HIM ABOUT IT!
LONG STORY FOR ANOTHER TIME. WHAT I WANT TO KNOW IS WHY KHAL LIED ABOUT THE ARTIFACT.
WHAT?! I—AH...
...I LIE VERY POORLY.
AND YET YOU STILL INSIST ON PLAYING CARDS.
WHAT'S GOING ON?
IF THAT SPHERE BE WHAT I BELIEVE...
...'TIS NOT A PROUD MOMENT IN MY PEOPLE'S HISTORY. I PROMISE TO TELL YE IF NEEDS BE.
GOOD ENOUGH. FOR NOW.
ADRIC!

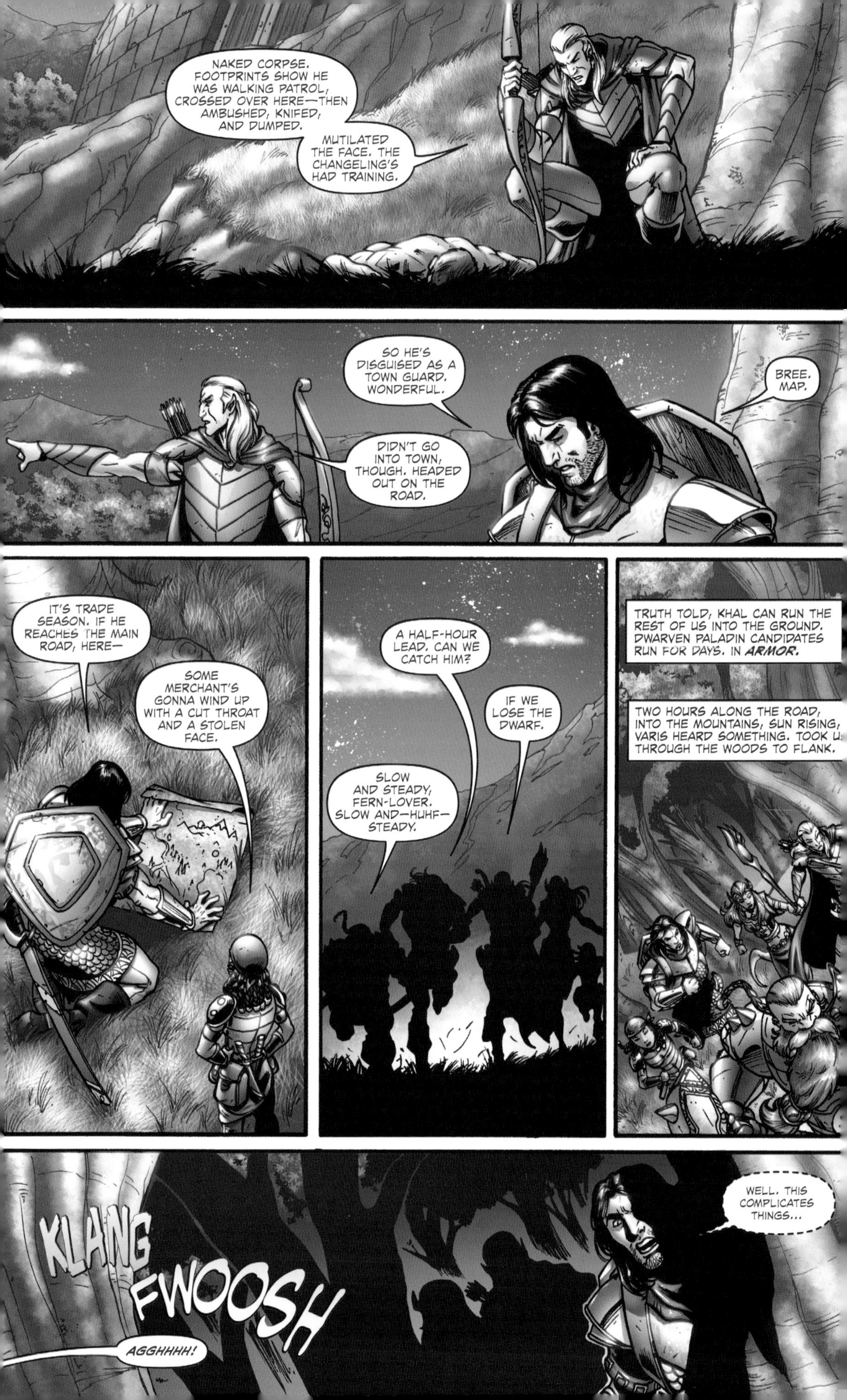
NAKED CORPSE. FOOTPRINTS SHOW HE WAS WALKING PATROL, CROSSED OVER HERE—THEN AMBUSHED, KNIFED, AND DUMPED.
MUTILATED THE FACE. THE CHANGELING'S HAD TRAINING.
SO HE'S DISGUISED AS A TOWN GUARD. WONDERFUL.
DIDN'T GO INTO TOWN, THOUGH. HEADED OUT ON THE ROAD.
BREE. MAP.
IT'S TRADE SEASON. IF HE REACHES THE MAIN ROAD, HERE—
SOME MERCHANT'S GONNA WIND UP WITH A CUT THROAT AND A STOLEN FACE.
A HALF-HOUR LEAD. CAN WE CATCH HIM?
IF WE LOSE THE DWARF.
SLOW AND STEADY, FERN-LOVER. SLOW AND—HUHF—STEADY.
TRUTH TOLD, KHAL CAN RUN THE REST OF US INTO THE GROUND. DWARVEN PALADIN CANDIDATES RUN FOR DAYS. IN *ARMOR.*
TWO HOURS ALONG THE ROAD, INTO THE MOUNTAINS, SUN RISING, VARIS HEARD SOMETHING. TOOK US THROUGH THE WOODS TO FLANK.
KLANG
FWOOSH
AGGHHHH!
WELL. THIS COMPLICATES THINGS...

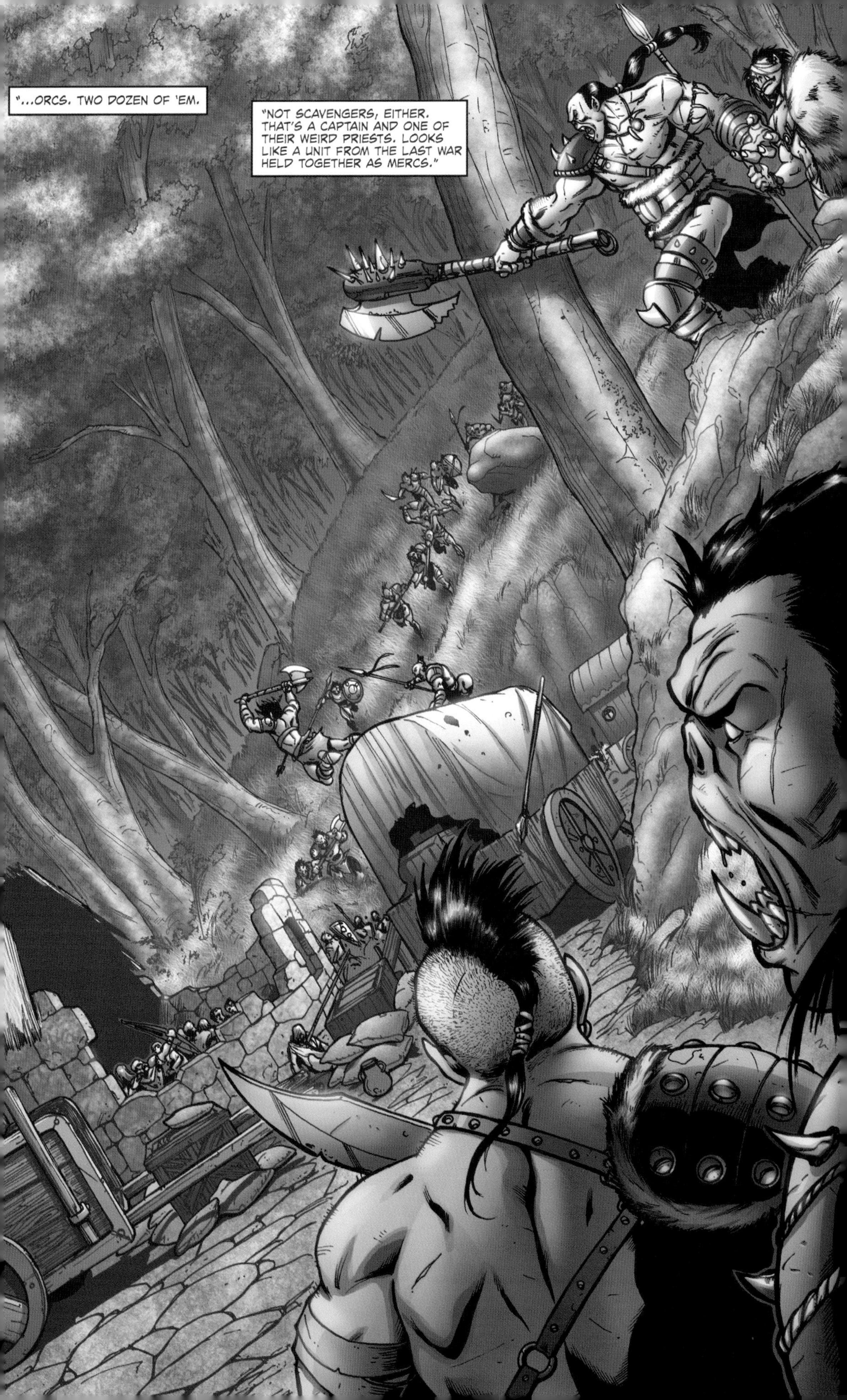
"...ORCS. TWO DOZEN OF 'EM.
"NOT SCAVENGERS, EITHER. THAT'S A CAPTAIN AND ONE OF THEIR WEIRD PRIESTS. LOOKS LIKE A UNIT FROM THE LAST WAR HELD TOGETHER AS MERCS."

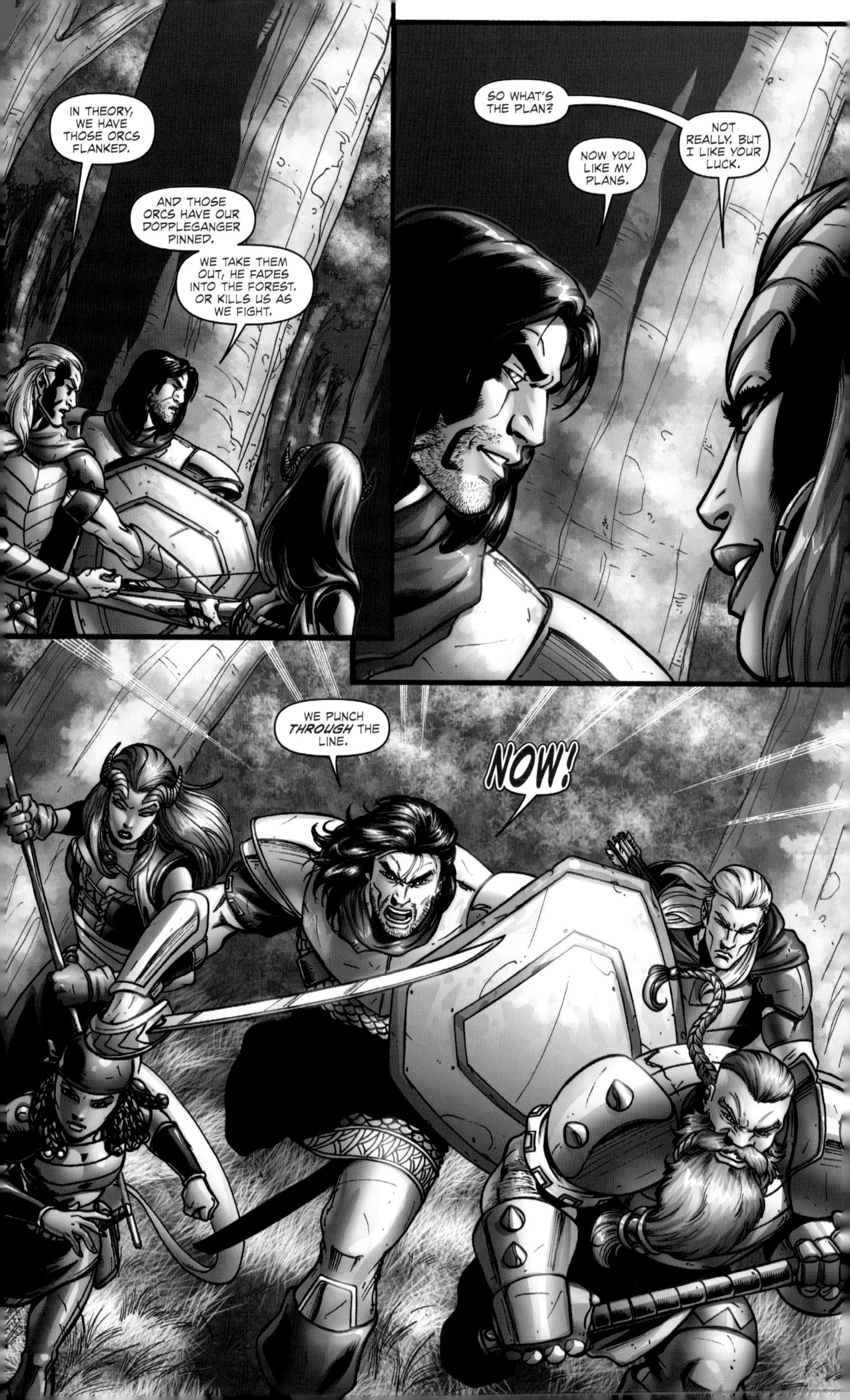

IN THEORY, WE HAVE THOSE ORCS FLANKED.
AND THOSE ORCS HAVE OUR DOPPLEGANGER PINNED.
WE TAKE THEM OUT, HE FADES INTO THE FOREST. OR KILLS US AS WE FIGHT.
SO WHAT'S THE PLAN?
NOW YOU LIKE MY PLANS.
NOT REALLY. BUT I LIKE YOUR LUCK.
WE PUNCH *THROUGH* THE LINE.
NOW!

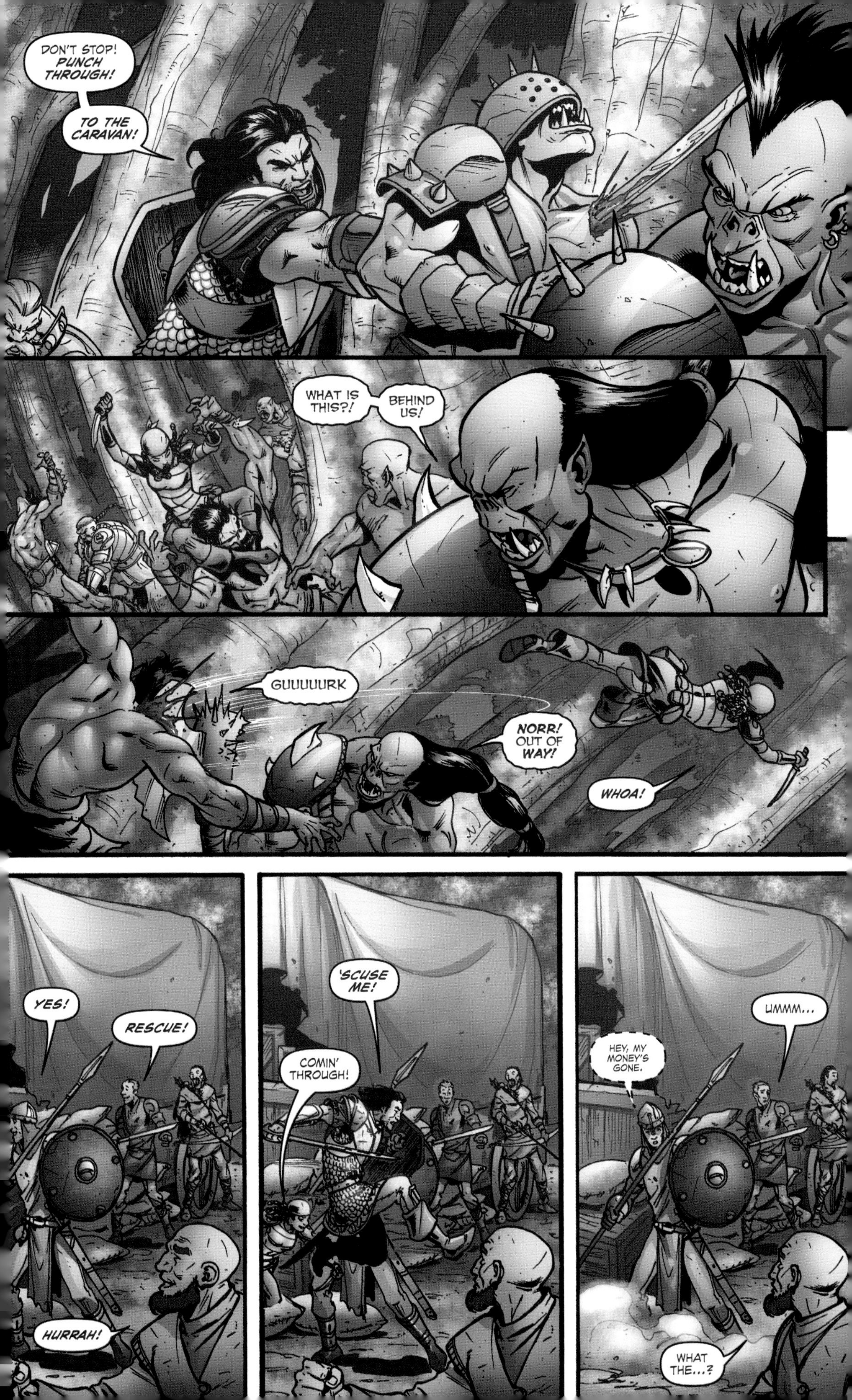
DON'T STOP! PUNCH THROUGH!
TO THE CARAVAN!
WHAT IS THIS?!
BEHIND US!
GUUUUURK
NORR! OUT OF WAY!
WHOA!
YES!
RESCUE!
HURRAH!
'SCUSE ME!
COMIN' THROUGH!
UMMM...
HEY, MY MONEY'S GONE.
WHAT THE...?

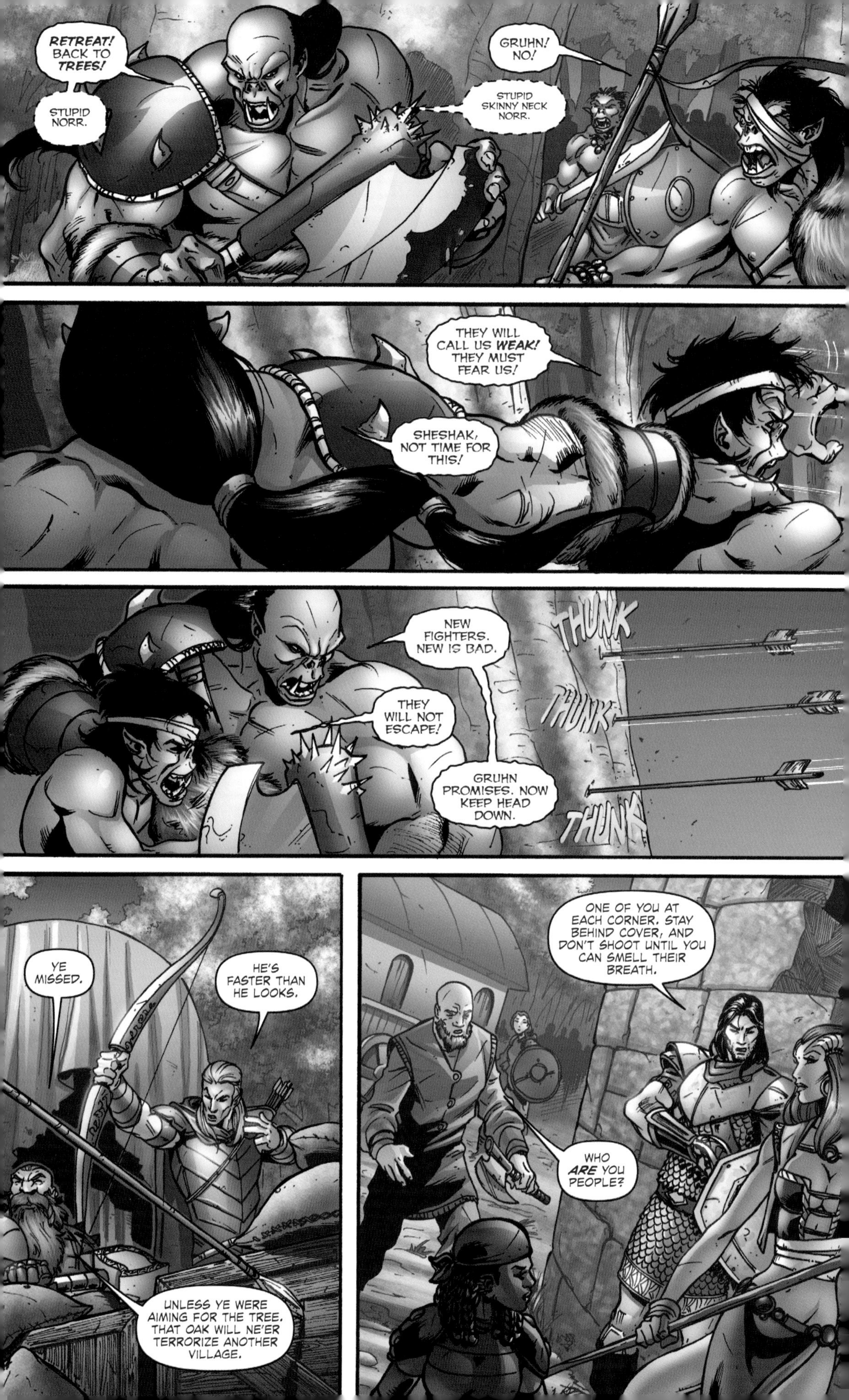
RETREAT! BACK TO TREES!
STUPID NORR.
GRUHN! NO!
STUPID SKINNY NECK NORR.
THEY WILL CALL US WEAK! THEY MUST FEAR US!
SHESHAK, NOT TIME FOR THIS!
NEW FIGHTERS. NEW IS BAD.
THEY WILL NOT ESCAPE!
GRUHN PROMISES. NOW KEEP HEAD DOWN.
THUNK
THUNK
THUNK
YE MISSED.
HE'S FASTER THAN HE LOOKS.
UNLESS YE WERE AIMING FOR THE TREE. THAT OAK WILL NE'ER TERRORIZE ANOTHER VILLAGE.
ONE OF YOU AT EACH CORNER. STAY BEHIND COVER, AND DON'T SHOOT UNTIL YOU CAN SMELL THEIR BREATH.
WHO ARE YOU PEOPLE?

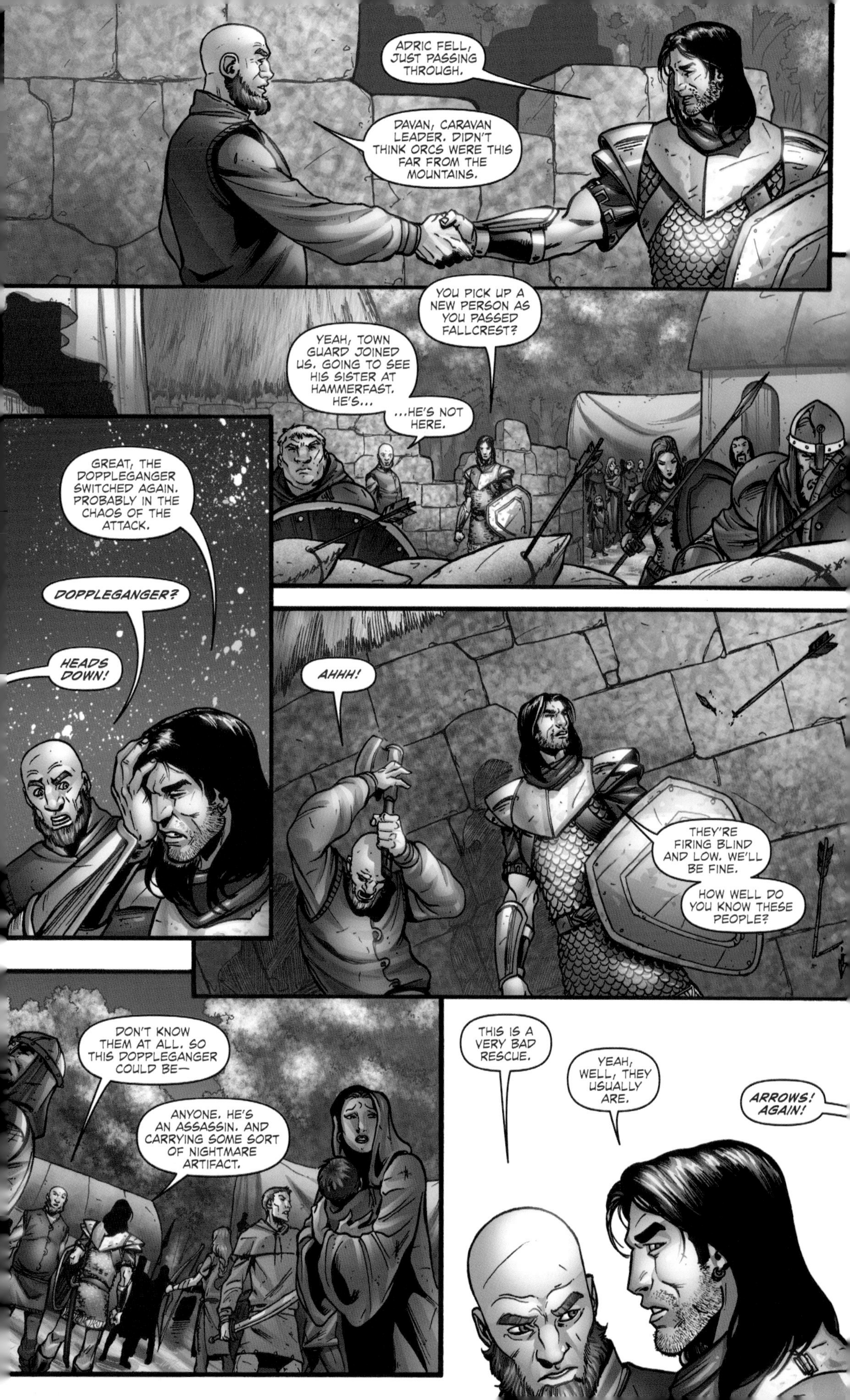
ADRIC FELL, JUST PASSING THROUGH.
DAVAN, CARAVAN LEADER. DIDN'T THINK ORCS WERE THIS FAR FROM THE MOUNTAINS.
YOU PICK UP A NEW PERSON AS YOU PASSED FALLCREST?
YEAH, TOWN GUARD JOINED US. GOING TO SEE HIS SISTER AT HAMMERFAST. HE'S...
...HE'S NOT HERE.
GREAT, THE DOPPLEGANGER SWITCHED AGAIN. PROBABLY IN THE CHAOS OF THE ATTACK.
DOPPLEGANGER?
HEADS DOWN!
AHHH!
THEY'RE FIRING BLIND AND LOW. WE'LL BE FINE.
HOW WELL DO YOU KNOW THESE PEOPLE?
DON'T KNOW THEM AT ALL. SO THIS DOPPLEGANGER COULD BE—
ANYONE. HE'S AN ASSASSIN. AND CARRYING SOME SORT OF NIGHTMARE ARTIFACT.
THIS IS A VERY BAD RESCUE.
YEAH, WELL, THEY USUALLY ARE.
ARROWS! AGAIN!

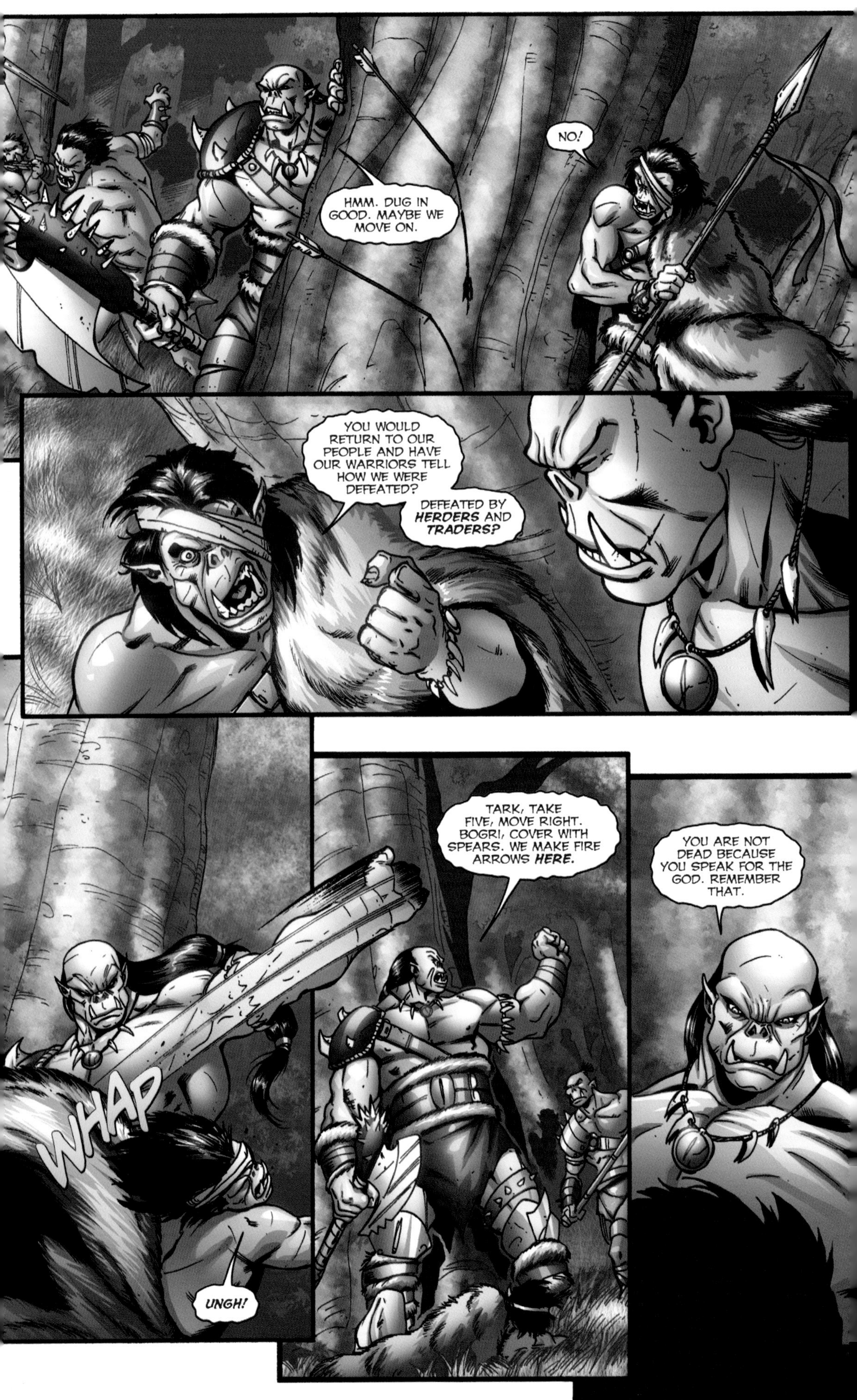
HMM. DUG IN GOOD. MAYBE WE MOVE ON.
NO!
YOU WOULD RETURN TO OUR PEOPLE AND HAVE OUR WARRIORS TELL HOW WE WERE DEFEATED?
DEFEATED BY HERDERS AND TRADERS?
WHAP
UNGH!
TARK, TAKE FIVE, MOVE RIGHT. BOGRI, COVER WITH SPEARS. WE MAKE FIRE ARROWS HERE.
YOU ARE NOT DEAD BECAUSE YOU SPEAK FOR THE GOD. REMEMBER THAT.

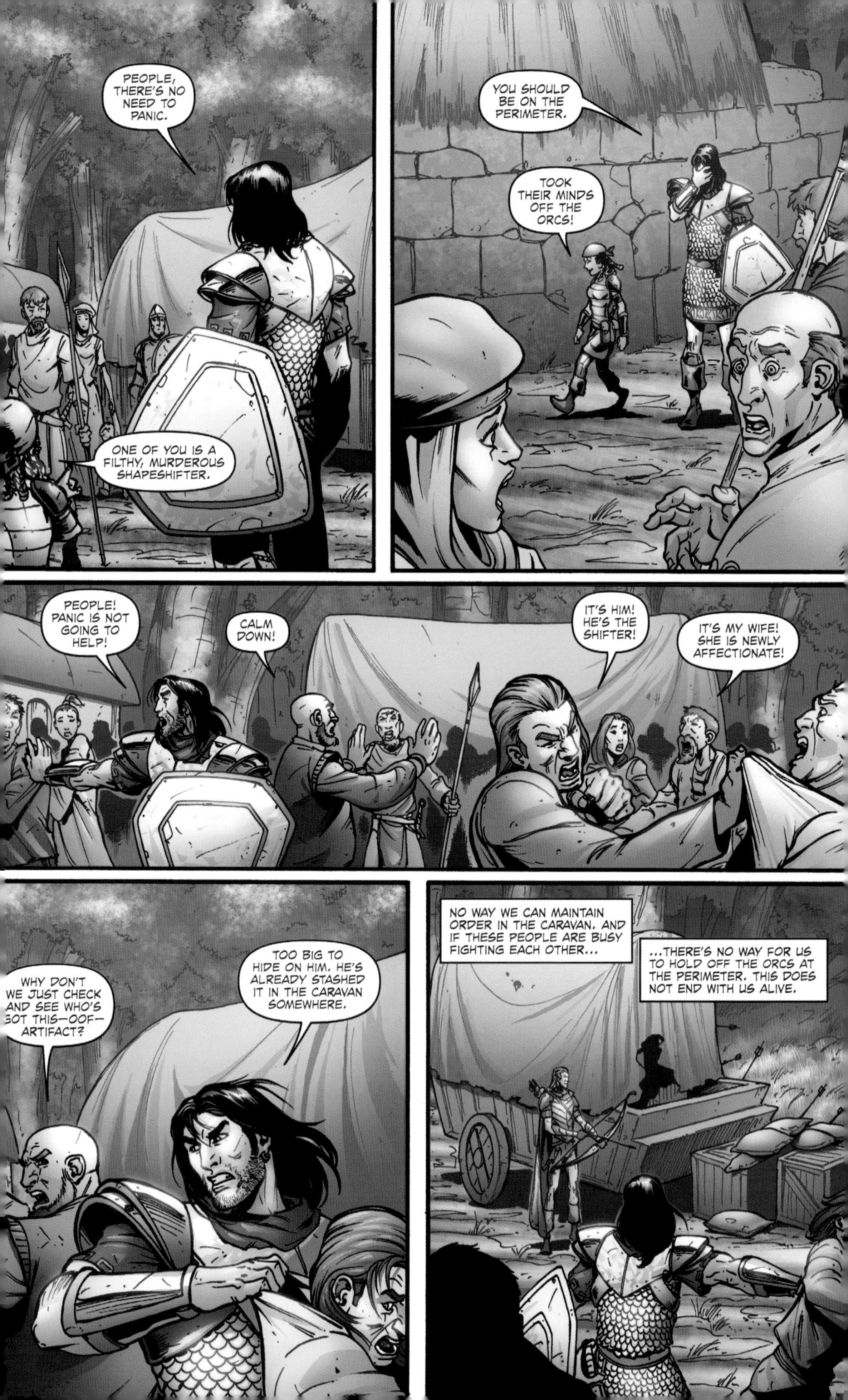
PEOPLE, THERE'S NO NEED TO PANIC.
ONE OF YOU IS A FILTHY, MURDEROUS SHAPESHIFTER.
YOU SHOULD BE ON THE PERIMETER.
TOOK THEIR MINDS OFF THE ORCS!
PEOPLE! PANIC IS NOT GOING TO HELP!
CALM DOWN!
IT'S HIM! HE'S THE SHIFTER!
IT'S MY WIFE! SHE IS NEWLY AFFECTIONATE!
WHY DON'T WE JUST CHECK AND SEE WHO'S GOT THIS—OOF—ARTIFACT?
TOO BIG TO HIDE ON HIM. HE'S ALREADY STASHED IT IN THE CARAVAN SOMEWHERE.
NO WAY WE CAN MAINTAIN ORDER IN THE CARAVAN. AND IF THESE PEOPLE ARE BUSY FIGHTING EACH OTHER...
...THERE'S NO WAY FOR US TO HOLD OFF THE ORCS AT THE PERIMETER. THIS DOES NOT END WITH US ALIVE.

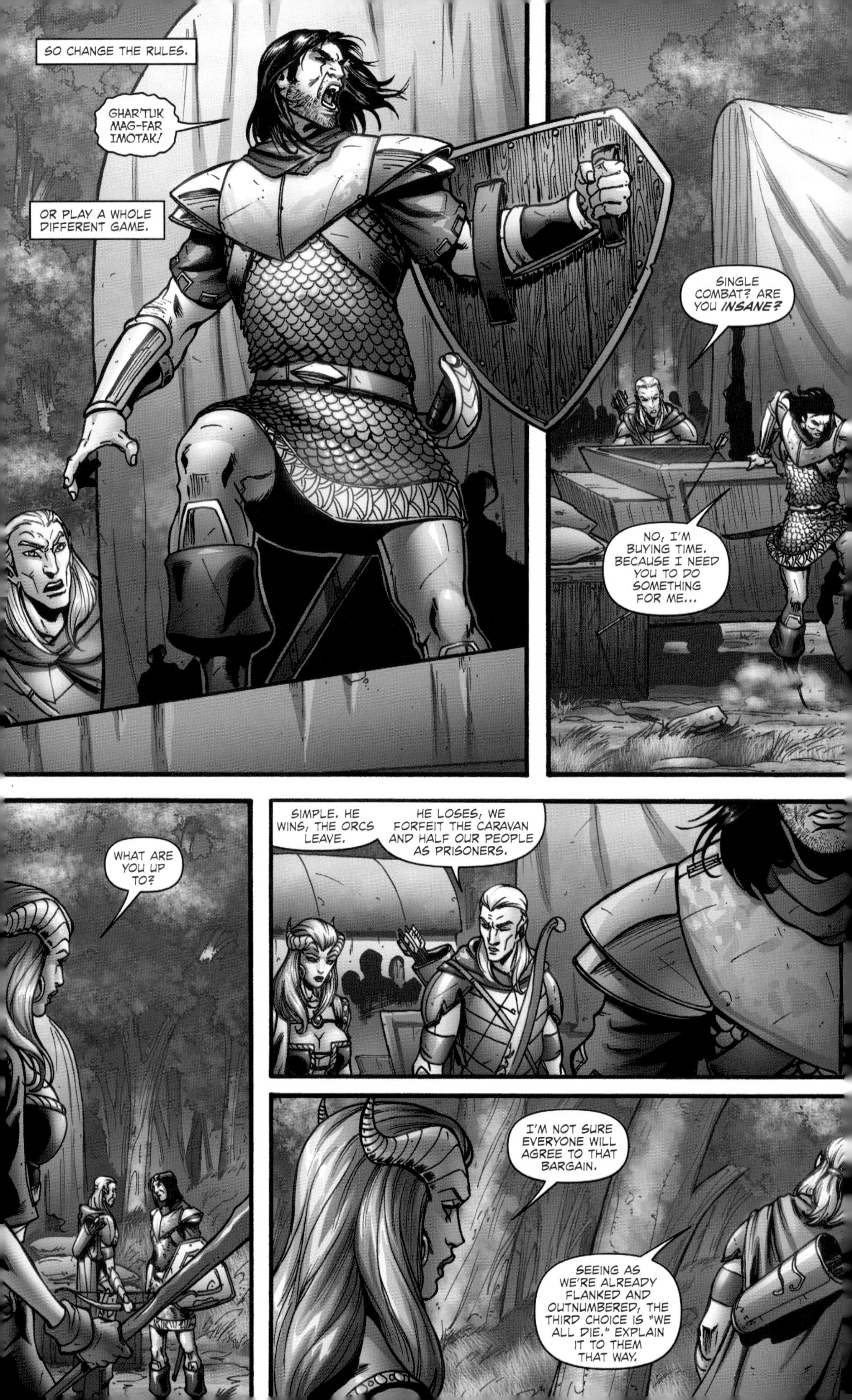
SO CHANGE THE RULES.
GHAR'TUK MAG-FAR IMOTAK!
OR PLAY A WHOLE DIFFERENT GAME.
SINGLE COMBAT? ARE YOU *INSANE?*
NO, I'M BUYING TIME. BECAUSE I NEED YOU TO DO SOMETHING FOR ME...
WHAT ARE YOU UP TO?
SIMPLE. HE WINS, THE ORCS LEAVE.
HE LOSES, WE FORFEIT THE CARAVAN AND HALF OUR PEOPLE AS PRISONERS.
I'M NOT SURE EVERYONE WILL AGREE TO THAT BARGAIN.
SEEING AS WE'RE ALREADY FLANKED AND OUTNUMBERED, THE THIRD CHOICE IS "WE ALL DIE." EXPLAIN IT TO THEM THAT WAY.

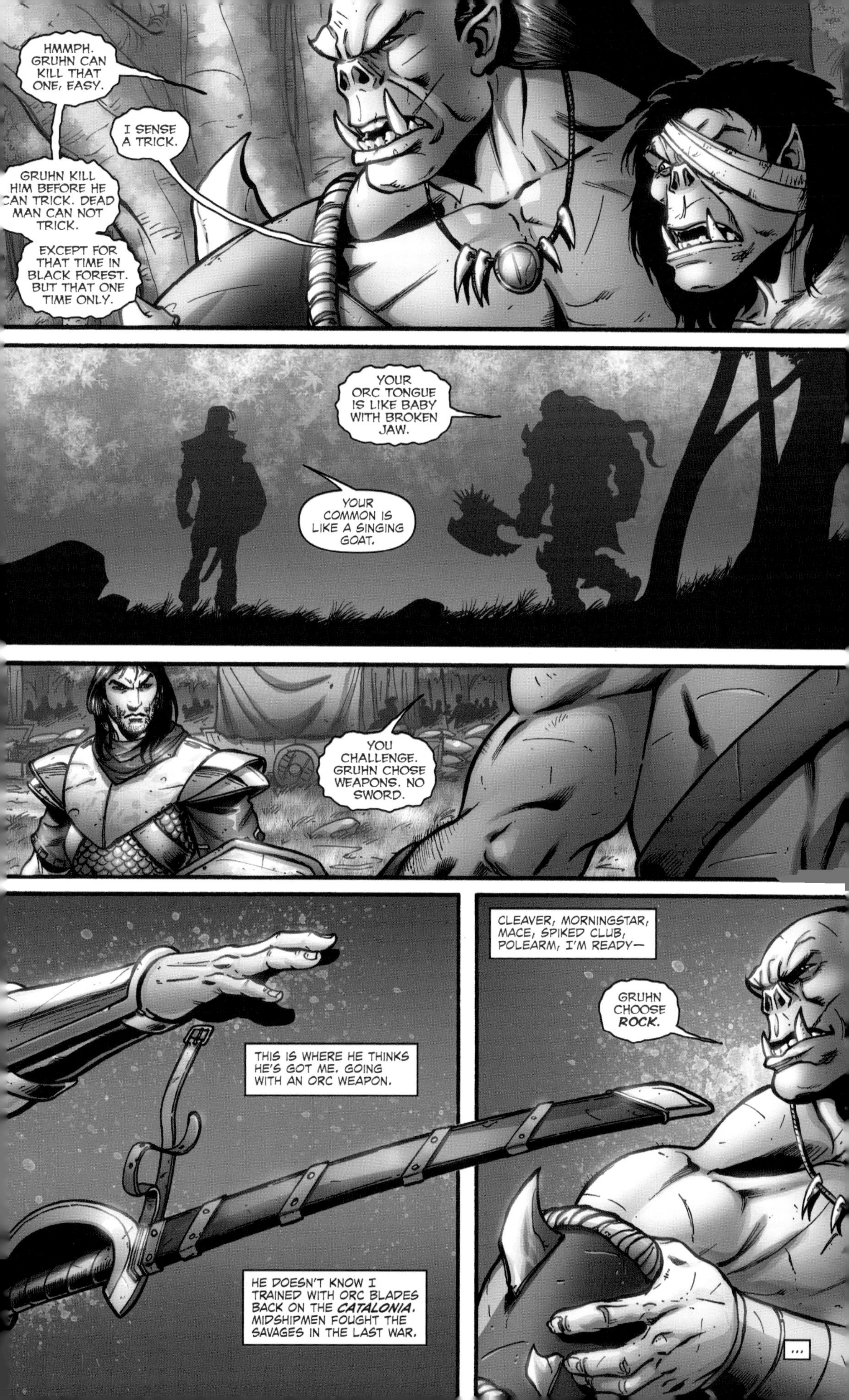
HMMPH. GRUHN CAN KILL THAT ONE, EASY.
I SENSE A TRICK.
GRUHN KILL HIM BEFORE HE CAN TRICK. DEAD MAN CAN NOT TRICK.
EXCEPT FOR THAT TIME IN BLACK FOREST. BUT THAT ONE TIME ONLY.
YOUR ORC TONGUE IS LIKE BABY WITH BROKEN JAW.
YOUR COMMON IS LIKE A SINGING GOAT.
YOU CHALLENGE. GRUHN CHOSE WEAPONS. NO SWORD.
THIS IS WHERE HE THINKS HE'S GOT ME. GOING WITH AN ORC WEAPON.
HE DOESN'T KNOW I TRAINED WITH ORC BLADES BACK ON THE *CATALONIA*. MIDSHIPMEN FOUGHT THE SAVAGES IN THE LAST WAR.
CLEAVER, MORNINGSTAR, MACE, SPIKED CLUB, POLEARM, I'M READY—
GRUHN CHOOSE ***ROCK***.
...

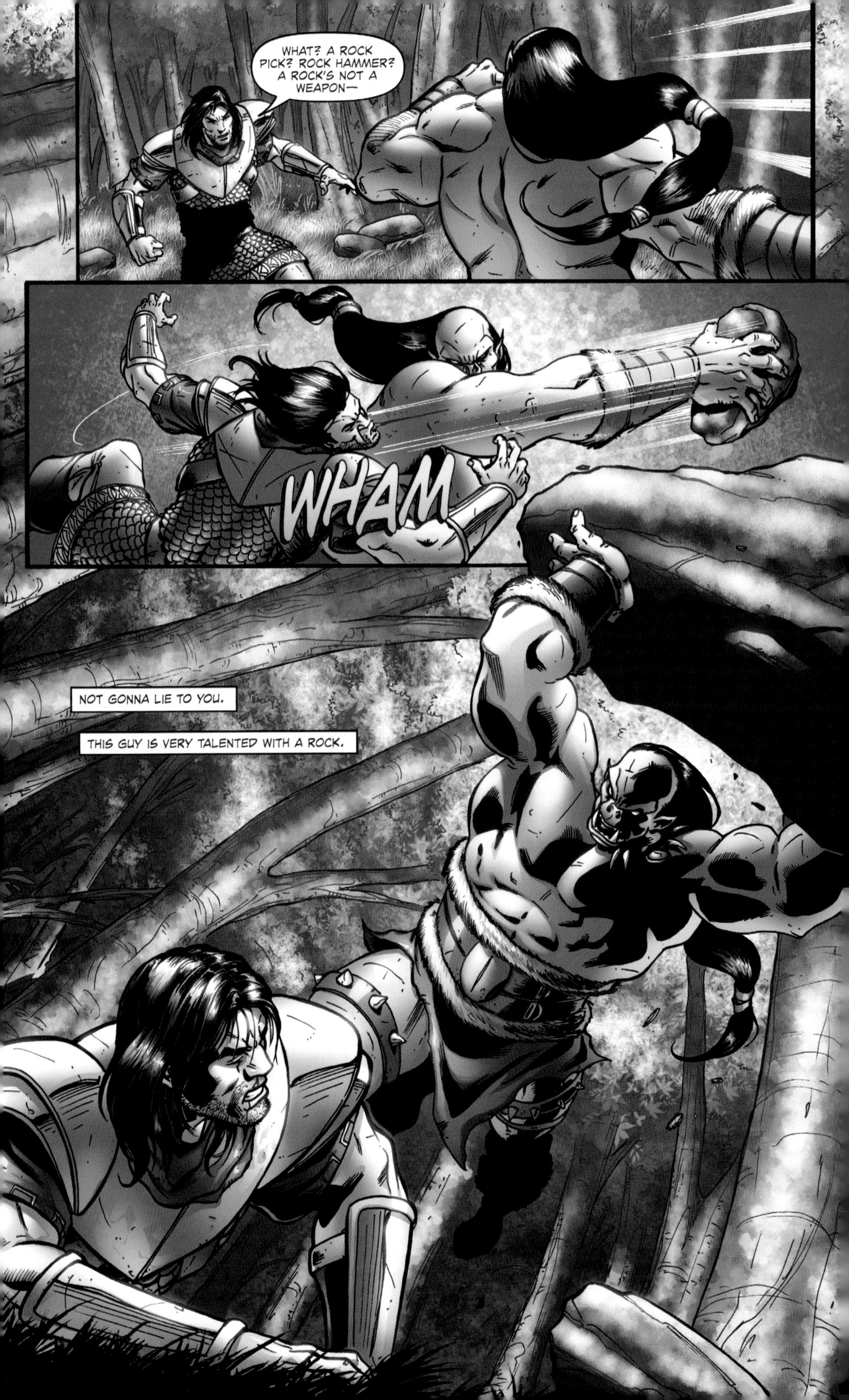
WHAT? A ROCK PICK? ROCK HAMMER? A ROCK'S NOT A WEAPON—
WHAM
NOT GONNA LIE TO YOU.
THIS GUY IS VERY TALENTED WITH A ROCK.

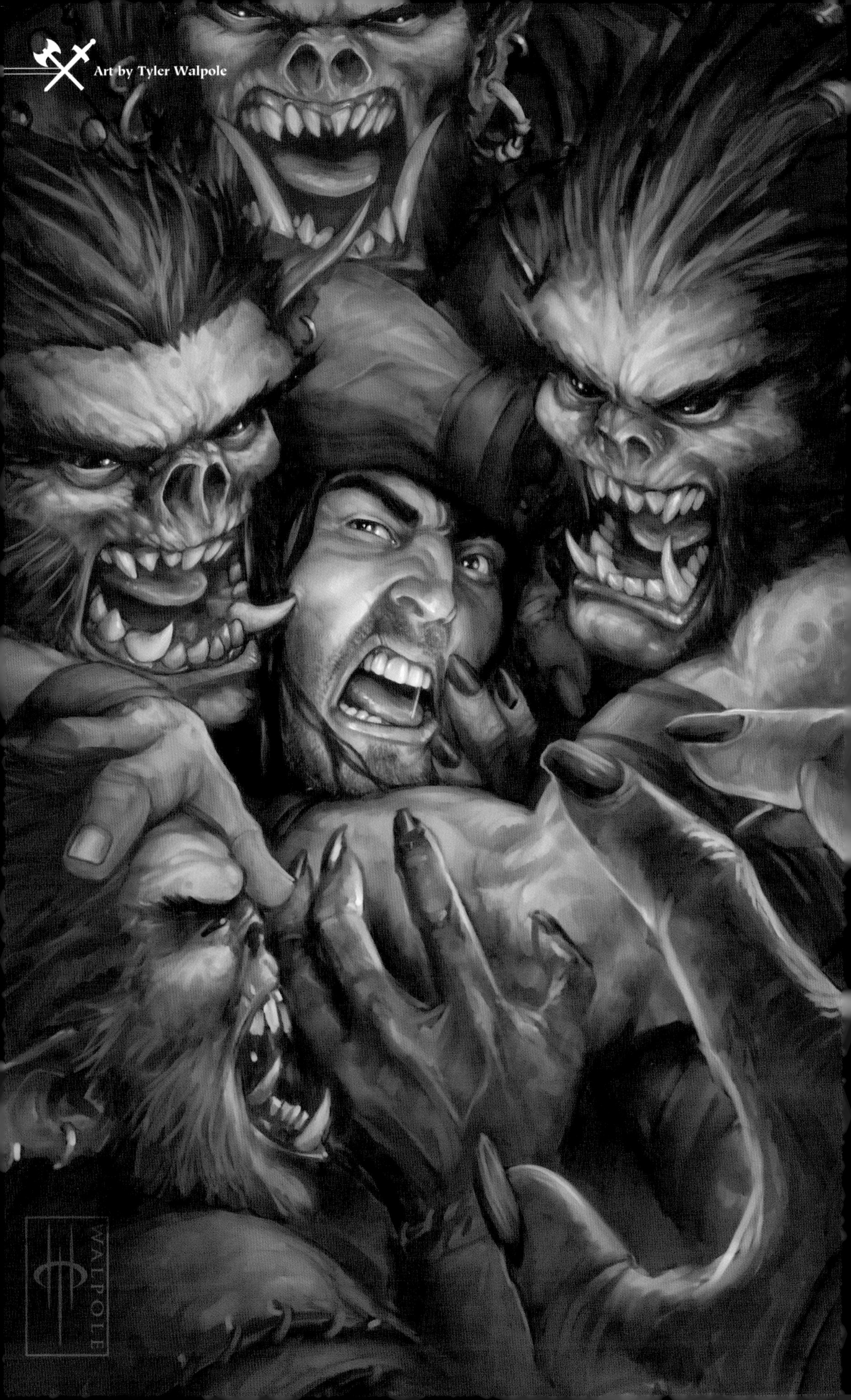
WALPOLE

Art by Tyler Walpole

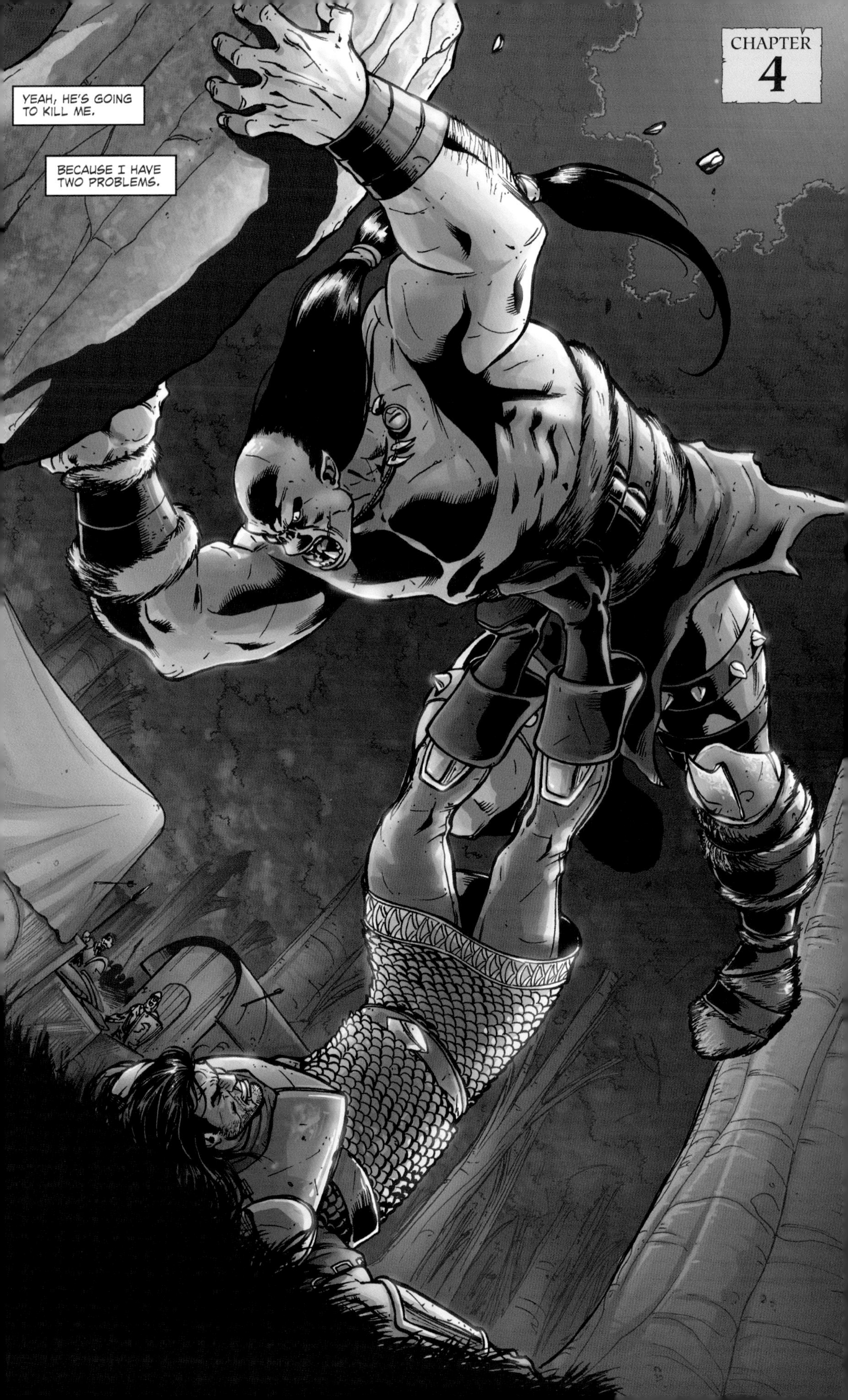
CHAPTER
4
YEAH, HE'S GOING TO KILL ME.
BECAUSE I HAVE TWO PROBLEMS.

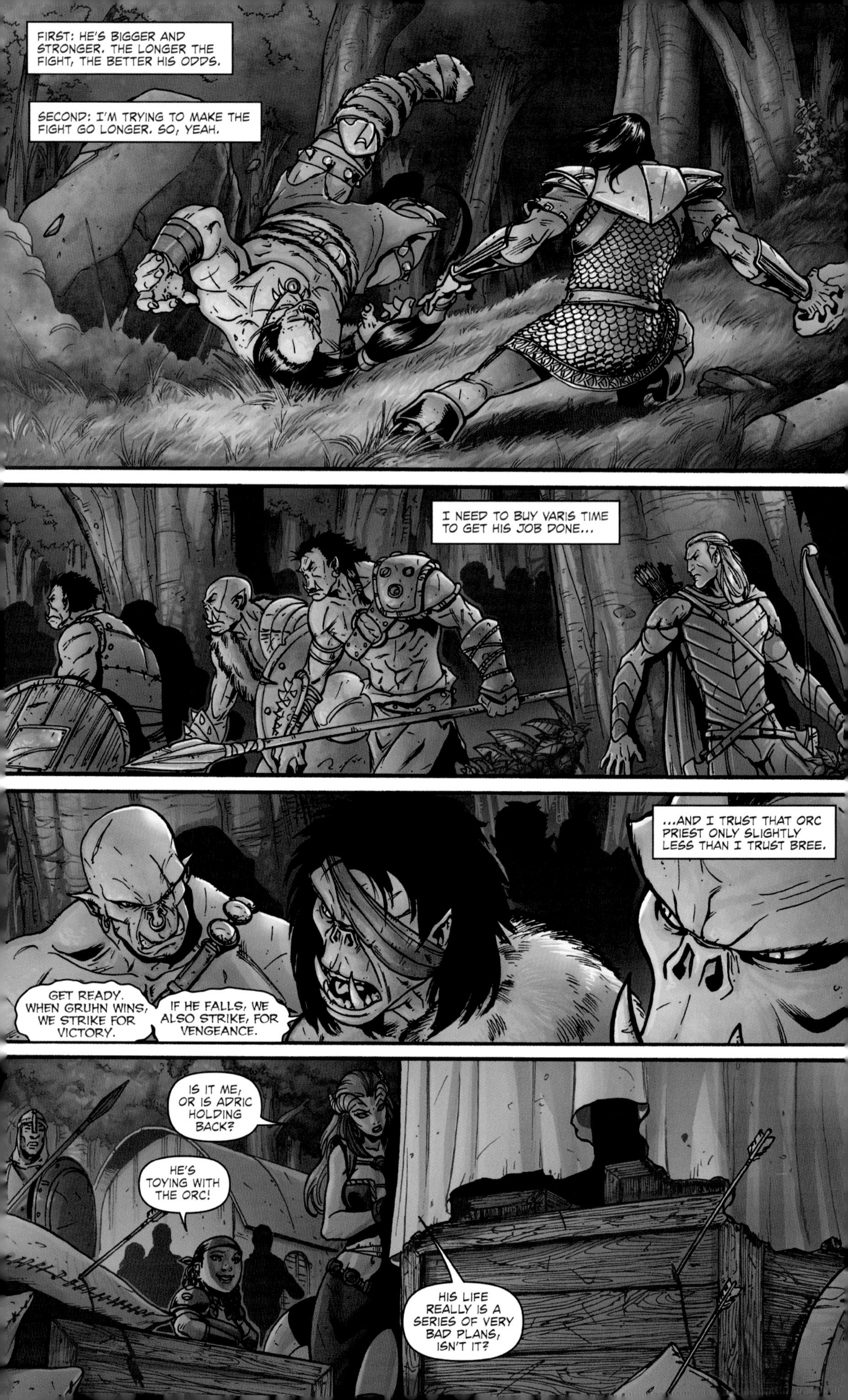
FIRST: HE'S BIGGER AND STRONGER. THE LONGER THE FIGHT, THE BETTER HIS ODDS.
SECOND: I'M TRYING TO MAKE THE FIGHT GO LONGER. SO, YEAH.
I NEED TO BUY VARIS TIME TO GET HIS JOB DONE...
...AND I TRUST THAT ORC PRIEST ONLY SLIGHTLY LESS THAN I TRUST BREE.
GET READY. WHEN GRUHN WINS, WE STRIKE FOR VICTORY.
IF HE FALLS, WE ALSO STRIKE, FOR VENGEANCE.
IS IT ME, OR IS ADRIC HOLDING BACK?
HE'S TOYING WITH THE ORC!
HIS LIFE REALLY IS A SERIES OF VERY BAD PLANS, ISN'T IT?

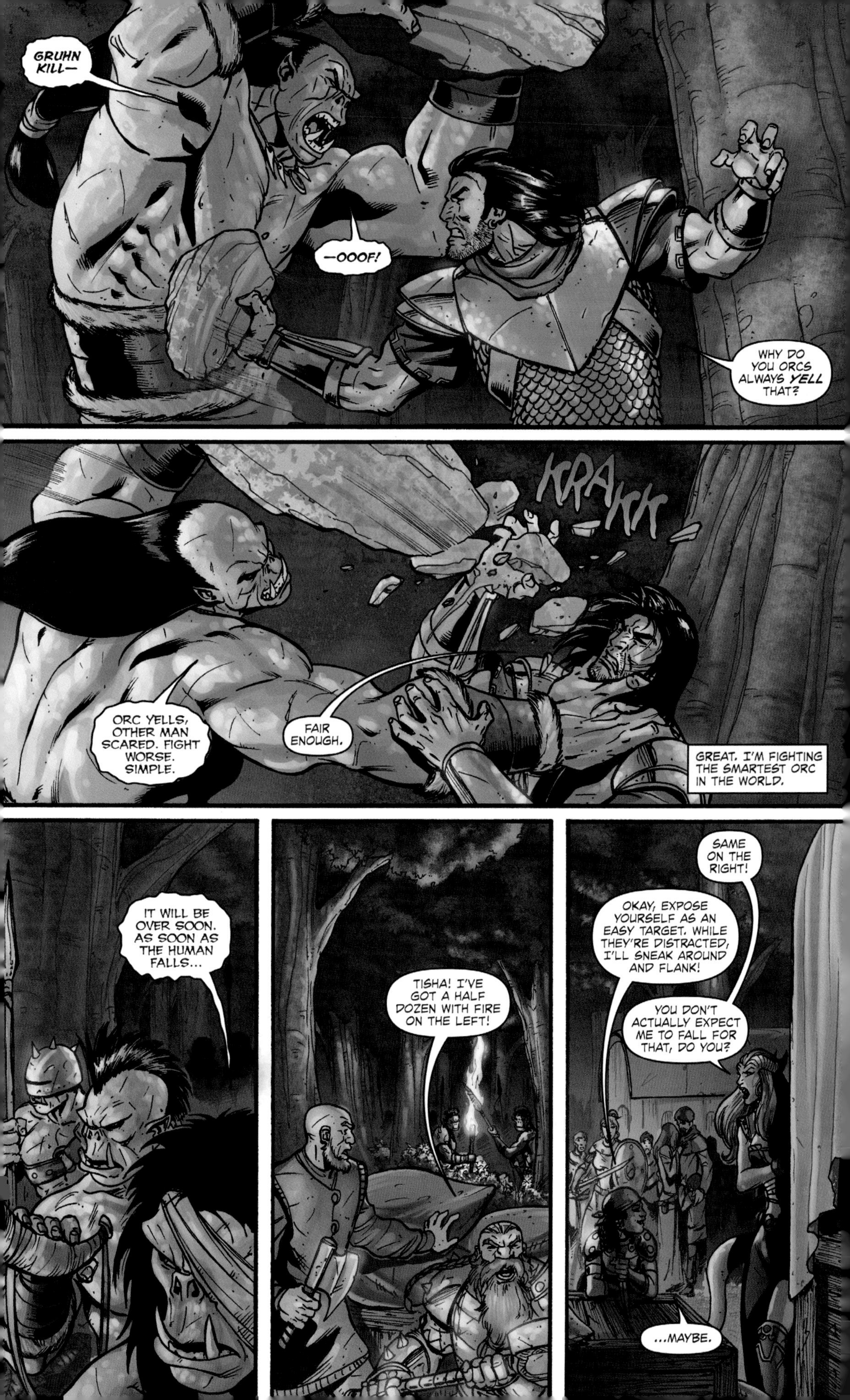
GRUHN KILL—
—OOOF!
WHY DO YOU ORCS ALWAYS *YELL* THAT?
KRAKK
ORC YELLS, OTHER MAN SCARED. FIGHT WORSE. SIMPLE.
FAIR ENOUGH.
GREAT. I'M FIGHTING THE SMARTEST ORC IN THE WORLD.
IT WILL BE OVER SOON. AS SOON AS THE HUMAN FALLS...
TISHA! I'VE GOT A HALF DOZEN WITH FIRE ON THE LEFT!
SAME ON THE RIGHT!
OKAY, EXPOSE YOURSELF AS AN EASY TARGET. WHILE THEY'RE DISTRACTED, I'LL SNEAK AROUND AND FLANK!
YOU DON'T ACTUALLY EXPECT ME TO FALL FOR THAT, DO YOU?
...MAYBE.

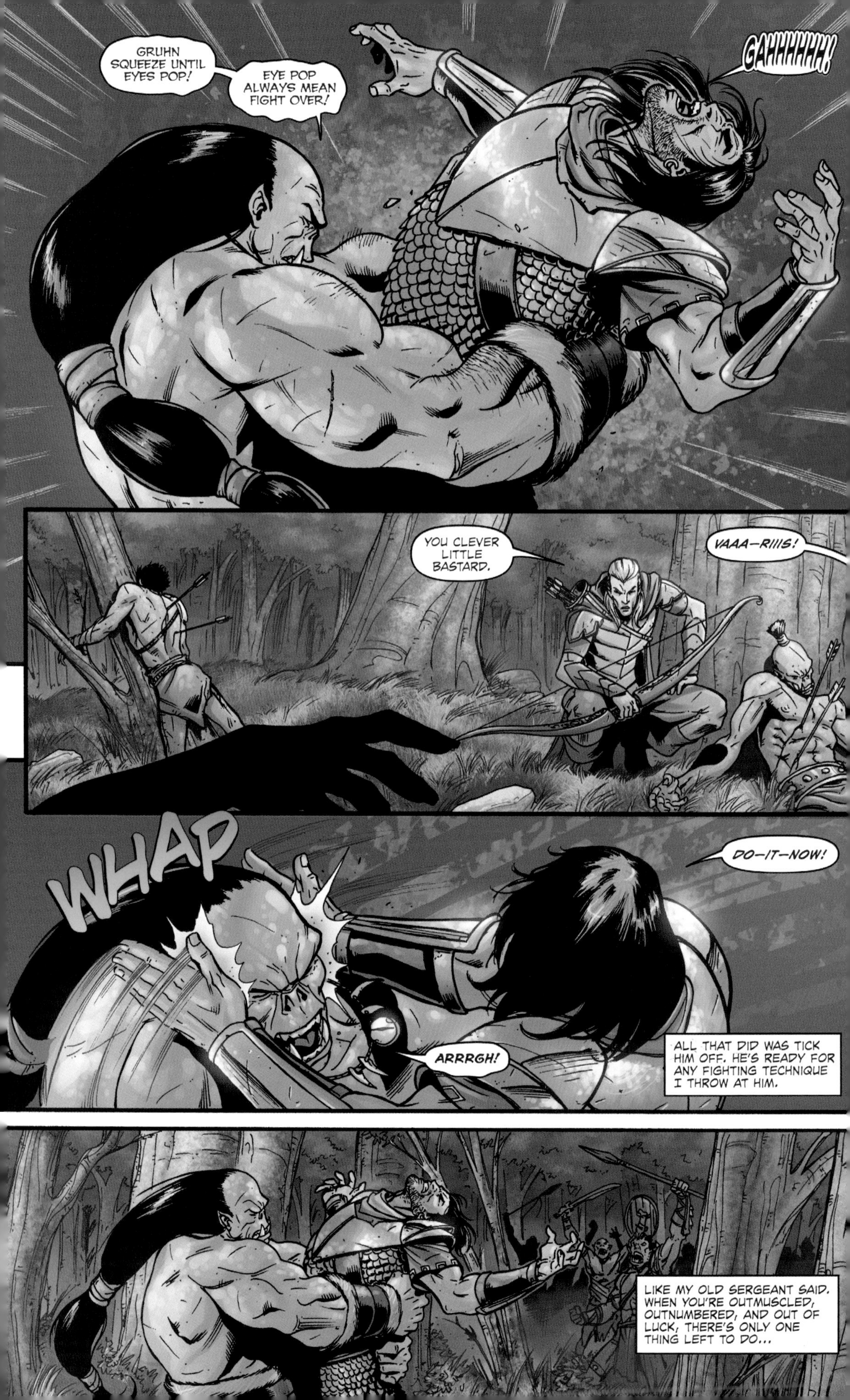
GRUHN SQUEEZE UNTIL EYES POP!
EYE POP ALWAYS MEAN FIGHT OVER!
GAHHHHHH!
YOU CLEVER LITTLE BASTARD.
VAAA—RIIIS!
WHAP
DO—IT—NOW!
ARRRGH!
ALL THAT DID WAS TICK HIM OFF. HE'S READY FOR ANY FIGHTING TECHNIQUE I THROW AT HIM.
LIKE MY OLD SERGEANT SAID. WHEN YOU'RE OUTMUSCLED, OUTNUMBERED, AND OUT OF LUCK, THERE'S ONLY ONE THING LEFT TO DO...

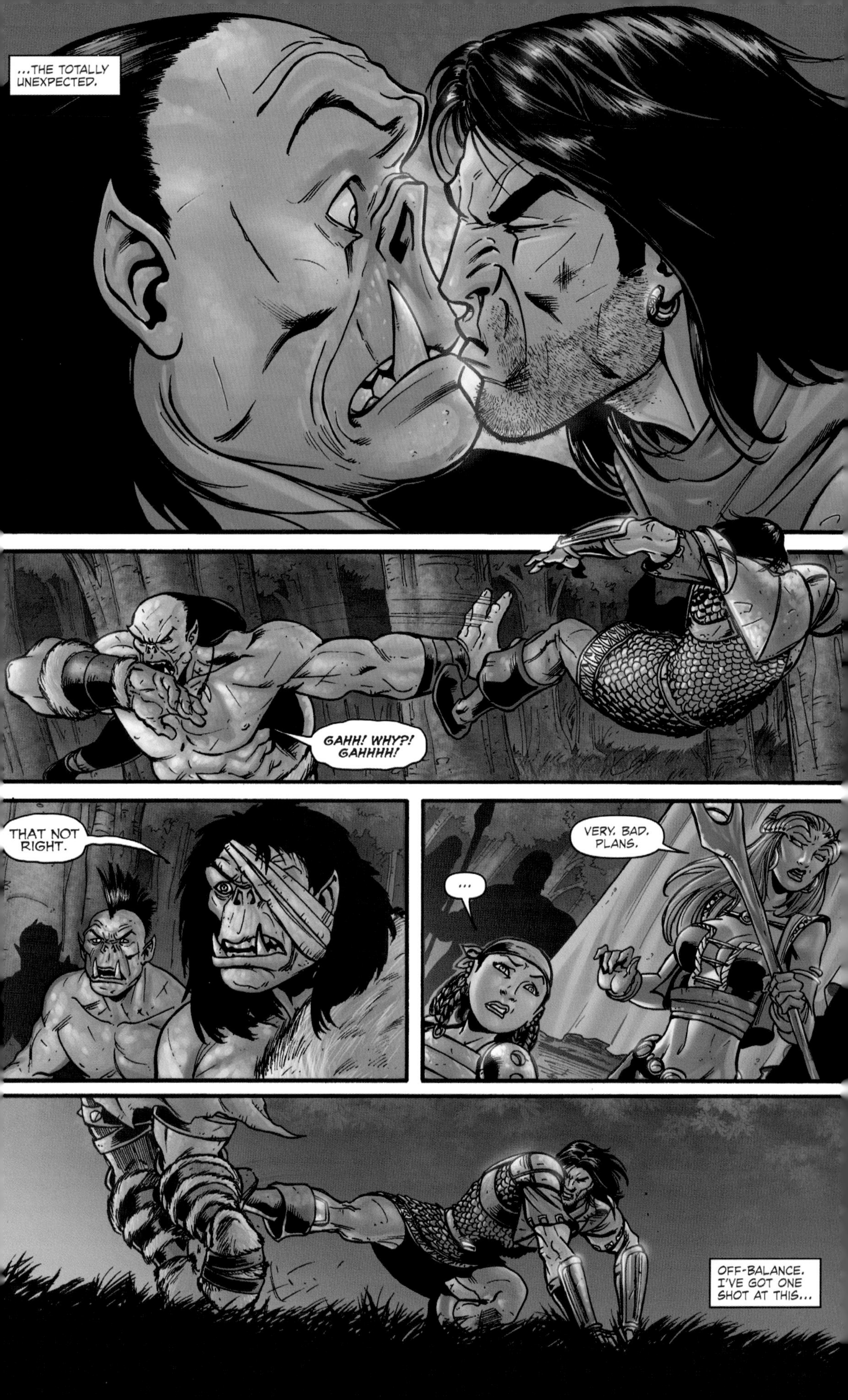
...THE TOTALLY UNEXPECTED.
GAHH! WHY?! GAHHHH!
THAT NOT RIGHT.
VERY. BAD. PLANS.
...
OFF-BALANCE. I'VE GOT ONE SHOT AT THIS...

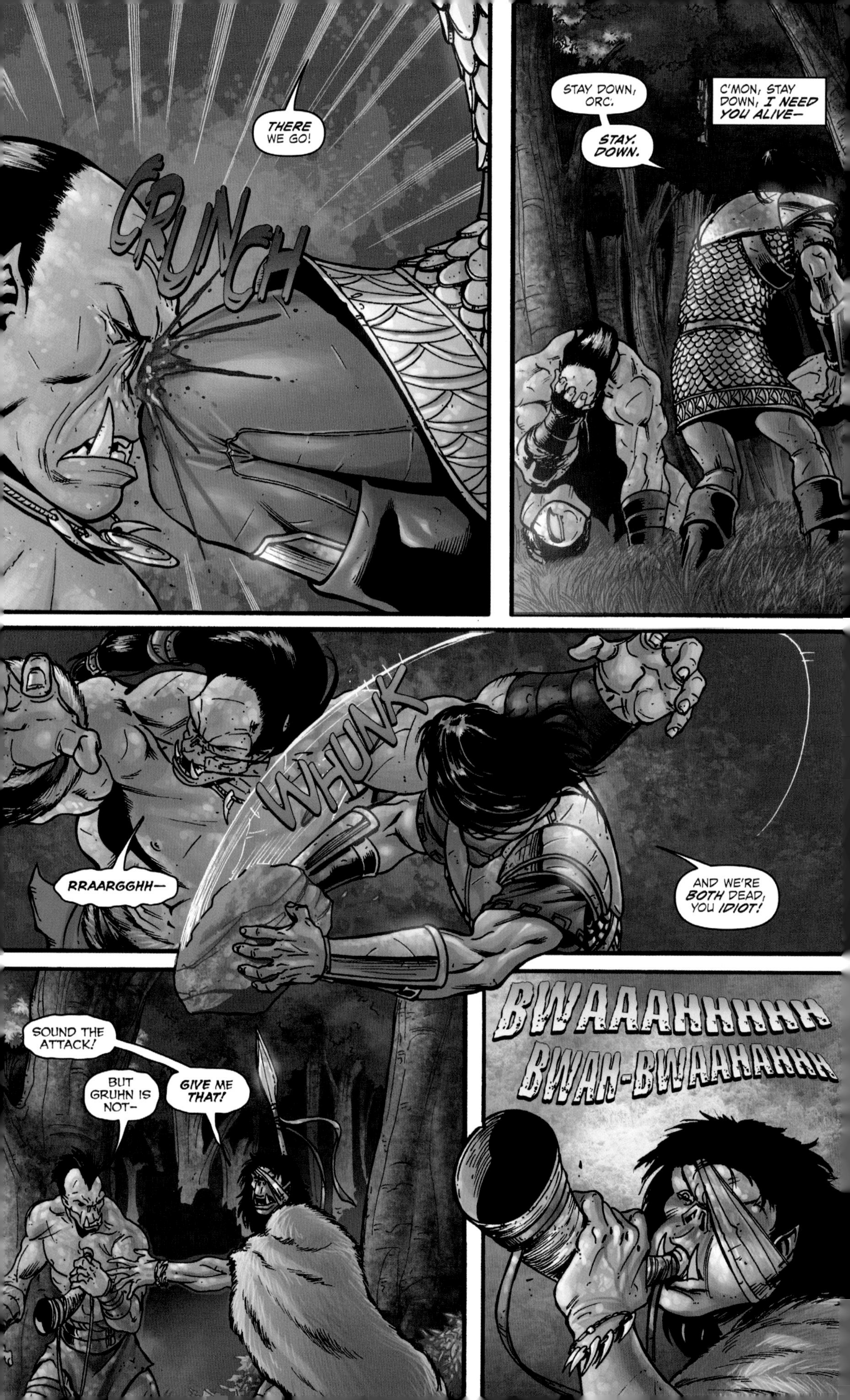
THERE WE GO!
CRUNCH
STAY DOWN, ORC.
STAY. DOWN.
C'MON, STAY DOWN, I NEED YOU ALIVE—
WHUNK
RRAARGGHH—
AND WE'RE BOTH DEAD, YOU IDIOT!
SOUND THE ATTACK!
BUT GRUHN IS NOT-
GIVE ME THAT!
BWAAAHHHHH
BWAH-BWAAHAHHH

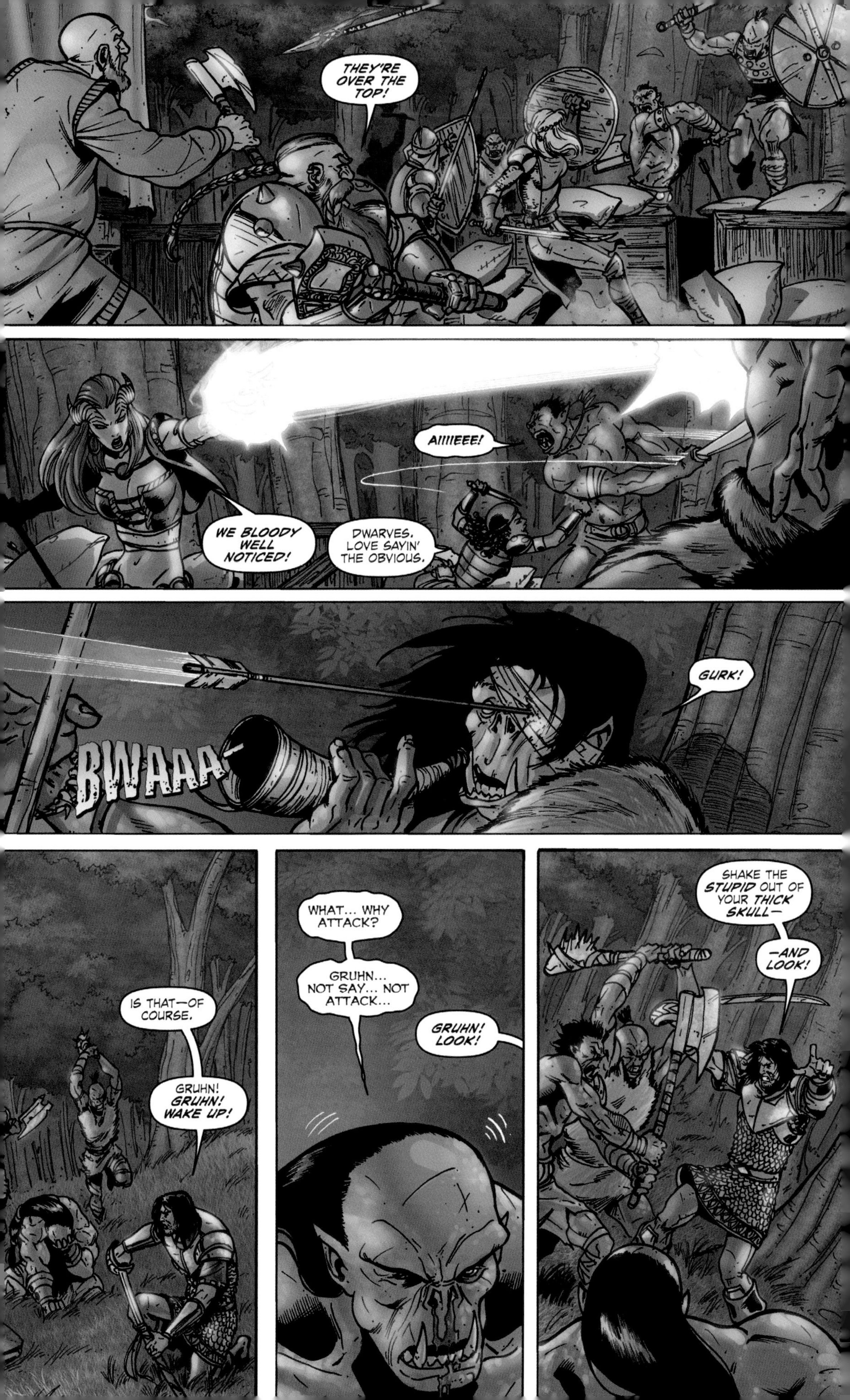
THEY'RE OVER THE TOP!
AIIIIEEE!
WE BLOODY WELL NOTICED!
DWARVES. LOVE SAYIN' THE OBVIOUS.
BWAAA
GURK!
IS THAT—OF COURSE.
GRUHN! GRUHN! WAKE UP!
WHAT... WHY ATTACK?
GRUHN... NOT SAY... NOT ATTACK...
GRUHN! LOOK!
SHAKE THE STUPID OUT OF YOUR THICK SKULL—
—AND LOOK!

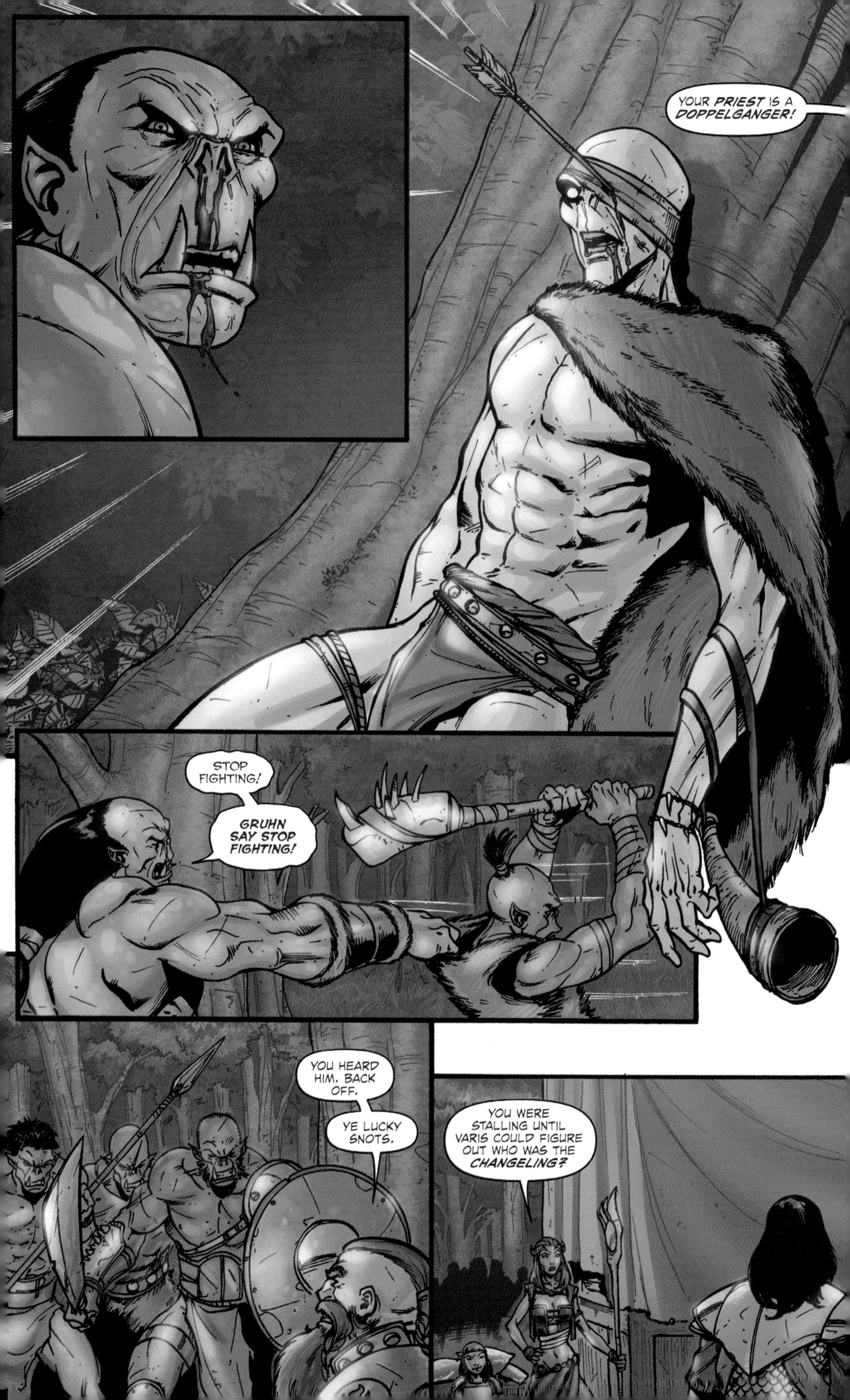
YOUR **PRIEST** IS A **DOPPELGANGER!**
STOP FIGHTING!
GRUHN SAY STOP FIGHTING!
YOU HEARD HIM. BACK OFF.
YE LUCKY SNOTS.
YOU WERE STALLING UNTIL VARIS COULD FIGURE OUT WHO WAS THE **CHANGELING?**

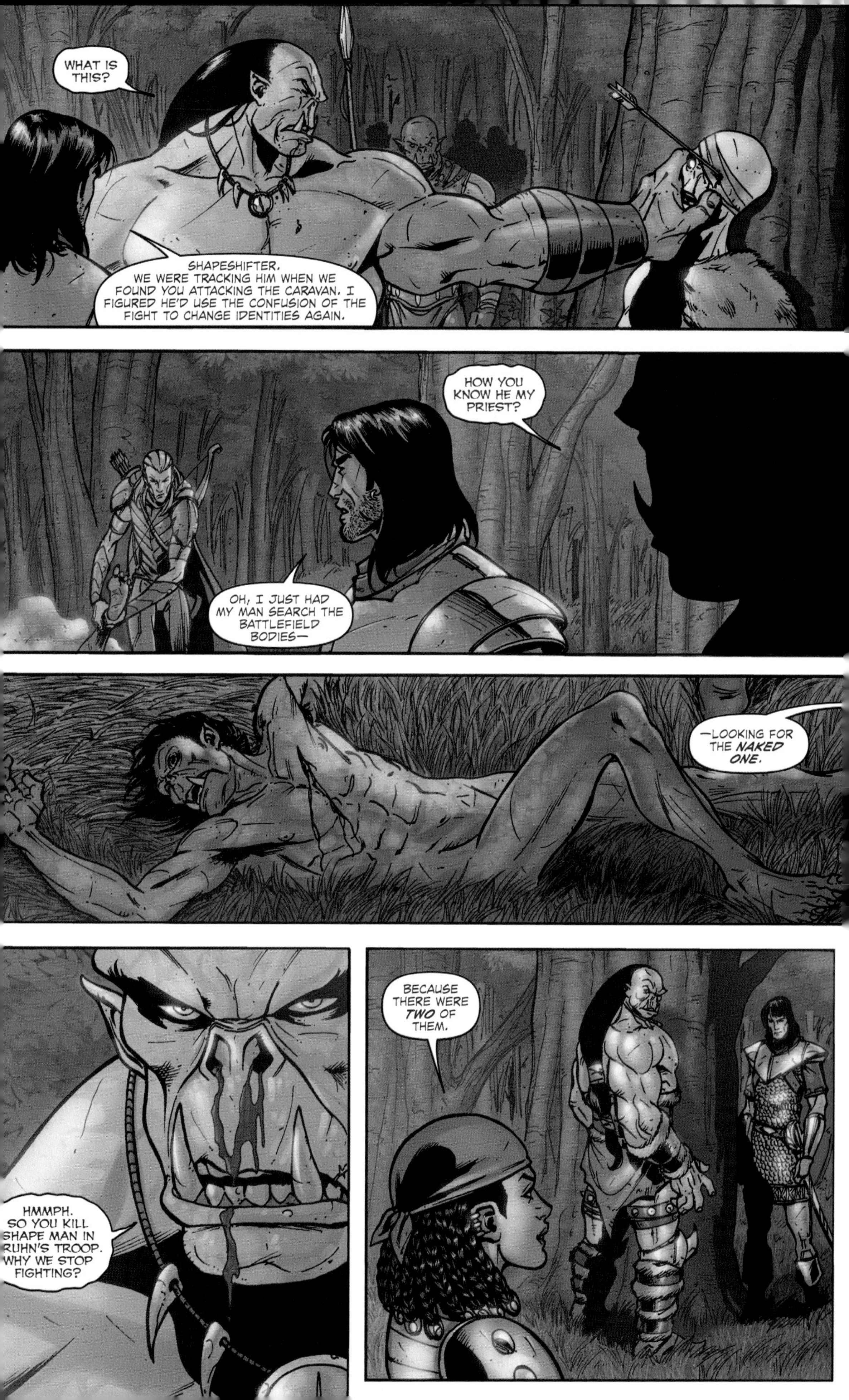
WHAT IS THIS?
SHAPESHIFTER. WE WERE TRACKING HIM WHEN WE FOUND YOU ATTACKING THE CARAVAN. I FIGURED HE'D USE THE CONFUSION OF THE FIGHT TO CHANGE IDENTITIES AGAIN.
HOW YOU KNOW HE MY PRIEST?
OH, I JUST HAD MY MAN SEARCH THE BATTLEFIELD BODIES—
—LOOKING FOR THE *NAKED ONE.*
HMMPH. SO YOU KILL SHAPE MAN IN RUHN'S TROOP. WHY WE STOP FIGHTING?
BECAUSE THERE WERE *TWO* OF THEM.

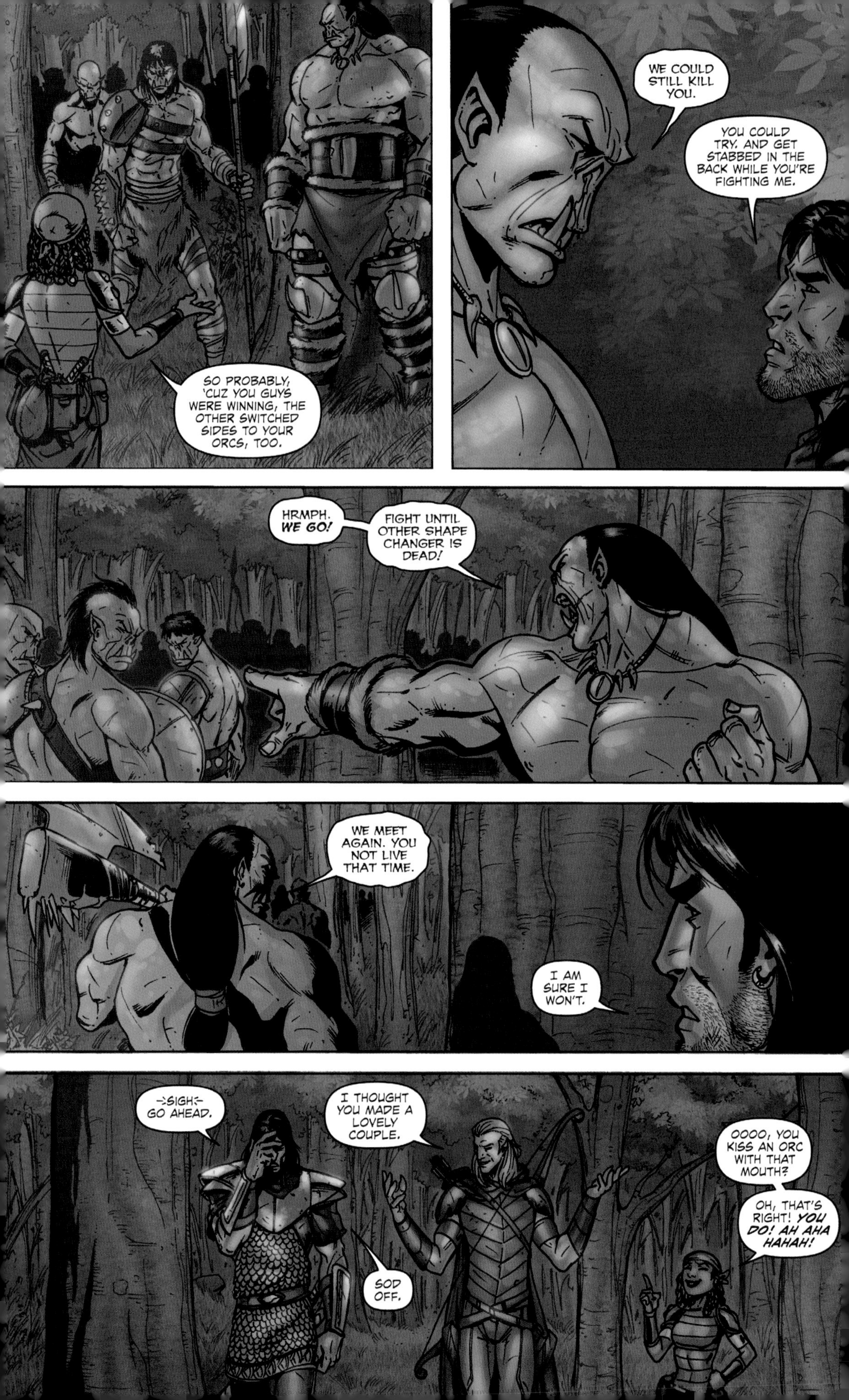
SO PROBABLY, 'CUZ YOU GUYS WERE WINNING, THE OTHER SWITCHED SIDES TO YOUR ORCS, TOO.
WE COULD STILL KILL YOU.
YOU COULD TRY. AND GET STABBED IN THE BACK WHILE YOU'RE FIGHTING ME.
HRMPH. **WE GO!**
FIGHT UNTIL OTHER SHAPE CHANGER IS DEAD!
WE MEET AGAIN. YOU NOT LIVE THAT TIME.
I AM SURE I WON'T.
~SIGH~ GO AHEAD.
I THOUGHT YOU MADE A LOVELY COUPLE.
SOD OFF.
OOOO, YOU KISS AN ORC WITH THAT MOUTH?
OH, THAT'S RIGHT! ***YOU DO! AH AHA HAHAH!***

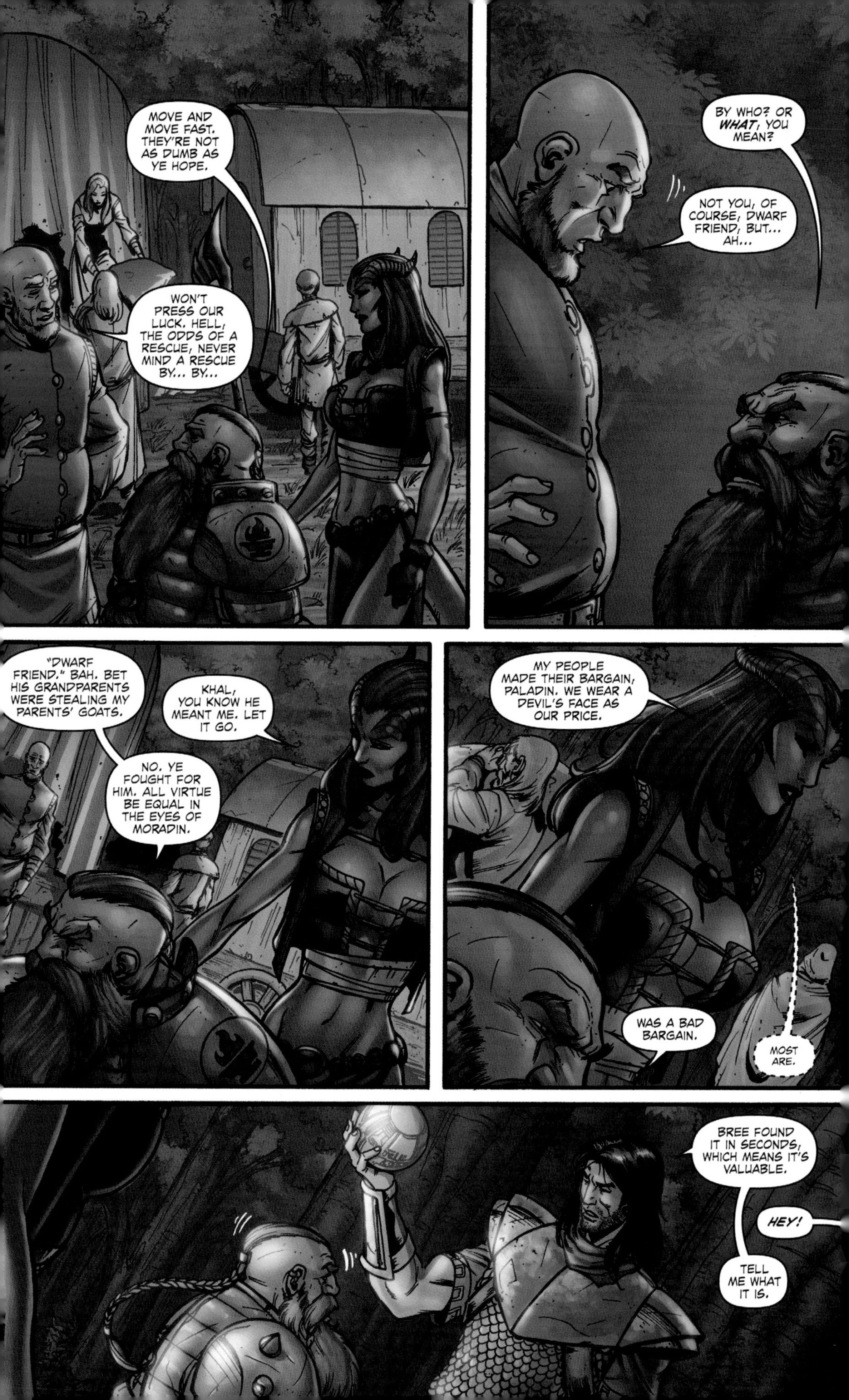
MOVE AND MOVE FAST. THEY'RE NOT AS DUMB AS YE HOPE.
WON'T PRESS OUR LUCK. HELL, THE ODDS OF A RESCUE, NEVER MIND A RESCUE BY... BY...
BY WHO? OR WHAT, YOU MEAN?
NOT YOU, OF COURSE, DWARF FRIEND, BUT... AH...
"DWARF FRIEND." BAH. BET HIS GRANDPARENTS WERE STEALING MY PARENTS' GOATS.
KHAL, YOU KNOW HE MEANT ME. LET IT GO.
NO. YE FOUGHT FOR HIM. ALL VIRTUE BE EQUAL IN THE EYES OF MORADIN.
MY PEOPLE MADE THEIR BARGAIN, PALADIN. WE WEAR A DEVIL'S FACE AS OUR PRICE.
WAS A BAD BARGAIN.
MOST ARE.
BREE FOUND IT IN SECONDS, WHICH MEANS IT'S VALUABLE.
HEY!
TELL ME WHAT IT IS.

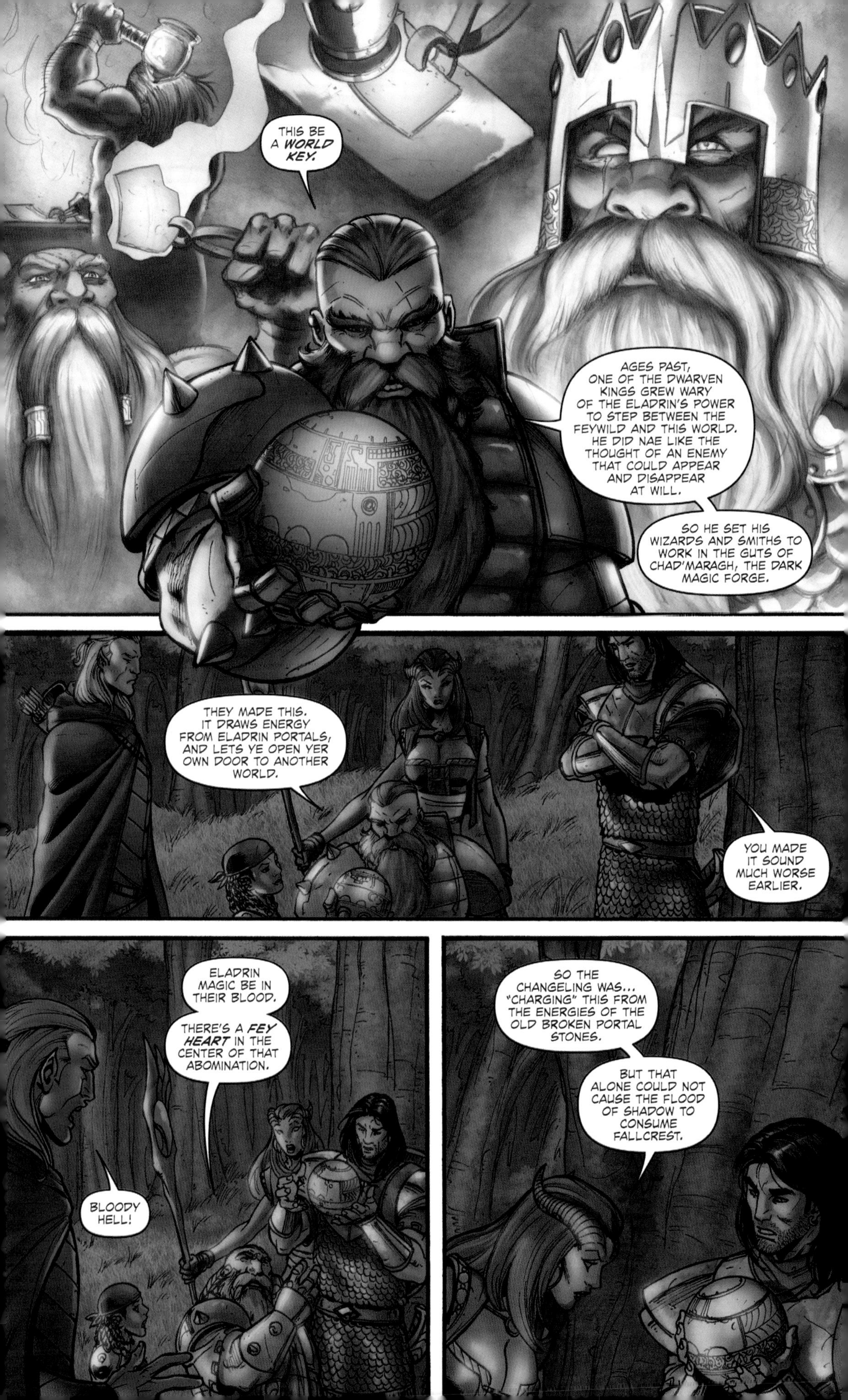
THIS BE A *WORLD KEY.*
AGES PAST, ONE OF THE DWARVEN KINGS GREW WARY OF THE ELADRIN'S POWER TO STEP BETWEEN THE FEYWILD AND THIS WORLD. HE DID NAE LIKE THE THOUGHT OF AN ENEMY THAT COULD APPEAR AND DISAPPEAR AT WILL.
SO HE SET HIS WIZARDS AND SMITHS TO WORK IN THE GUTS OF CHAD'MARAGH, THE DARK MAGIC FORGE.
THEY MADE THIS. IT DRAWS ENERGY FROM ELADRIN PORTALS, AND LETS YE OPEN YER OWN DOOR TO ANOTHER WORLD.
YOU MADE IT SOUND MUCH WORSE EARLIER.
ELADRIN MAGIC BE IN THEIR BLOOD.
THERE'S A *FEY HEART* IN THE CENTER OF THAT ABOMINATION.
BLOODY HELL!
SO THE CHANGELING WAS... "CHARGING" THIS FROM THE ENERGIES OF THE OLD BROKEN PORTAL STONES.
BUT THAT ALONE COULD NOT CAUSE THE FLOOD OF SHADOW TO CONSUME FALLCREST.

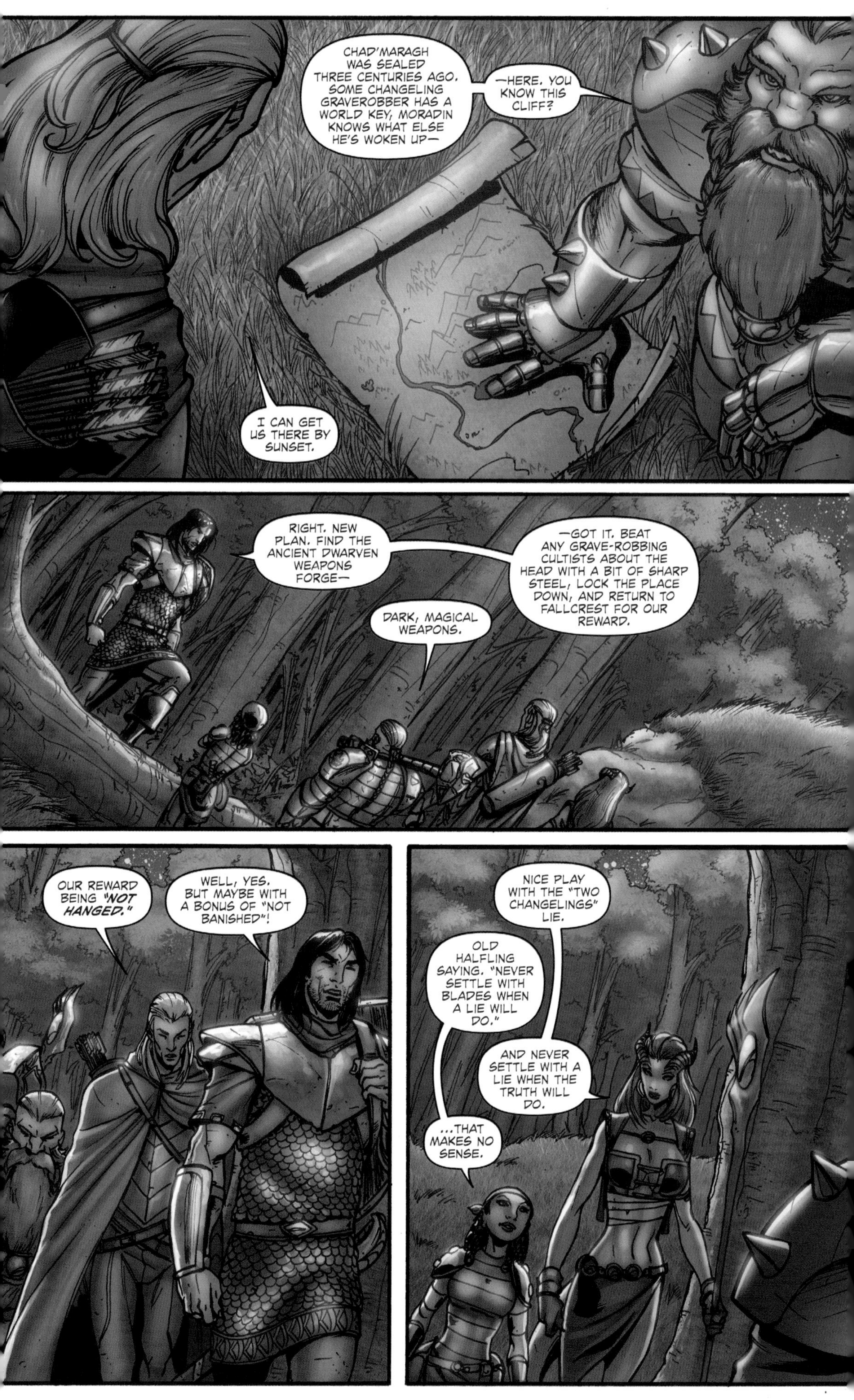
CHAD'MARAGH WAS SEALED THREE CENTURIES AGO. SOME CHANGELING GRAVEROBBER HAS A WORLD KEY; MORADIN KNOWS WHAT ELSE HE'S WOKEN UP—
—HERE. YOU KNOW THIS CLIFF?
I CAN GET US THERE BY SUNSET.
RIGHT. NEW PLAN. FIND THE ANCIENT DWARVEN WEAPONS FORGE—
—GOT IT. BEAT ANY GRAVE-ROBBING CULTISTS ABOUT THE HEAD WITH A BIT OF SHARP STEEL, LOCK THE PLACE DOWN, AND RETURN TO FALLCREST FOR OUR REWARD.
DARK, MAGICAL WEAPONS.
OUR REWARD BEING ***"NOT HANGED."***
WELL, YES. BUT MAYBE WITH A BONUS OF "NOT BANISHED"!
NICE PLAY WITH THE "TWO CHANGELINGS" LIE.
OLD HALFLING SAYING. "NEVER SETTLE WITH BLADES WHEN A LIE WILL DO."
AND NEVER SETTLE WITH A LIE WHEN THE TRUTH WILL DO.
...THAT MAKES NO SENSE.

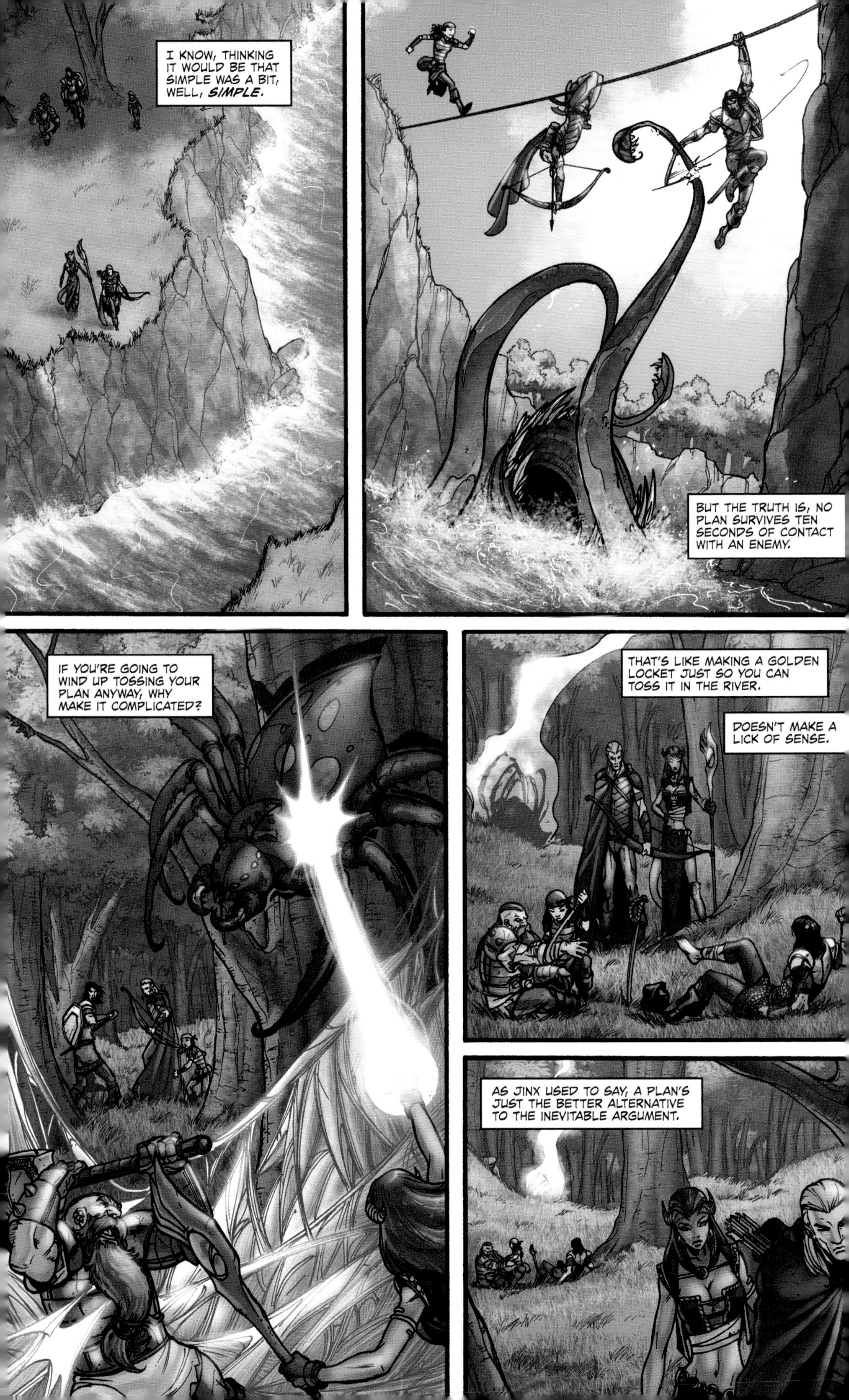
I KNOW, THINKING IT WOULD BE THAT SIMPLE WAS A BIT, WELL, SIMPLE.
BUT THE TRUTH IS, NO PLAN SURVIVES TEN SECONDS OF CONTACT WITH AN ENEMY.
IF YOU'RE GOING TO WIND UP TOSSING YOUR PLAN ANYWAY, WHY MAKE IT COMPLICATED?
THAT'S LIKE MAKING A GOLDEN LOCKET JUST SO YOU CAN TOSS IT IN THE RIVER.
DOESN'T MAKE A LICK OF SENSE.
AS JINX USED TO SAY, A PLAN'S JUST THE BETTER ALTERNATIVE TO THE INEVITABLE ARGUMENT.

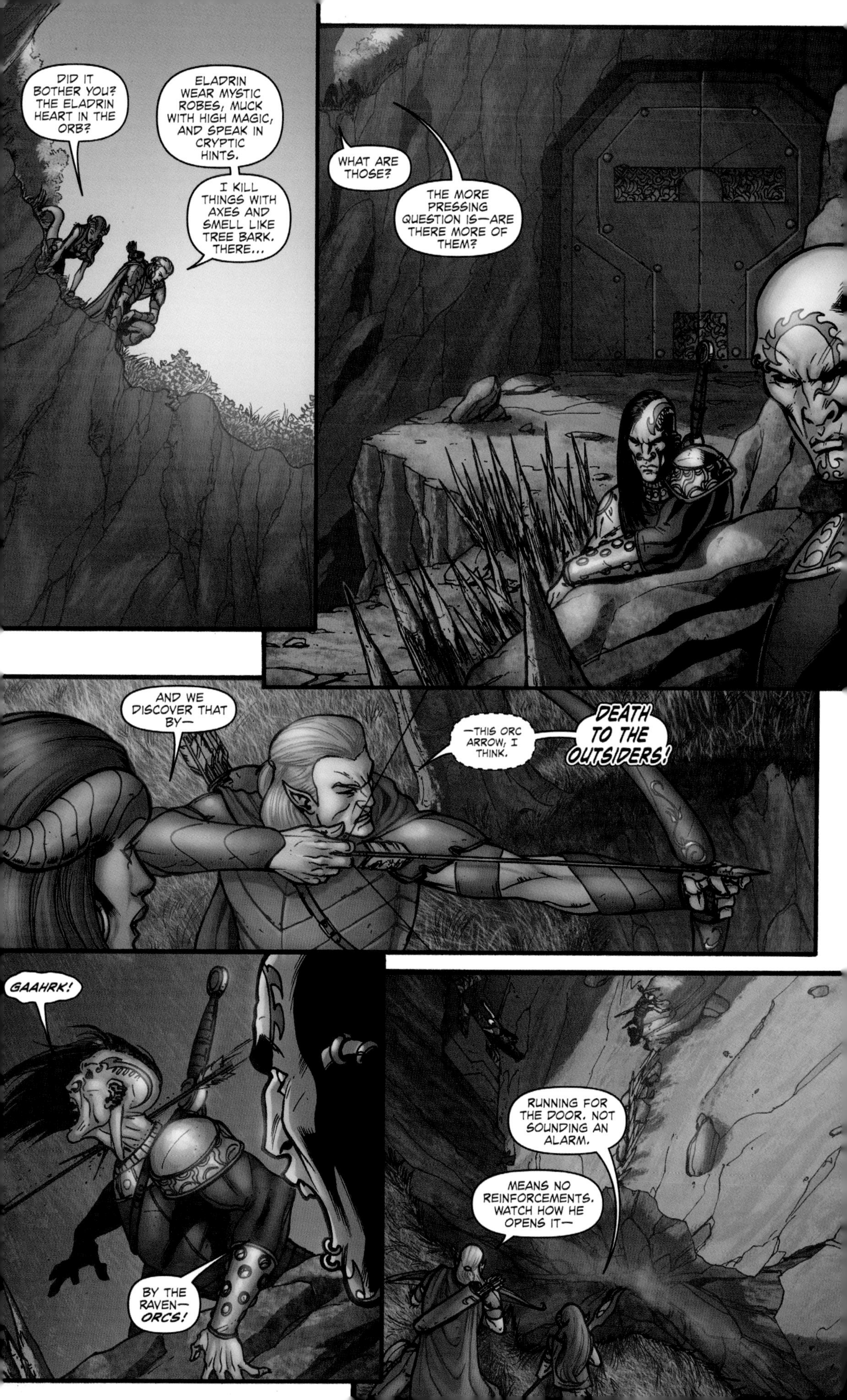
DID IT BOTHER YOU? THE ELADRIN HEART IN THE ORB?
ELADRIN WEAR MYSTIC ROBES, MUCK WITH HIGH MAGIC, AND SPEAK IN CRYPTIC HINTS.
I KILL THINGS WITH AXES AND SMELL LIKE TREE BARK. THERE...
WHAT ARE THOSE?
THE MORE PRESSING QUESTION IS—ARE THERE MORE OF THEM?
AND WE DISCOVER THAT BY—
—THIS ORC ARROW, I THINK.
DEATH TO THE OUTSIDERS!
GAAHRK!
BY THE RAVEN—ORCS!
RUNNING FOR THE DOOR. NOT SOUNDING AN ALARM.
MEANS NO REINFORCEMENTS. WATCH HOW HE OPENS IT—

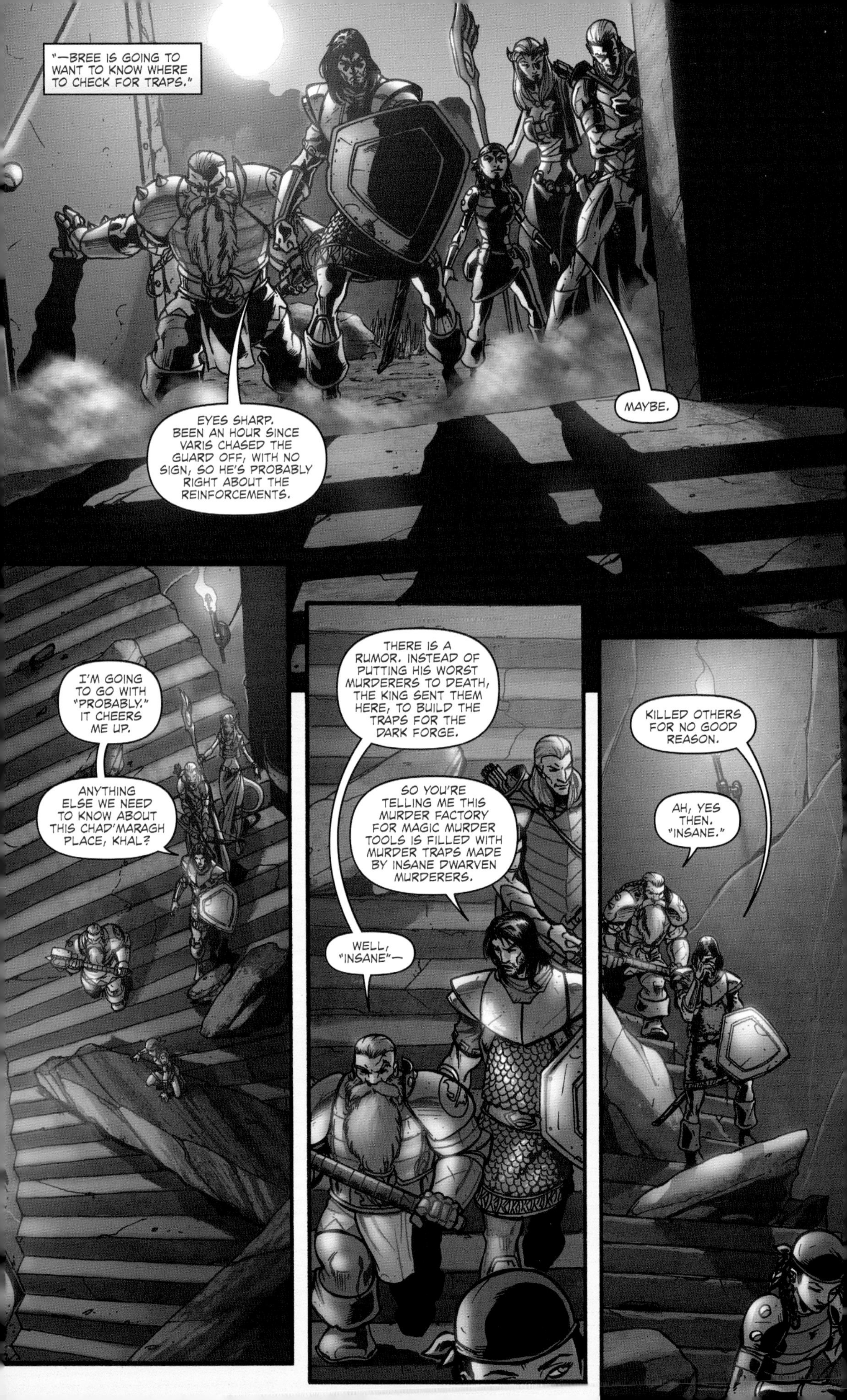
"—BREE IS GOING TO WANT TO KNOW WHERE TO CHECK FOR TRAPS."
EYES SHARP. BEEN AN HOUR SINCE VARIS CHASED THE GUARD OFF, WITH NO SIGN, SO HE'S PROBABLY RIGHT ABOUT THE REINFORCEMENTS.
MAYBE.
I'M GOING TO GO WITH "PROBABLY." IT CHEERS ME UP.
ANYTHING ELSE WE NEED TO KNOW ABOUT THIS CHAD'MARAGH PLACE, KHAL?
THERE IS A RUMOR. INSTEAD OF PUTTING HIS WORST MURDERERS TO DEATH, THE KING SENT THEM HERE, TO BUILD THE TRAPS FOR THE DARK FORGE.
SO YOU'RE TELLING ME THIS MURDER FACTORY FOR MAGIC MURDER TOOLS IS FILLED WITH MURDER TRAPS MADE BY INSANE DWARVEN MURDERERS.
WELL, "INSANE"—
KILLED OTHERS FOR NO GOOD REASON.
AH, YES THEN. "INSANE."

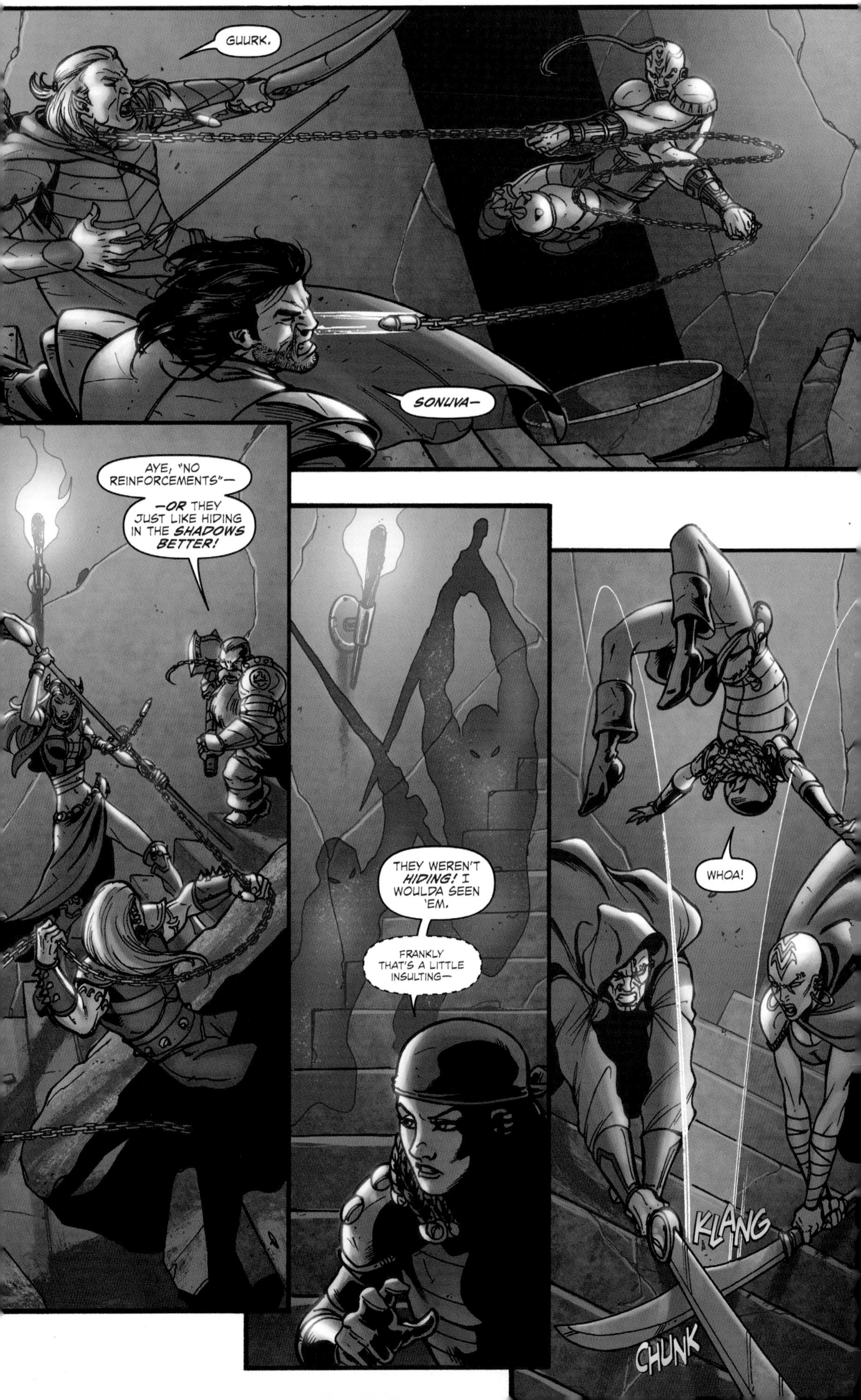

GUURK.
SONUVA—
AYE, "NO REINFORCEMENTS"—
—OR THEY JUST LIKE HIDING IN THE SHADOWS BETTER!
THEY WEREN'T HIDING! I WOULDA SEEN 'EM.
FRANKLY THAT'S A LITTLE INSULTING—
WHOA!
KLANG
CHUNK

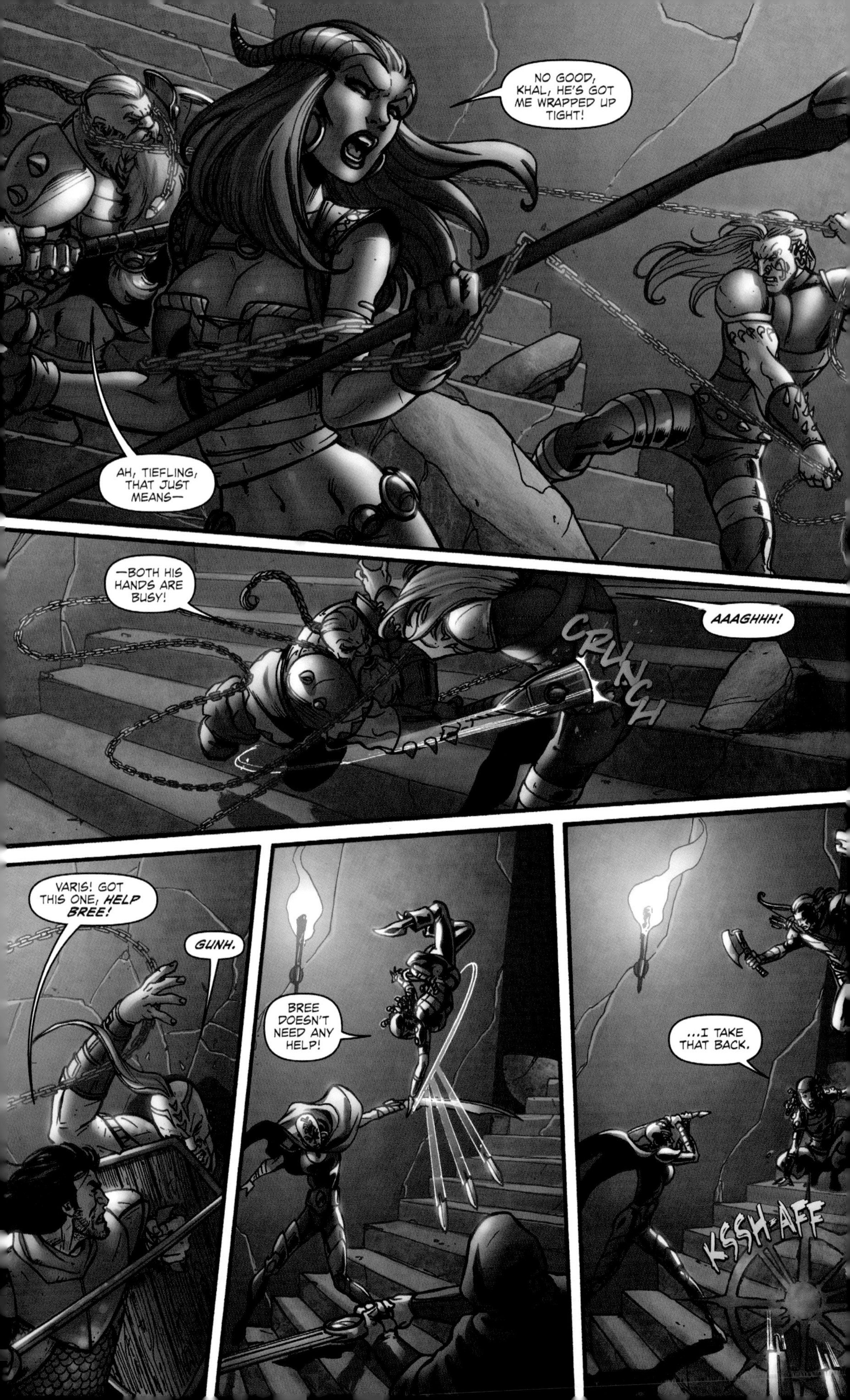
NO GOOD, KHAL, HE'S GOT ME WRAPPED UP TIGHT!
AH, TIEFLING, THAT JUST MEANS—
—BOTH HIS HANDS ARE BUSY!
CRUNCH
AAAGHHH!
VARIS! GOT THIS ONE, HELP BREE!
GUNH.
BREE DOESN'T NEED ANY HELP!
...I TAKE THAT BACK.
KSSH-AFF

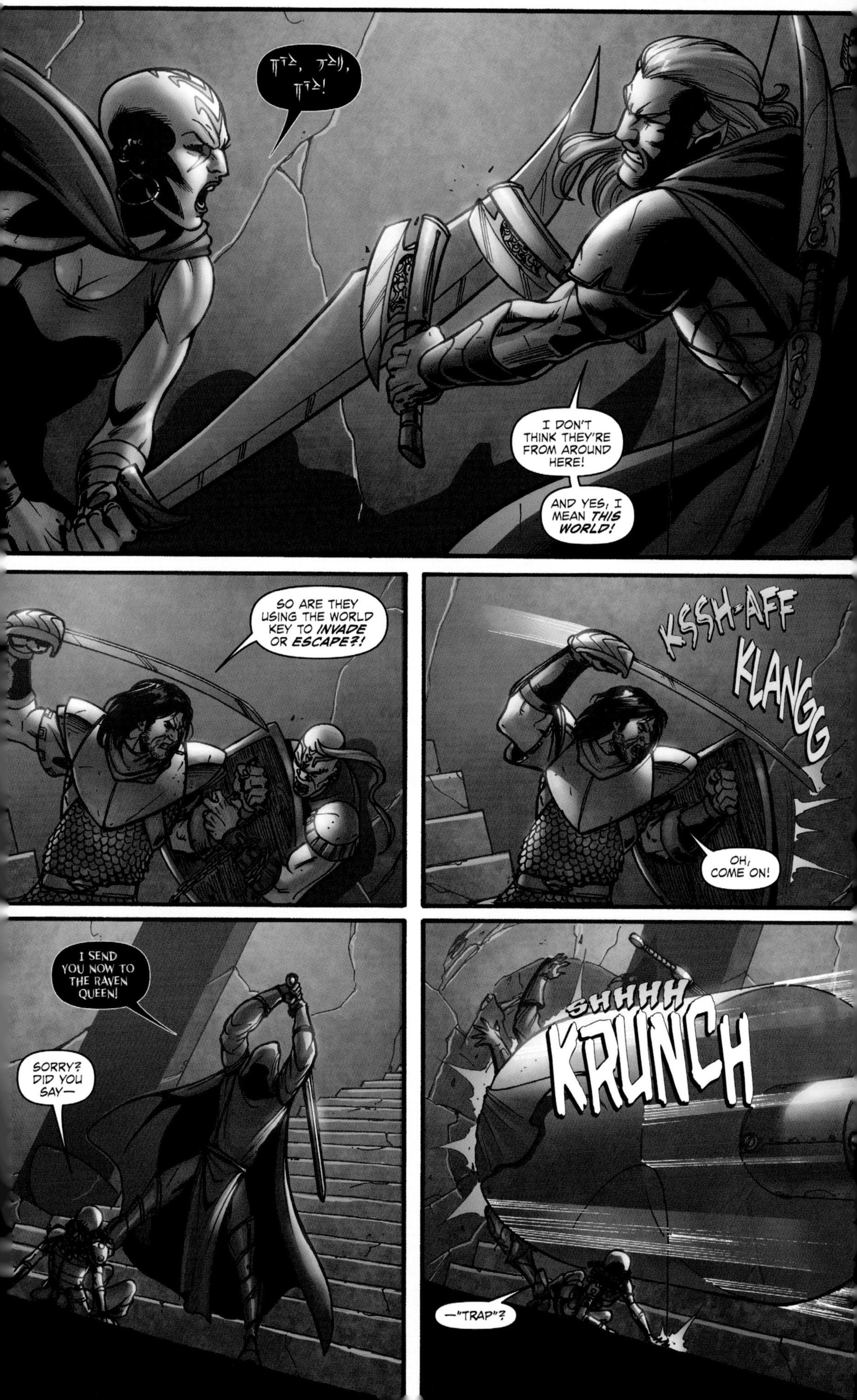
I DON'T THINK THEY'RE FROM AROUND HERE!
AND YES, I MEAN *THIS WORLD!*
SO ARE THEY USING THE WORLD KEY TO *INVADE* OR *ESCAPE?!*
KSSH-AFF
KLANGG
OH, COME ON!
I SEND YOU NOW TO THE RAVEN QUEEN!
SORRY? DID YOU SAY—
SHHHH
KRUNCH
—"TRAP"?

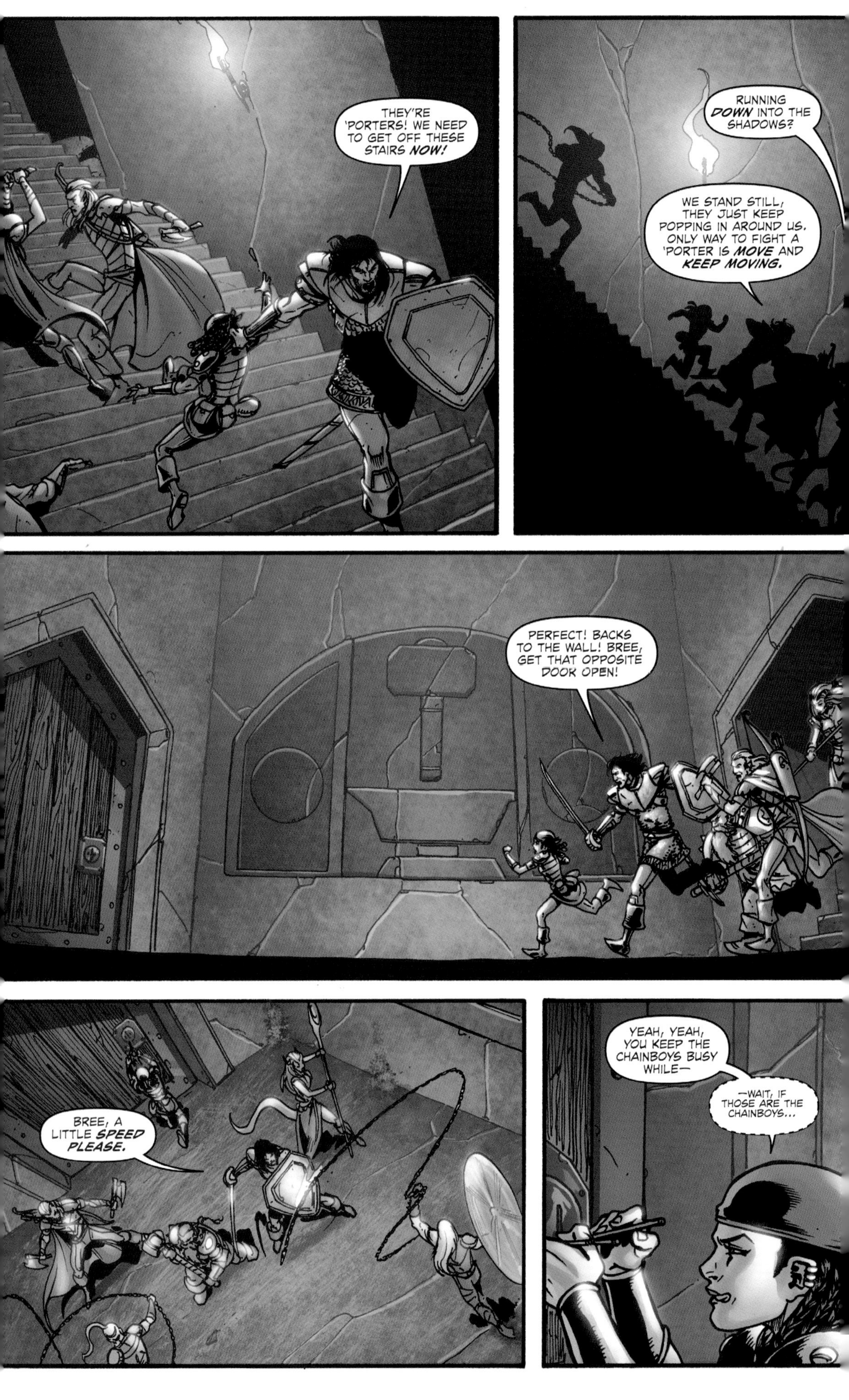
THEY'RE 'PORTERS! WE NEED TO GET OFF THESE STAIRS NOW!
RUNNING DOWN INTO THE SHADOWS?
WE STAND STILL, THEY JUST KEEP POPPING IN AROUND US. ONLY WAY TO FIGHT A 'PORTER IS MOVE AND KEEP MOVING.
PERFECT! BACKS TO THE WALL! BREE, GET THAT OPPOSITE DOOR OPEN!
BREE, A LITTLE SPEED PLEASE.
YEAH, YEAH, YOU KEEP THE CHAINBOYS BUSY WHILE—
—WAIT, IF THOSE ARE THE CHAINBOYS...

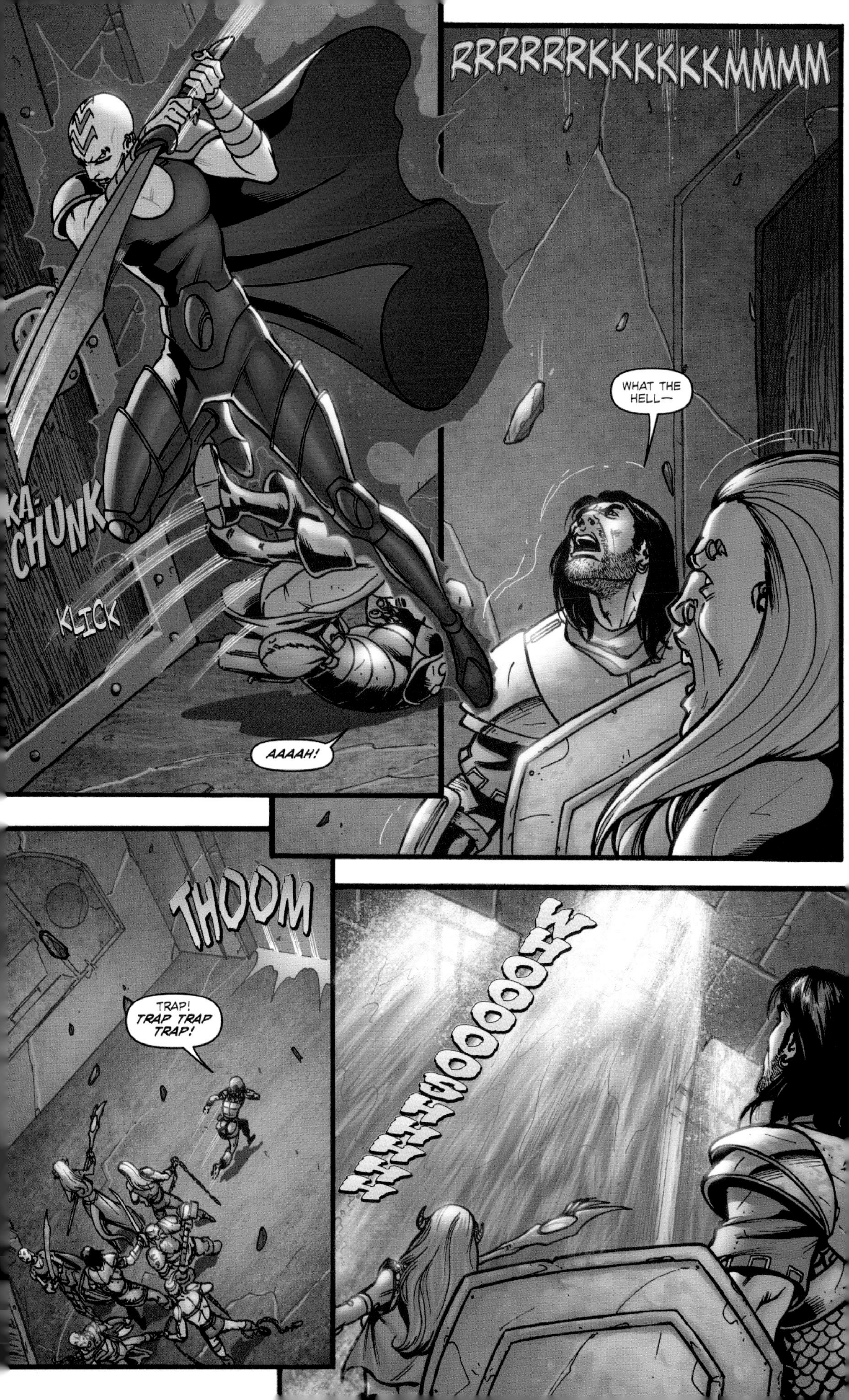
KA-CHUNK
KLICK
AAAAH!
RRRRRRKKKKKKMMMM
WHAT THE HELL—
THOOM
TRAP! TRAP TRAP TRAP!
WHOOOOOOSHHHH

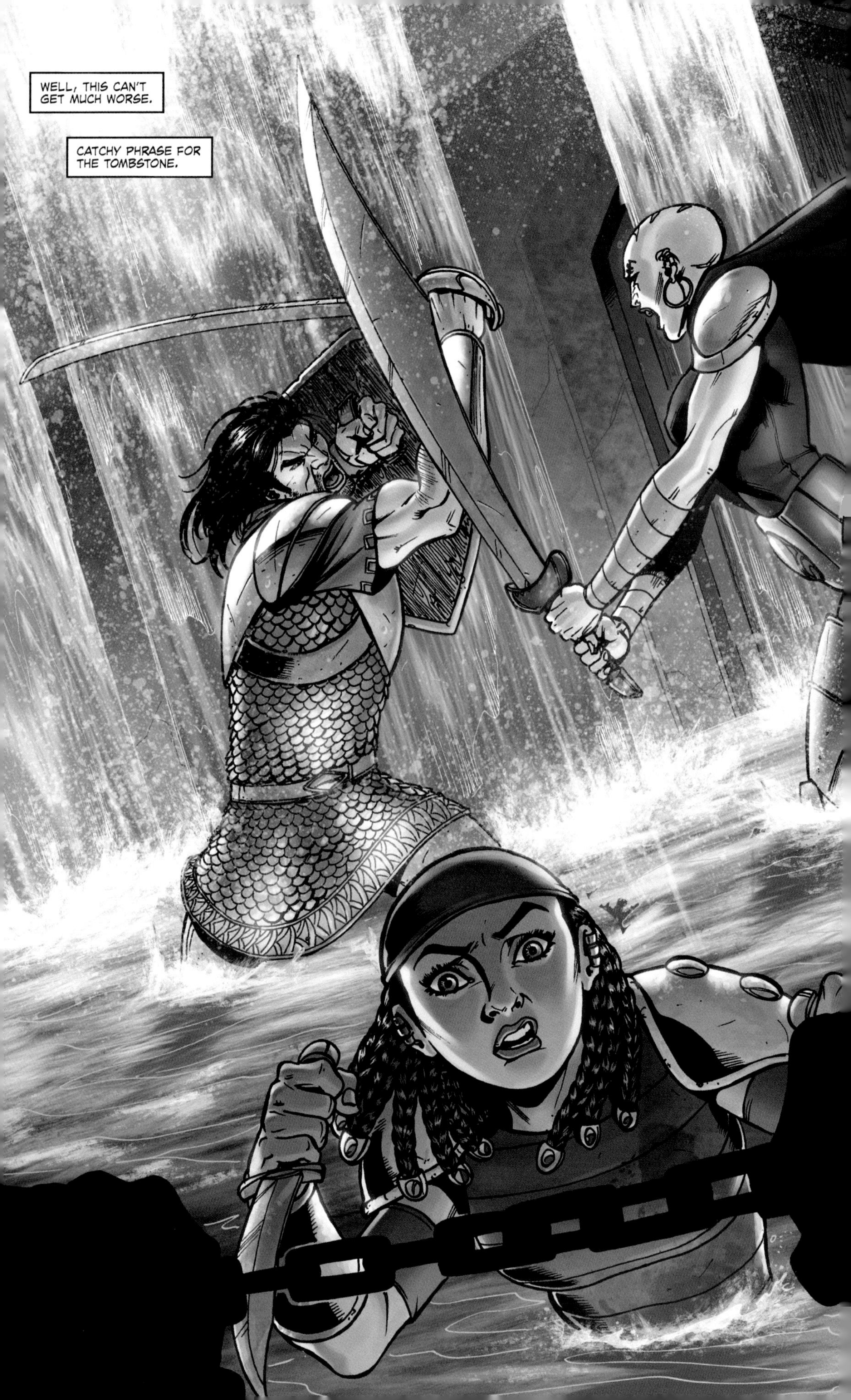
WELL, THIS CAN'T GET MUCH WORSE.
CATCHY PHRASE FOR THE TOMBSTONE.

Art by Tyler Walpole

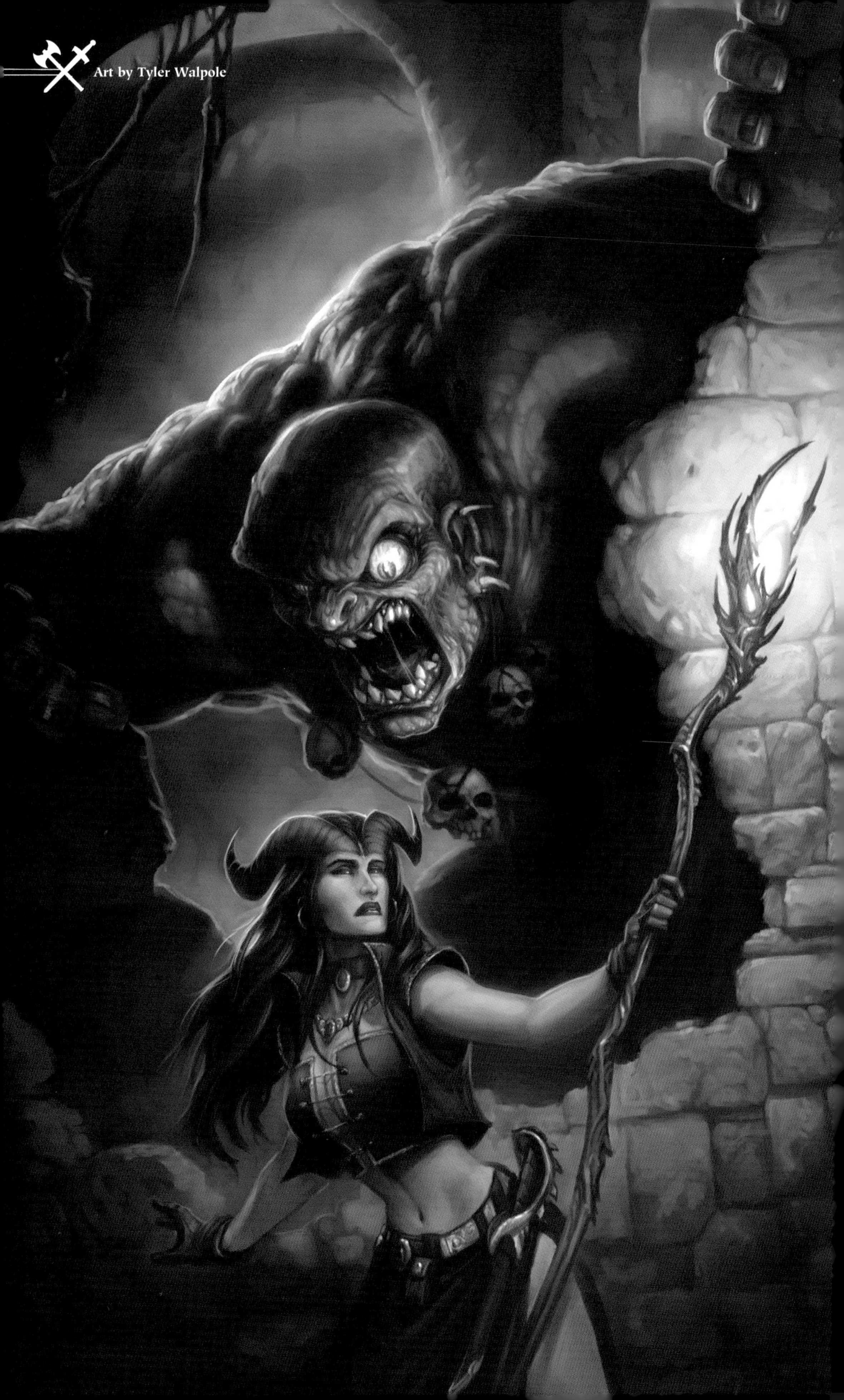

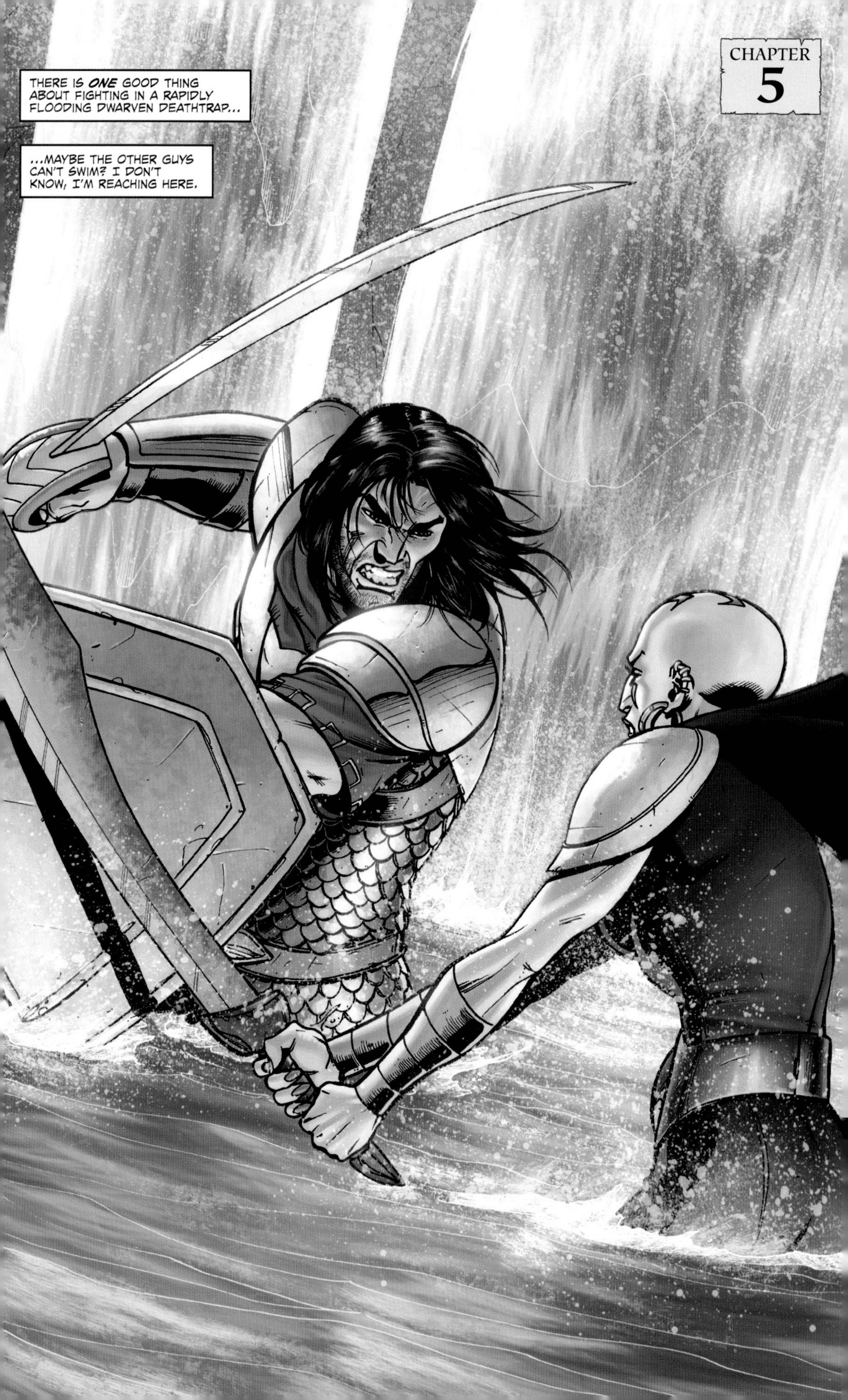
THERE IS ONE GOOD THING ABOUT FIGHTING IN A RAPIDLY FLOODING DWARVEN DEATHTRAP...
...MAYBE THE OTHER GUYS CAN'T SWIM? I DON'T KNOW, I'M REACHING HERE.
CHAPTER 5

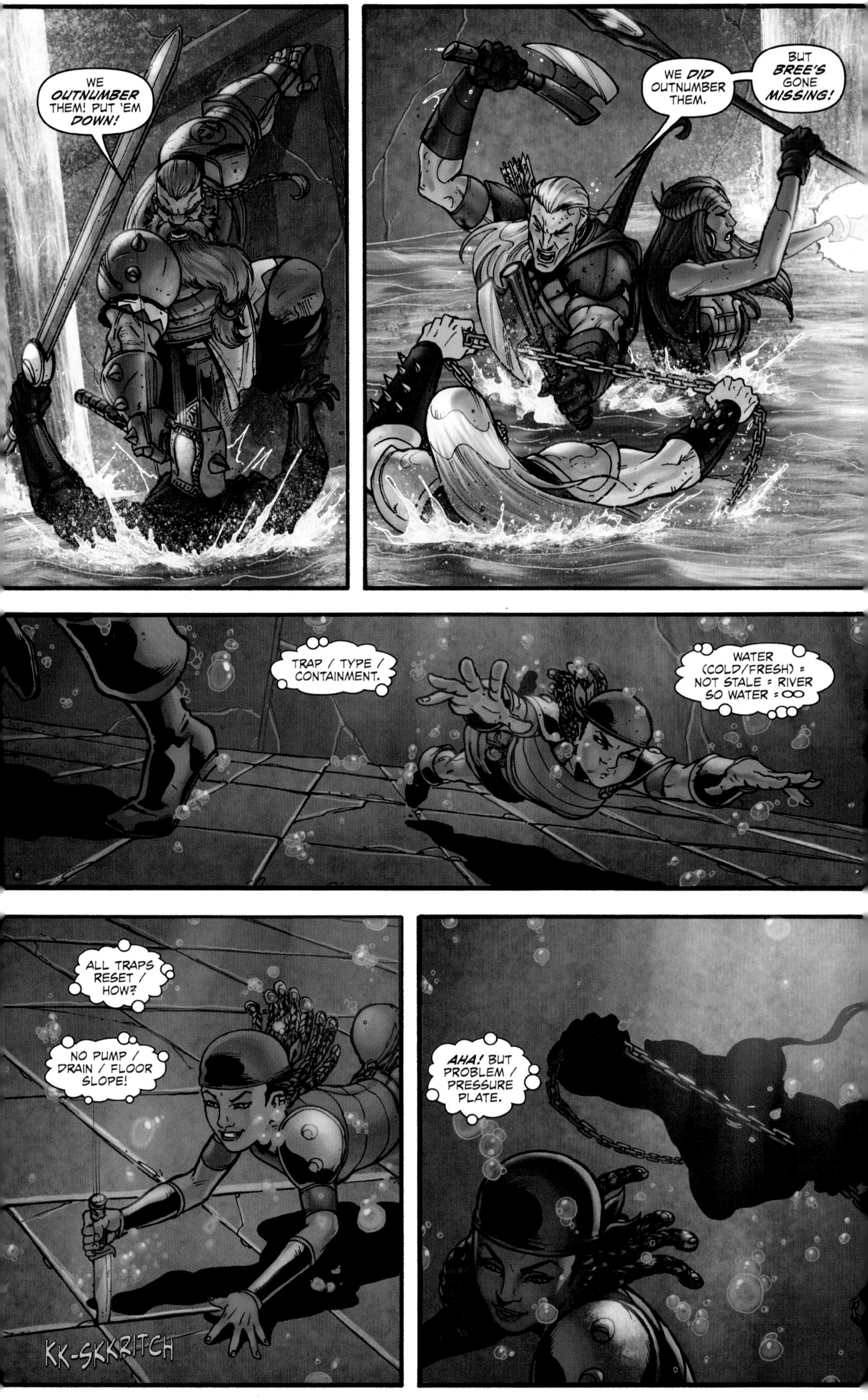
WE OUTNUMBER THEM! PUT 'EM DOWN!
WE DID OUTNUMBER THEM.
BUT BREE'S GONE MISSING!
TRAP / TYPE / CONTAINMENT.
WATER (COLD/FRESH) = NOT STALE = RIVER SO WATER = ∞
ALL TRAPS RESET / HOW?
NO PUMP / DRAIN / FLOOR SLOPE!
KK-SKKRITCH
AHA! BUT PROBLEM / PRESSURE PLATE.

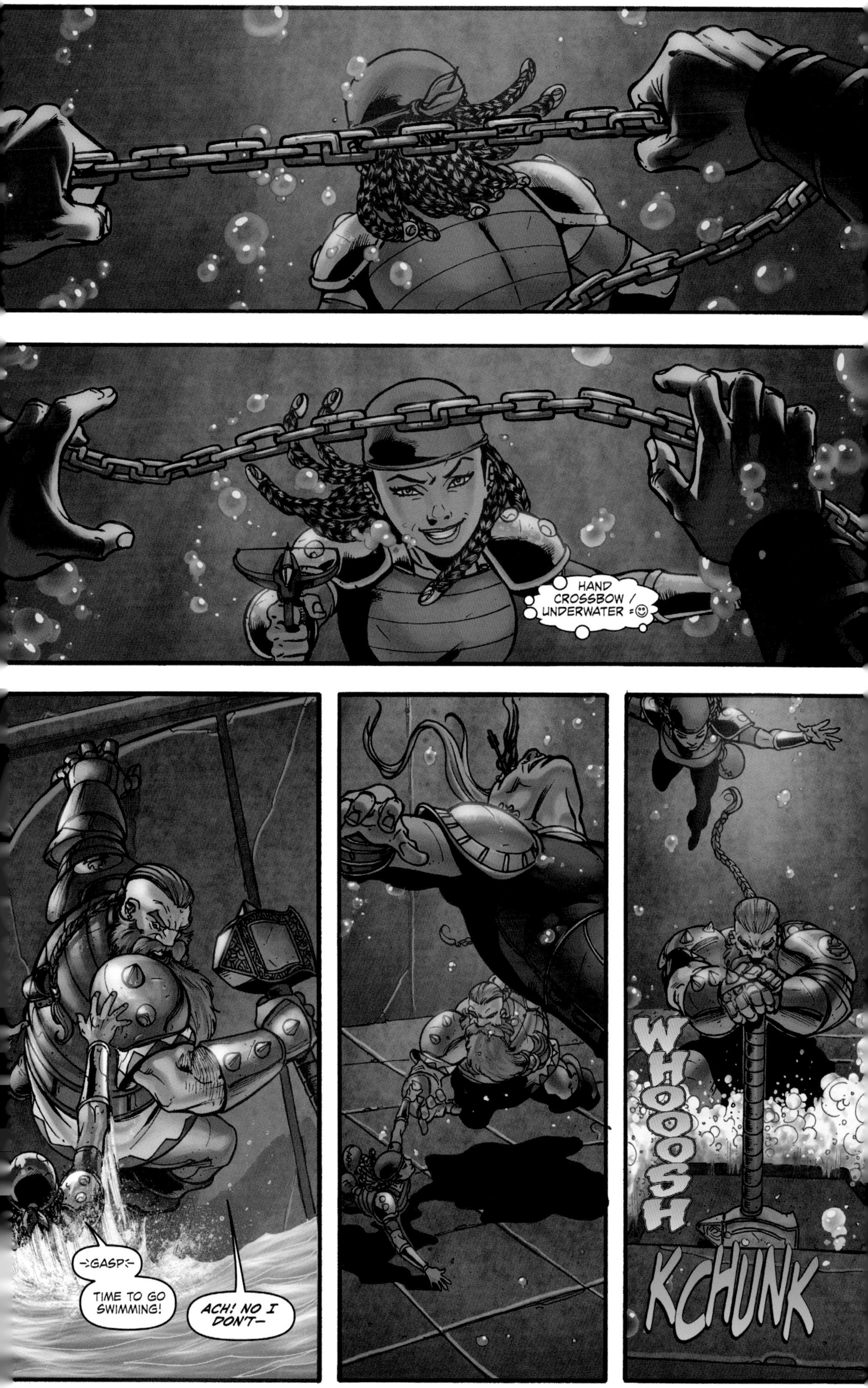
HAND
CROSSBOW /
UNDERWATER = ☺
-GASP-
TIME TO GO
SWIMMING!
ACH! NO I
DON'T--
WHOOSH
KCHUNK

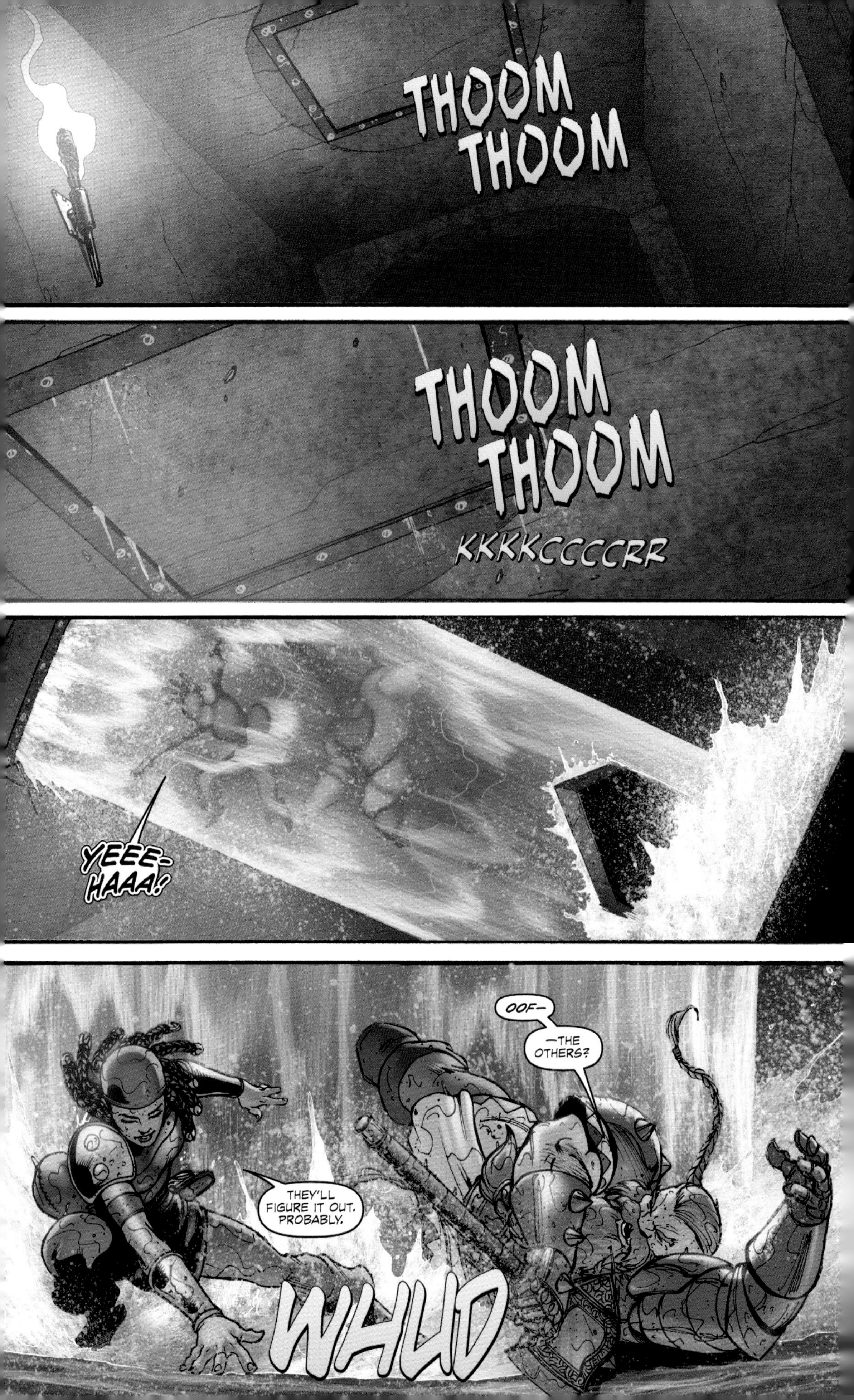
THOOM
THOOM
THOOM
THOOM
KKKKCCCCRR
YEEE-HAAA!
OOF—
—THE OTHERS?
THEY'LL FIGURE IT OUT. PROBABLY.
WHUD

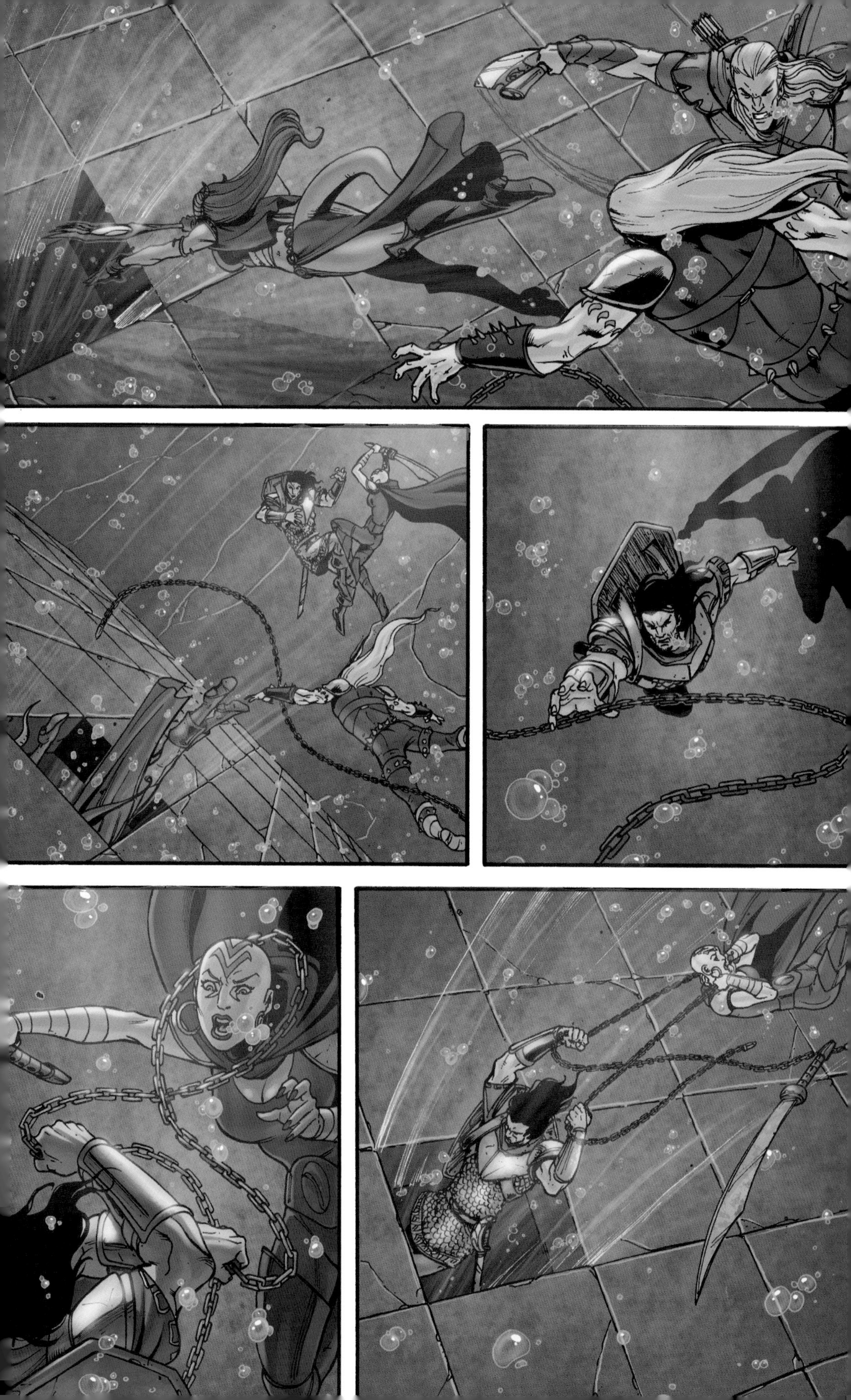

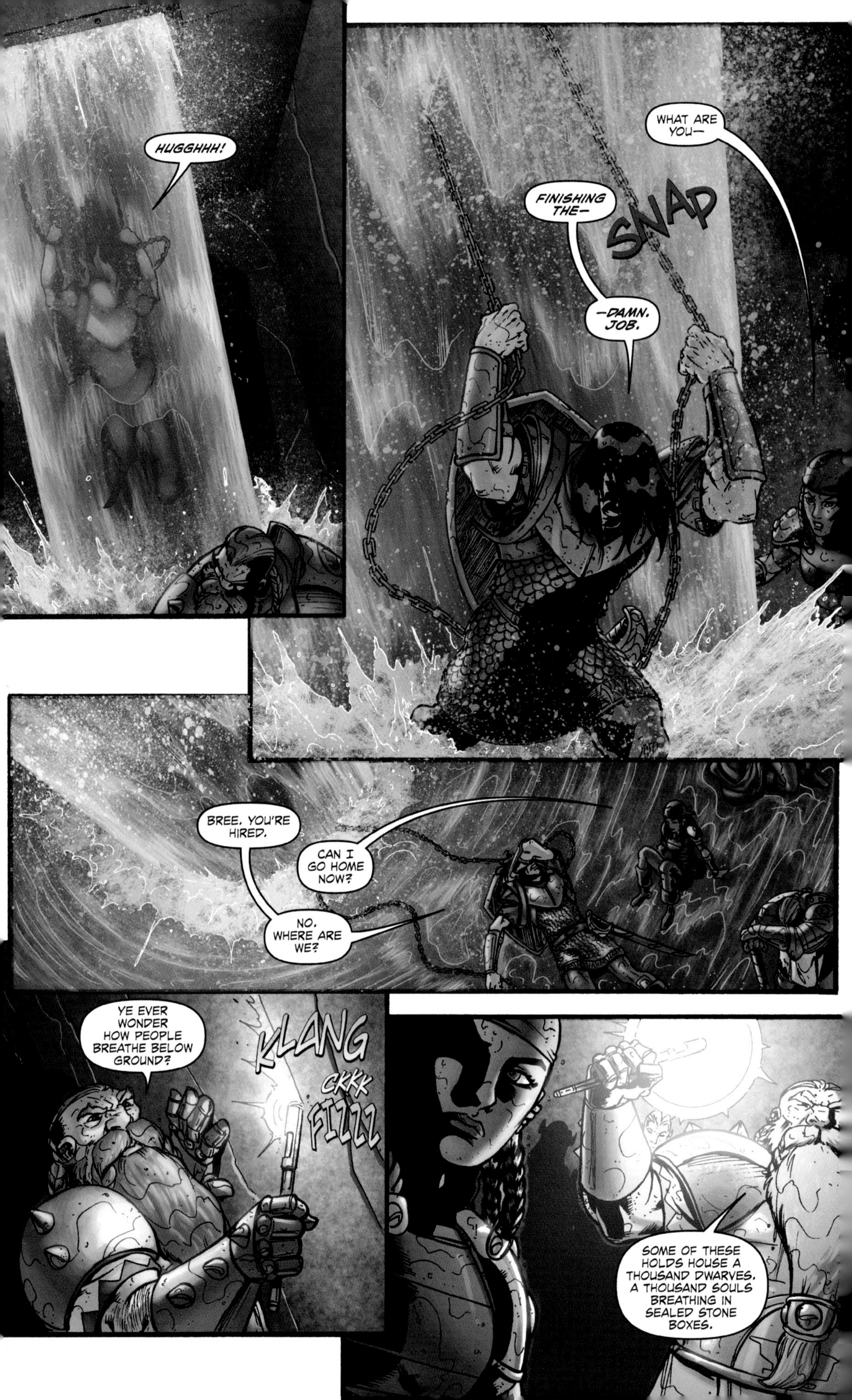
HUGGHHH!
WHAT ARE YOU—
FINISHING THE—
SNAP
—DAMN. JOB.
BREE. YOU'RE HIRED.
CAN I GO HOME NOW?
NO. WHERE ARE WE?
YE EVER WONDER HOW PEOPLE BREATHE BELOW GROUND?
KLANG
CKKK
FIZZZ
SOME OF THESE HOLDS HOUSE A THOUSAND DWARVES. A THOUSAND SOULS BREATHING IN SEALED STONE BOXES.

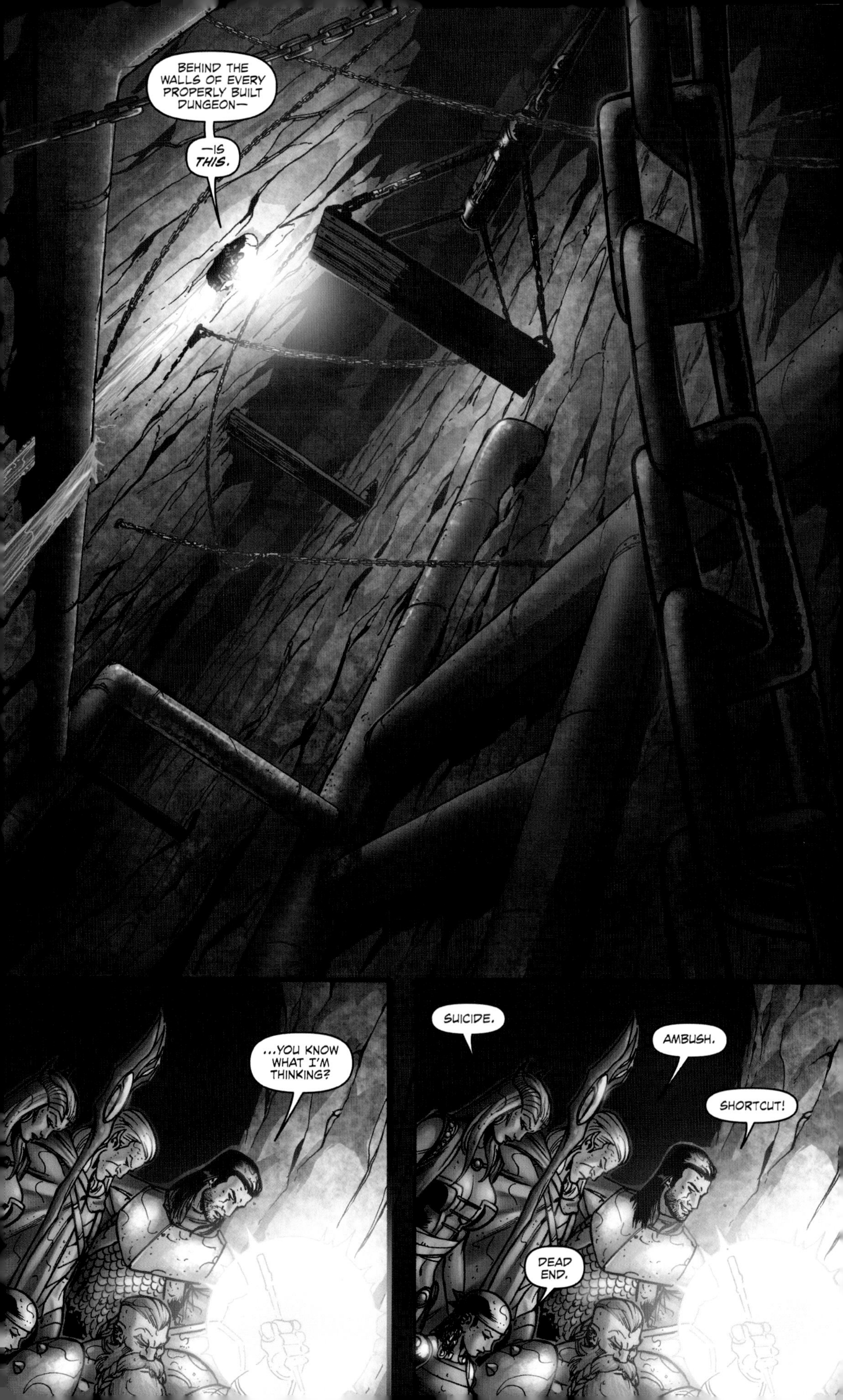
BEHIND THE WALLS OF EVERY PROPERLY BUILT DUNGEON—
—IS *THIS*.
...YOU KNOW WHAT I'M THINKING?
SUICIDE.
AMBUSH.
SHORTCUT!
DEAD END.

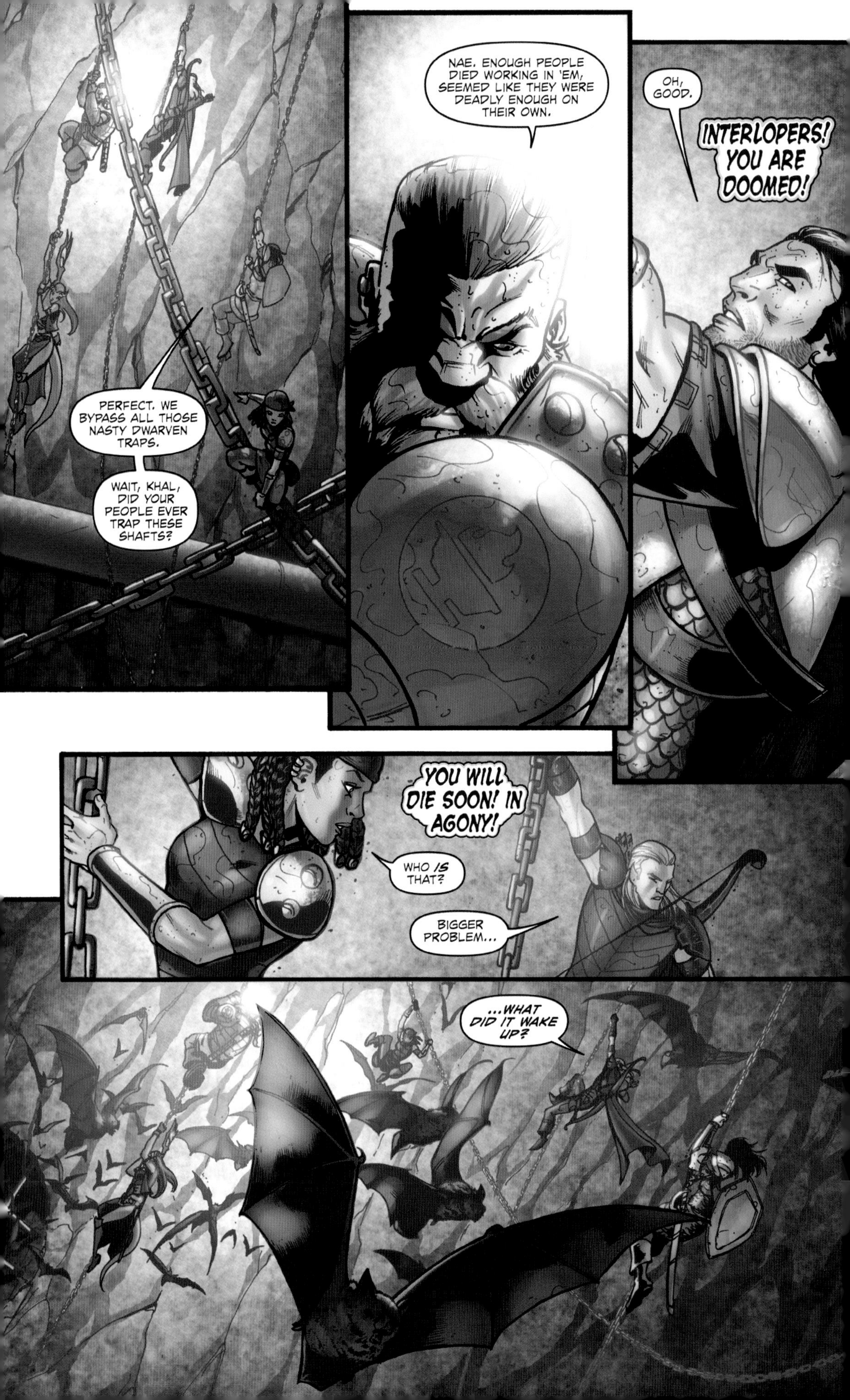
PERFECT. WE BYPASS ALL THOSE NASTY DWARVEN TRAPS.
WAIT, KHAL, DID YOUR PEOPLE EVER TRAP THESE SHAFTS?
NAE. ENOUGH PEOPLE DIED WORKING IN 'EM, SEEMED LIKE THEY WERE DEADLY ENOUGH ON THEIR OWN.
OH, GOOD.
INTERLOPERS! YOU ARE DOOMED!
YOU WILL DIE SOON! IN AGONY!
WHO *IS* THAT?
BIGGER PROBLEM...
...WHAT DID IT WAKE UP?

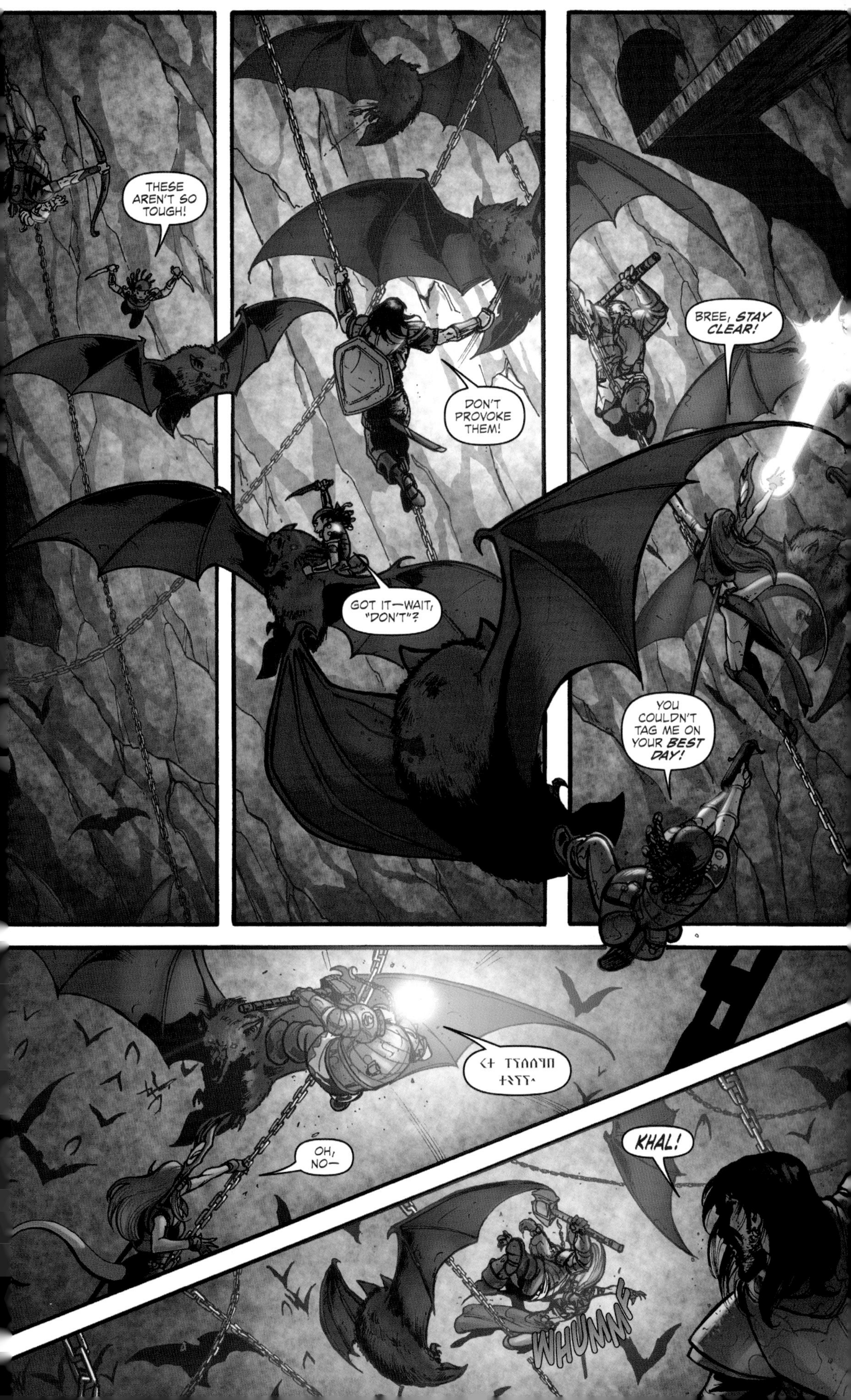
THESE AREN'T SO TOUGH!
DON'T PROVOKE THEM!
GOT IT—WAIT, "DON'T"?
BREE, STAY CLEAR!
YOU COULDN'T TAG ME ON YOUR BEST DAY!
OH, NO—
KHAL!
WHUMMF

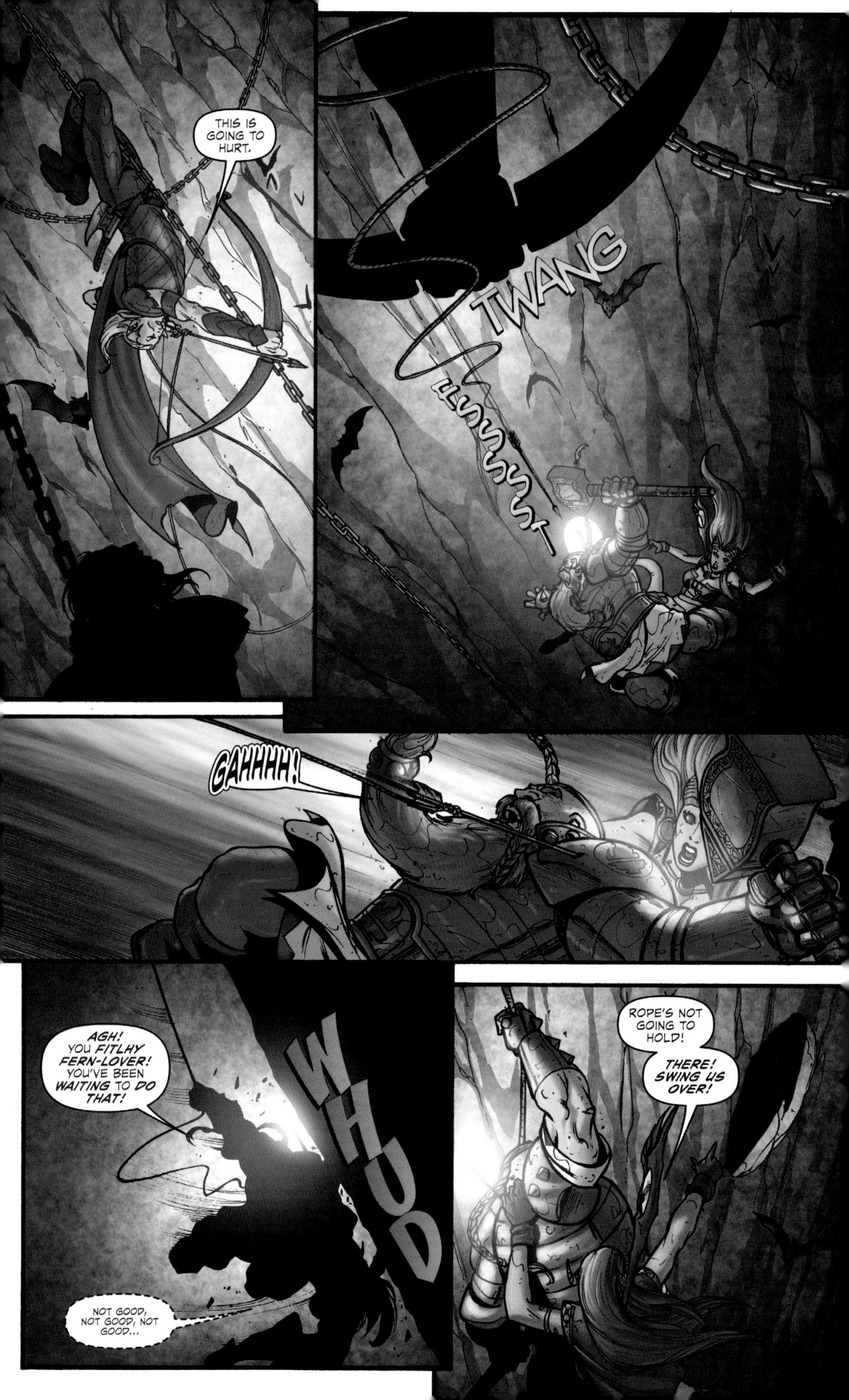

THIS IS GOING TO HURT.
TWANG
FSSSSSST
GAHHHH!
AGH! YOU FITLHY FERN-LOVER! YOU'VE BEEN WAITING TO DO THAT!
WHUD
NOT GOOD, NOT GOOD, NOT GOOD...
ROPE'S NOT GOING TO HOLD!
THERE! SWING US OVER!

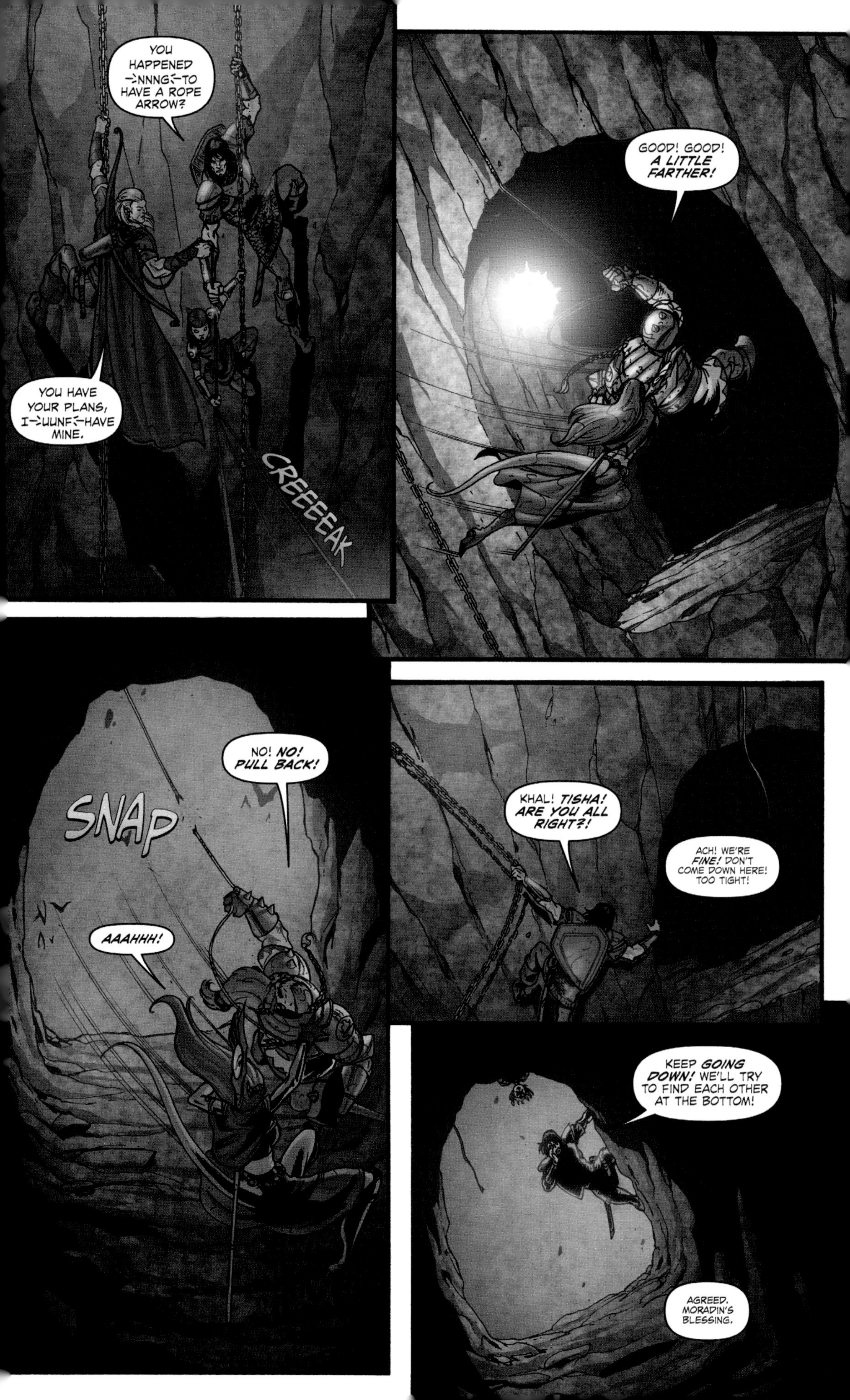
YOU HAPPENED —NNNG— TO HAVE A ROPE ARROW?
YOU HAVE YOUR PLANS, I —UUNF— HAVE MINE.
CREEEEAK
GOOD! GOOD! A LITTLE FARTHER!
NO! NO! PULL BACK!
SNAP
AAAHHH!
KHAL! TISHA! ARE YOU ALL RIGHT?!
ACH! WE'RE FINE! DON'T COME DOWN HERE! TOO TIGHT!
KEEP GOING DOWN! WE'LL TRY TO FIND EACH OTHER AT THE BOTTOM!
AGREED. MORADIN'S BLESSING.

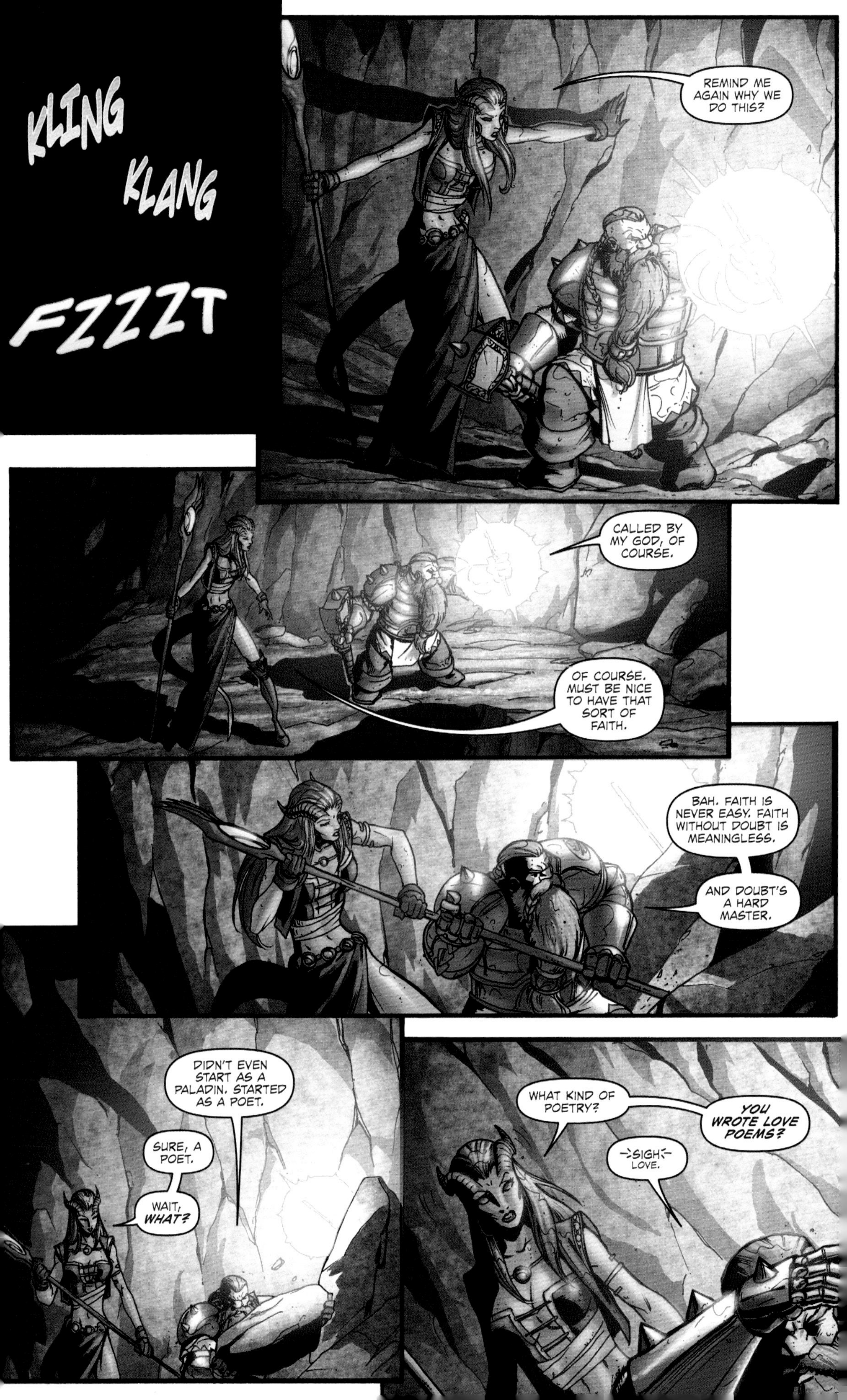
KLING
KLANG
FZZZT
REMIND ME AGAIN WHY WE DO THIS?
CALLED BY MY GOD, OF COURSE.
OF COURSE. MUST BE NICE TO HAVE THAT SORT OF FAITH.
BAH. FAITH IS NEVER EASY. FAITH WITHOUT DOUBT IS MEANINGLESS.
AND DOUBT'S A HARD MASTER.
DIDN'T EVEN START AS A PALADIN. STARTED AS A POET.
SURE, A POET.
WAIT, *WHAT?*
WHAT KIND OF POETRY?
YOU WROTE LOVE POEMS?
-SIGH- LOVE.

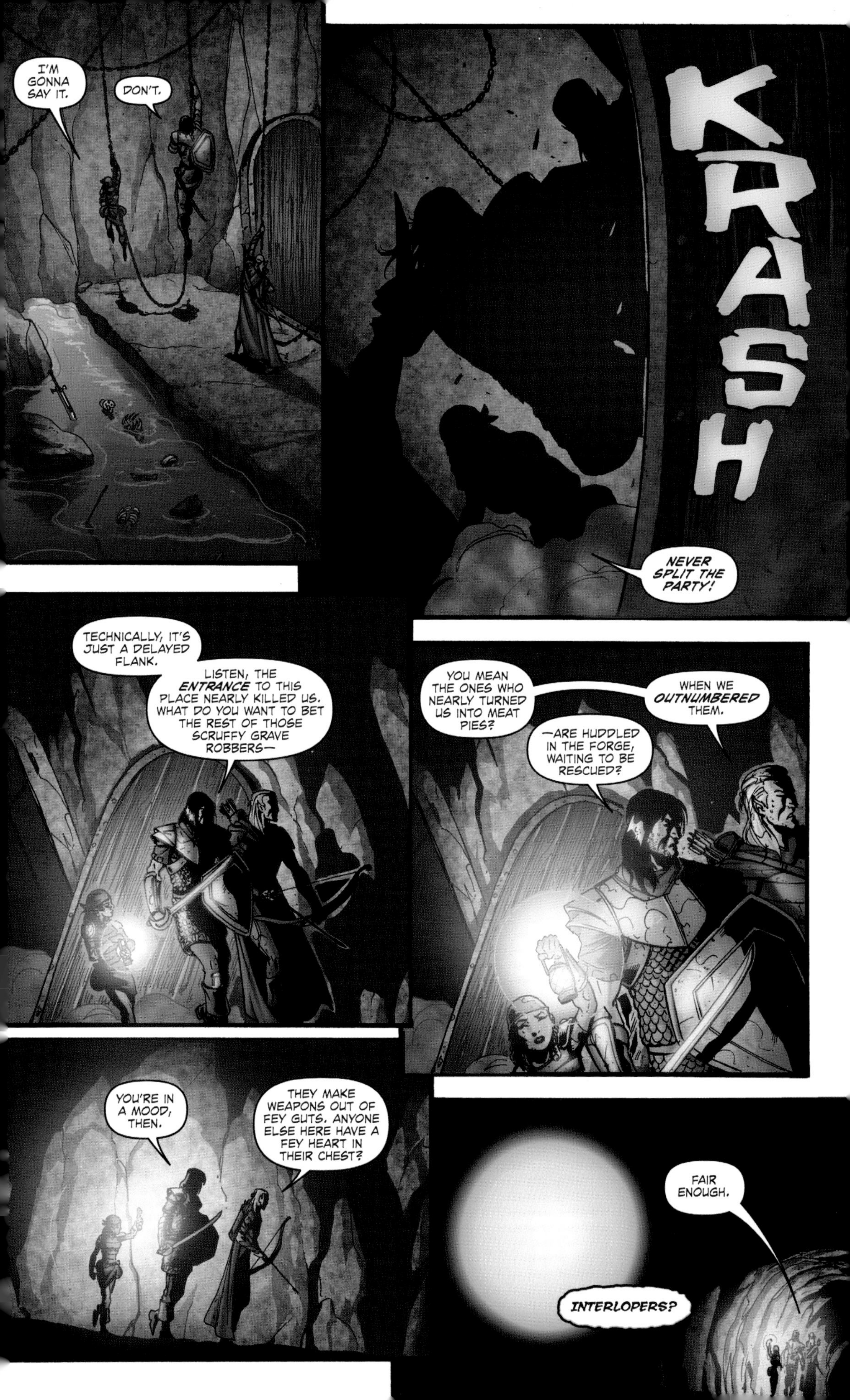
I'M GONNA SAY IT.
DON'T.
KRASH
NEVER SPLIT THE PARTY!
TECHNICALLY, IT'S JUST A DELAYED FLANK.
LISTEN, THE ENTRANCE TO THIS PLACE NEARLY KILLED US. WHAT DO YOU WANT TO BET THE REST OF THOSE SCRUFFY GRAVE ROBBERS—
YOU MEAN THE ONES WHO NEARLY TURNED US INTO MEAT PIES?
WHEN WE OUTNUMBERED THEM.
—ARE HUDDLED IN THE FORGE, WAITING TO BE RESCUED?
YOU'RE IN A MOOD, THEN.
THEY MAKE WEAPONS OUT OF FEY GUTS. ANYONE ELSE HERE HAVE A FEY HEART IN THEIR CHEST?
FAIR ENOUGH.
INTERLOPERS?

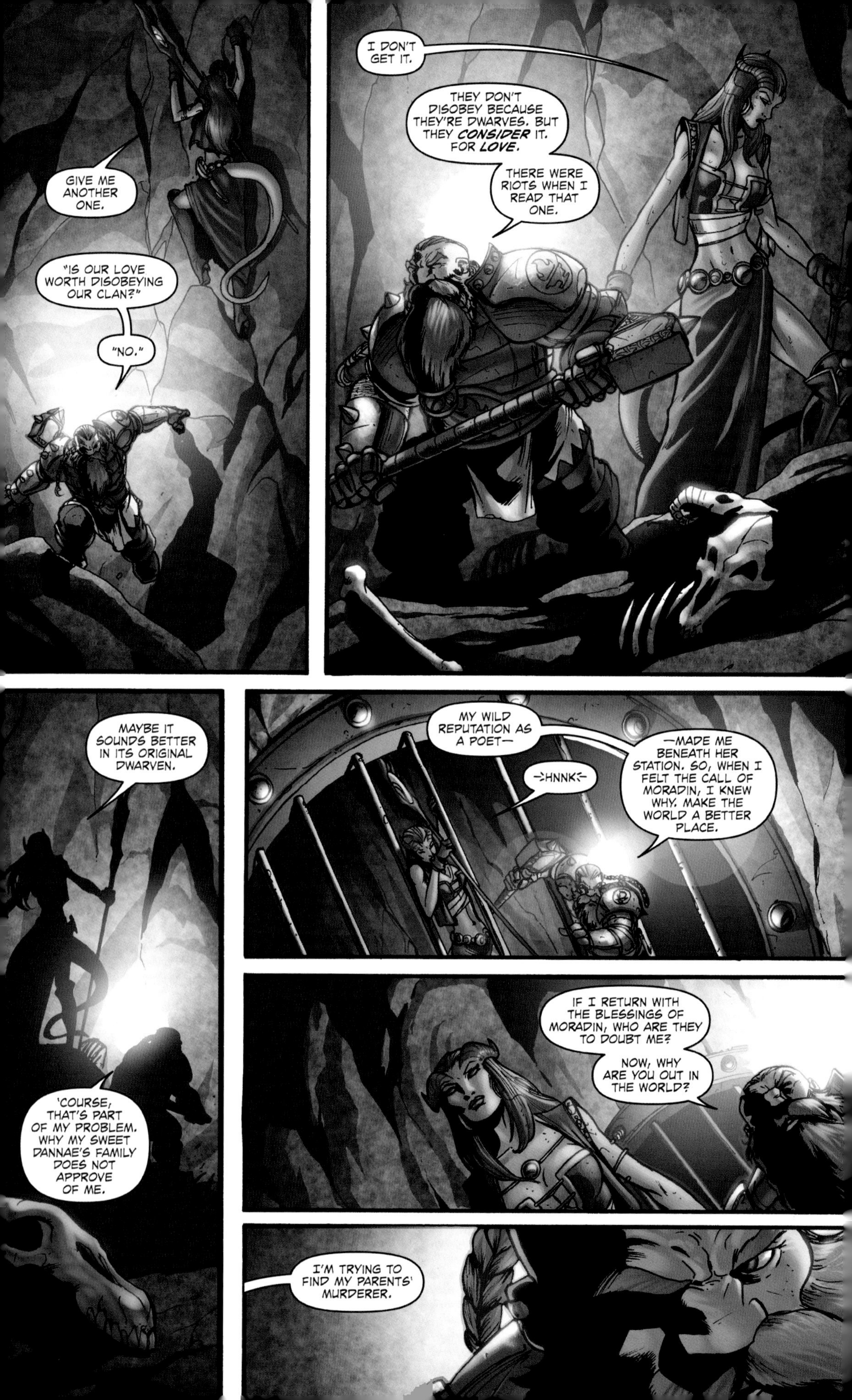
GIVE ME ANOTHER ONE.
"IS OUR LOVE WORTH DISOBEYING OUR CLAN?"
"NO."
I DON'T GET IT.
THEY DON'T DISOBEY BECAUSE THEY'RE DWARVES. BUT THEY CONSIDER IT. FOR LOVE.
THERE WERE RIOTS WHEN I READ THAT ONE.
MAYBE IT SOUNDS BETTER IN ITS ORIGINAL DWARVEN.
'COURSE, THAT'S PART OF MY PROBLEM. WHY MY SWEET DANNAE'S FAMILY DOES NOT APPROVE OF ME.
MY WILD REPUTATION AS A POET—
—HNNK—
—MADE ME BENEATH HER STATION. SO, WHEN I FELT THE CALL OF MORADIN, I KNEW WHY. MAKE THE WORLD A BETTER PLACE.
IF I RETURN WITH THE BLESSINGS OF MORADIN, WHO ARE THEY TO DOUBT ME?
NOW, WHY ARE YOU OUT IN THE WORLD?
I'M TRYING TO FIND MY PARENTS' MURDERER.

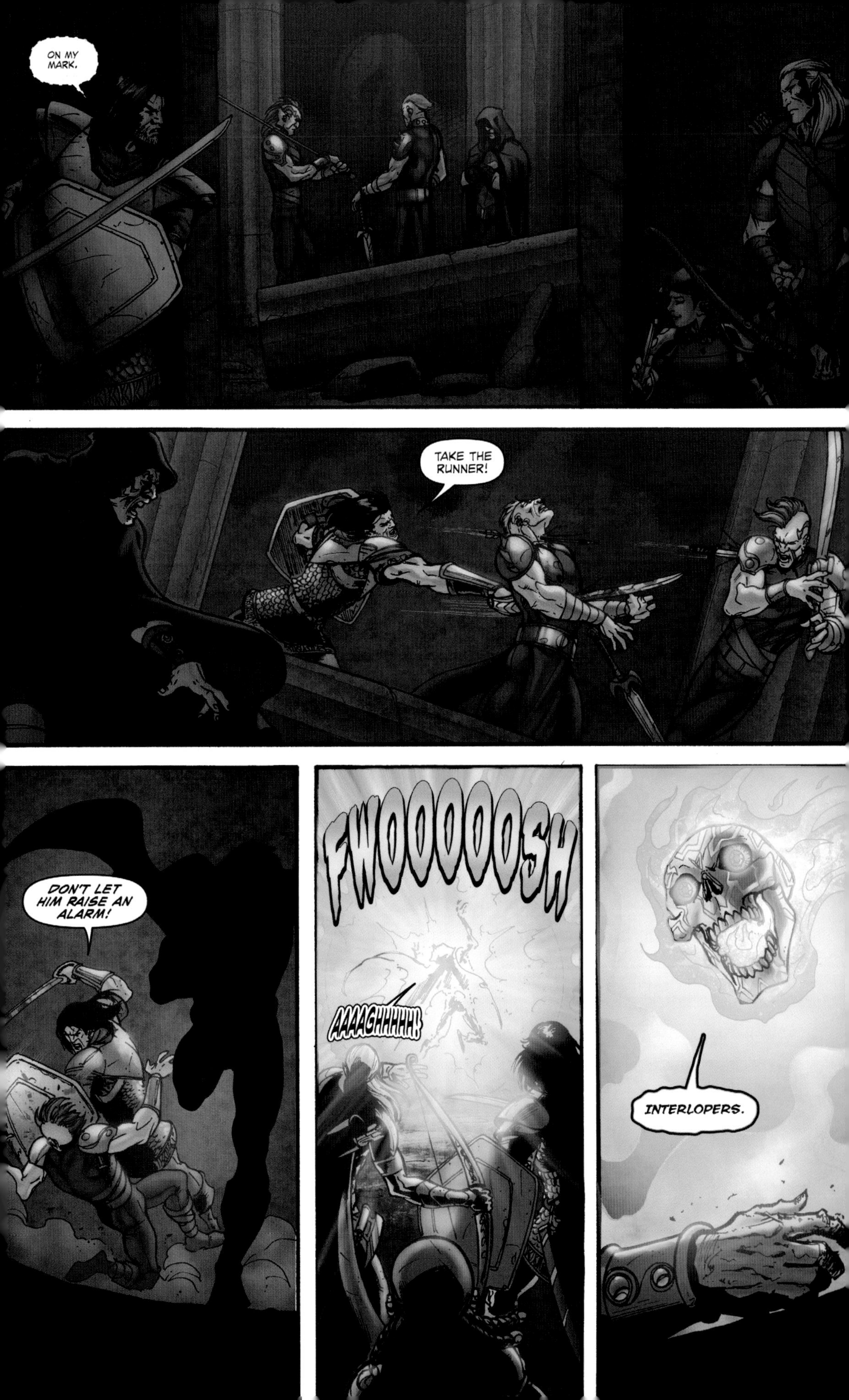
ON MY MARK.
TAKE THE RUNNER!
DON'T LET HIM RAISE AN ALARM!
FWOOOOOSH
AAAAGHHHHH!
INTERLOPERS.

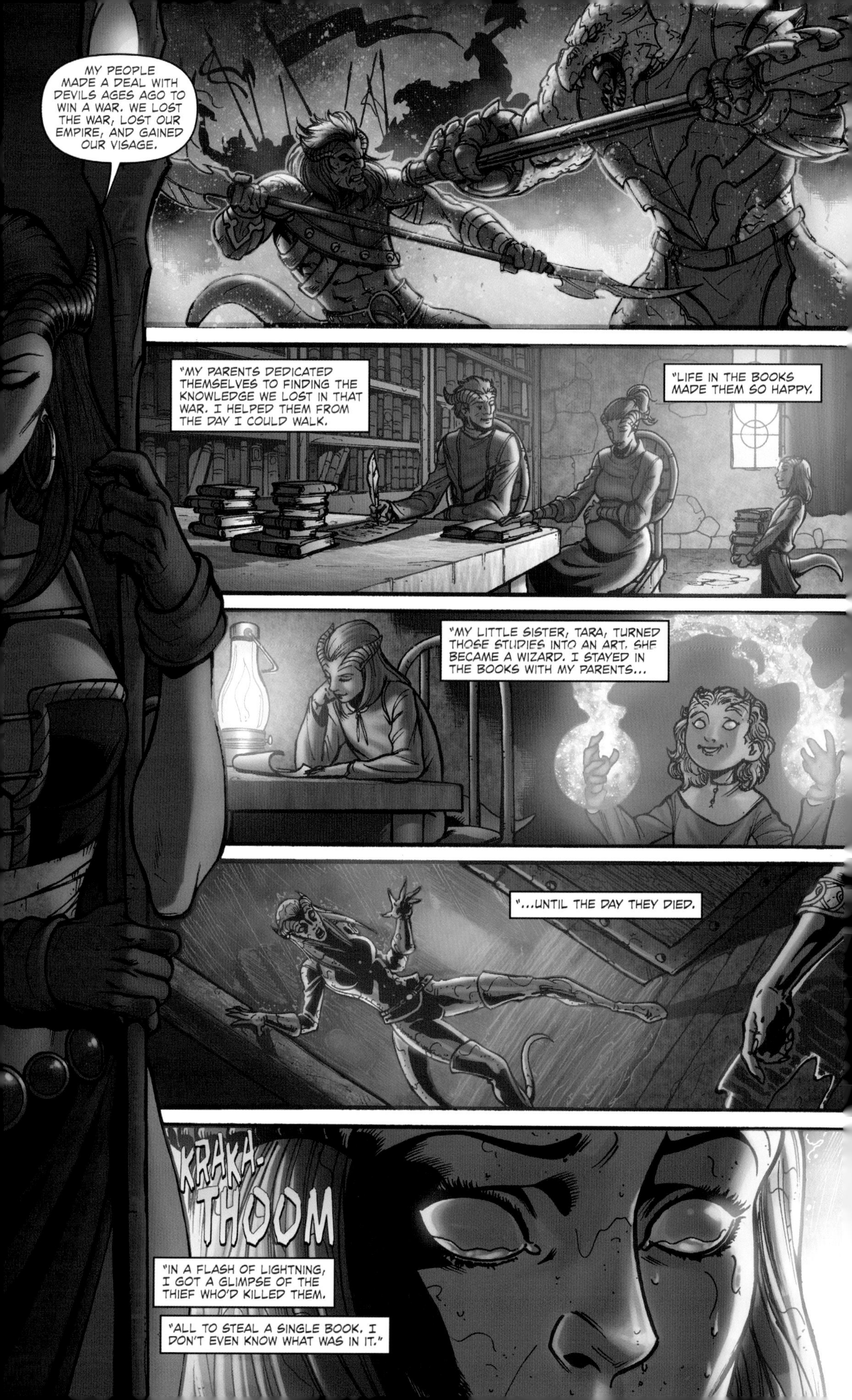
MY PEOPLE MADE A DEAL WITH DEVILS AGES AGO TO WIN A WAR. WE LOST THE WAR, LOST OUR EMPIRE, AND GAINED OUR VISAGE.
"MY PARENTS DEDICATED THEMSELVES TO FINDING THE KNOWLEDGE WE LOST IN THAT WAR. I HELPED THEM FROM THE DAY I COULD WALK.
"LIFE IN THE BOOKS MADE THEM SO HAPPY.
"MY LITTLE SISTER, TARA, TURNED THOSE STUDIES INTO AN ART. SHE BECAME A WIZARD. I STAYED IN THE BOOKS WITH MY PARENTS...
"...UNTIL THE DAY THEY DIED.
KRAKA-THOOM
"IN A FLASH OF LIGHTNING, I GOT A GLIMPSE OF THE THIEF WHO'D KILLED THEM.
"ALL TO STEAL A SINGLE BOOK. I DON'T EVEN KNOW WHAT WAS IN IT."

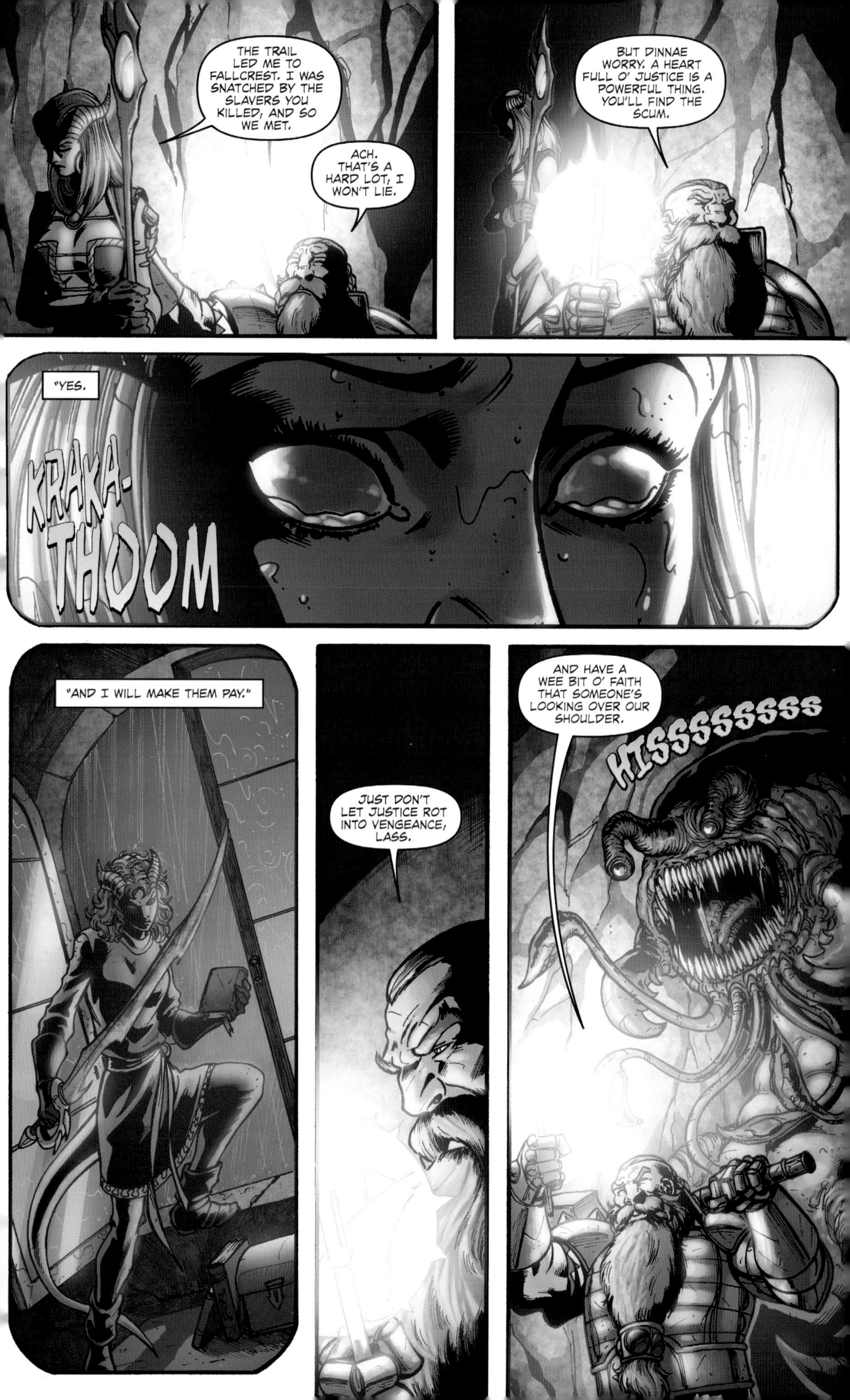
THE TRAIL LED ME TO FALLCREST. I WAS SNATCHED BY THE SLAVERS YOU KILLED, AND SO WE MET.
ACH. THAT'S A HARD LOT, I WON'T LIE.
BUT DINNAE WORRY. A HEART FULL O' JUSTICE IS A POWERFUL THING. YOU'LL FIND THE SCUM.
"YES.
KRAKA-THOOM
"AND I WILL MAKE THEM PAY."
JUST DON'T LET JUSTICE ROT INTO VENGEANCE, LASS.
AND HAVE A WEE BIT O' FAITH THAT SOMEONE'S LOOKING OVER OUR SHOULDER.
HISSSSSSSS

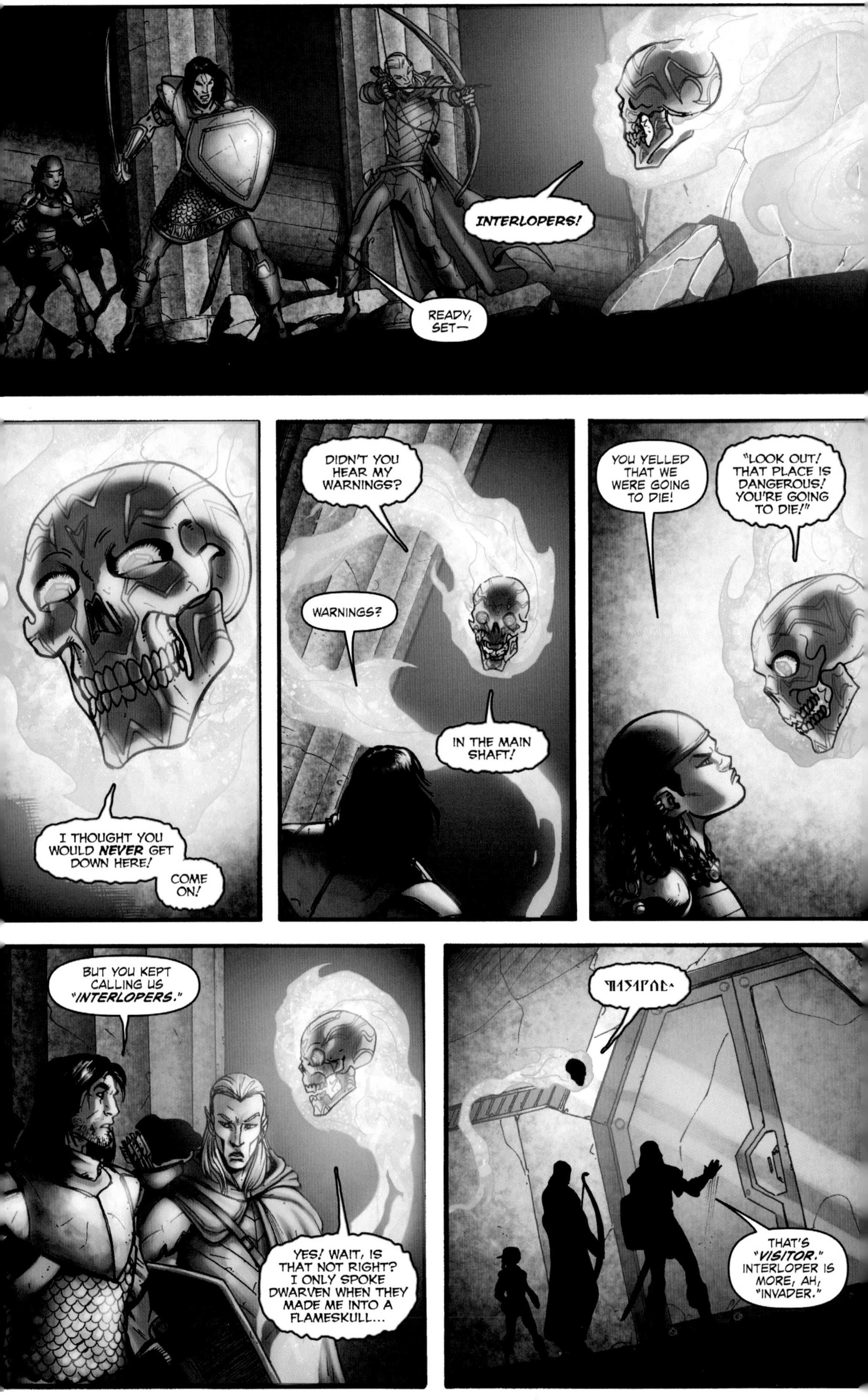
INTERLOPERS!
READY, SET—
I THOUGHT YOU WOULD NEVER GET DOWN HERE!
COME ON!
DIDN'T YOU HEAR MY WARNINGS?
WARNINGS?
IN THE MAIN SHAFT!
YOU YELLED THAT WE WERE GOING TO DIE!
"LOOK OUT! THAT PLACE IS DANGEROUS! YOU'RE GOING TO DIE!"
BUT YOU KEPT CALLING US "INTERLOPERS."
YES! WAIT, IS THAT NOT RIGHT? I ONLY SPOKE DWARVEN WHEN THEY MADE ME INTO A FLAMESKULL...
THAT'S "VISITOR." INTERLOPER IS MORE, AH, "INVADER."

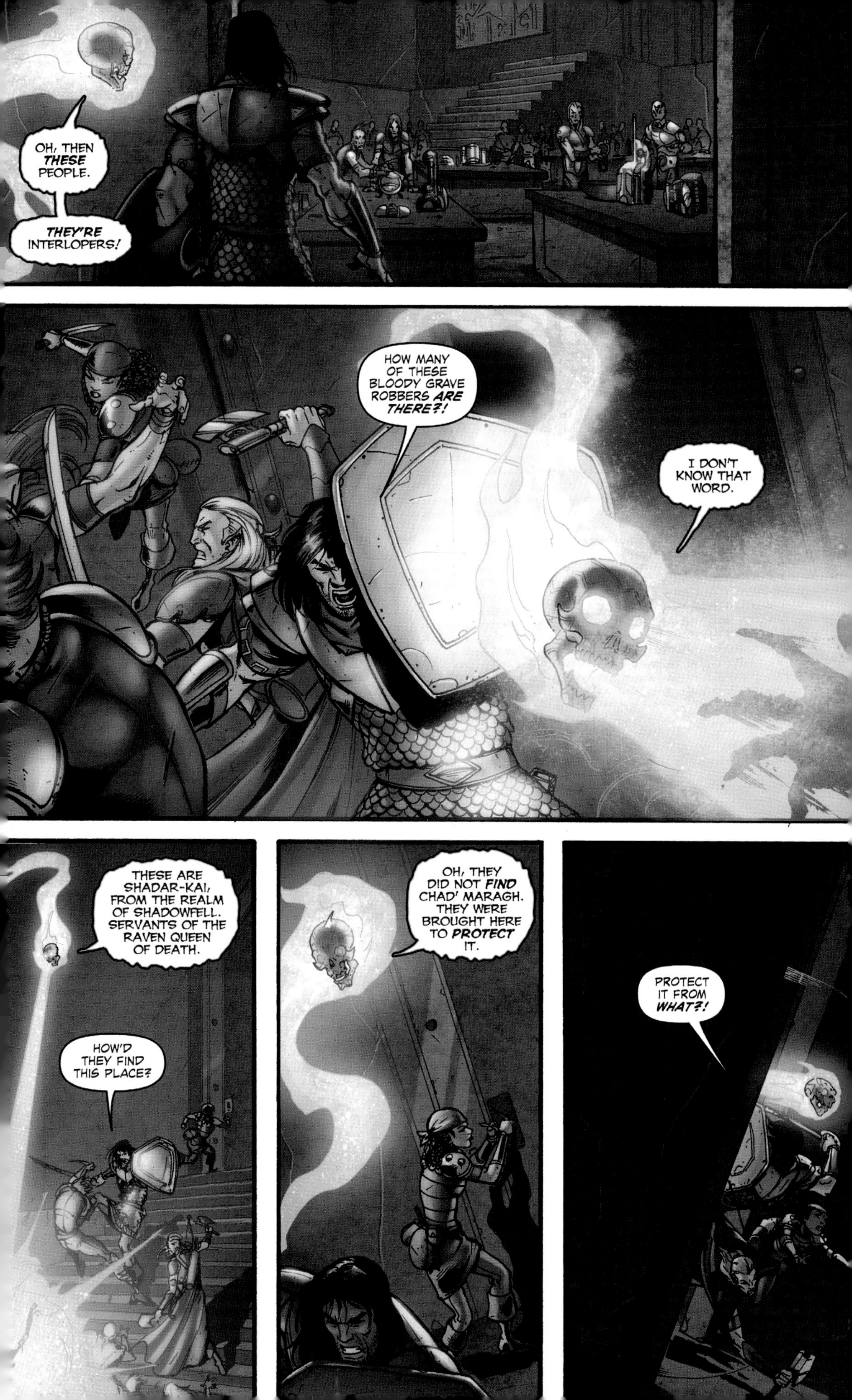
OH, THEN *THESE* PEOPLE.
THEY'RE INTERLOPERS!
HOW MANY OF THESE BLOODY GRAVE ROBBERS *ARE THERE?!*
I DON'T KNOW THAT WORD.
THESE ARE SHADAR-KAI, FROM THE REALM OF SHADOWFELL. SERVANTS OF THE RAVEN QUEEN OF DEATH.
HOW'D THEY FIND THIS PLACE?
OH, THEY DID NOT *FIND* CHAD' MARAGH. THEY WERE BROUGHT HERE TO *PROTECT* IT.
PROTECT IT FROM *WHAT?!*

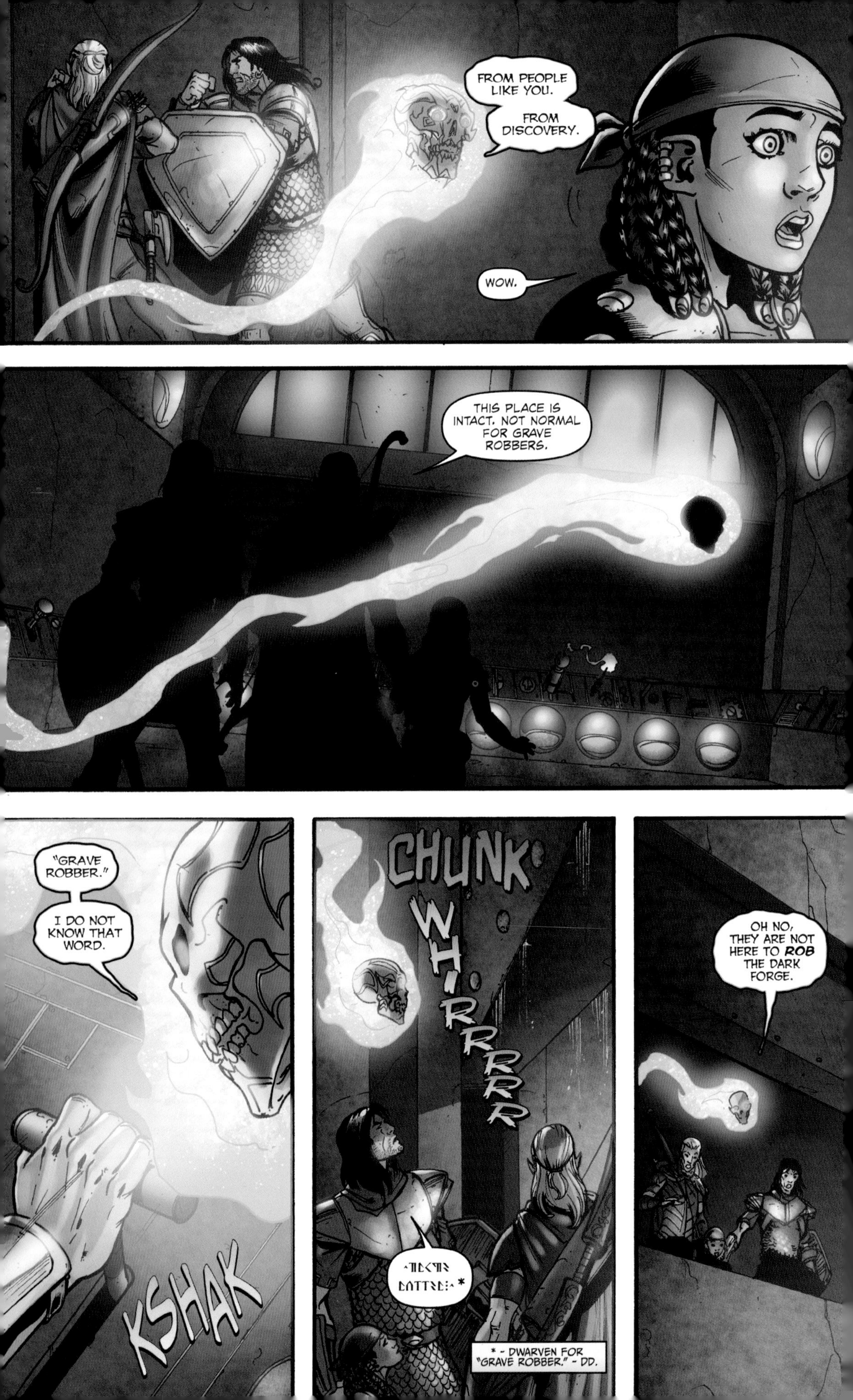
FROM PEOPLE LIKE YOU.
FROM DISCOVERY.
WOW.
THIS PLACE IS INTACT. NOT NORMAL FOR GRAVE ROBBERS.
"GRAVE ROBBER."
I DO NOT KNOW THAT WORD.
KSHAK
CHUNK
WHIRRRRR
* - DWARVEN FOR "GRAVE ROBBER." - DD.
OH NO, THEY ARE NOT HERE TO ROB THE DARK FORGE.

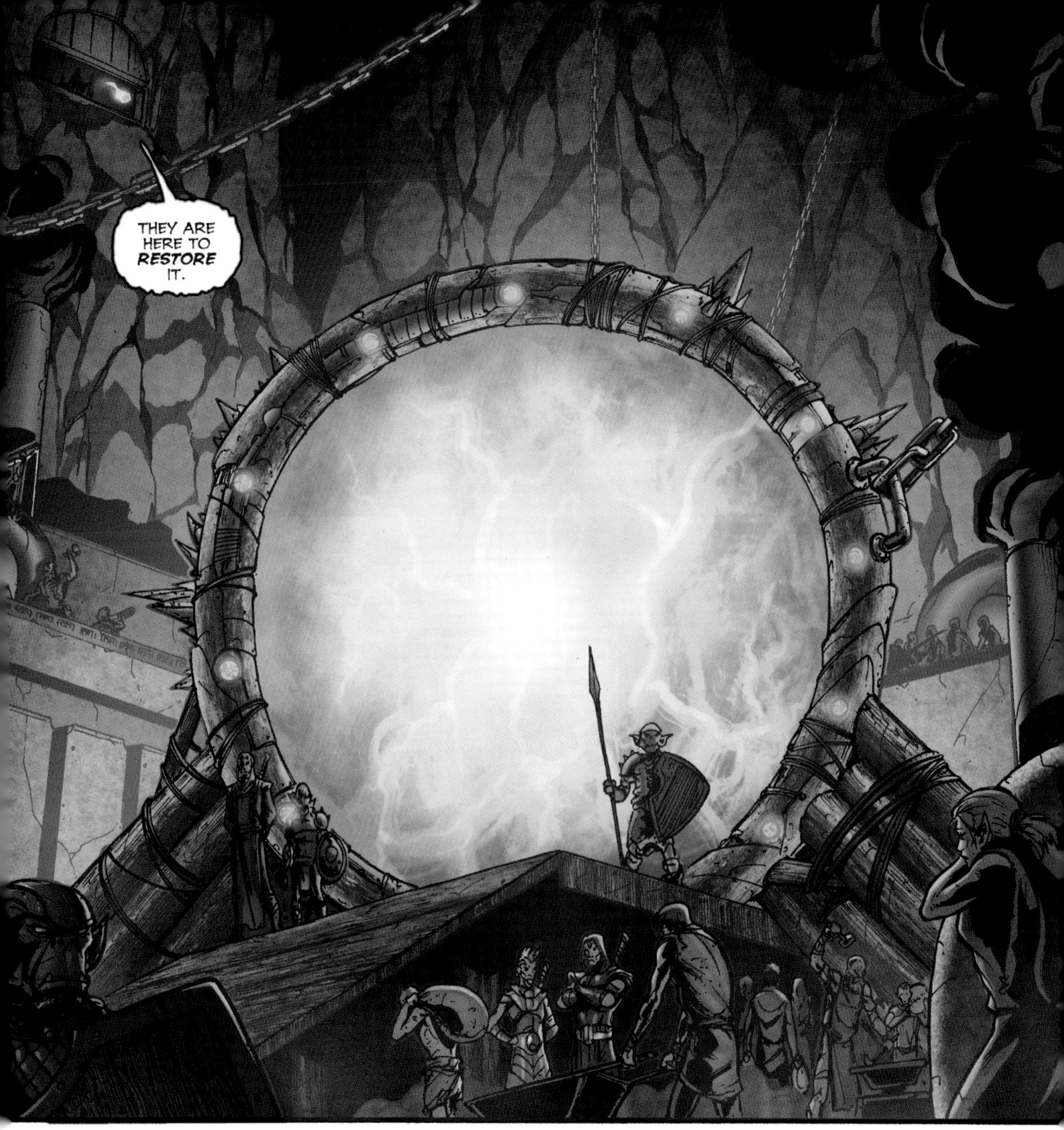
THEY ARE HERE TO RESTORE IT.

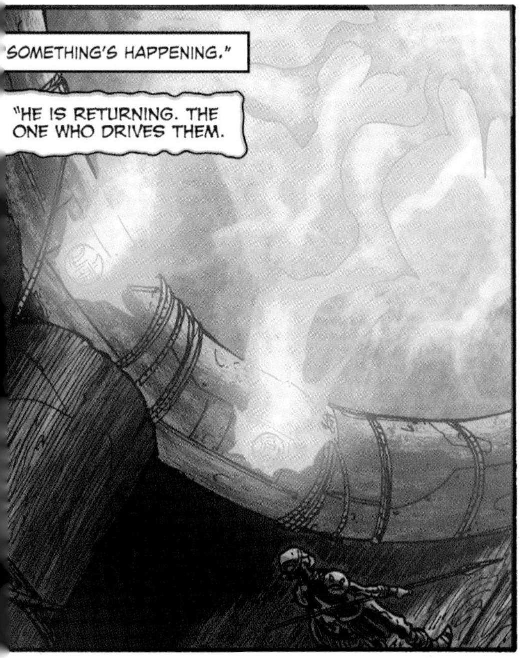
"SOMETHING'S HAPPENING."
"HE IS RETURNING. THE ONE WHO DRIVES THEM.

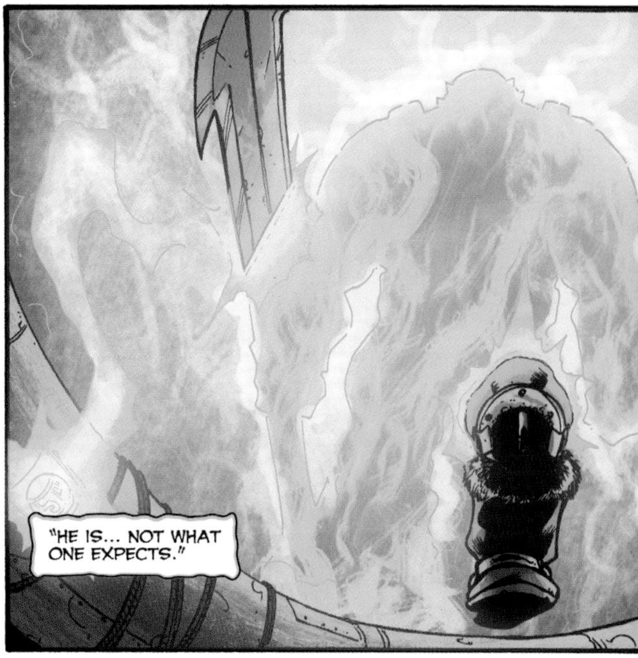
"HE IS... NOT WHAT ONE EXPECTS."

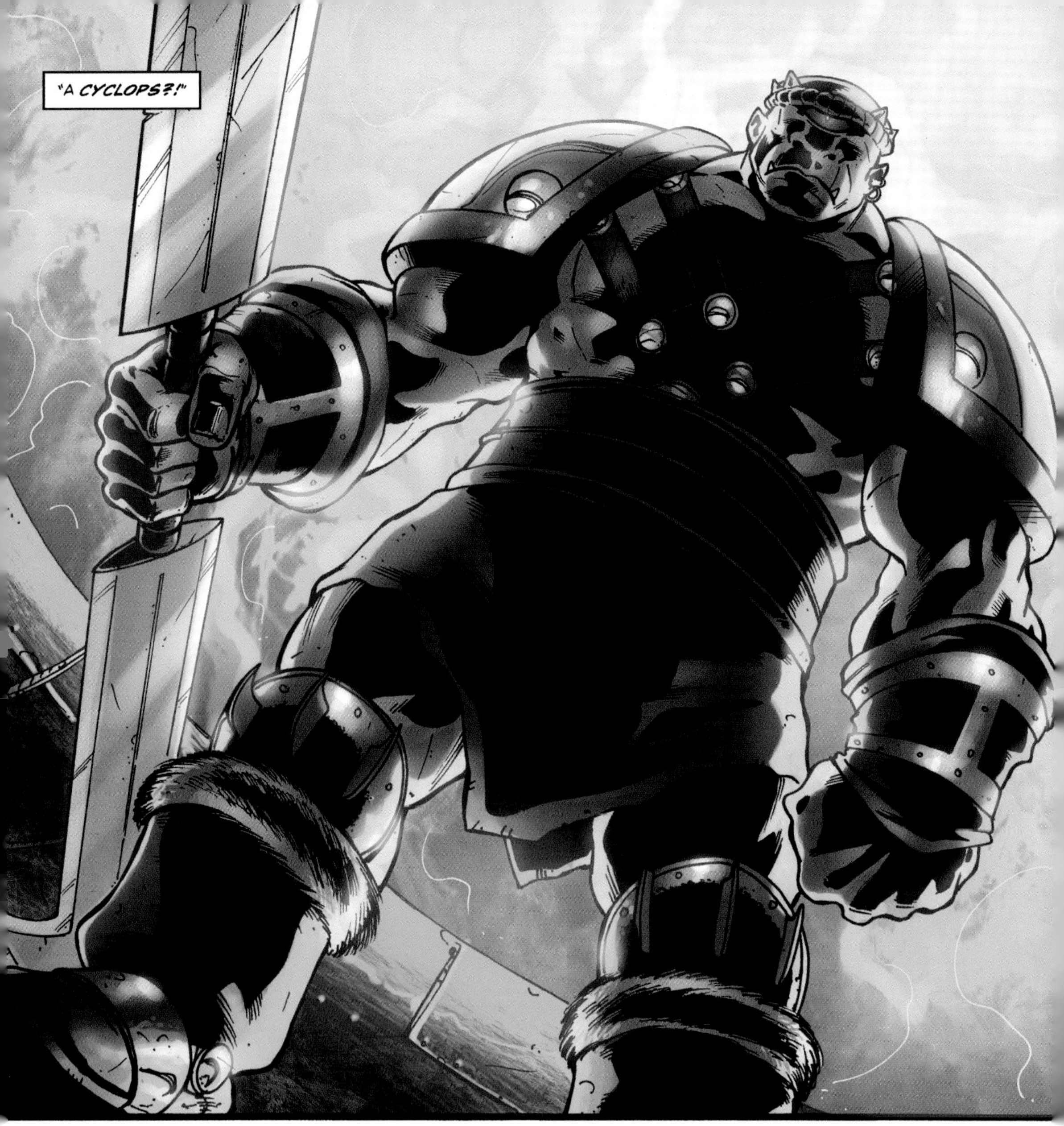
"A CYCLOPS?!"

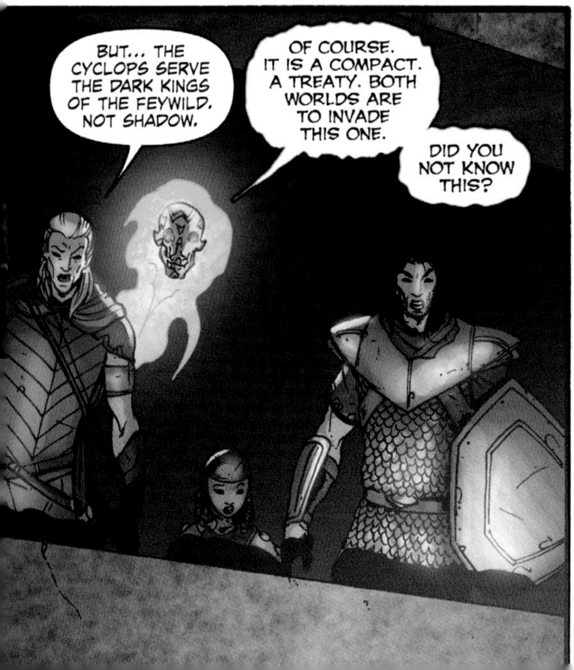
BUT... THE CYCLOPS SERVE THE DARK KINGS OF THE FEYWILD. NOT SHADOW.
OF COURSE. IT IS A COMPACT. A TREATY. BOTH WORLDS ARE TO INVADE THIS ONE.
DID YOU NOT KNOW THIS?

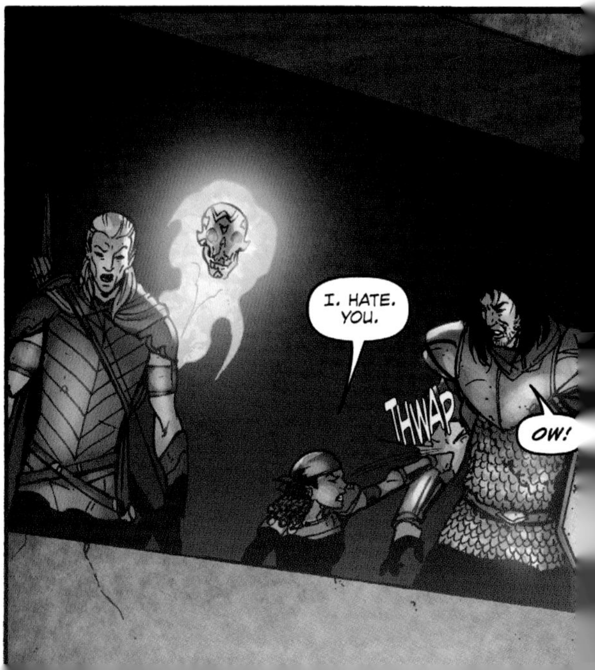
I. HATE. YOU.
THWAP
OW!

Art by Tyler Walpole

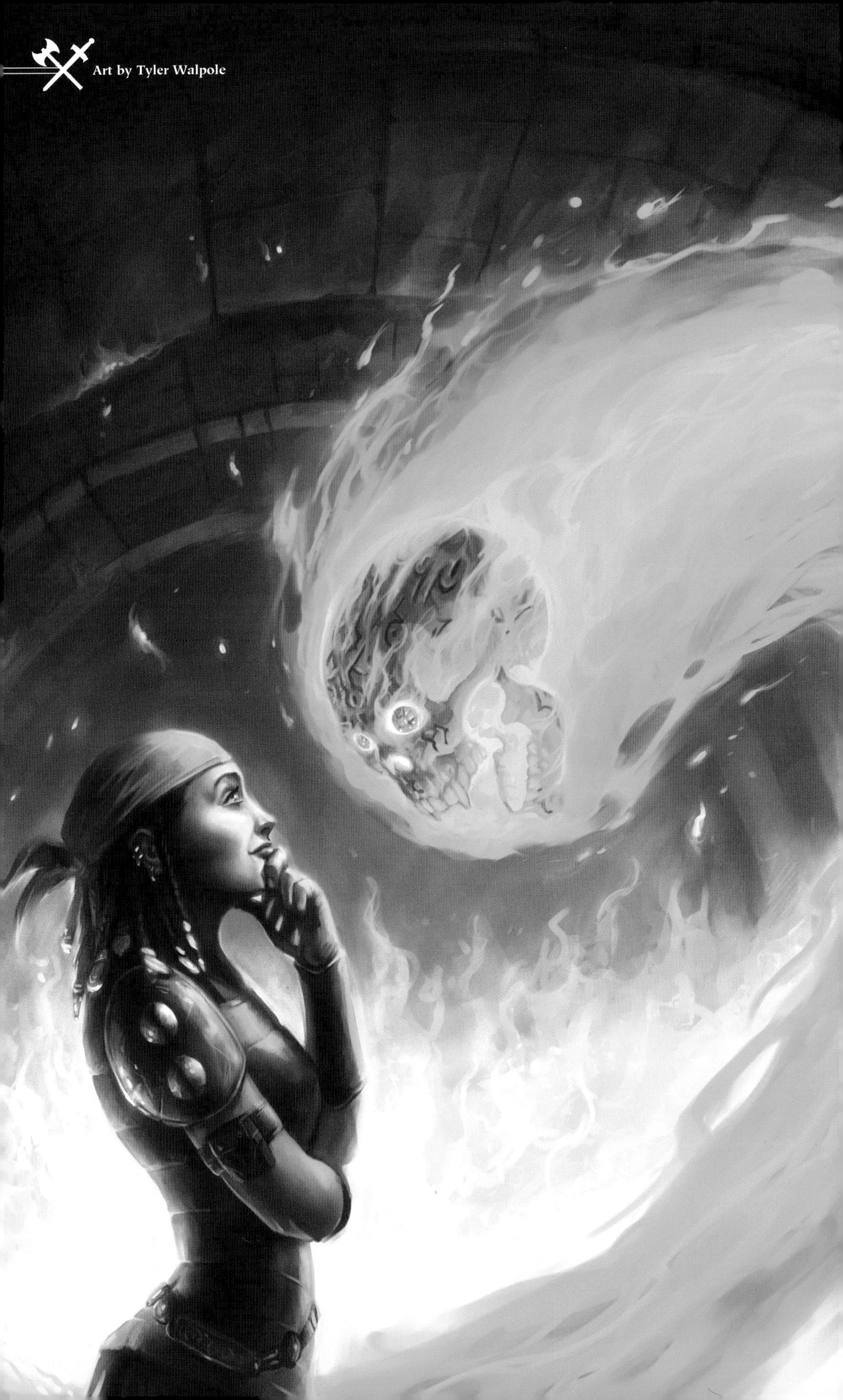

CHAPTER 6

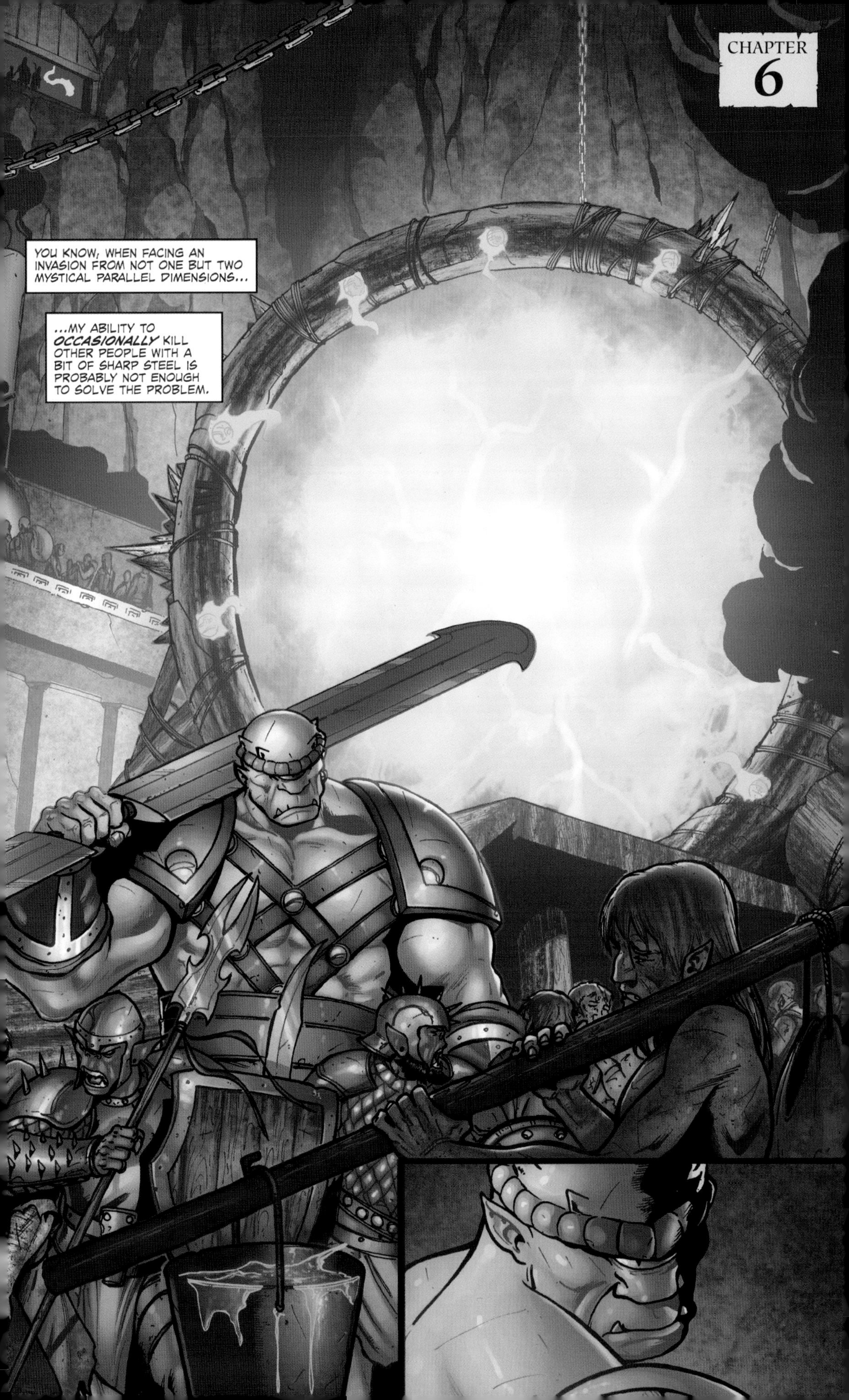
YOU KNOW, WHEN FACING AN INVASION FROM NOT ONE BUT TWO MYSTICAL PARALLEL DIMENSIONS...
...MY ABILITY TO OCCASIONALLY KILL OTHER PEOPLE WITH A BIT OF SHARP STEEL IS PROBABLY NOT ENOUGH TO SOLVE THE PROBLEM.

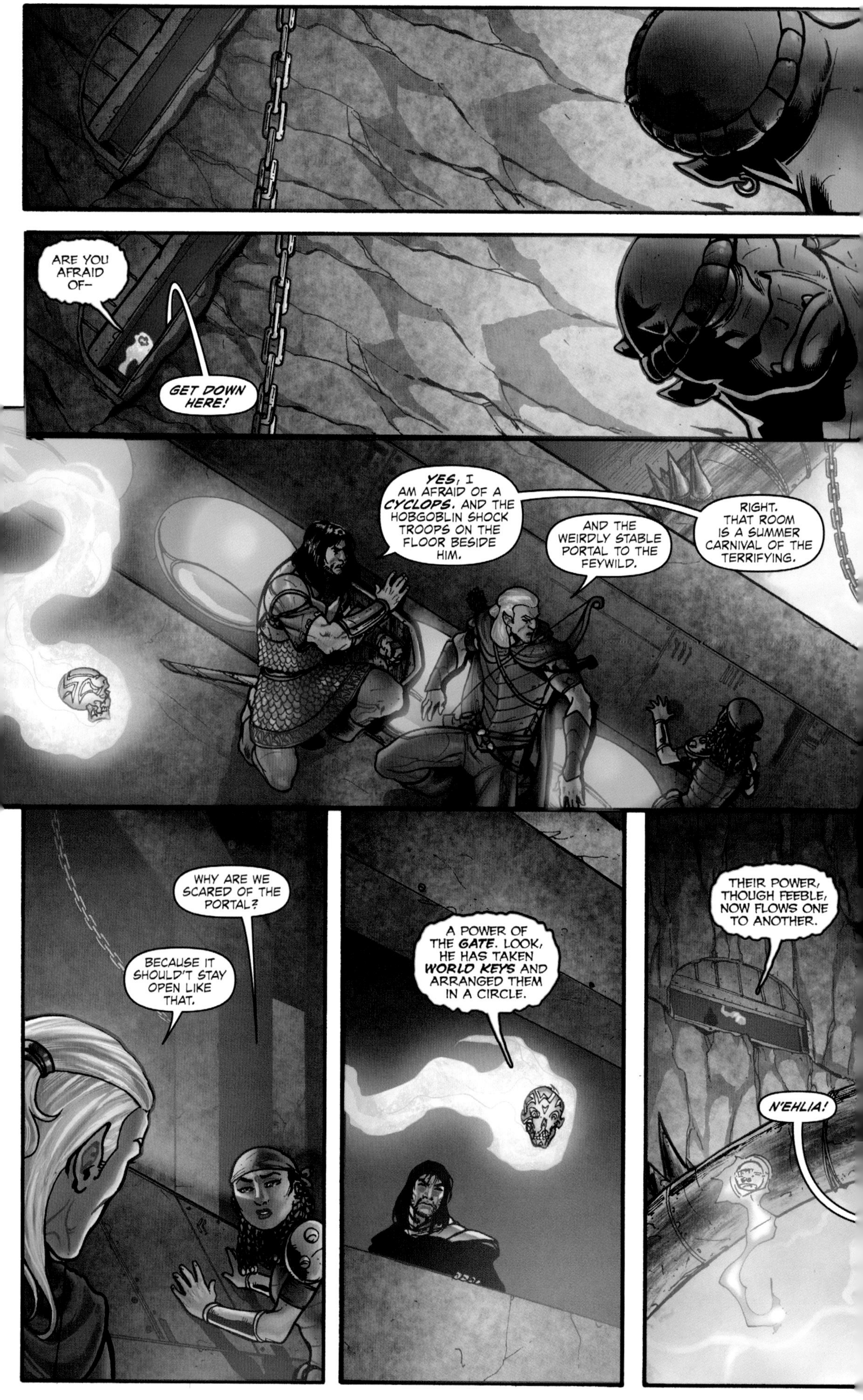
ARE YOU AFRAID OF–
GET DOWN HERE!
YES, I AM AFRAID OF A CYCLOPS. AND THE HOBGOBLIN SHOCK TROOPS ON THE FLOOR BESIDE HIM.
AND THE WEIRDLY STABLE PORTAL TO THE FEYWILD.
RIGHT. THAT ROOM IS A SUMMER CARNIVAL OF THE TERRIFYING.
WHY ARE WE SCARED OF THE PORTAL?
BECAUSE IT SHOULDN'T STAY OPEN LIKE THAT.
A POWER OF THE GATE. LOOK, HE HAS TAKEN WORLD KEYS AND ARRANGED THEM IN A CIRCLE.
THEIR POWER, THOUGH FEEBLE, NOW FLOWS ONE TO ANOTHER.
N'EHLIA!

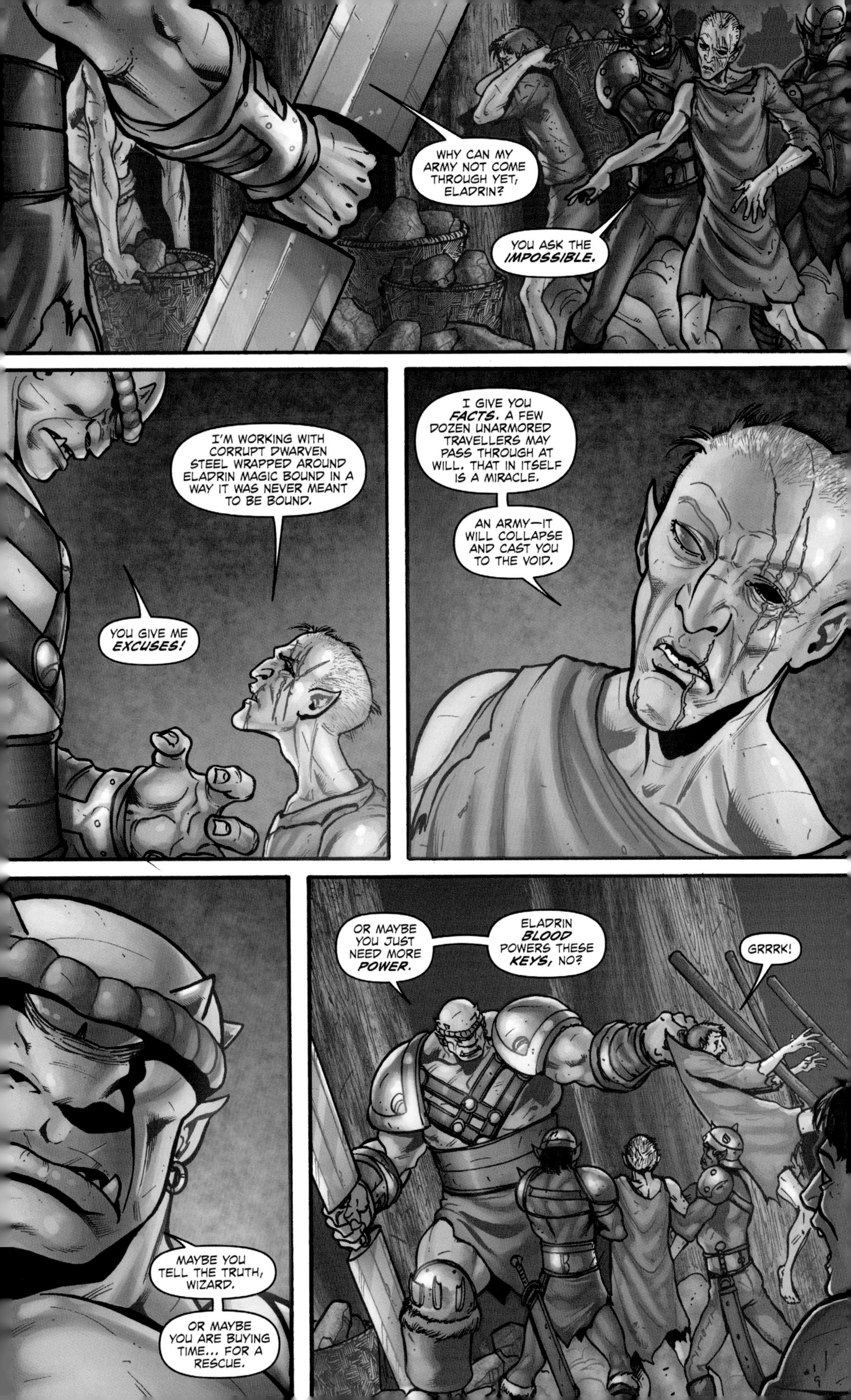

WHY CAN MY ARMY NOT COME THROUGH YET, ELADRIN?
YOU ASK THE *IMPOSSIBLE.*
I'M WORKING WITH CORRUPT DWARVEN STEEL WRAPPED AROUND ELADRIN MAGIC BOUND IN A WAY IT WAS NEVER MEANT TO BE BOUND.
YOU GIVE ME *EXCUSES!*
I GIVE YOU *FACTS.* A FEW DOZEN UNARMORED TRAVELLERS MAY PASS THROUGH AT WILL. THAT IN ITSELF IS A MIRACLE.
AN ARMY—IT WILL COLLAPSE AND CAST YOU TO THE VOID.
MAYBE YOU TELL THE TRUTH, WIZARD.
OR MAYBE YOU ARE BUYING TIME... FOR A RESCUE.
OR MAYBE YOU JUST NEED MORE *POWER.*
ELADRIN *BLOOD* POWERS THESE *KEYS,* NO?
GRRRK!

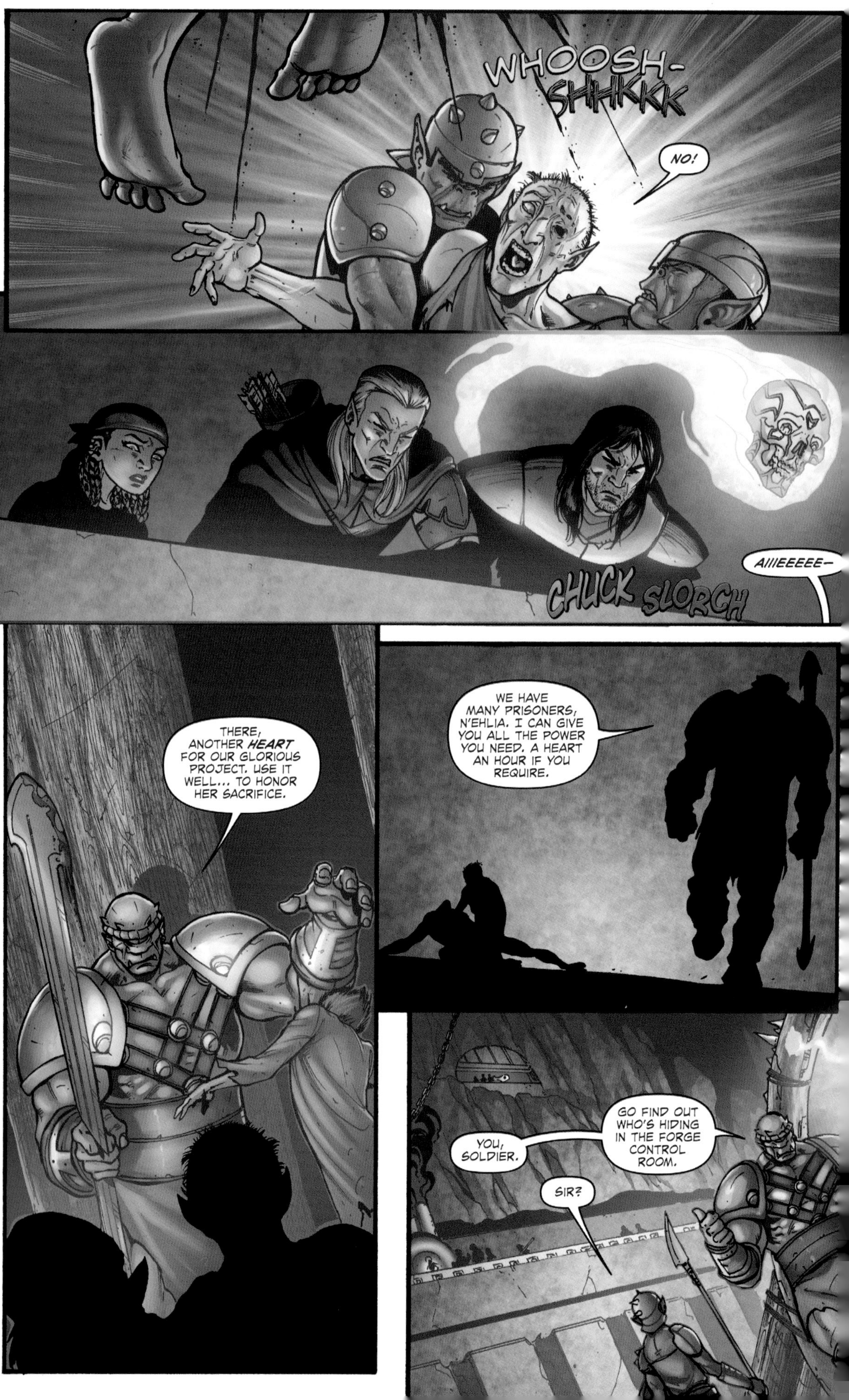
WHOOSH-
SHHKKK
NO!
AIIIEEEEE—
CHUCK SLORCH
THERE, ANOTHER HEART FOR OUR GLORIOUS PROJECT. USE IT WELL... TO HONOR HER SACRIFICE.
WE HAVE MANY PRISONERS, N'EHLIA. I CAN GIVE YOU ALL THE POWER YOU NEED. A HEART AN HOUR IF YOU REQUIRE.
YOU, SOLDIER.
GO FIND OUT WHO'S HIDING IN THE FORGE CONTROL ROOM.
SIR?

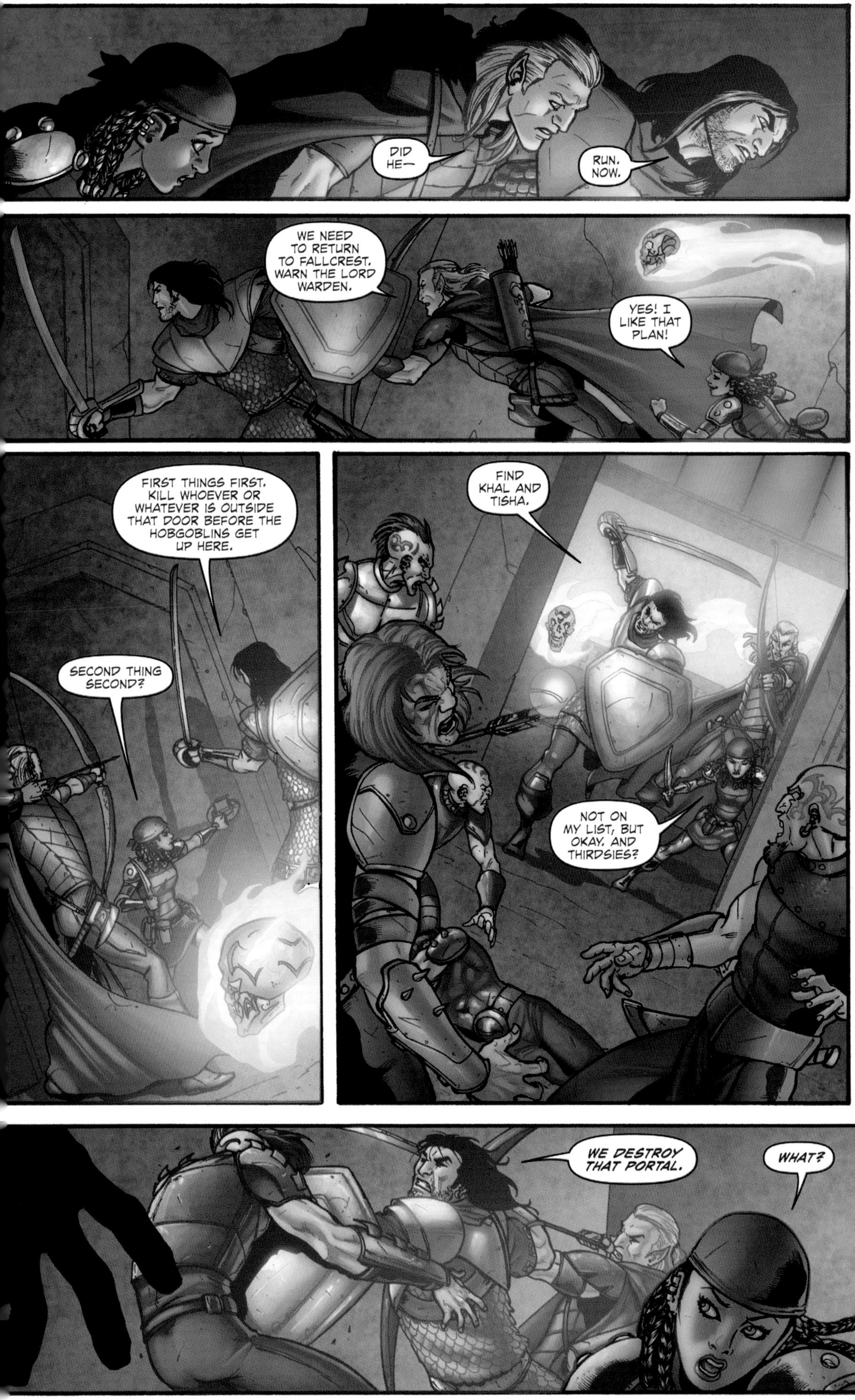
DID HE—
RUN. NOW.
WE NEED TO RETURN TO FALLCREST. WARN THE LORD WARDEN.
YES! I LIKE THAT PLAN!
FIRST THINGS FIRST. KILL WHOEVER OR WHATEVER IS OUTSIDE THAT DOOR BEFORE THE HOBGOBLINS GET UP HERE.
SECOND THING SECOND?
FIND KHAL AND TISHA.
NOT ON MY LIST, BUT OKAY. AND THIRDSIES?
WE DESTROY THAT PORTAL.
WHAT?

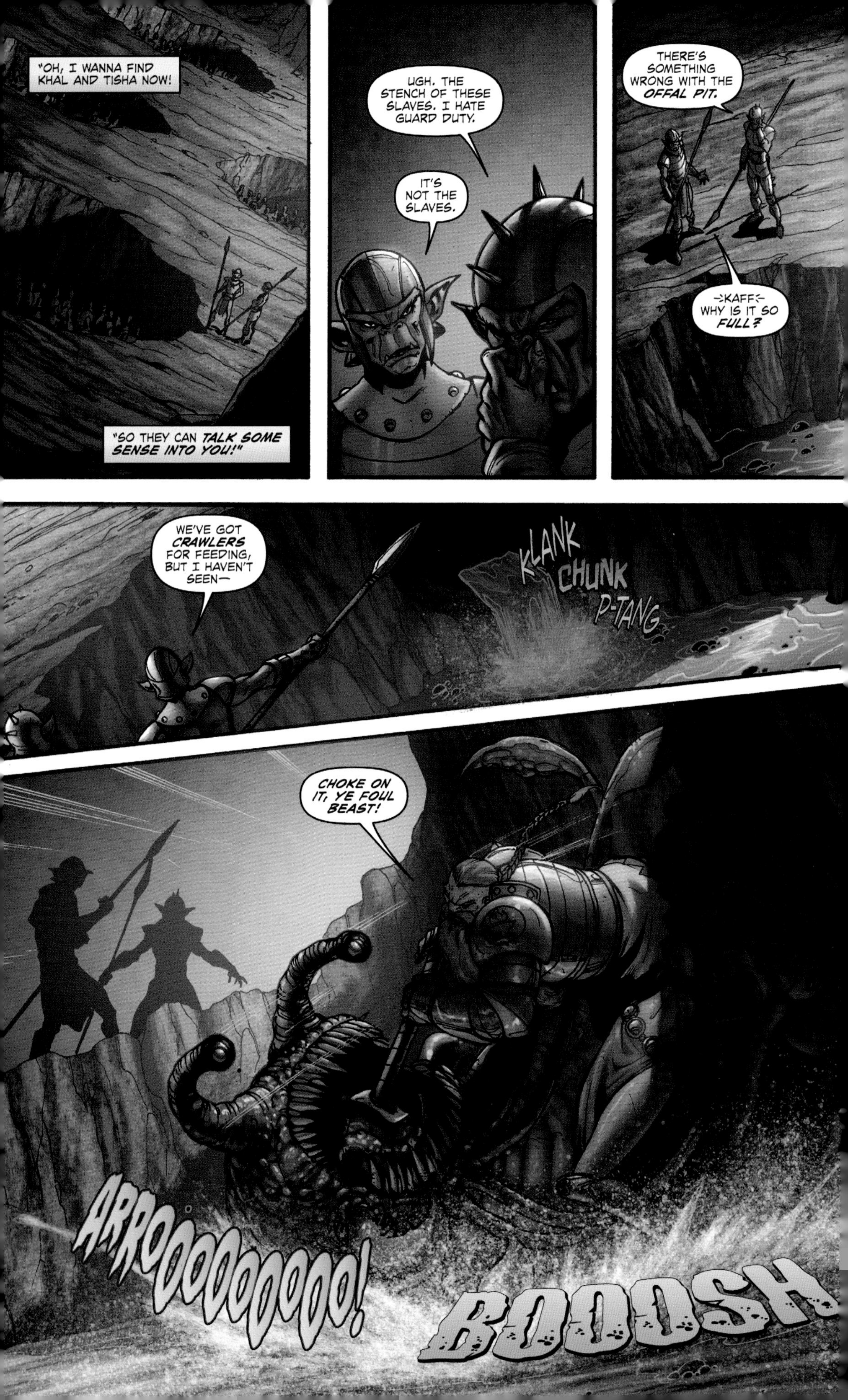
"OH, I WANNA FIND KHAL AND TISHA NOW!
"SO THEY CAN TALK SOME SENSE INTO YOU!"
UGH. THE STENCH OF THESE SLAVES. I HATE GUARD DUTY.
IT'S NOT THE SLAVES.
THERE'S SOMETHING WRONG WITH THE OFFAL PIT.
-KAFF- WHY IS IT SO FULL?
WE'VE GOT CRAWLERS FOR FEEDING, BUT I HAVEN'T SEEN—
KLANK
CHUNK
P-TANG
CHOKE ON IT, YE FOUL BEAST!
ARROOOOOOOOOO!
BOOOSH

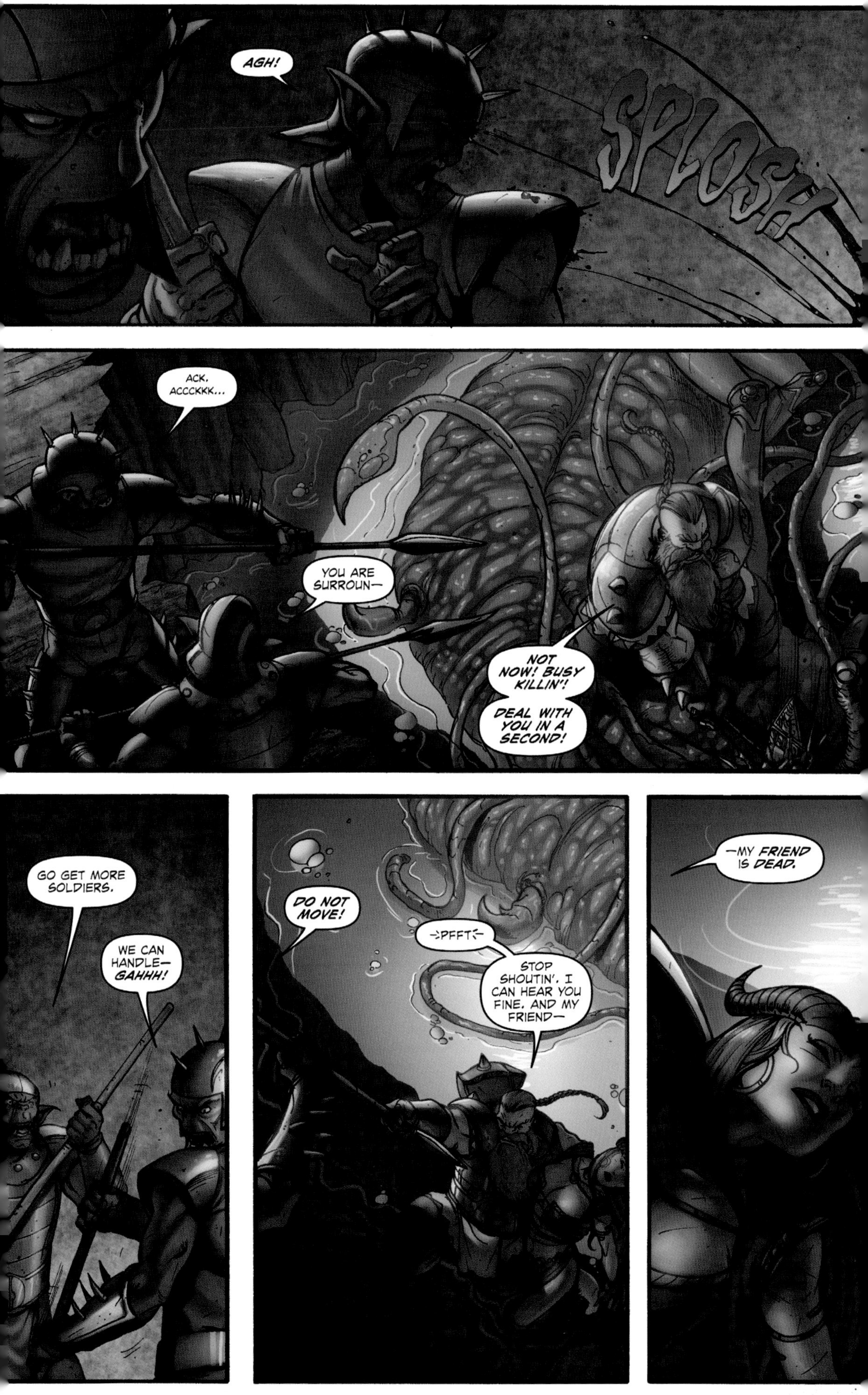
AGH!
SPLOSH
ACK. ACCCKKK...
YOU ARE SURROUN—
NOT NOW! BUSY KILLIN'!
DEAL WITH YOU IN A SECOND!
GO GET MORE SOLDIERS.
WE CAN HANDLE— GAHHH!
DO NOT MOVE!
—PFFT—
STOP SHOUTIN'. I CAN HEAR YOU FINE. AND MY FRIEND—
—MY FRIEND IS DEAD.

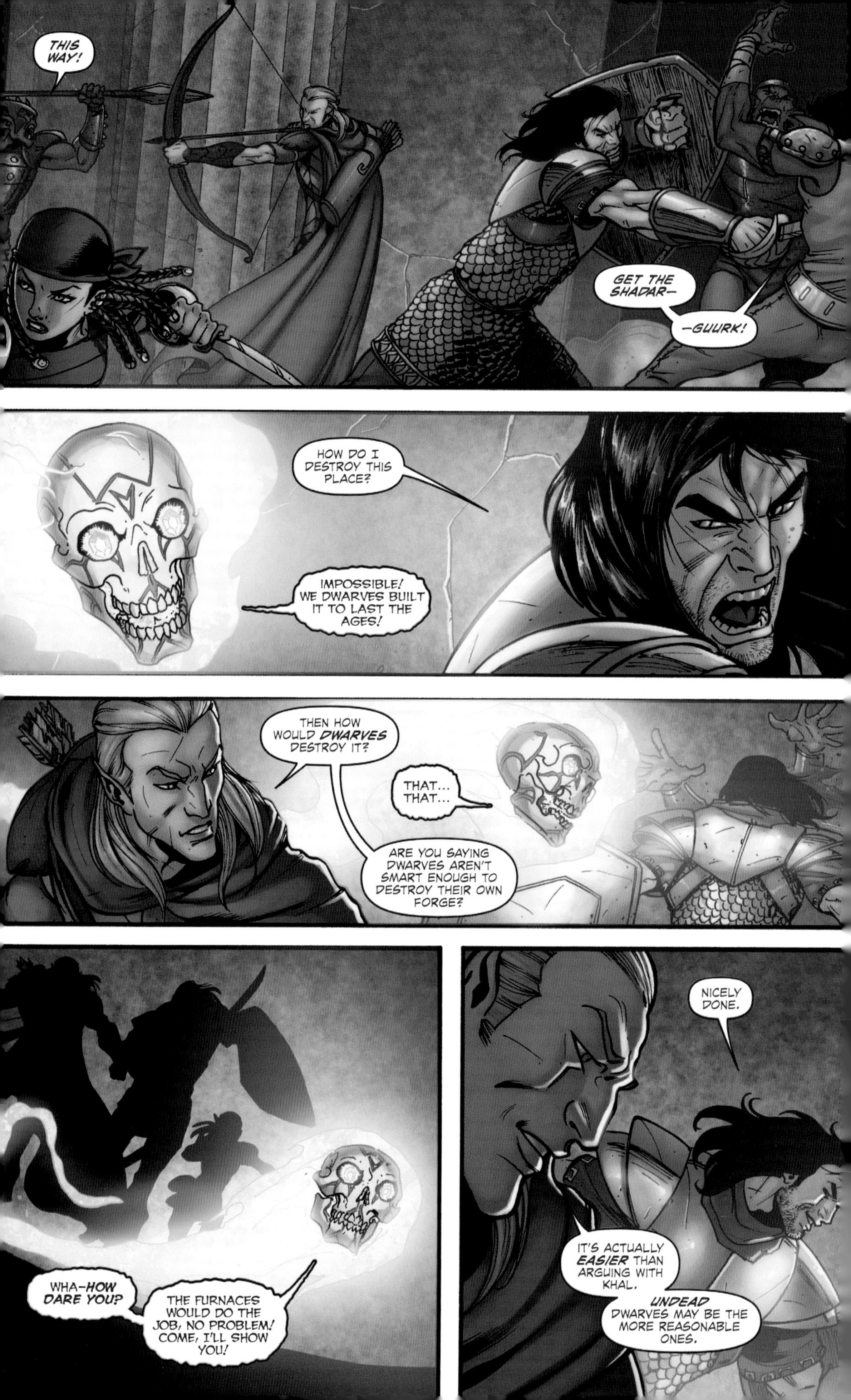
THIS WAY!
GET THE SHADAR—
—GUURK!
HOW DO I DESTROY THIS PLACE?
IMPOSSIBLE! WE DWARVES BUILT IT TO LAST THE AGES!
THEN HOW WOULD DWARVES DESTROY IT?
THAT... THAT...
ARE YOU SAYING DWARVES AREN'T SMART ENOUGH TO DESTROY THEIR OWN FORGE?
WHA—HOW DARE YOU?
THE FURNACES WOULD DO THE JOB, NO PROBLEM! COME, I'LL SHOW YOU!
NICELY DONE.
IT'S ACTUALLY EASIER THAN ARGUING WITH KHAL.
UNDEAD DWARVES MAY BE THE MORE REASONABLE ONES.

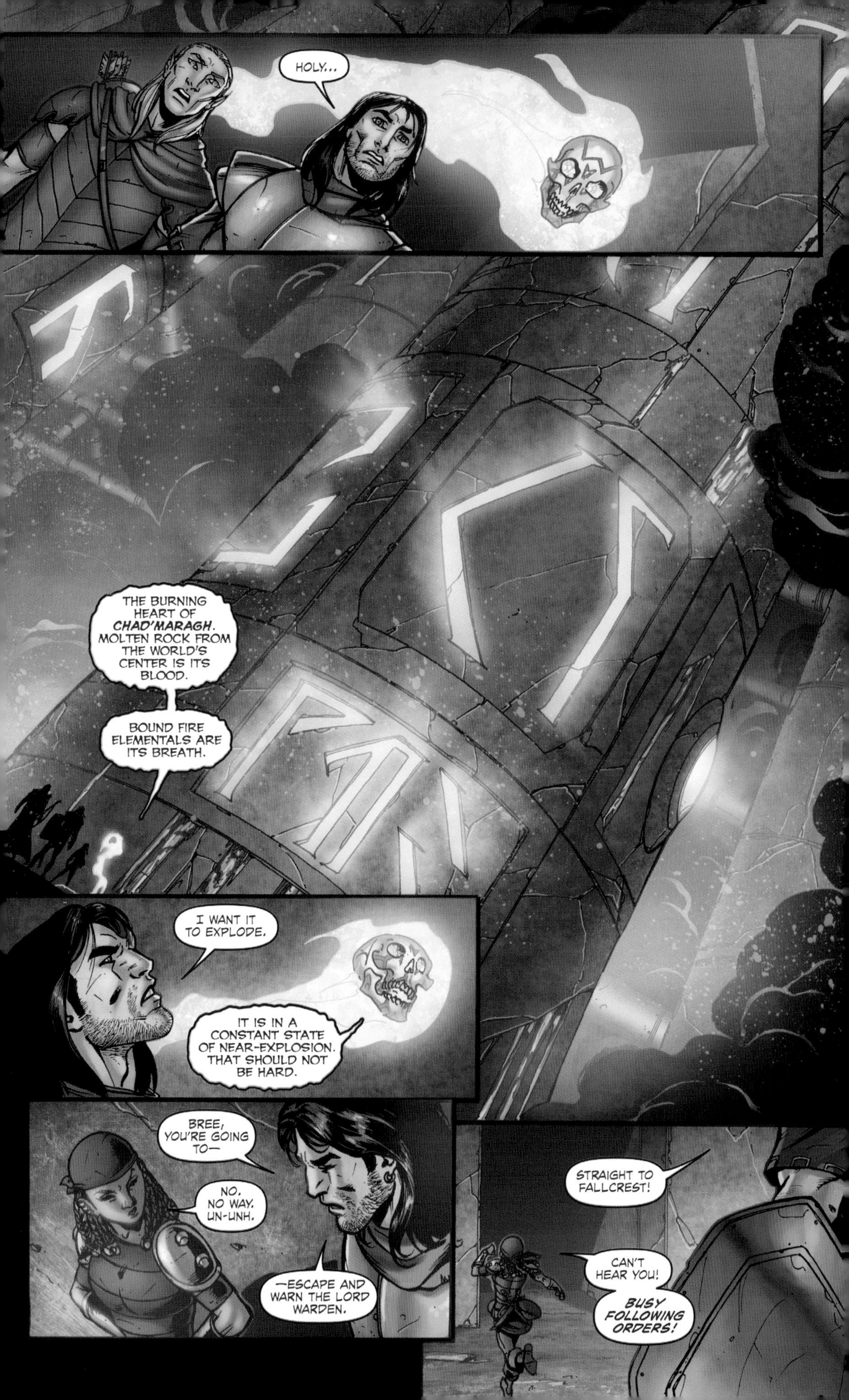
HOLY...
THE BURNING HEART OF **CHAD'MARAGH**. MOLTEN ROCK FROM THE WORLD'S CENTER IS ITS BLOOD.
BOUND FIRE ELEMENTALS ARE ITS BREATH.
I WANT IT TO EXPLODE.
IT IS IN A CONSTANT STATE OF NEAR-EXPLOSION. THAT SHOULD NOT BE HARD.
BREE, YOU'RE GOING TO—
NO. NO WAY. UN-UNH.
—ESCAPE AND WARN THE LORD WARDEN.
STRAIGHT TO FALLCREST!
CAN'T HEAR YOU!
BUSY FOLLOWING ORDERS!

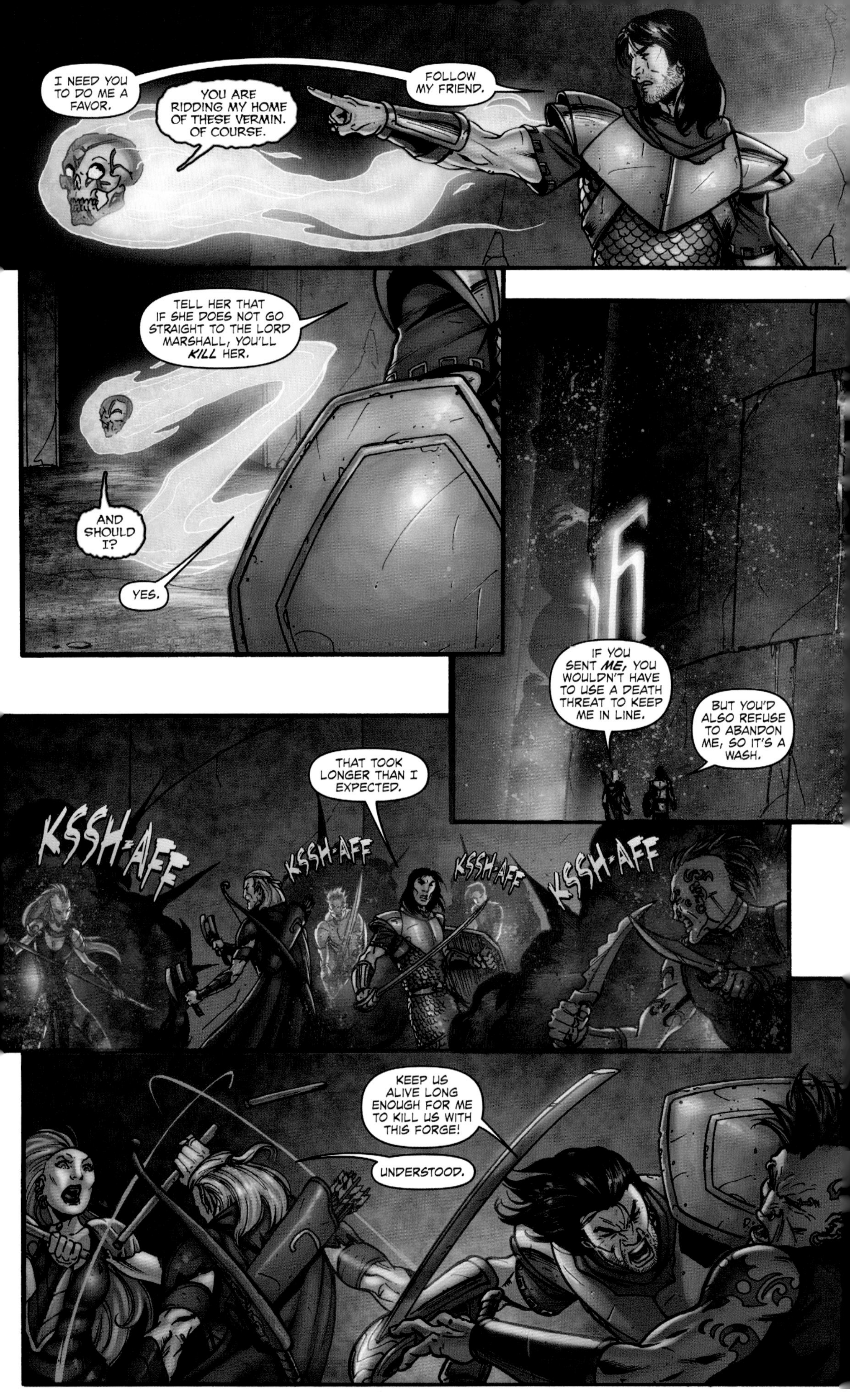
I NEED YOU TO DO ME A FAVOR.
YOU ARE RIDDING MY HOME OF THESE VERMIN. OF COURSE.
FOLLOW MY FRIEND.
TELL HER THAT IF SHE DOES NOT GO STRAIGHT TO THE LORD MARSHALL, YOU'LL KILL HER.
AND SHOULD I?
YES.
IF YOU SENT ME, YOU WOULDN'T HAVE TO USE A DEATH THREAT TO KEEP ME IN LINE.
BUT YOU'D ALSO REFUSE TO ABANDON ME, SO IT'S A WASH.
KSSH-AFF
THAT TOOK LONGER THAN I EXPECTED.
KSSH-AFF
KSSH-AFF
KSSH-AFF
KEEP US ALIVE LONG ENOUGH FOR ME TO KILL US WITH THIS FORGE!
UNDERSTOOD.

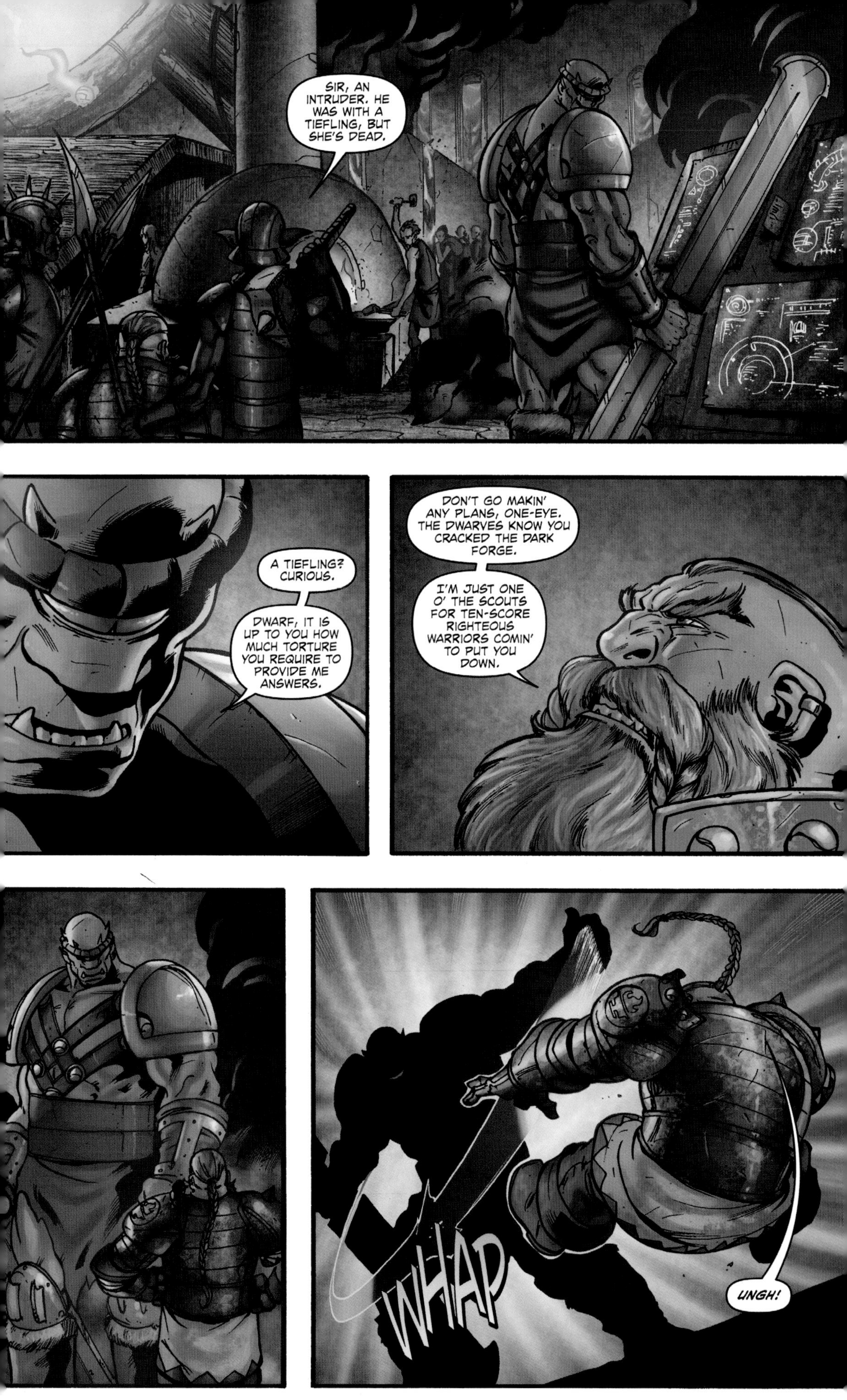
SIR, AN INTRUDER. HE WAS WITH A TIEFLING, BUT SHE'S DEAD.
A TIEFLING? CURIOUS.
DWARF, IT IS UP TO YOU HOW MUCH TORTURE YOU REQUIRE TO PROVIDE ME ANSWERS.
DON'T GO MAKIN' ANY PLANS, ONE-EYE. THE DWARVES KNOW YOU CRACKED THE DARK FORGE.
I'M JUST ONE O' THE SCOUTS FOR TEN-SCORE RIGHTEOUS WARRIORS COMIN' TO PUT YOU DOWN.
WHAP
UNGH!

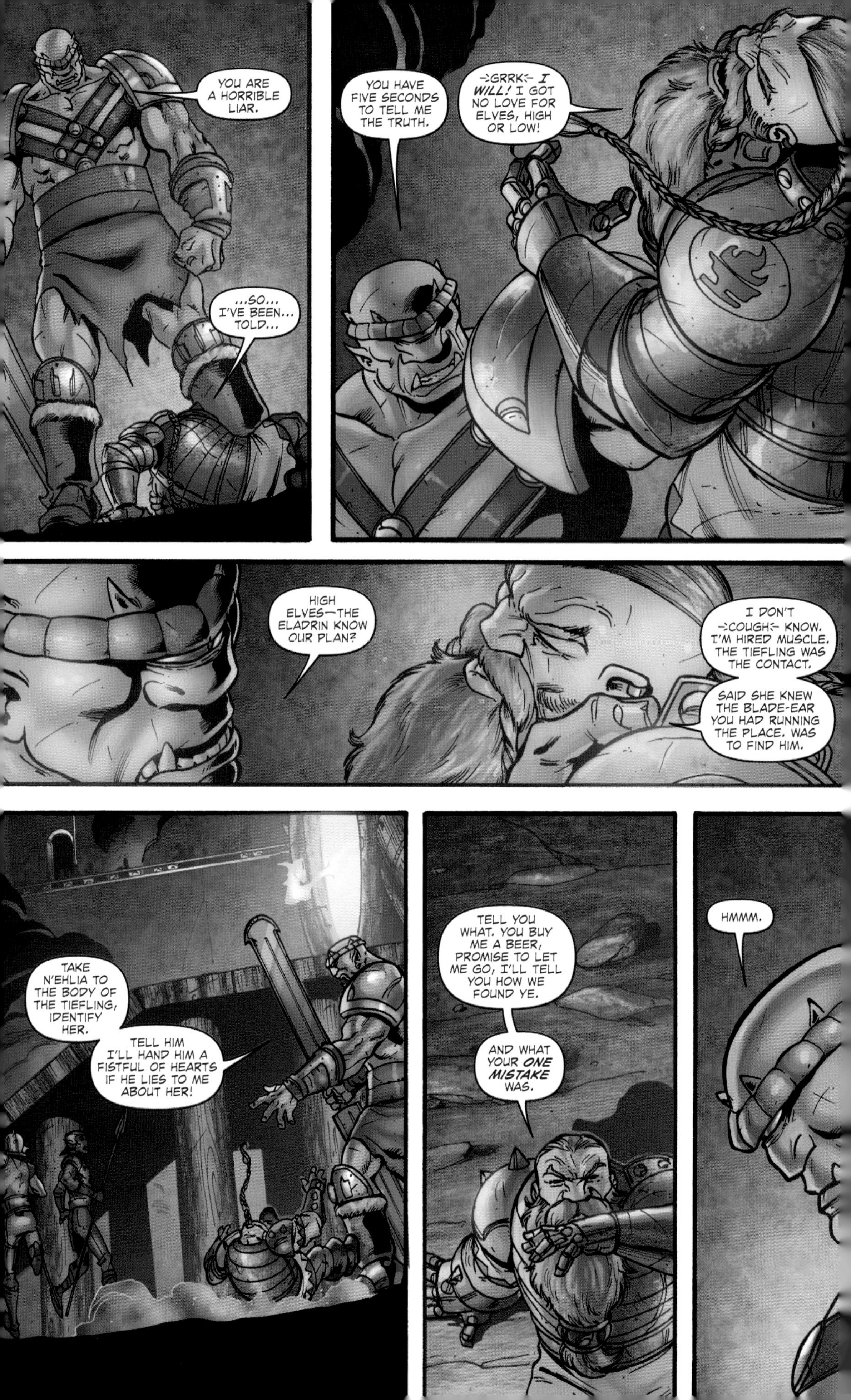

YOU ARE A HORRIBLE LIAR.
...SO... I'VE BEEN... TOLD...
YOU HAVE FIVE SECONDS TO TELL ME THE TRUTH.
-GRRK- I WILL! I GOT NO LOVE FOR ELVES, HIGH OR LOW!
HIGH ELVES—THE ELADRIN KNOW OUR PLAN?
I DON'T -COUGH- KNOW. I'M HIRED MUSCLE. THE TIEFLING WAS THE CONTACT.
SAID SHE KNEW THE BLADE-EAR YOU HAD RUNNING THE PLACE. WAS TO FIND HIM.
TAKE N'EHLIA TO THE BODY OF THE TIEFLING, IDENTIFY HER.
TELL HIM I'LL HAND HIM A FISTFUL OF HEARTS IF HE LIES TO ME ABOUT HER!
TELL YOU WHAT. YOU BUY ME A BEER, PROMISE TO LET ME GO, I'LL TELL YOU HOW WE FOUND YE.
AND WHAT YOUR ONE MISTAKE WAS.
HMMM.

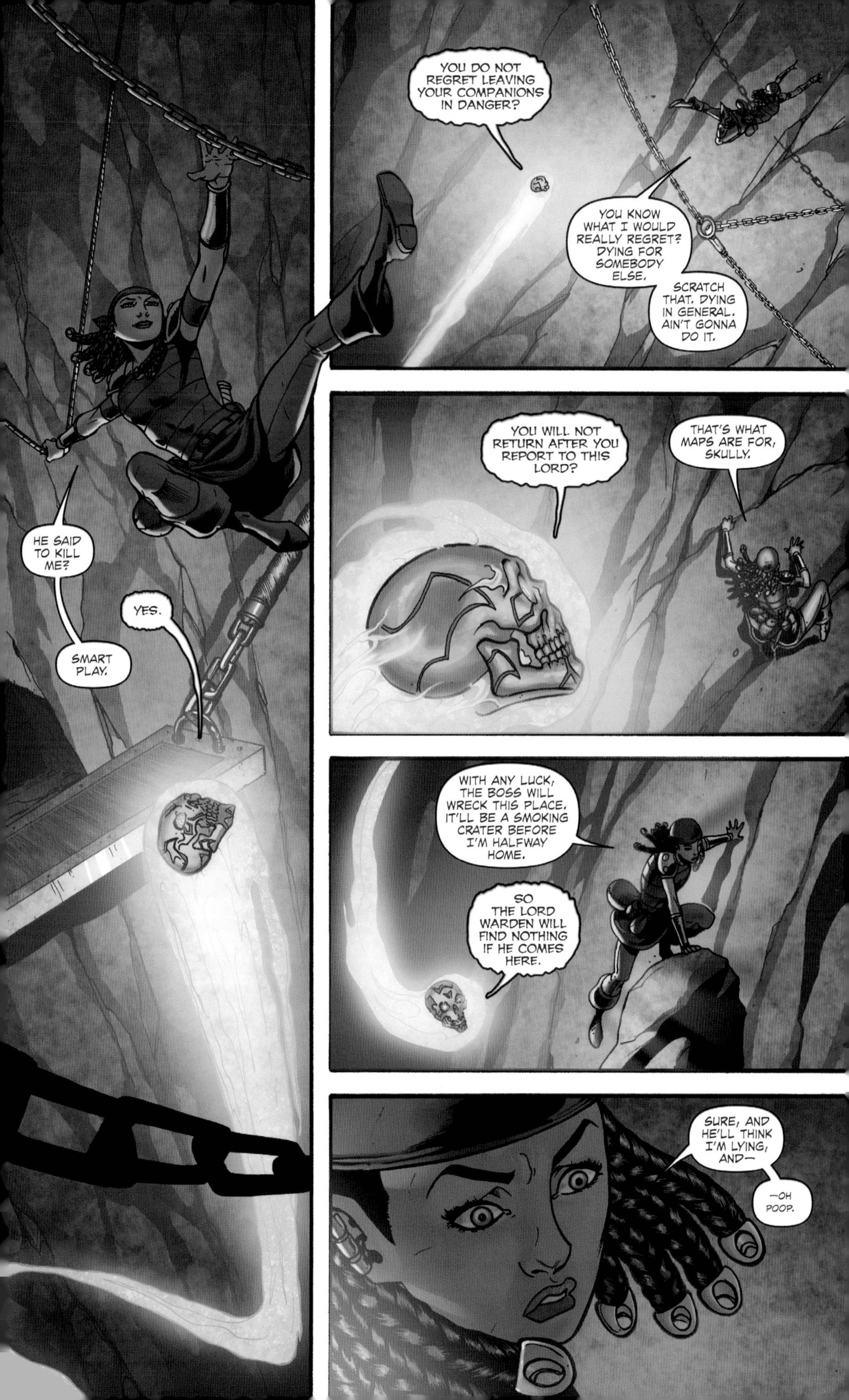
HE SAID TO KILL ME?
YES.
SMART PLAY.
YOU DO NOT REGRET LEAVING YOUR COMPANIONS IN DANGER?
YOU KNOW WHAT I WOULD REALLY REGRET? DYING FOR SOMEBODY ELSE.
SCRATCH THAT. DYING IN GENERAL. AIN'T GONNA DO IT.
YOU WILL NOT RETURN AFTER YOU REPORT TO THIS LORD?
THAT'S WHAT MAPS ARE FOR, SKULLY.
WITH ANY LUCK, THE BOSS WILL WRECK THIS PLACE. IT'LL BE A SMOKING CRATER BEFORE I'M HALFWAY HOME.
SO THE LORD WARDEN WILL FIND NOTHING IF HE COMES HERE.
SURE, AND HE'LL THINK I'M LYING, AND—
—OH POOP.

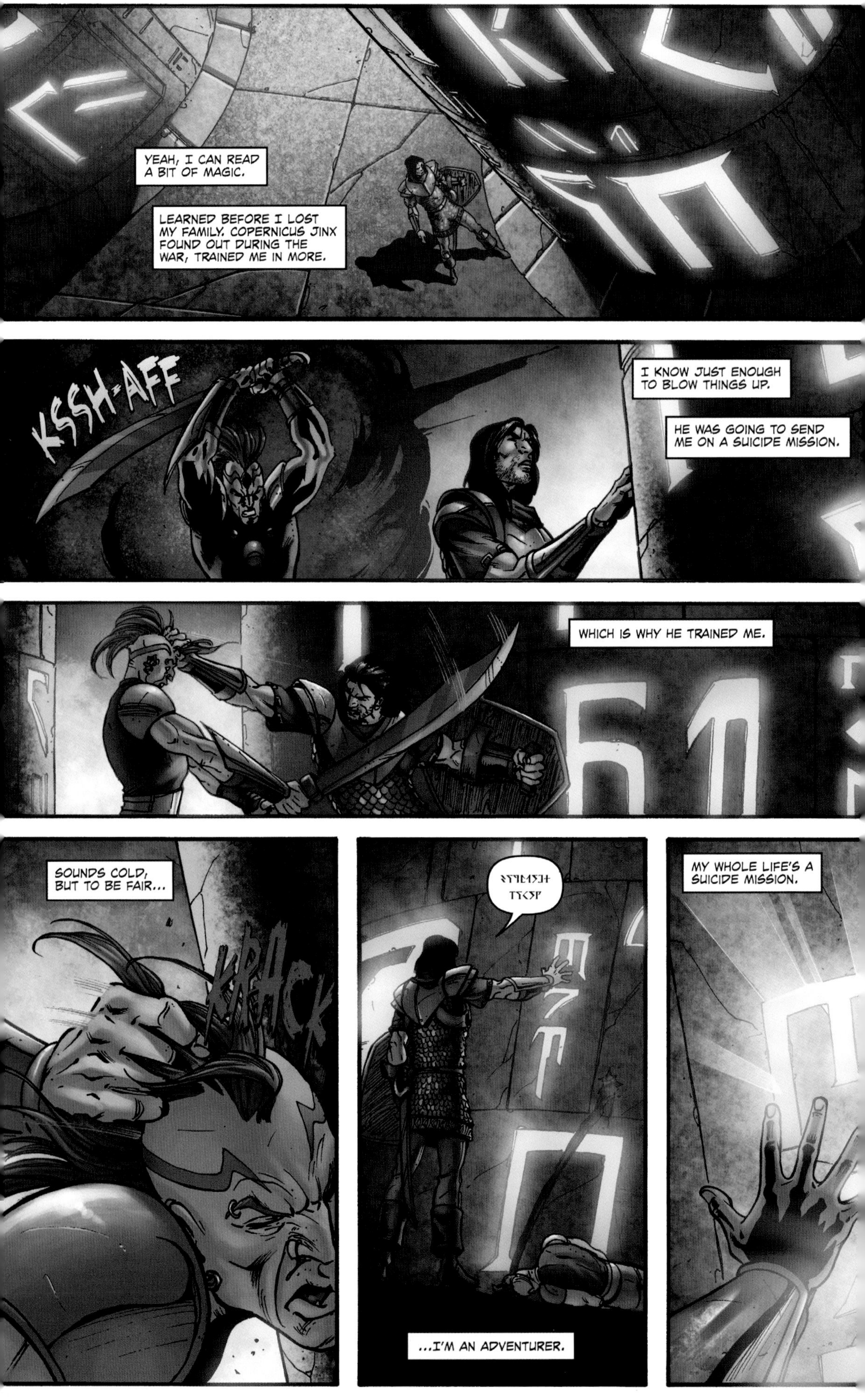
YEAH, I CAN READ A BIT OF MAGIC.
LEARNED BEFORE I LOST MY FAMILY. COPERNICUS JINX FOUND OUT DURING THE WAR, TRAINED ME IN MORE.
KSSH-AFF
I KNOW JUST ENOUGH TO BLOW THINGS UP.
HE WAS GOING TO SEND ME ON A SUICIDE MISSION.
WHICH IS WHY HE TRAINED ME.
SOUNDS COLD, BUT TO BE FAIR...
KRACK
...I'M AN ADVENTURER.
MY WHOLE LIFE'S A SUICIDE MISSION.

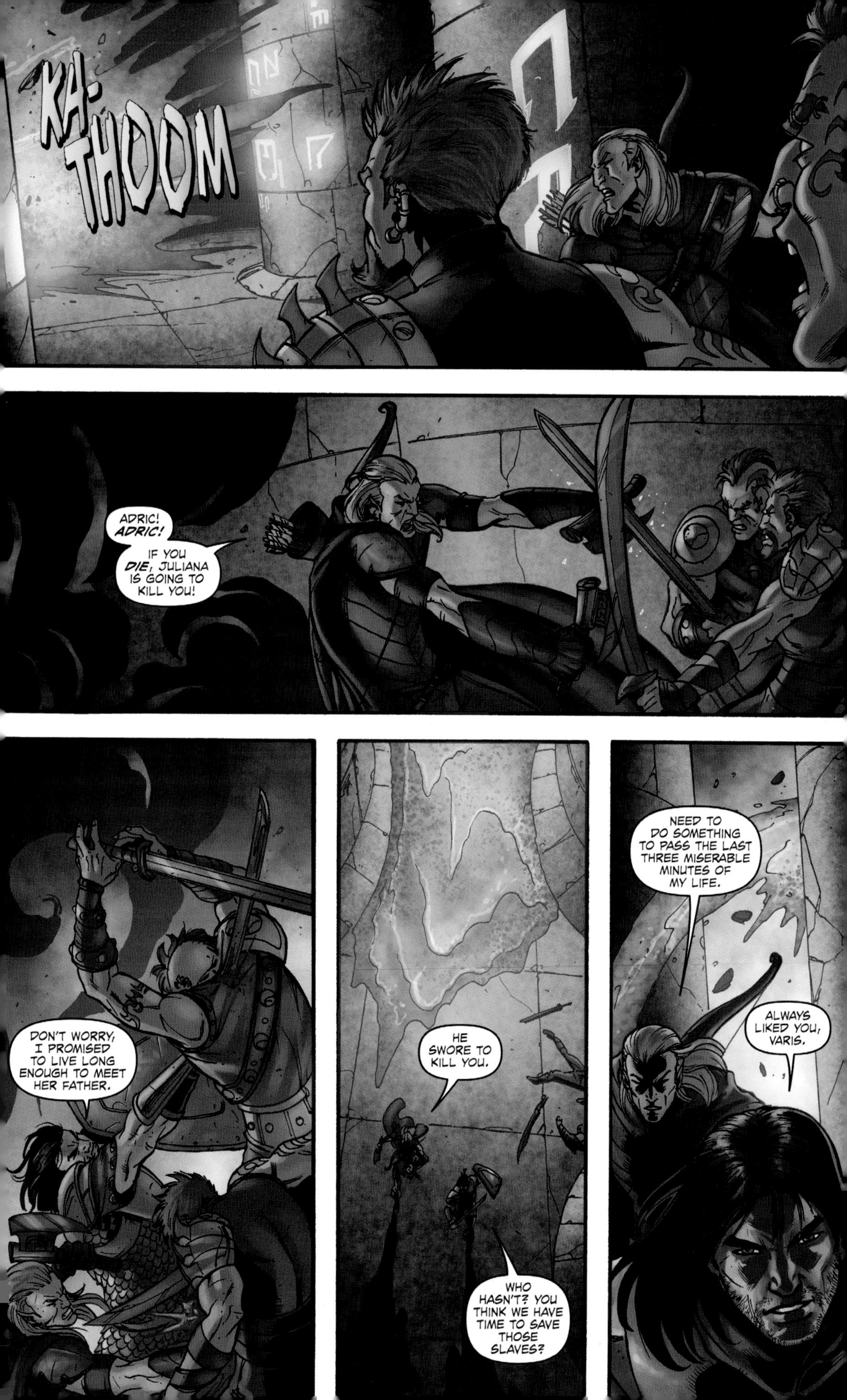
KA-THOOM
ADRIC! ADRIC!
IF YOU DIE, JULIANA IS GOING TO KILL YOU!
DON'T WORRY, I PROMISED TO LIVE LONG ENOUGH TO MEET HER FATHER.
HE SWORE TO KILL YOU.
WHO HASN'T? YOU THINK WE HAVE TIME TO SAVE THOSE SLAVES?
NEED TO DO SOMETHING TO PASS THE LAST THREE MISERABLE MINUTES OF MY LIFE.
ALWAYS LIKED YOU, VARIS.

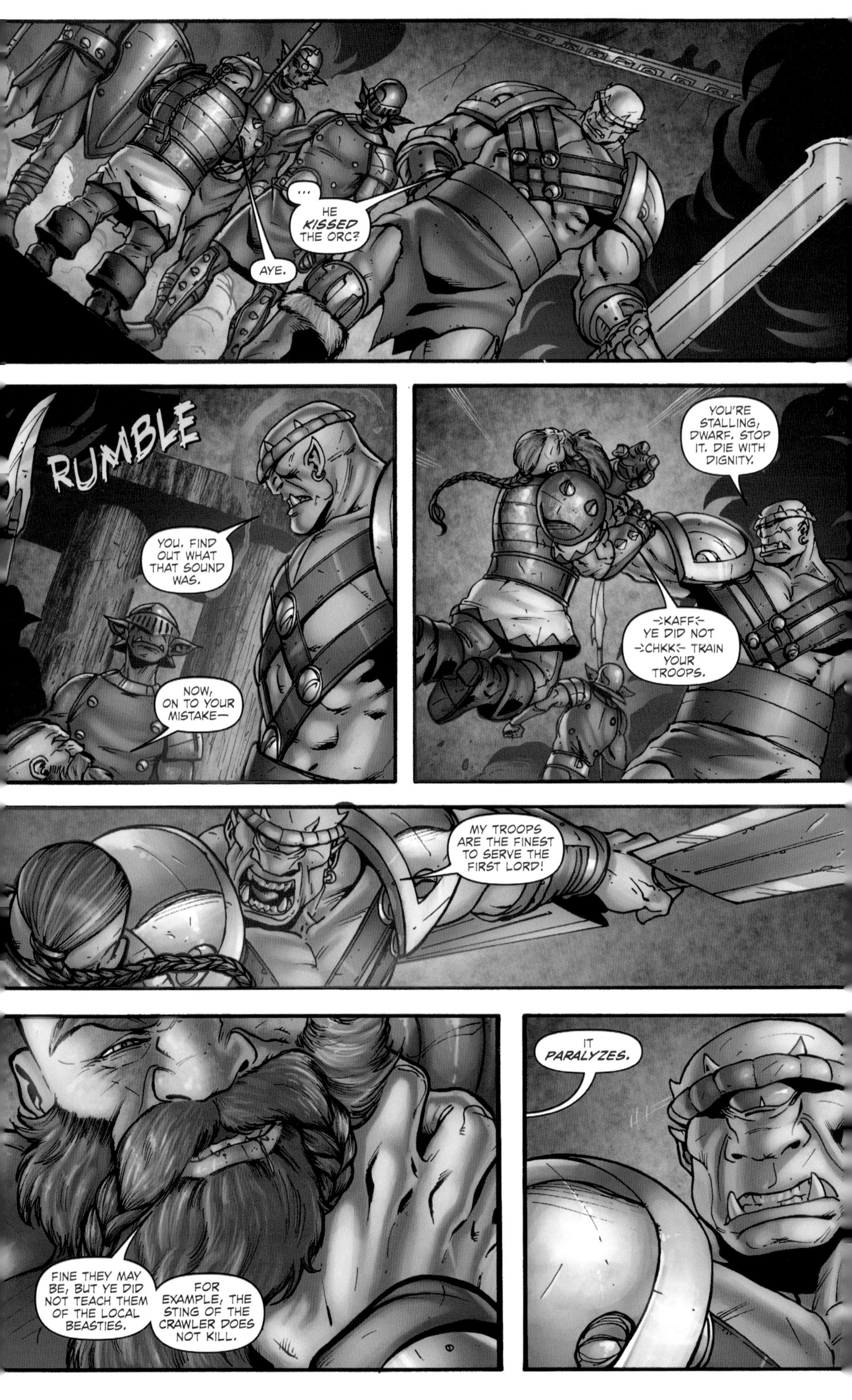
...
HE KISSED THE ORC?
AYE.
RUMBLE
YOU. FIND OUT WHAT THAT SOUND WAS.
NOW, ON TO YOUR MISTAKE—
YOU'RE STALLING, DWARF. STOP IT. DIE WITH DIGNITY.
-KAFF- YE DID NOT -CHKK- TRAIN YOUR TROOPS.
MY TROOPS ARE THE FINEST TO SERVE THE FIRST LORD!
FINE THEY MAY BE, BUT YE DID NOT TEACH THEM OF THE LOCAL BEASTIES.
FOR EXAMPLE, THE STING OF THE CRAWLER DOES NOT KILL.
IT PARALYZES.

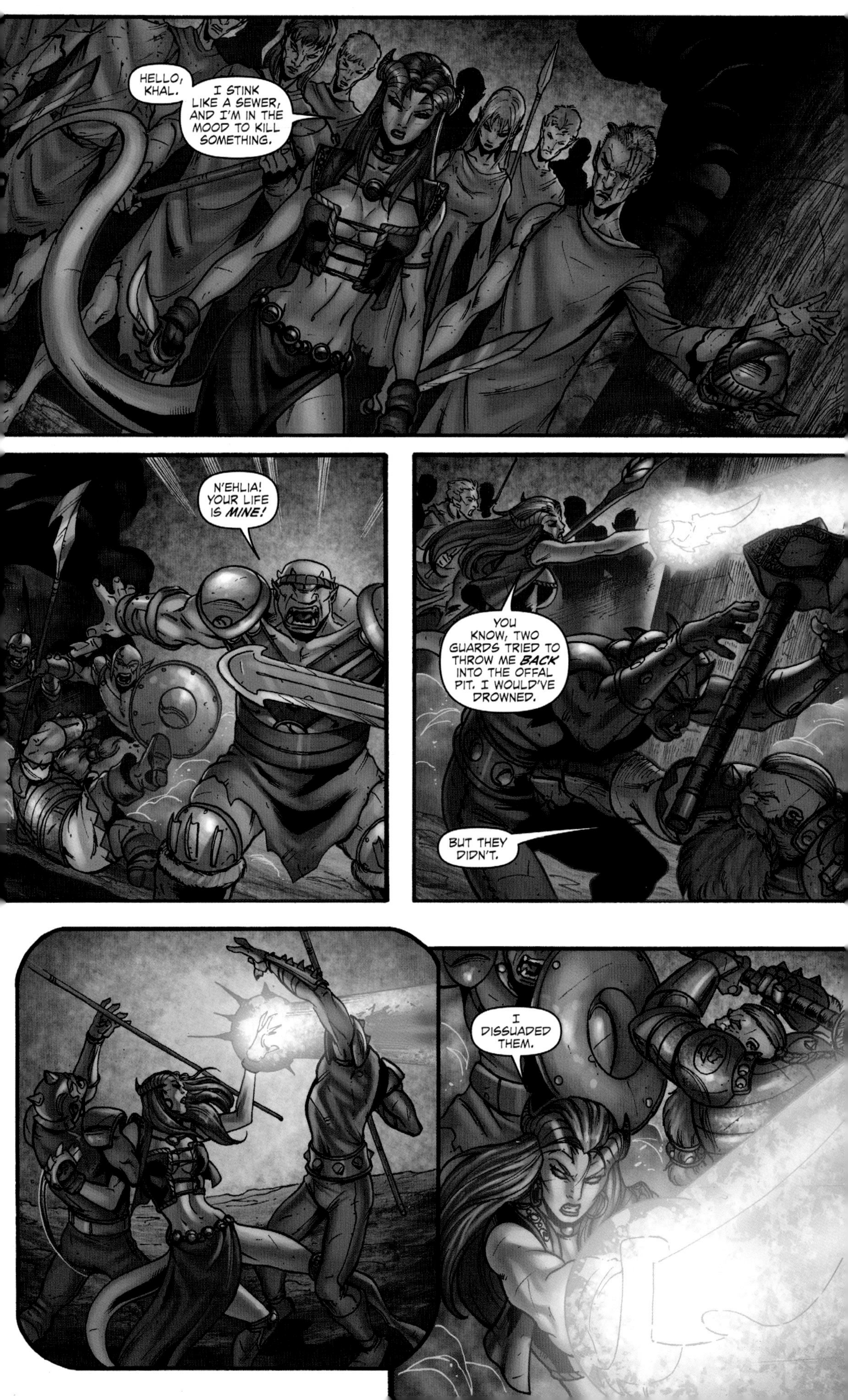
HELLO, KHAL.
I STINK LIKE A SEWER, AND I'M IN THE MOOD TO KILL SOMETHING.
N'EHLIA! YOUR LIFE IS *MINE!*
YOU KNOW, TWO GUARDS TRIED TO THROW ME *BACK* INTO THE OFFAL PIT. I WOULD'VE DROWNED.
BUT THEY DIDN'T.
I DISSUADED THEM.

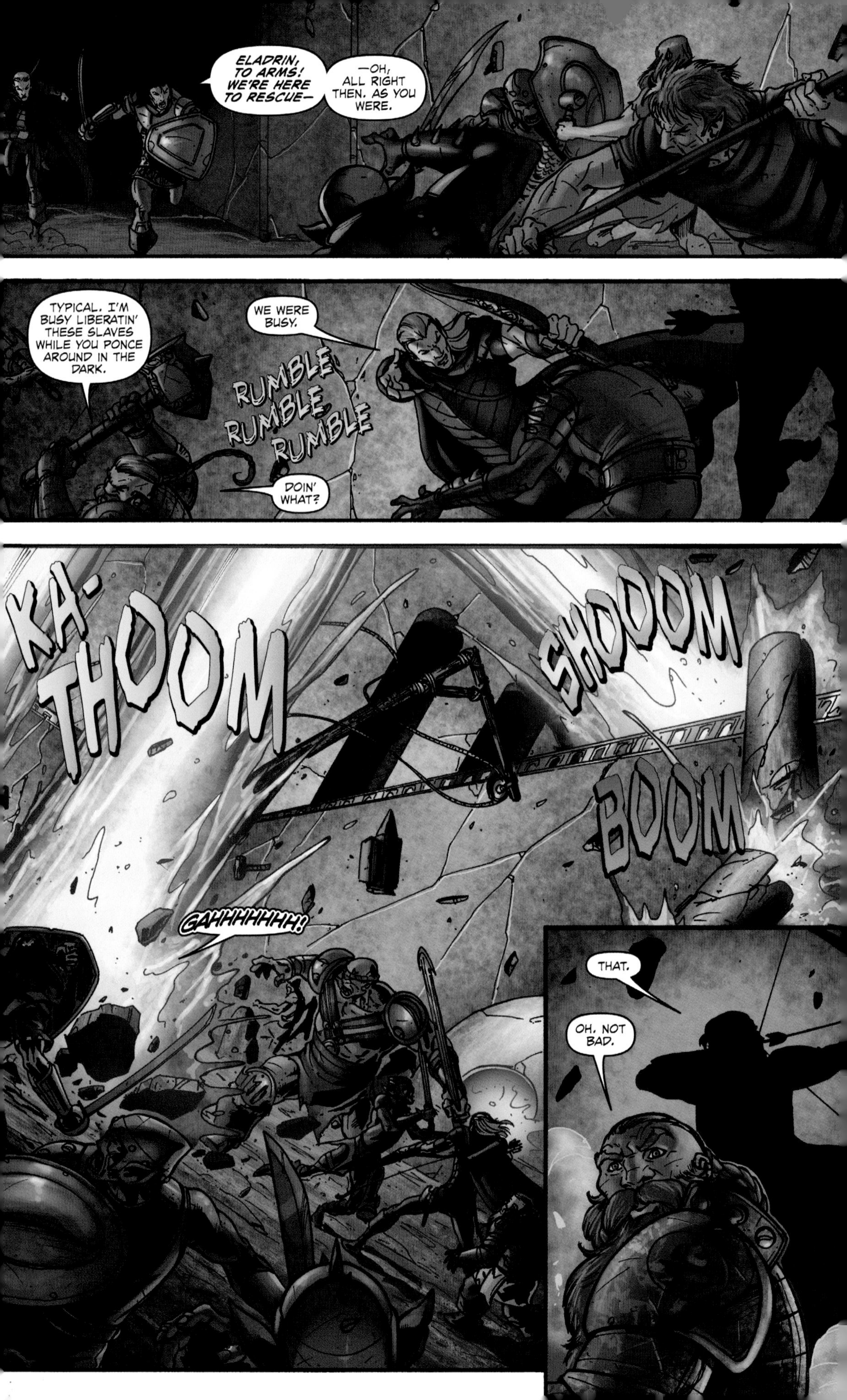
ELADRIN, TO ARMS! WE'RE HERE TO RESCUE—
—OH, ALL RIGHT THEN. AS YOU WERE.
TYPICAL. I'M BUSY LIBERATIN' THESE SLAVES WHILE YOU PONCE AROUND IN THE DARK.
WE WERE BUSY.
RUMBLE RUMBLE RUMBLE
DOIN' WHAT?
KA-THOOM
SHOOOM
BOOM
GAHHHHHHH!
THAT.
OH, NOT BAD.

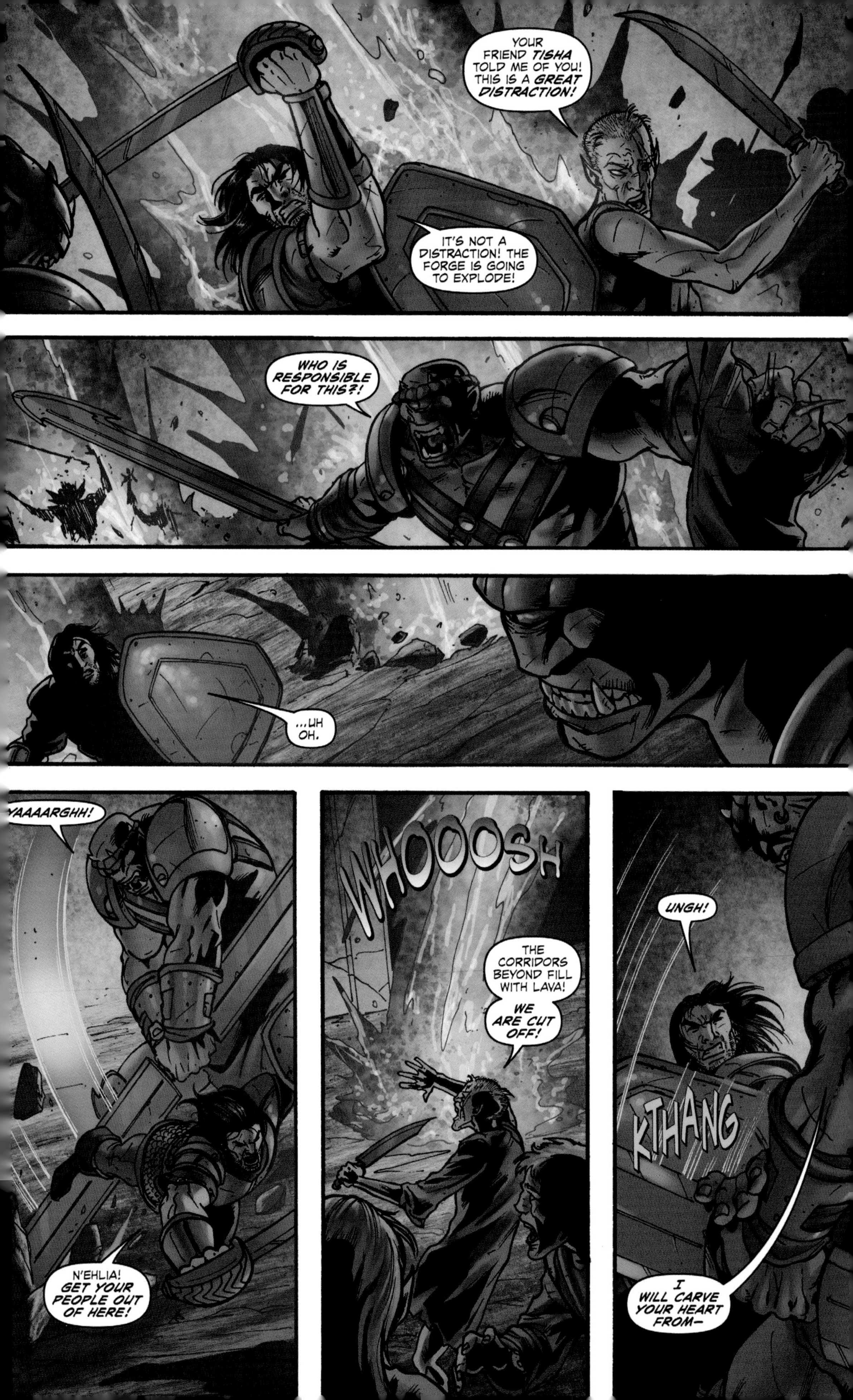
YOUR FRIEND TISHA TOLD ME OF YOU! THIS IS A GREAT DISTRACTION!
IT'S NOT A DISTRACTION! THE FORGE IS GOING TO EXPLODE!
WHO IS RESPONSIBLE FOR THIS?!
...UH OH.
YAAAARGHH!
N'EHLIA! GET YOUR PEOPLE OUT OF HERE!
WHOOOSH
THE CORRIDORS BEYOND FILL WITH LAVA!
WE ARE CUT OFF!
UNGH!
KTHANG
I WILL CARVE YOUR HEART FROM—

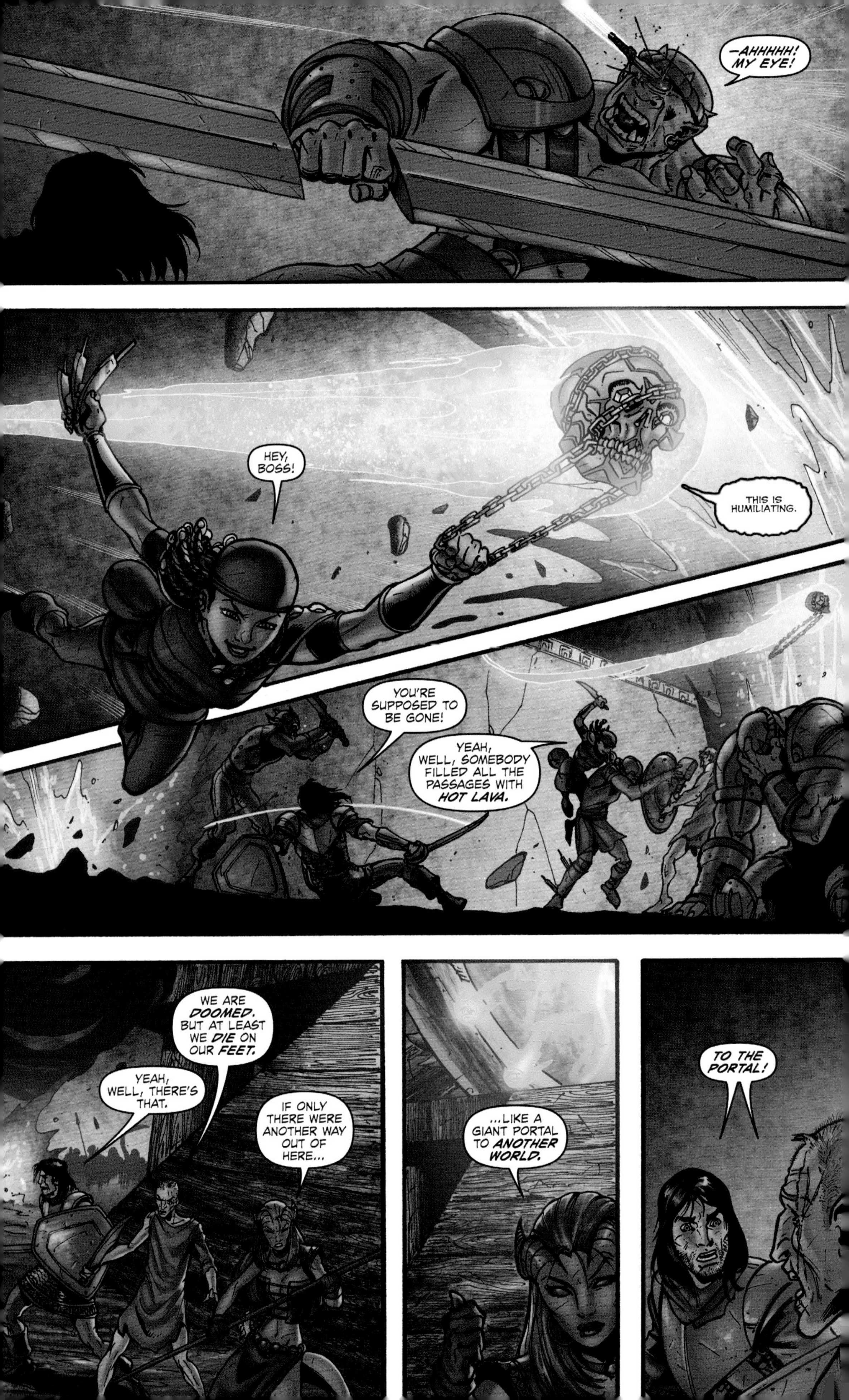
—AHHHHH! MY EYE!
HEY, BOSS!
THIS IS HUMILIATING.
YOU'RE SUPPOSED TO BE GONE!
YEAH, WELL, SOMEBODY FILLED ALL THE PASSAGES WITH HOT LAVA.
WE ARE DOOMED. BUT AT LEAST WE DIE ON OUR FEET.
YEAH, WELL, THERE'S THAT.
IF ONLY THERE WERE ANOTHER WAY OUT OF HERE...
...LIKE A GIANT PORTAL TO ANOTHER WORLD.
TO THE PORTAL!

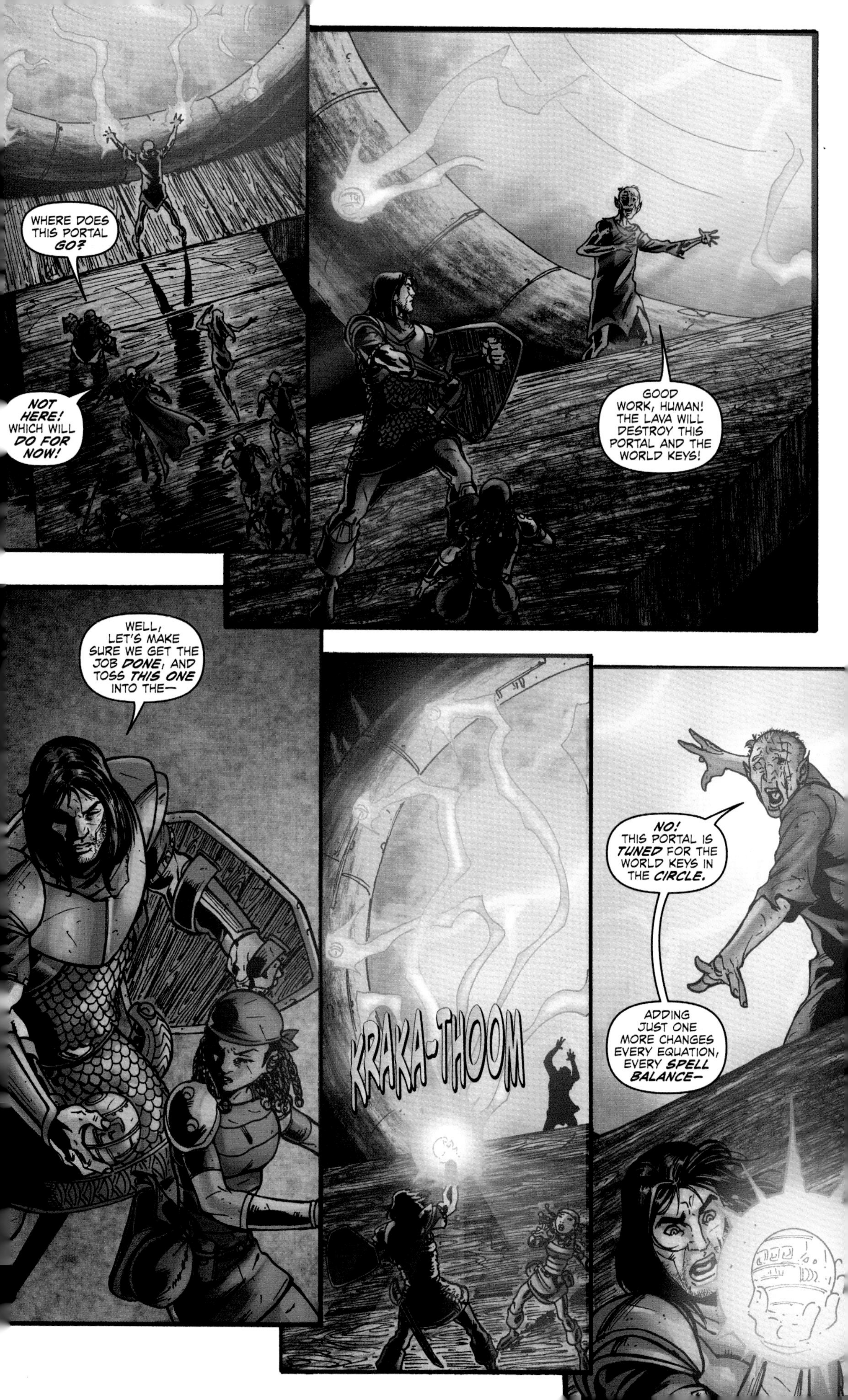
WHERE DOES THIS PORTAL GO?
NOT HERE! WHICH WILL DO FOR NOW!
GOOD WORK, HUMAN! THE LAVA WILL DESTROY THIS PORTAL AND THE WORLD KEYS!
WELL, LET'S MAKE SURE WE GET THE JOB DONE; AND TOSS THIS ONE INTO THE—
KRAKA-THOOM
NO! THIS PORTAL IS TUNED FOR THE WORLD KEYS IN THE CIRCLE.
ADDING JUST ONE MORE CHANGES EVERY EQUATION, EVERY SPELL BALANCE—

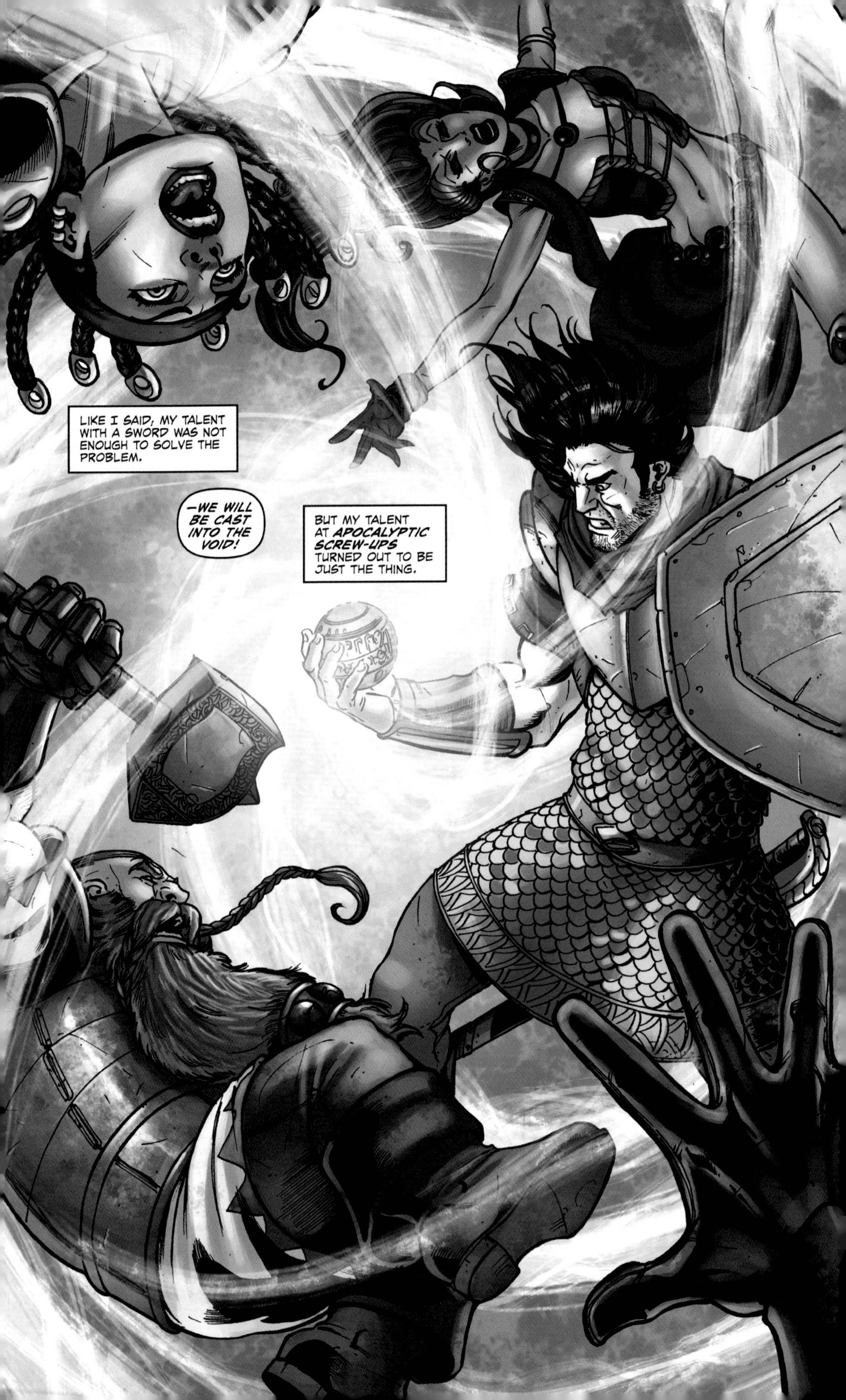
LIKE I SAID, MY TALENT WITH A SWORD WAS NOT ENOUGH TO SOLVE THE PROBLEM.
—WE WILL BE CAST INTO THE VOID!
BUT MY TALENT AT APOCALYPTIC SCREW-UPS TURNED OUT TO BE JUST THE THING.

Art by Tyler Walpole

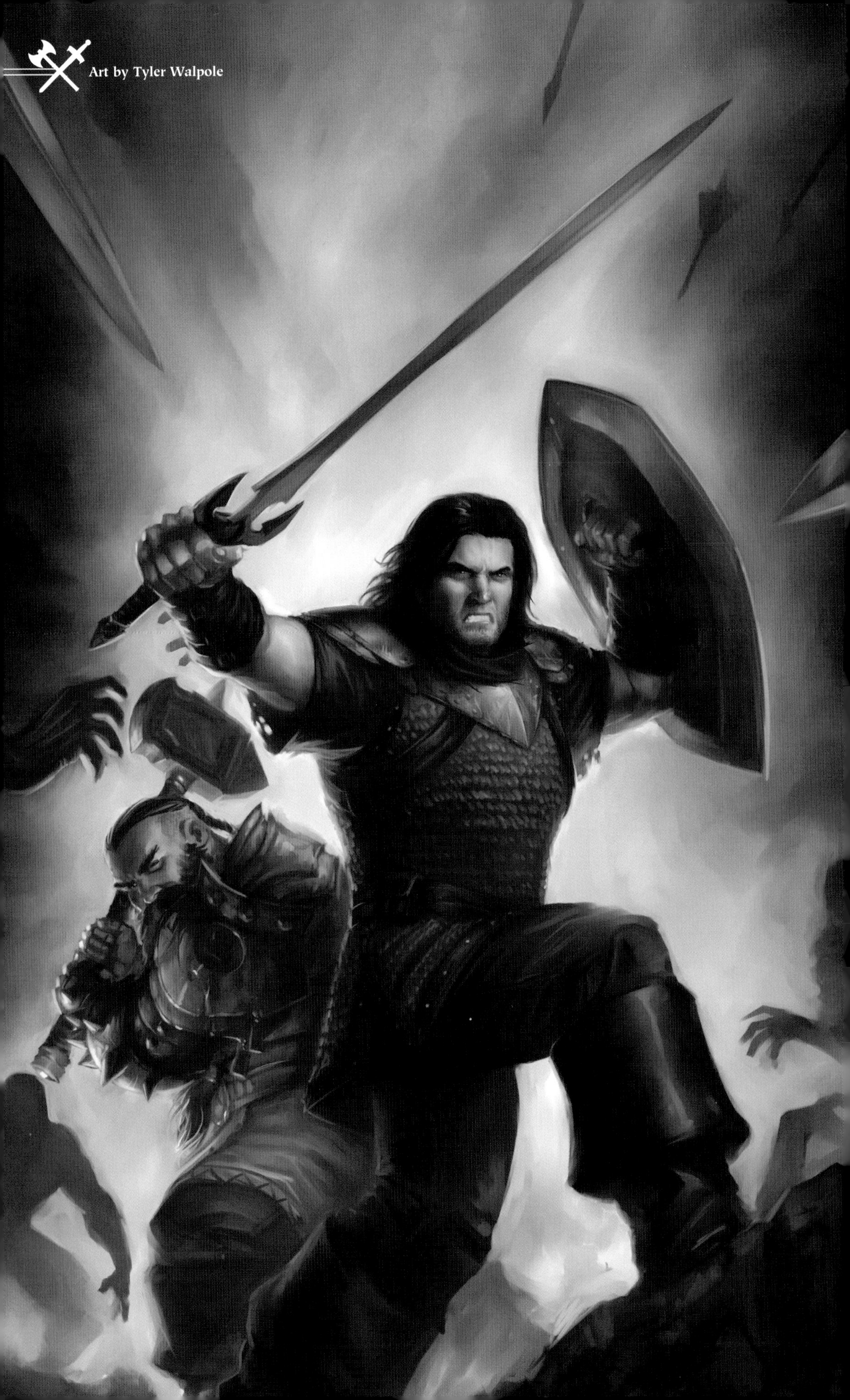

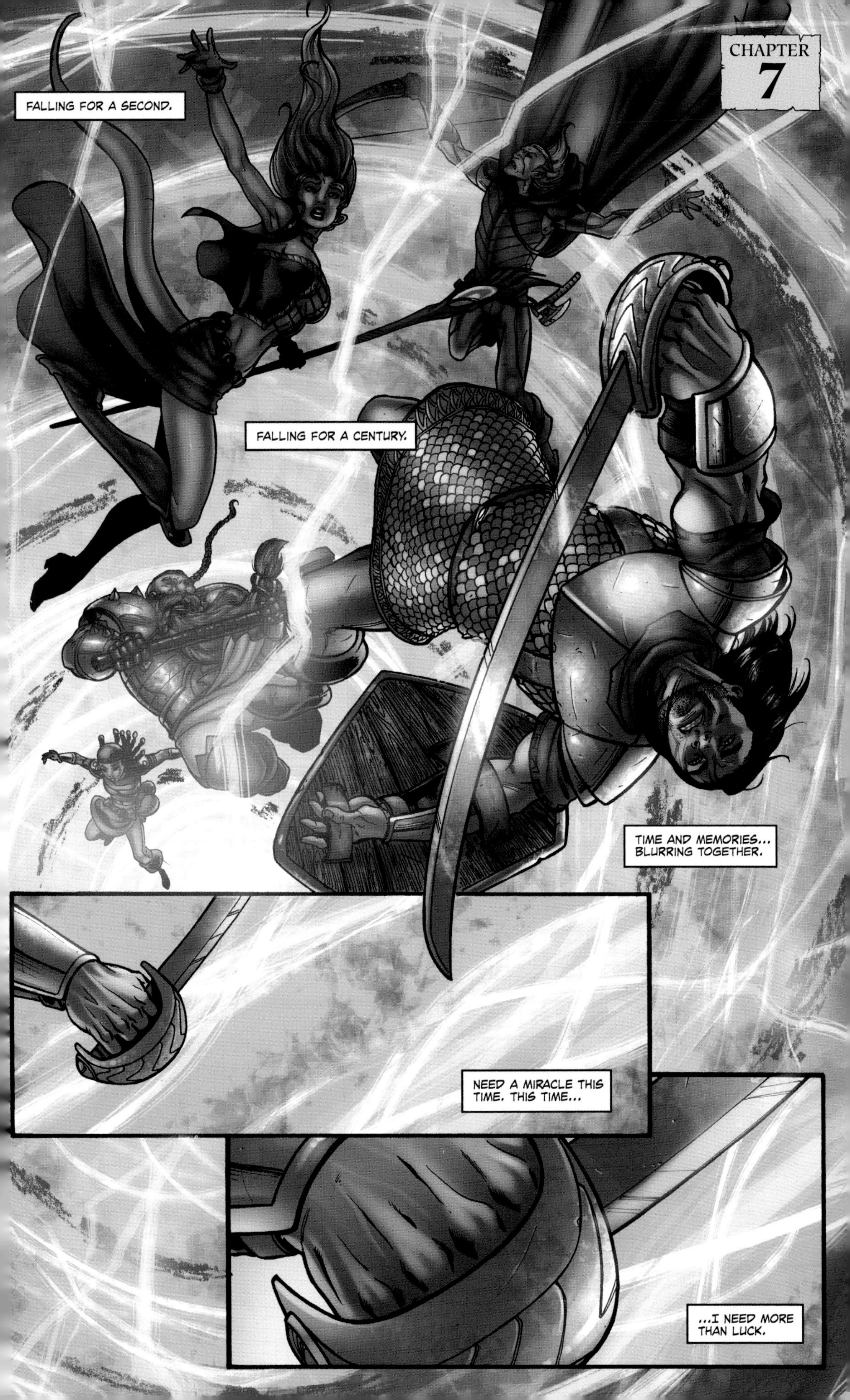
CHAPTER 7
FALLING FOR A SECOND.
FALLING FOR A CENTURY.
TIME AND MEMORIES... BLURRING TOGETHER.
NEED A MIRACLE THIS TIME. THIS TIME...
...I NEED MORE THAN LUCK.

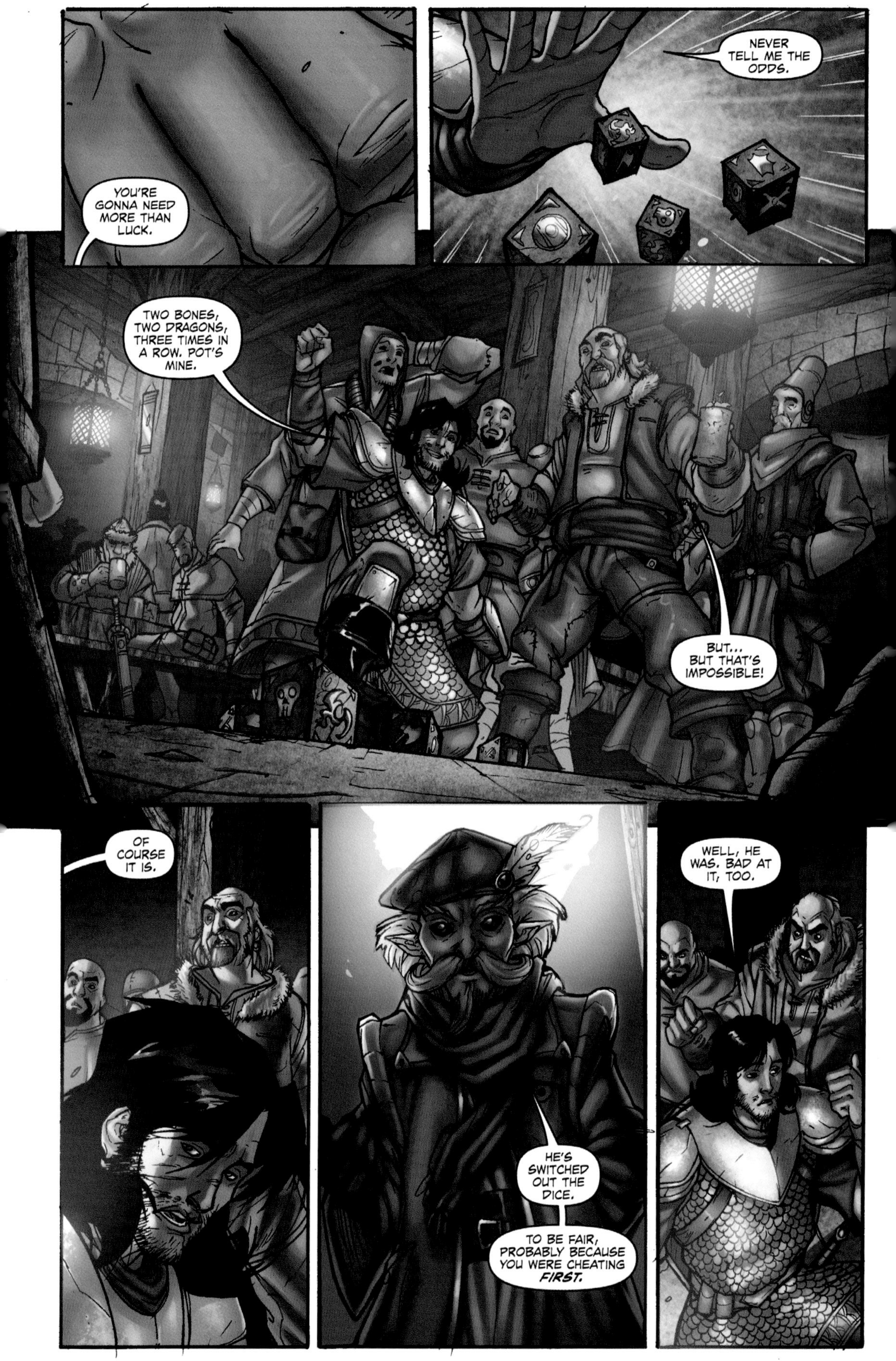
YOU'RE GONNA NEED MORE THAN LUCK.
NEVER TELL ME THE ODDS.
TWO BONES, TWO DRAGONS, THREE TIMES IN A ROW. POT'S MINE.
BUT... BUT THAT'S IMPOSSIBLE!
OF COURSE IT IS.
HE'S SWITCHED OUT THE DICE.
TO BE FAIR, PROBABLY BECAUSE YOU WERE CHEATING *FIRST.*
WELL, HE WAS. BAD AT IT, TOO.

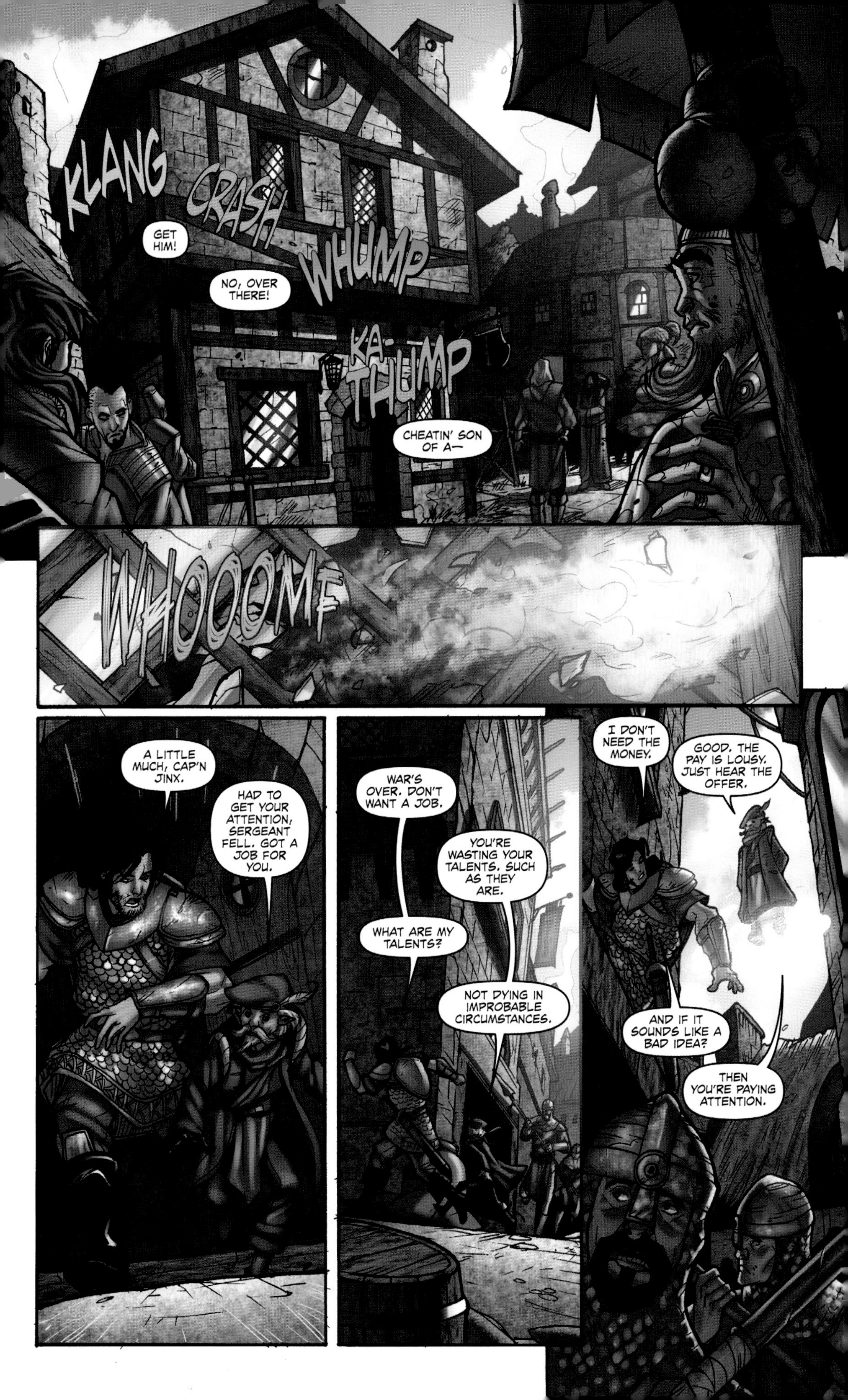
KLANG
CRASH
GET HIM!
NO, OVER THERE!
WHUMP
KA-THUMP
CHEATIN' SON OF A—
WHOOOMF
A LITTLE MUCH, CAP'N JINX.
HAD TO GET YOUR ATTENTION, SERGEANT FELL. GOT A JOB FOR YOU.
WAR'S OVER. DON'T WANT A JOB.
YOU'RE WASTING YOUR TALENTS. SUCH AS THEY ARE.
WHAT ARE MY TALENTS?
NOT DYING IN IMPROBABLE CIRCUMSTANCES.
I DON'T NEED THE MONEY.
GOOD. THE PAY IS LOUSY. JUST HEAR THE OFFER.
AND IF IT SOUNDS LIKE A BAD IDEA?
THEN YOU'RE PAYING ATTENTION.

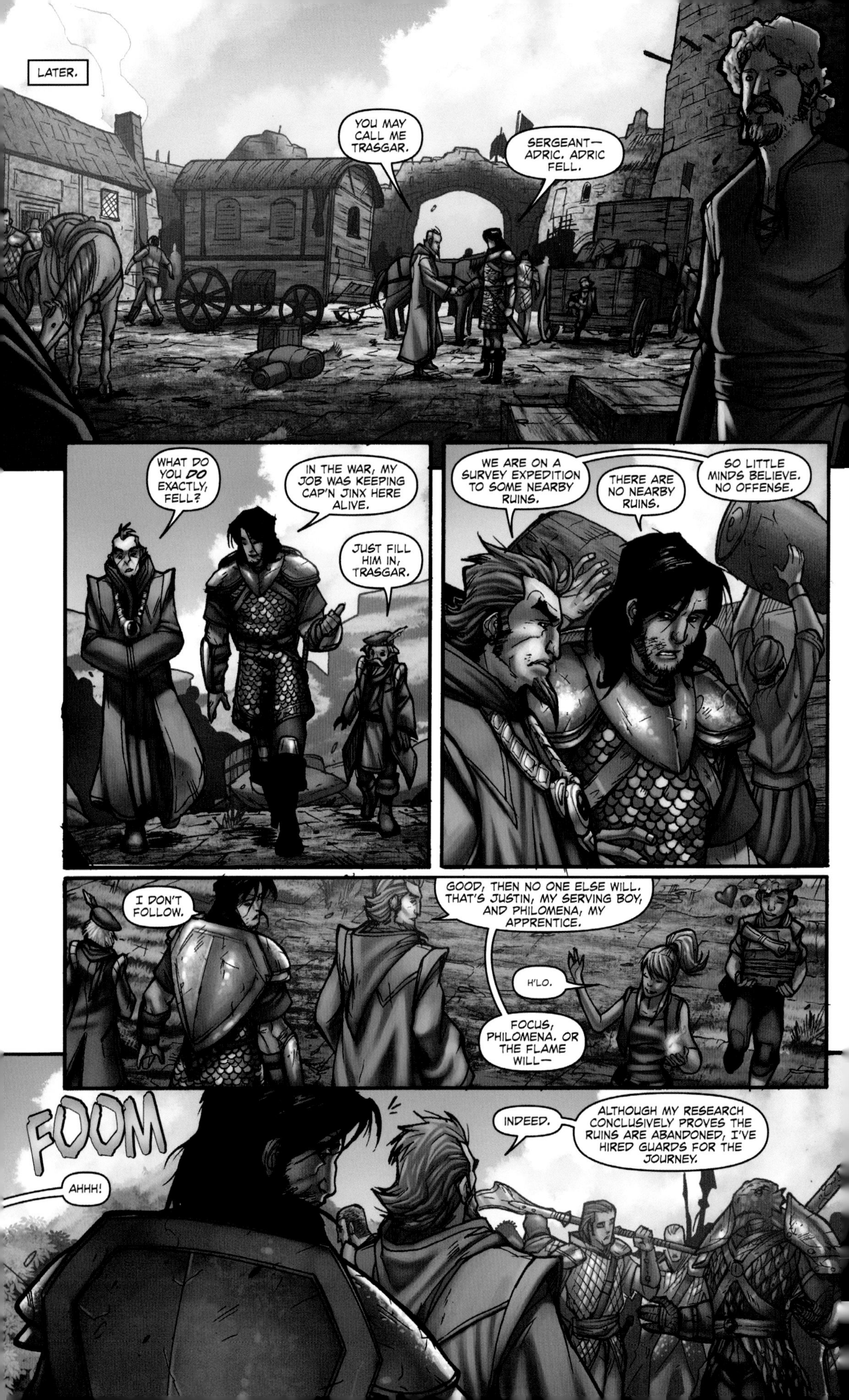
LATER.
YOU MAY CALL ME TRASGAR.
SERGEANT— ADRIC. ADRIC FELL.
WHAT DO YOU *DO* EXACTLY, FELL?
IN THE WAR, MY JOB WAS KEEPING CAP'N JINX HERE ALIVE.
JUST FILL HIM IN, TRASGAR.
WE ARE ON A SURVEY EXPEDITION TO SOME NEARBY RUINS.
THERE ARE NO NEARBY RUINS.
SO LITTLE MINDS BELIEVE. NO OFFENSE.
I DON'T FOLLOW.
GOOD, THEN NO ONE ELSE WILL. THAT'S JUSTIN, MY SERVING BOY, AND PHILOMENA, MY APPRENTICE.
H'LO.
FOCUS, PHILOMENA. OR THE FLAME WILL—
FOOM
AHHH!
INDEED.
ALTHOUGH MY RESEARCH CONCLUSIVELY PROVES THE RUINS ARE ABANDONED, I'VE HIRED GUARDS FOR THE JOURNEY.

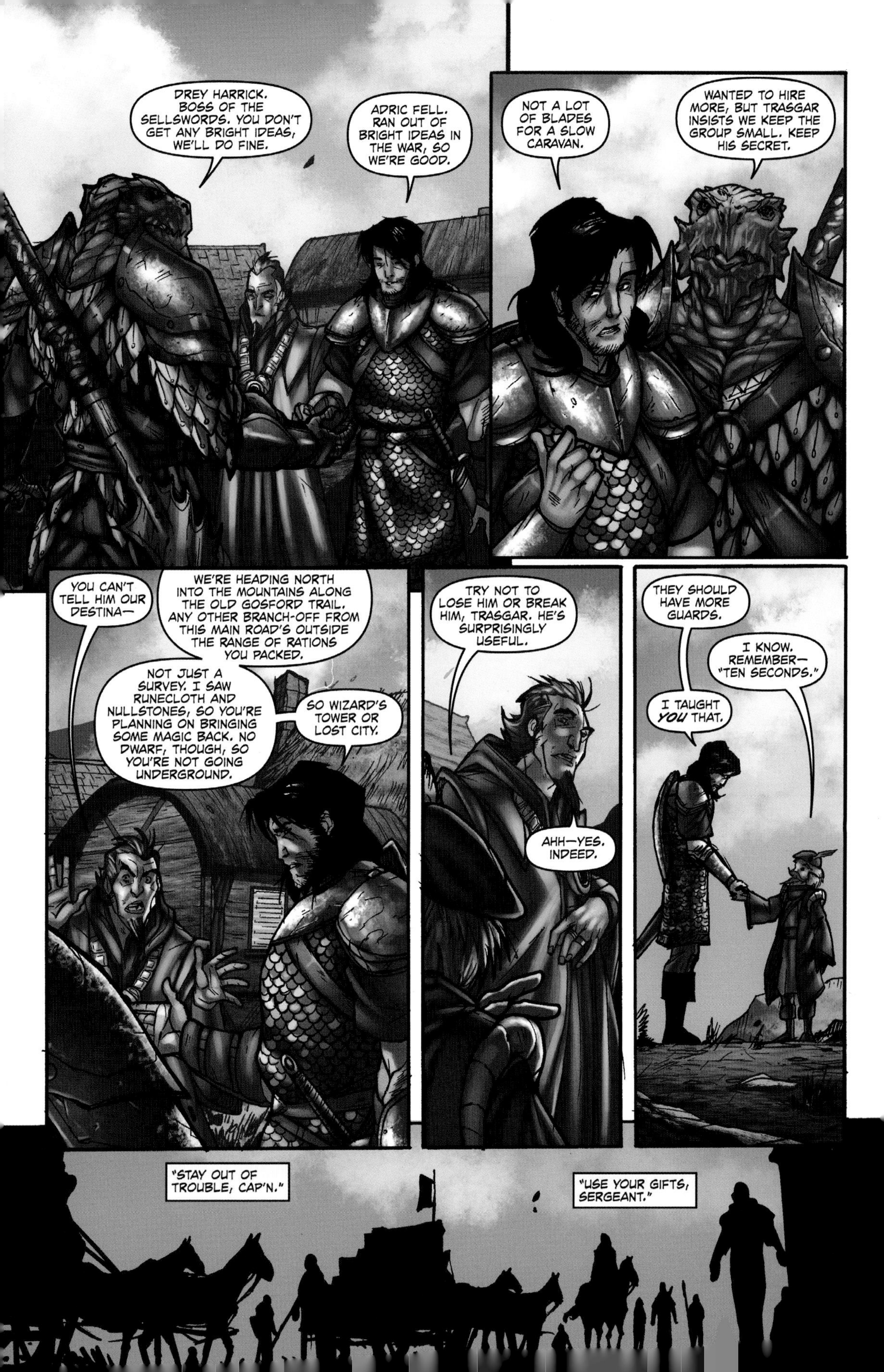
DREY HARRICK. BOSS OF THE SELLSWORDS. YOU DON'T GET ANY BRIGHT IDEAS, WE'LL DO FINE.
ADRIC FELL. RAN OUT OF BRIGHT IDEAS IN THE WAR, SO WE'RE GOOD.
NOT A LOT OF BLADES FOR A SLOW CARAVAN.
WANTED TO HIRE MORE, BUT TRASGAR INSISTS WE KEEP THE GROUP SMALL. KEEP HIS SECRET.
YOU CAN'T TELL HIM OUR DESTINA—
WE'RE HEADING NORTH INTO THE MOUNTAINS ALONG THE OLD GOSFORD TRAIL. ANY OTHER BRANCH-OFF FROM THIS MAIN ROAD'S OUTSIDE THE RANGE OF RATIONS YOU PACKED.
NOT JUST A SURVEY. I SAW RUNECLOTH AND NULLSTONES, SO YOU'RE PLANNING ON BRINGING SOME MAGIC BACK. NO DWARF, THOUGH, SO YOU'RE NOT GOING UNDERGROUND.
SO WIZARD'S TOWER OR LOST CITY.
TRY NOT TO LOSE HIM OR BREAK HIM, TRASGAR. HE'S SURPRISINGLY USEFUL.
AHH—YES. INDEED.
THEY SHOULD HAVE MORE GUARDS.
I KNOW. REMEMBER— "TEN SECONDS."
I TAUGHT *YOU* THAT.
"STAY OUT OF TROUBLE, CAP'N."
"USE YOUR GIFTS, SERGEANT."

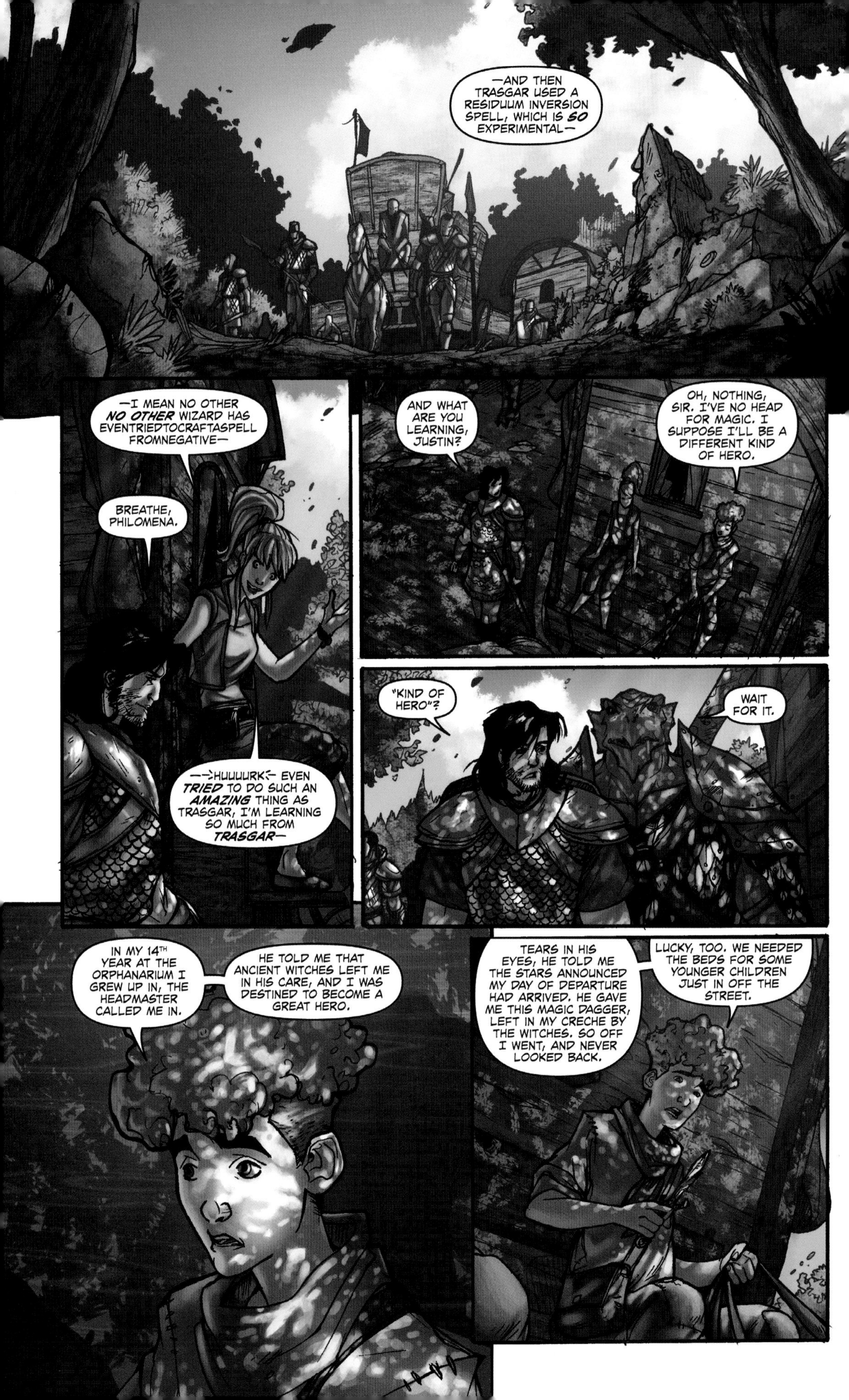
—AND THEN TRASGAR USED A RESIDUUM INVERSION SPELL, WHICH IS SO EXPERIMENTAL—
—I MEAN NO OTHER NO OTHER WIZARD HAS EVENTRIEDTOCRAFTASPELL FROMNEGATIVE—
BREATHE, PHILOMENA.
—HUUUURK— EVEN TRIED TO DO SUCH AN AMAZING THING AS TRASGAR, I'M LEARNING SO MUCH FROM TRASGAR—
AND WHAT ARE YOU LEARNING, JUSTIN?
OH, NOTHING, SIR. I'VE NO HEAD FOR MAGIC. I SUPPOSE I'LL BE A DIFFERENT KIND OF HERO.
"KIND OF HERO"?
WAIT FOR IT.
IN MY 14TH YEAR AT THE ORPHANARIUM I GREW UP IN, THE HEADMASTER CALLED ME IN.
HE TOLD ME THAT ANCIENT WITCHES LEFT ME IN HIS CARE, AND I WAS DESTINED TO BECOME A GREAT HERO.
TEARS IN HIS EYES, HE TOLD ME THE STARS ANNOUNCED MY DAY OF DEPARTURE HAD ARRIVED. HE GAVE ME THIS MAGIC DAGGER, LEFT IN MY CRECHE BY THE WITCHES. SO OFF I WENT, AND NEVER LOOKED BACK.
LUCKY, TOO. WE NEEDED THE BEDS FOR SOME YOUNGER CHILDREN JUST IN OFF THE STREET.

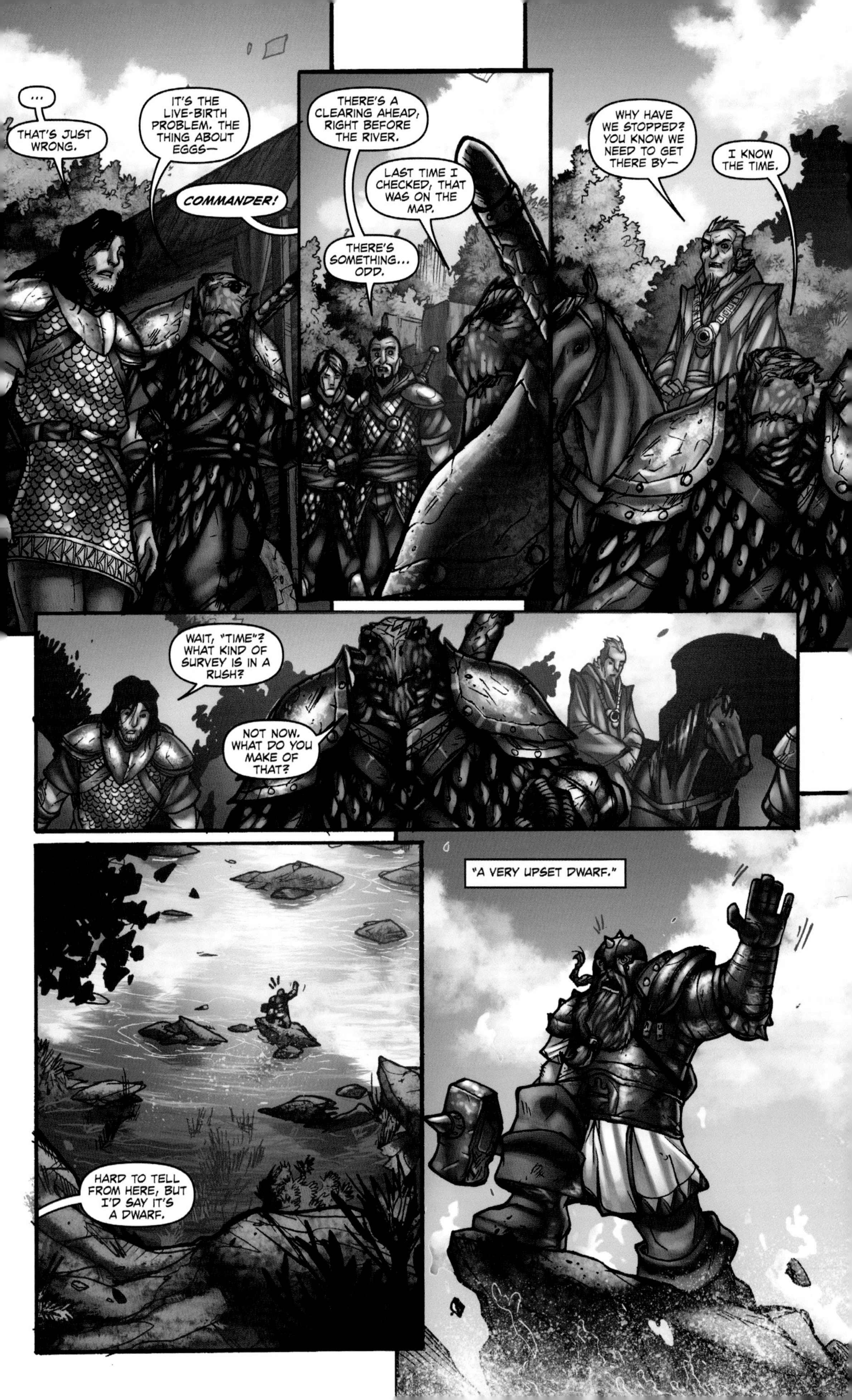
...
THAT'S JUST WRONG.
IT'S THE LIVE-BIRTH PROBLEM. THE THING ABOUT EGGS—
COMMANDER!
THERE'S A CLEARING AHEAD, RIGHT BEFORE THE RIVER.
LAST TIME I CHECKED, THAT WAS ON THE MAP.
THERE'S SOMETHING... ODD.
WHY HAVE WE STOPPED? YOU KNOW WE NEED TO GET THERE BY—
I KNOW THE TIME.
WAIT, "TIME"? WHAT KIND OF SURVEY IS IN A RUSH?
NOT NOW. WHAT DO YOU MAKE OF THAT?
HARD TO TELL FROM HERE, BUT I'D SAY IT'S A DWARF.
"A VERY UPSET DWARF."

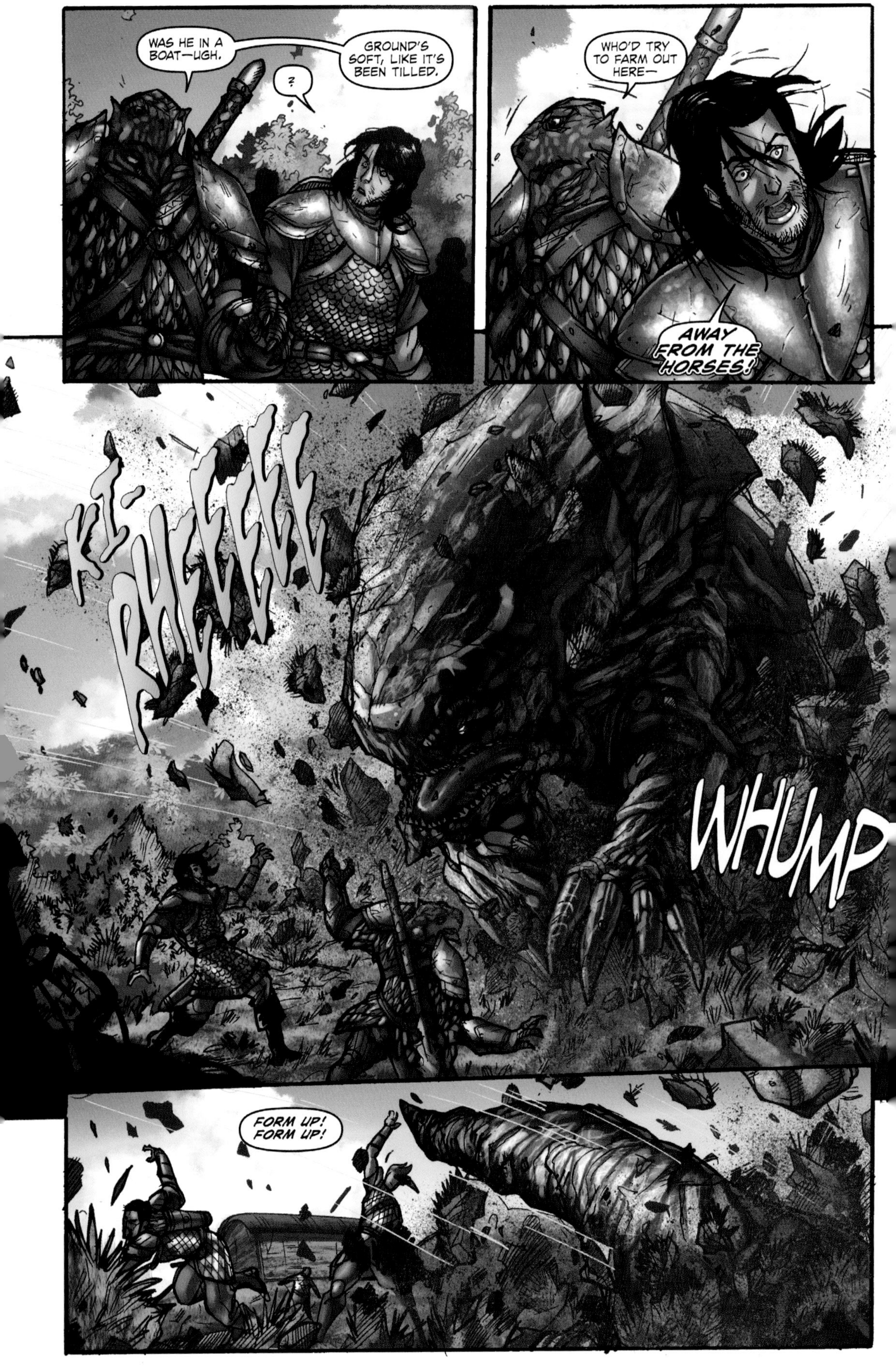
WAS HE IN A BOAT—UGH.
GROUND'S SOFT, LIKE IT'S BEEN TILLED.
?
WHO'D TRY TO FARM OUT HERE—
AWAY FROM THE HORSES!
KI-RHEEEE
WHUMP
FORM UP! FORM UP!

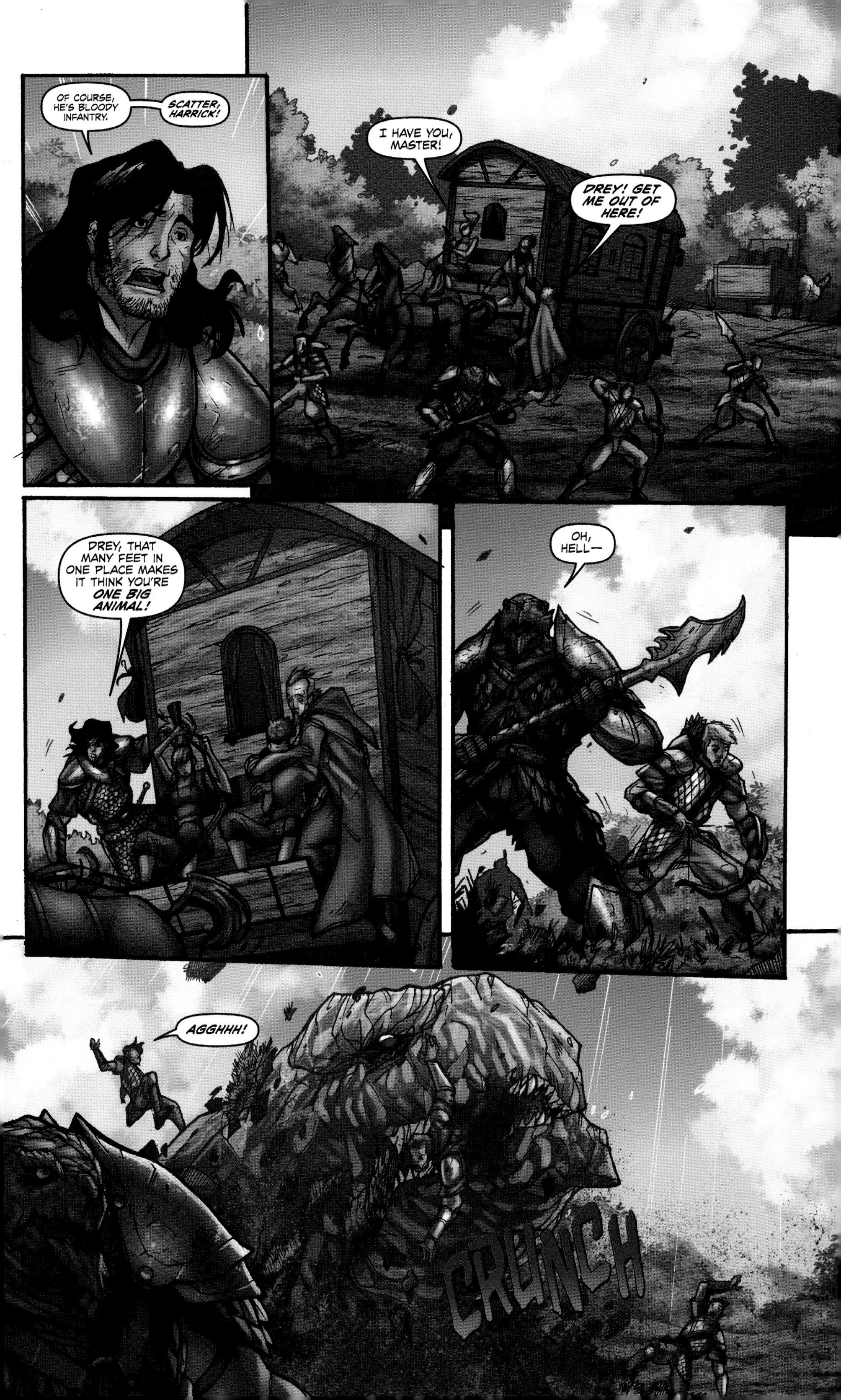
OF COURSE, HE'S BLOODY INFANTRY.
SCATTER, HARRICK!
I HAVE YOU, MASTER!
DREY! GET ME OUT OF HERE!
DREY, THAT MANY FEET IN ONE PLACE MAKES IT THINK YOU'RE ONE BIG ANIMAL!
OH, HELL—
AGGHHH!
CRUNCH

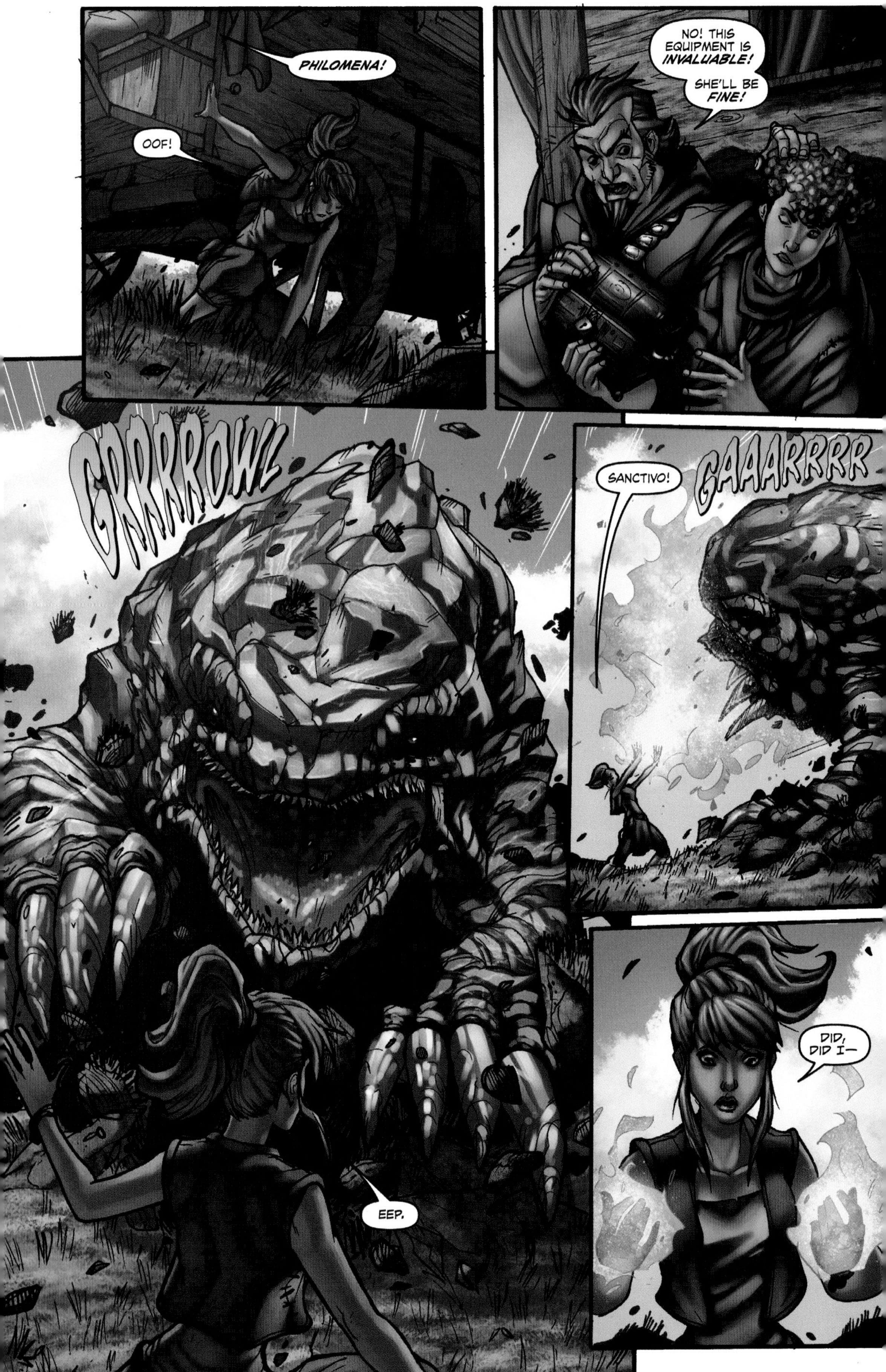
PHILOMENA!
OOF!
NO! THIS EQUIPMENT IS INVALUABLE!
SHE'LL BE FINE!
GRRRROWL
EEP.
SANCTIVO!
GAAARRRR
DID, DID I—

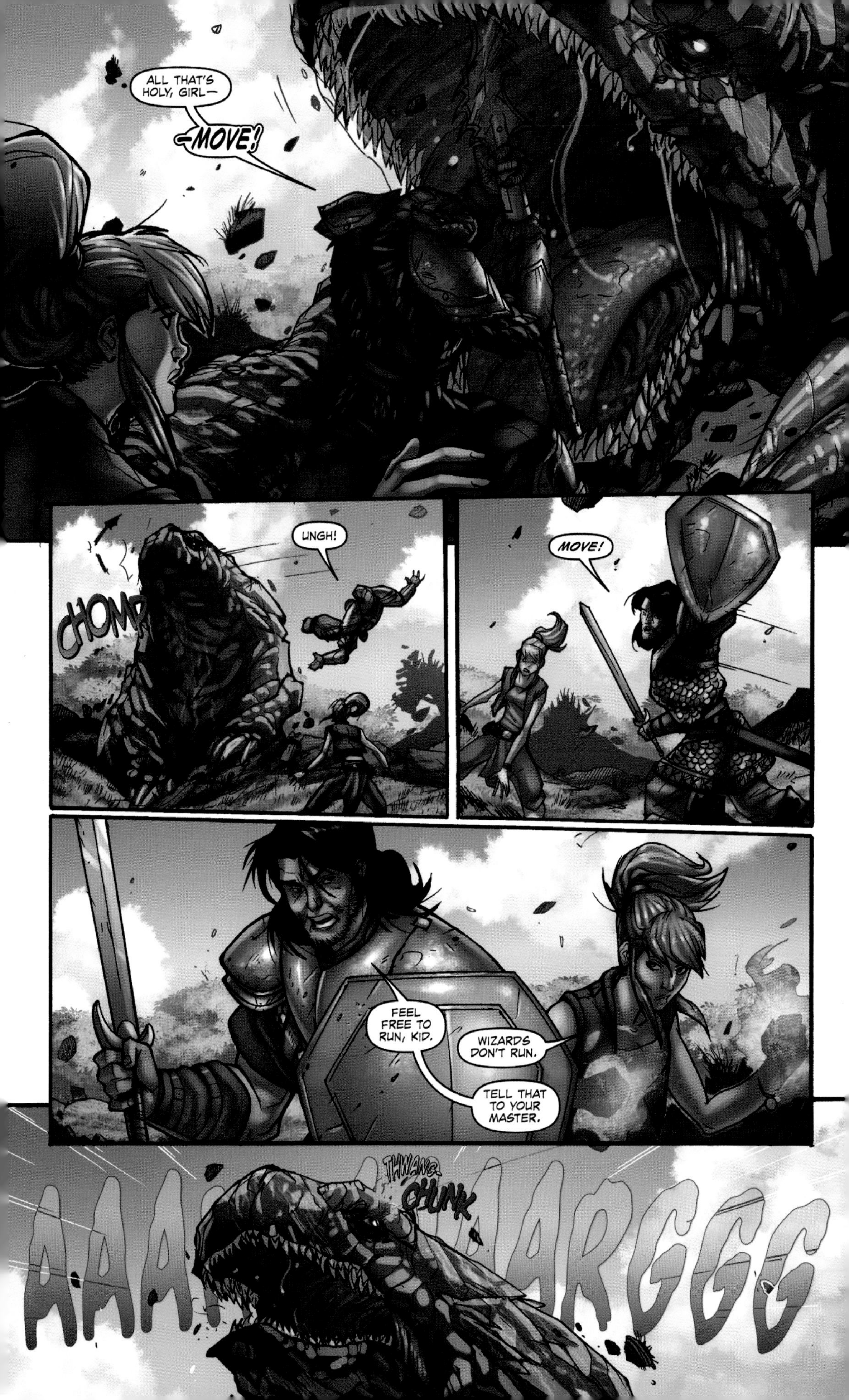
ALL THAT'S HOLY, GIRL—
—MOVE!
CHOMP
UNGH!
MOVE!
FEEL FREE TO RUN, KID.
WIZARDS DON'T RUN.
TELL THAT TO YOUR MASTER.
THWANG-CHUNK
ARGGG

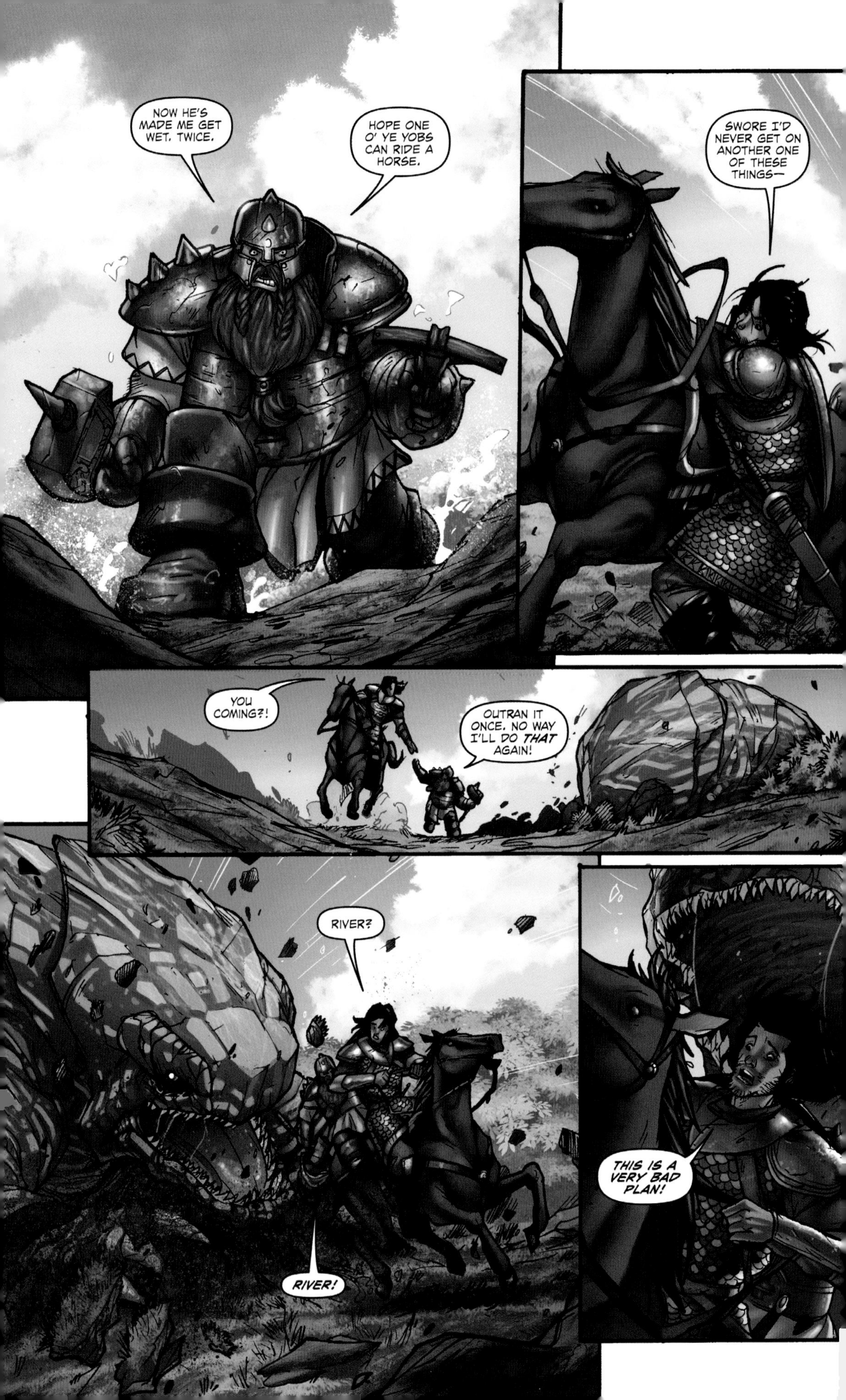
NOW HE'S MADE ME GET WET. TWICE.
HOPE ONE O' YE YOBS CAN RIDE A HORSE.
SWORE I'D NEVER GET ON ANOTHER ONE OF THESE THINGS—
YOU COMING?!
OUTRAN IT ONCE. NO WAY I'LL DO *THAT* AGAIN!
RIVER?
RIVER!
THIS IS A VERY BAD PLAN!

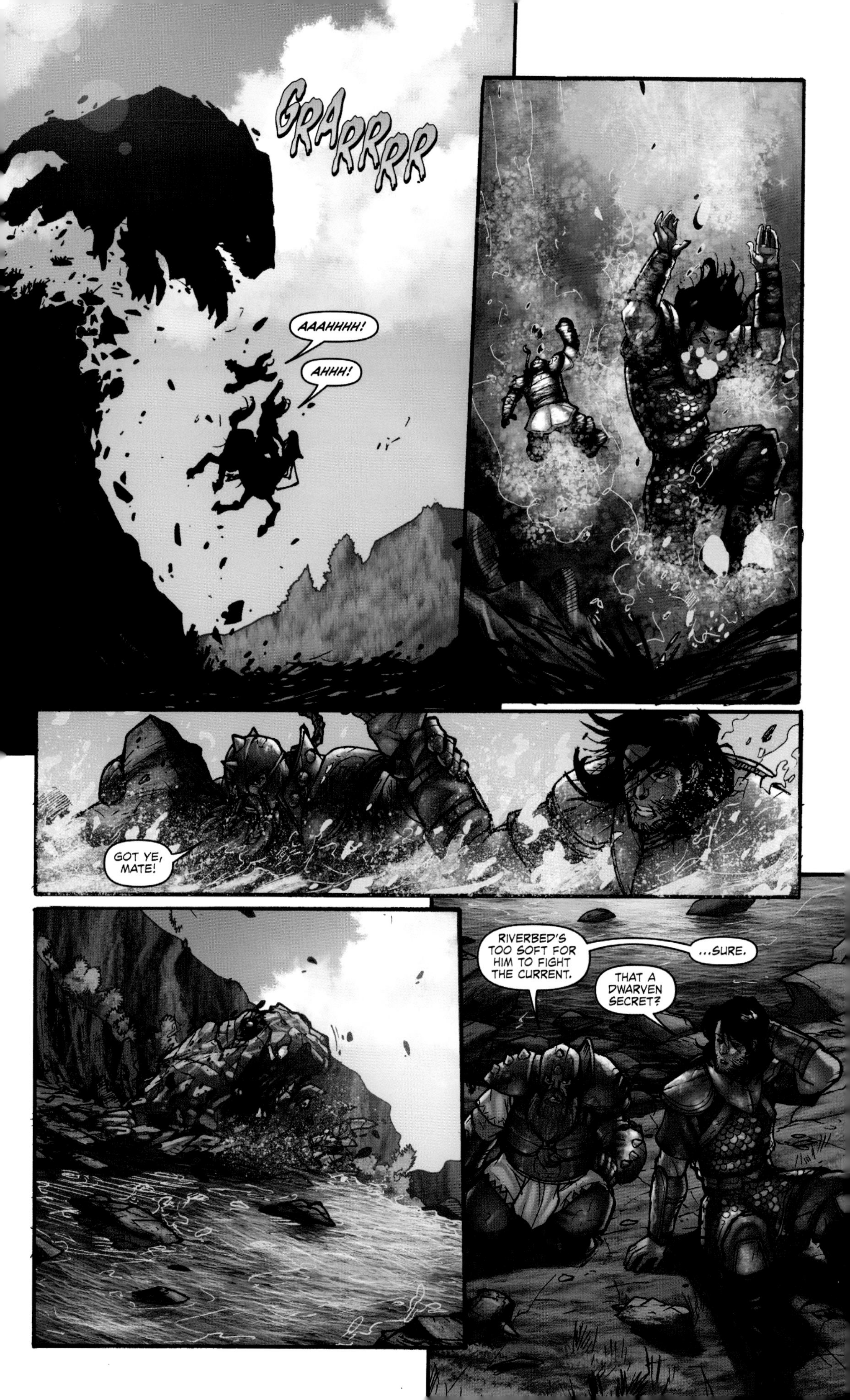
GRARRRRR
AAAHHHH!
AHHH!
GOT YE, MATE!
RIVERBED'S TOO SOFT FOR HIM TO FIGHT THE CURRENT.
THAT A DWARVEN SECRET?
...SURE.

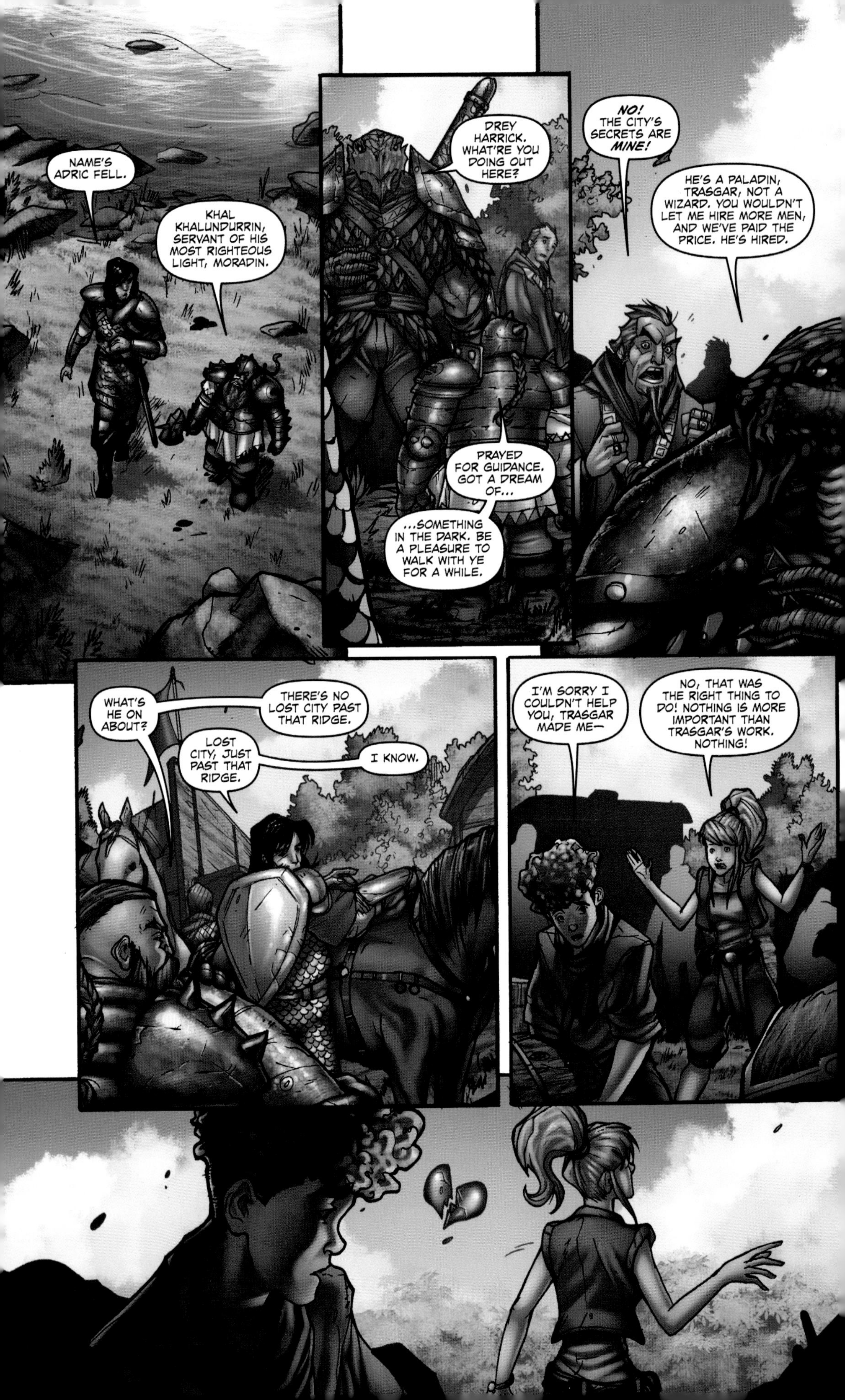
NAME'S ADRIC FELL.
KHAL KHALUNDURRIN, SERVANT OF HIS MOST RIGHTEOUS LIGHT, MORADIN.
DREY HARRICK. WHAT'RE YOU DOING OUT HERE?
PRAYED FOR GUIDANCE. GOT A DREAM OF...
...SOMETHING IN THE DARK. BE A PLEASURE TO WALK WITH YE FOR A WHILE.
NO! THE CITY'S SECRETS ARE MINE!
HE'S A PALADIN, TRASGAR, NOT A WIZARD. YOU WOULDN'T LET ME HIRE MORE MEN, AND WE'VE PAID THE PRICE. HE'S HIRED.
WHAT'S HE ON ABOUT?
THERE'S NO LOST CITY PAST THAT RIDGE.
LOST CITY, JUST PAST THAT RIDGE.
I KNOW.
I'M SORRY I COULDN'T HELP YOU, TRASGAR MADE ME—
NO, THAT WAS THE RIGHT THING TO DO! NOTHING IS MORE IMPORTANT THAN TRASGAR'S WORK. NOTHING!

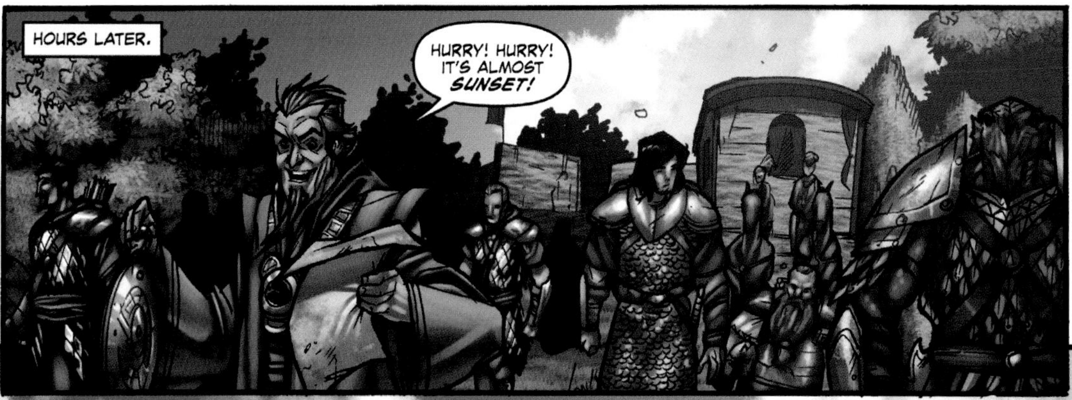
HOURS LATER.
HURRY! HURRY! IT'S ALMOST SUNSET!

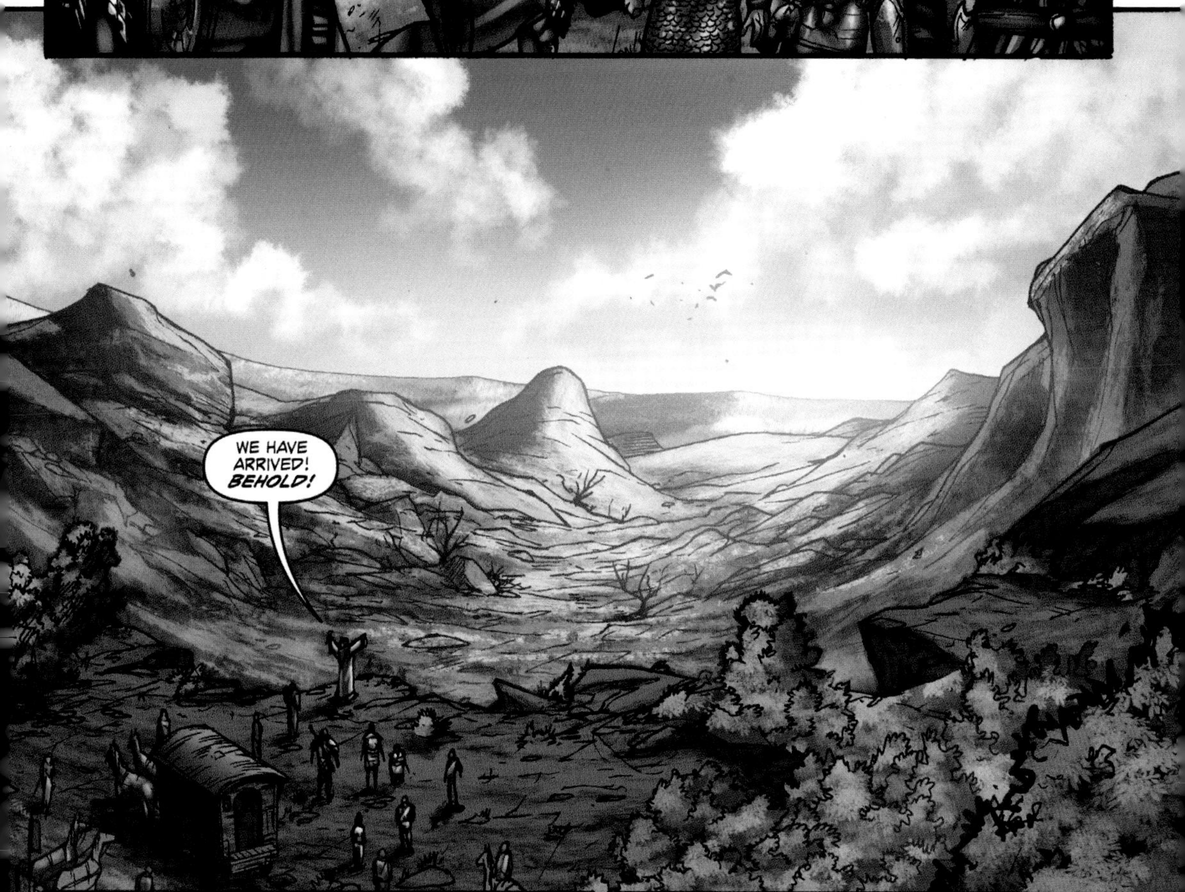
WE HAVE ARRIVED! BEHOLD!

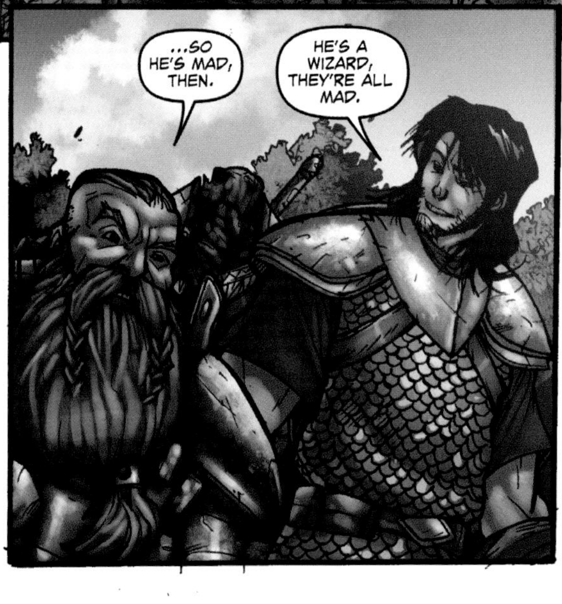
...SO HE'S MAD, THEN.
HE'S A WIZARD, THEY'RE ALL MAD.

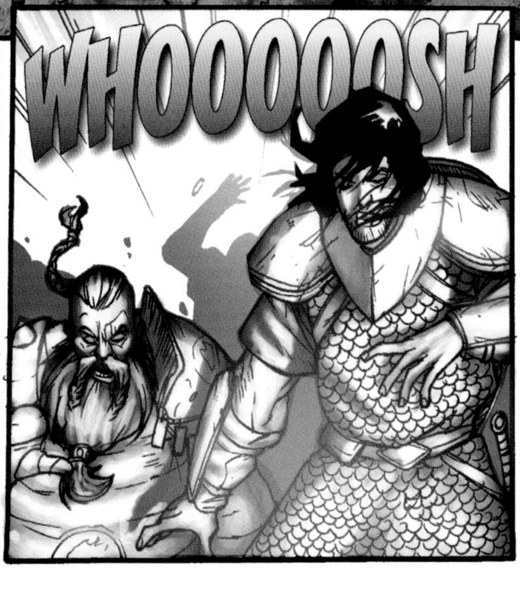
WHOOOOOOSH

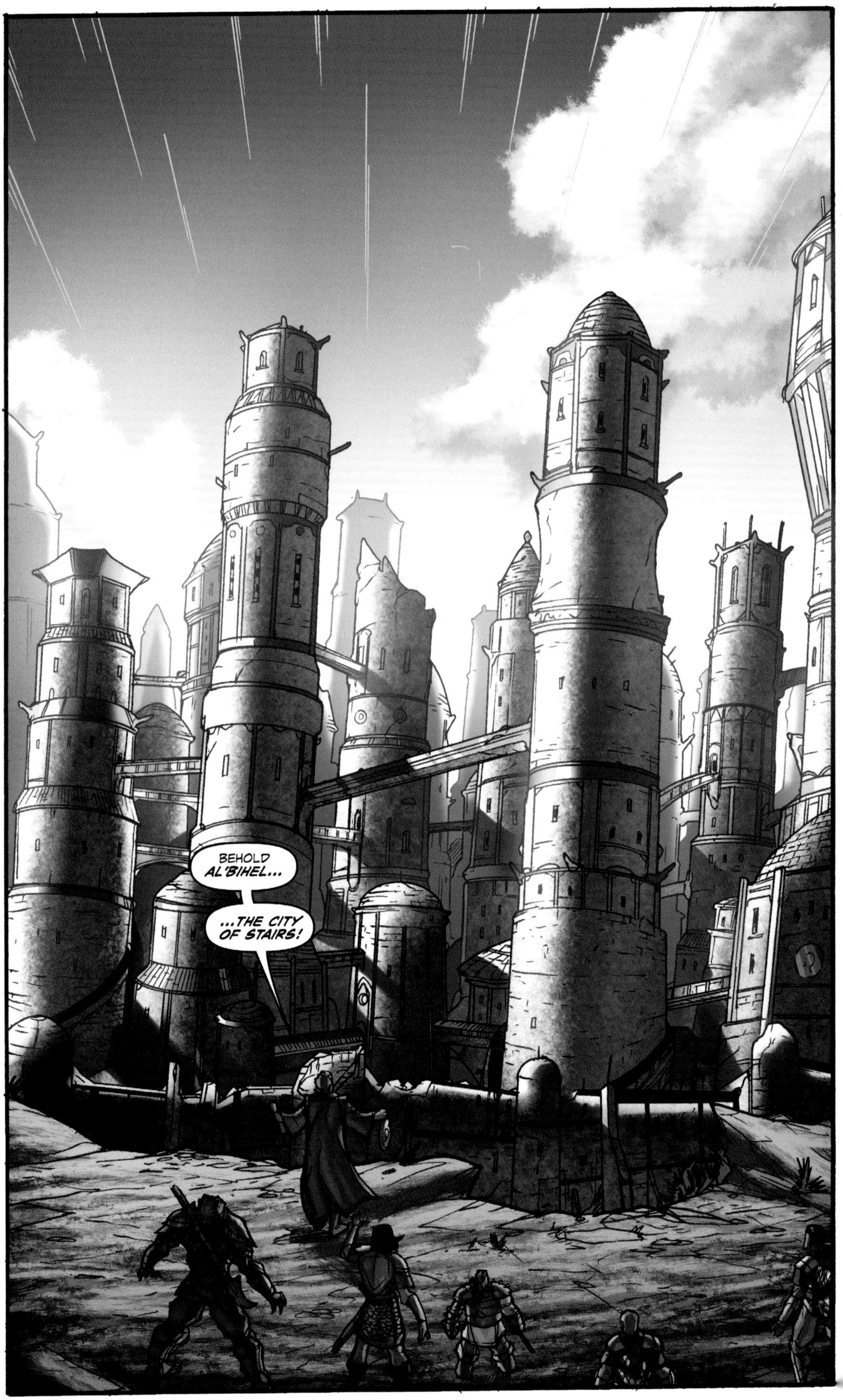
BEHOLD AL'BIHEL...
...THE CITY OF STAIRS!

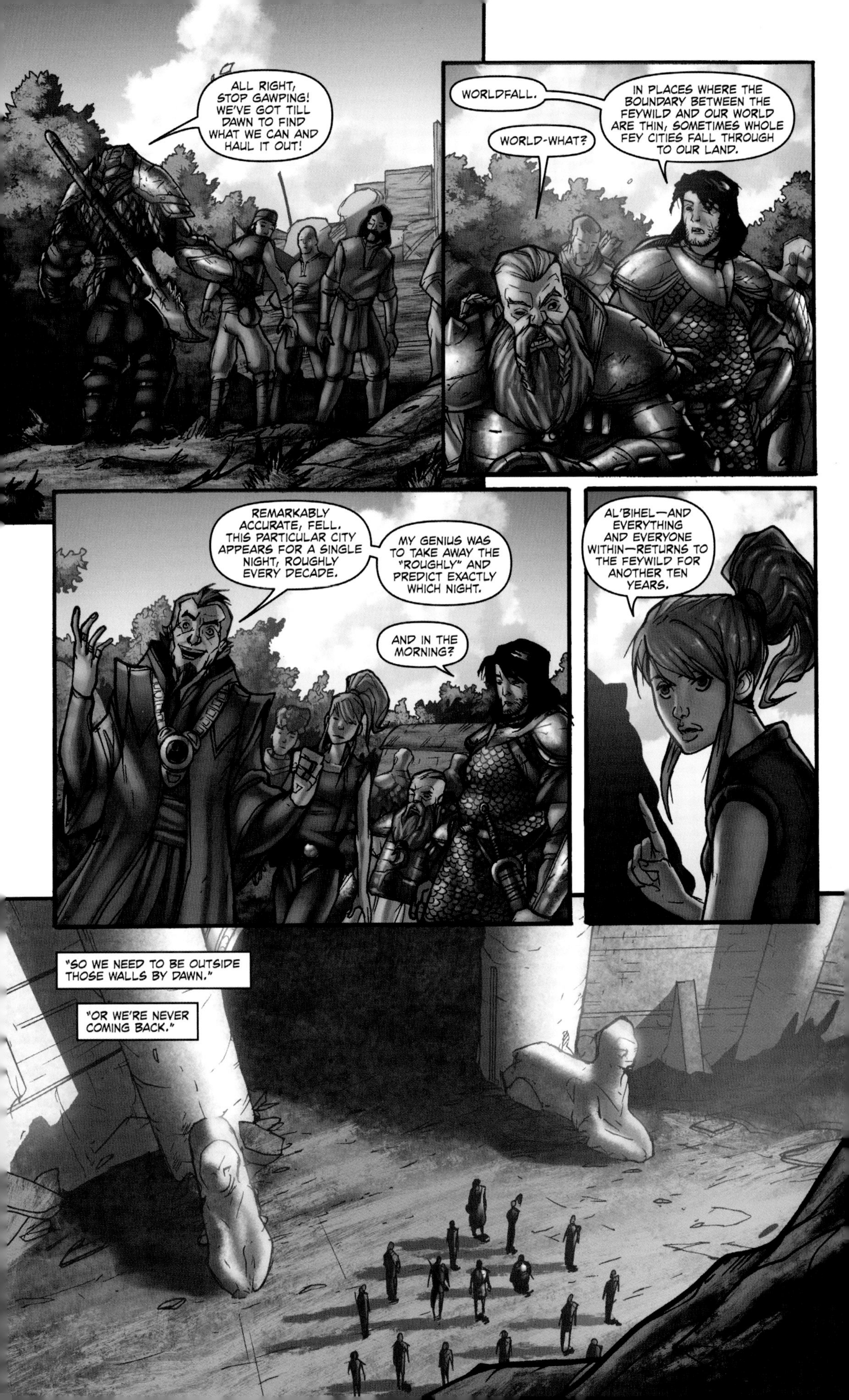
ALL RIGHT, STOP GAWPING! WE'VE GOT TILL DAWN TO FIND WHAT WE CAN AND HAUL IT OUT!
WORLDFALL.
WORLD-WHAT?
IN PLACES WHERE THE BOUNDARY BETWEEN THE FEYWILD AND OUR WORLD ARE THIN, SOMETIMES WHOLE FEY CITIES FALL THROUGH TO OUR LAND.
REMARKABLY ACCURATE, FELL. THIS PARTICULAR CITY APPEARS FOR A SINGLE NIGHT, ROUGHLY EVERY DECADE.
MY GENIUS WAS TO TAKE AWAY THE "ROUGHLY" AND PREDICT EXACTLY WHICH NIGHT.
AND IN THE MORNING?
AL'BIHEL—AND EVERYTHING AND EVERYONE WITHIN—RETURNS TO THE FEYWILD FOR ANOTHER TEN YEARS.
"SO WE NEED TO BE OUTSIDE THOSE WALLS BY DAWN."
"OR WE'RE NEVER COMING BACK."

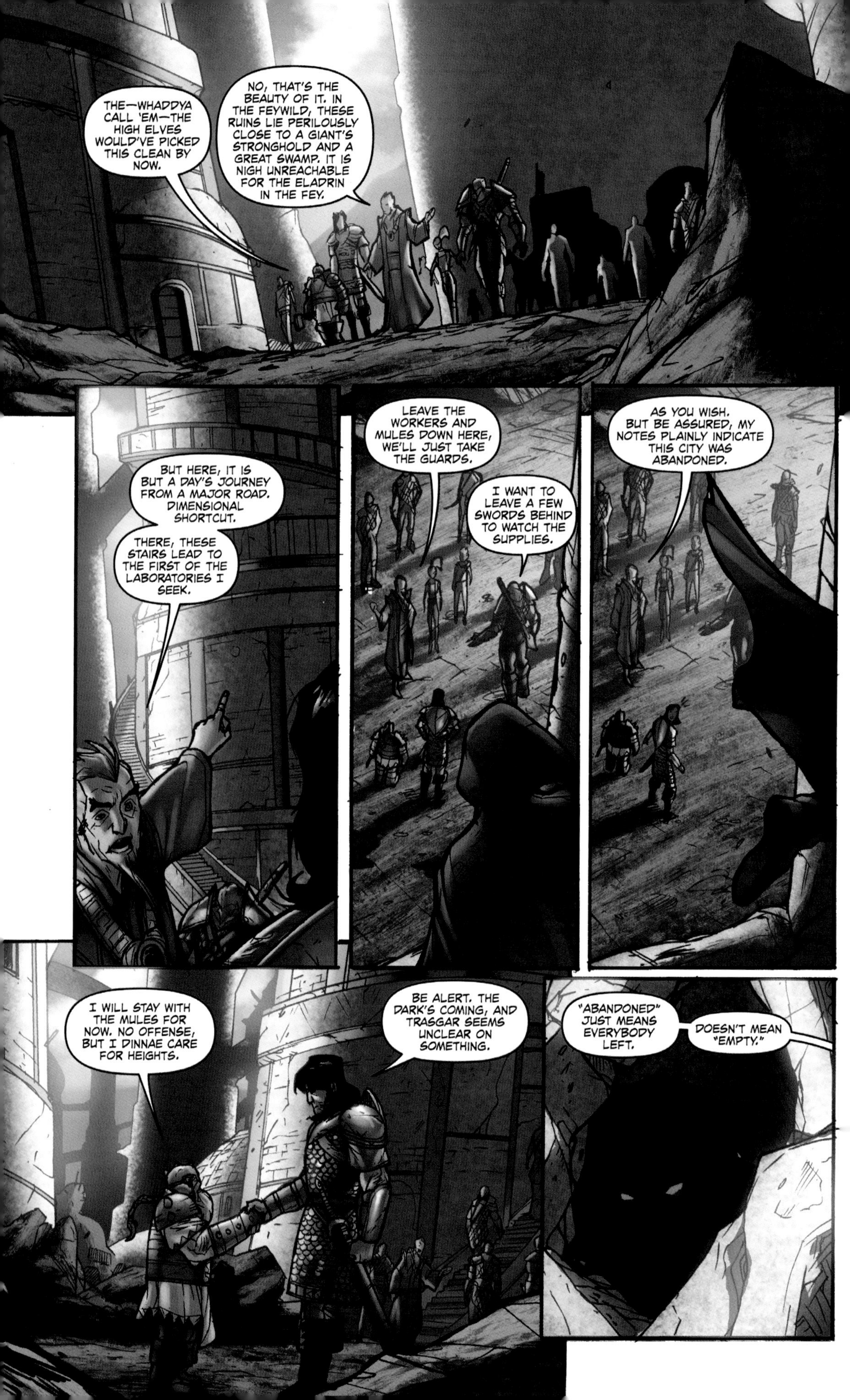
THE—WHADDYA CALL 'EM—THE HIGH ELVES WOULD'VE PICKED THIS CLEAN BY NOW.
NO, THAT'S THE BEAUTY OF IT. IN THE FEYWILD, THESE RUINS LIE PERILOUSLY CLOSE TO A GIANT'S STRONGHOLD AND A GREAT SWAMP. IT IS NIGH UNREACHABLE FOR THE ELADRIN IN THE FEY.
BUT HERE, IT IS BUT A DAY'S JOURNEY FROM A MAJOR ROAD. DIMENSIONAL SHORTCUT.
THERE, THESE STAIRS LEAD TO THE FIRST OF THE LABORATORIES I SEEK.
LEAVE THE WORKERS AND MULES DOWN HERE, WE'LL JUST TAKE THE GUARDS.
I WANT TO LEAVE A FEW SWORDS BEHIND TO WATCH THE SUPPLIES.
AS YOU WISH. BUT BE ASSURED, MY NOTES PLAINLY INDICATE THIS CITY WAS ABANDONED.
I WILL STAY WITH THE MULES FOR NOW. NO OFFENSE, BUT I DINNAE CARE FOR HEIGHTS.
BE ALERT. THE DARK'S COMING, AND TRASGAR SEEMS UNCLEAR ON SOMETHING.
"ABANDONED" JUST MEANS EVERYBODY LEFT.
DOESN'T MEAN "EMPTY."

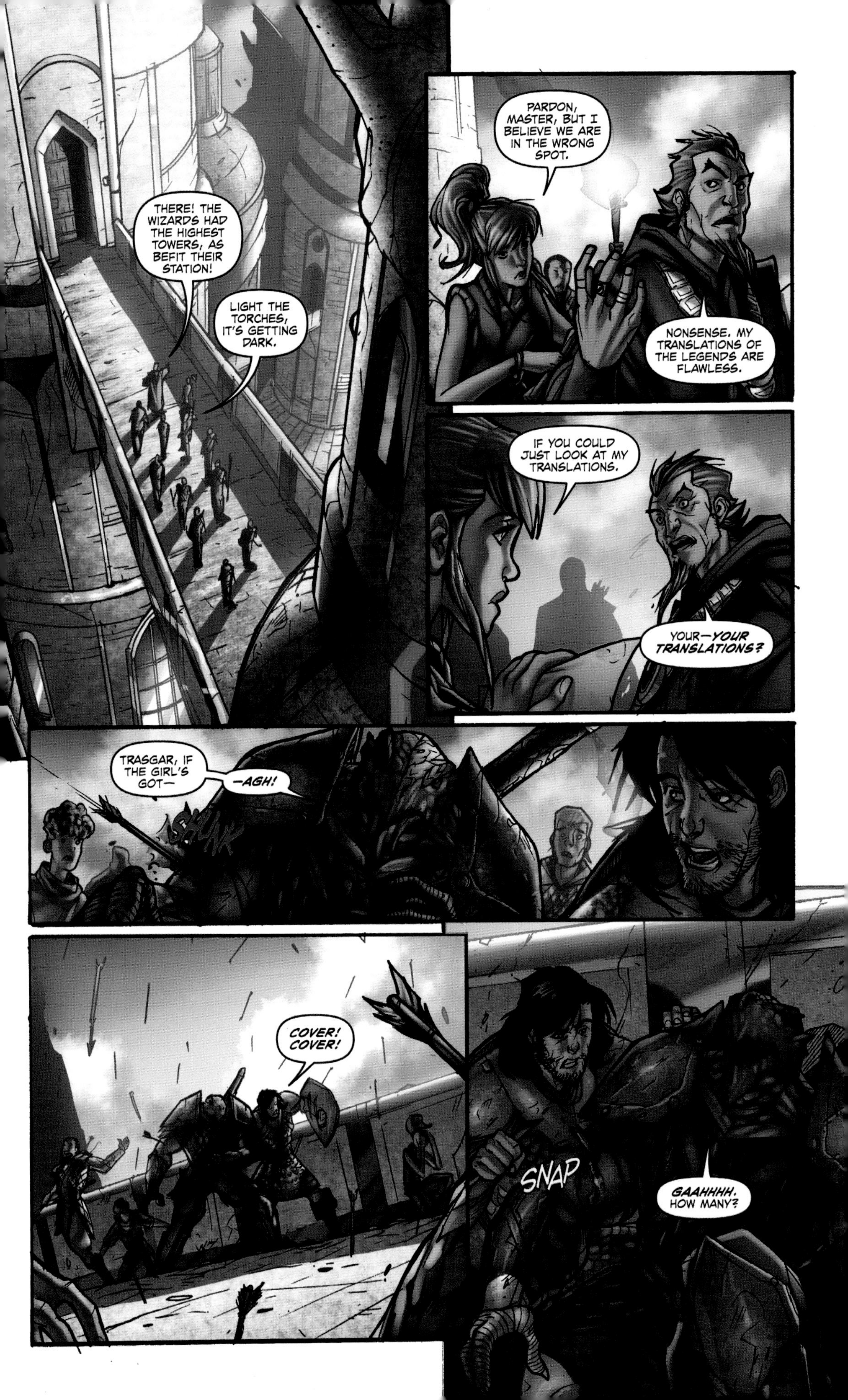
THERE! THE WIZARDS HAD THE HIGHEST TOWERS, AS BEFIT THEIR STATION!
LIGHT THE TORCHES, IT'S GETTING DARK.
PARDON, MASTER, BUT I BELIEVE WE ARE IN THE WRONG SPOT.
NONSENSE. MY TRANSLATIONS OF THE LEGENDS ARE FLAWLESS.
IF YOU COULD JUST LOOK AT MY TRANSLATIONS.
YOUR—YOUR TRANSLATIONS?
TRASGAR, IF THE GIRL'S GOT—
—AGH!
SHUNK
COVER! COVER!
SNAP
GAAHHHH. HOW MANY?

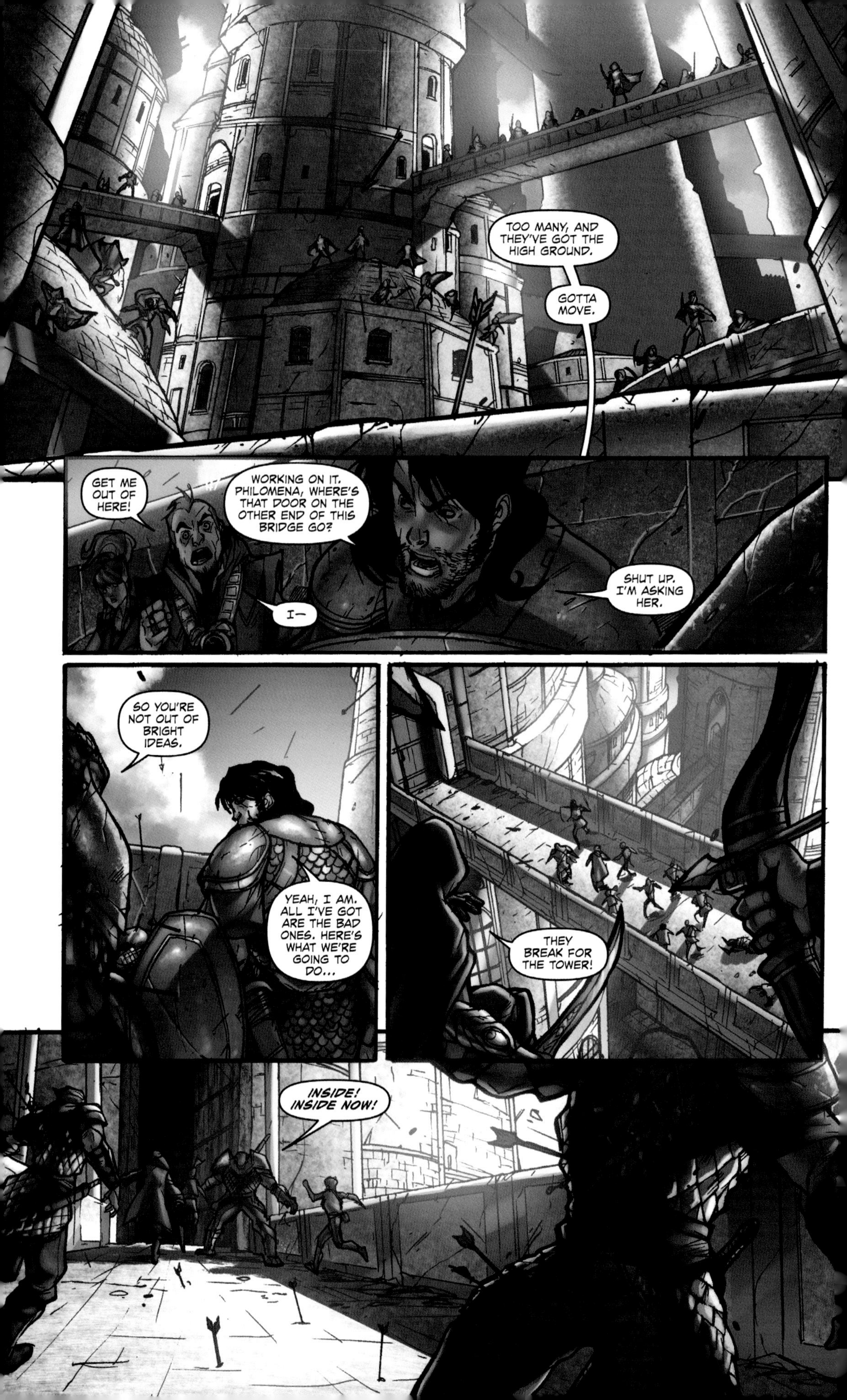
TOO MANY, AND THEY'VE GOT THE HIGH GROUND.
GOTTA MOVE.
GET ME OUT OF HERE!
WORKING ON IT. PHILOMENA, WHERE'S THAT DOOR ON THE OTHER END OF THIS BRIDGE GO?
I—
SHUT UP. I'M ASKING HER.
SO YOU'RE NOT OUT OF BRIGHT IDEAS.
YEAH, I AM. ALL I'VE GOT ARE THE BAD ONES. HERE'S WHAT WE'RE GOING TO DO...
THEY BREAK FOR THE TOWER!
INSIDE! INSIDE NOW!

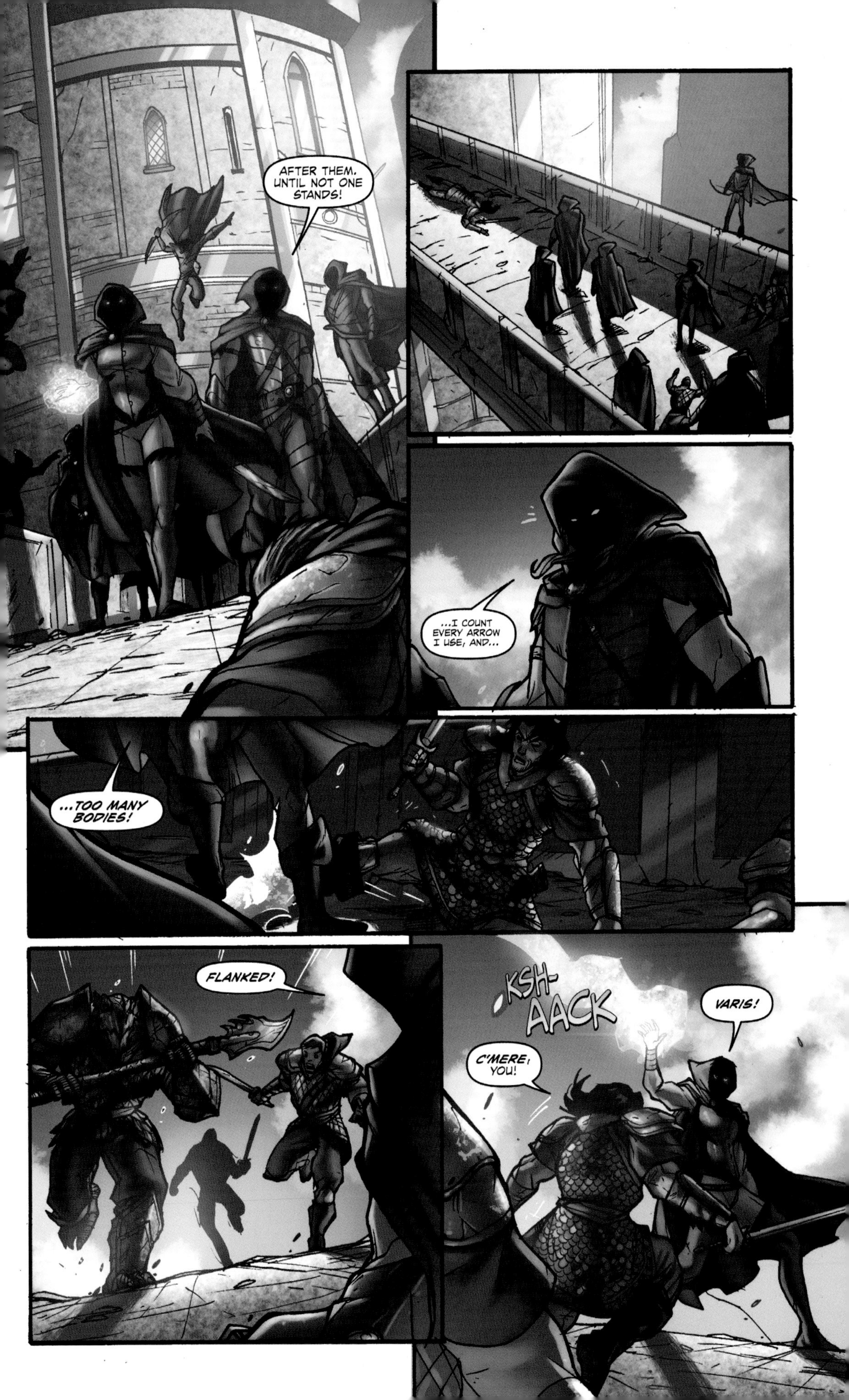
AFTER THEM. UNTIL NOT ONE STANDS!
...I COUNT EVERY ARROW I USE, AND...
...TOO MANY BODIES!
FLANKED!
KSH-AACK
VARIS!
C'MERE, YOU!

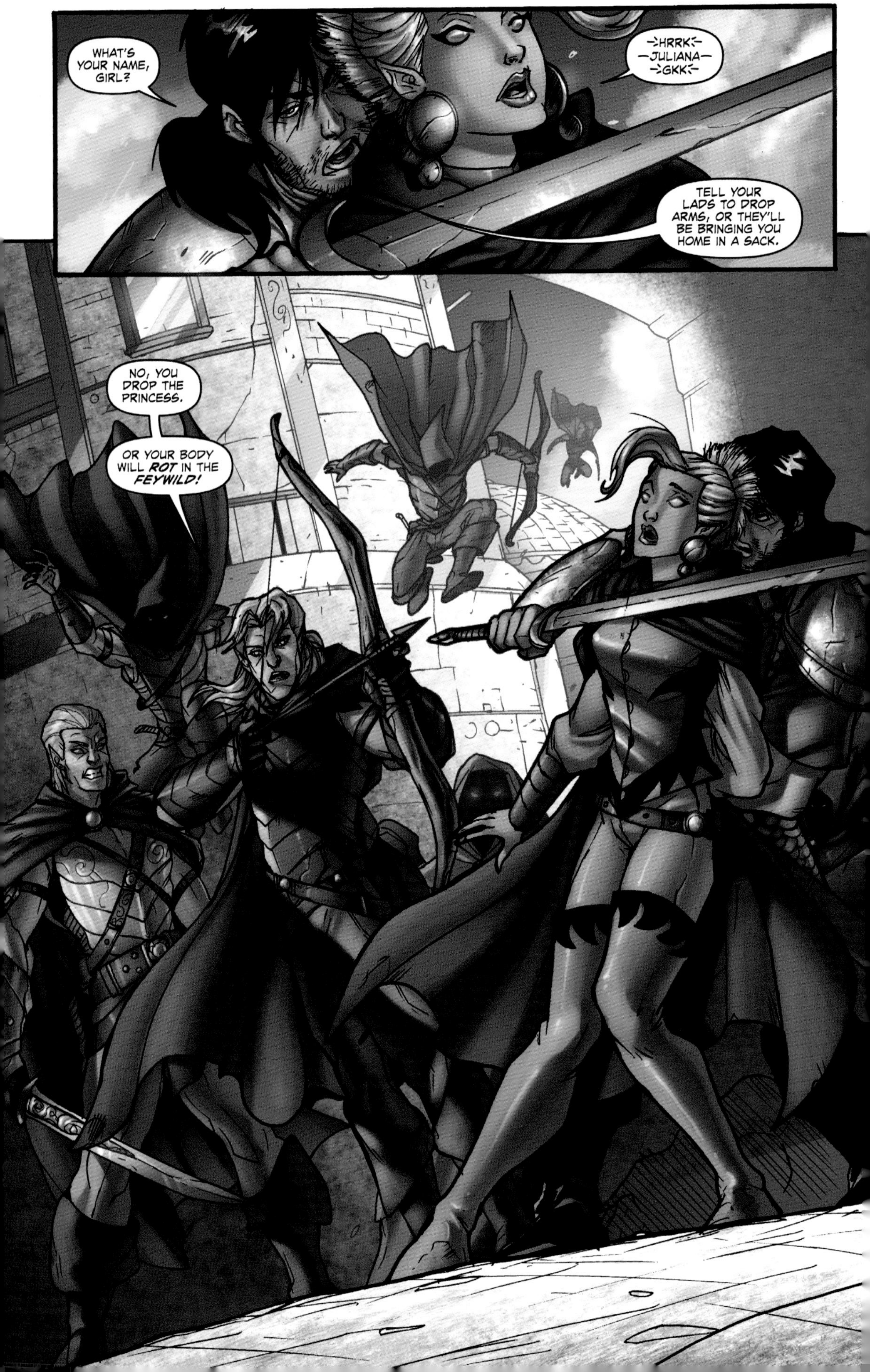
WHAT'S YOUR NAME, GIRL?
-HRRK- -JULIANA- -GKK-
TELL YOUR LADS TO DROP ARMS, OR THEY'LL BE BRINGING YOU HOME IN A SACK.
NO, YOU DROP THE PRINCESS.
OR YOUR BODY WILL ROT IN THE FEYWILD!

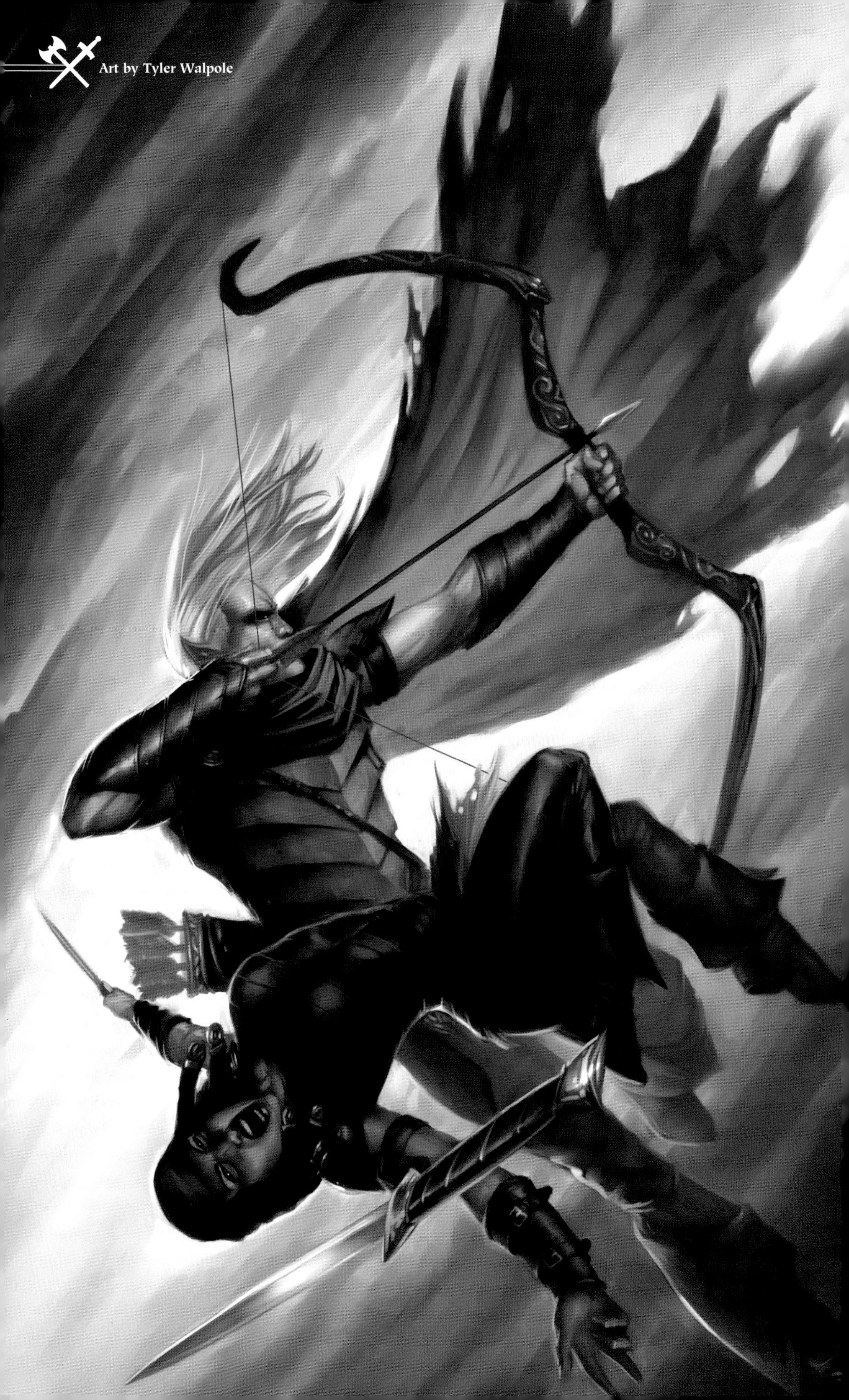

Art by Tyler Walpole

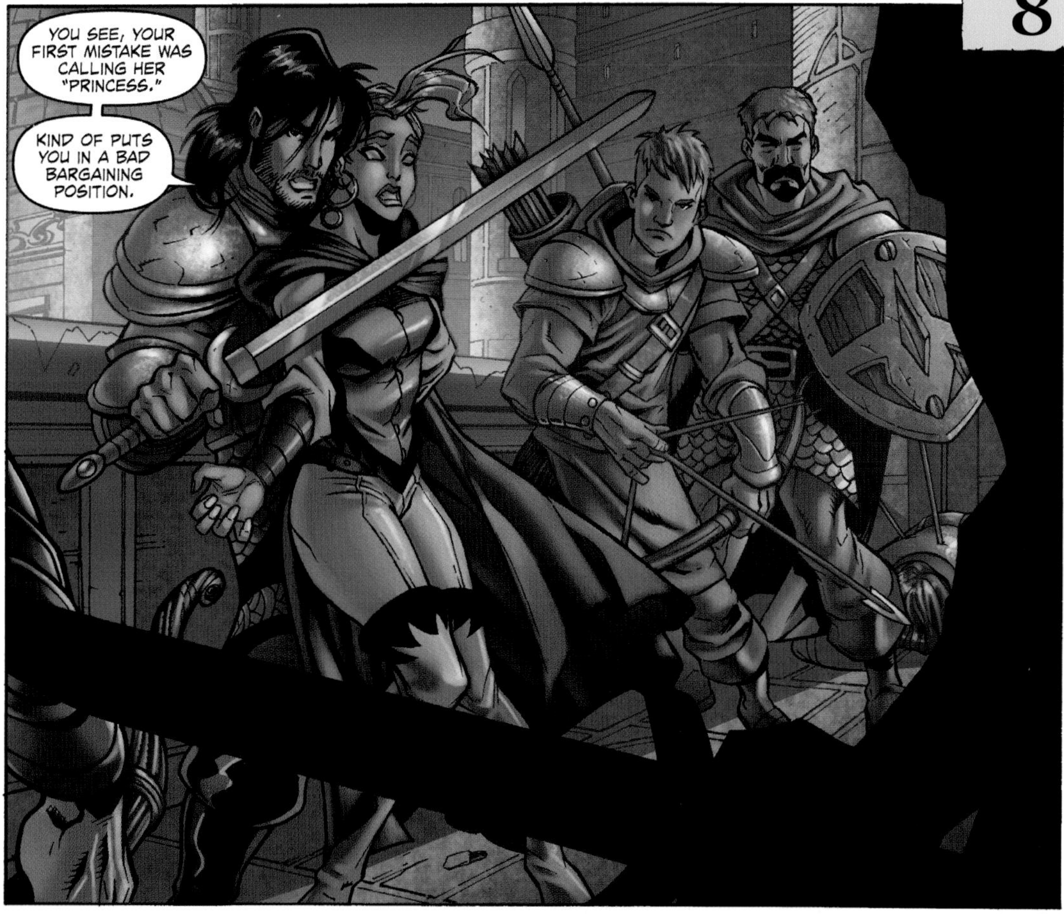
YOU SEE, YOUR FIRST MISTAKE WAS CALLING HER "PRINCESS."
KIND OF PUTS YOU IN A BAD BARGAINING POSITION.

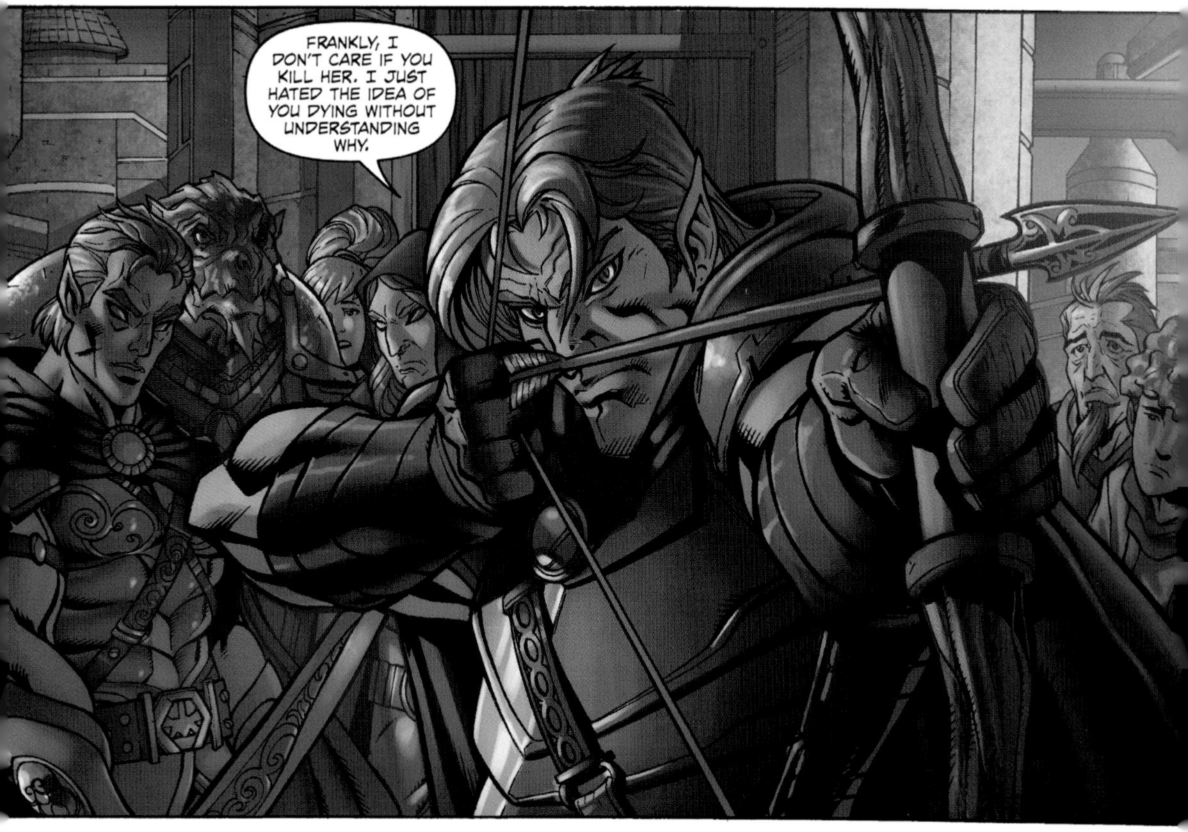
FRANKLY, I DON'T CARE IF YOU KILL HER. I JUST HATED THE IDEA OF YOU DYING WITHOUT UNDERSTANDING WHY.

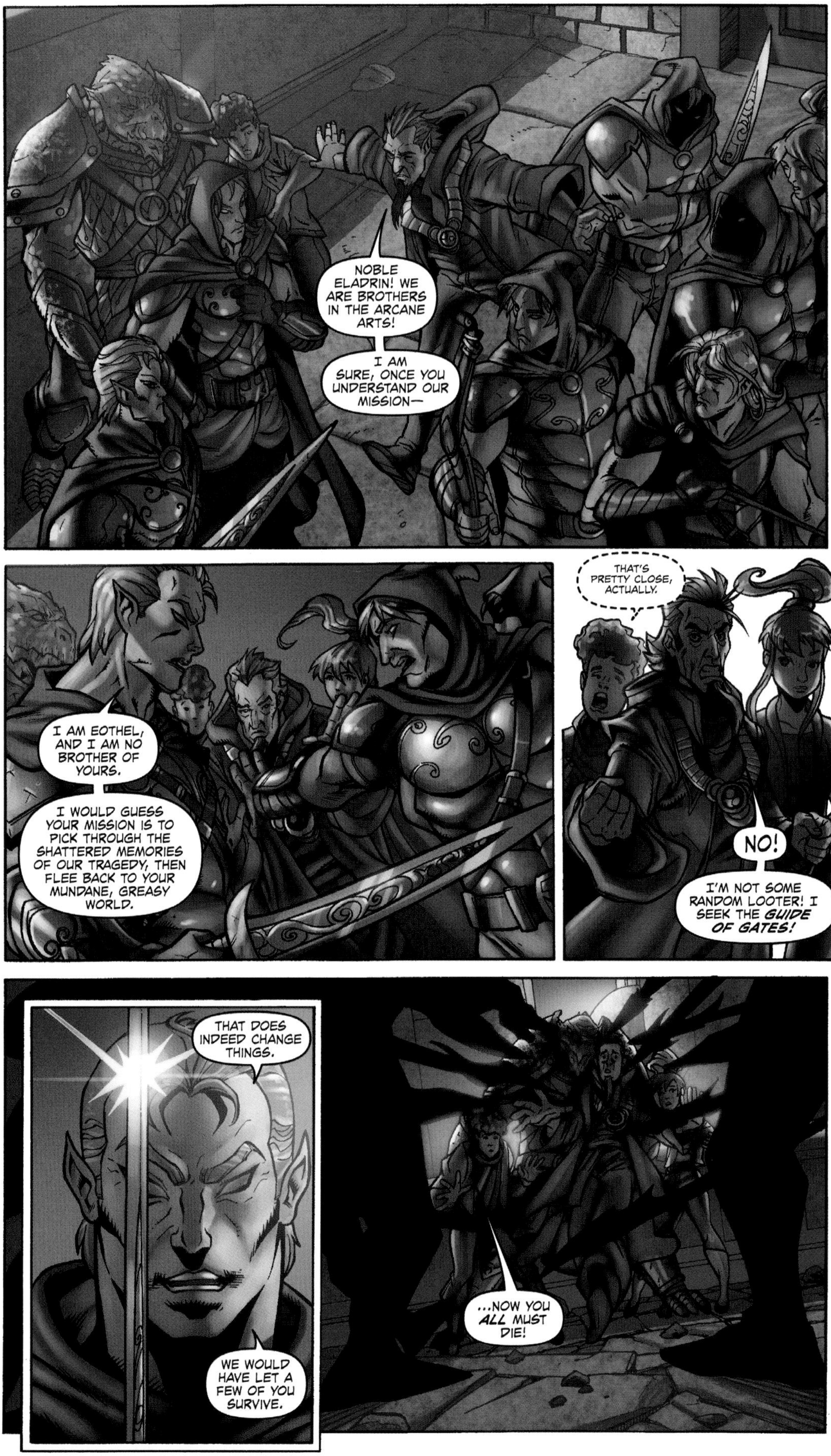
NOBLE ELADRIN! WE ARE BROTHERS IN THE ARCANE ARTS!
I AM SURE, ONCE YOU UNDERSTAND OUR MISSION—
I AM EOTHEL, AND I AM NO BROTHER OF YOURS.
I WOULD GUESS YOUR MISSION IS TO PICK THROUGH THE SHATTERED MEMORIES OF OUR TRAGEDY, THEN FLEE BACK TO YOUR MUNDANE, GREASY WORLD.
THAT'S PRETTY CLOSE, ACTUALLY.
NO!
I'M NOT SOME RANDOM LOOTER! I SEEK THE *GUIDE OF GATES!*
THAT DOES INDEED CHANGE THINGS.
WE WOULD HAVE LET A FEW OF YOU SURVIVE.
...NOW YOU *ALL* MUST DIE!

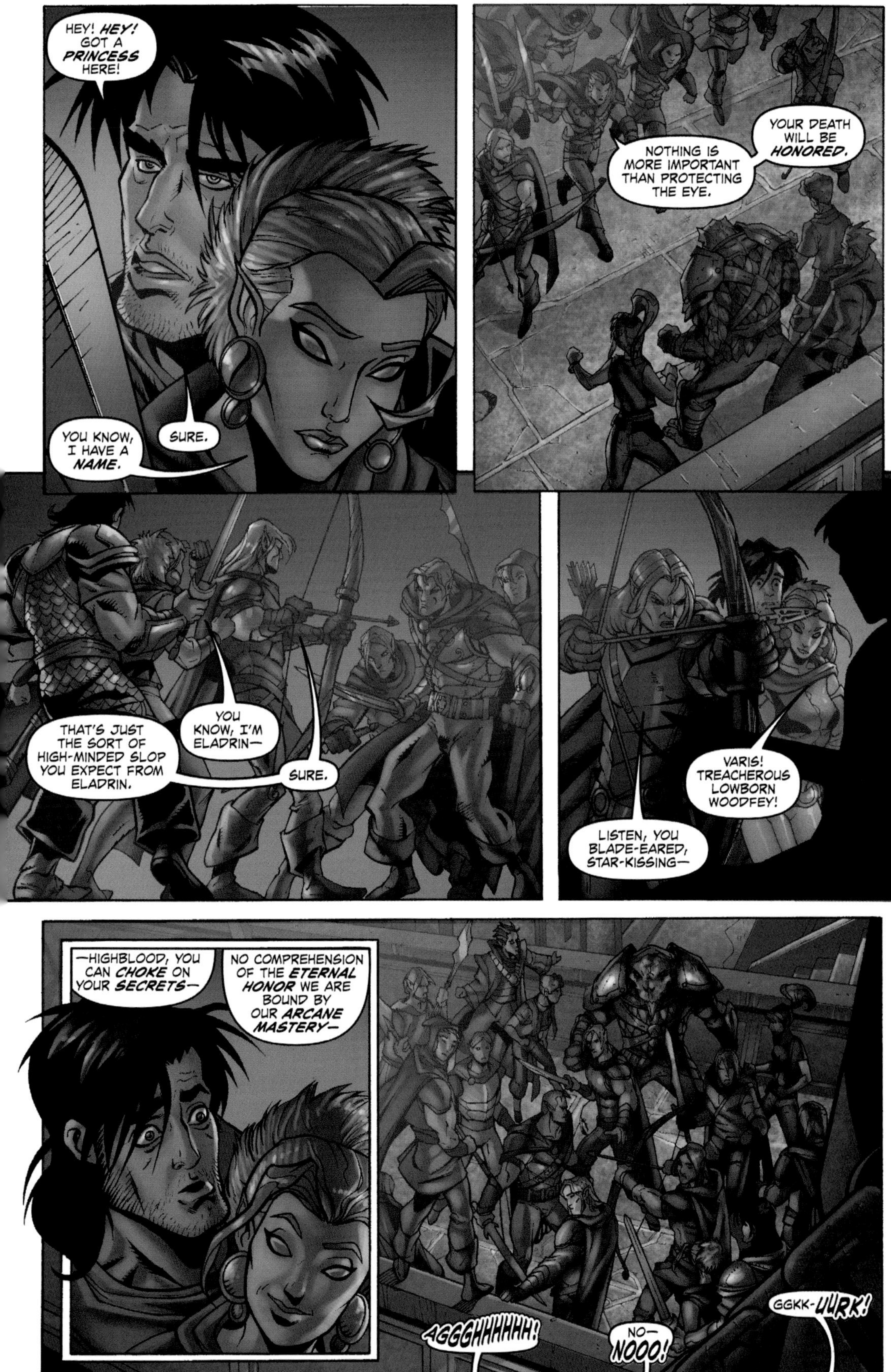
HEY! HEY! GOT A PRINCESS HERE!
YOU KNOW, I HAVE A NAME.
SURE.
NOTHING IS MORE IMPORTANT THAN PROTECTING THE EYE.
YOUR DEATH WILL BE HONORED.
THAT'S JUST THE SORT OF HIGH-MINDED SLOP YOU EXPECT FROM ELADRIN.
YOU KNOW, I'M ELADRIN—
SURE.
VARIS! TREACHEROUS LOWBORN WOODFEY!
LISTEN, YOU BLADE-EARED, STAR-KISSING—
—HIGHBLOOD, YOU CAN CHOKE ON YOUR SECRETS—
NO COMPREHENSION OF THE ETERNAL HONOR WE ARE BOUND BY OUR ARCANE MASTERY—
AGGGHHHHHH!
NO— NOOO!
GGKK-UURK!

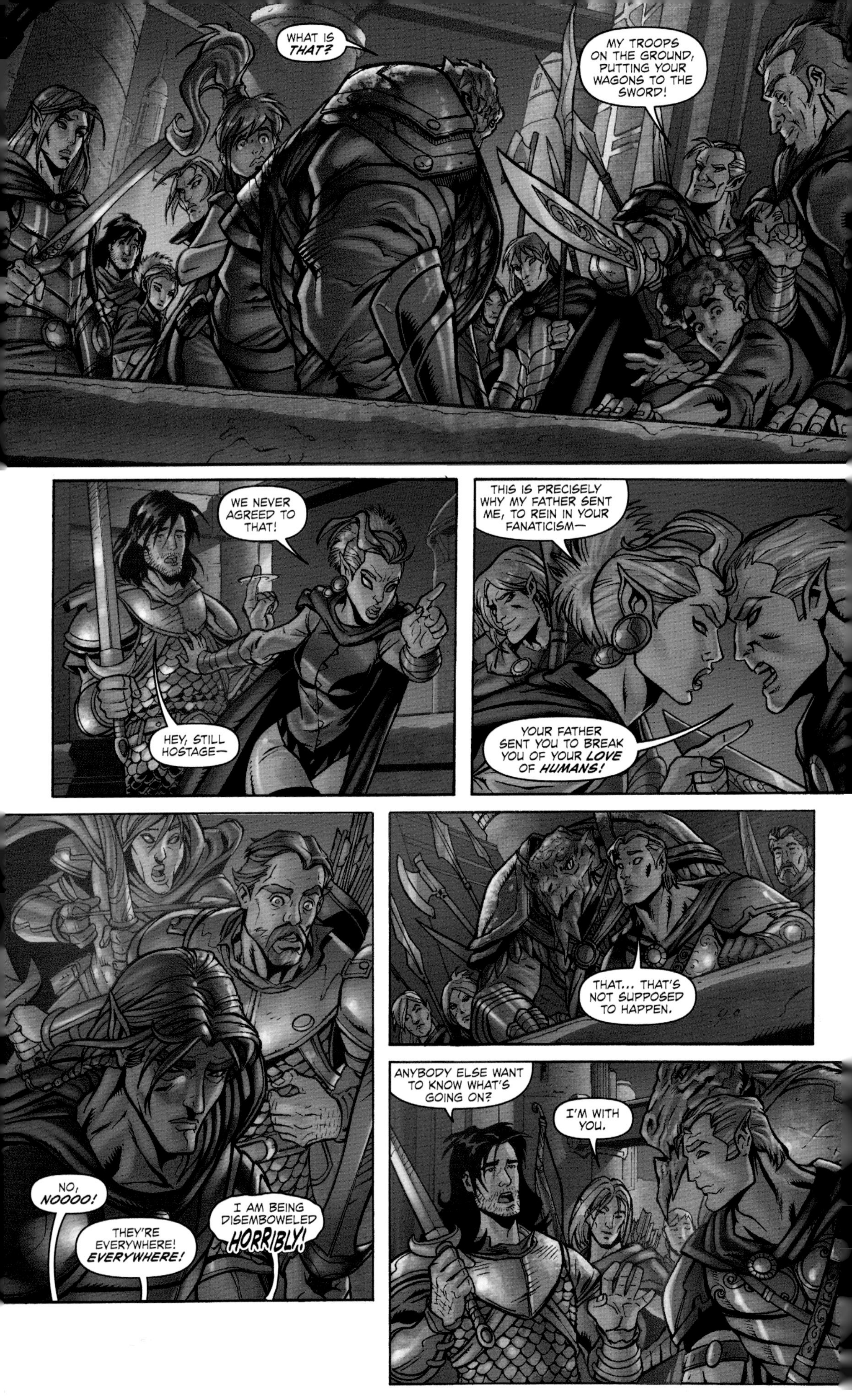
WHAT IS THAT?
MY TROOPS ON THE GROUND, PUTTING YOUR WAGONS TO THE SWORD!
WE NEVER AGREED TO THAT!
HEY, STILL HOSTAGE—
THIS IS PRECISELY WHY MY FATHER SENT ME, TO REIN IN YOUR FANATICISM—
YOUR FATHER SENT YOU TO BREAK YOU OF YOUR LOVE OF HUMANS!
NO, NOOOO!
THEY'RE EVERYWHERE! EVERYWHERE!
I AM BEING DISEMBOWELED HORRIBLY!
THAT... THAT'S NOT SUPPOSED TO HAPPEN.
ANYBODY ELSE WANT TO KNOW WHAT'S GOING ON?
I'M WITH YOU.

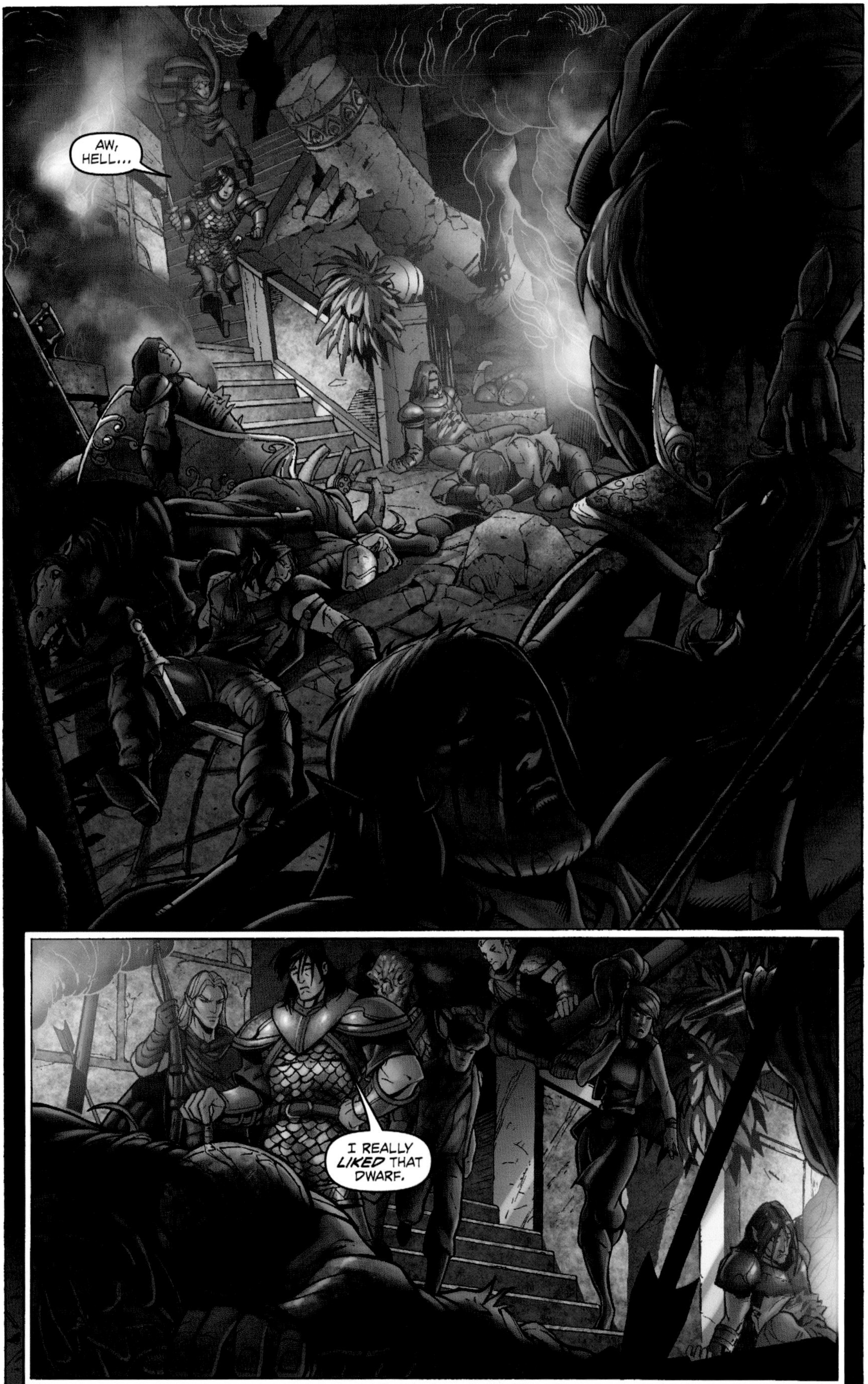
AW, HELL...
I REALLY LIKED THAT DWARF.

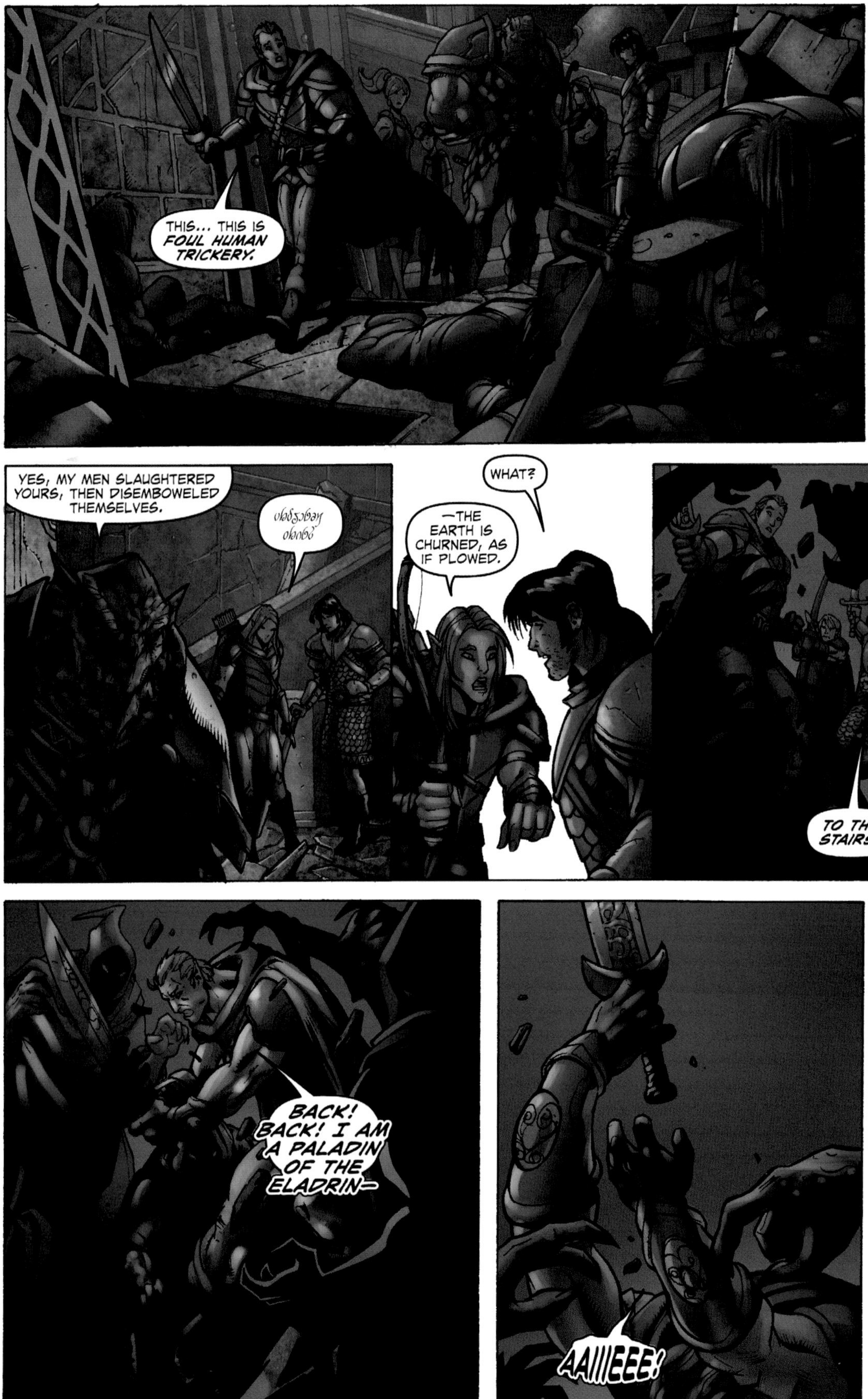
THIS... THIS IS FOUL HUMAN TRICKERY.
YES, MY MEN SLAUGHTERED YOURS, THEN DISEMBOWELED THEMSELVES.
—THE EARTH IS CHURNED, AS IF PLOWED.
WHAT?
TO THE STAIRS!
BACK! BACK! I AM A PALADIN OF THE ELADRIN—
AAIIIEEE!

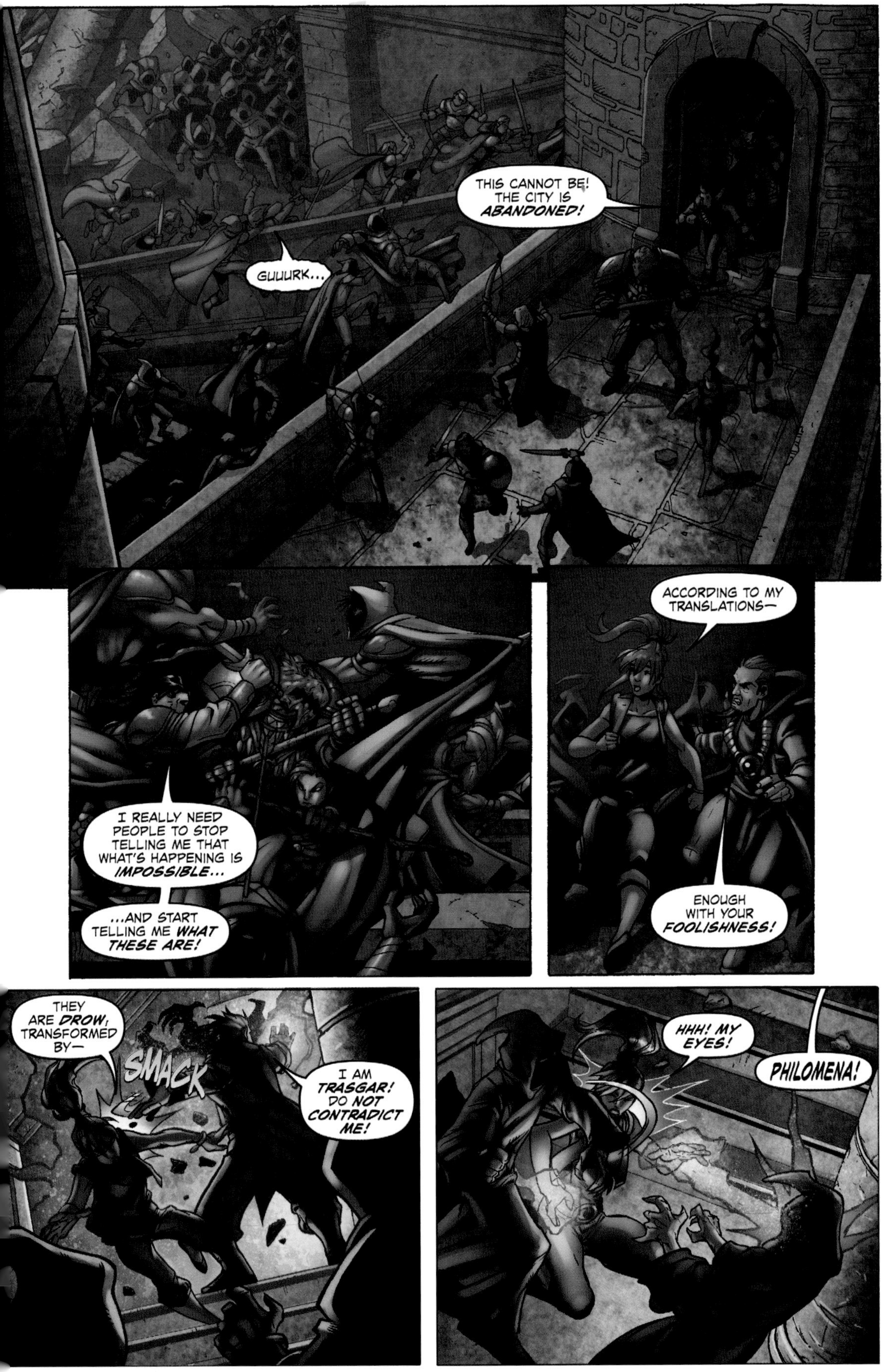
THIS CANNOT BE! THE CITY IS ABANDONED!
GUUURK...
I REALLY NEED PEOPLE TO STOP TELLING ME THAT WHAT'S HAPPENING IS IMPOSSIBLE...
...AND START TELLING ME WHAT THESE ARE!
ACCORDING TO MY TRANSLATIONS—
ENOUGH WITH YOUR FOOLISHNESS!
THEY ARE DROW, TRANSFORMED BY—
SMACK
I AM TRASGAR! DO NOT CONTRADICT ME!
HHH! MY EYES!
PHILOMENA!

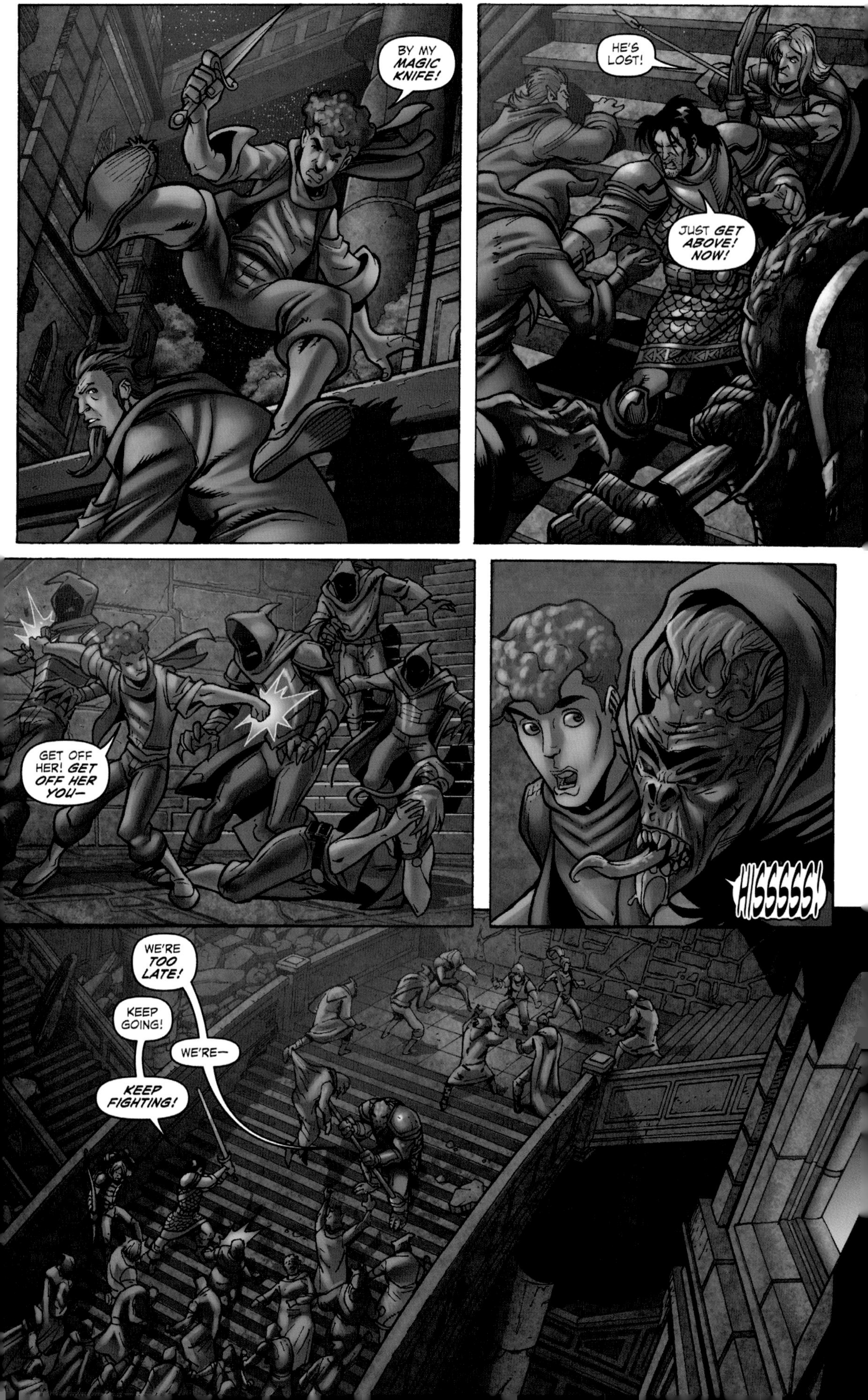
BY MY MAGIC KNIFE!
HE'S LOST!
JUST GET ABOVE! NOW!
GET OFF HER! GET OFF HER YOU—
HISSSSS!
WE'RE TOO LATE!
WE'RE—
KEEP GOING!
KEEP FIGHTING!

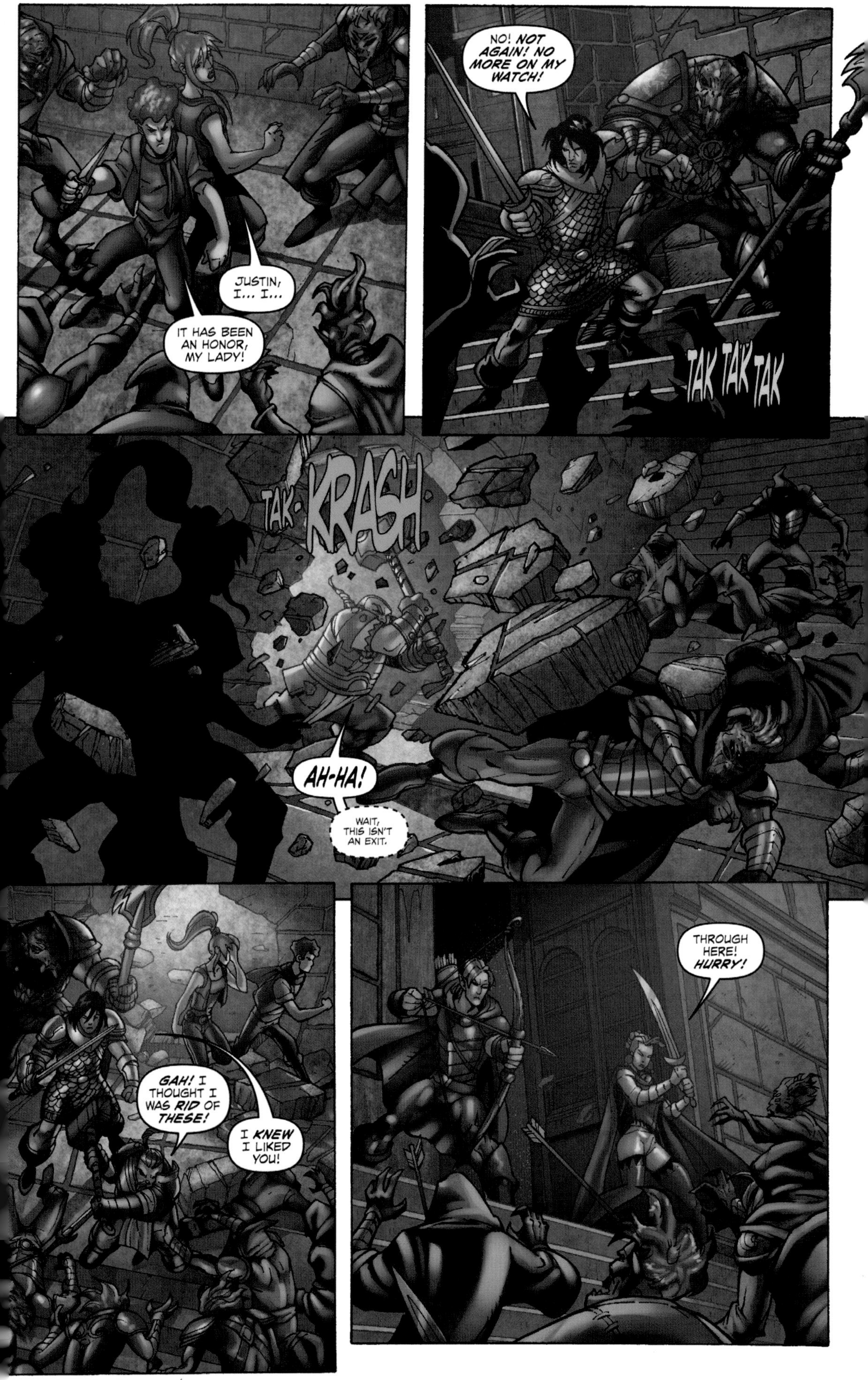
JUSTIN, I... I...
IT HAS BEEN AN HONOR, MY LADY!
NO! NOT AGAIN! NO MORE ON MY WATCH!
TAK TAK TAK
TAK-KRASH
AH-HA!
WAIT, THIS ISN'T AN EXIT.
GAH! I THOUGHT I WAS RID OF THESE!
I KNEW I LIKED YOU!
THROUGH HERE! HURRY!

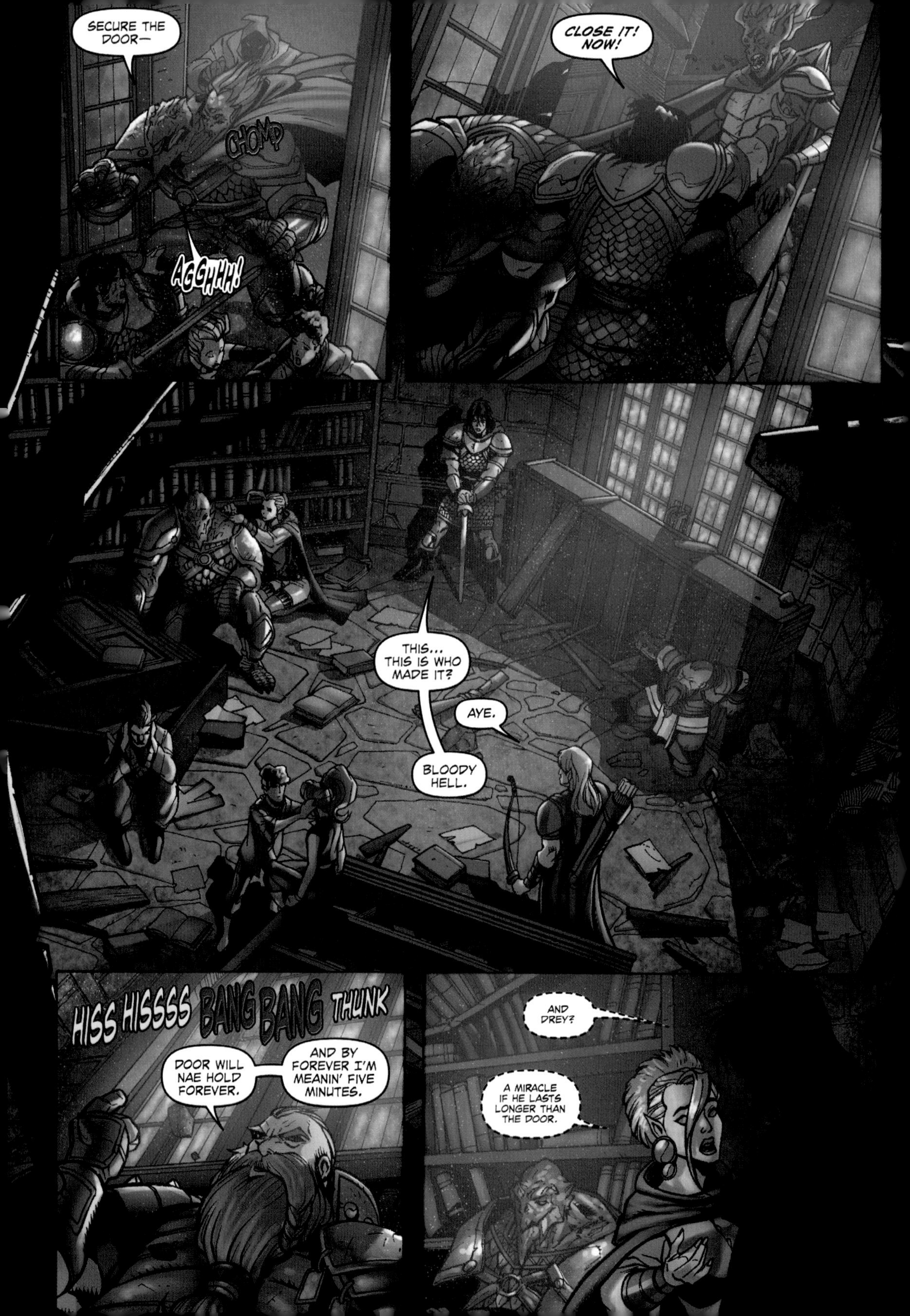

SECURE THE DOOR—
CHOMP
AGGHHH!
CLOSE IT! NOW!
THIS... THIS IS WHO MADE IT?
AYE.
BLOODY HELL.
HISS HISSSS BANG BANG THUNK
DOOR WILL NAE HOLD FOREVER.
AND BY FOREVER I'M MEANIN' FIVE MINUTES.
AND DREY?
A MIRACLE IF HE LASTS LONGER THAN THE DOOR.

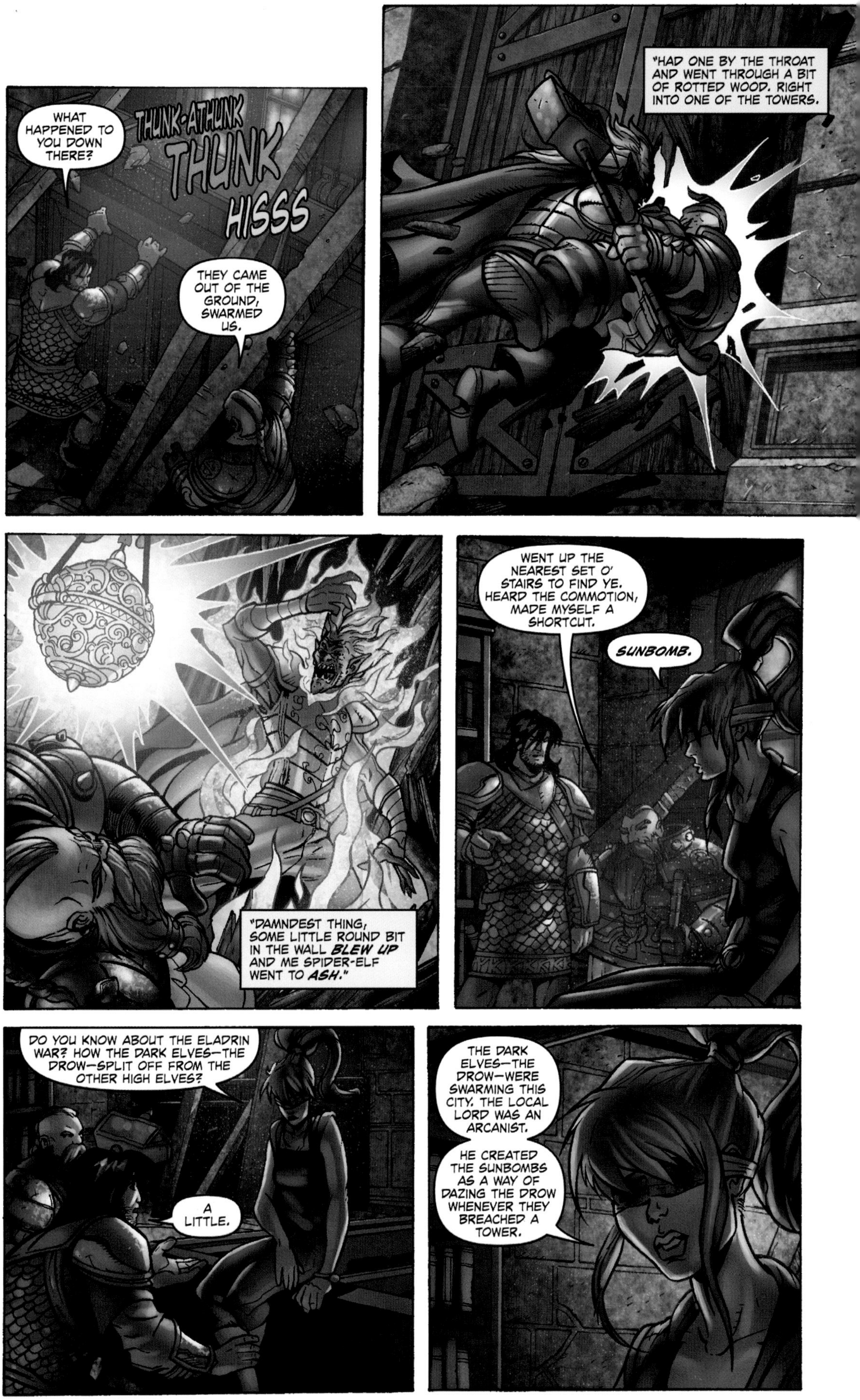
WHAT HAPPENED TO YOU DOWN THERE?
THUNK-ATHUNK
THUNK
HISSS
THEY CAME OUT OF THE GROUND, SWARMED US.
"HAD ONE BY THE THROAT AND WENT THROUGH A BIT OF ROTTED WOOD. RIGHT INTO ONE OF THE TOWERS.
"DAMNDEST THING, SOME LITTLE ROUND BIT IN THE WALL BLEW UP AND ME SPIDER-ELF WENT TO ASH."
WENT UP THE NEAREST SET O' STAIRS TO FIND YE. HEARD THE COMMOTION, MADE MYSELF A SHORTCUT.
SUNBOMB.
DO YOU KNOW ABOUT THE ELADRIN WAR? HOW THE DARK ELVES—THE DROW—SPLIT OFF FROM THE OTHER HIGH ELVES?
A LITTLE.
THE DARK ELVES—THE DROW—WERE SWARMING THIS CITY. THE LOCAL LORD WAS AN ARCANIST.
HE CREATED THE SUNBOMBS AS A WAY OF DAZING THE DROW WHENEVER THEY BREACHED A TOWER.

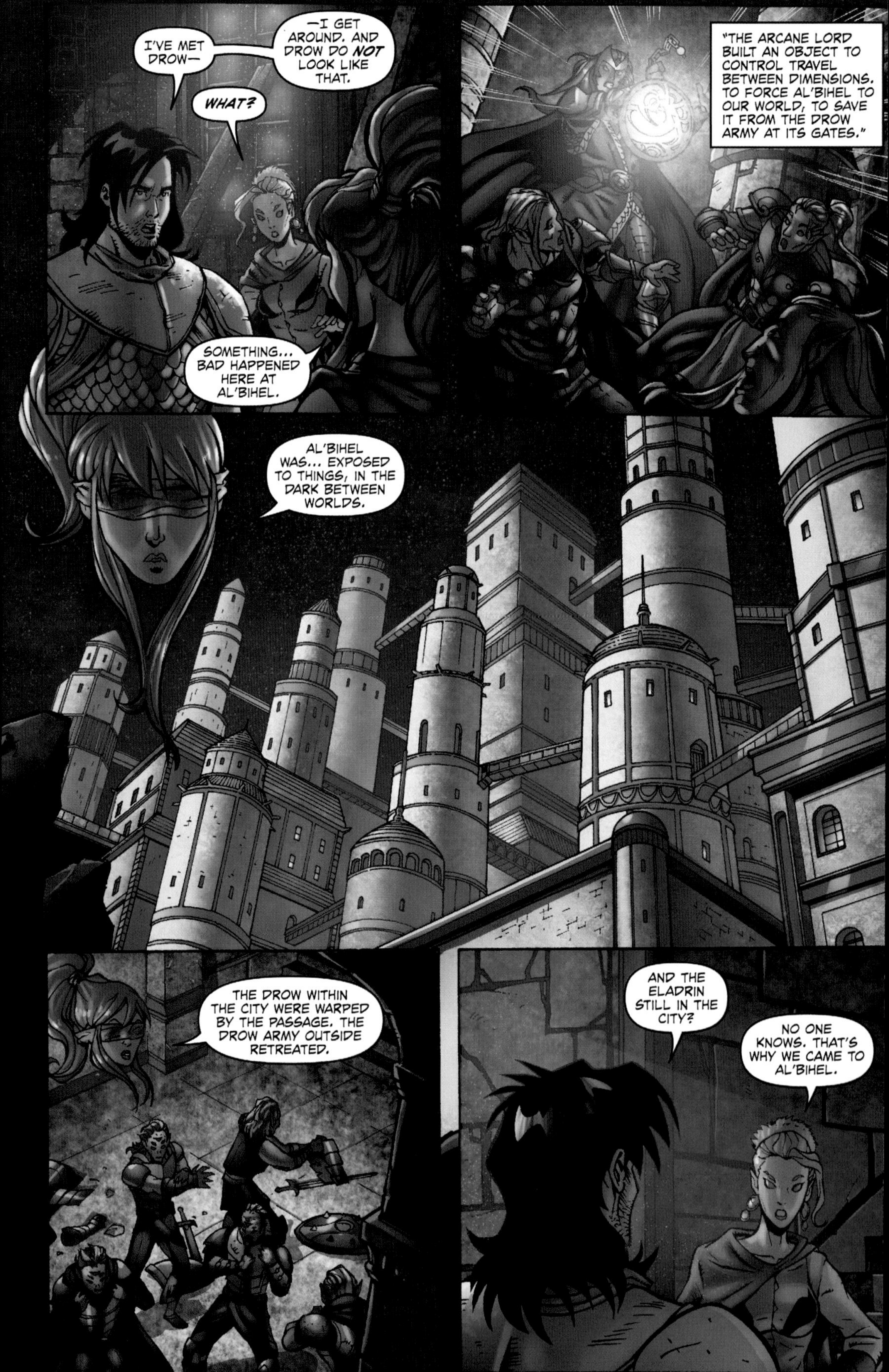
I'VE MET DROW—
—I GET AROUND. AND DROW DO *NOT* LOOK LIKE THAT.
WHAT?
SOMETHING... BAD HAPPENED HERE AT AL'BIHEL.
"THE ARCANE LORD BUILT AN OBJECT TO CONTROL TRAVEL BETWEEN DIMENSIONS. TO FORCE AL'BIHEL TO OUR WORLD, TO SAVE IT FROM THE DROW ARMY AT ITS GATES."
AL'BIHEL WAS... EXPOSED TO THINGS, IN THE DARK BETWEEN WORLDS.
THE DROW WITHIN THE CITY WERE WARPED BY THE PASSAGE. THE DROW ARMY OUTSIDE RETREATED.
AND THE ELADRIN STILL IN THE CITY?
NO ONE KNOWS. THAT'S WHY WE CAME TO AL'BIHEL.

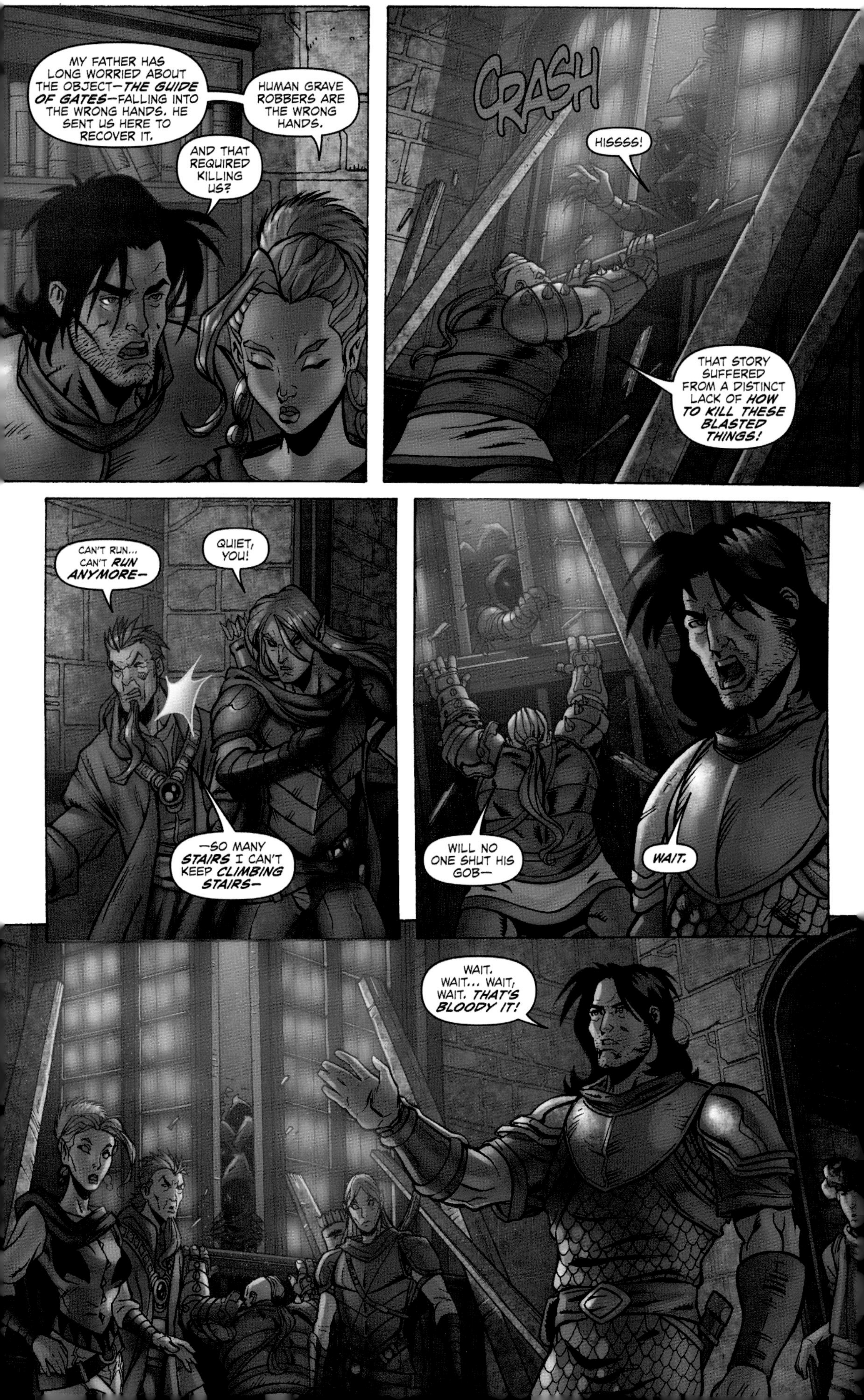
MY FATHER HAS LONG WORRIED ABOUT THE OBJECT—THE GUIDE OF GATES—FALLING INTO THE WRONG HANDS. HE SENT US HERE TO RECOVER IT.
HUMAN GRAVE ROBBERS ARE THE WRONG HANDS.
AND THAT REQUIRED KILLING US?
CRASH
HISSSS!
THAT STORY SUFFERED FROM A DISTINCT LACK OF HOW TO KILL THESE BLASTED THINGS!
CAN'T RUN... CAN'T RUN ANYMORE—
QUIET, YOU!
—SO MANY STAIRS I CAN'T KEEP CLIMBING STAIRS—
WILL NO ONE SHUT HIS GOB—
WAIT.
WAIT. WAIT... WAIT, WAIT. THAT'S BLOODY IT!

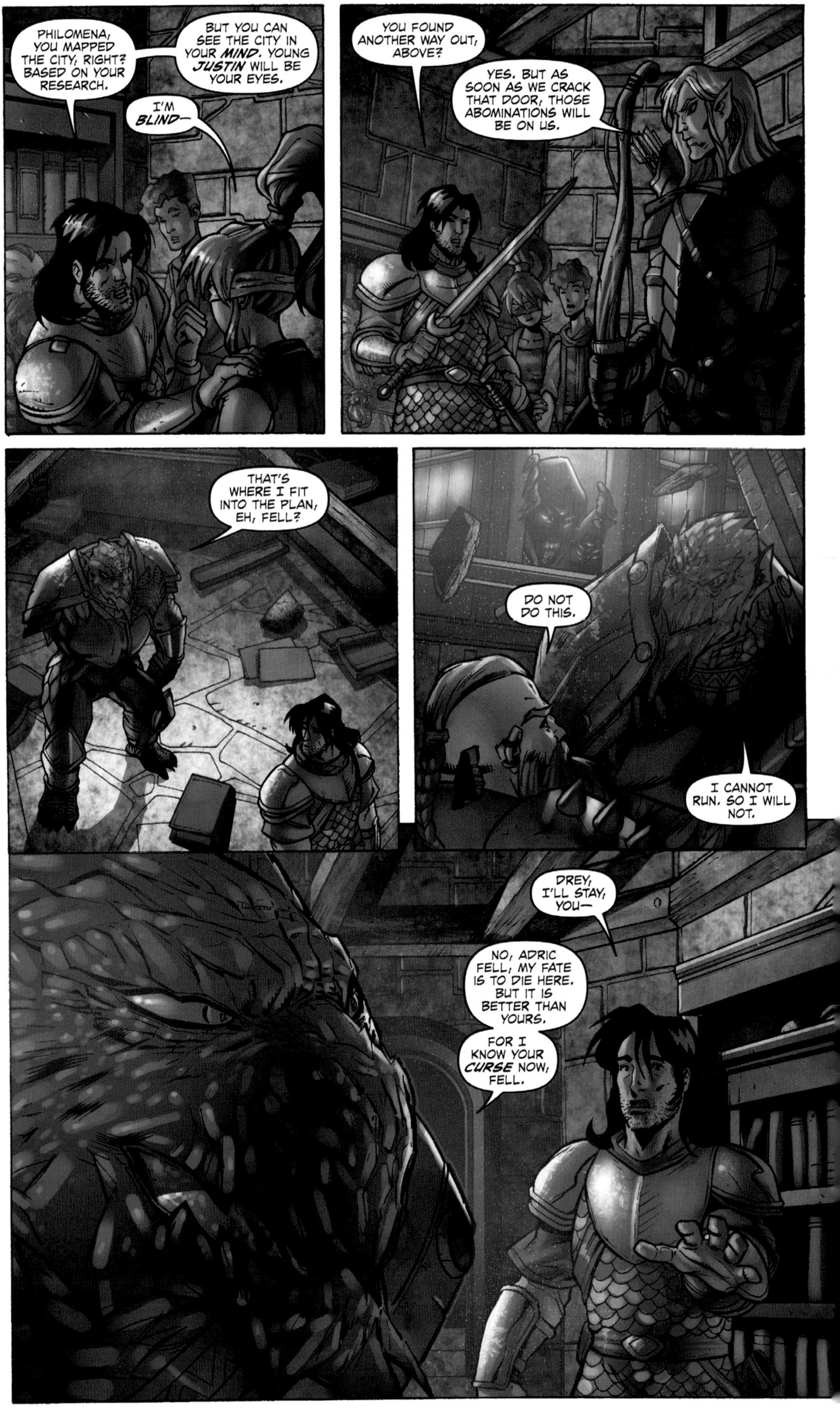
PHILOMENA, YOU MAPPED THE CITY, RIGHT? BASED ON YOUR RESEARCH.
I'M *BLIND*—
BUT YOU CAN SEE THE CITY IN YOUR *MIND*. YOUNG *JUSTIN* WILL BE YOUR EYES.
YOU FOUND ANOTHER WAY OUT, ABOVE?
YES. BUT AS SOON AS WE CRACK THAT DOOR, THOSE ABOMINATIONS WILL BE ON US.
THAT'S WHERE I FIT INTO THE PLAN, EH, FELL?
DO NOT DO THIS.
I CANNOT RUN. SO I WILL NOT.
DREY, I'LL STAY, YOU—
NO, ADRIC FELL, MY FATE IS TO DIE HERE. BUT IT IS BETTER THAN YOURS.
FOR I KNOW YOUR *CURSE* NOW, FELL.

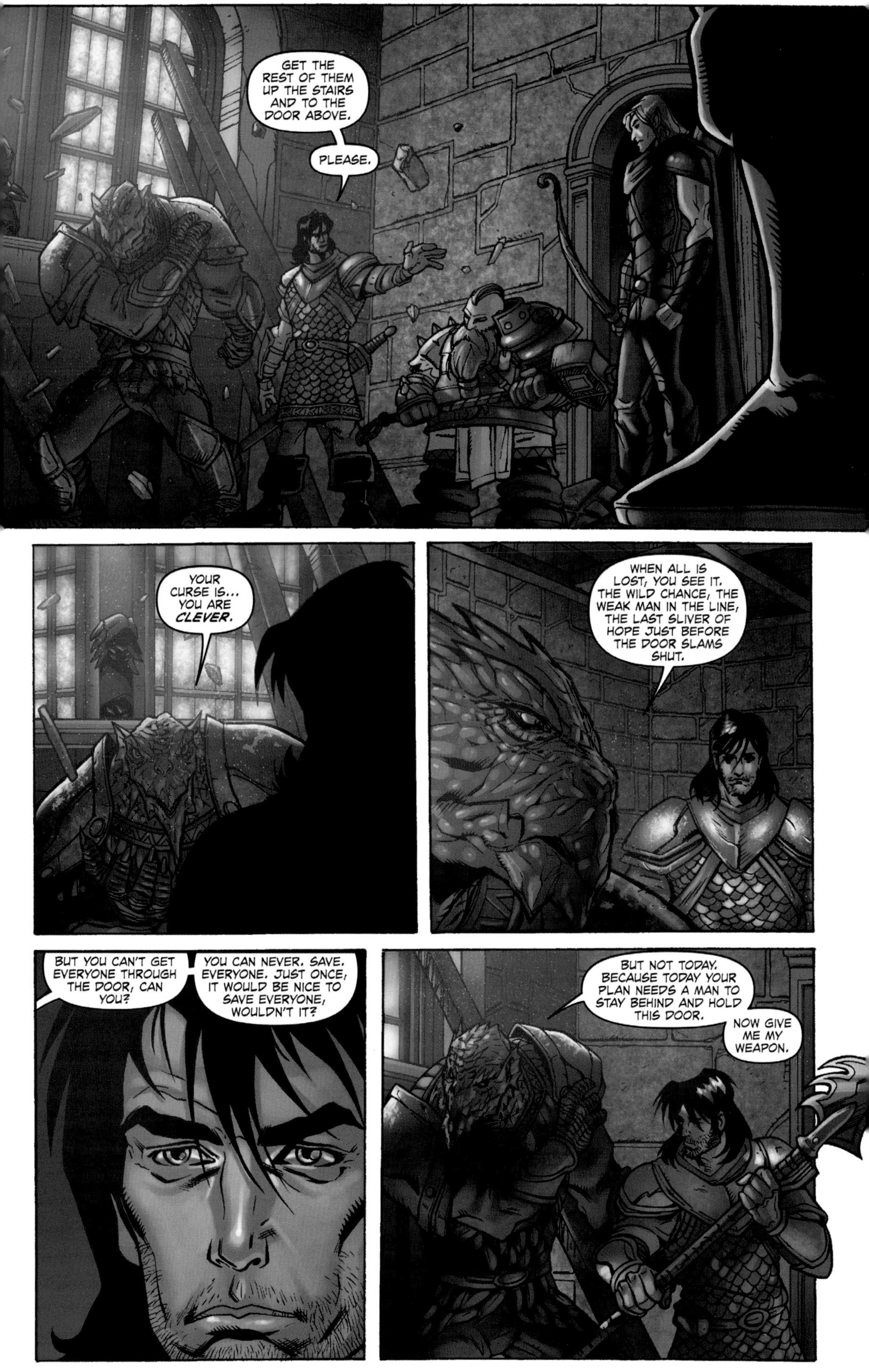
GET THE REST OF THEM UP THE STAIRS AND TO THE DOOR ABOVE.
PLEASE.
YOUR CURSE IS... YOU ARE *CLEVER.*
WHEN ALL IS LOST, YOU SEE IT. THE WILD CHANCE, THE WEAK MAN IN THE LINE, THE LAST SLIVER OF HOPE JUST BEFORE THE DOOR SLAMS SHUT.
BUT YOU CAN'T GET EVERYONE THROUGH THE DOOR, CAN YOU?
YOU CAN NEVER. SAVE. EVERYONE. JUST ONCE, IT WOULD BE NICE TO SAVE EVERYONE, WOULDN'T IT?
BUT NOT TODAY. BECAUSE TODAY YOUR PLAN NEEDS A MAN TO STAY BEHIND AND HOLD THIS DOOR.
NOW GIVE ME MY WEAPON.

HISS
THUNK
CRAASSHHH

GODS BE WITH YOU, DREY HARRICK.

GET OUT OF HERE, FELL. I'M BUSY—

—SHOWING THIS *FILTH* HOW A *DRAGONBORN DIES!*

OPEN IT!

WHERE IS—

HE BOUGHT US MAYBE A *MINUTE! JUST OPEN IT!*

HISS
KRASH GARRR CHUNK

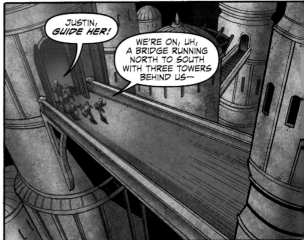

JUSTIN, *GUIDE HER!*

WE'RE ON, UH, A BRIDGE RUNNING NORTH TO SOUTH WITH THREE TOWERS BEHIND US—

IT'S OKAY, JUSTIN, I KNOW WHERE WE ARE.

BUT WHERE ARE WE *GOING?*

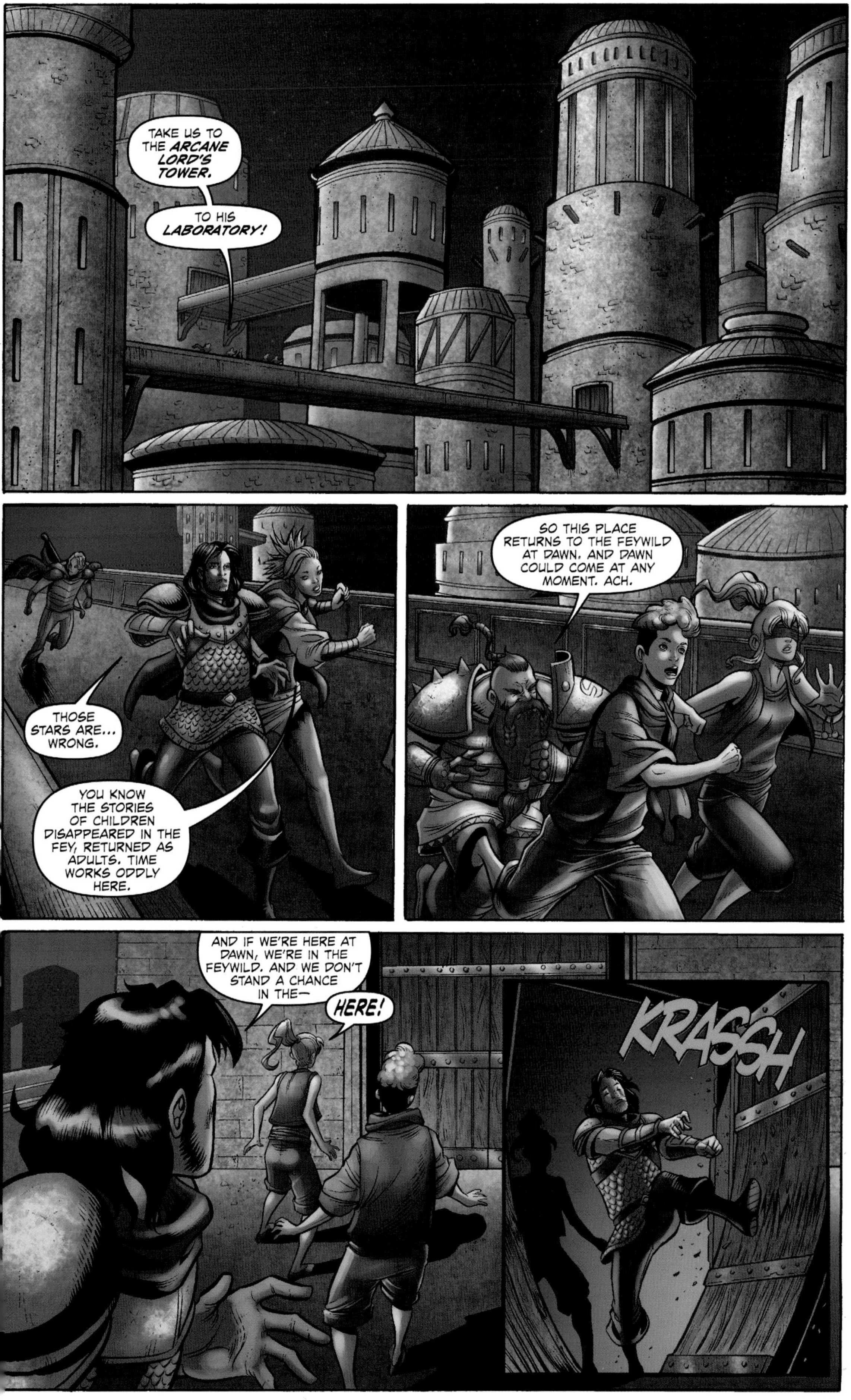
TAKE US TO THE *ARCANE LORD'S TOWER.*
TO HIS *LABORATORY!*
THOSE STARS ARE... WRONG.
YOU KNOW THE STORIES OF CHILDREN DISAPPEARED IN THE FEY, RETURNED AS ADULTS. TIME WORKS ODDLY HERE.
SO THIS PLACE RETURNS TO THE FEYWILD AT DAWN. AND DAWN COULD COME AT ANY MOMENT. ACH.
AND IF WE'RE HERE AT DAWN, WE'RE IN THE FEYWILD. AND WE DON'T STAND A CHANCE IN THE—
HERE!
KRASSH

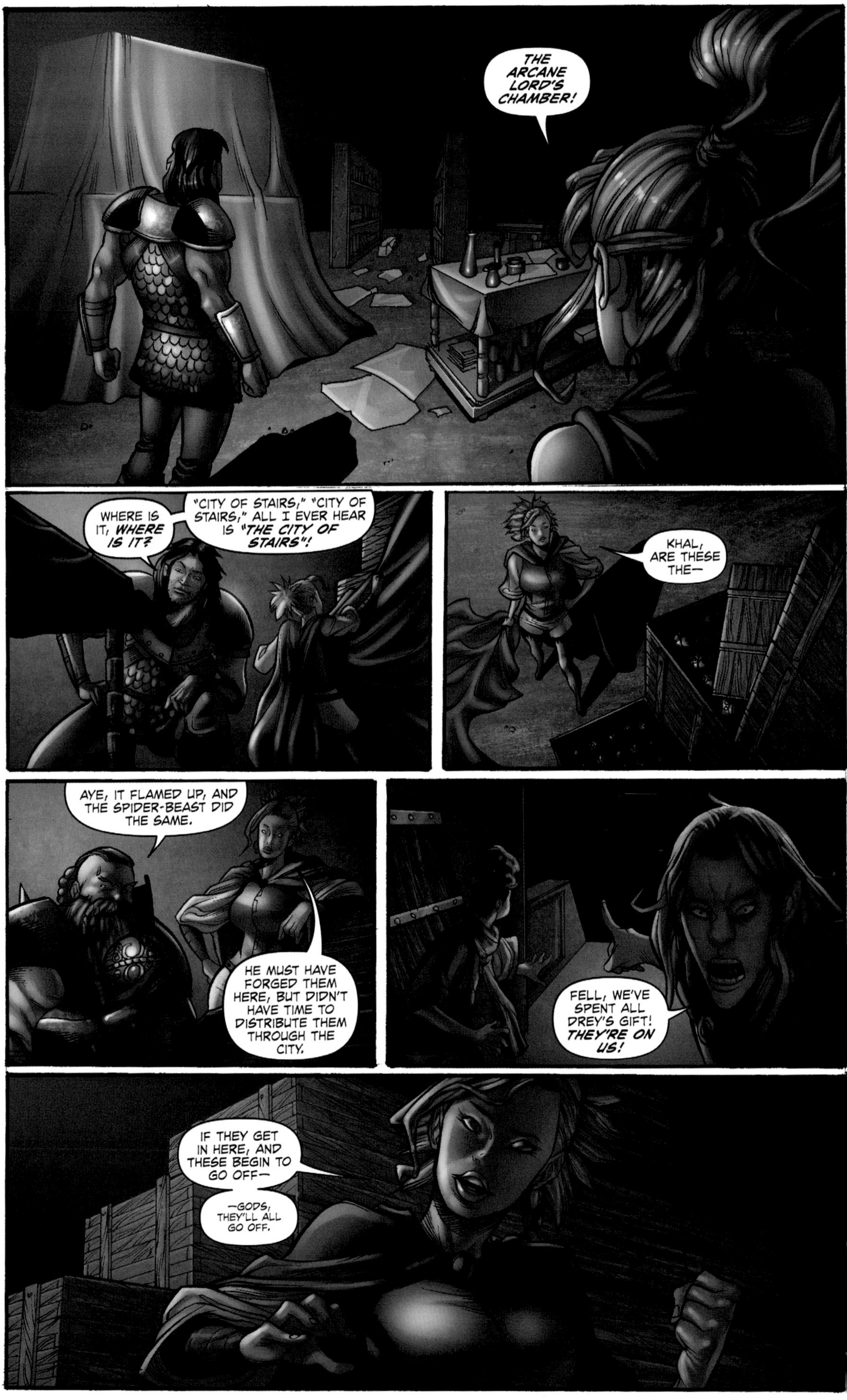
THE ARCANE LORD'S CHAMBER!
WHERE IS IT, WHERE IS IT?
"CITY OF STAIRS," "CITY OF STAIRS," ALL I EVER HEAR IS "THE CITY OF STAIRS"!
KHAL, ARE THESE THE—
AYE, IT FLAMED UP, AND THE SPIDER-BEAST DID THE SAME.
HE MUST HAVE FORGED THEM HERE, BUT DIDN'T HAVE TIME TO DISTRIBUTE THEM THROUGH THE CITY.
FELL, WE'VE SPENT ALL DREY'S GIFT! THEY'RE ON US!
IF THEY GET IN HERE, AND THESE BEGIN TO GO OFF—
—GODS, THEY'LL ALL GO OFF.

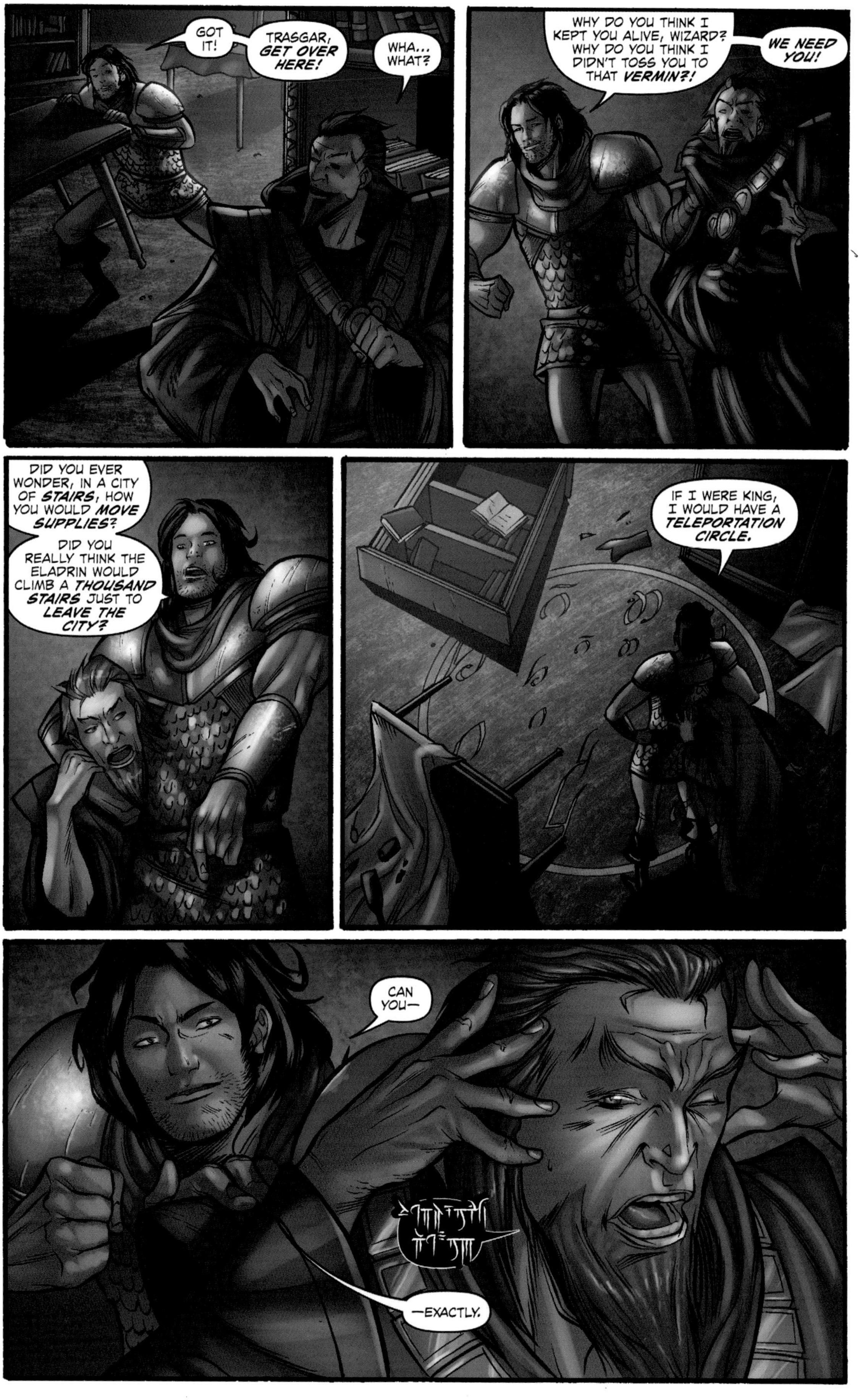
GOT IT!
TRASGAR, GET OVER HERE!
WHA... WHAT?
WHY DO YOU THINK I KEPT YOU ALIVE, WIZARD? WHY DO YOU THINK I DIDN'T TOSS YOU TO THAT VERMIN?!
WE NEED YOU!
DID YOU EVER WONDER, IN A CITY OF STAIRS, HOW YOU WOULD MOVE SUPPLIES?
DID YOU REALLY THINK THE ELADRIN WOULD CLIMB A THOUSAND STAIRS JUST TO LEAVE THE CITY?
IF I WERE KING, I WOULD HAVE A TELEPORTATION CIRCLE.
CAN YOU—
—EXACTLY.

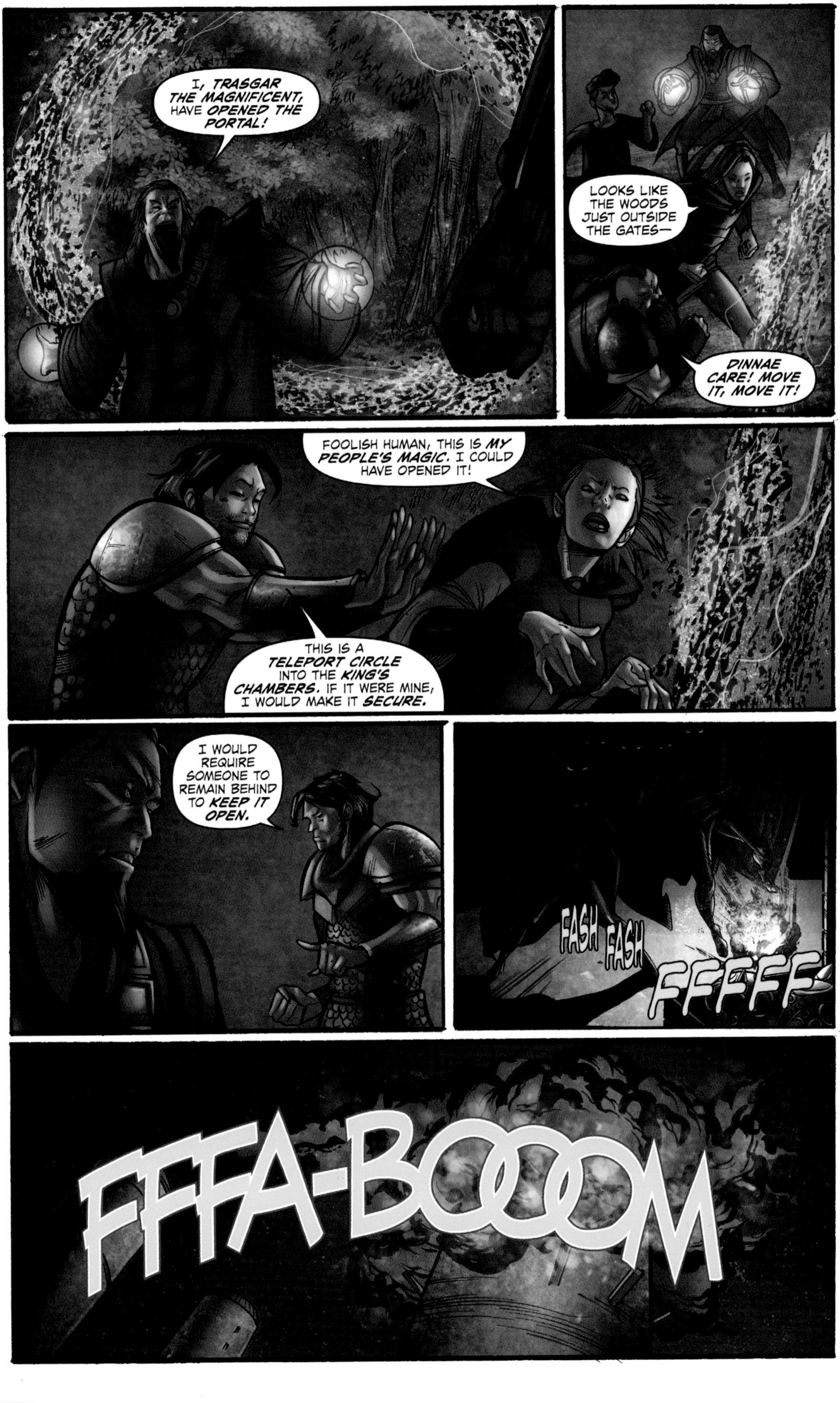
I, TRASGAR THE MAGNIFICENT, HAVE OPENED THE PORTAL!
LOOKS LIKE THE WOODS JUST OUTSIDE THE GATES—
DINNAE CARE! MOVE IT, MOVE IT!
FOOLISH HUMAN, THIS IS MY PEOPLE'S MAGIC. I COULD HAVE OPENED IT!
THIS IS A TELEPORT CIRCLE INTO THE KING'S CHAMBERS. IF IT WERE MINE, I WOULD MAKE IT SECURE.
I WOULD REQUIRE SOMEONE TO REMAIN BEHIND TO KEEP IT OPEN.
FASH
FASH
FFFFF
FFFA-BOOOM

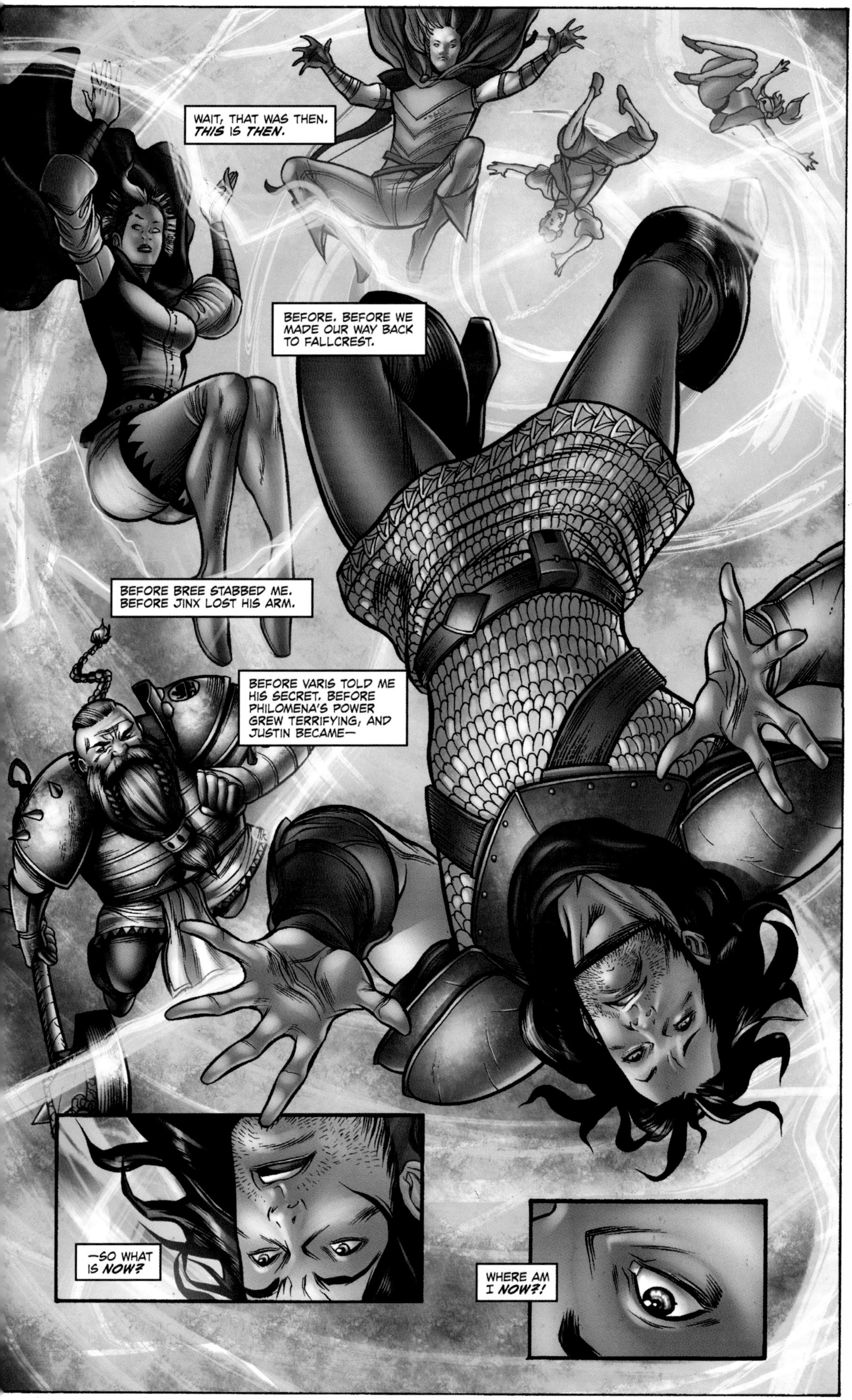

WAIT, THAT WAS THEN. *THIS* IS *THEN.*
BEFORE. BEFORE WE MADE OUR WAY BACK TO FALLCREST.
BEFORE BREE STABBED ME. BEFORE JINX LOST HIS ARM.
BEFORE VARIS TOLD ME HIS SECRET. BEFORE PHILOMENA'S POWER GREW TERRIFYING, AND JUSTIN BECAME—
—SO WHAT IS *NOW?*
WHERE AM I *NOW?!*

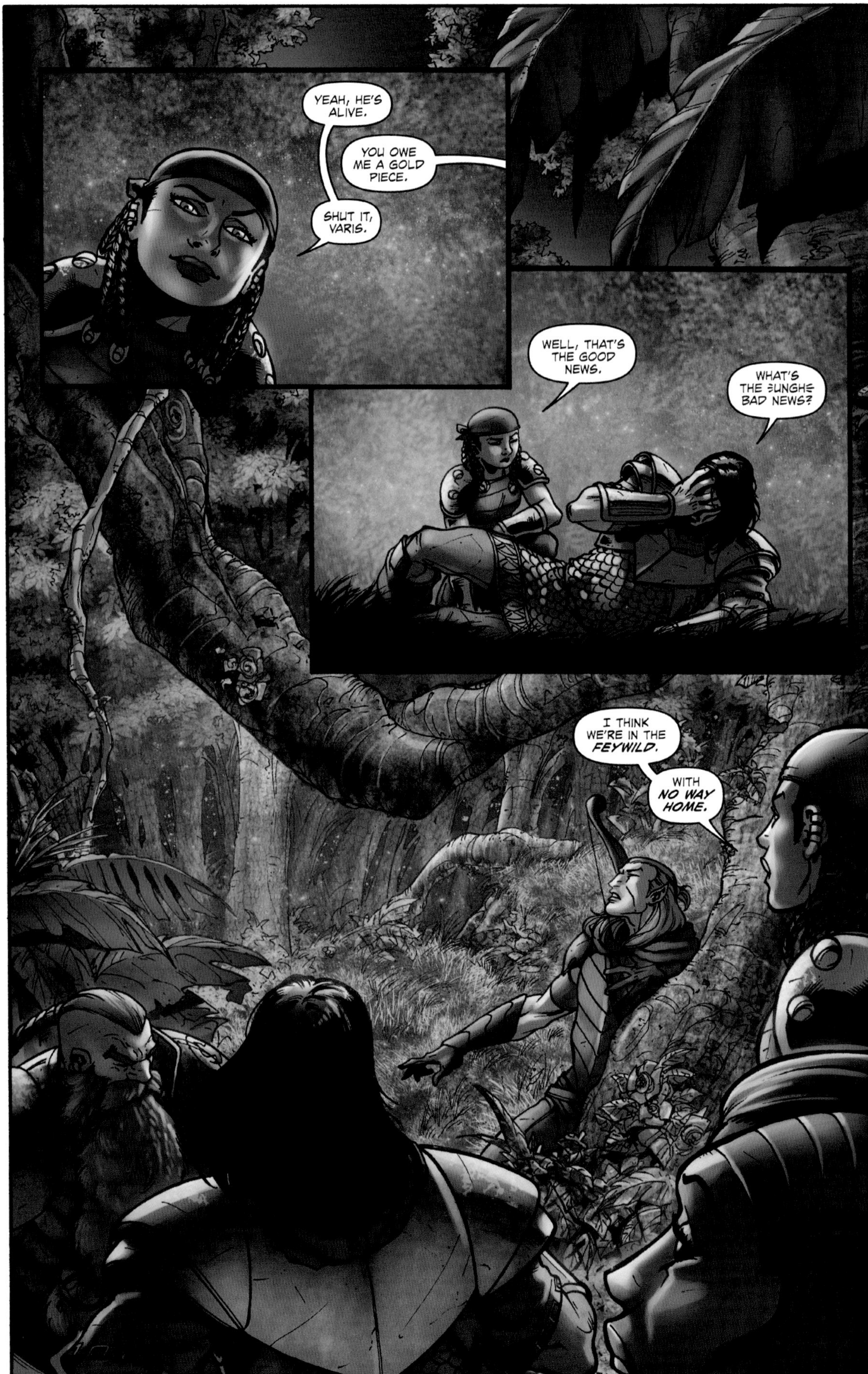
YEAH, HE'S ALIVE.
YOU OWE ME A GOLD PIECE.
SHUT IT, VARIS.
WELL, THAT'S THE GOOD NEWS.
WHAT'S THE =UNGH= BAD NEWS?
I THINK WE'RE IN THE *FEYWILD*.
WITH ***NO WAY HOME.***

Art by Tyler Walpole

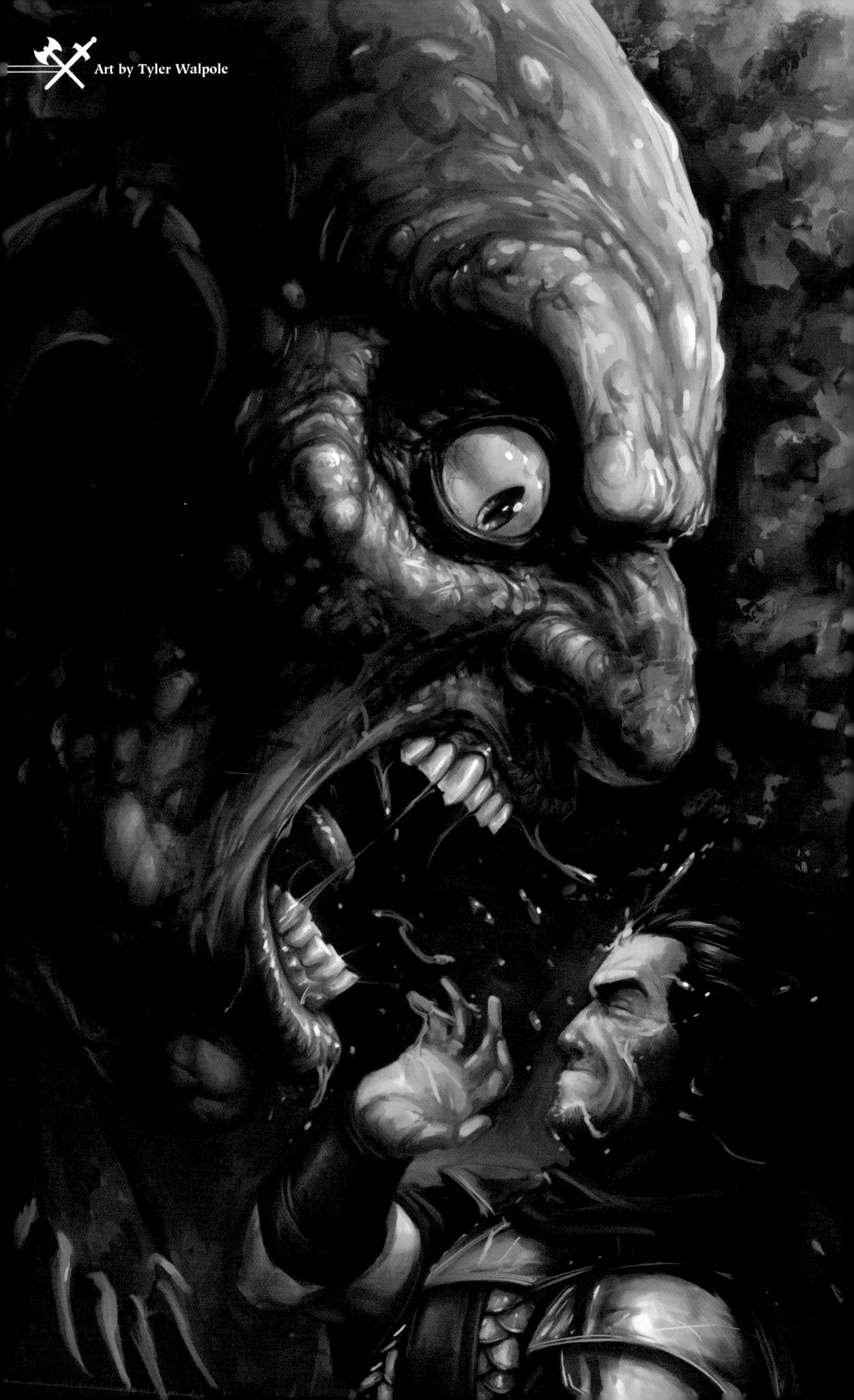

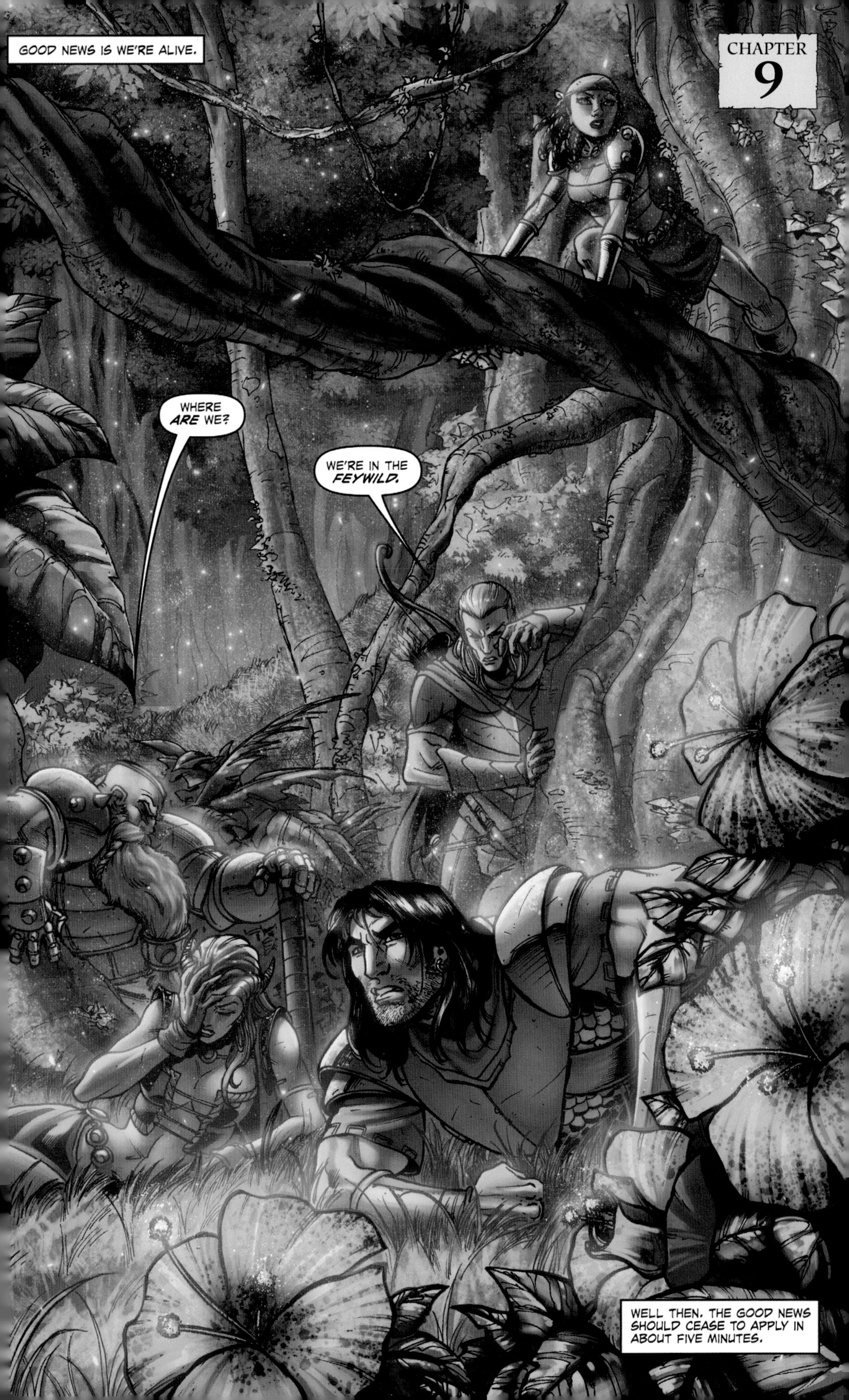
GOOD NEWS IS WE'RE ALIVE.
CHAPTER 9
WHERE *ARE* WE?
WE'RE IN THE *FEYWILD.*
WELL THEN. THE GOOD NEWS SHOULD CEASE TO APPLY IN ABOUT FIVE MINUTES.

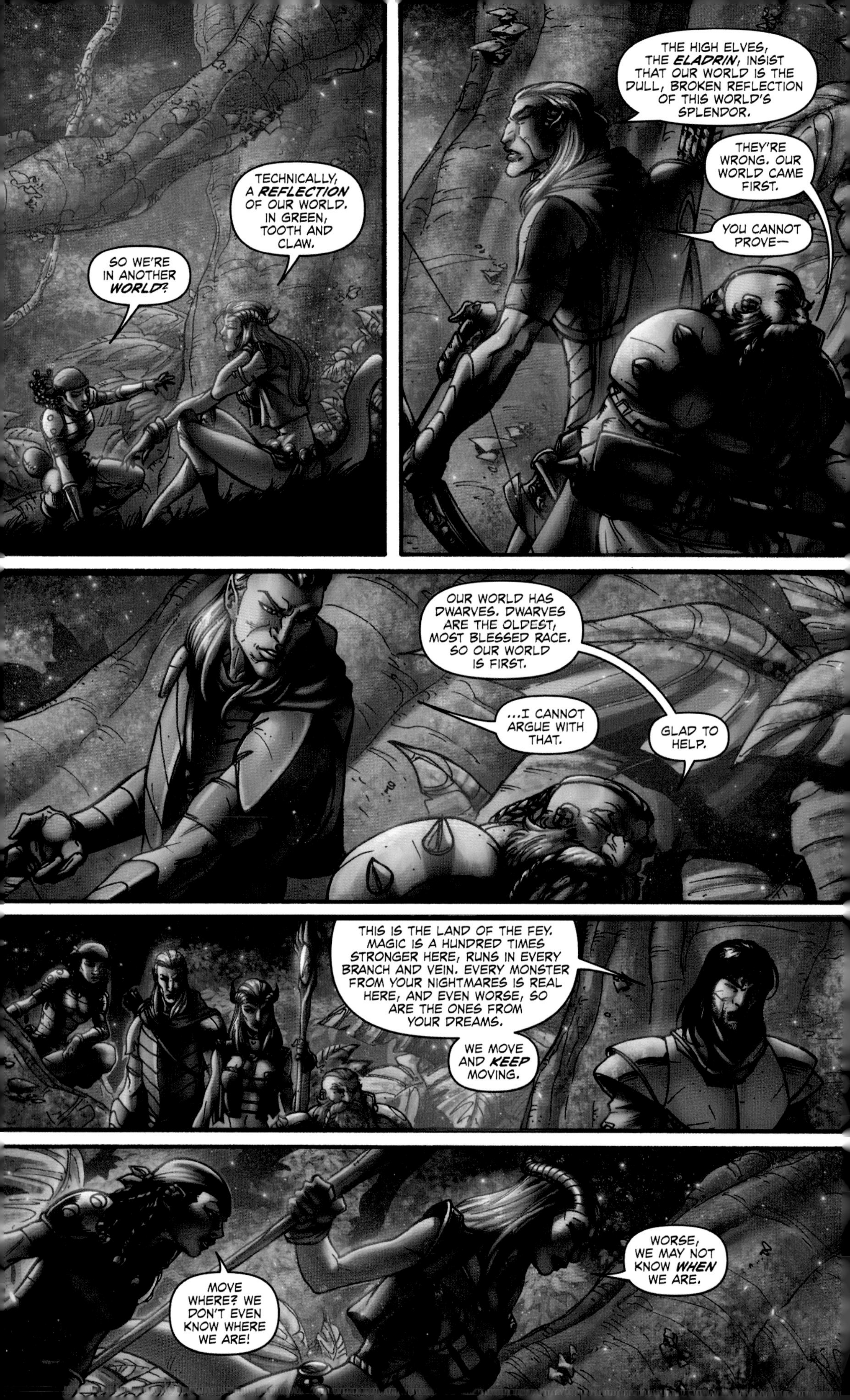

TECHNICALLY, A REFLECTION OF OUR WORLD. IN GREEN, TOOTH AND CLAW.
SO WE'RE IN ANOTHER WORLD?
THE HIGH ELVES, THE ELADRIN, INSIST THAT OUR WORLD IS THE DULL, BROKEN REFLECTION OF THIS WORLD'S SPLENDOR.
THEY'RE WRONG. OUR WORLD CAME FIRST.
YOU CANNOT PROVE—
OUR WORLD HAS DWARVES. DWARVES ARE THE OLDEST, MOST BLESSED RACE. SO OUR WORLD IS FIRST.
...I CANNOT ARGUE WITH THAT.
GLAD TO HELP.
THIS IS THE LAND OF THE FEY. MAGIC IS A HUNDRED TIMES STRONGER HERE, RUNS IN EVERY BRANCH AND VEIN. EVERY MONSTER FROM YOUR NIGHTMARES IS REAL HERE, AND EVEN WORSE, SO ARE THE ONES FROM YOUR DREAMS.
WE MOVE AND KEEP MOVING.
MOVE WHERE? WE DON'T EVEN KNOW WHERE WE ARE!
WORSE, WE MAY NOT KNOW WHEN WE ARE.

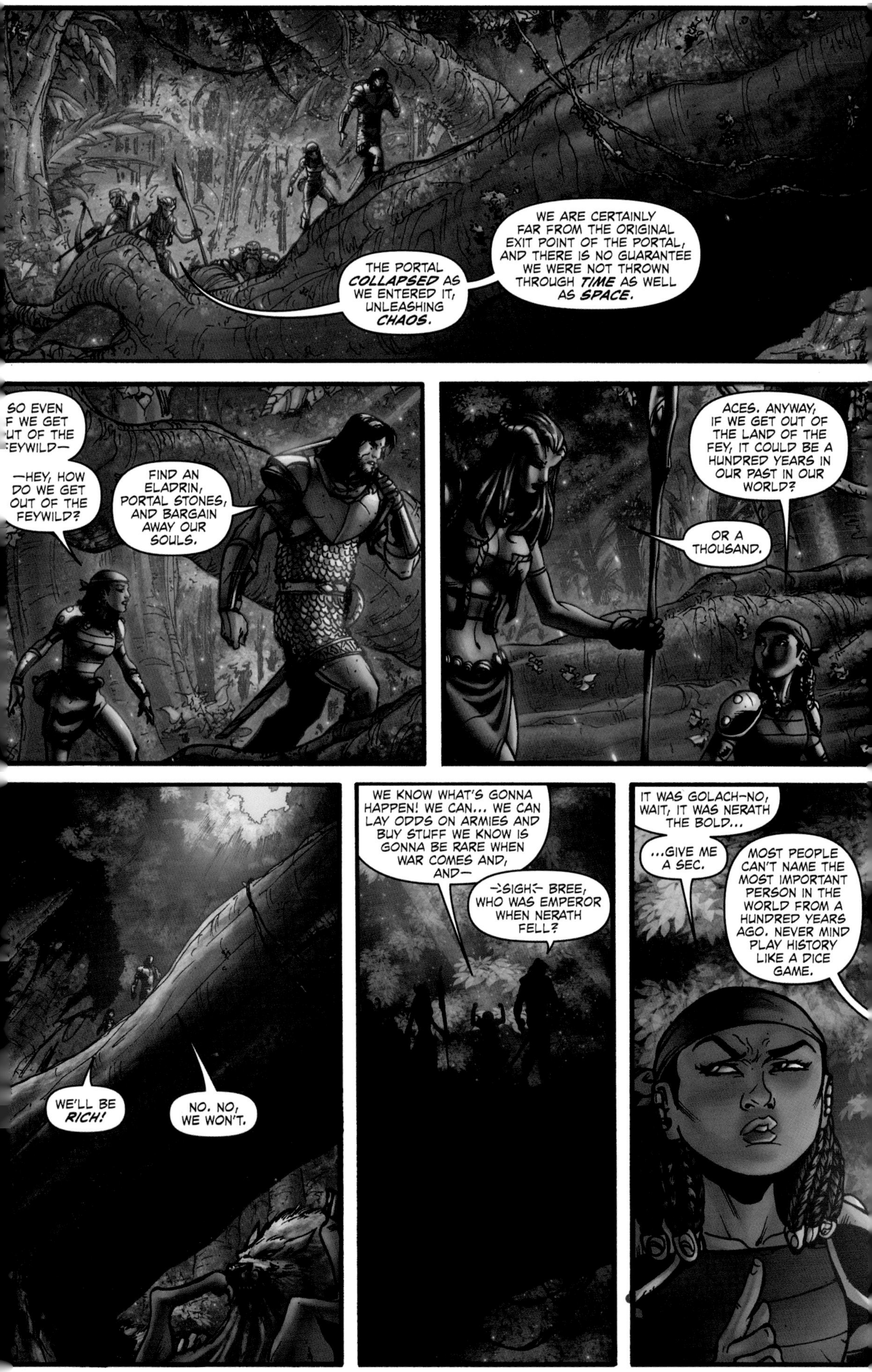
THE PORTAL *COLLAPSED* AS WE ENTERED IT, UNLEASHING *CHAOS*.
WE ARE CERTAINLY FAR FROM THE ORIGINAL EXIT POINT OF THE PORTAL, AND THERE IS NO GUARANTEE WE WERE NOT THROWN THROUGH *TIME* AS WELL AS *SPACE*.
SO EVEN F WE GET UT OF THE EYWILD—
—HEY, HOW DO WE GET OUT OF THE FEYWILD?
FIND AN ELADRIN, PORTAL STONES, AND BARGAIN AWAY OUR SOULS.
ACES. ANYWAY, IF WE GET OUT OF THE LAND OF THE FEY, IT COULD BE A HUNDRED YEARS IN OUR PAST IN OUR WORLD?
OR A THOUSAND.
WE'LL BE *RICH!*
NO. NO, WE WON'T.
WE KNOW WHAT'S GONNA HAPPEN! WE CAN... WE CAN LAY ODDS ON ARMIES AND BUY STUFF WE KNOW IS GONNA BE RARE WHEN WAR COMES AND, AND—
-SIGH- BREE, WHO WAS EMPEROR WHEN NERATH FELL?
IT WAS GOLACH—NO, WAIT, IT WAS NERATH THE BOLD...
...GIVE ME A SEC.
MOST PEOPLE CAN'T NAME THE MOST IMPORTANT PERSON IN THE WORLD FROM A HUNDRED YEARS AGO. NEVER MIND PLAY HISTORY LIKE A DICE GAME.

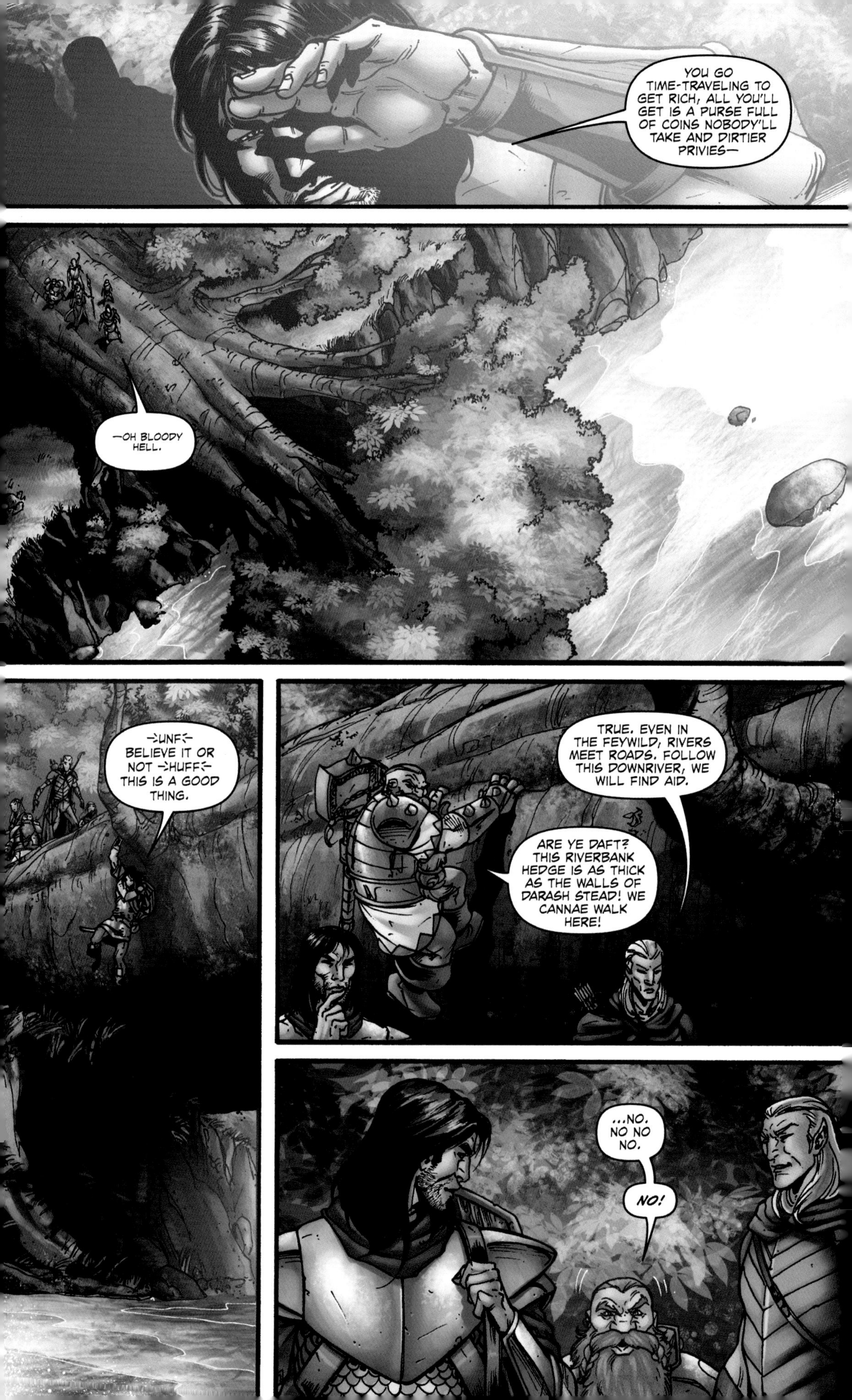
YOU GO TIME-TRAVELING TO GET RICH, ALL YOU'LL GET IS A PURSE FULL OF COINS NOBODY'LL TAKE AND DIRTIER PRIVIES—
—OH BLOODY HELL.
-UNF- BELIEVE IT OR NOT -HUFF- THIS IS A GOOD THING.
TRUE. EVEN IN THE FEYWILD, RIVERS MEET ROADS. FOLLOW THIS DOWNRIVER, WE WILL FIND AID.
ARE YE DAFT? THIS RIVERBANK HEDGE IS AS THICK AS THE WALLS OF DARASH STEAD! WE CANNAE WALK HERE!
...NO. NO NO NO.
NO!

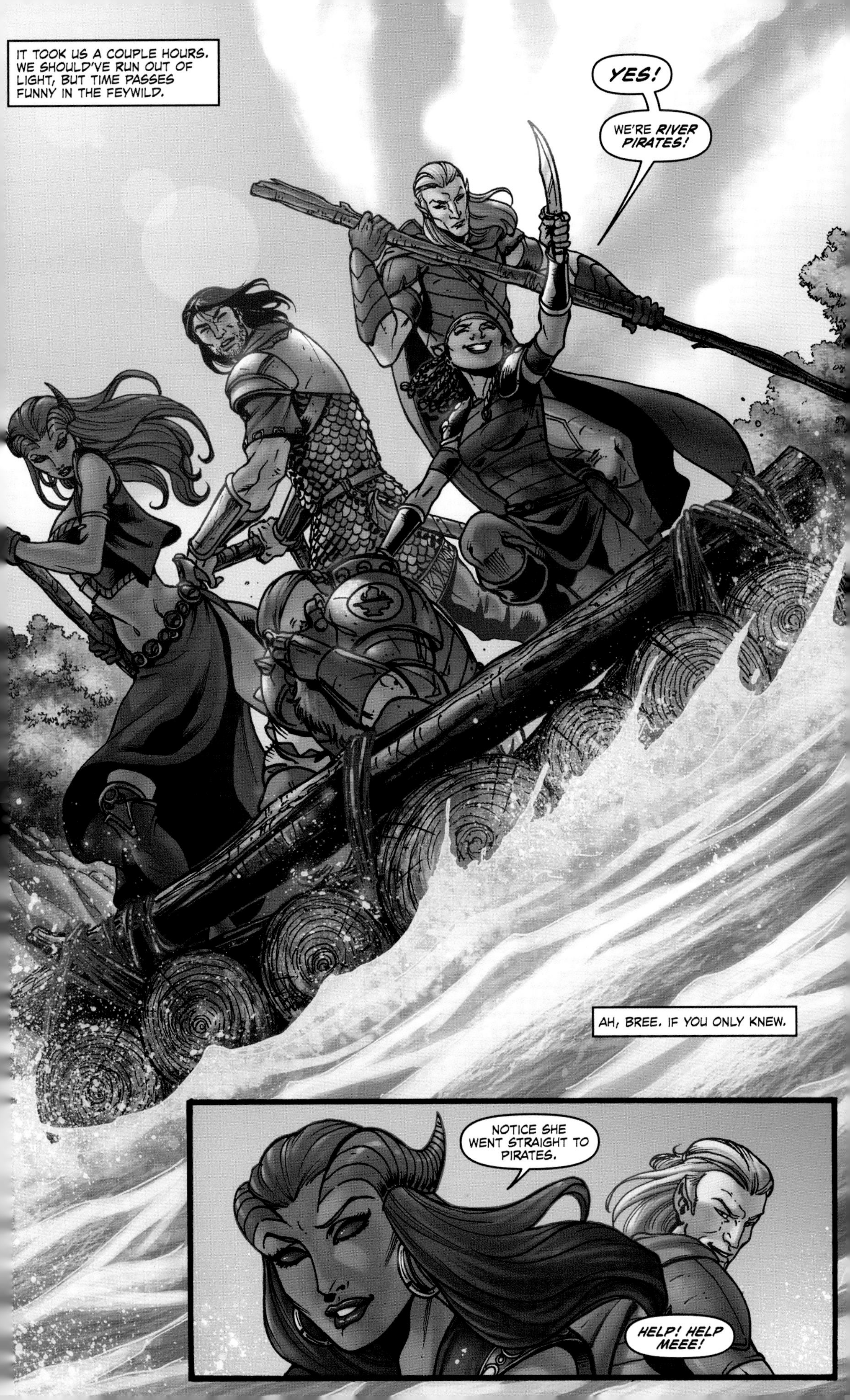
IT TOOK US A COUPLE HOURS. WE SHOULD'VE RUN OUT OF LIGHT, BUT TIME PASSES FUNNY IN THE FEYWILD.
YES!
WE'RE RIVER PIRATES!
AH, BREE. IF YOU ONLY KNEW.
NOTICE SHE WENT STRAIGHT TO PIRATES.
HELP! HELP MEEE!

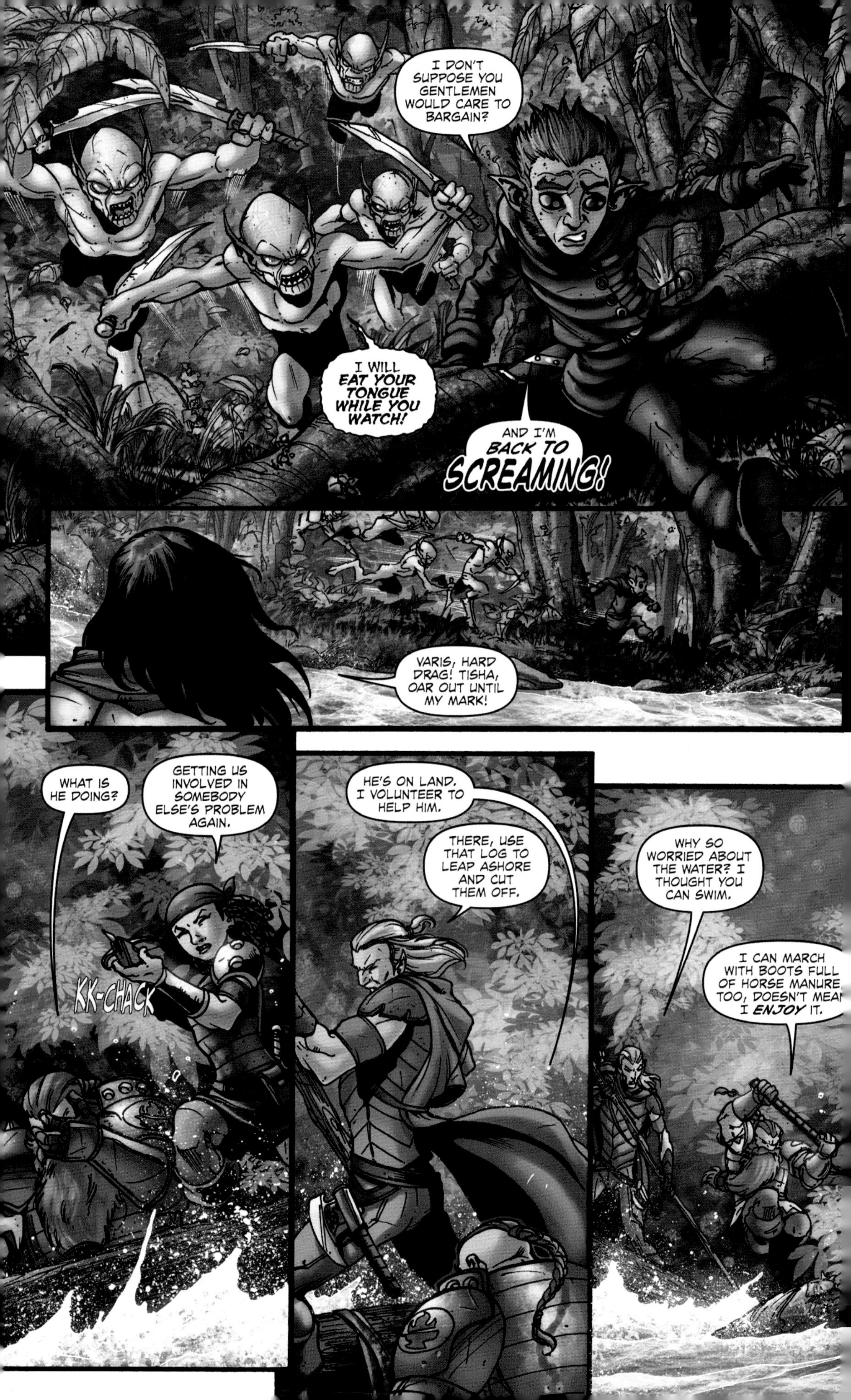
I DON'T SUPPOSE YOU GENTLEMEN WOULD CARE TO BARGAIN?
I WILL EAT YOUR TONGUE WHILE YOU WATCH!
AND I'M BACK TO SCREAMING!
VARIS, HARD DRAG! TISHA, OAR OUT UNTIL MY MARK!
WHAT IS HE DOING?
GETTING US INVOLVED IN SOMEBODY ELSE'S PROBLEM AGAIN.
KK-CHACK
HE'S ON LAND. I VOLUNTEER TO HELP HIM.
THERE, USE THAT LOG TO LEAP ASHORE AND CUT THEM OFF.
WHY SO WORRIED ABOUT THE WATER? I THOUGHT YOU CAN SWIM.
I CAN MARCH WITH BOOTS FULL OF HORSE MANURE TOO, DOESN'T MEAN I ENJOY IT.

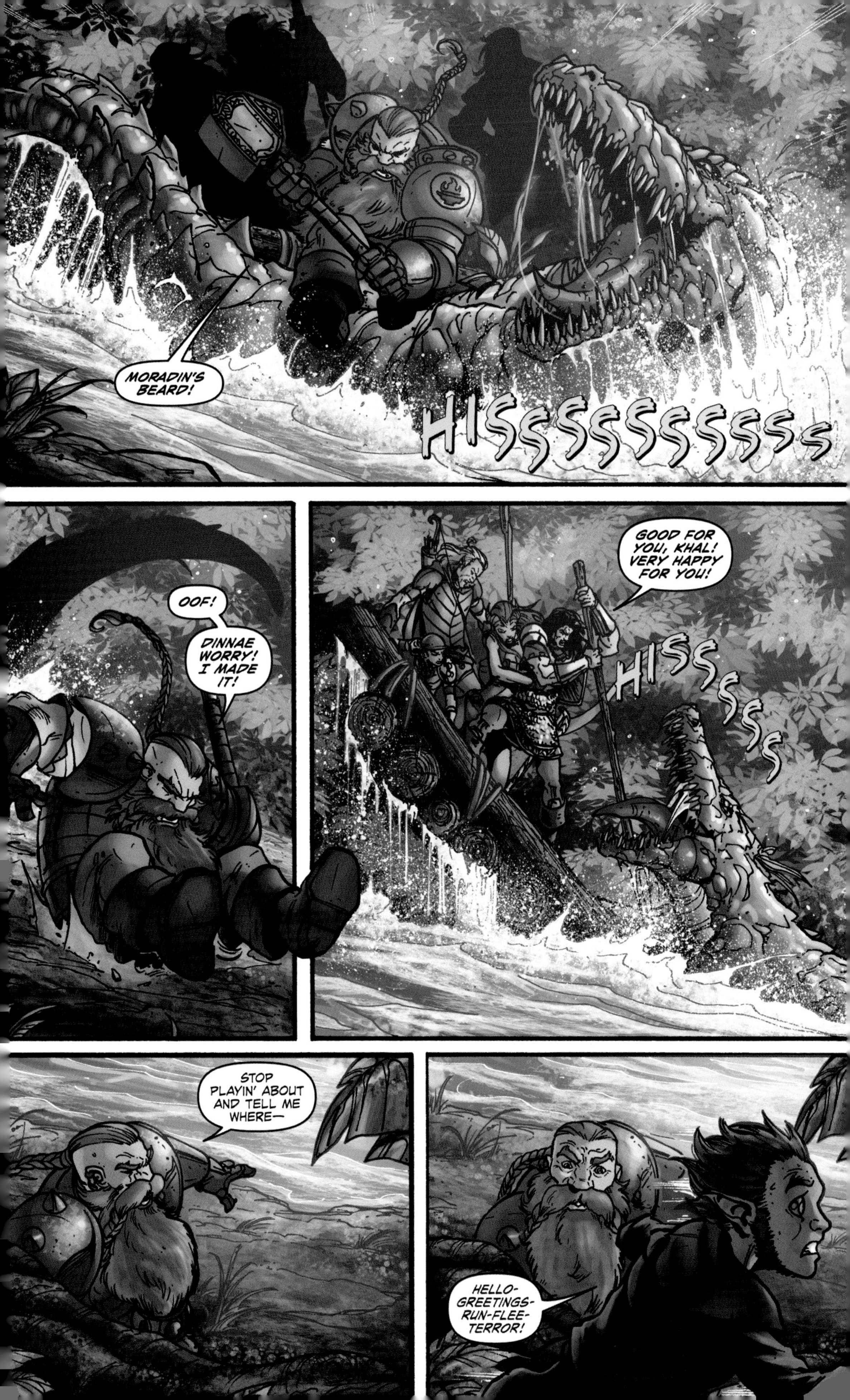
MORADIN'S BEARD!
HISSSSSSSSSSS
OOF!
DINNAE WORRY! I MADE IT!
GOOD FOR YOU, KHAL! VERY HAPPY FOR YOU!
HISSSSSS
STOP PLAYIN' ABOUT AND TELL ME WHERE—
HELLO-GREETINGS-RUN-FLEE-TERROR!

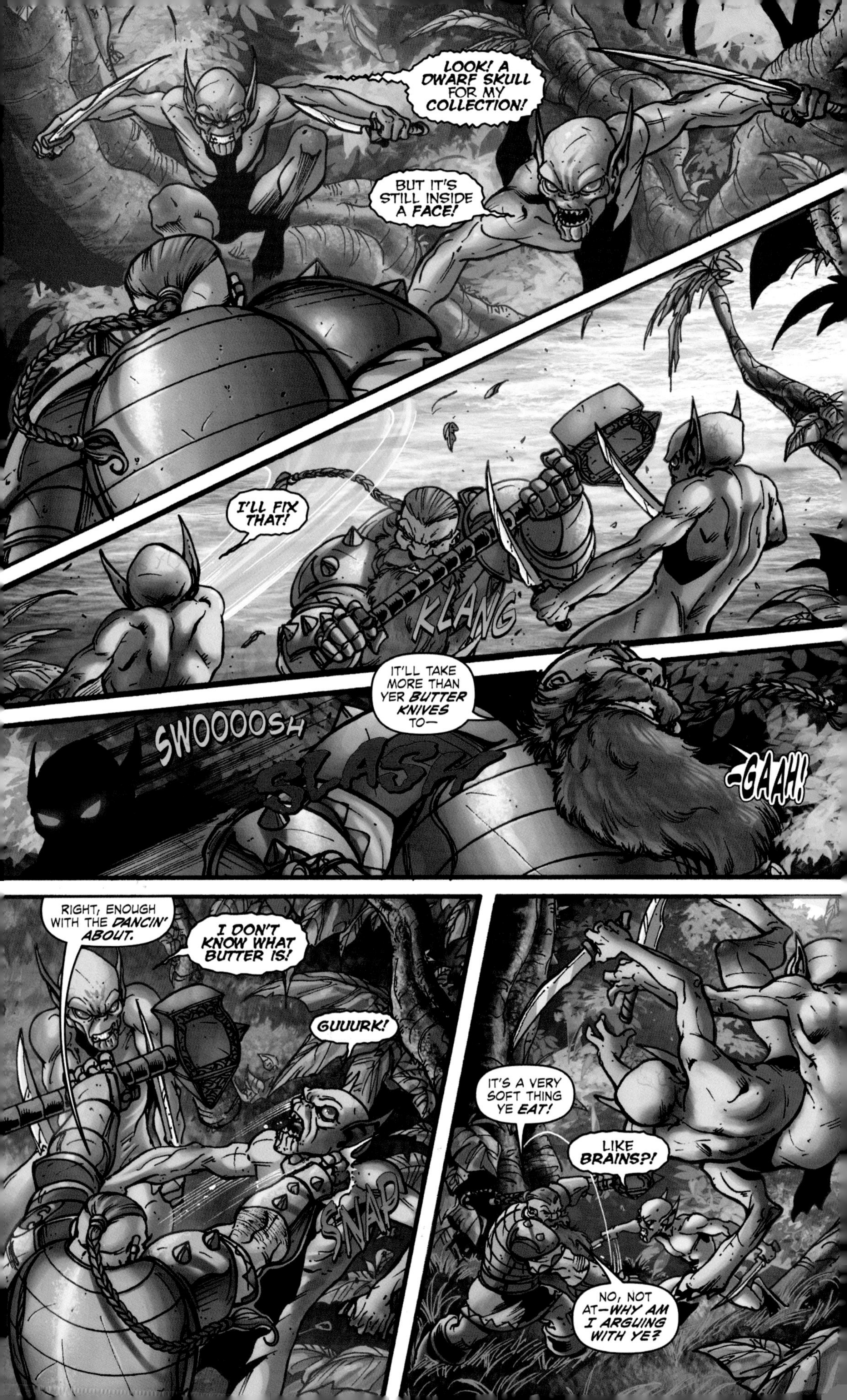
LOOK! A DWARF SKULL FOR MY COLLECTION!
BUT IT'S STILL INSIDE A FACE!
I'LL FIX THAT!
KLANG
IT'LL TAKE MORE THAN YER BUTTER KNIVES TO—
SWOOOOSH
SLASH
-GAAH!
RIGHT, ENOUGH WITH THE DANCIN' ABOUT.
I DON'T KNOW WHAT BUTTER IS!
GUUURK!
SNAP
IT'S A VERY SOFT THING YE EAT!
LIKE BRAINS?!
NO, NOT AT—WHY AM I ARGUING WITH YE?

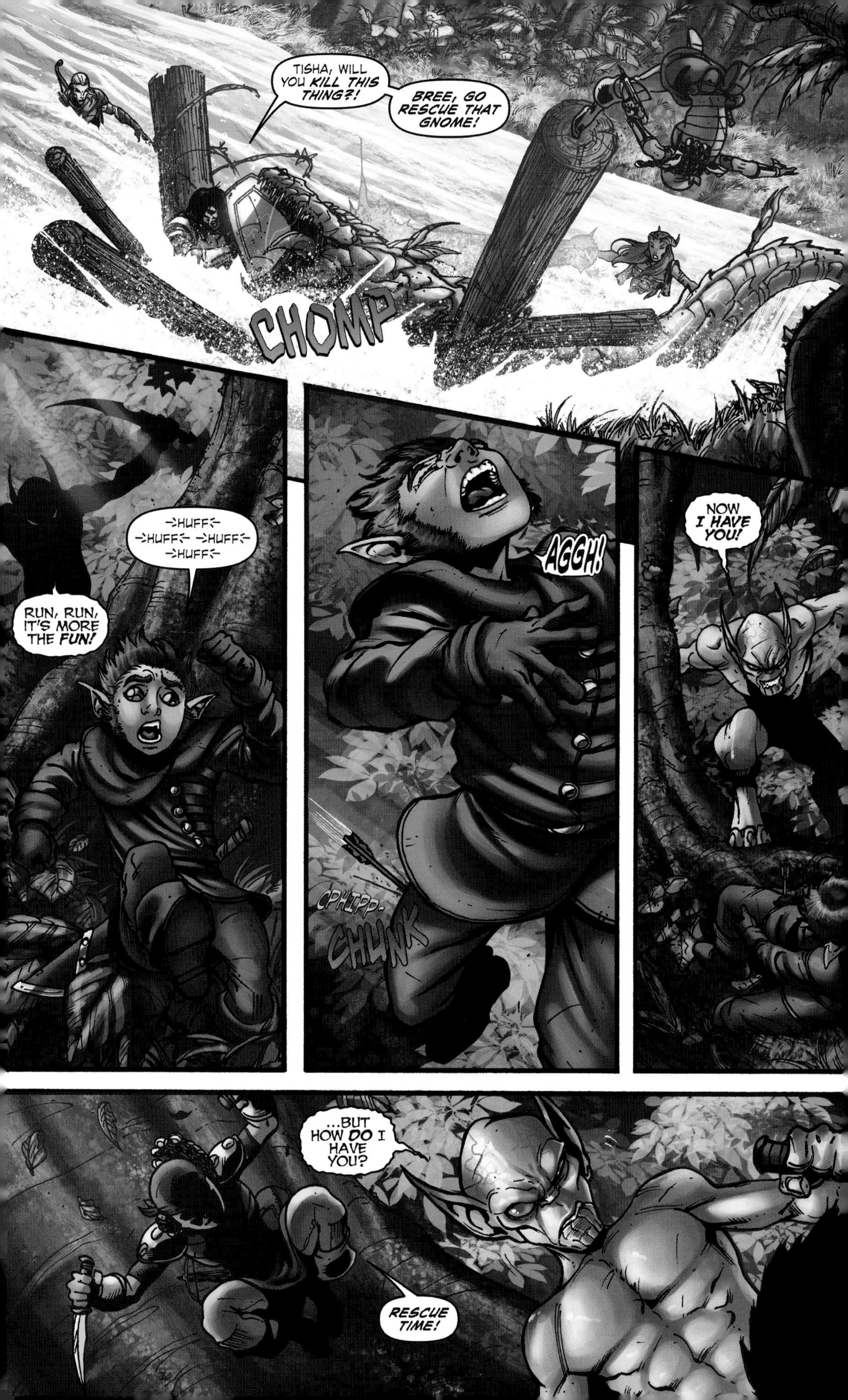
TISHA, WILL YOU KILL THIS THING?!
BREE, GO RESCUE THAT GNOME!
CHOMP
RUN, RUN, IT'S MORE THE FUN!
HUFF HUFF HUFF HUFF
AGGH!
CPHIPP-CHUNK
NOW I HAVE YOU!
...BUT HOW DO I HAVE YOU?
RESCUE TIME!

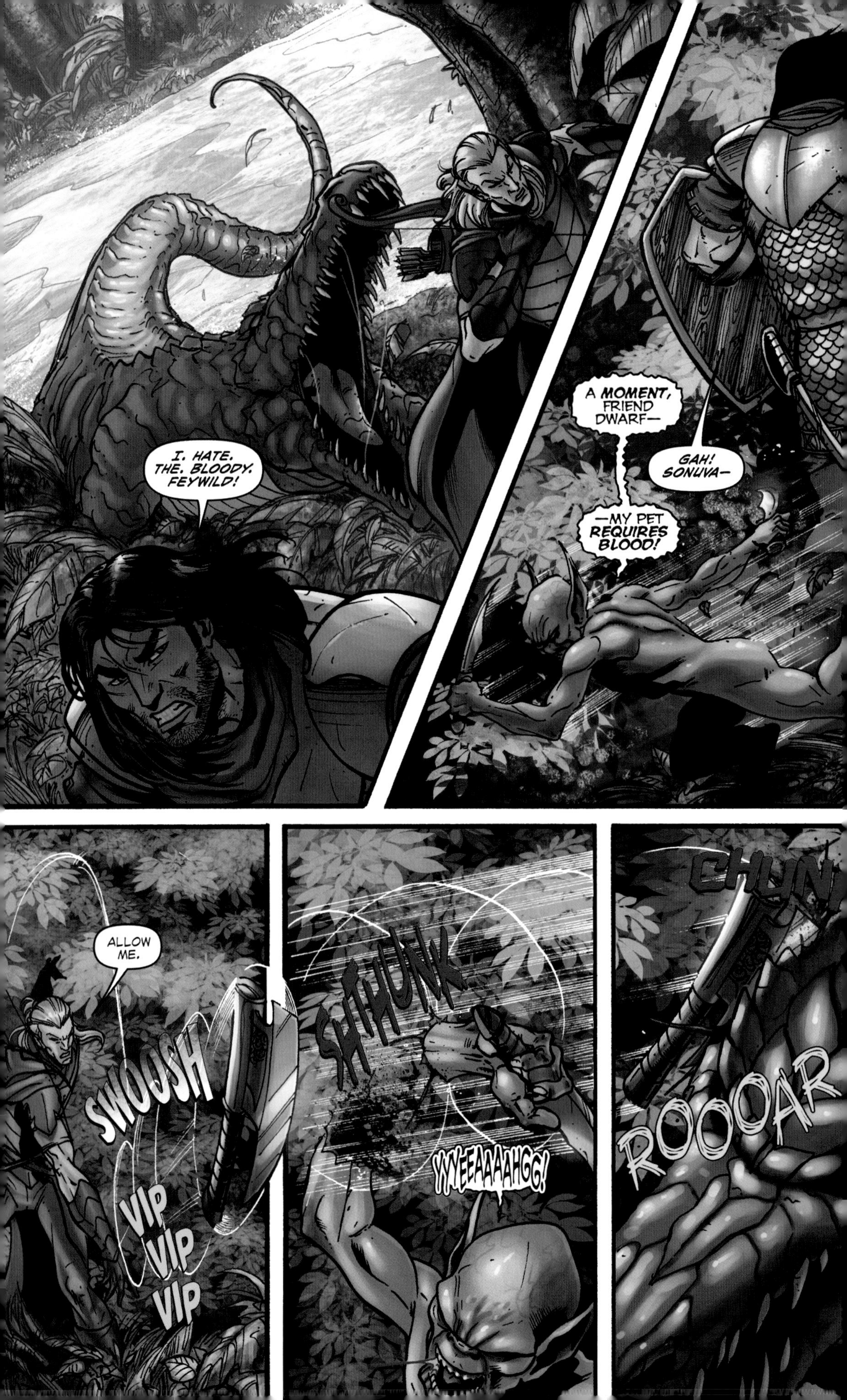
I. HATE. THE. BLOODY. FEYWILD!
A MOMENT, FRIEND DWARF—
GAH! SONUVA—
—MY PET REQUIRES BLOOD!
ALLOW ME.
SWOOSH
VIP
VIP
VIP
SHTHUNK
YYYEEAAAAHGG!
CHUN
ROOOAR

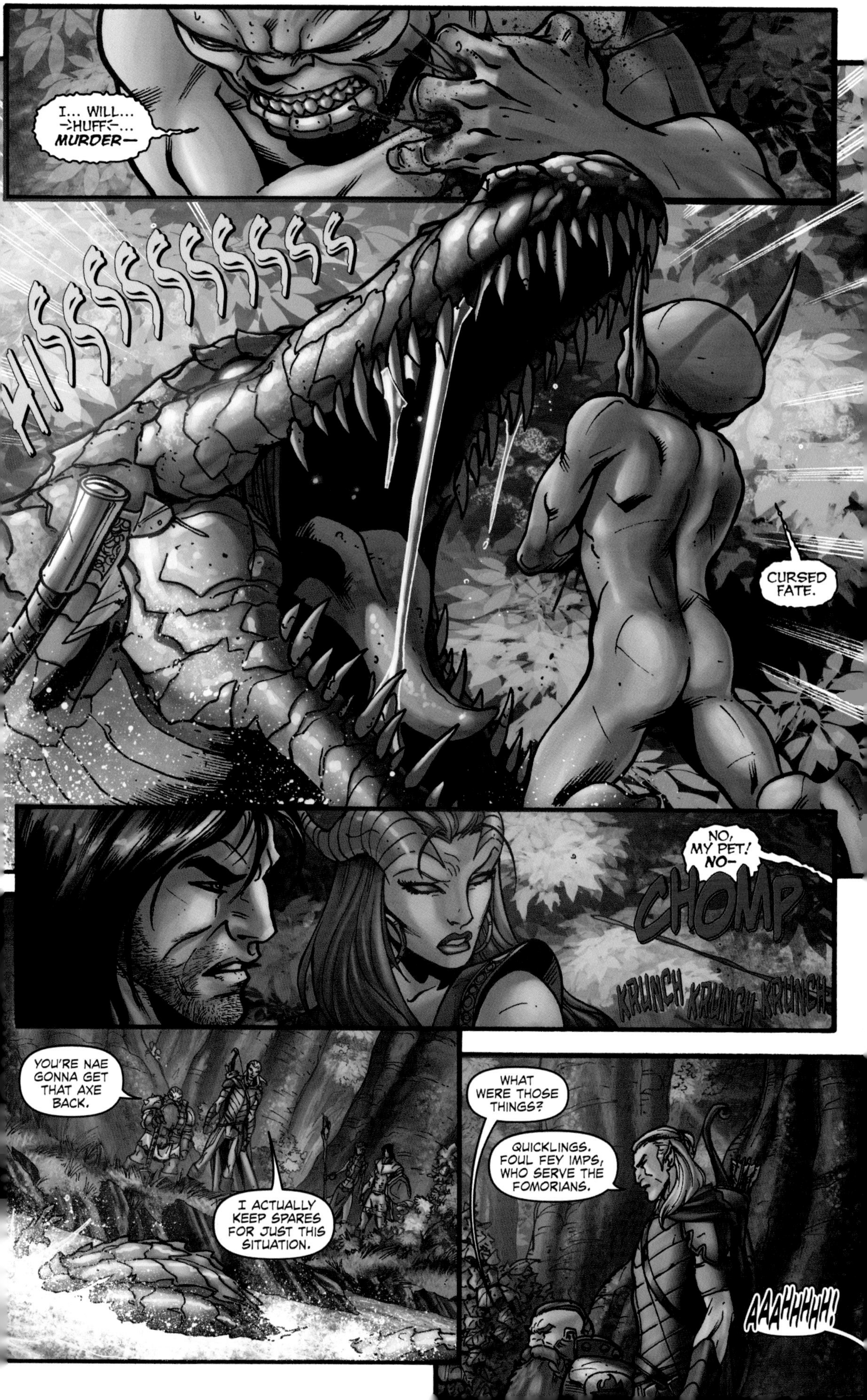
I... WILL... ~HUFF~... MURDER—
HISSSSSSSSSS
CURSED FATE.
NO, MY PET! NO—
CHOMP
KRUNCH KRUNCH KRUNCH
YOU'RE NAE GONNA GET THAT AXE BACK.
I ACTUALLY KEEP SPARES FOR JUST THIS SITUATION.
WHAT WERE THOSE THINGS?
QUICKLINGS. FOUL FEY IMPS, WHO SERVE THE FOMORIANS.
AAAHHHHH!

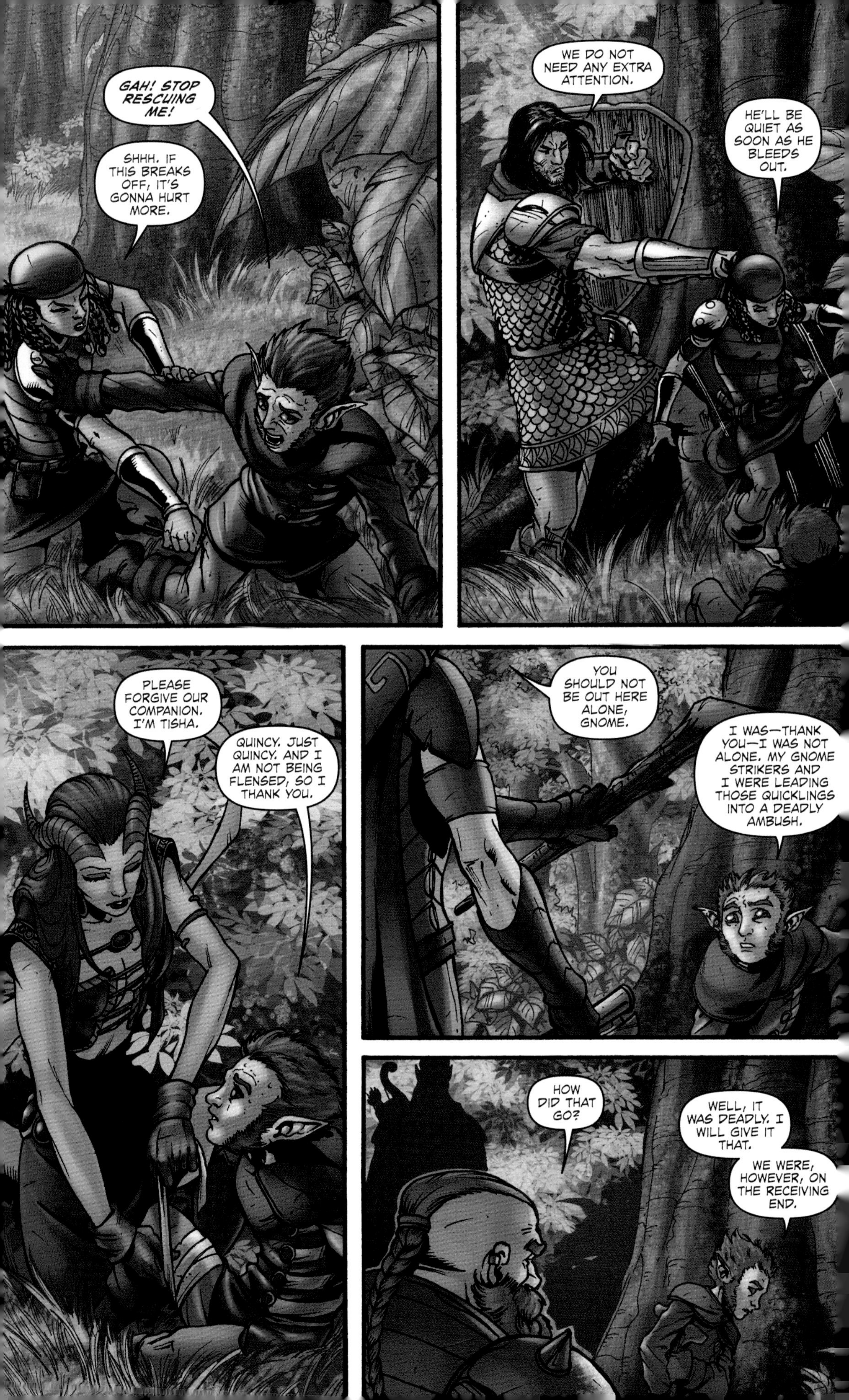
GAH! STOP RESCUING ME!
SHHH. IF THIS BREAKS OFF, IT'S GONNA HURT MORE.
WE DO NOT NEED ANY EXTRA ATTENTION.
HE'LL BE QUIET AS SOON AS HE BLEEDS OUT.
PLEASE FORGIVE OUR COMPANION. I'M TISHA.
QUINCY. JUST QUINCY. AND I AM NOT BEING FLENSED, SO I THANK YOU.
YOU SHOULD NOT BE OUT HERE ALONE, GNOME.
I WAS—THANK YOU—I WAS NOT ALONE. MY GNOME STRIKERS AND I WERE LEADING THOSE QUICKLINGS INTO A DEADLY AMBUSH.
HOW DID THAT GO?
WELL, IT WAS DEADLY. I WILL GIVE IT THAT.
WE WERE, HOWEVER, ON THE RECEIVING END.

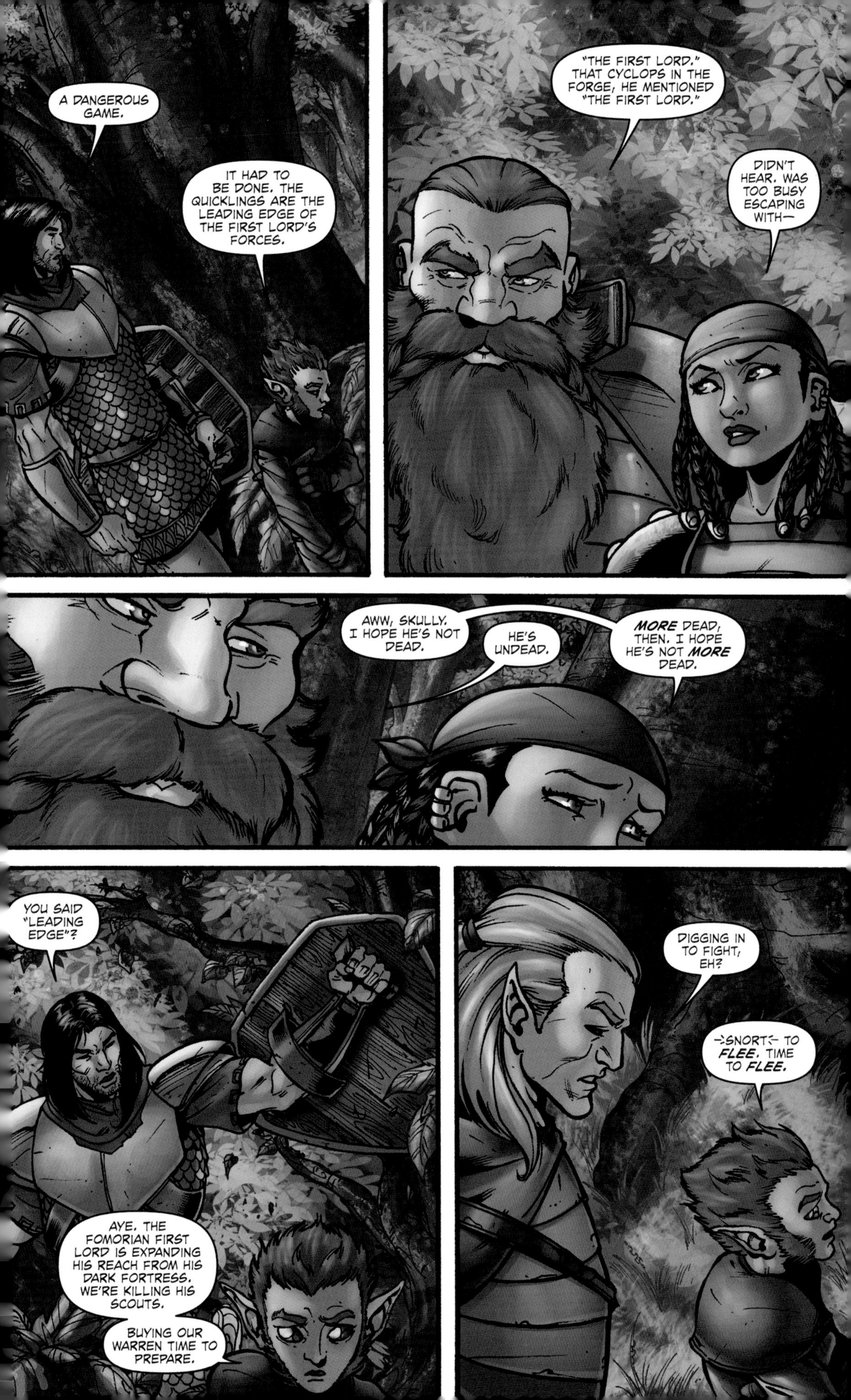
A DANGEROUS GAME.
IT HAD TO BE DONE. THE QUICKLINGS ARE THE LEADING EDGE OF THE FIRST LORD'S FORCES.
"THE FIRST LORD." THAT CYCLOPS IN THE FORGE, HE MENTIONED "THE FIRST LORD."
DIDN'T HEAR. WAS TOO BUSY ESCAPING WITH—
AWW, SKULLY. I HOPE HE'S NOT DEAD.
HE'S UNDEAD.
MORE DEAD, THEN. I HOPE HE'S NOT *MORE* DEAD.
YOU SAID "LEADING EDGE"?
AYE. THE FOMORIAN FIRST LORD IS EXPANDING HIS REACH FROM HIS DARK FORTRESS. WE'RE KILLING HIS SCOUTS.
BUYING OUR WARREN TIME TO PREPARE.
DIGGING IN TO FIGHT, EH?
>SNORT< TO *FLEE.* TIME TO *FLEE.*

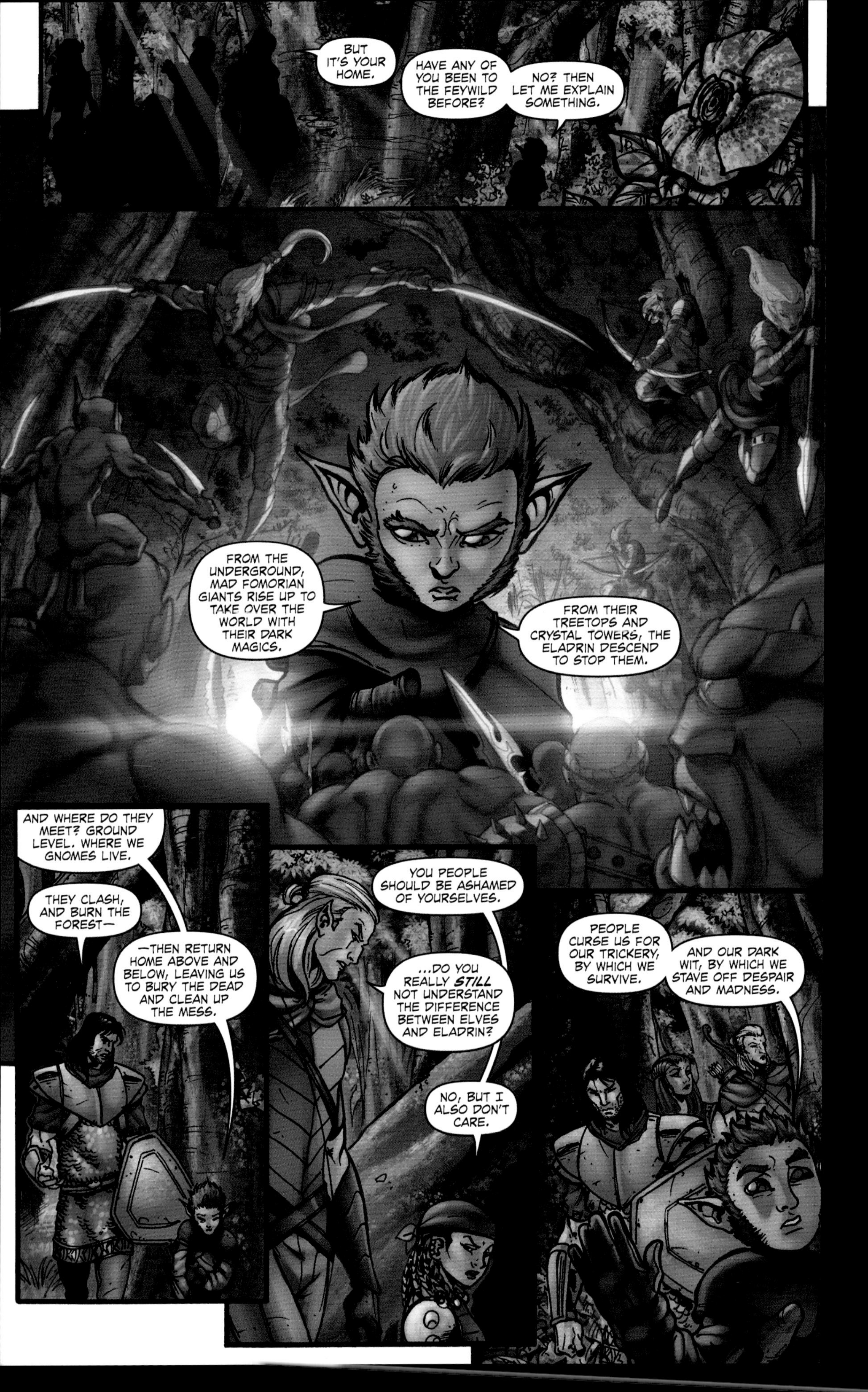
BUT IT'S YOUR HOME.
HAVE ANY OF YOU BEEN TO THE FEYWILD BEFORE?
NO? THEN LET ME EXPLAIN SOMETHING.
FROM THE UNDERGROUND, MAD FOMORIAN GIANTS RISE UP TO TAKE OVER THE WORLD WITH THEIR DARK MAGICS.
FROM THEIR TREETOPS AND CRYSTAL TOWERS, THE ELADRIN DESCEND TO STOP THEM.
AND WHERE DO THEY MEET? GROUND LEVEL. WHERE WE GNOMES LIVE.
THEY CLASH, AND BURN THE FOREST—
—THEN RETURN HOME ABOVE AND BELOW, LEAVING US TO BURY THE DEAD AND CLEAN UP THE MESS.
YOU PEOPLE SHOULD BE ASHAMED OF YOURSELVES.
...DO YOU REALLY *STILL* NOT UNDERSTAND THE DIFFERENCE BETWEEN ELVES AND ELADRIN?
NO, BUT I ALSO DON'T CARE.
PEOPLE CURSE US FOR OUR TRICKERY, BY WHICH WE SURVIVE.
AND OUR DARK WIT, BY WHICH WE STAVE OFF DESPAIR AND MADNESS.

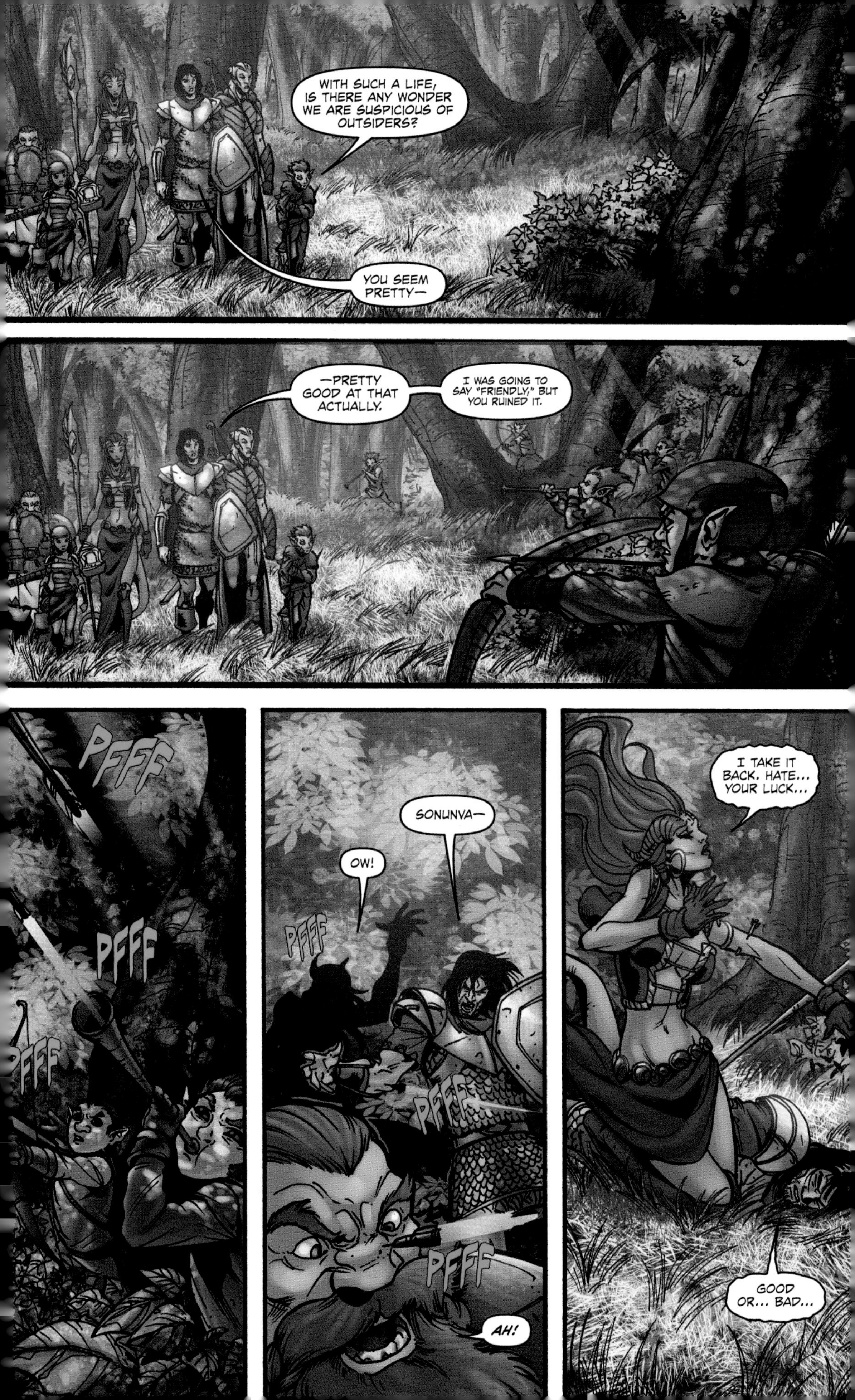
WITH SUCH A LIFE, IS THERE ANY WONDER WE ARE SUSPICIOUS OF OUTSIDERS?
YOU SEEM PRETTY—
—PRETTY GOOD AT THAT ACTUALLY.
I WAS GOING TO SAY "FRIENDLY," BUT YOU RUINED IT.
PFFF
PFFF
PFFF
SONUNVA—
OW!
PFFF
PFFF
PFFF
AH!
I TAKE IT BACK. HATE... YOUR LUCK...
GOOD OR... BAD...

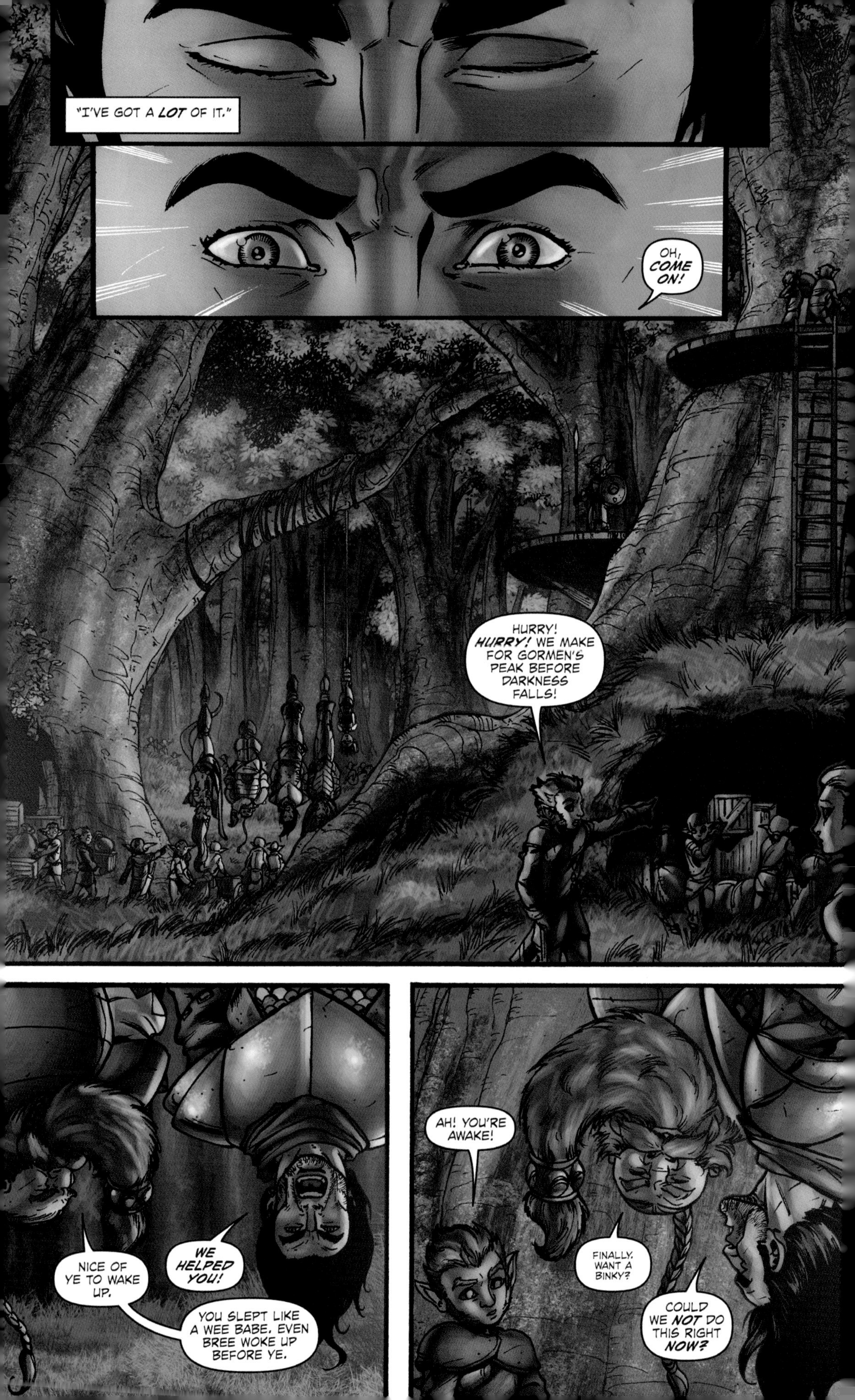
"I'VE GOT A LOT OF IT."
OH, COME ON!
HURRY! HURRY! WE MAKE FOR GORMEN'S PEAK BEFORE DARKNESS FALLS!
NICE OF YE TO WAKE UP.
WE HELPED YOU!
YOU SLEPT LIKE A WEE BABE. EVEN BREE WOKE UP BEFORE YE.
AH! YOU'RE AWAKE!
FINALLY. WANT A BINKY?
COULD WE NOT DO THIS RIGHT NOW?

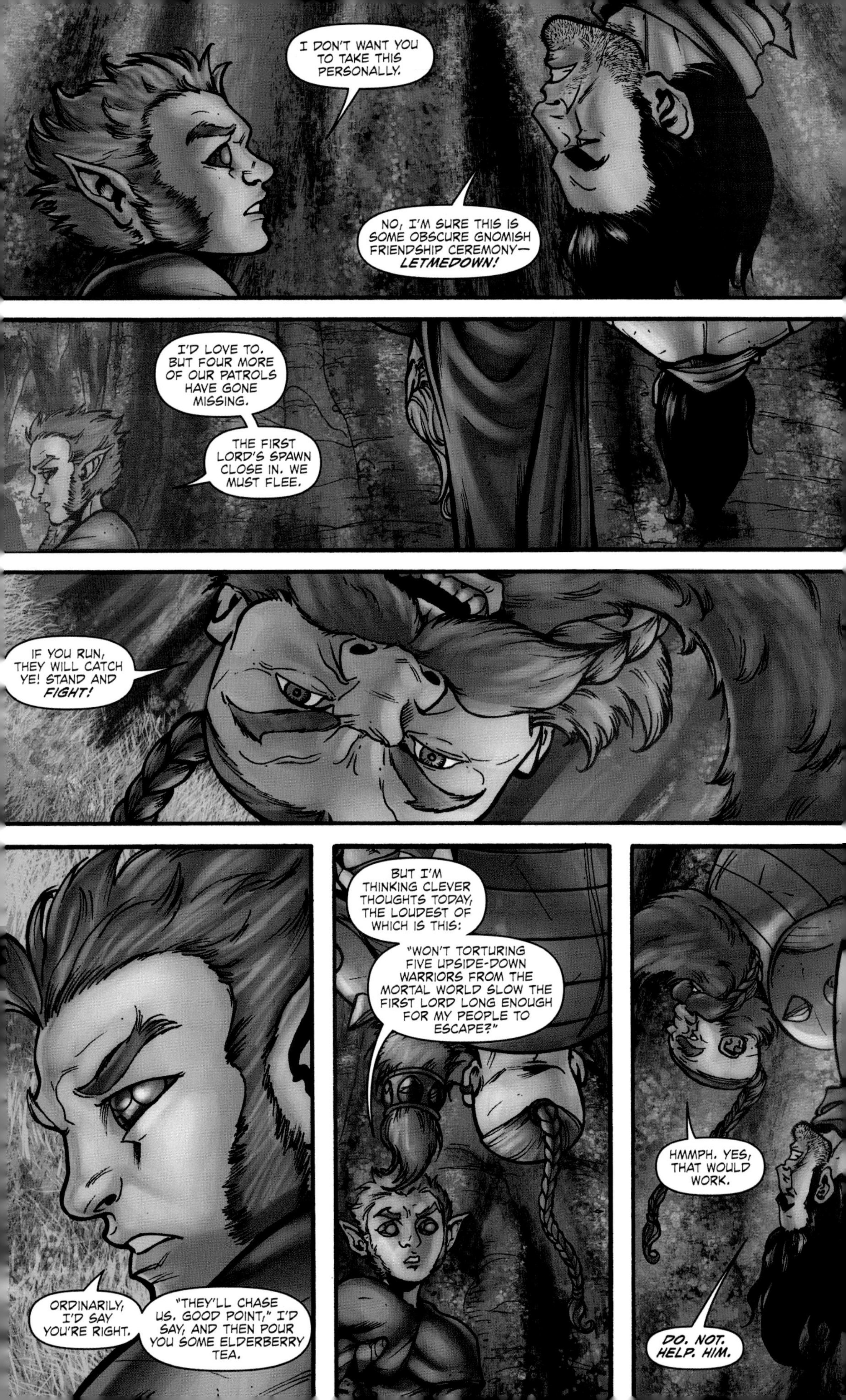

I DON'T WANT YOU TO TAKE THIS PERSONALLY.
NO, I'M SURE THIS IS SOME OBSCURE GNOMISH FRIENDSHIP CEREMONY—*LETMEDOWN!*
I'D LOVE TO. BUT FOUR MORE OF OUR PATROLS HAVE GONE MISSING.
THE FIRST LORD'S SPAWN CLOSE IN. WE MUST FLEE.
IF YOU RUN, THEY WILL CATCH YE! STAND AND *FIGHT!*
ORDINARILY, I'D SAY YOU'RE RIGHT.
"THEY'LL CHASE US. GOOD POINT," I'D SAY, AND THEN POUR YOU SOME ELDERBERRY TEA.
BUT I'M THINKING CLEVER THOUGHTS TODAY, THE LOUDEST OF WHICH IS THIS:
"WON'T TORTURING FIVE UPSIDE-DOWN WARRIORS FROM THE MORTAL WORLD SLOW THE FIRST LORD LONG ENOUGH FOR MY PEOPLE TO ESCAPE?"
HMMPH. YES, THAT WOULD WORK.
DO. NOT. HELP. HIM.

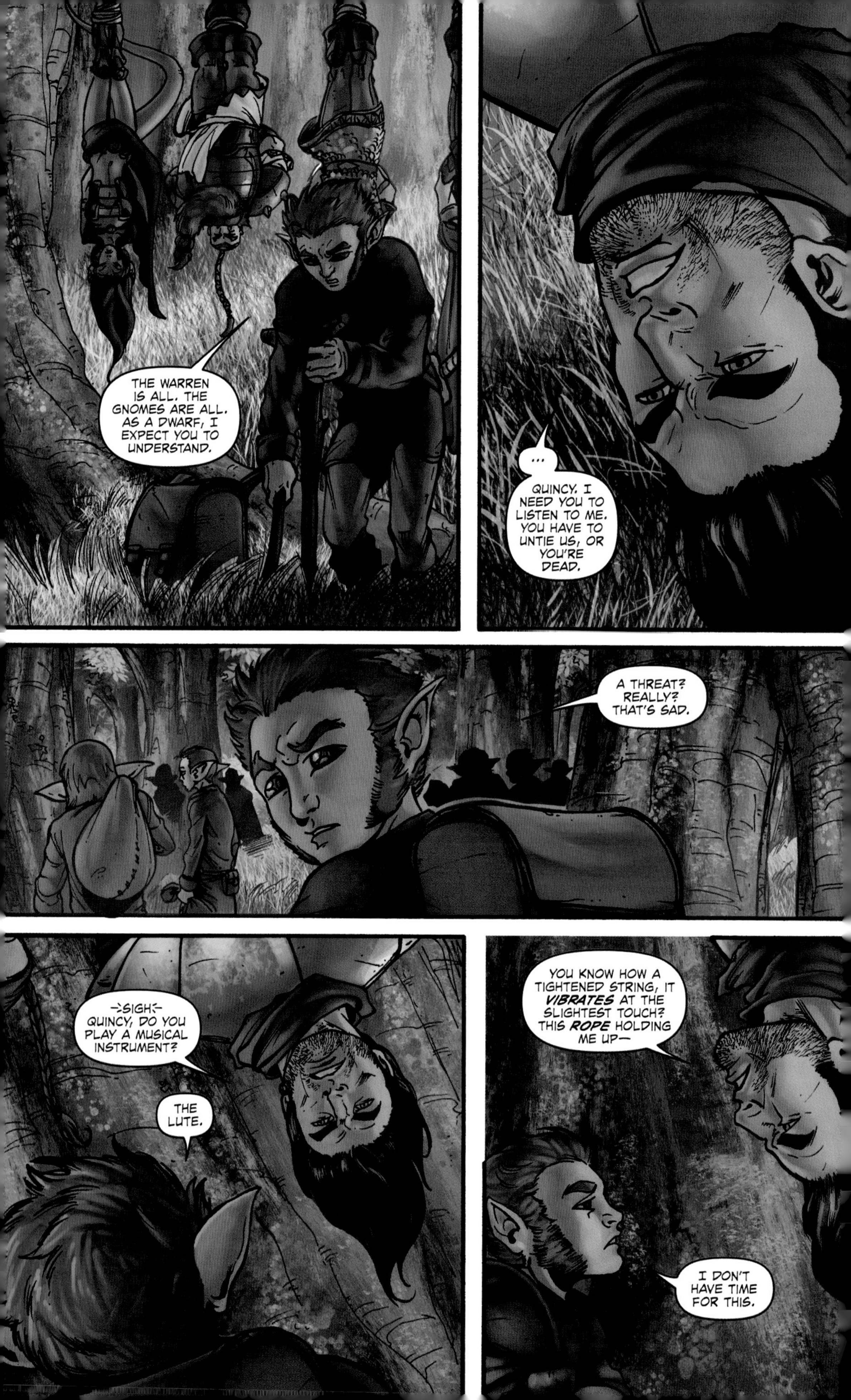
THE WARREN IS ALL. THE GNOMES ARE ALL. AS A DWARF, I EXPECT YOU TO UNDERSTAND.
...
QUINCY. I NEED YOU TO LISTEN TO ME. YOU HAVE TO UNTIE US, OR YOU'RE DEAD.
A THREAT? REALLY? THAT'S SAD.
—SIGH— QUINCY, DO YOU PLAY A MUSICAL INSTRUMENT?
THE LUTE.
YOU KNOW HOW A TIGHTENED STRING, IT VIBRATES AT THE SLIGHTEST TOUCH? THIS ROPE HOLDING ME UP—
I DON'T HAVE TIME FOR THIS.

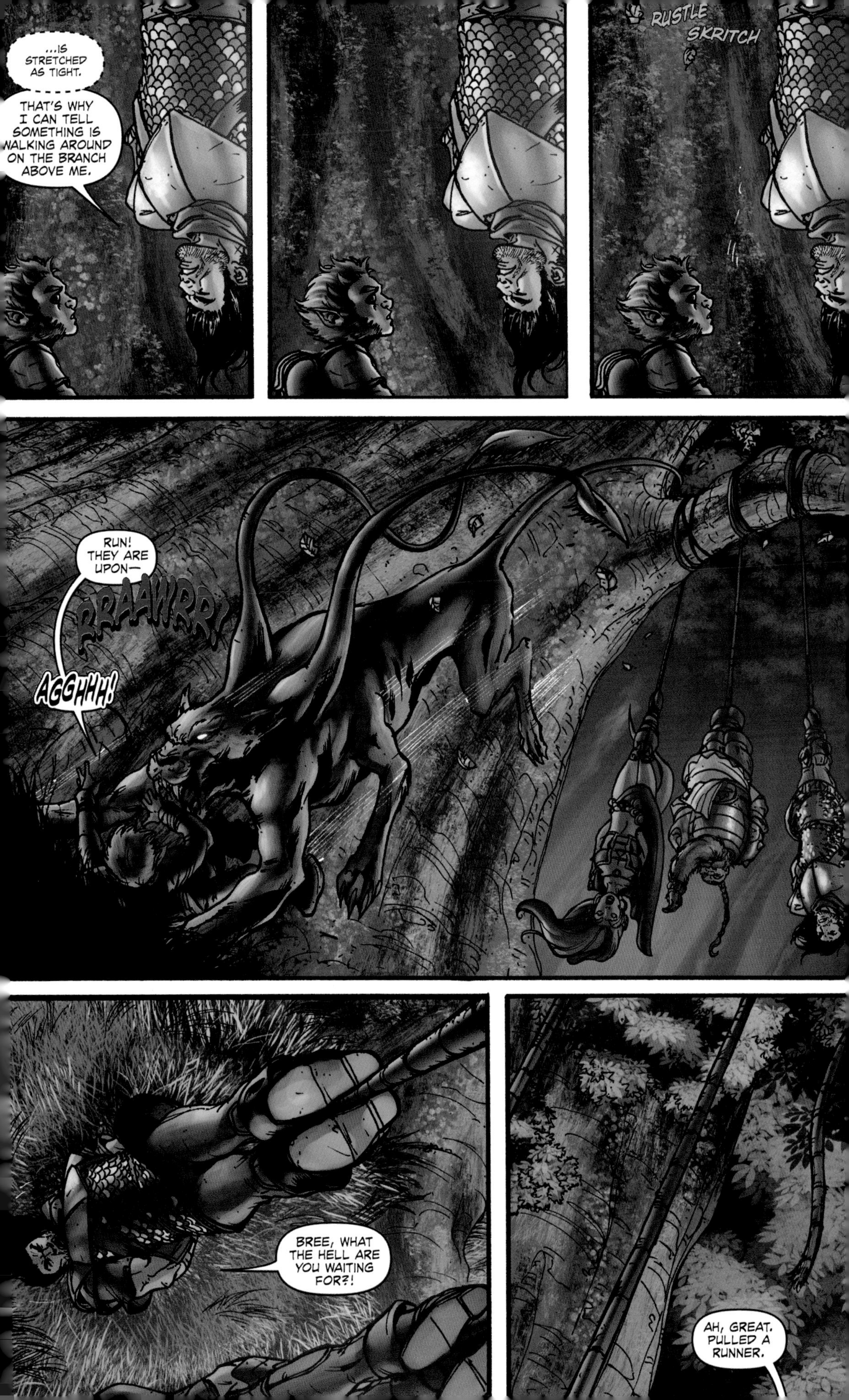
...IS STRETCHED AS TIGHT.
THAT'S WHY I CAN TELL SOMETHING IS WALKING AROUND ON THE BRANCH ABOVE ME.
RUSTLE
SKRITCH
RUN! THEY ARE UPON—
BRAAWRR!
AGGHHH!
BREE, WHAT THE HELL ARE YOU WAITING FOR?!
AH, GREAT. PULLED A RUNNER.

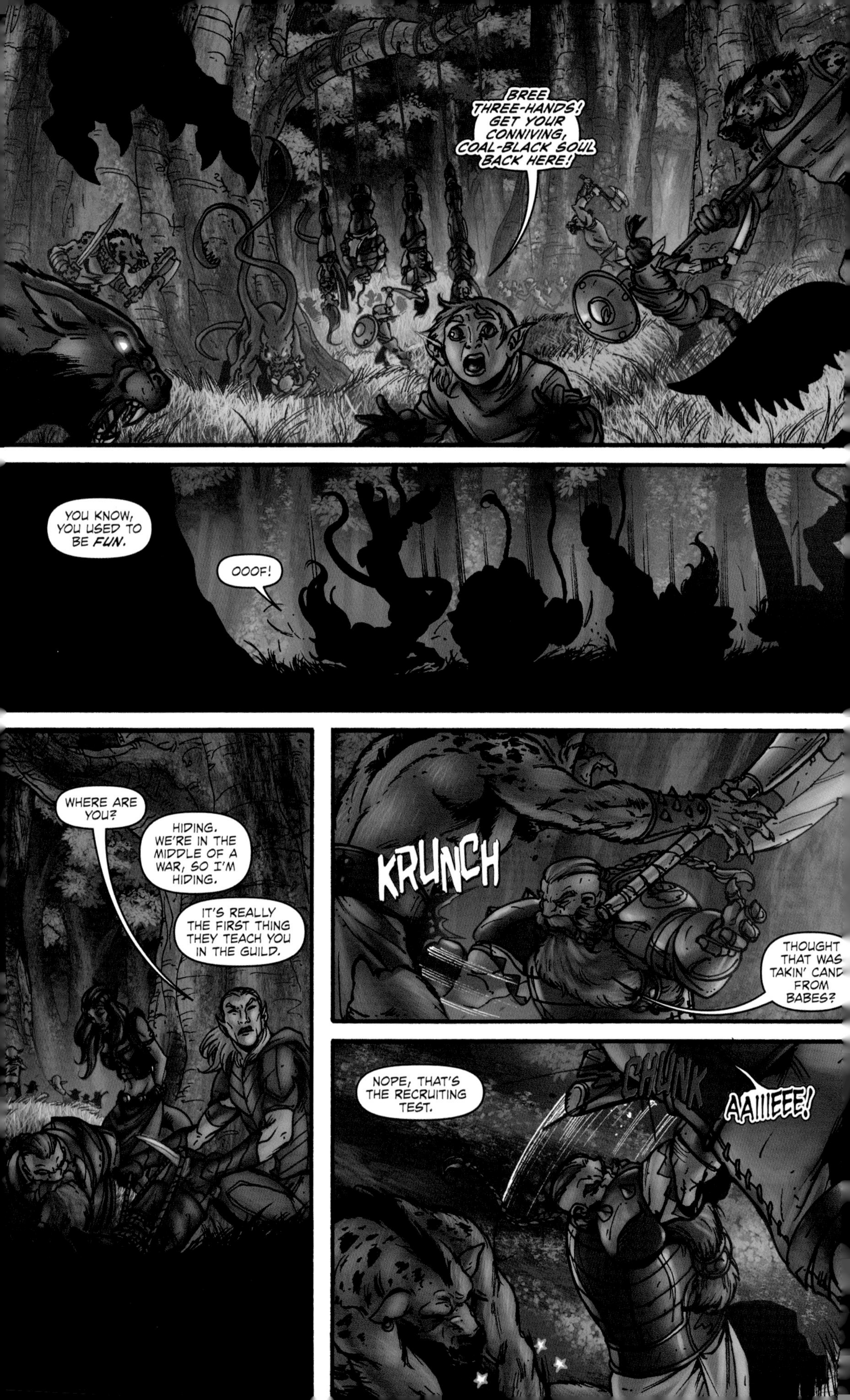
BREE THREE-HANDS! GET YOUR CONNIVING, COAL-BLACK SOUL BACK HERE!
YOU KNOW, YOU USED TO BE *FUN*.
OOOF!
WHERE ARE YOU?
HIDING. WE'RE IN THE MIDDLE OF A WAR, SO I'M HIDING.
IT'S REALLY THE FIRST THING THEY TEACH YOU IN THE GUILD.
KRUNCH
THOUGHT THAT WAS TAKIN' CAND FROM BABES?
NOPE, THAT'S THE RECRUITING TEST.
CHUNK
AAIIIEEE!

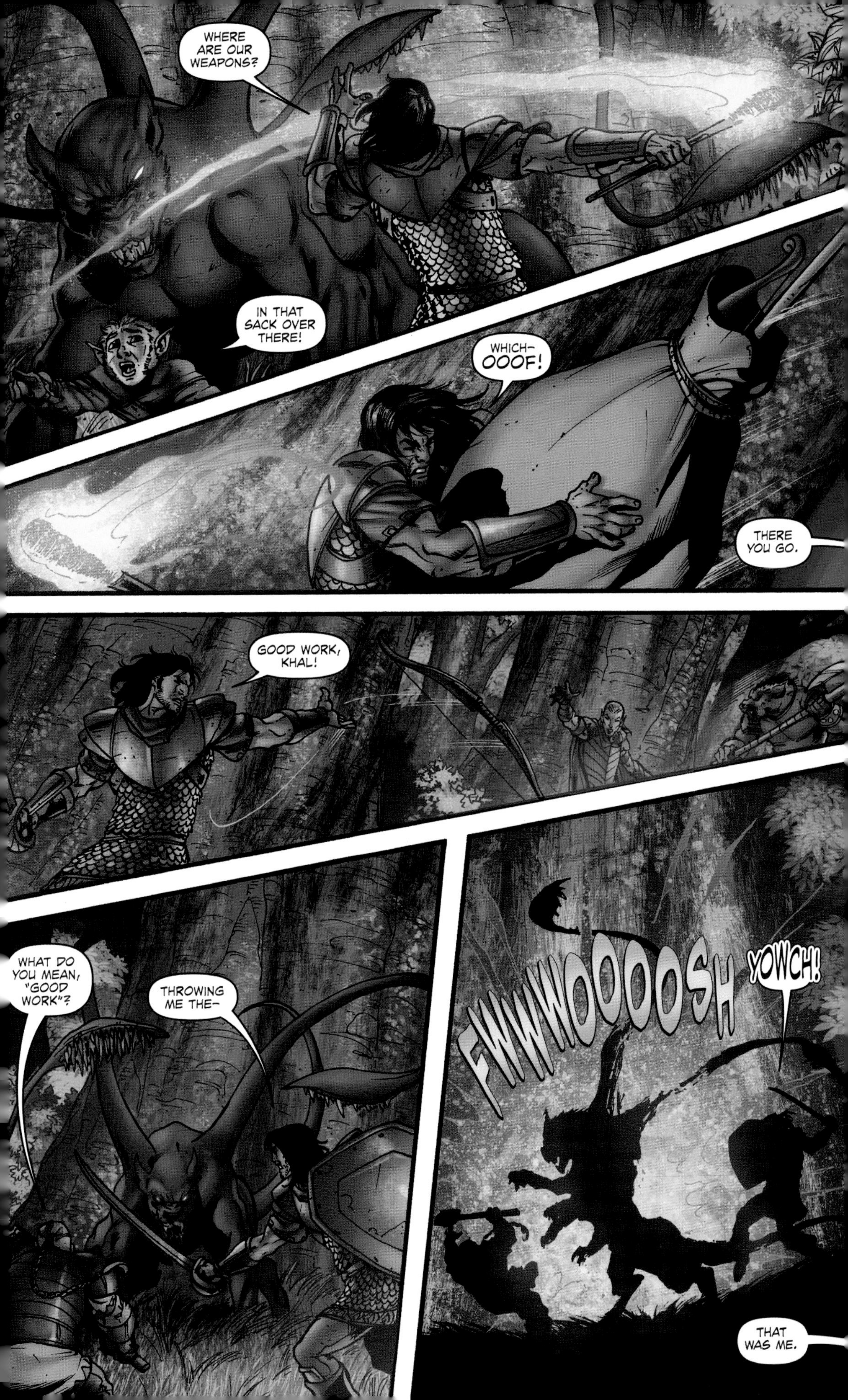
WHERE ARE OUR WEAPONS?
IN THAT SACK OVER THERE!
WHICH- OOOF!
THERE YOU GO.
GOOD WORK, KHAL!
WHAT DO YOU MEAN, "GOOD WORK"?
THROWING ME THE-
FWWWOOOOSH
YOWCH!
THAT WAS ME.

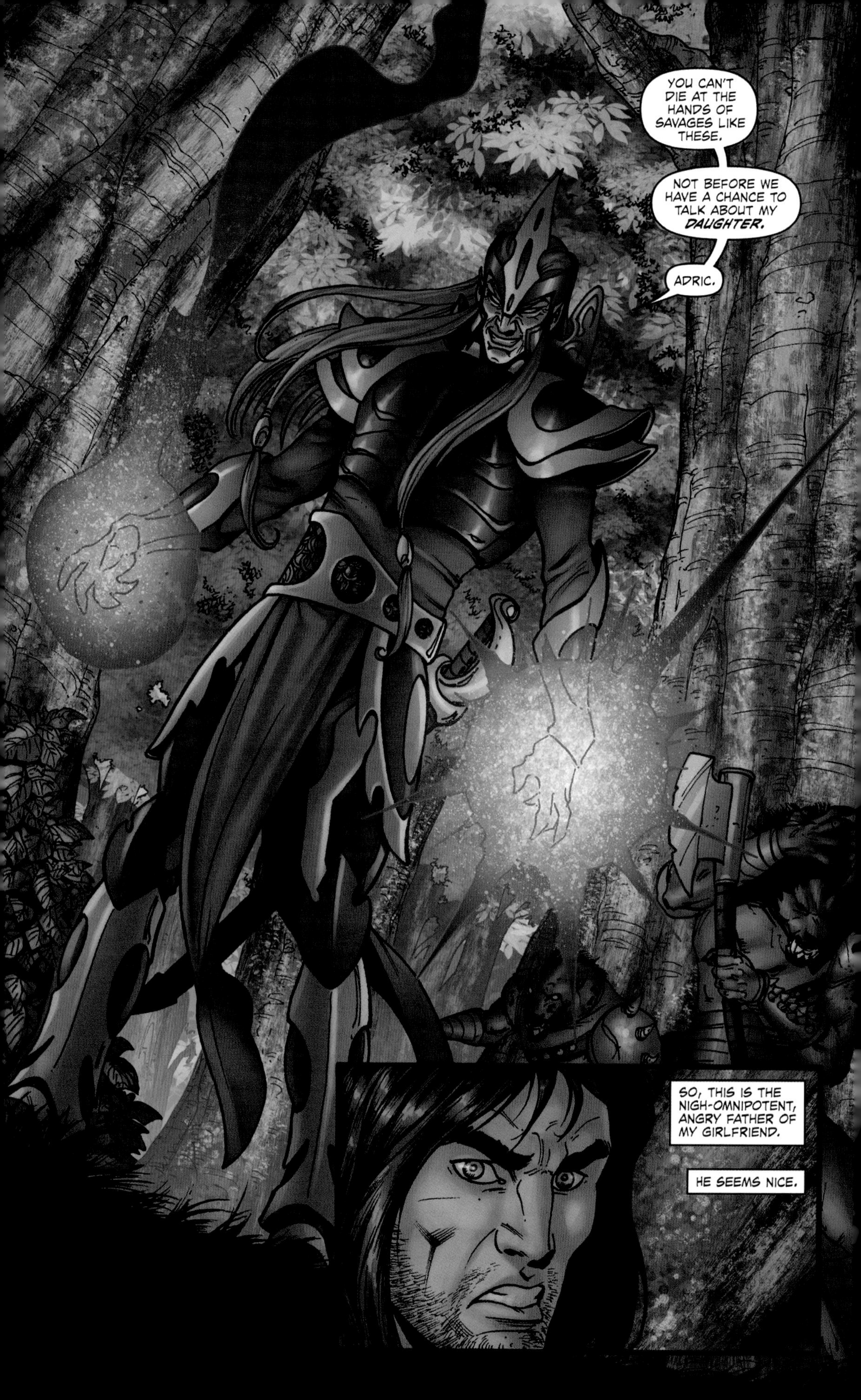
YOU CAN'T DIE AT THE HANDS OF SAVAGES LIKE THESE.
NOT BEFORE WE HAVE A CHANCE TO TALK ABOUT MY DAUGHTER.
ADRIC.
SO, THIS IS THE NIGH-OMNIPOTENT, ANGRY FATHER OF MY GIRLFRIEND.
HE SEEMS NICE.

Art by Tyler Walpole

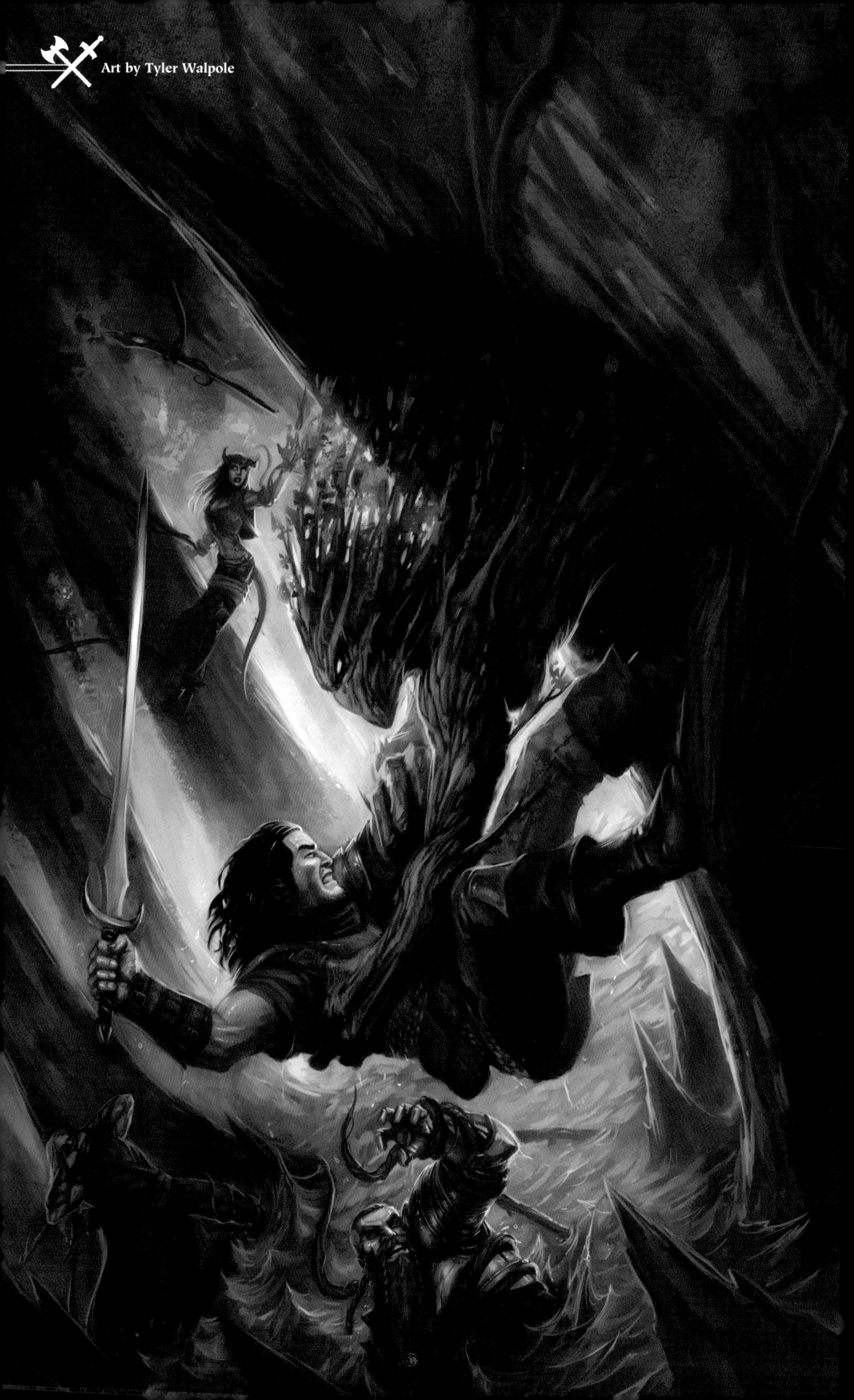

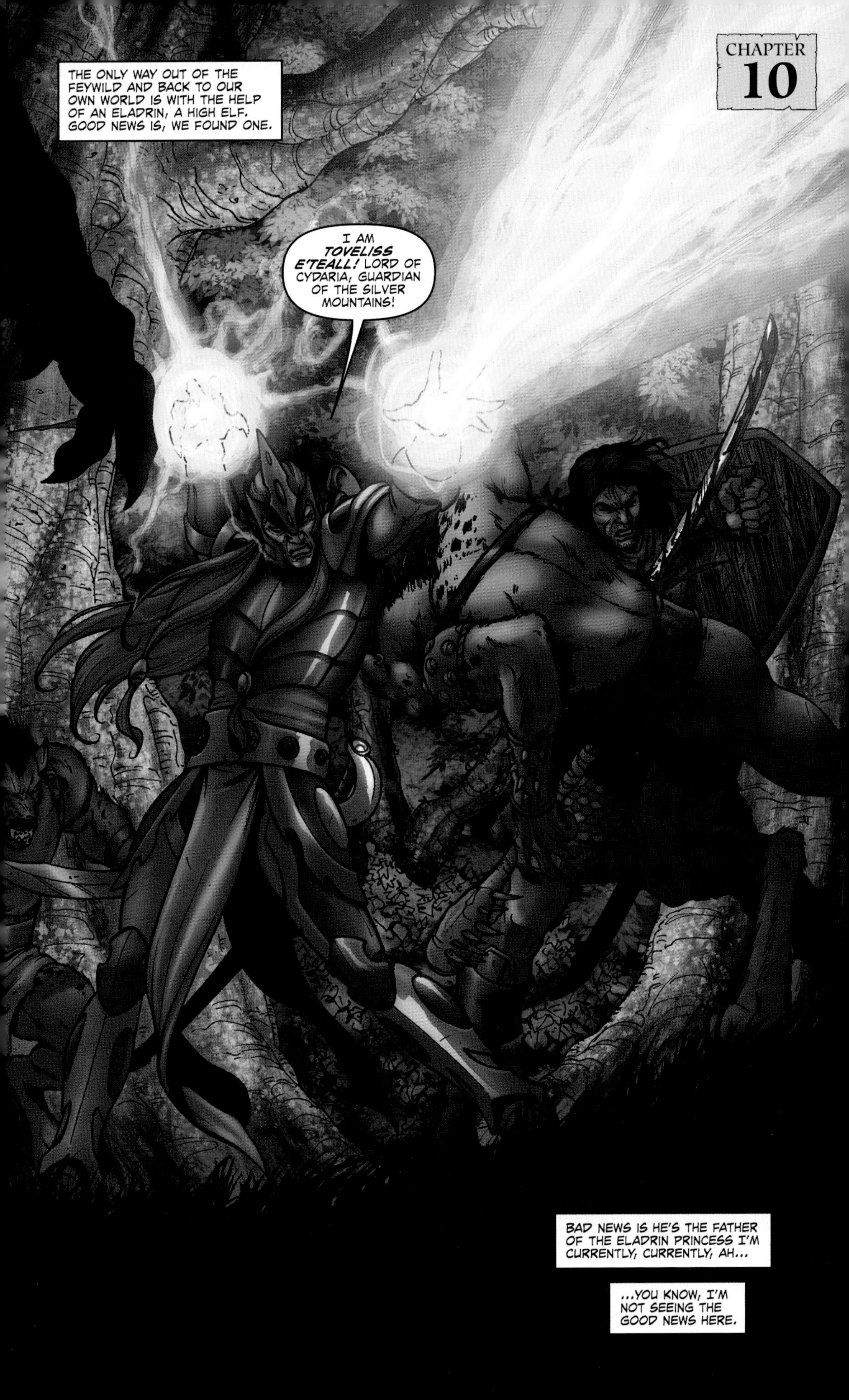
CHAPTER 10
THE ONLY WAY OUT OF THE FEYWILD AND BACK TO OUR OWN WORLD IS WITH THE HELP OF AN ELADRIN, A HIGH ELF. GOOD NEWS IS, WE FOUND ONE.
I AM TOVELISS E'TEALL! LORD OF CYDARIA, GUARDIAN OF THE SILVER MOUNTAINS!
BAD NEWS IS HE'S THE FATHER OF THE ELADRIN PRINCESS I'M CURRENTLY, CURRENTLY, AH...
...YOU KNOW, I'M NOT SEEING THE GOOD NEWS HERE.

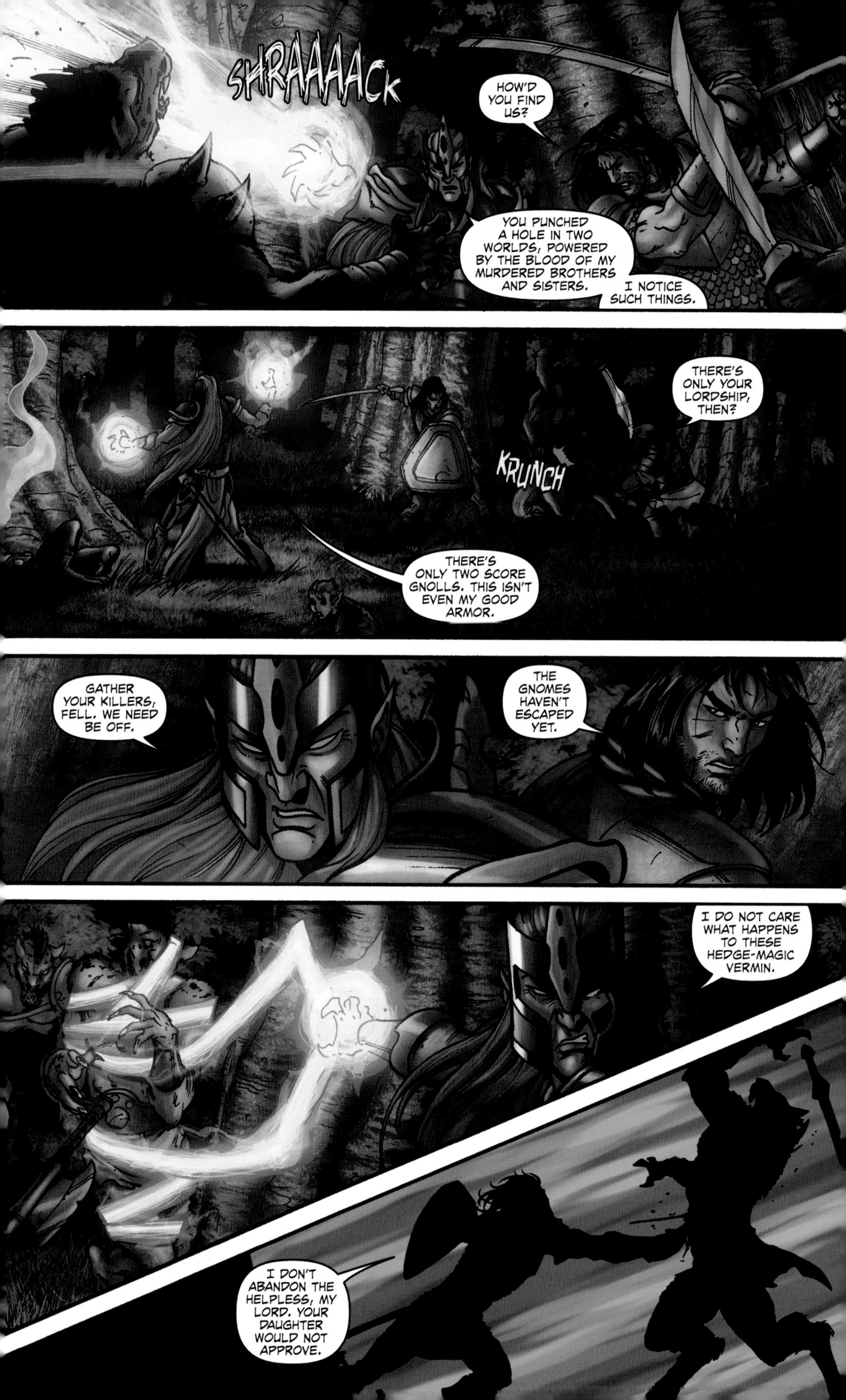
SHRAAAACK
HOW'D YOU FIND US?
YOU PUNCHED A HOLE IN TWO WORLDS, POWERED BY THE BLOOD OF MY MURDERED BROTHERS AND SISTERS.
I NOTICE SUCH THINGS.
THERE'S ONLY YOUR LORDSHIP, THEN?
KRUNCH
THERE'S ONLY TWO SCORE GNOLLS. THIS ISN'T EVEN MY GOOD ARMOR.
GATHER YOUR KILLERS, FELL. WE NEED BE OFF.
THE GNOMES HAVEN'T ESCAPED YET.
I DO NOT CARE WHAT HAPPENS TO THESE HEDGE-MAGIC VERMIN.
I DON'T ABANDON THE HELPLESS, MY LORD. YOUR DAUGHTER WOULD NOT APPROVE.

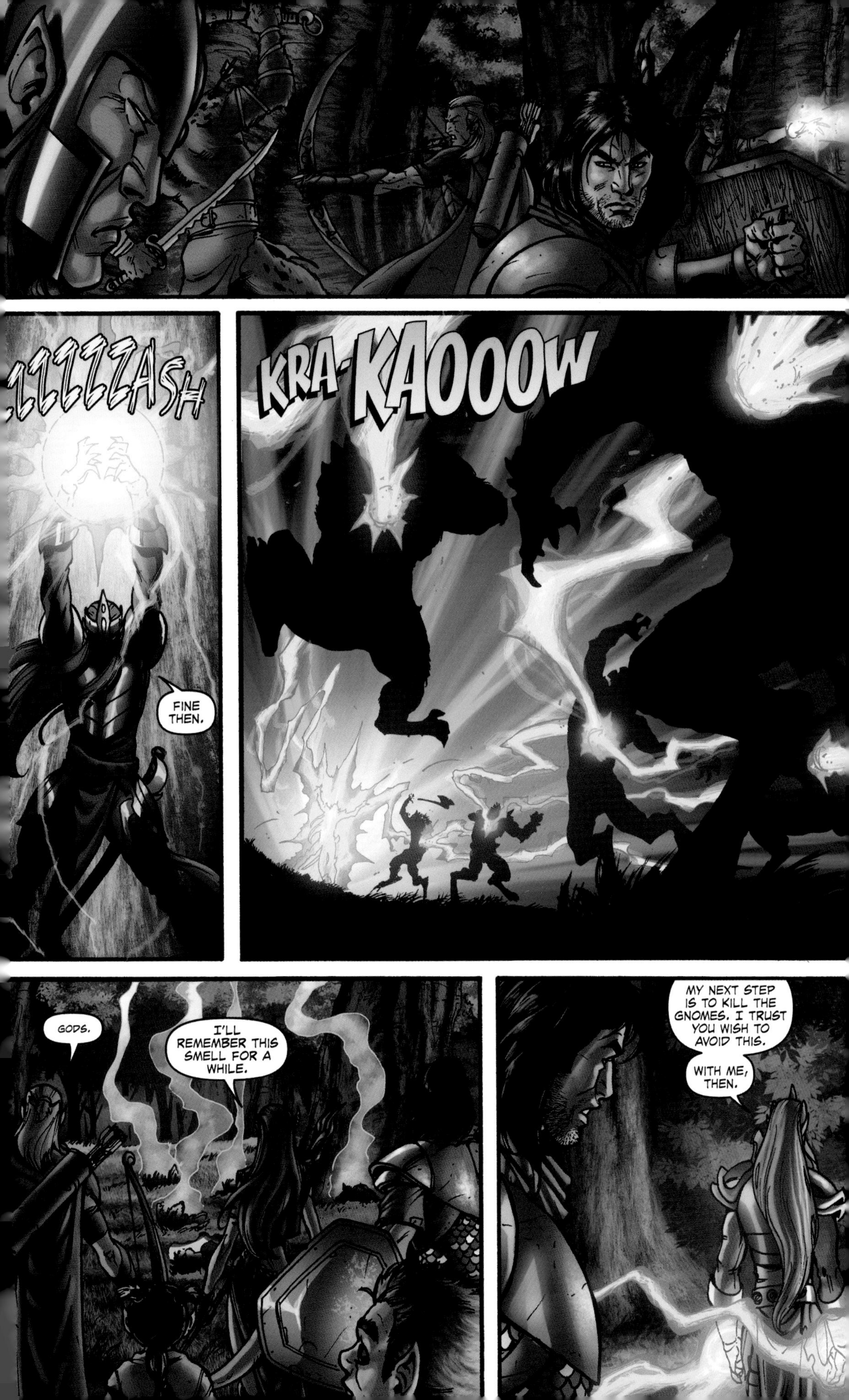
ZZZZZZASH
FINE THEN.
KRA-KAOOOW
GODS.
I'LL REMEMBER THIS SMELL FOR A WHILE.
MY NEXT STEP IS TO KILL THE GNOMES. I TRUST YOU WISH TO AVOID THIS.
WITH ME, THEN.

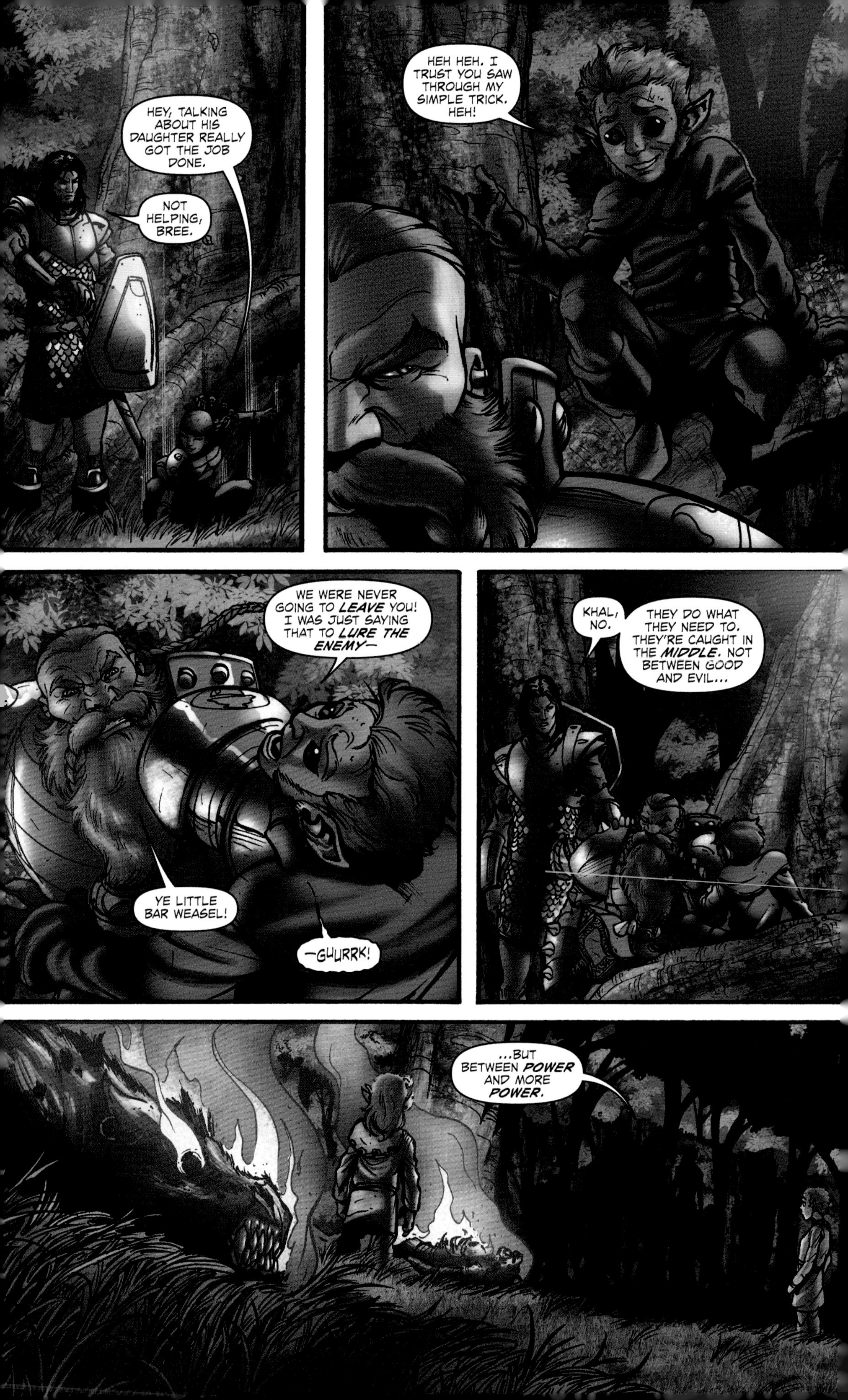
HEY, TALKING ABOUT HIS DAUGHTER REALLY GOT THE JOB DONE.
NOT HELPING, BREE.
HEH HEH. I TRUST YOU SAW THROUGH MY SIMPLE TRICK. HEH!
WE WERE NEVER GOING TO LEAVE YOU! I WAS JUST SAYING THAT TO LURE THE ENEMY—
YE LITTLE BAR WEASEL!
—GUURRK!
KHAL, NO.
THEY DO WHAT THEY NEED TO. THEY'RE CAUGHT IN THE MIDDLE. NOT BETWEEN GOOD AND EVIL...
...BUT BETWEEN POWER AND MORE POWER.

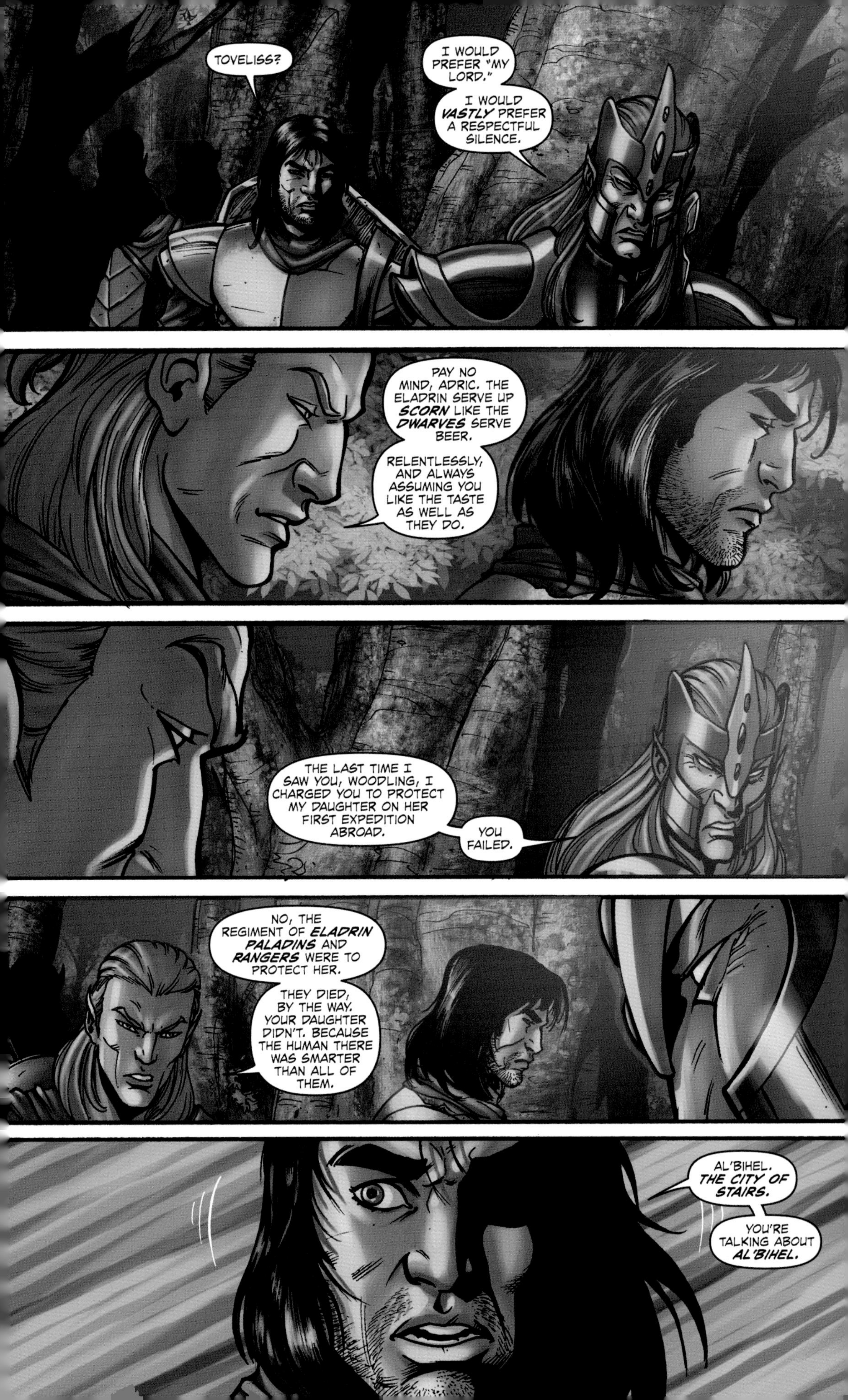
TOVELISS?
I WOULD PREFER "MY LORD."
I WOULD *VASTLY* PREFER A RESPECTFUL SILENCE.
PAY NO MIND, ADRIC. THE ELADRIN SERVE UP *SCORN* LIKE THE *DWARVES* SERVE BEER.
RELENTLESSLY, AND ALWAYS ASSUMING YOU LIKE THE TASTE AS WELL AS THEY DO.
THE LAST TIME I SAW YOU, WOODLING, I CHARGED YOU TO PROTECT MY DAUGHTER ON HER FIRST EXPEDITION ABROAD.
YOU FAILED.
NO, THE REGIMENT OF *ELADRIN PALADINS* AND *RANGERS* WERE TO PROTECT HER.
THEY DIED, BY THE WAY. YOUR DAUGHTER DIDN'T. BECAUSE THE HUMAN THERE WAS SMARTER THAN ALL OF THEM.
AL'BIHEL. *THE CITY OF STAIRS.*
YOU'RE TALKING ABOUT *AL'BIHEL.*

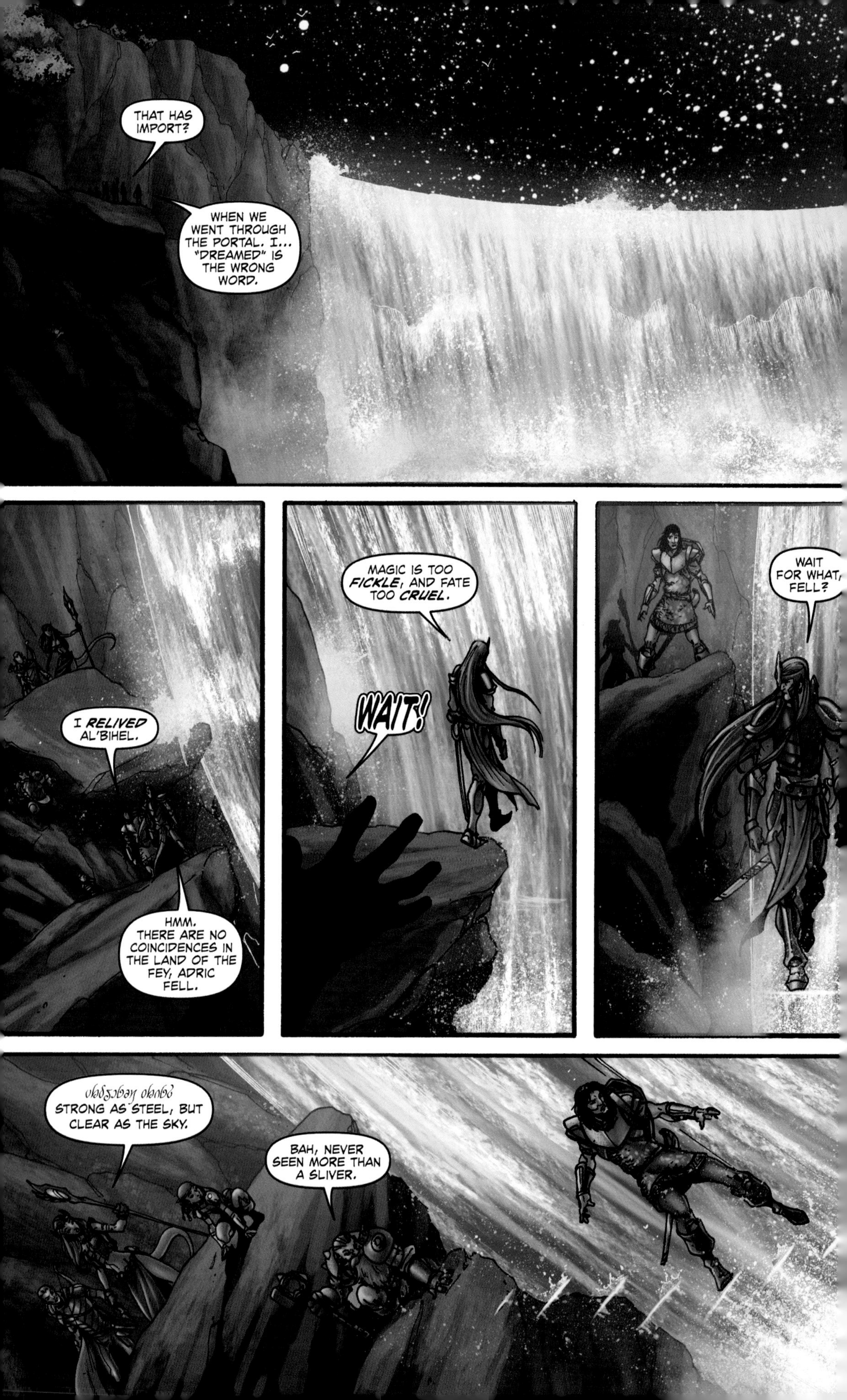
THAT HAS IMPORT?
WHEN WE WENT THROUGH THE PORTAL. I... "DREAMED" IS THE WRONG WORD.
I RELIVED AL'BIHEL.
HMM. THERE ARE NO COINCIDENCES IN THE LAND OF THE FEY, ADRIC FELL.
MAGIC IS TOO FICKLE, AND FATE TOO CRUEL.
WAIT!
WAIT FOR WHAT, FELL?
STRONG AS STEEL, BUT CLEAR AS THE SKY.
BAH, NEVER SEEN MORE THAN A SLIVER.

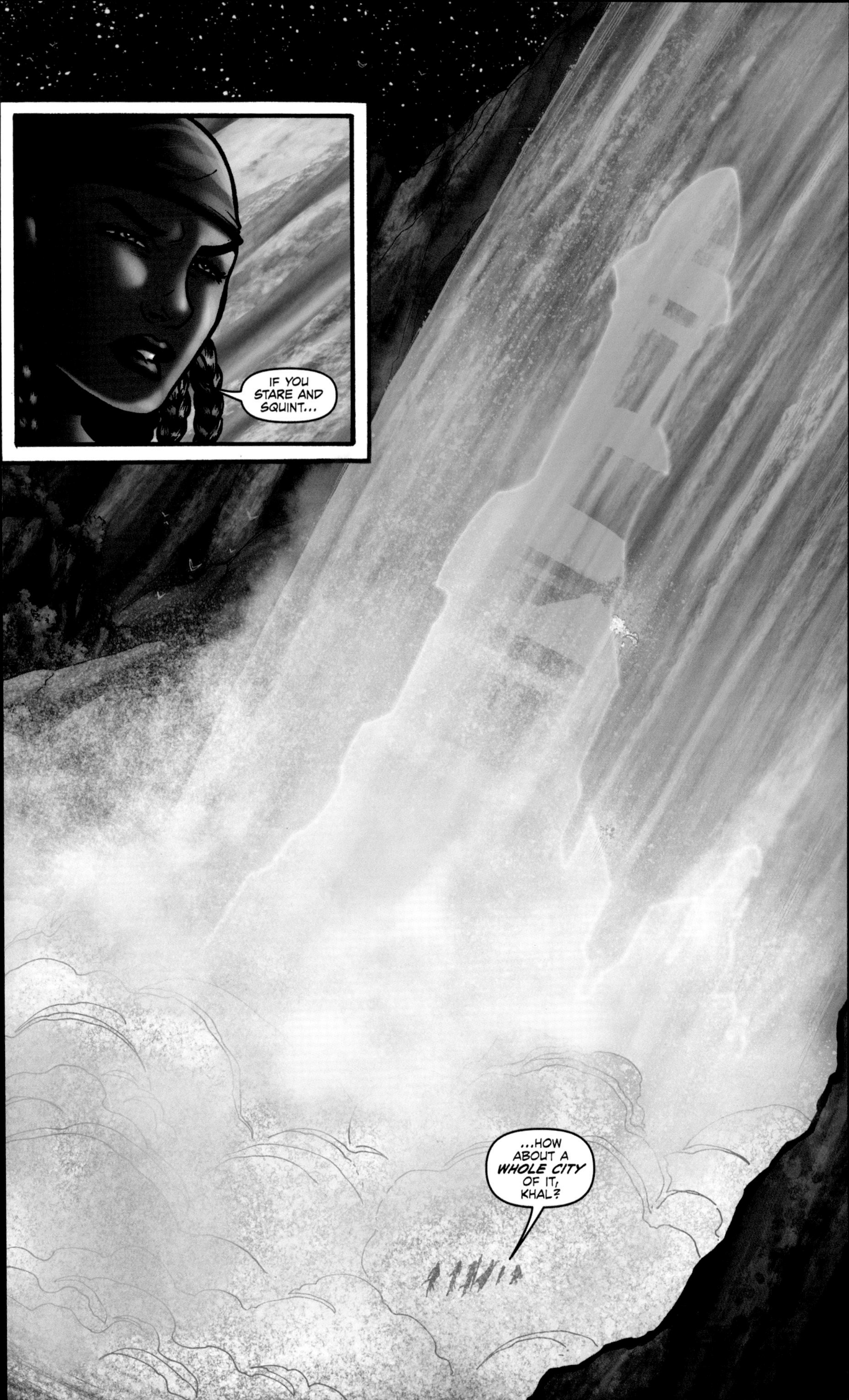
IF YOU
STARE AND
SQUINT...
...HOW
ABOUT A
WHOLE CITY
OF IT,
KHAL?

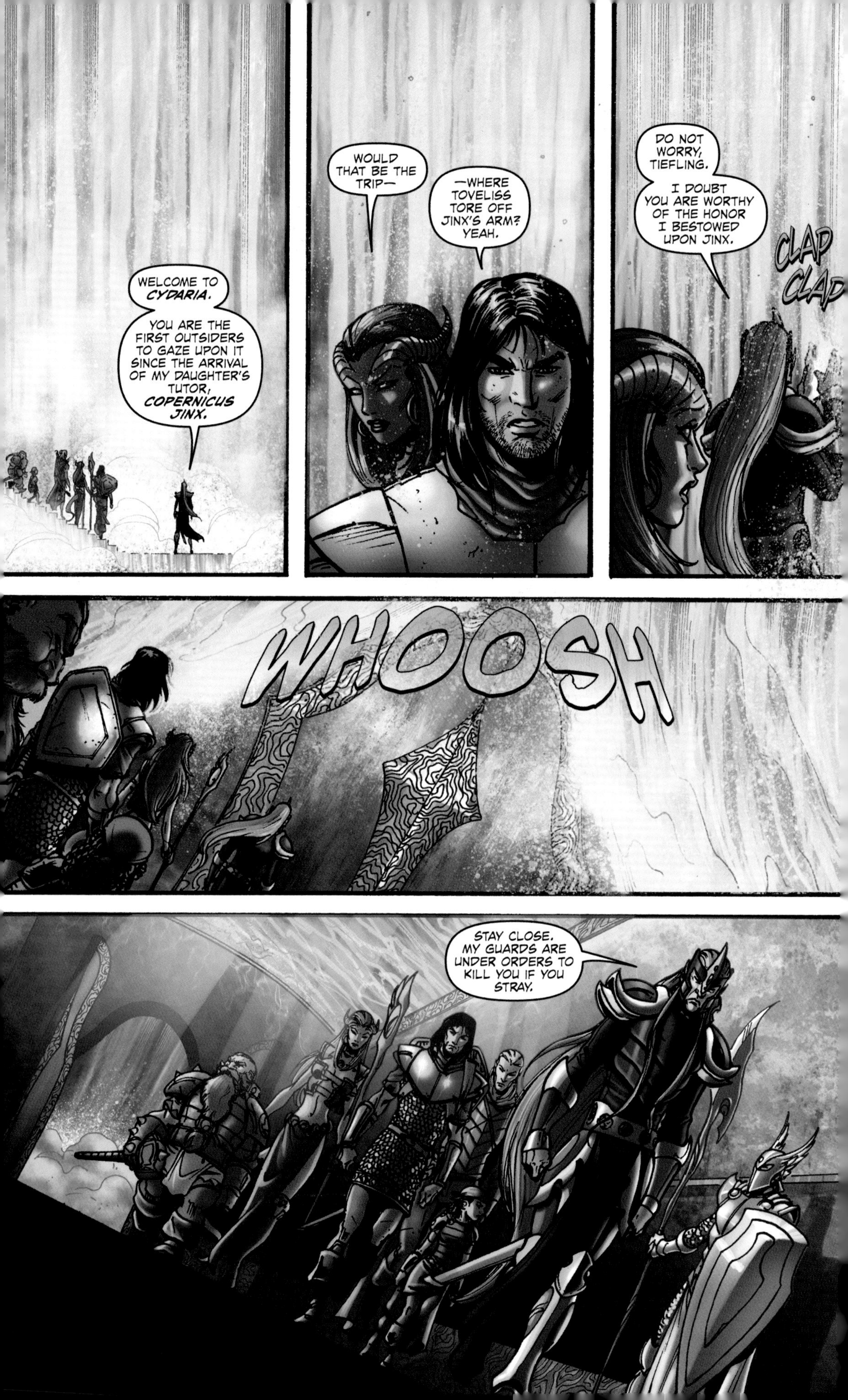
WELCOME TO CYDARIA.
YOU ARE THE FIRST OUTSIDERS TO GAZE UPON IT SINCE THE ARRIVAL OF MY DAUGHTER'S TUTOR, COPERNICUS JINX.
WOULD THAT BE THE TRIP—
—WHERE TOVELISS TORE OFF JINX'S ARM? YEAH.
DO NOT WORRY, TIEFLING.
I DOUBT YOU ARE WORTHY OF THE HONOR I BESTOWED UPON JINX.
CLAP CLAP
WHOOSH
STAY CLOSE. MY GUARDS ARE UNDER ORDERS TO KILL YOU IF YOU STRAY.

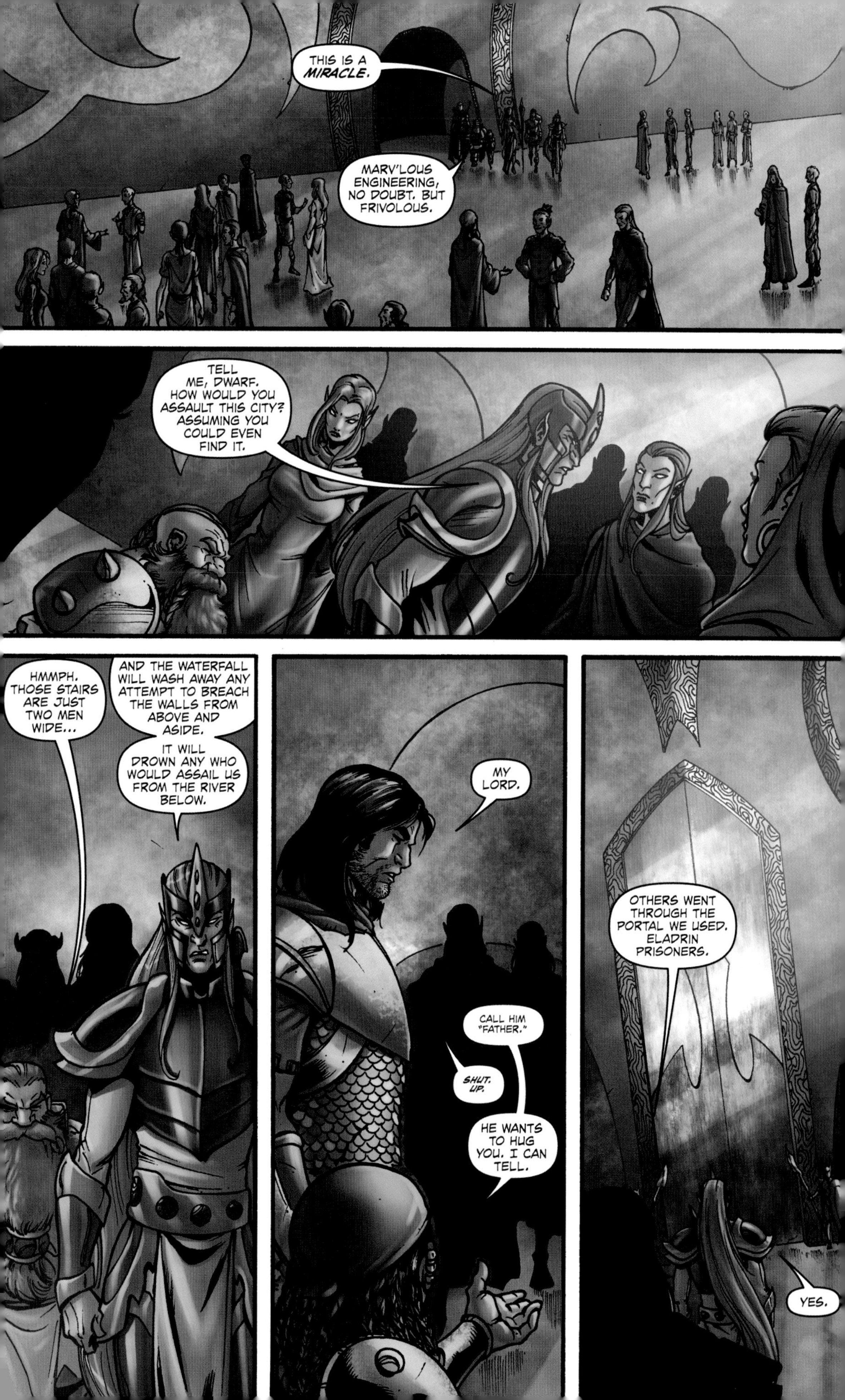
THIS IS A *MIRACLE*.
MARV'LOUS ENGINEERING, NO DOUBT. BUT FRIVOLOUS.
TELL ME, DWARF. HOW WOULD YOU ASSAULT THIS CITY? ASSUMING YOU COULD EVEN FIND IT.
HMMPH. THOSE STAIRS ARE JUST TWO MEN WIDE...
AND THE WATERFALL WILL WASH AWAY ANY ATTEMPT TO BREACH THE WALLS FROM ABOVE AND ASIDE.
IT WILL DROWN ANY WHO WOULD ASSAIL US FROM THE RIVER BELOW.
MY LORD.
CALL HIM "FATHER."
SHUT. UP.
HE WANTS TO HUG YOU. I CAN TELL.
OTHERS WENT THROUGH THE PORTAL WE USED. ELADRIN PRISONERS.
YES.

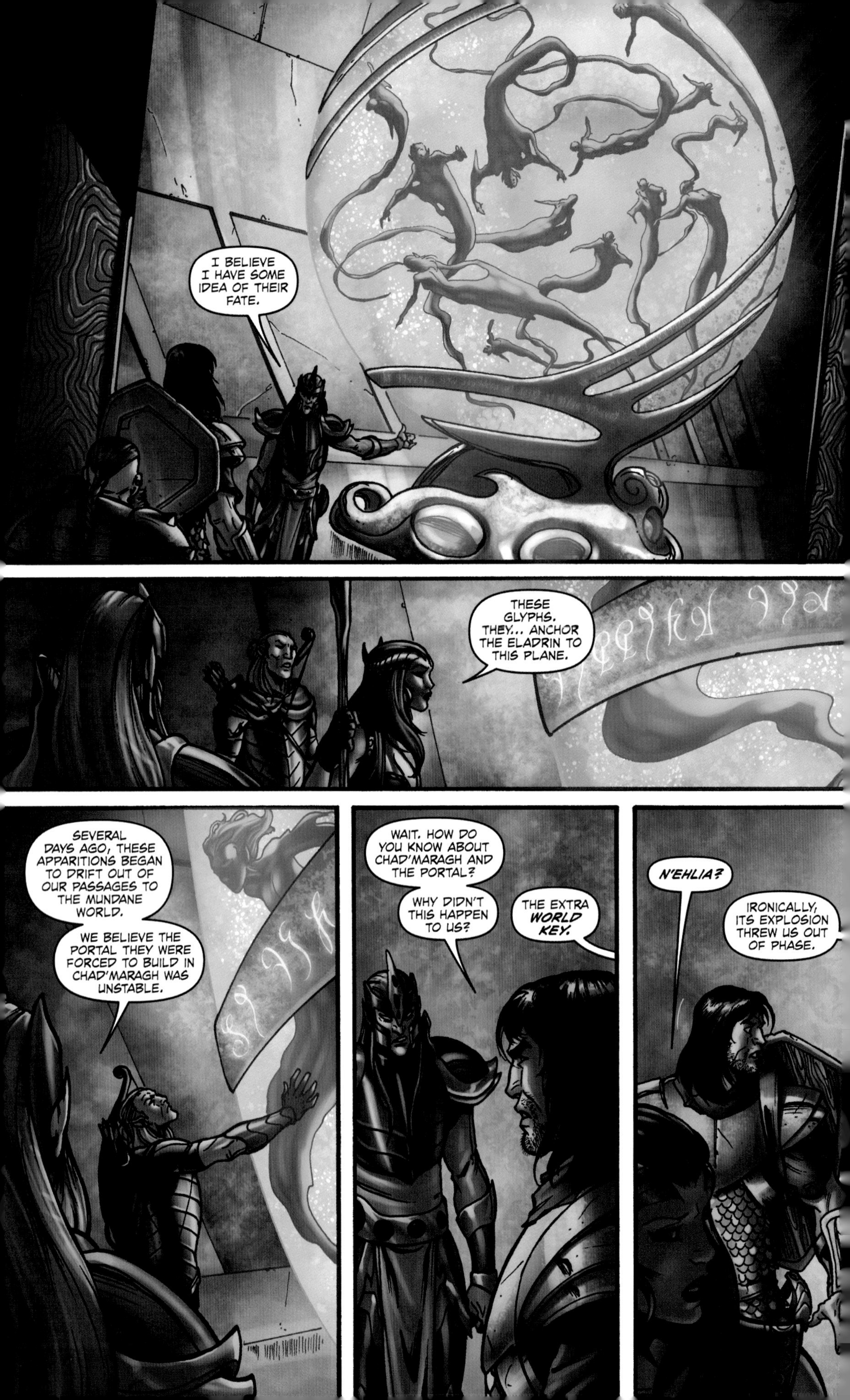
I BELIEVE I HAVE SOME IDEA OF THEIR FATE.
THESE GLYPHS. THEY... ANCHOR THE ELADRIN TO THIS PLANE.
SEVERAL DAYS AGO, THESE APPARITIONS BEGAN TO DRIFT OUT OF OUR PASSAGES TO THE MUNDANE WORLD.
WE BELIEVE THE PORTAL THEY WERE FORCED TO BUILD IN CHAD'MARAGH WAS UNSTABLE.
WAIT. HOW DO YOU KNOW ABOUT CHAD'MARAGH AND THE PORTAL?
WHY DIDN'T THIS HAPPEN TO US?
THE EXTRA *WORLD KEY.*
N'EHLIA?
IRONICALLY, ITS EXPLOSION THREW US OUT OF PHASE.

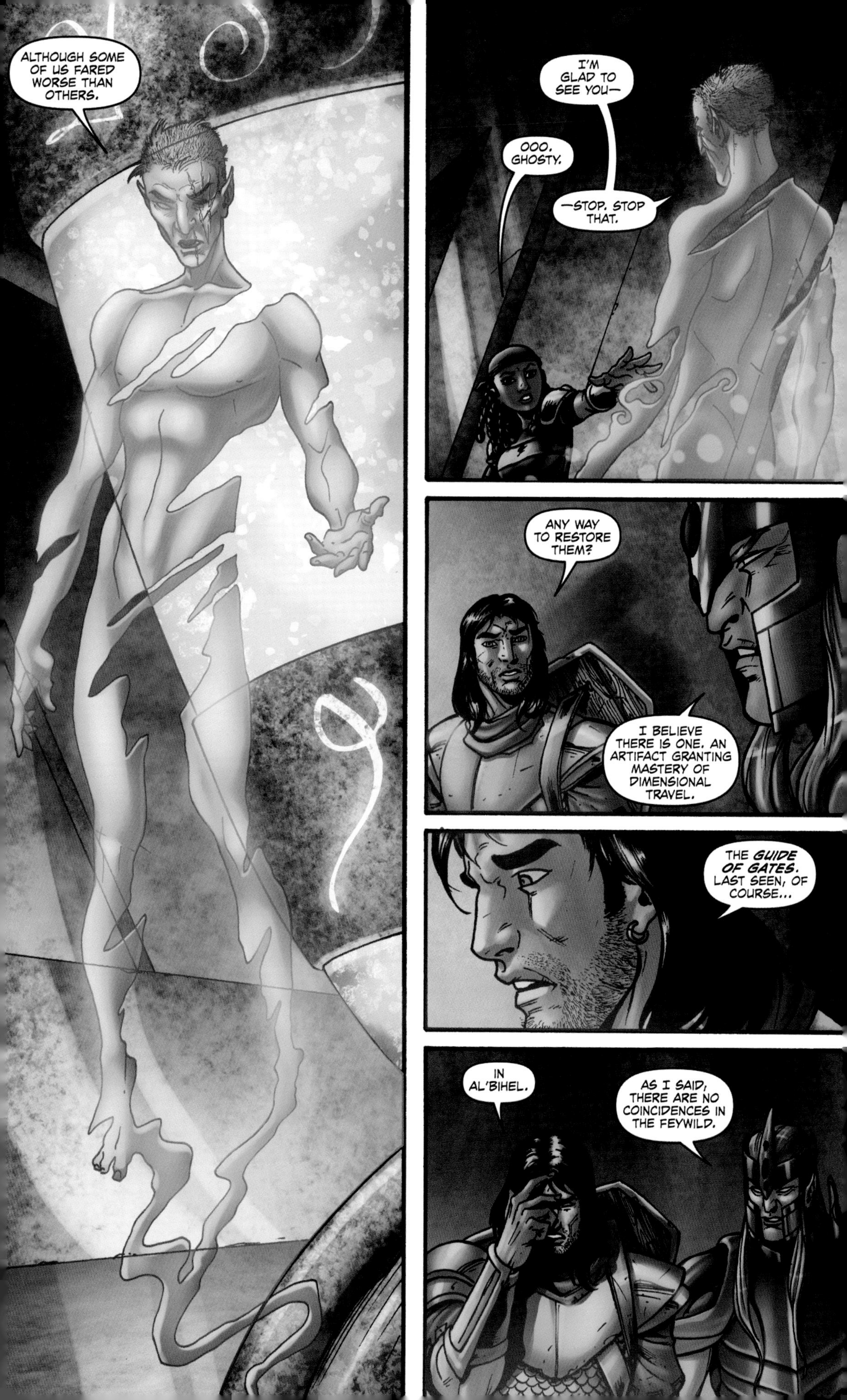
ALTHOUGH SOME OF US FARED WORSE THAN OTHERS.
I'M GLAD TO SEE YOU—
OOO. GHOSTY.
—STOP. STOP THAT.
ANY WAY TO RESTORE THEM?
I BELIEVE THERE IS ONE. AN ARTIFACT GRANTING MASTERY OF DIMENSIONAL TRAVEL.
THE *GUIDE OF GATES*. LAST SEEN, OF COURSE...
IN AL'BIHEL.
AS I SAID, THERE ARE NO COINCIDENCES IN THE FEYWILD.

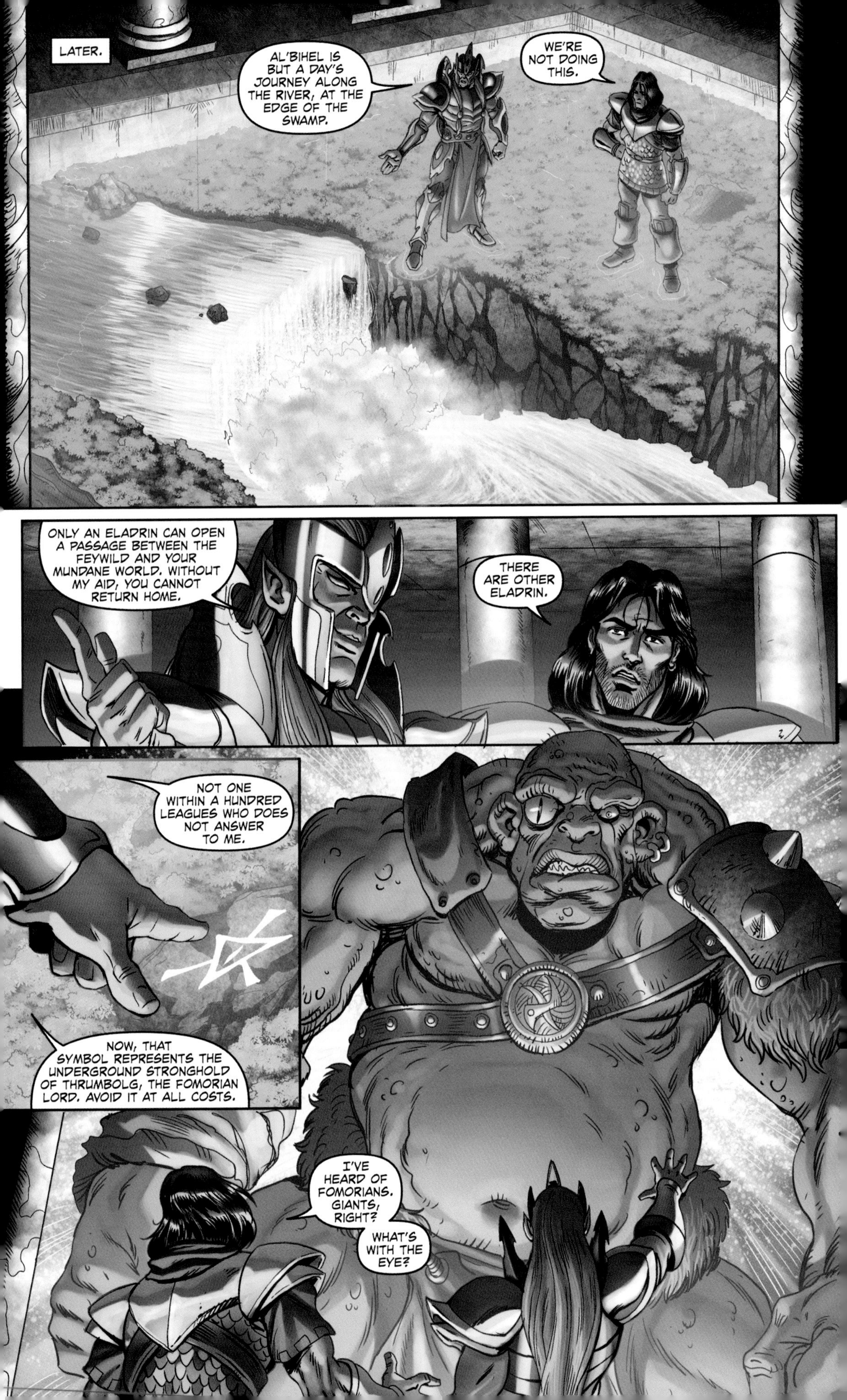
LATER.
AL'BIHEL IS BUT A DAY'S JOURNEY ALONG THE RIVER, AT THE EDGE OF THE SWAMP.
WE'RE NOT DOING THIS.
ONLY AN ELADRIN CAN OPEN A PASSAGE BETWEEN THE FEYWILD AND YOUR MUNDANE WORLD. WITHOUT MY AID, YOU CANNOT RETURN HOME.
THERE ARE OTHER ELADRIN.
NOT ONE WITHIN A HUNDRED LEAGUES WHO DOES NOT ANSWER TO ME.
NOW, THAT SYMBOL REPRESENTS THE UNDERGROUND STRONGHOLD OF THRUMBOLG, THE FOMORIAN LORD. AVOID IT AT ALL COSTS.
I'VE HEARD OF FOMORIANS. GIANTS, RIGHT?
WHAT'S WITH THE EYE?

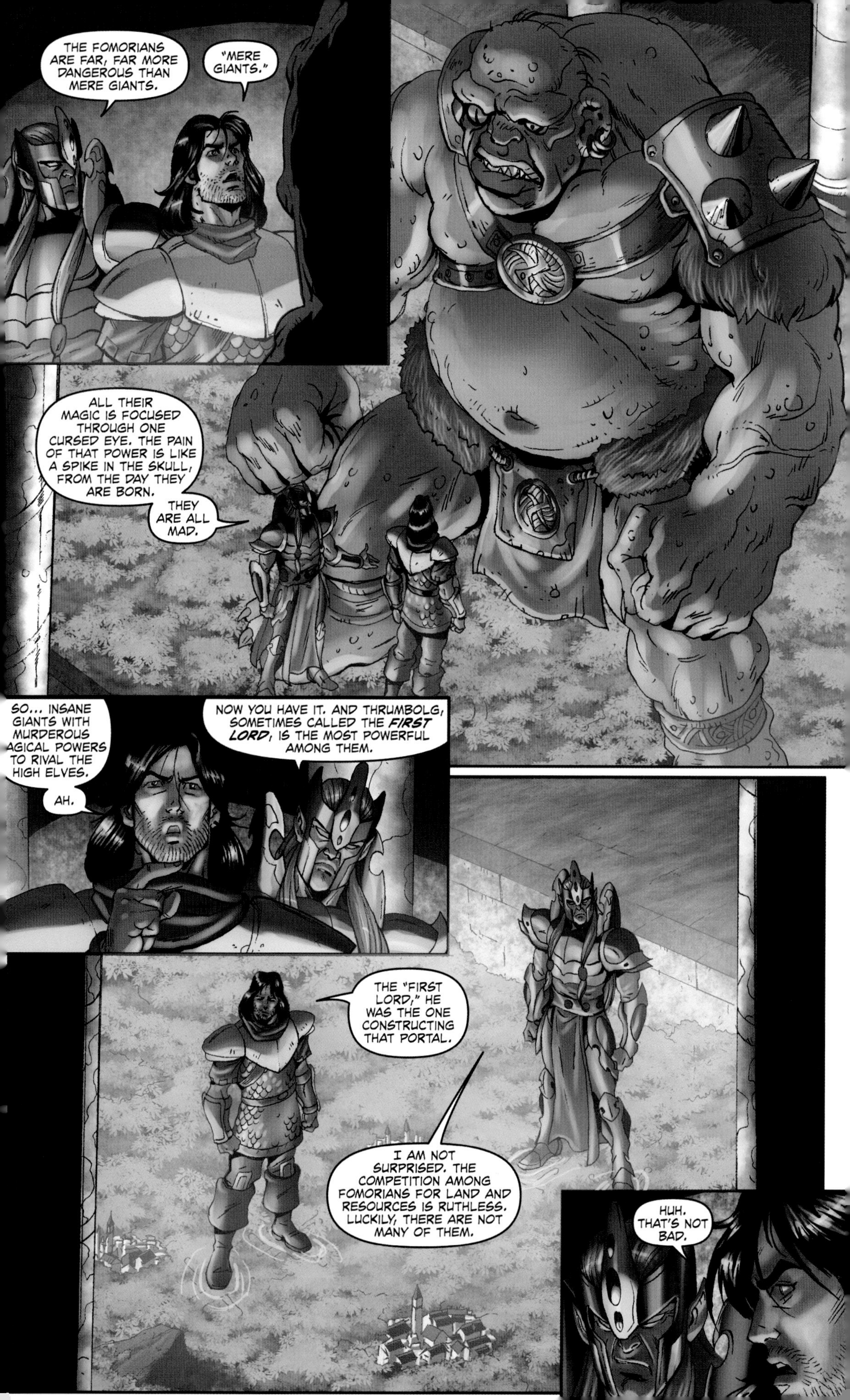
THE FOMORIANS ARE FAR, FAR MORE DANGEROUS THAN MERE GIANTS.
"MERE GIANTS."
ALL THEIR MAGIC IS FOCUSED THROUGH ONE CURSED EYE. THE PAIN OF THAT POWER IS LIKE A SPIKE IN THE SKULL, FROM THE DAY THEY ARE BORN.
THEY ARE ALL MAD.
SO... INSANE GIANTS WITH MURDEROUS AGICAL POWERS TO RIVAL THE HIGH ELVES.
AH.
NOW YOU HAVE IT. AND THRUMBOLG, SOMETIMES CALLED THE FIRST LORD, IS THE MOST POWERFUL AMONG THEM.
THE "FIRST LORD," HE WAS THE ONE CONSTRUCTING THAT PORTAL.
I AM NOT SURPRISED. THE COMPETITION AMONG FOMORIANS FOR LAND AND RESOURCES IS RUTHLESS. LUCKILY, THERE ARE NOT MANY OF THEM.
HUH. THAT'S NOT BAD.

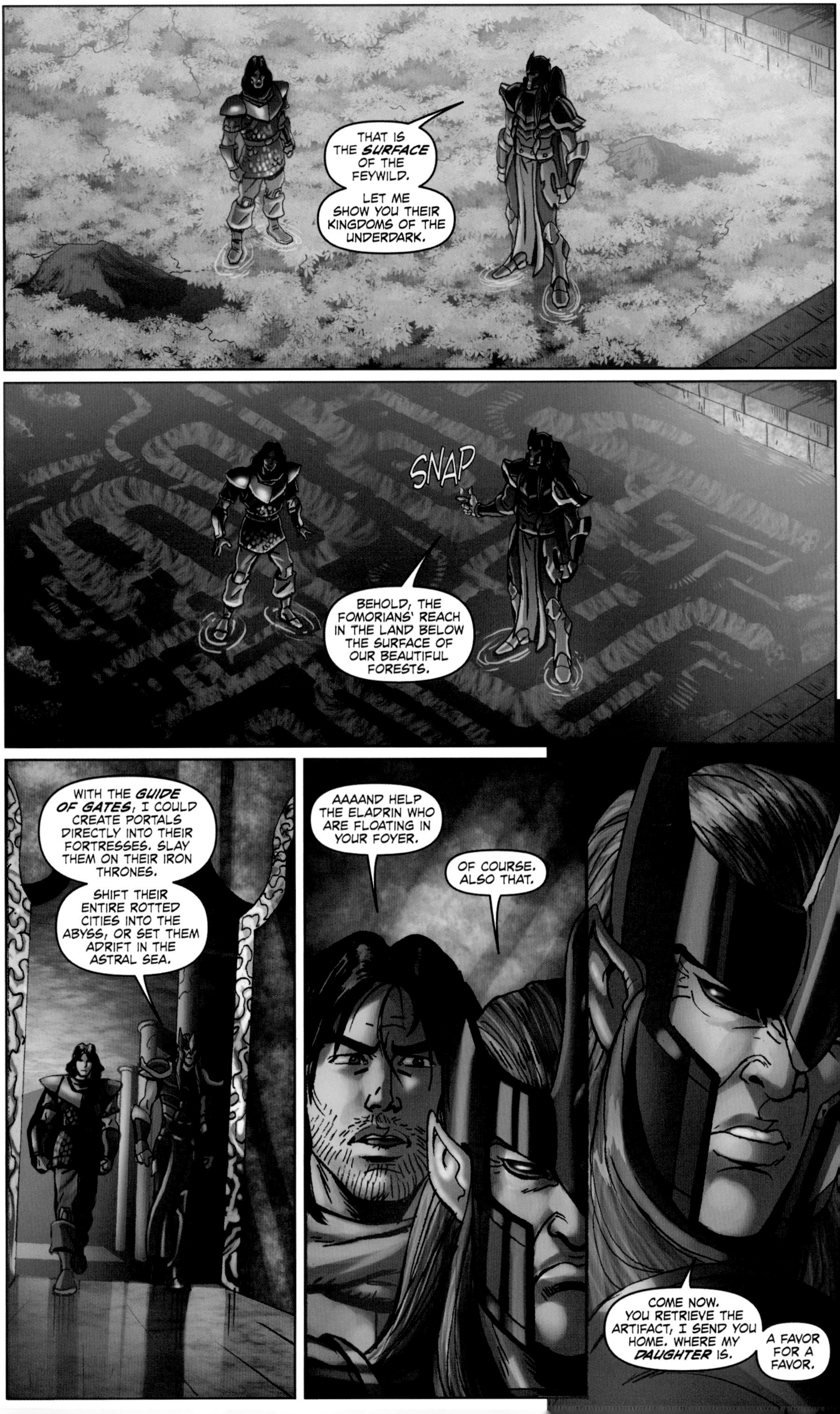
THAT IS THE SURFACE OF THE FEYWILD.
LET ME SHOW YOU THEIR KINGDOMS OF THE UNDERDARK.
SNAP
BEHOLD, THE FOMORIANS' REACH IN THE LAND BELOW THE SURFACE OF OUR BEAUTIFUL FORESTS.
WITH THE GUIDE OF GATES, I COULD CREATE PORTALS DIRECTLY INTO THEIR FORTRESSES. SLAY THEM ON THEIR IRON THRONES.
SHIFT THEIR ENTIRE ROTTED CITIES INTO THE ABYSS, OR SET THEM ADRIFT IN THE ASTRAL SEA.
AAAAND HELP THE ELADRIN WHO ARE FLOATING IN YOUR FOYER.
OF COURSE. ALSO THAT.
COME NOW. YOU RETRIEVE THE ARTIFACT, I SEND YOU HOME. WHERE MY DAUGHTER IS.
A FAVOR FOR A FAVOR.

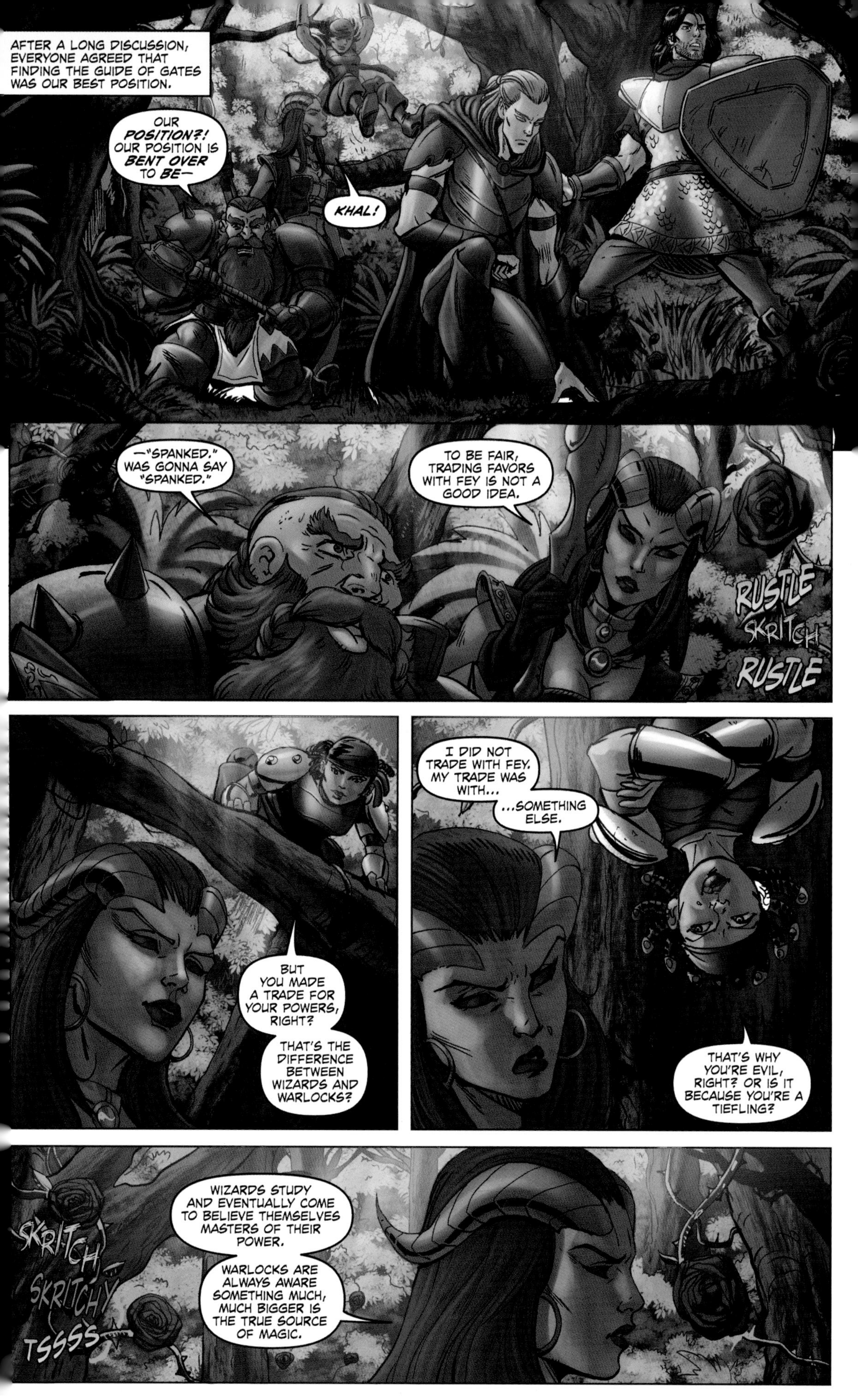
AFTER A LONG DISCUSSION, EVERYONE AGREED THAT FINDING THE GUIDE OF GATES WAS OUR BEST POSITION.
OUR *POSITION?!* OUR POSITION IS *BENT OVER* TO *BE*—
KHAL!
—"SPANKED." WAS GONNA SAY "SPANKED."
TO BE FAIR, TRADING FAVORS WITH FEY IS NOT A GOOD IDEA.
RUSTLE
SKRITCH
RUSTLE
BUT YOU MADE A TRADE FOR YOUR POWERS, RIGHT?
THAT'S THE DIFFERENCE BETWEEN WIZARDS AND WARLOCKS?
I DID NOT TRADE WITH FEY. MY TRADE WAS WITH...
...SOMETHING ELSE.
THAT'S WHY YOU'RE EVIL, RIGHT? OR IS IT BECAUSE YOU'RE A TIEFLING?
SKRITCH
SKRITCH
TSSSS
WIZARDS STUDY AND EVENTUALLY COME TO BELIEVE THEMSELVES MASTERS OF THEIR POWER.
WARLOCKS ARE ALWAYS AWARE SOMETHING MUCH, MUCH BIGGER IS THE TRUE SOURCE OF MAGIC.

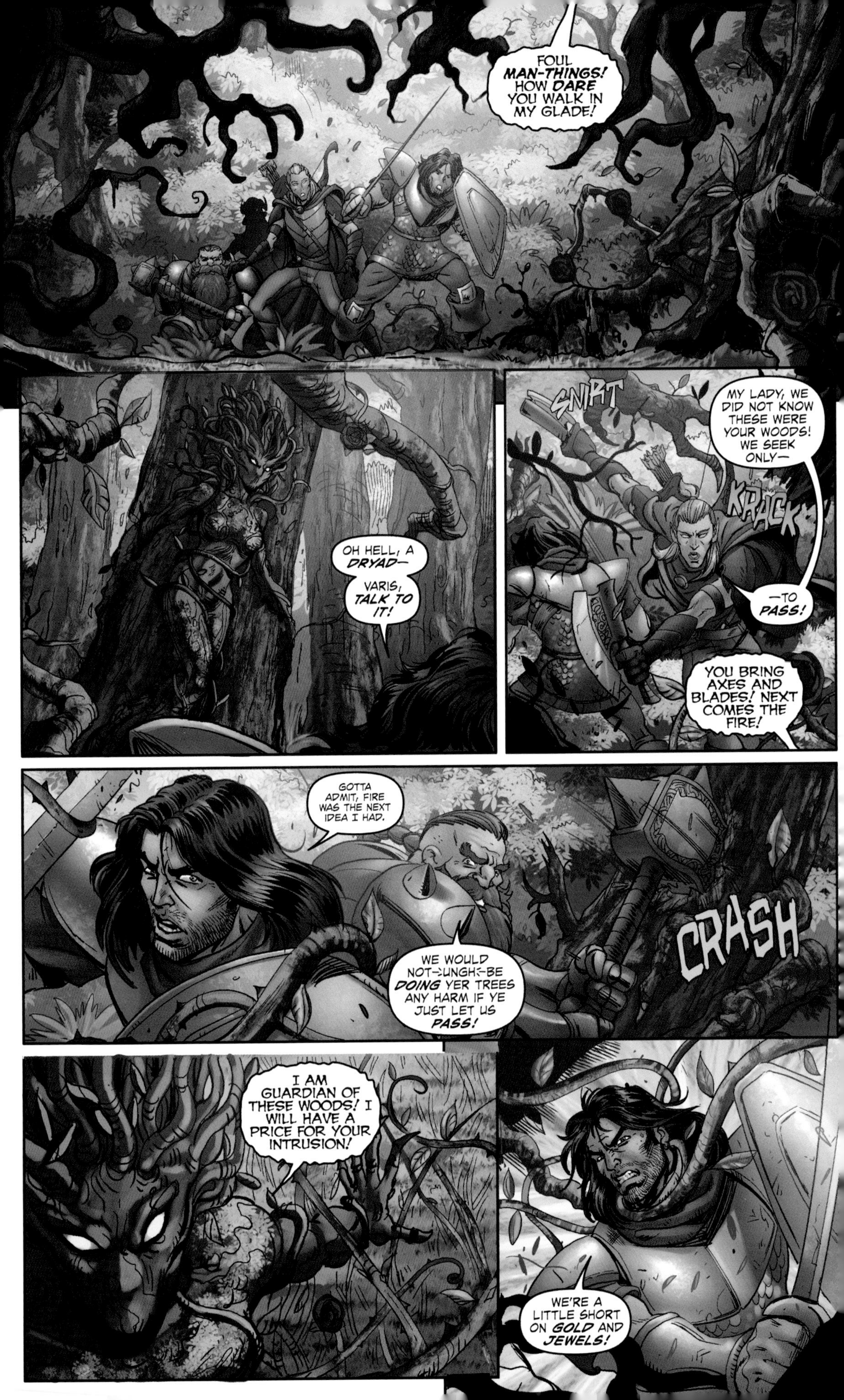
FOUL MAN-THINGS! HOW DARE YOU WALK IN MY GLADE!
OH HELL, A DRYAD—
VARIS, TALK TO IT!
SNIRT
MY LADY, WE DID NOT KNOW THESE WERE YOUR WOODS! WE SEEK ONLY—
KRACK
—TO PASS!
YOU BRING AXES AND BLADES! NEXT COMES THE FIRE!
GOTTA ADMIT, FIRE WAS THE NEXT IDEA I HAD.
WE WOULD NOT—UNGH—BE DOING YER TREES ANY HARM IF YE JUST LET US PASS!
CRASH
I AM GUARDIAN OF THESE WOODS! I WILL HAVE A PRICE FOR YOUR INTRUSION!
WE'RE A LITTLE SHORT ON GOLD AND JEWELS!

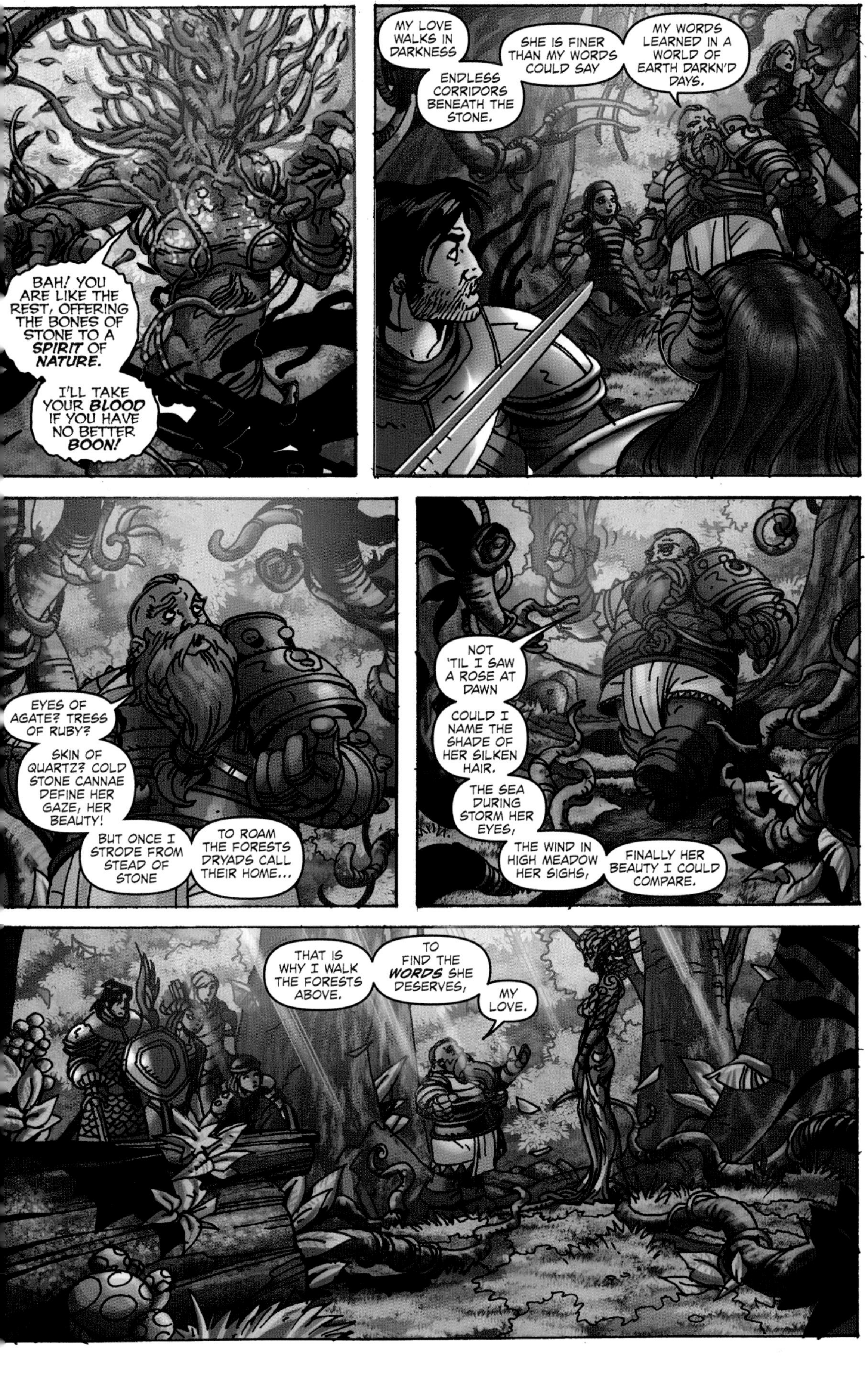
BAH! YOU ARE LIKE THE REST, OFFERING THE BONES OF STONE TO A SPIRIT OF NATURE.
I'LL TAKE YOUR BLOOD IF YOU HAVE NO BETTER BOON!
MY LOVE WALKS IN DARKNESS
ENDLESS CORRIDORS BENEATH THE STONE.
SHE IS FINER THAN MY WORDS COULD SAY
MY WORDS LEARNED IN A WORLD OF EARTH DARKN'D DAYS.
EYES OF AGATE? TRESS OF RUBY?
SKIN OF QUARTZ? COLD STONE CANNAE DEFINE HER GAZE, HER BEAUTY!
BUT ONCE I STRODE FROM STEAD OF STONE
TO ROAM THE FORESTS DRYADS CALL THEIR HOME...
NOT 'TIL I SAW A ROSE AT DAWN
COULD I NAME THE SHADE OF HER SILKEN HAIR.
THE SEA DURING STORM HER EYES,
THE WIND IN HIGH MEADOW HER SIGHS,
FINALLY HER BEAUTY I COULD COMPARE.
THAT IS WHY I WALK THE FORESTS ABOVE.
TO FIND THE WORDS SHE DESERVES,
MY LOVE.

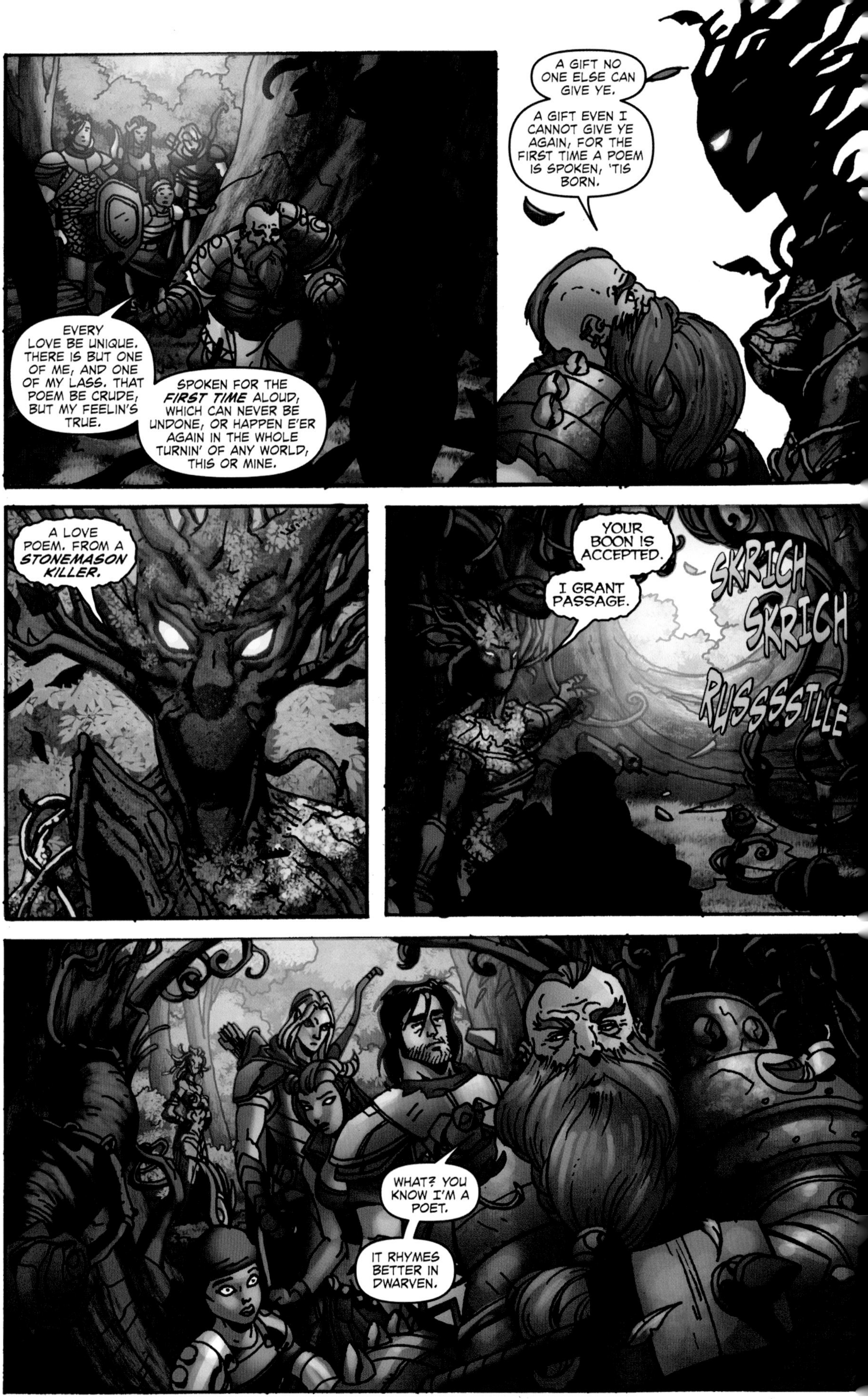

EVERY LOVE BE UNIQUE. THERE IS BUT ONE OF ME, AND ONE OF MY LASS. THAT POEM BE CRUDE, BUT MY FEELIN'S TRUE.
SPOKEN FOR THE FIRST TIME ALOUD, WHICH CAN NEVER BE UNDONE, OR HAPPEN E'ER AGAIN IN THE WHOLE TURNIN' OF ANY WORLD, THIS OR MINE.
A GIFT NO ONE ELSE CAN GIVE YE.
A GIFT EVEN I CANNOT GIVE YE AGAIN, FOR THE FIRST TIME A POEM IS SPOKEN, 'TIS BORN.
A LOVE POEM. FROM A STONEMASON KILLER.
YOUR BOON IS ACCEPTED.
I GRANT PASSAGE.
SKRICH
SKRICH
RUSSSSTLE
WHAT? YOU KNOW I'M A POET.
IT RHYMES BETTER IN DWARVEN.

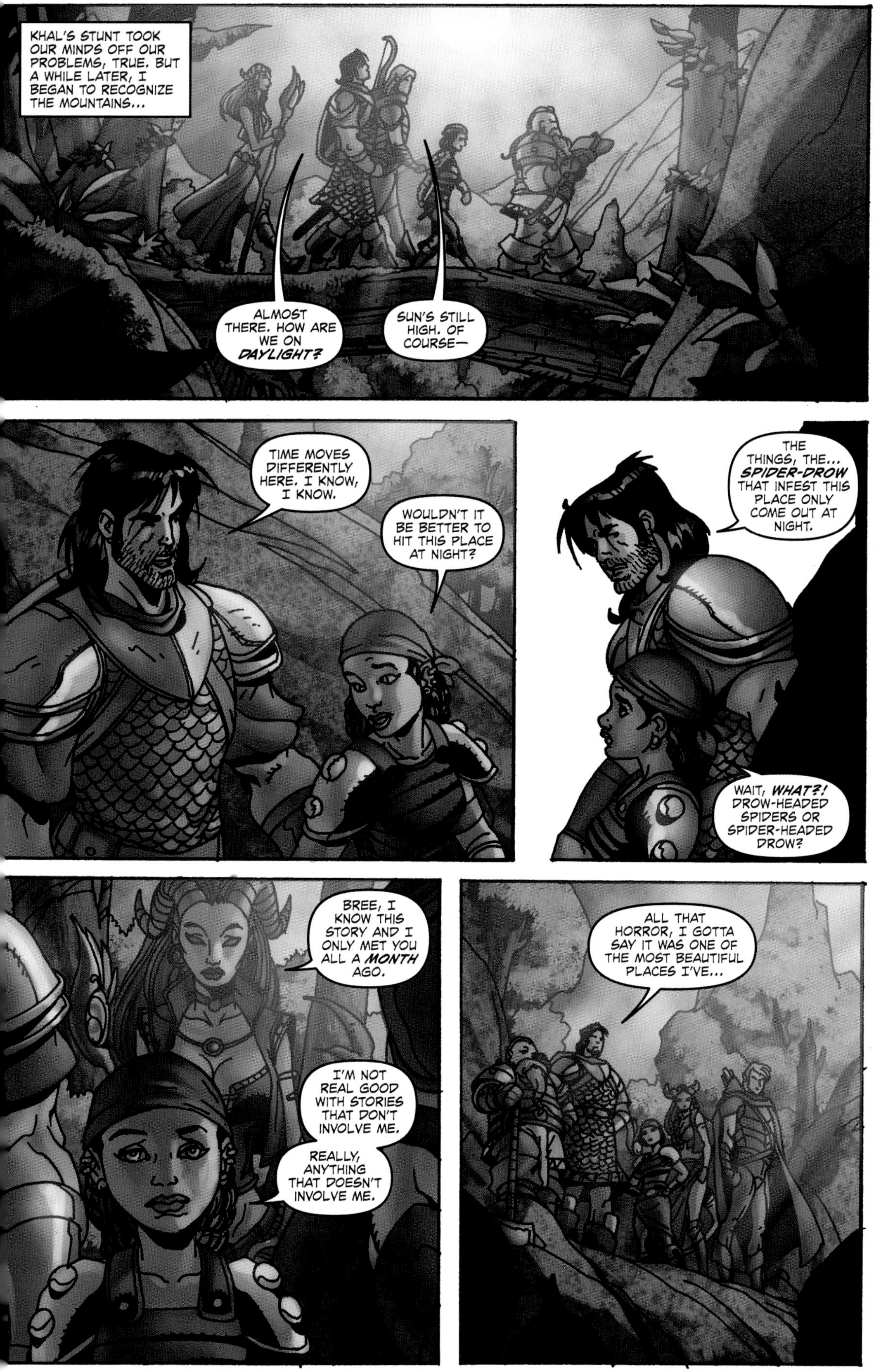
KHAL'S STUNT TOOK OUR MINDS OFF OUR PROBLEMS, TRUE. BUT A WHILE LATER, I BEGAN TO RECOGNIZE THE MOUNTAINS...
ALMOST THERE. HOW ARE WE ON *DAYLIGHT?*
SUN'S STILL HIGH. OF COURSE—
TIME MOVES DIFFERENTLY HERE. I KNOW, I KNOW.
WOULDN'T IT BE BETTER TO HIT THIS PLACE AT NIGHT?
THE THINGS, THE... *SPIDER-DROW* THAT INFEST THIS PLACE ONLY COME OUT AT NIGHT.
WAIT, *WHAT?!* DROW-HEADED SPIDERS OR SPIDER-HEADED DROW?
BREE, I KNOW THIS STORY AND I ONLY MET YOU ALL A *MONTH* AGO.
I'M NOT REAL GOOD WITH STORIES THAT DON'T INVOLVE ME.
REALLY, ANYTHING THAT DOESN'T INVOLVE ME.
ALL THAT HORROR, I GOTTA SAY IT WAS ONE OF THE MOST BEAUTIFUL PLACES I'VE...

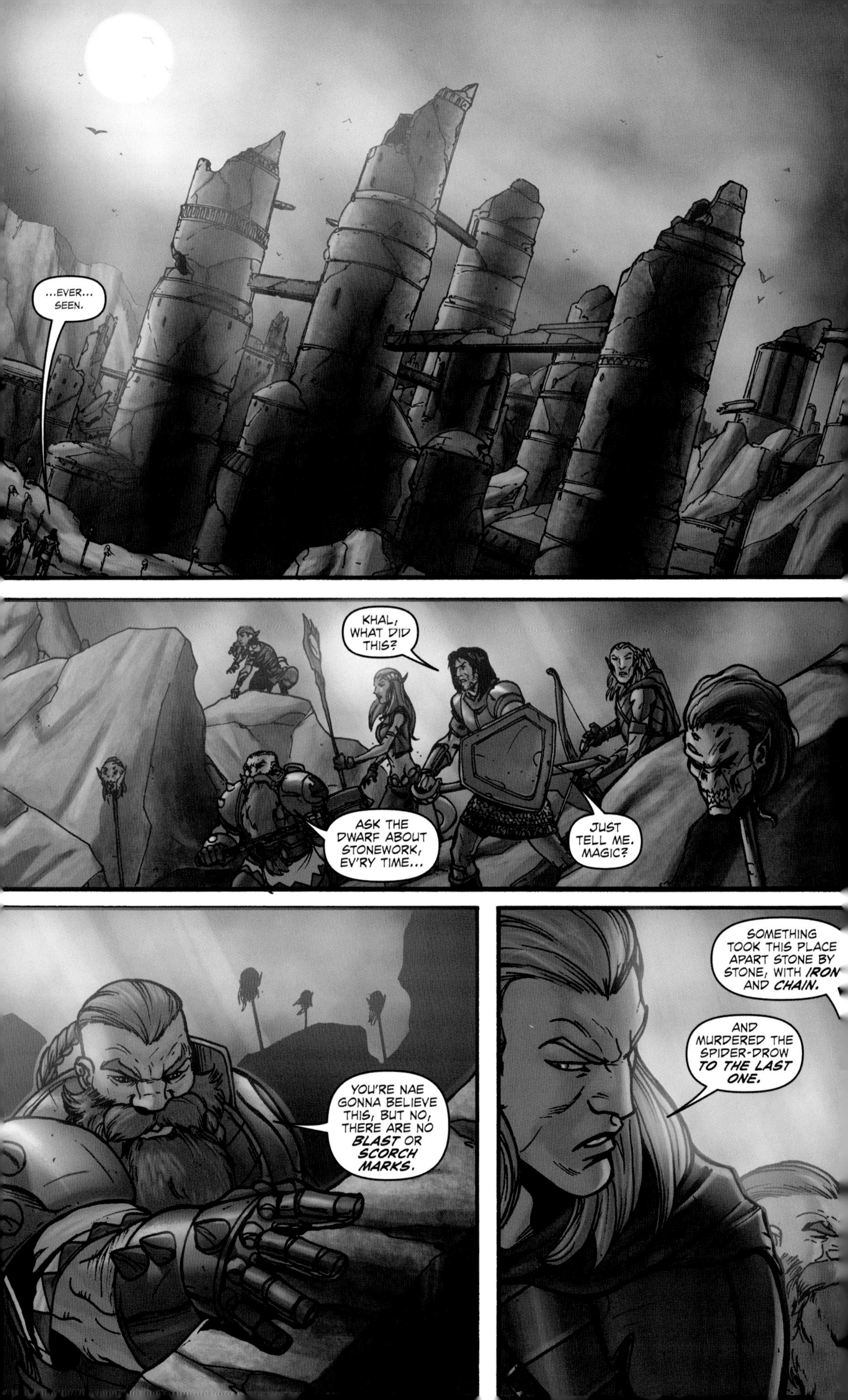
...EVER... SEEN.
KHAL, WHAT DID THIS?
ASK THE DWARF ABOUT STONEWORK, EV'RY TIME...
JUST TELL ME. MAGIC?
YOU'RE NAE GONNA BELIEVE THIS, BUT NO, THERE ARE NO BLAST OR SCORCH MARKS.
SOMETHING TOOK THIS PLACE APART STONE BY STONE, WITH IRON AND CHAIN.
AND MURDERED THE SPIDER-DROW TO THE LAST ONE.

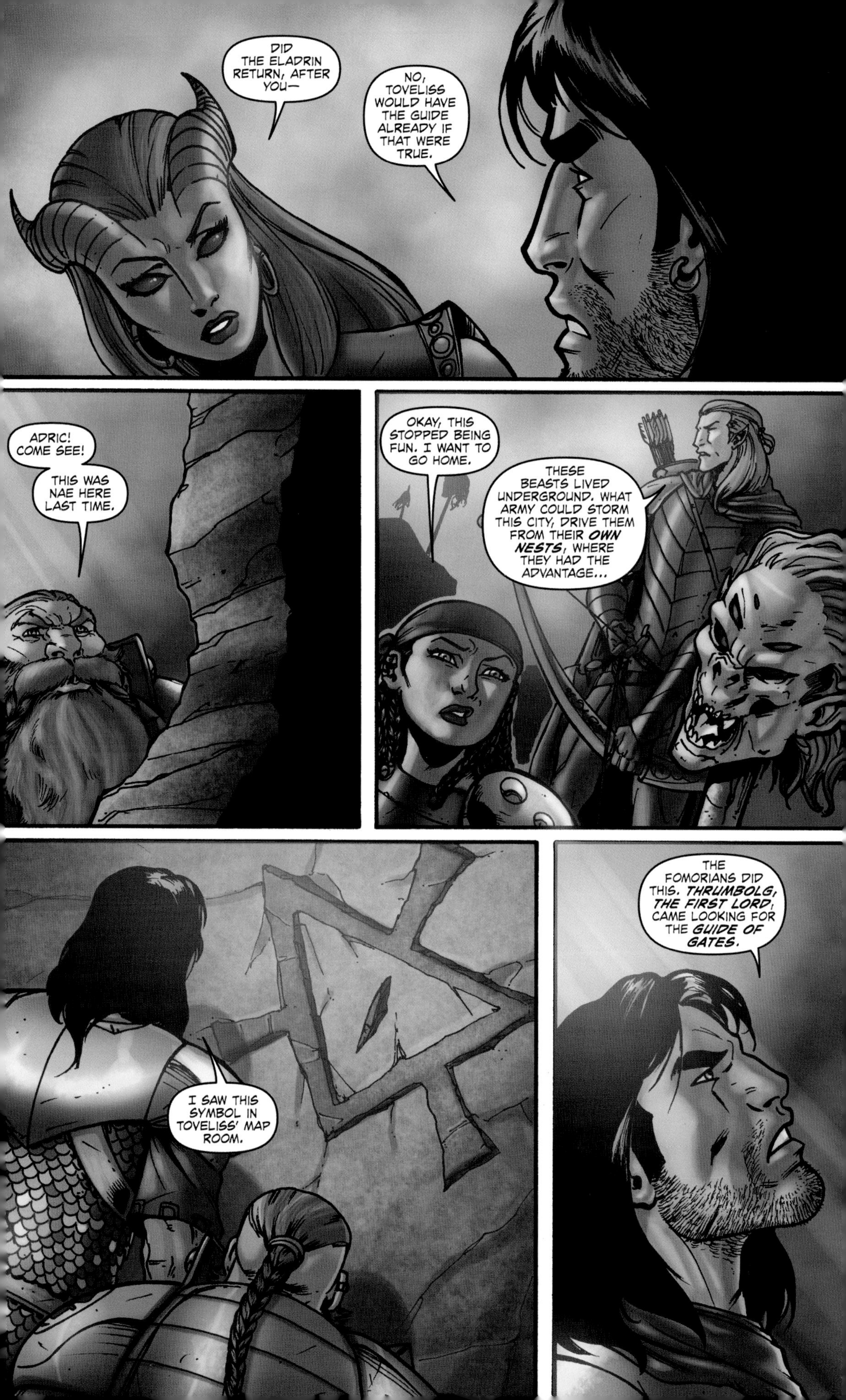

DID THE ELADRIN RETURN, AFTER YOU—
NO, TOVELISS WOULD HAVE THE GUIDE ALREADY IF THAT WERE TRUE.
ADRIC! COME SEE!
THIS WAS NAE HERE LAST TIME.
OKAY, THIS STOPPED BEING FUN. I WANT TO GO HOME.
THESE BEASTS LIVED UNDERGROUND. WHAT ARMY COULD STORM THIS CITY, DRIVE THEM FROM THEIR OWN NESTS, WHERE THEY HAD THE ADVANTAGE...
I SAW THIS SYMBOL IN TOVELISS' MAP ROOM.
THE FOMORIANS DID THIS. THRUMBOLG, THE FIRST LORD, CAME LOOKING FOR THE GUIDE OF GATES.

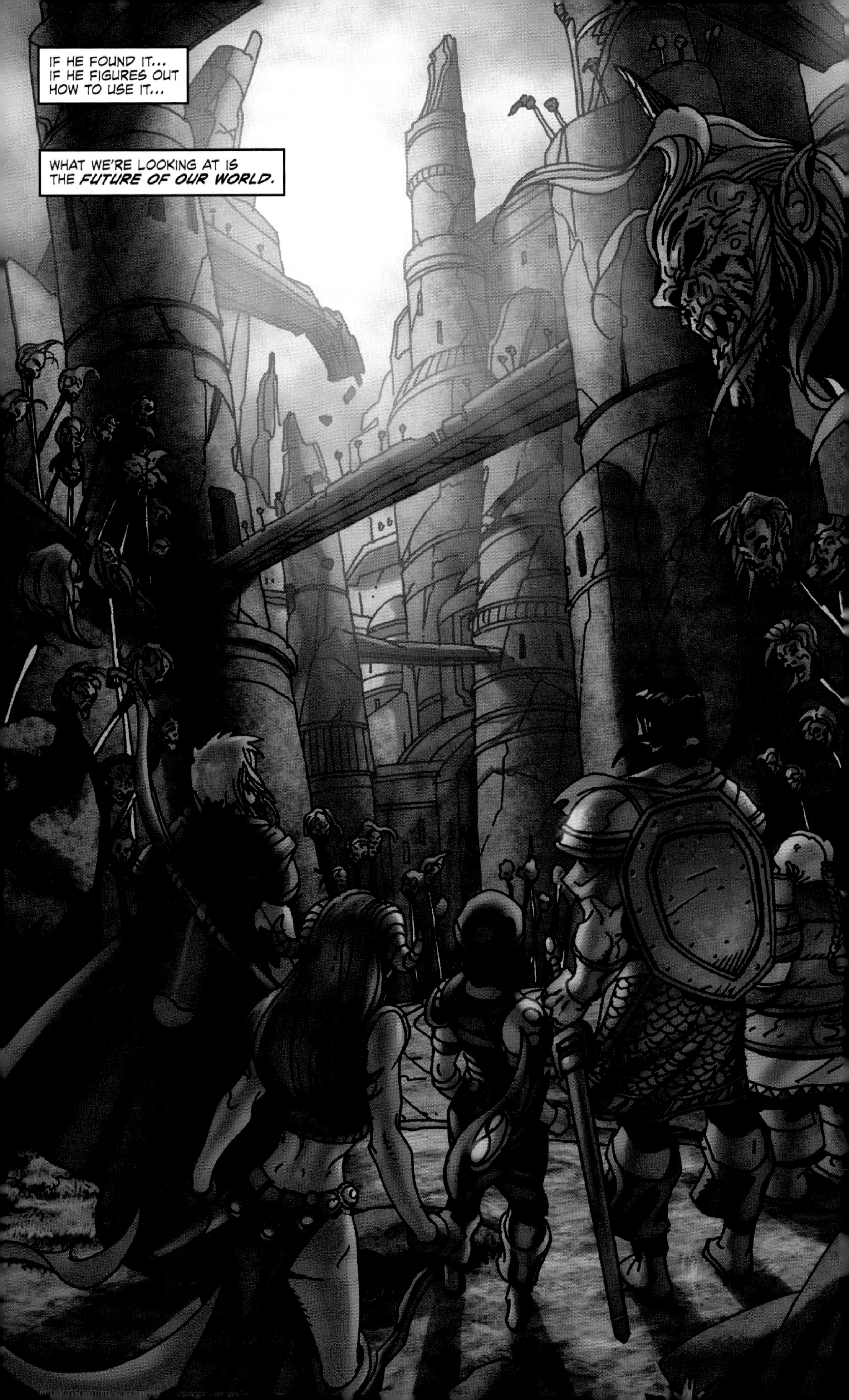
IF HE FOUND IT...
IF HE FIGURES OUT
HOW TO USE IT...
WHAT WE'RE LOOKING AT IS
THE *FUTURE OF OUR WORLD.*

Art by Tyler Walpole

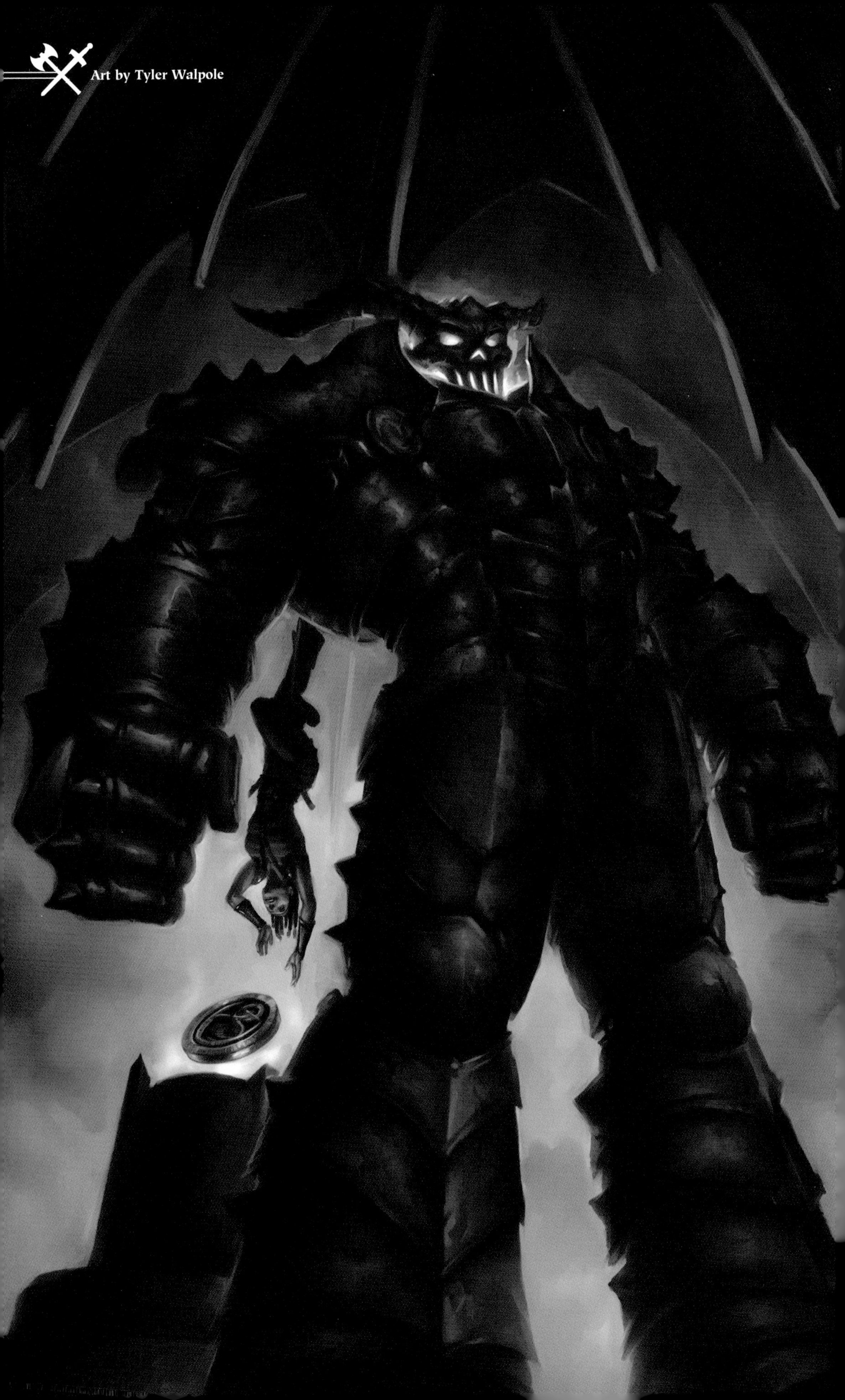

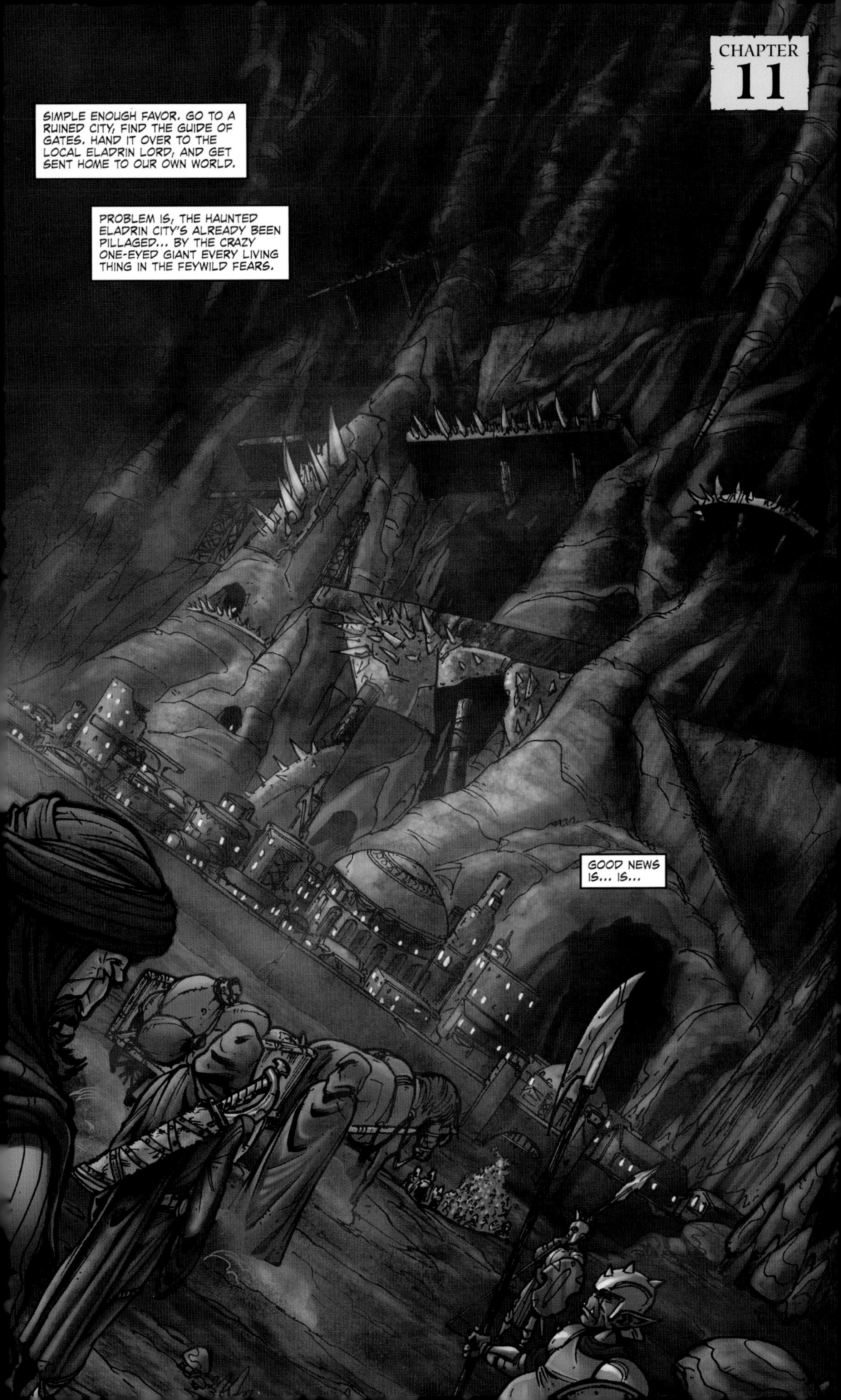
CHAPTER 11
SIMPLE ENOUGH FAVOR. GO TO A RUINED CITY, FIND THE GUIDE OF GATES. HAND IT OVER TO THE LOCAL ELADRIN LORD, AND GET SENT HOME TO OUR OWN WORLD.
PROBLEM IS, THE HAUNTED ELADRIN CITY'S ALREADY BEEN PILLAGED... BY THE CRAZY ONE-EYED GIANT EVERY LIVING THING IN THE FEYWILD FEARS.
GOOD NEWS IS... IS...

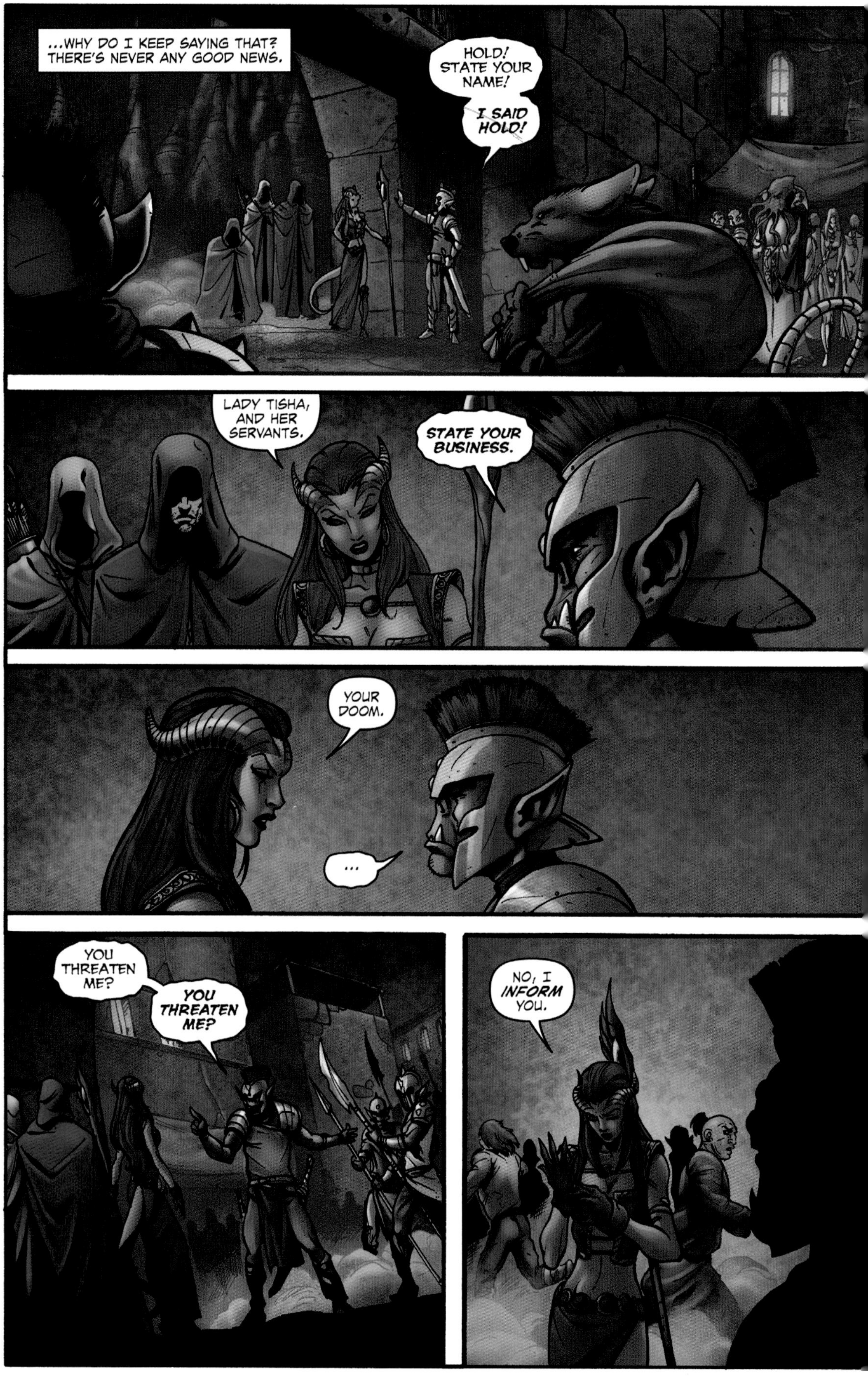
...WHY DO I KEEP SAYING THAT? THERE'S NEVER ANY GOOD NEWS.
HOLD! STATE YOUR NAME!
I SAID HOLD!
LADY TISHA, AND HER SERVANTS.
STATE YOUR BUSINESS.
YOUR DOOM.
...
YOU THREATEN ME?
YOU THREATEN ME?
NO, I INFORM YOU.

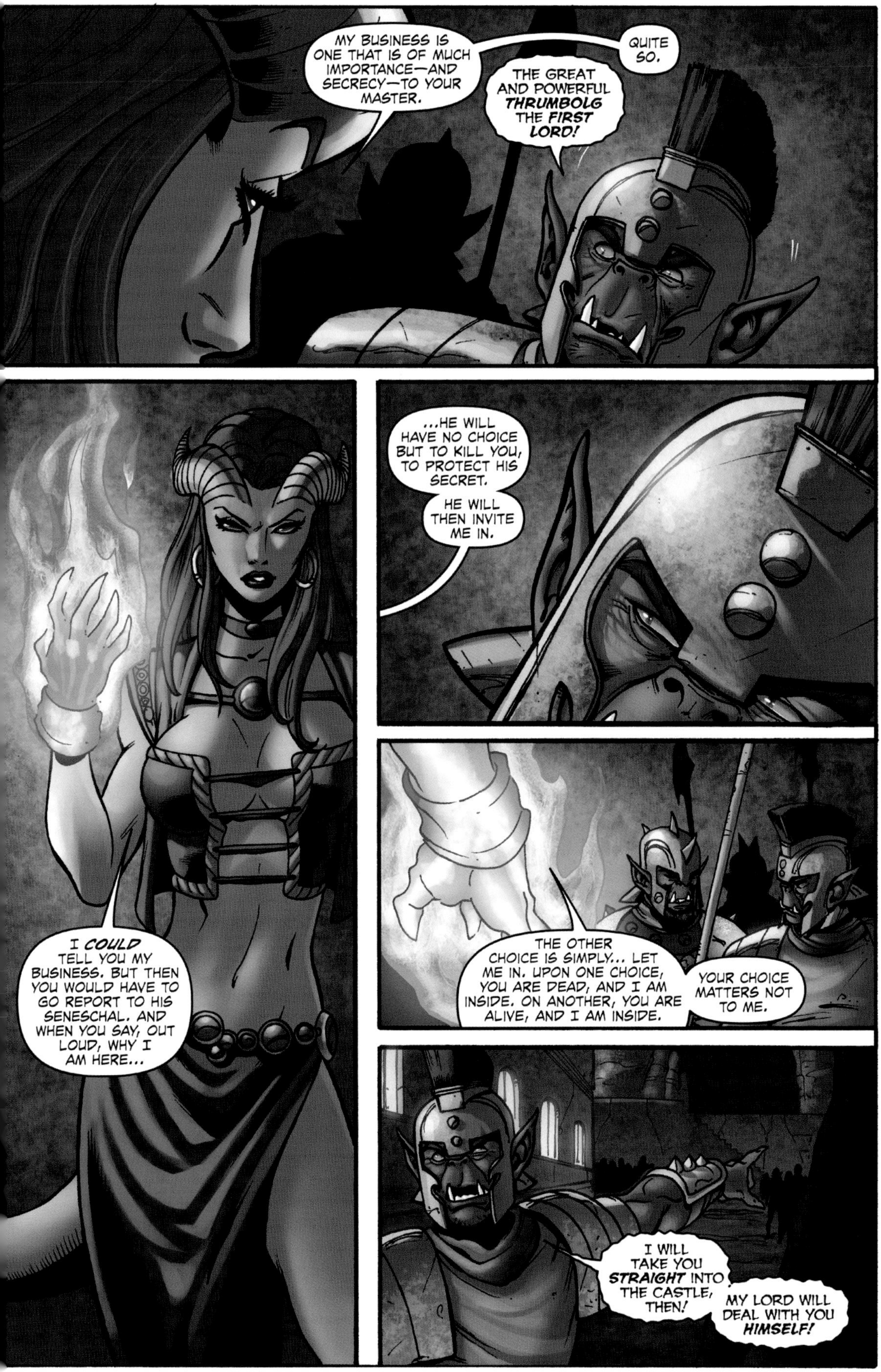

MY BUSINESS IS ONE THAT IS OF MUCH IMPORTANCE—AND SECRECY—TO YOUR MASTER.
QUITE SO.
THE GREAT AND POWERFUL **THRUMBOLG** THE **FIRST LORD!**
I **COULD** TELL YOU MY BUSINESS. BUT THEN YOU WOULD HAVE TO GO REPORT TO HIS SENESCHAL. AND WHEN YOU SAY, OUT LOUD, WHY I AM HERE...
...HE WILL HAVE NO CHOICE BUT TO KILL YOU, TO PROTECT HIS SECRET.
HE WILL THEN INVITE ME IN.
THE OTHER CHOICE IS SIMPLY... LET ME IN. UPON ONE CHOICE, YOU ARE DEAD, AND I AM INSIDE. ON ANOTHER, YOU ARE ALIVE, AND I AM INSIDE.
YOUR CHOICE MATTERS NOT TO ME.
I WILL TAKE YOU **STRAIGHT** INTO THE CASTLE, THEN!
MY LORD WILL DEAL WITH YOU **HIMSELF!**

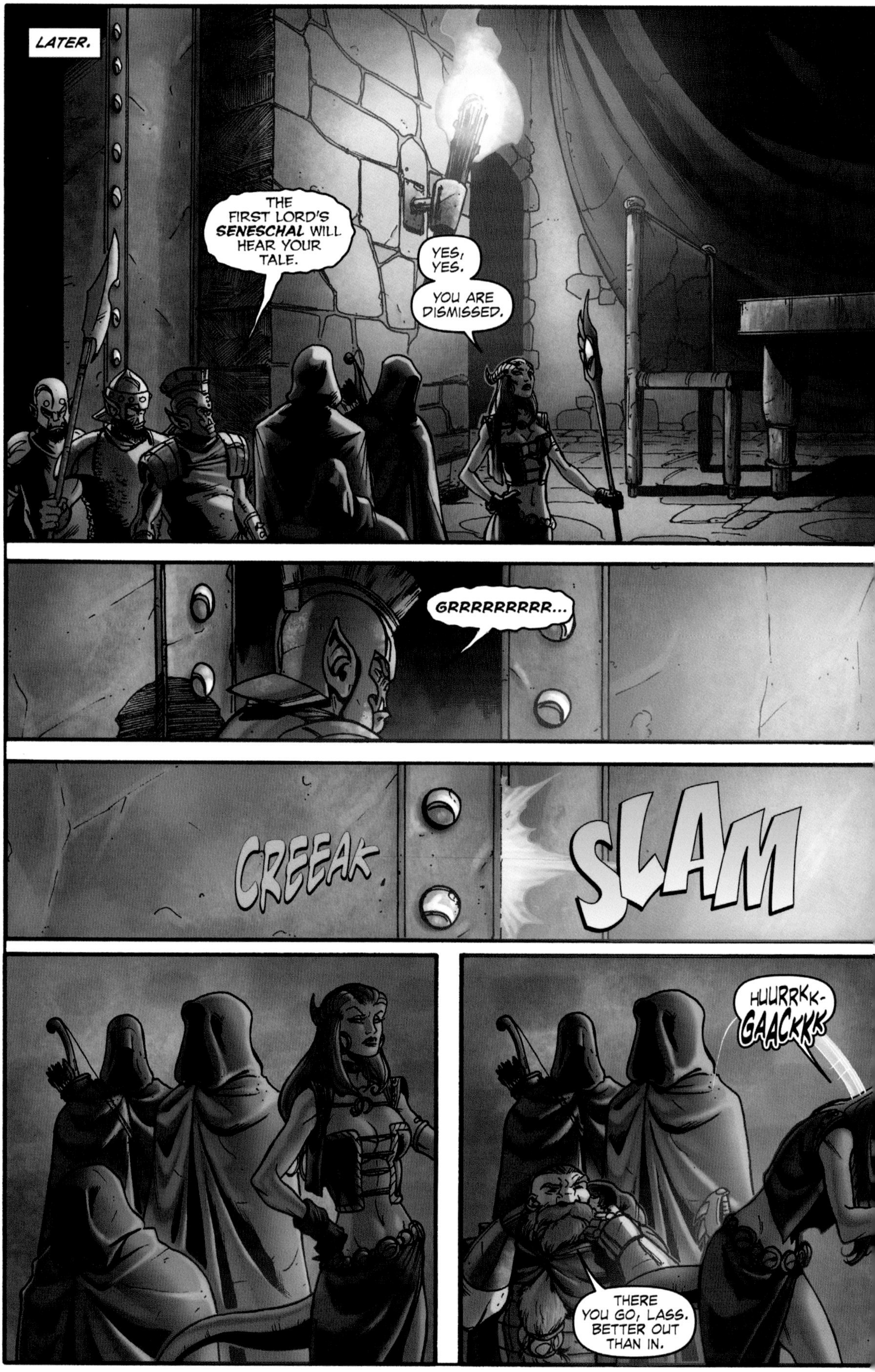
LATER.
THE FIRST LORD'S SENESCHAL WILL HEAR YOUR TALE.
YES, YES.
YOU ARE DISMISSED.
GRRRRRRRRR...
CREEAK
SLAM
HUURRKK-GAACKKK
THERE YOU GO, LASS. BETTER OUT THAN IN.

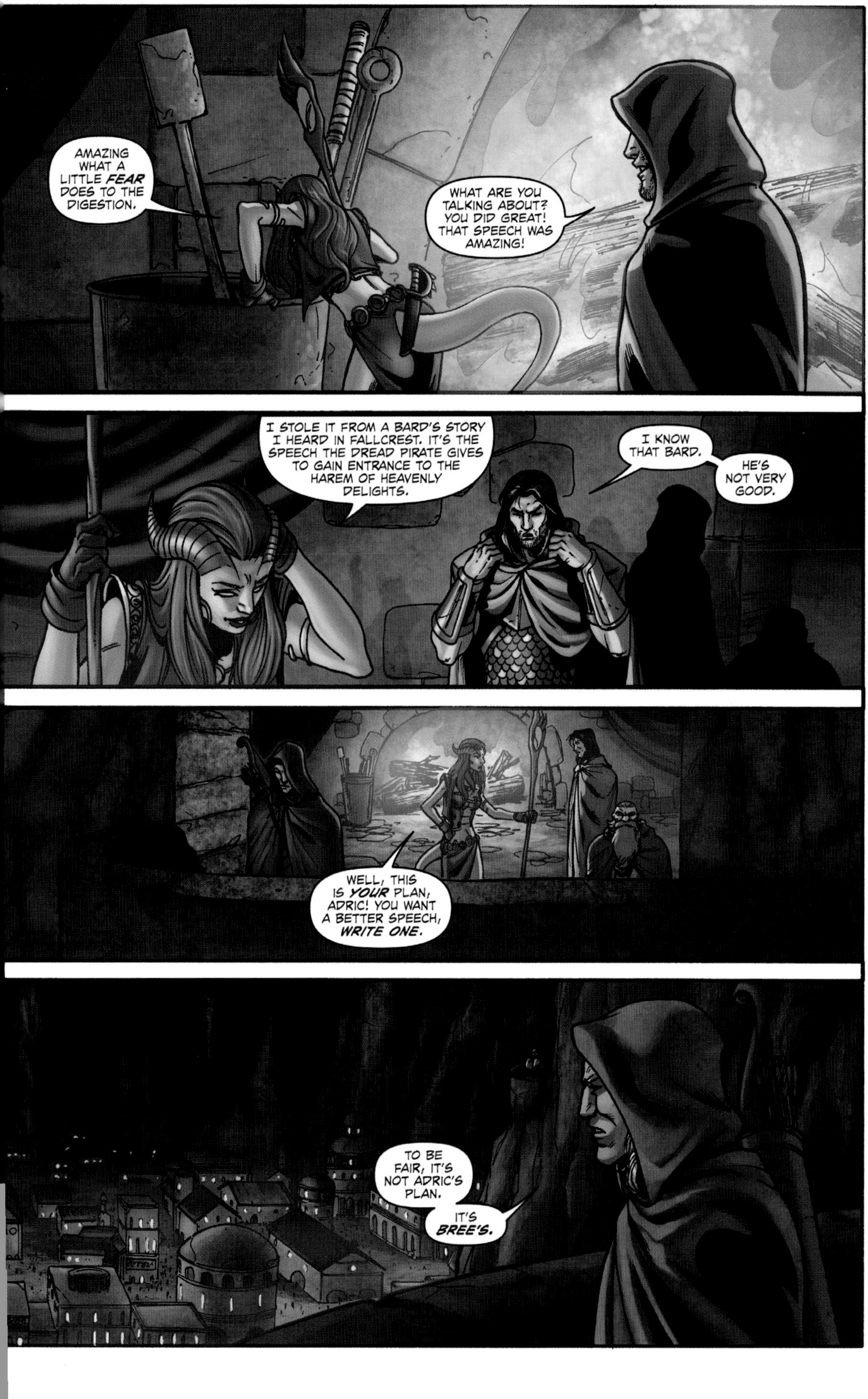
AMAZING WHAT A LITTLE FEAR DOES TO THE DIGESTION.
WHAT ARE YOU TALKING ABOUT? YOU DID GREAT! THAT SPEECH WAS AMAZING!
I STOLE IT FROM A BARD'S STORY I HEARD IN FALLCREST. IT'S THE SPEECH THE DREAD PIRATE GIVES TO GAIN ENTRANCE TO THE HAREM OF HEAVENLY DELIGHTS.
I KNOW THAT BARD.
HE'S NOT VERY GOOD.
WELL, THIS IS YOUR PLAN, ADRIC! YOU WANT A BETTER SPEECH, WRITE ONE.
TO BE FAIR, IT'S NOT ADRIC'S PLAN.
IT'S BREE'S.

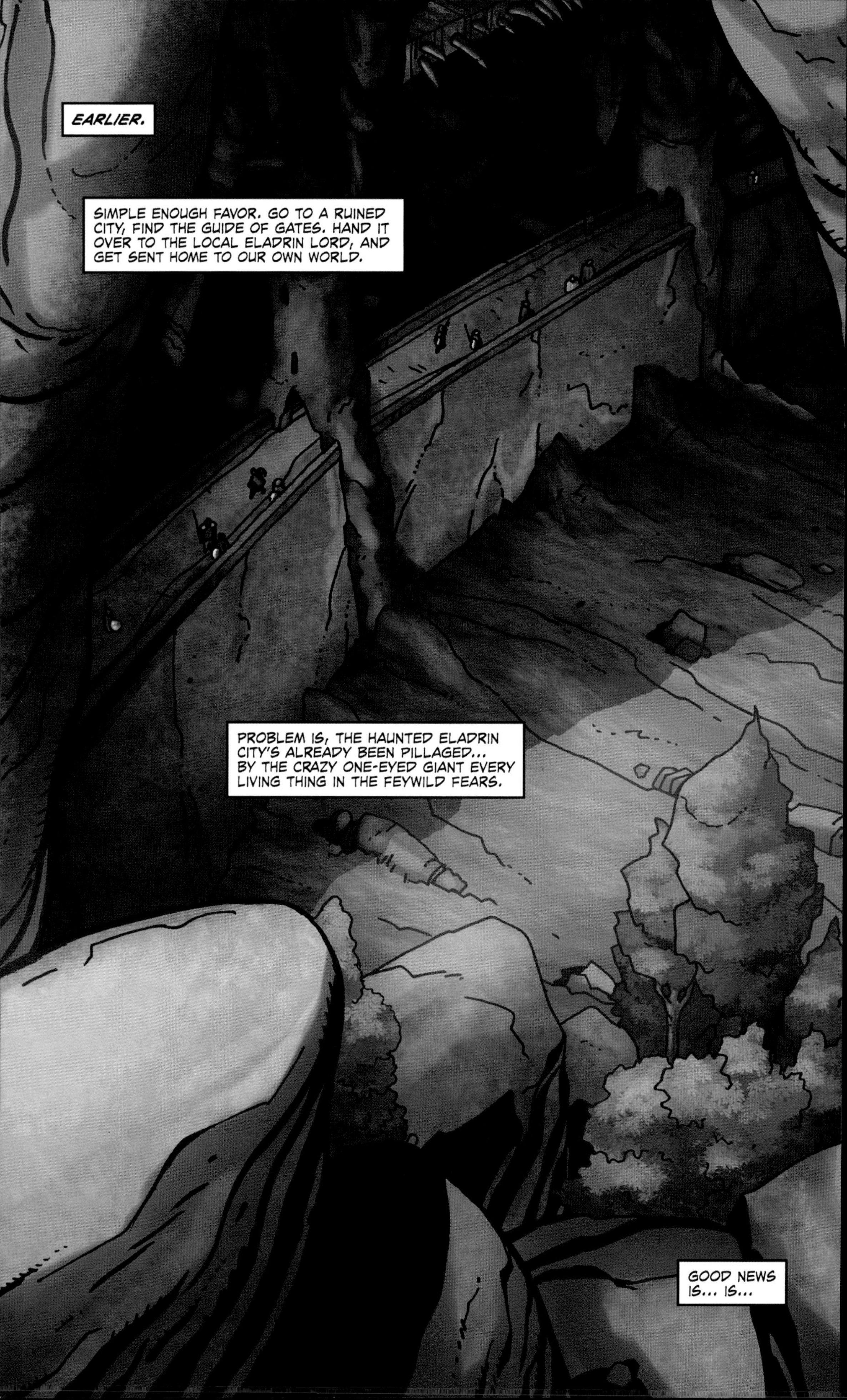
EARLIER.
SIMPLE ENOUGH FAVOR. GO TO A RUINED CITY, FIND THE GUIDE OF GATES. HAND IT OVER TO THE LOCAL ELADRIN LORD, AND GET SENT HOME TO OUR OWN WORLD.
PROBLEM IS, THE HAUNTED ELADRIN CITY'S ALREADY BEEN PILLAGED... BY THE CRAZY ONE-EYED GIANT EVERY LIVING THING IN THE FEYWILD FEARS.
GOOD NEWS IS... IS...

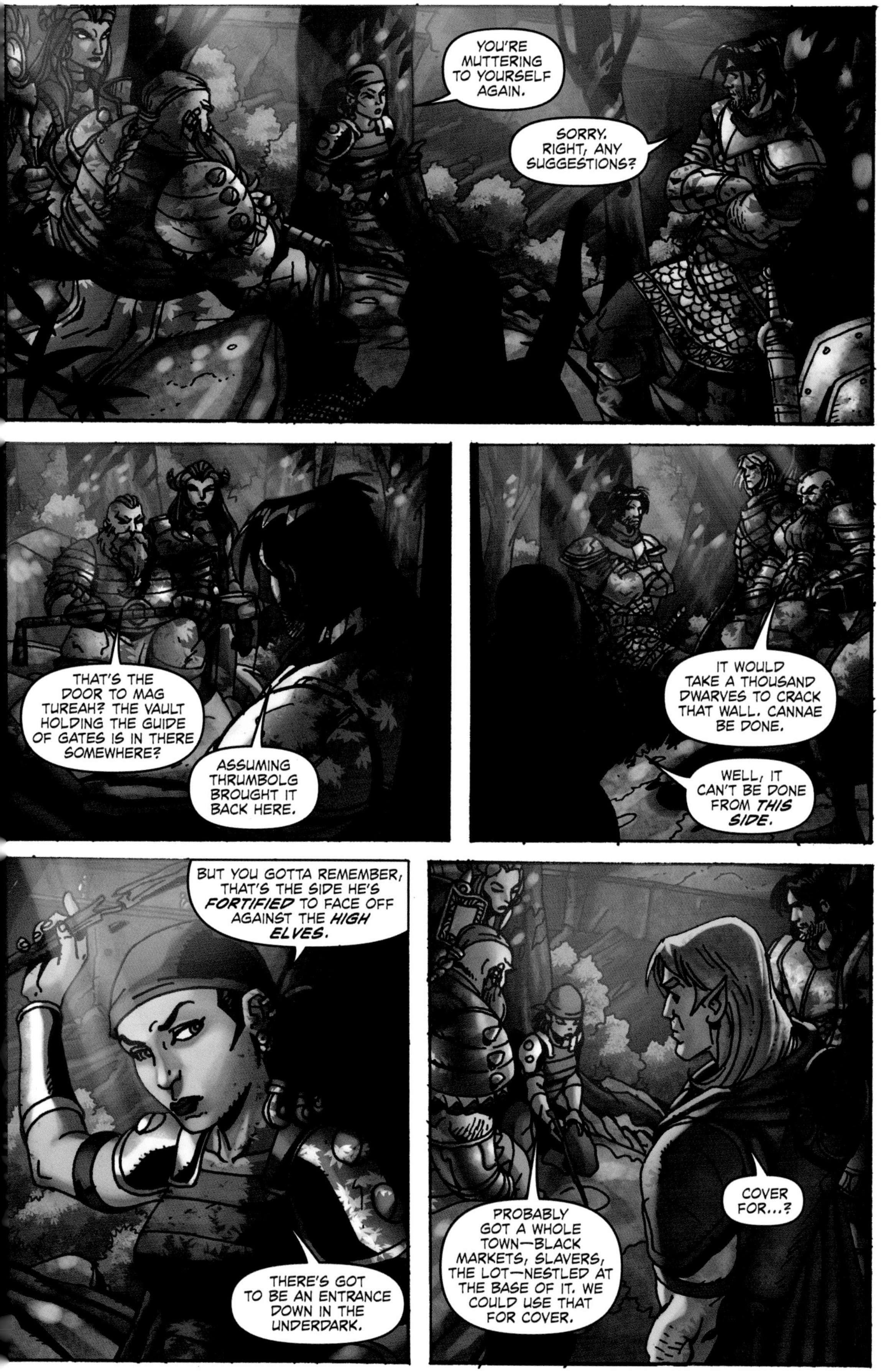

YOU'RE MUTTERING TO YOURSELF AGAIN.
SORRY. RIGHT, ANY SUGGESTIONS?
THAT'S THE DOOR TO MAG TUREAH? THE VAULT HOLDING THE GUIDE OF GATES IS IN THERE SOMEWHERE?
ASSUMING THRUMBOLG BROUGHT IT BACK HERE.
IT WOULD TAKE A THOUSAND DWARVES TO CRACK THAT WALL. CANNAE BE DONE.
WELL, IT CAN'T BE DONE FROM *THIS SIDE*.
BUT YOU GOTTA REMEMBER, THAT'S THE SIDE HE'S *FORTIFIED* TO FACE OFF AGAINST THE *HIGH ELVES*.
THERE'S GOT TO BE AN ENTRANCE DOWN IN THE UNDERDARK.
PROBABLY GOT A WHOLE TOWN—BLACK MARKETS, SLAVERS, THE LOT—NESTLED AT THE BASE OF IT. WE COULD USE THAT FOR COVER.
COVER FOR...?

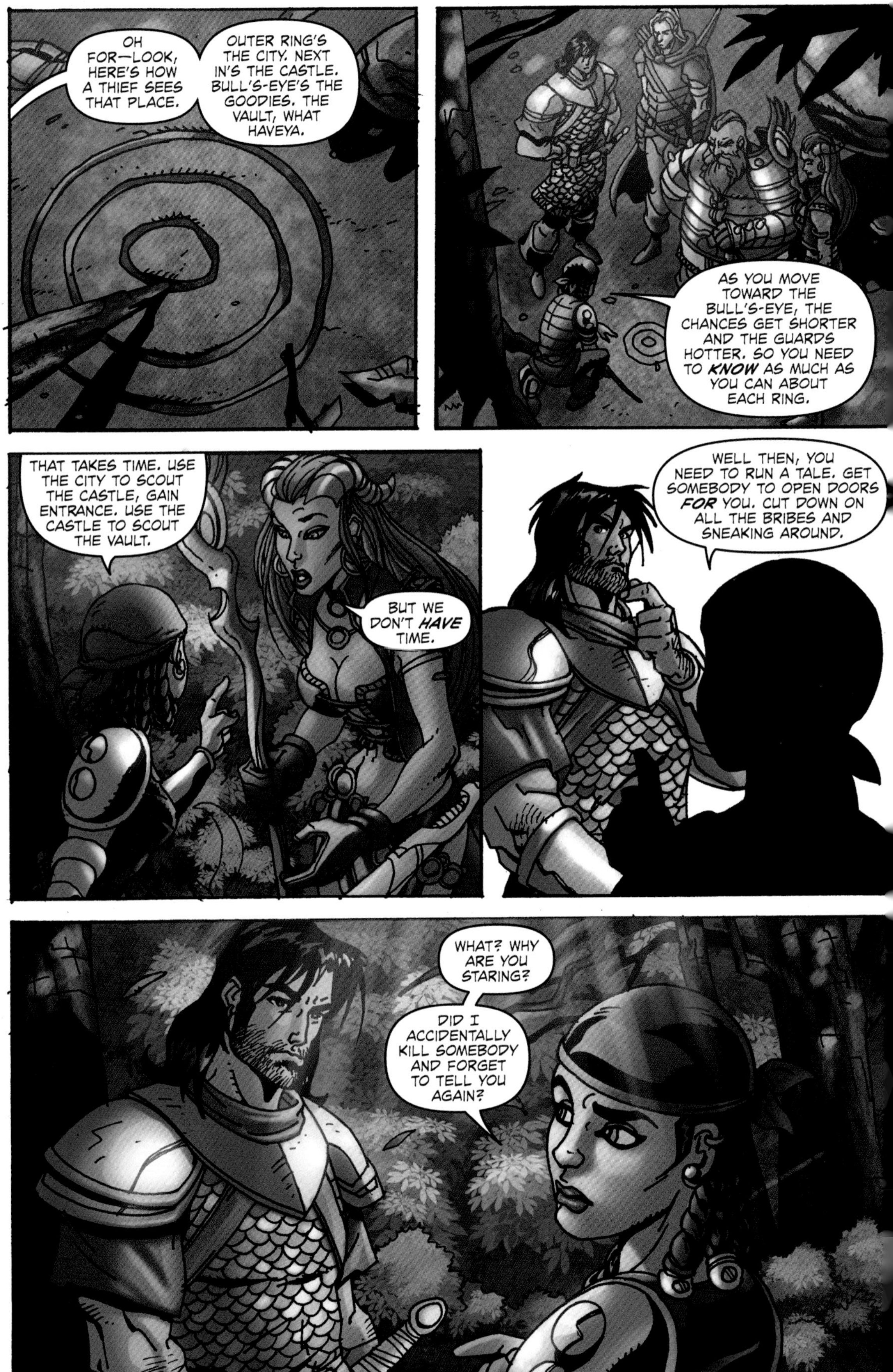
OH FOR—LOOK, HERE'S HOW A THIEF SEES THAT PLACE.
OUTER RING'S THE CITY. NEXT IN'S THE CASTLE. BULL'S-EYE'S THE GOODIES. THE VAULT, WHAT HAVEYA.
AS YOU MOVE TOWARD THE BULL'S-EYE, THE CHANCES GET SHORTER AND THE GUARDS HOTTER. SO YOU NEED TO KNOW AS MUCH AS YOU CAN ABOUT EACH RING.
THAT TAKES TIME. USE THE CITY TO SCOUT THE CASTLE, GAIN ENTRANCE. USE THE CASTLE TO SCOUT THE VAULT.
BUT WE DON'T HAVE TIME.
WELL THEN, YOU NEED TO RUN A TALE. GET SOMEBODY TO OPEN DOORS FOR YOU. CUT DOWN ON ALL THE BRIBES AND SNEAKING AROUND.
WHAT? WHY ARE YOU STARING?
DID I ACCIDENTALLY KILL SOMEBODY AND FORGET TO TELL YOU AGAIN?

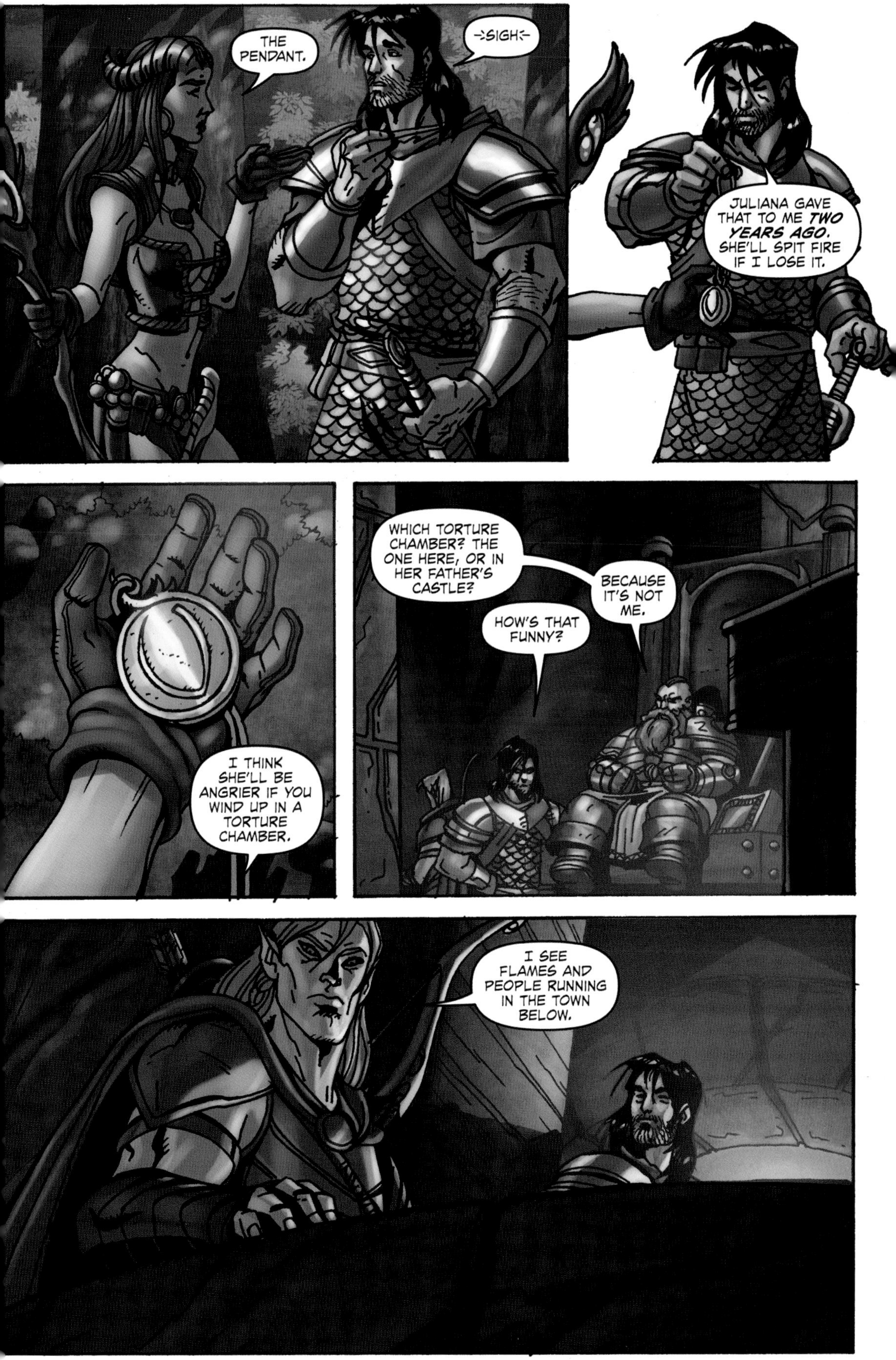
THE PENDANT.
-SIGH-
JULIANA GAVE THAT TO ME TWO YEARS AGO. SHE'LL SPIT FIRE IF I LOSE IT.
I THINK SHE'LL BE ANGRIER IF YOU WIND UP IN A TORTURE CHAMBER.
WHICH TORTURE CHAMBER? THE ONE HERE, OR IN HER FATHER'S CASTLE?
HOW'S THAT FUNNY?
BECAUSE IT'S NOT ME.
I SEE FLAMES AND PEOPLE RUNNING IN THE TOWN BELOW.

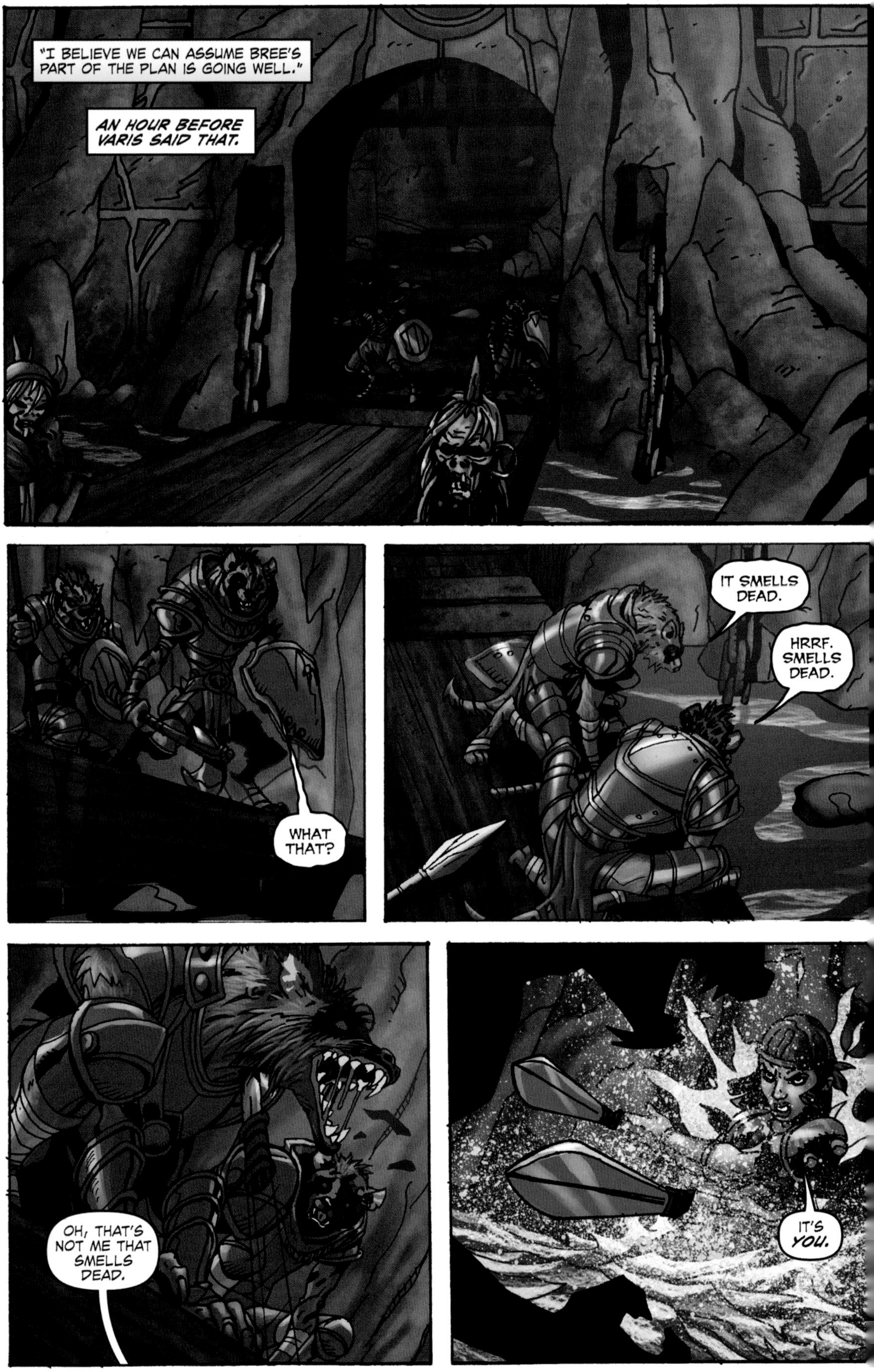
"I BELIEVE WE CAN ASSUME BREE'S PART OF THE PLAN IS GOING WELL."
AN HOUR BEFORE VARIS SAID THAT.
WHAT THAT?
IT SMELLS DEAD.
HRRF. SMELLS DEAD.
OH, THAT'S NOT ME THAT SMELLS DEAD.
IT'S YOU.

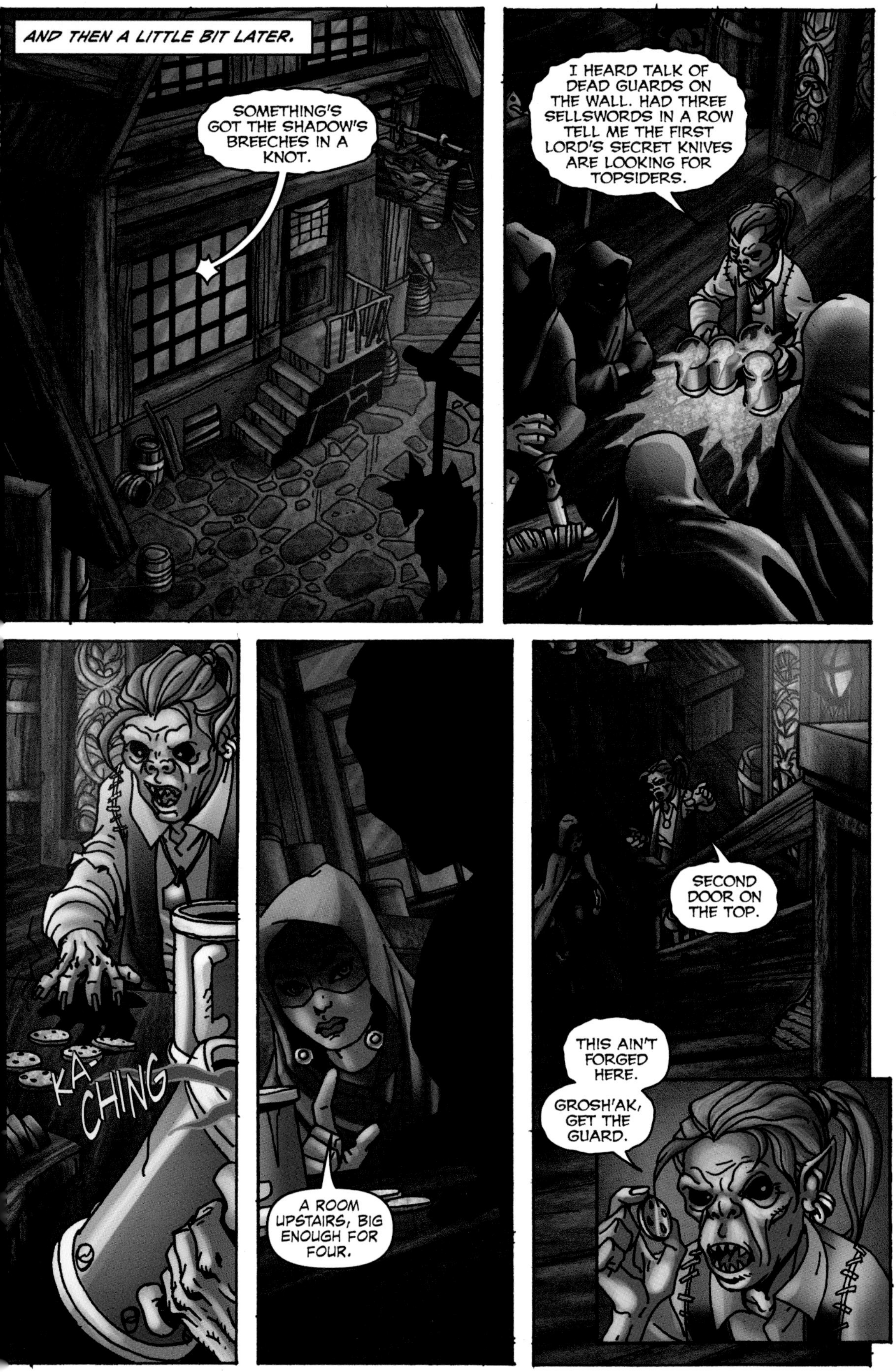
AND THEN A LITTLE BIT LATER.
SOMETHING'S GOT THE SHADOW'S BREECHES IN A KNOT.
I HEARD TALK OF DEAD GUARDS ON THE WALL. HAD THREE SELLSWORDS IN A ROW TELL ME THE FIRST LORD'S SECRET KNIVES ARE LOOKING FOR TOPSIDERS.
KA-CHING
A ROOM UPSTAIRS, BIG ENOUGH FOR FOUR.
SECOND DOOR ON THE TOP.
THIS AIN'T FORGED HERE.
GROSH'AK, GET THE GUARD.

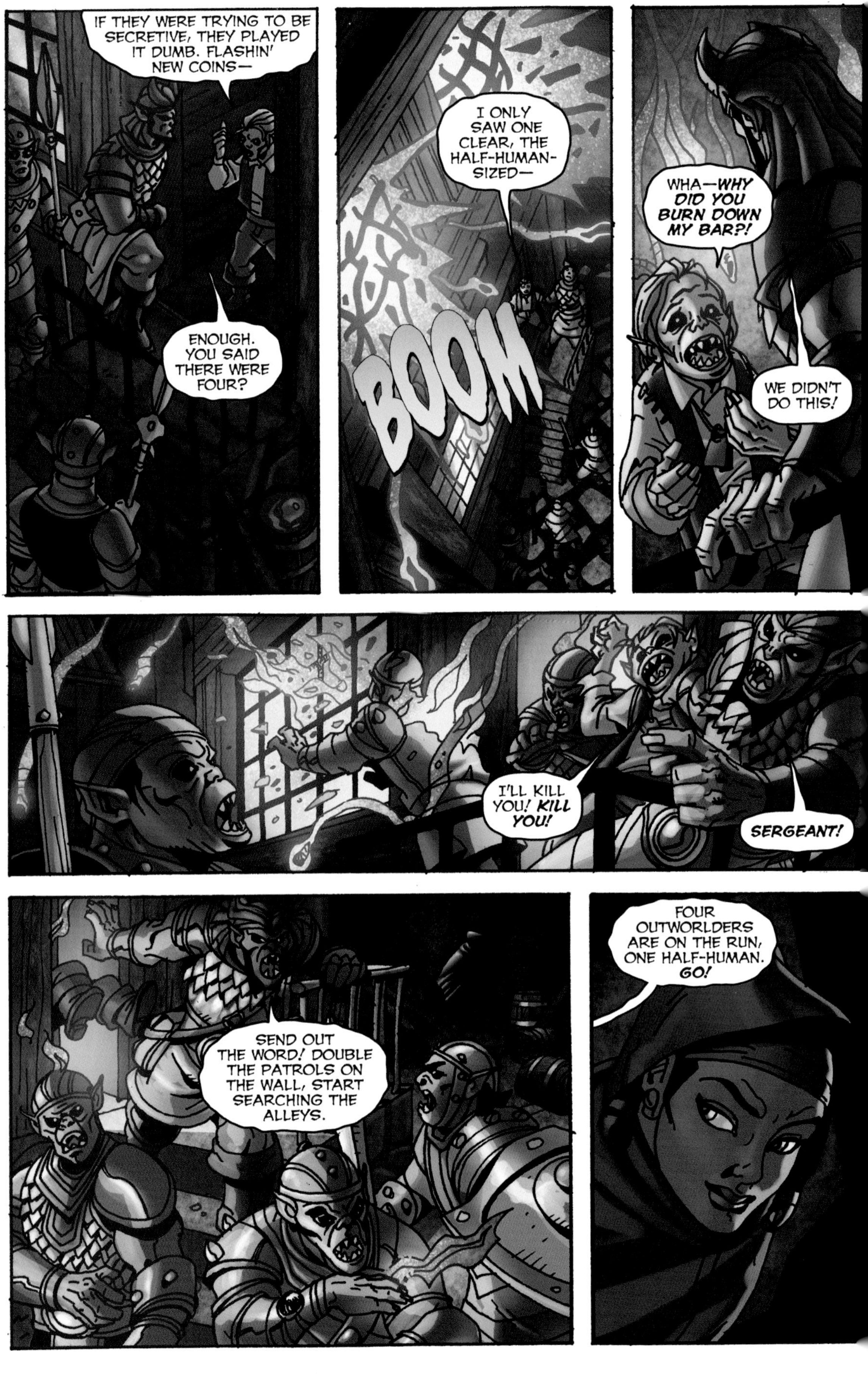
IF THEY WERE TRYING TO BE SECRETIVE, THEY PLAYED IT DUMB. FLASHIN' NEW COINS—
ENOUGH. YOU SAID THERE WERE FOUR?
I ONLY SAW ONE CLEAR, THE HALF-HUMAN-SIZED—
BOOM
WHA—WHY DID YOU BURN DOWN MY BAR?!
WE DIDN'T DO THIS!
I'LL KILL YOU! KILL YOU!
SERGEANT!
SEND OUT THE WORD! DOUBLE THE PATROLS ON THE WALL, START SEARCHING THE ALLEYS.
FOUR OUTWORLDERS ARE ON THE RUN, ONE HALF-HUMAN. GO!

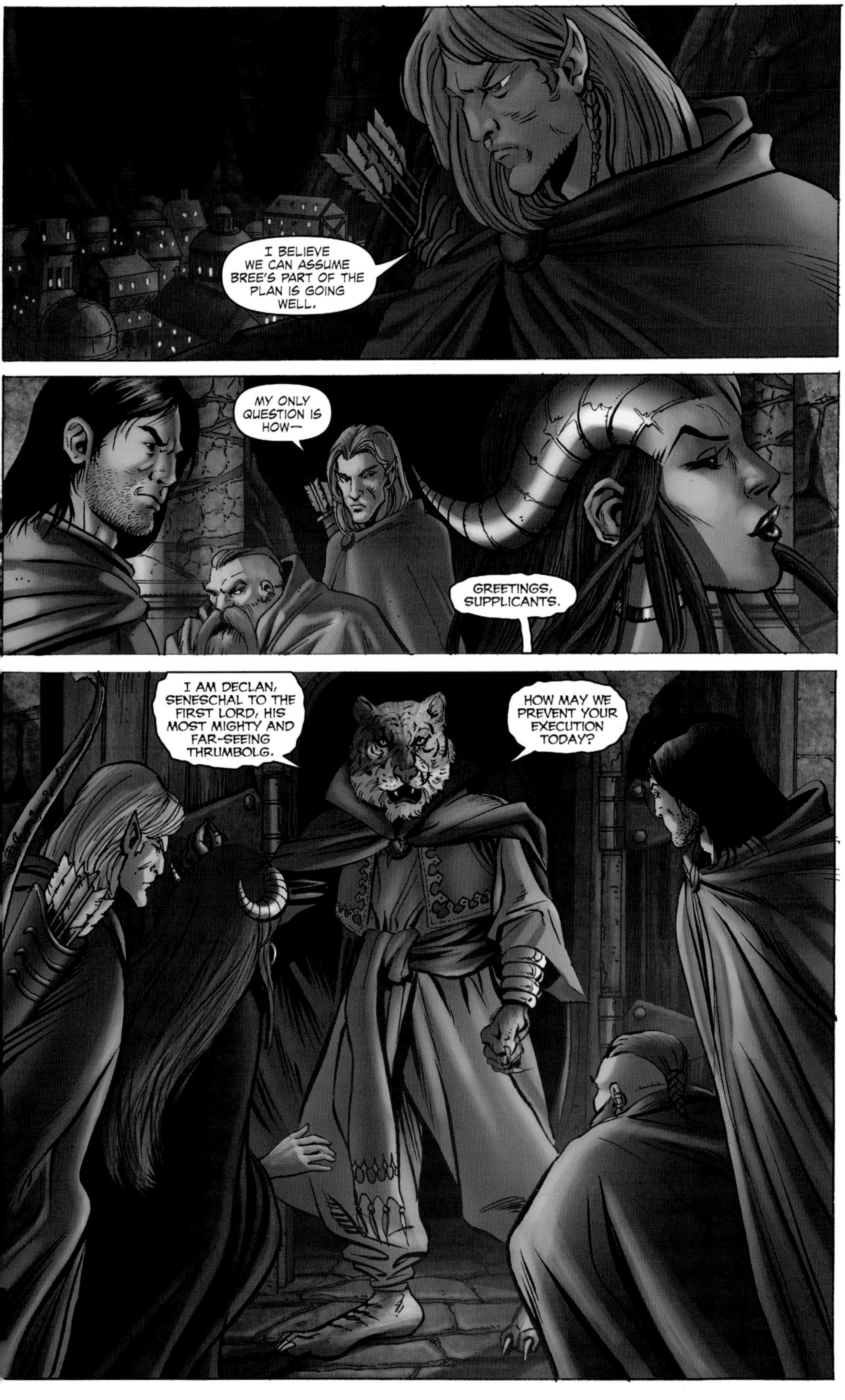
I BELIEVE WE CAN ASSUME BREE'S PART OF THE PLAN IS GOING WELL.
MY ONLY QUESTION IS HOW—
GREETINGS, SUPPLICANTS.
I AM DECLAN, SENESCHAL TO THE FIRST LORD, HIS MOST MIGHTY AND FAR-SEEING THRUMBOLG.
HOW MAY WE PREVENT YOUR EXECUTION TODAY?

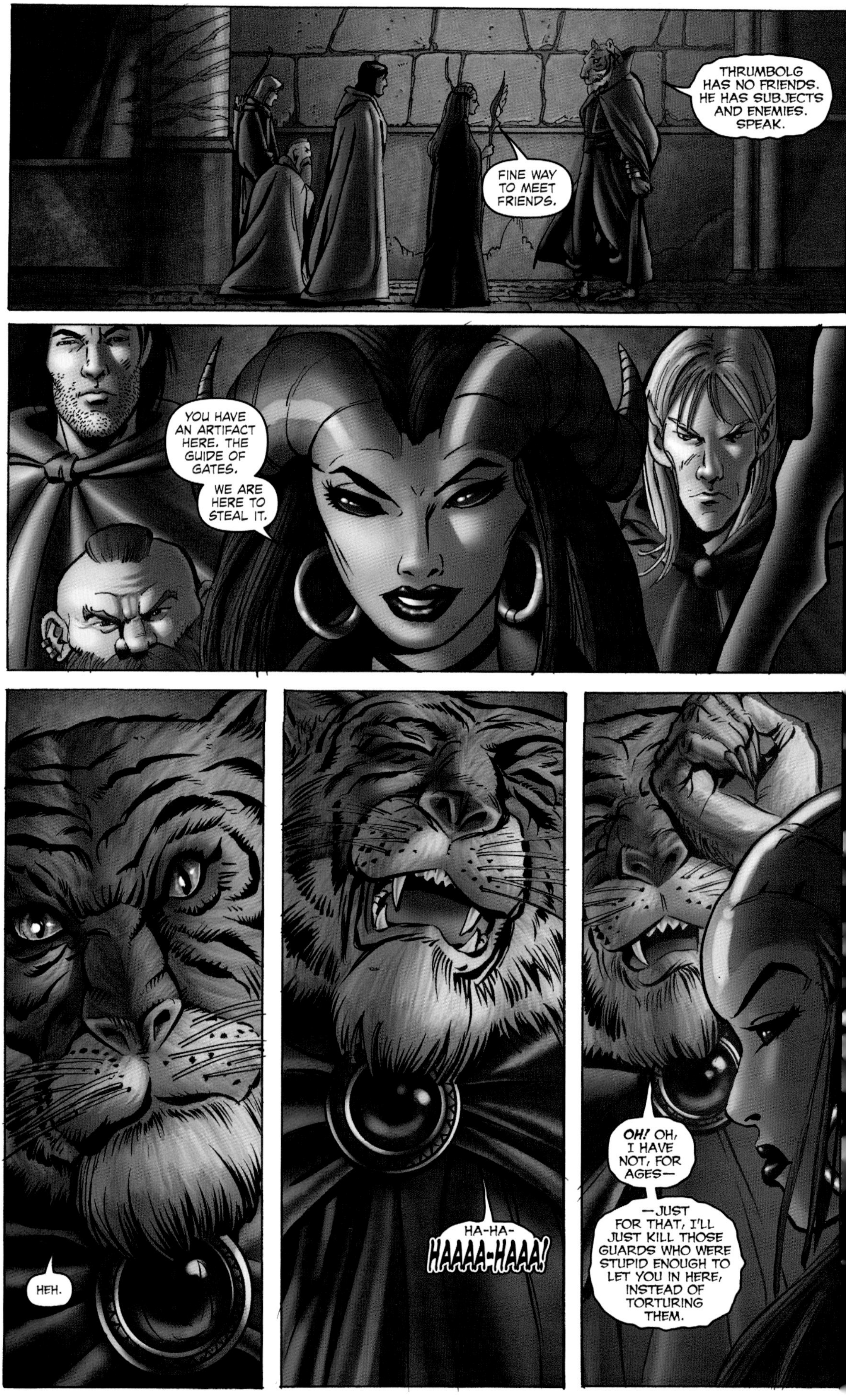

THRUMBOLG HAS NO FRIENDS. HE HAS SUBJECTS AND ENEMIES. SPEAK.
FINE WAY TO MEET FRIENDS.
YOU HAVE AN ARTIFACT HERE. THE GUIDE OF GATES.
WE ARE HERE TO STEAL IT.
HEH.
HA-HA-
HAAAA-HAAA!
OH! OH, I HAVE NOT, FOR AGES—
—JUST FOR THAT, I'LL JUST KILL THOSE GUARDS WHO WERE STUPID ENOUGH TO LET YOU IN HERE, INSTEAD OF TORTURING THEM.

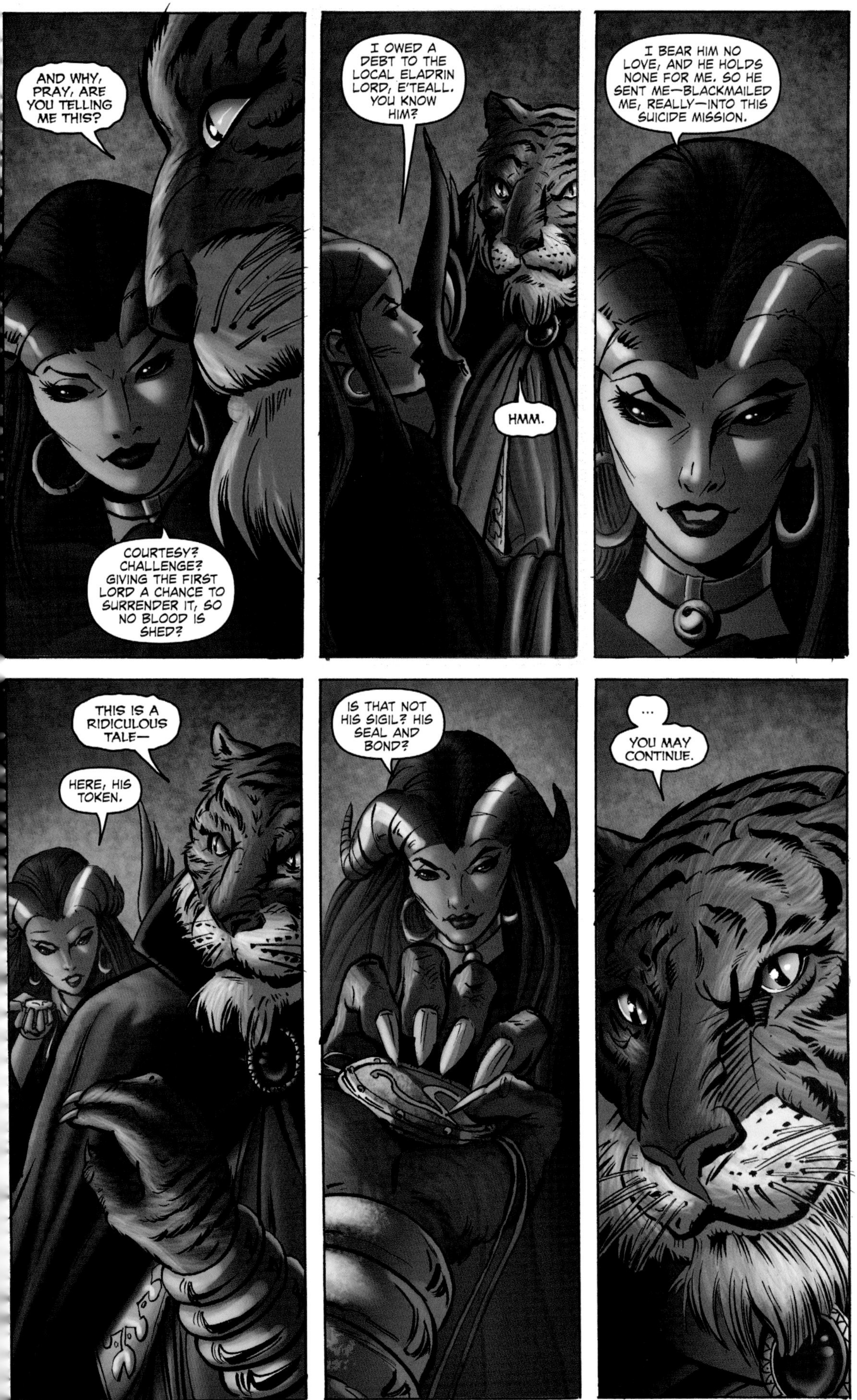
AND WHY, PRAY, ARE YOU TELLING ME THIS?
COURTESY? CHALLENGE? GIVING THE FIRST LORD A CHANCE TO SURRENDER IT, SO NO BLOOD IS SHED?
I OWED A DEBT TO THE LOCAL ELADRIN LORD, E'TEALL. YOU KNOW HIM?
HMM.
I BEAR HIM NO LOVE, AND HE HOLDS NONE FOR ME. SO HE SENT ME—BLACKMAILED ME, REALLY—INTO THIS SUICIDE MISSION.
THIS IS A RIDICULOUS TALE—
HERE, HIS TOKEN.
IS THAT NOT HIS SIGIL? HIS SEAL AND BOND?
...
YOU MAY CONTINUE.

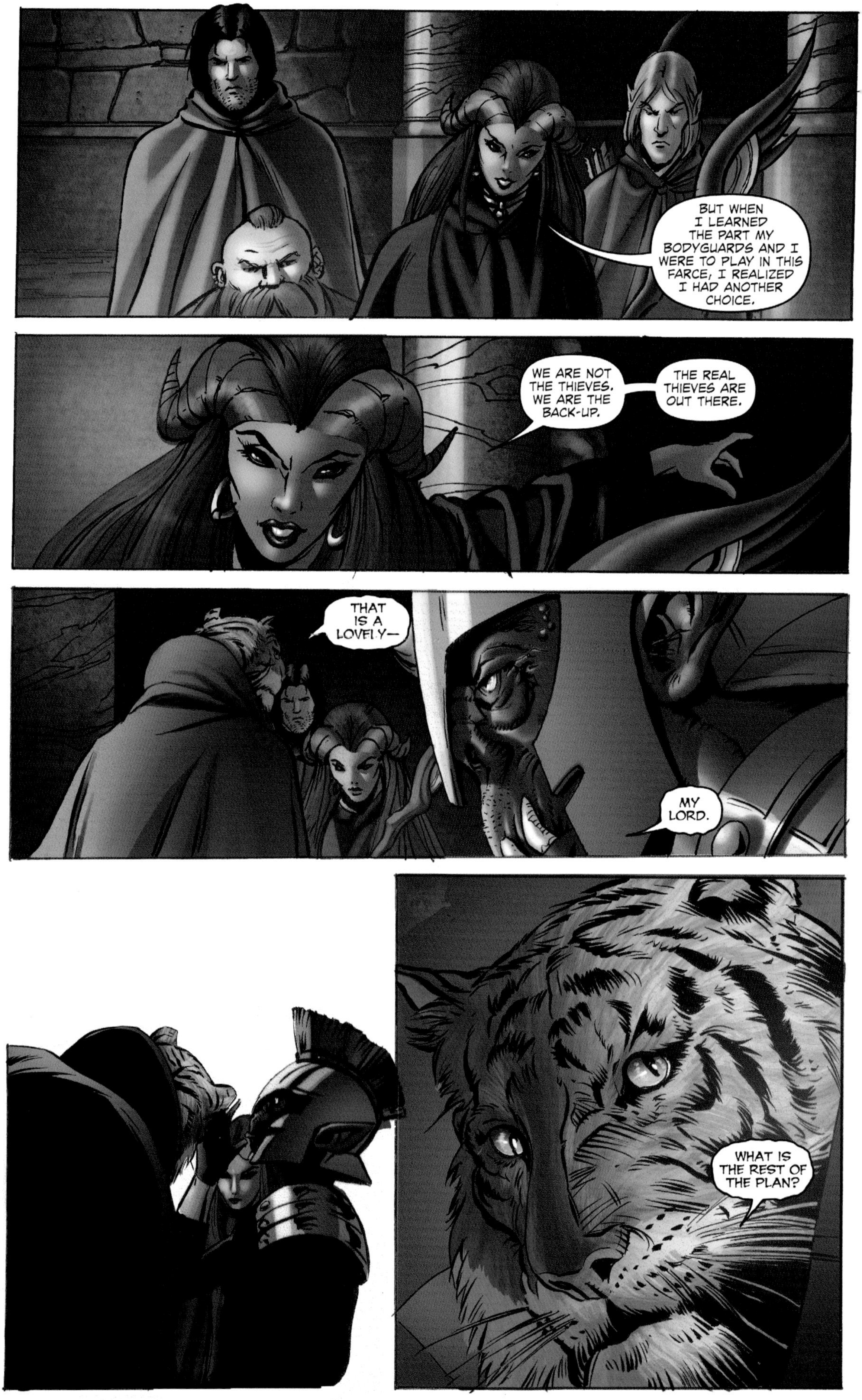
BUT WHEN I LEARNED THE PART MY BODYGUARDS AND I WERE TO PLAY IN THIS FARCE, I REALIZED I HAD ANOTHER CHOICE.
WE ARE NOT THE THIEVES. WE ARE THE BACK-UP.
THE REAL THIEVES ARE OUT THERE.
THAT IS A LOVELY—
MY LORD.
WHAT IS THE REST OF THE PLAN?

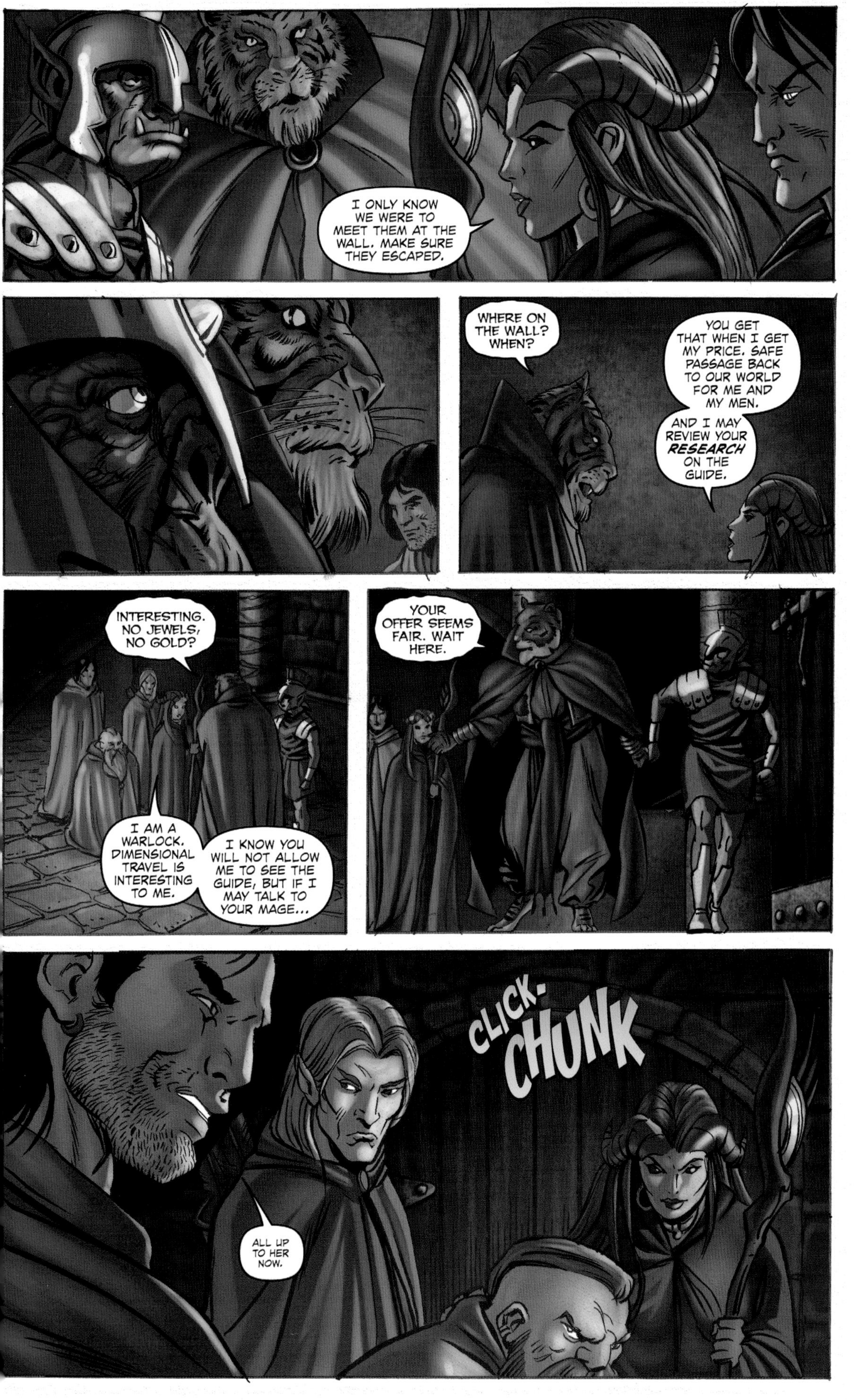
I ONLY KNOW WE WERE TO MEET THEM AT THE WALL. MAKE SURE THEY ESCAPED.
WHERE ON THE WALL? WHEN?
YOU GET THAT WHEN I GET MY PRICE. SAFE PASSAGE BACK TO OUR WORLD FOR ME AND MY MEN.
AND I MAY REVIEW YOUR RESEARCH ON THE GUIDE.
INTERESTING. NO JEWELS, NO GOLD?
I AM A WARLOCK. DIMENSIONAL TRAVEL IS INTERESTING TO ME.
I KNOW YOU WILL NOT ALLOW ME TO SEE THE GUIDE, BUT IF I MAY TALK TO YOUR MAGE...
YOUR OFFER SEEMS FAIR. WAIT HERE.
CLICK-CHUNK
ALL UP TO HER NOW.

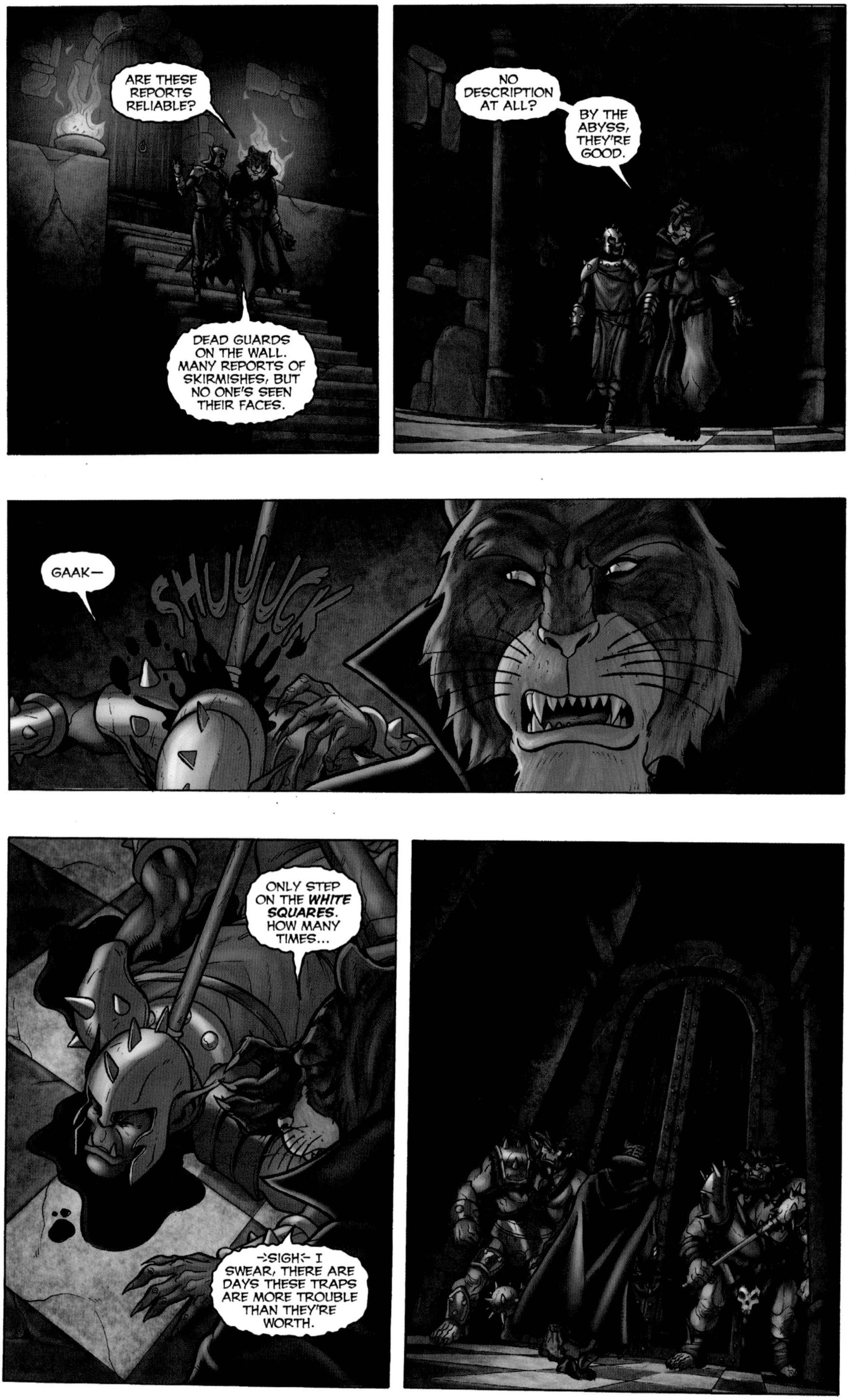

ARE THESE REPORTS RELIABLE?
DEAD GUARDS ON THE WALL. MANY REPORTS OF SKIRMISHES, BUT NO ONE'S SEEN THEIR FACES.
NO DESCRIPTION AT ALL?
BY THE ABYSS, THEY'RE GOOD.
GAAK—
SHUUUCK
ONLY STEP ON THE *WHITE SQUARES*. HOW MANY TIMES...
-SIGH- I SWEAR, THERE ARE DAYS THESE TRAPS ARE MORE TROUBLE THAN THEY'RE WORTH.

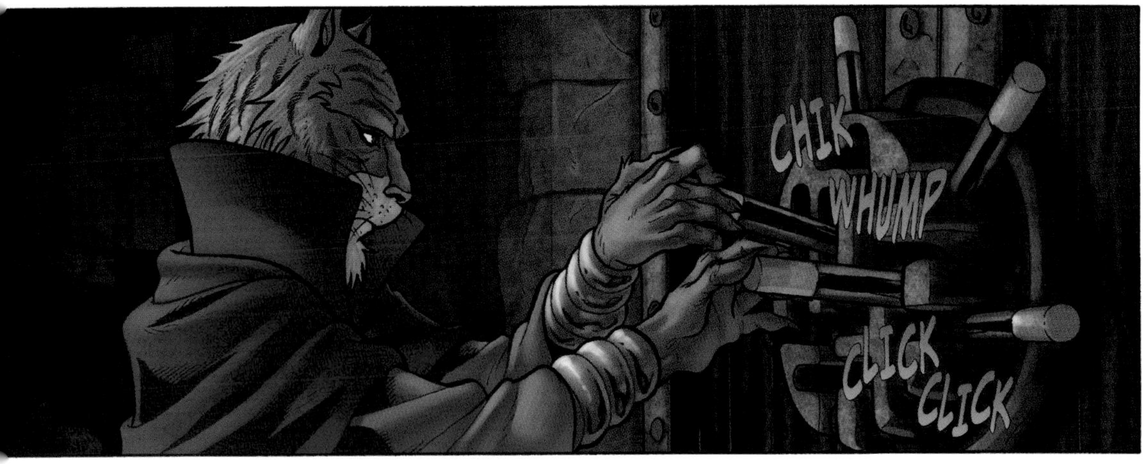
CHIK
WHUMP
CLICK
CLICK

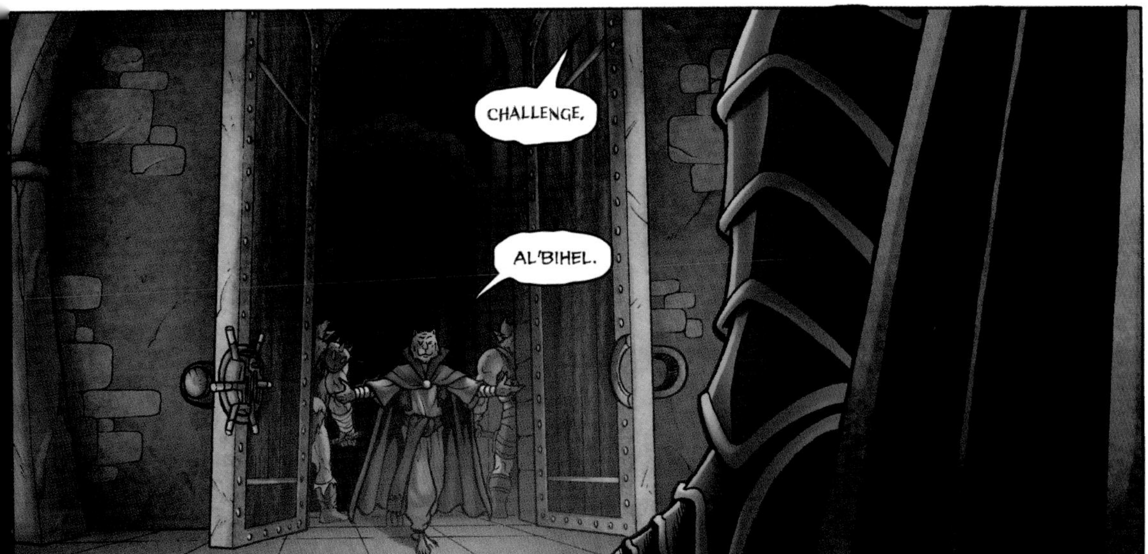
CHALLENGE.
AL'BIHEL.

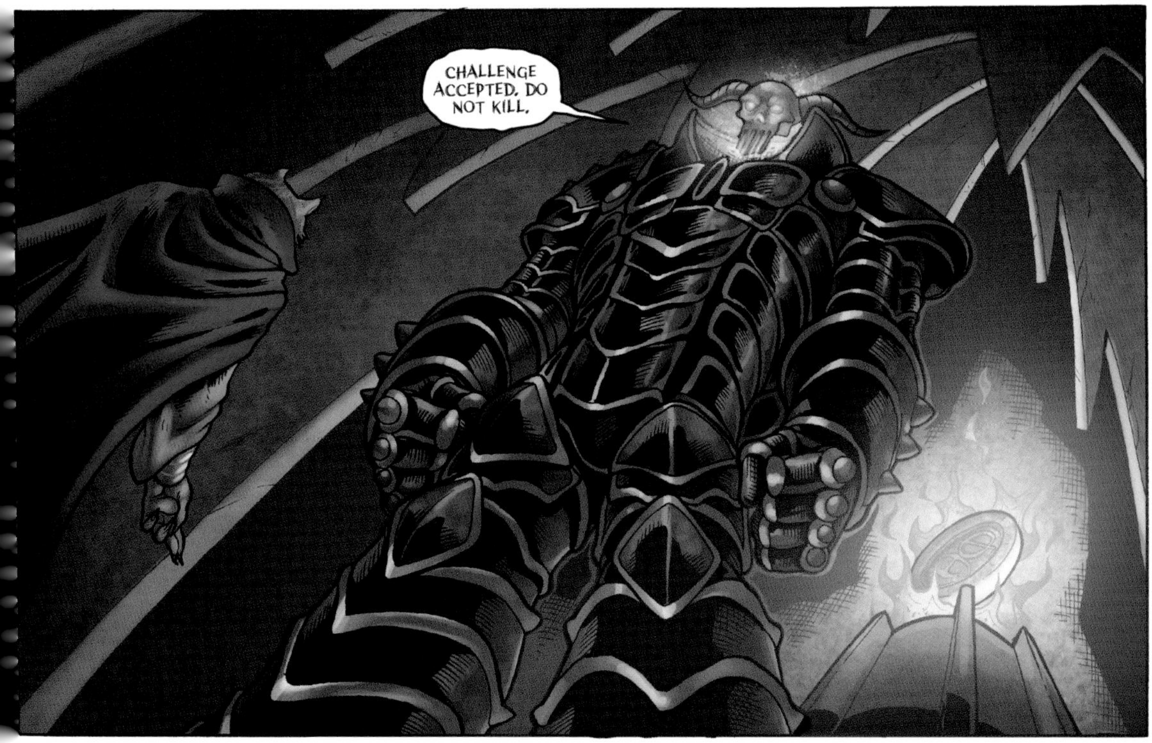
CHALLENGE ACCEPTED. DO NOT KILL.

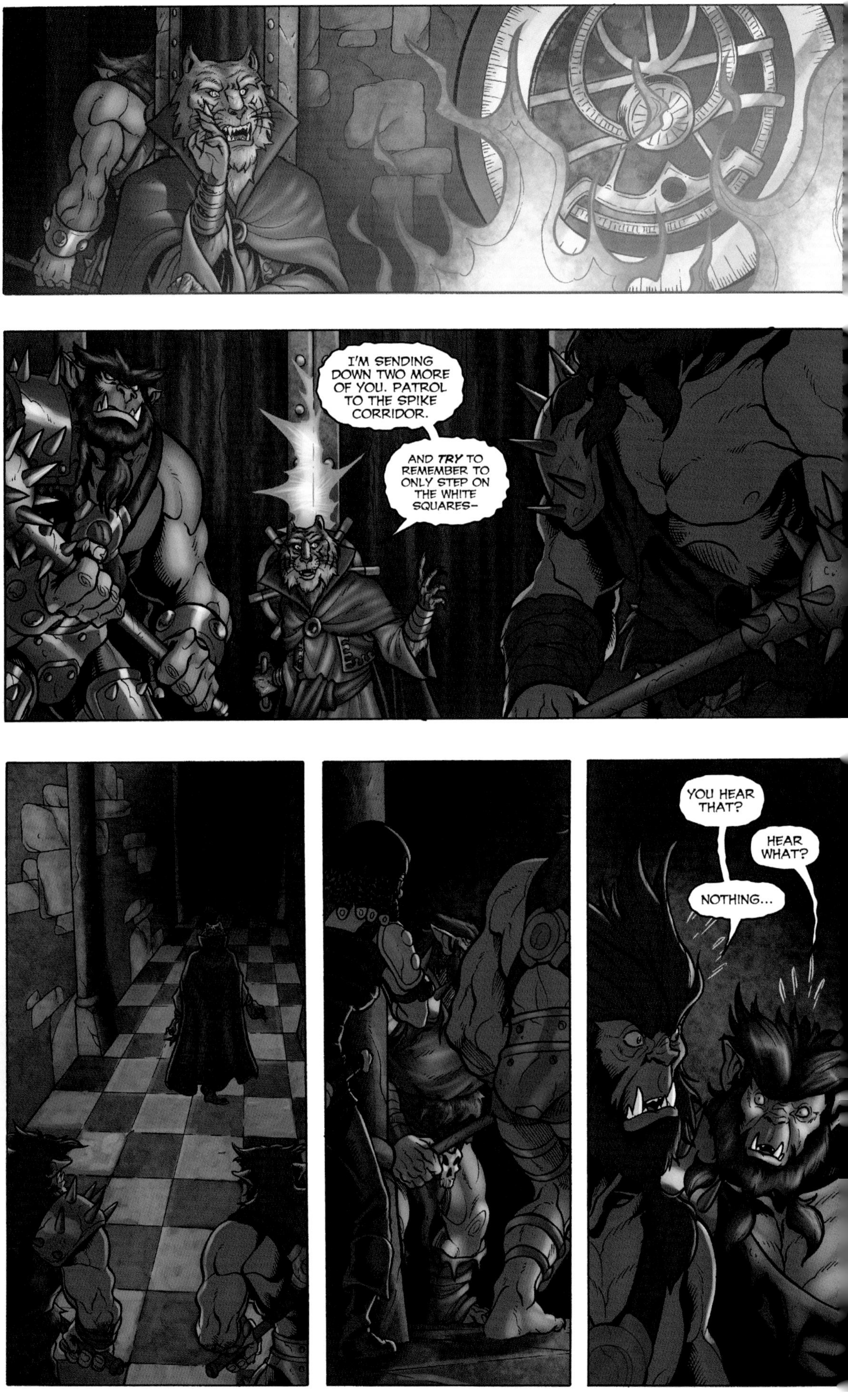
I'M SENDING DOWN TWO MORE OF YOU. PATROL TO THE SPIKE CORRIDOR.
AND TRY TO REMEMBER TO ONLY STEP ON THE WHITE SQUARES–
YOU HEAR THAT?
HEAR WHAT?
NOTHING...

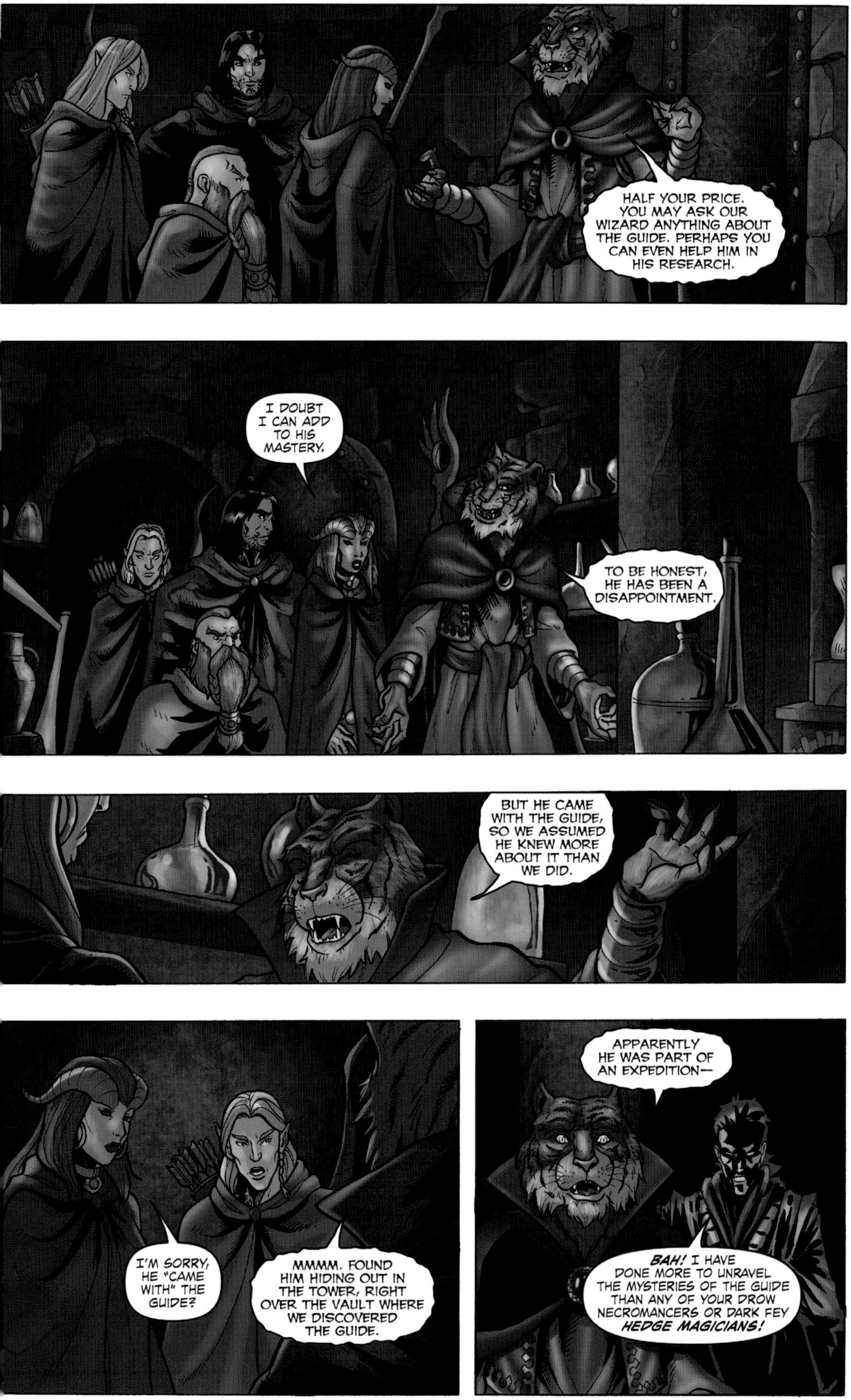
HALF YOUR PRICE. YOU MAY ASK OUR WIZARD ANYTHING ABOUT THE GUIDE. PERHAPS YOU CAN EVEN HELP HIM IN HIS RESEARCH.
I DOUBT I CAN ADD TO HIS MASTERY.
TO BE HONEST, HE HAS BEEN A DISAPPOINTMENT.
BUT HE CAME WITH THE GUIDE, SO WE ASSUMED HE KNEW MORE ABOUT IT THAN WE DID.
I'M SORRY, HE "CAME WITH" THE GUIDE?
MMMM. FOUND HIM HIDING OUT IN THE TOWER, RIGHT OVER THE VAULT WHERE WE DISCOVERED THE GUIDE.
APPARENTLY HE WAS PART OF AN EXPEDITION—
BAH! I HAVE DONE MORE TO UNRAVEL THE MYSTERIES OF THE GUIDE THAN ANY OF YOUR DROW NECROMANCERS OR DARK FEY ***HEDGE MAGICIANS!***

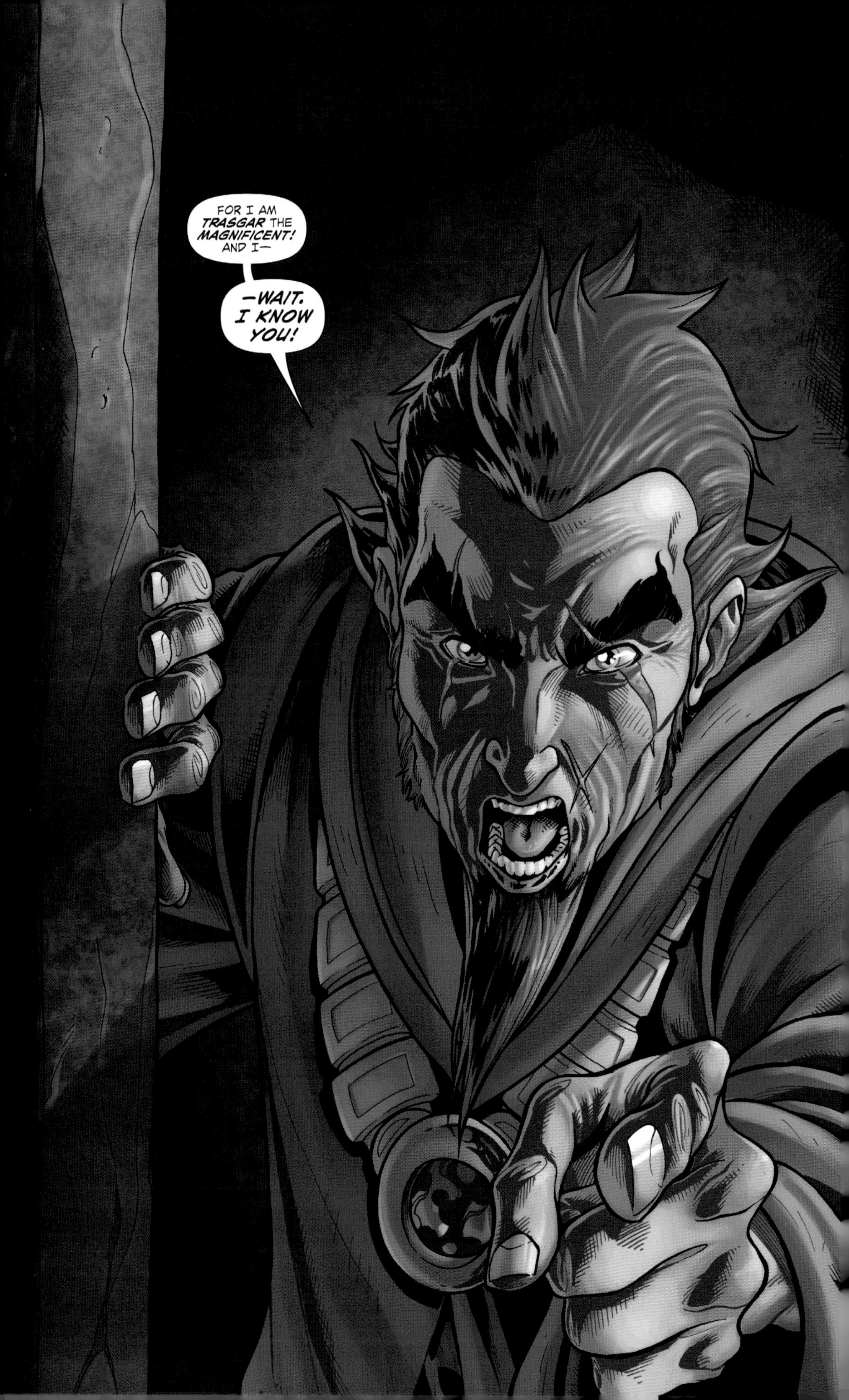
FOR I AM TRASGAR THE MAGNIFICENT! AND I—
—WAIT. I KNOW YOU!

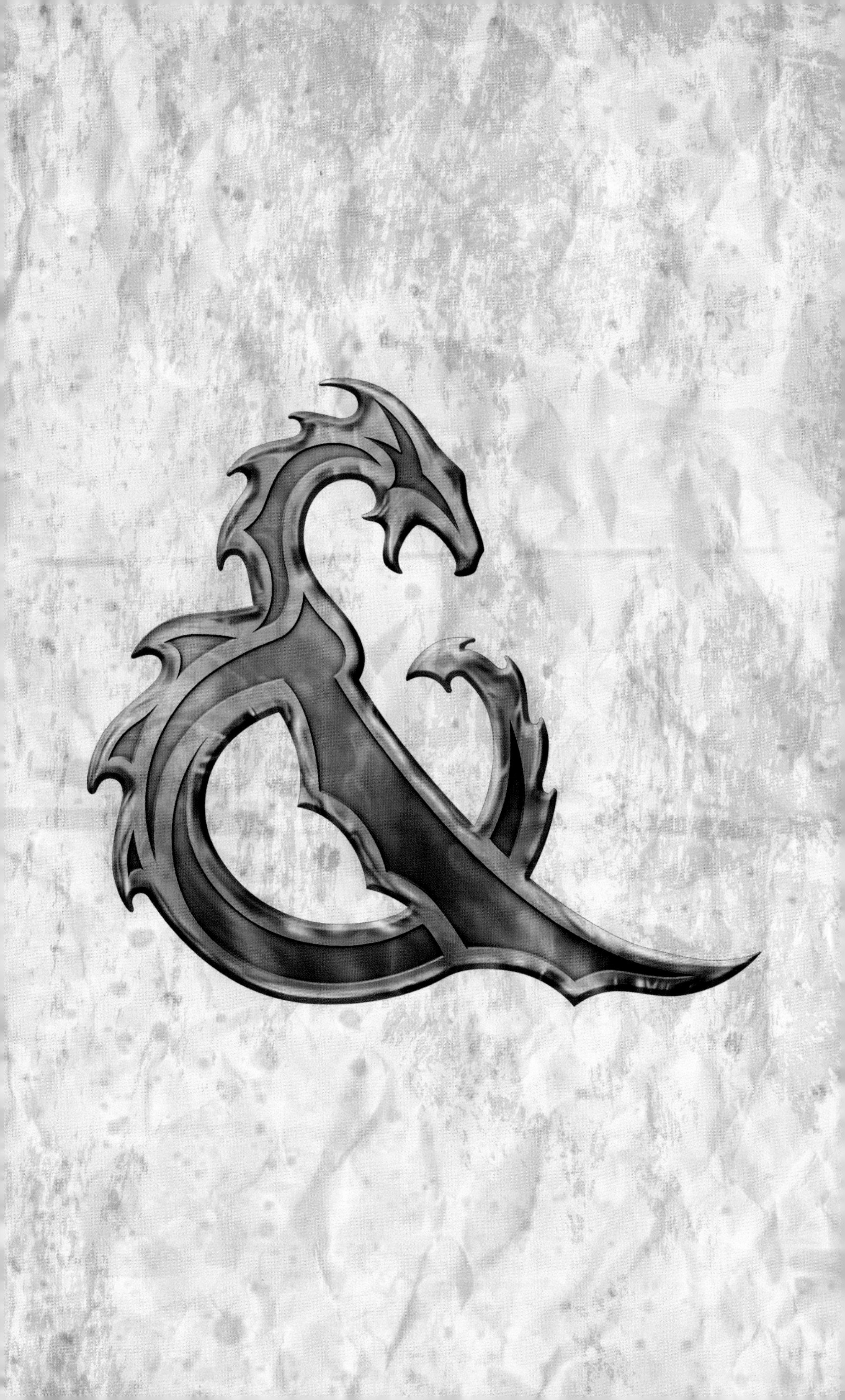

Art by Tyler Walpole

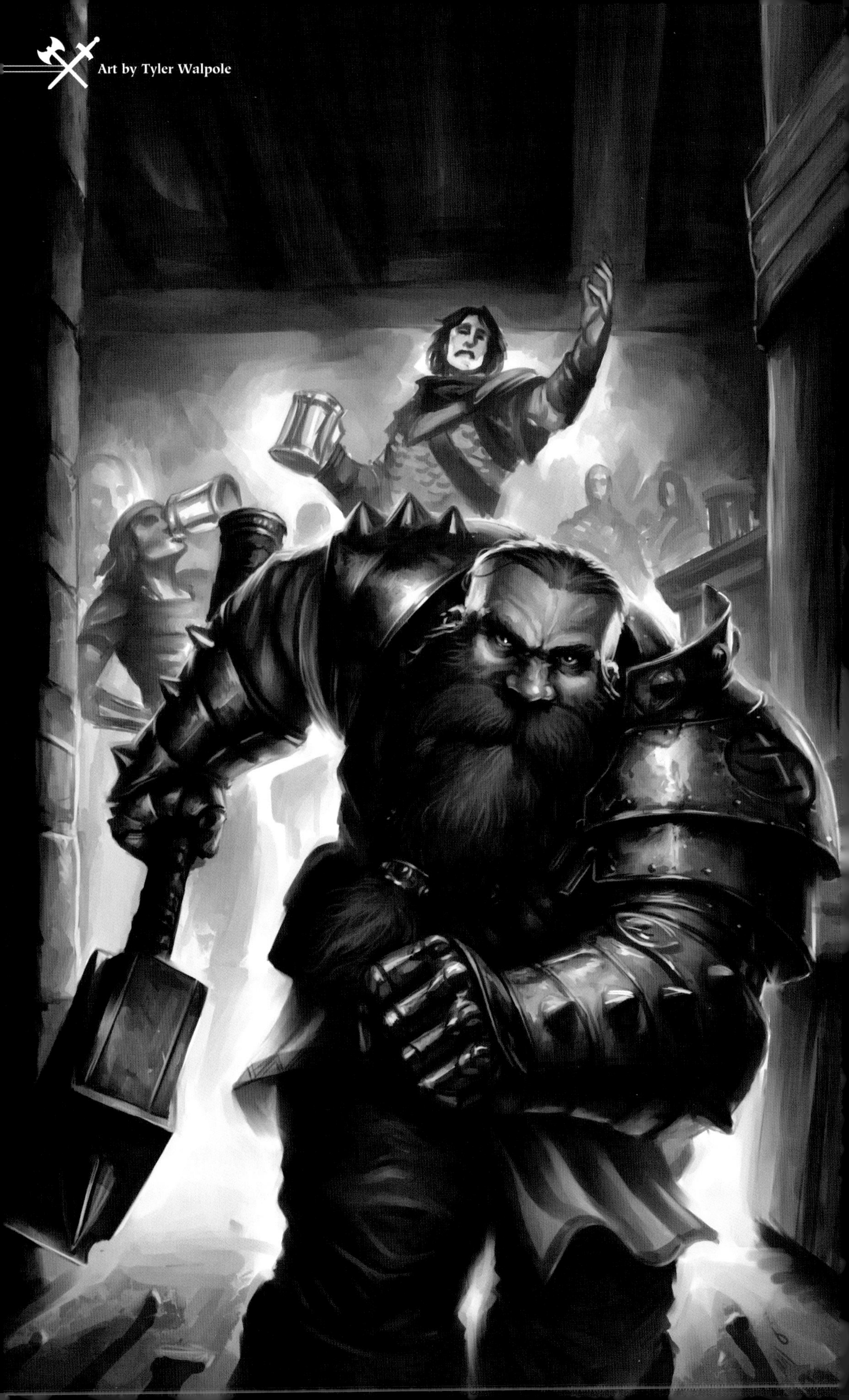

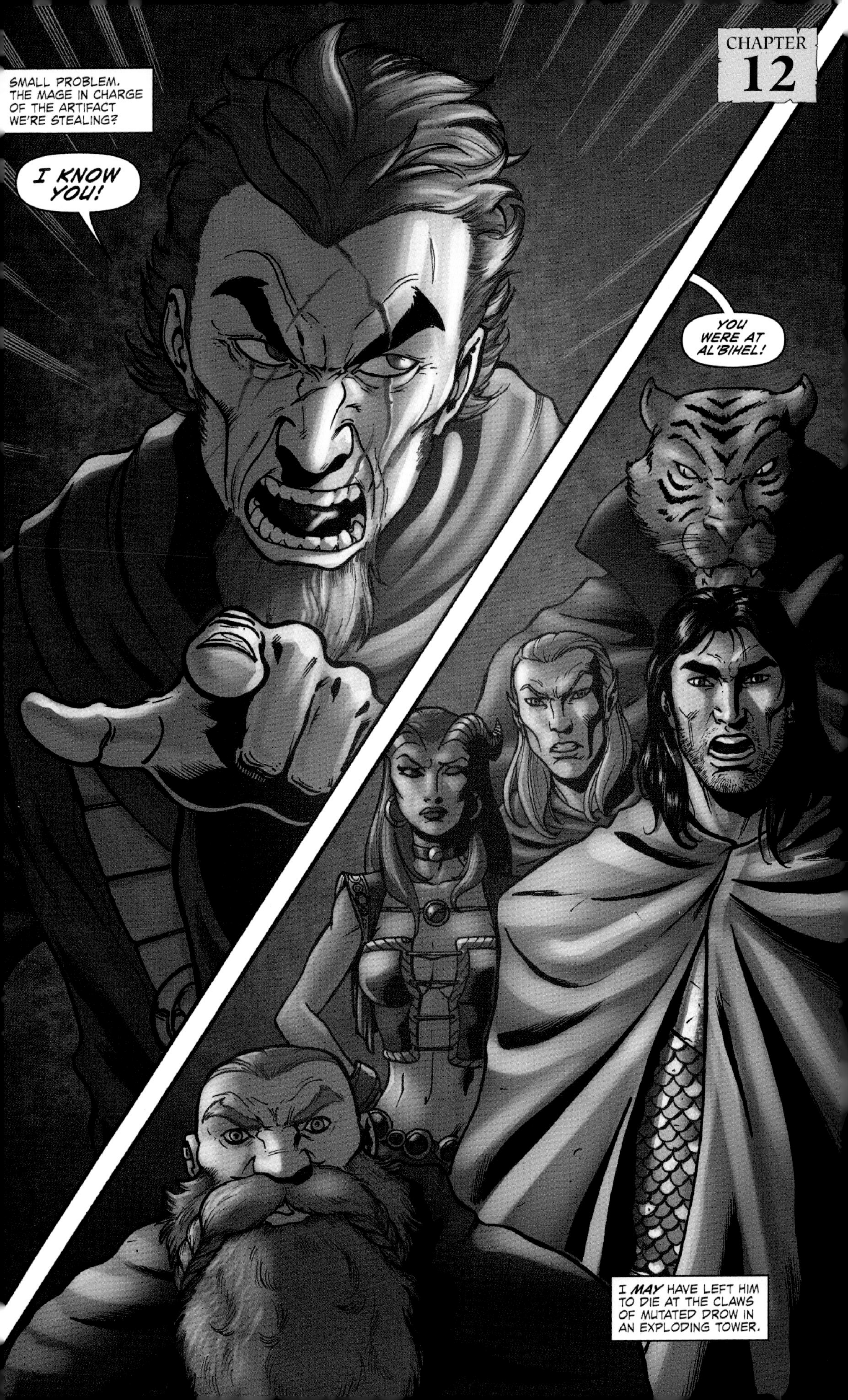
CHAPTER 12
SMALL PROBLEM. THE MAGE IN CHARGE OF THE ARTIFACT WE'RE STEALING?
I KNOW YOU!
YOU WERE AT AL'BIHEL!
I *MAY* HAVE LEFT HIM TO DIE AT THE CLAWS OF MUTATED DROW IN AN EXPLODING TOWER.

YOU CAME WITH THE FORCES OF THE ELADRIN! YOU WERE THEIR ELVEN SCOUT!

I NEVER FORGET A *VOICE!*

THERE IS A SIMPLE EXPLANATION. I TOLD YOU I WAS HERE AT THE BEHEST OF THE ELADRIN LORD.

THE WOOD-ELF HAS WORKED AS HIS SCOUT FOR YEARS. HE IS MY SCOUT FOR THIS MISSION, AS HE WAS FOR THE EXPEDITION YOUR BLIND MAGE SPEAKS OF.

HMM. THEN A SIMPLE TEST. SPEAK, SO THIS MAGE MAY TELL ME IF HE RECOGNIZES YOU AS WELL.

MY NAME IS ULRIC THE LAME FROM... SOUTH. OF HERE... INGTON.

ᛁᛅᚠ ᛏᛁᚱᚠᛁᚵᛁᛁ ᛁᛁᚨᛋ ᚴᚨᛋᛅᚠ ᛥᛏᚴᛁᚨ ᛏᚴᛌᛅᚠᛁᚱᛥ, ᛁᛁᚨᛋ ᚲᛅᛚᚨᛁᚲᛋᚠ ᛁᛁᛁᚠ:✱

*I'M BETTING YOU DON'T SPEAK DWARVEN, YOU ARROGANT GIT.

NO! I WAS HOPING ONE WOULD BE *ADRIC FELL*, THE IMPOTENT, BRAIN-ADDLED SELLSWORD FOOL WHO *PANICKED* AND *BETRAYED* ME!

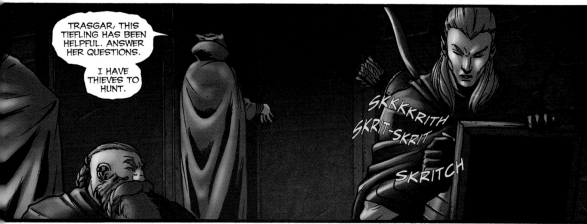

TRASGAR, THIS TIEFLING HAS BEEN HELPFUL. ANSWER HER QUESTIONS.

I HAVE THIEVES TO HUNT.

SKKKKRITH
SKRIT-SKRIT
SKRITCH

AH, ANOTHER SUPPLICANT SEEKING KNOWLEDGE FROM MY VAST EXPERIENCE!

YES. I HAVE QUESTIONS ABOUT THE *GUIDE OF GATES*.

GET HIM INTO THE NEXT ROOM

THANK YOU. MANY MEN WHO FONDLE MY NOSE TELL ME SO. MAY WE STEP INTO YOUR INNER SANCTUM?

A *TIEFLING!* AND A BEAUTY IF I MAY SAY SO.

I WOULD KNOW OF THE GUIDE'S—

—THAT IS MY TAIL. DO NOT FEEL THAT. EVER.

VARIS, KEEP AN EYE OUT BEHIND. KHAL, IF WE HIT ANY RESISTANCE, YOU PUNCH THROUGH THE CENTER, I'LL CATCH THE FLANKERS.

BREE, YOU CAN COME OUT NOW.

WORKED LIKE A CHARM. HE WENT STRAIGHT TO THE GUIDE TO MAKE SURE IT'S SAFE. I GOT EVERYTHING.

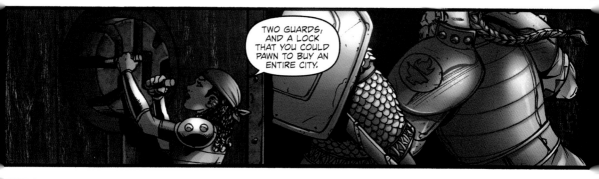

TWO GUARDS, AND A LOCK THAT YOU COULD PAWN TO BUY AN ENTIRE CITY.

OH, STEP ON THE WHITE SQUARES ONLY!

CLANK

SONUVA— BREE!

THERE'S A BIG GOLEM IN THE VAULT WHERE THE GUIDE'S KEPT, TOO. A KIND I'VE NEVER SEEN BEFORE.

SO, THIS SHOULD BE FUN.

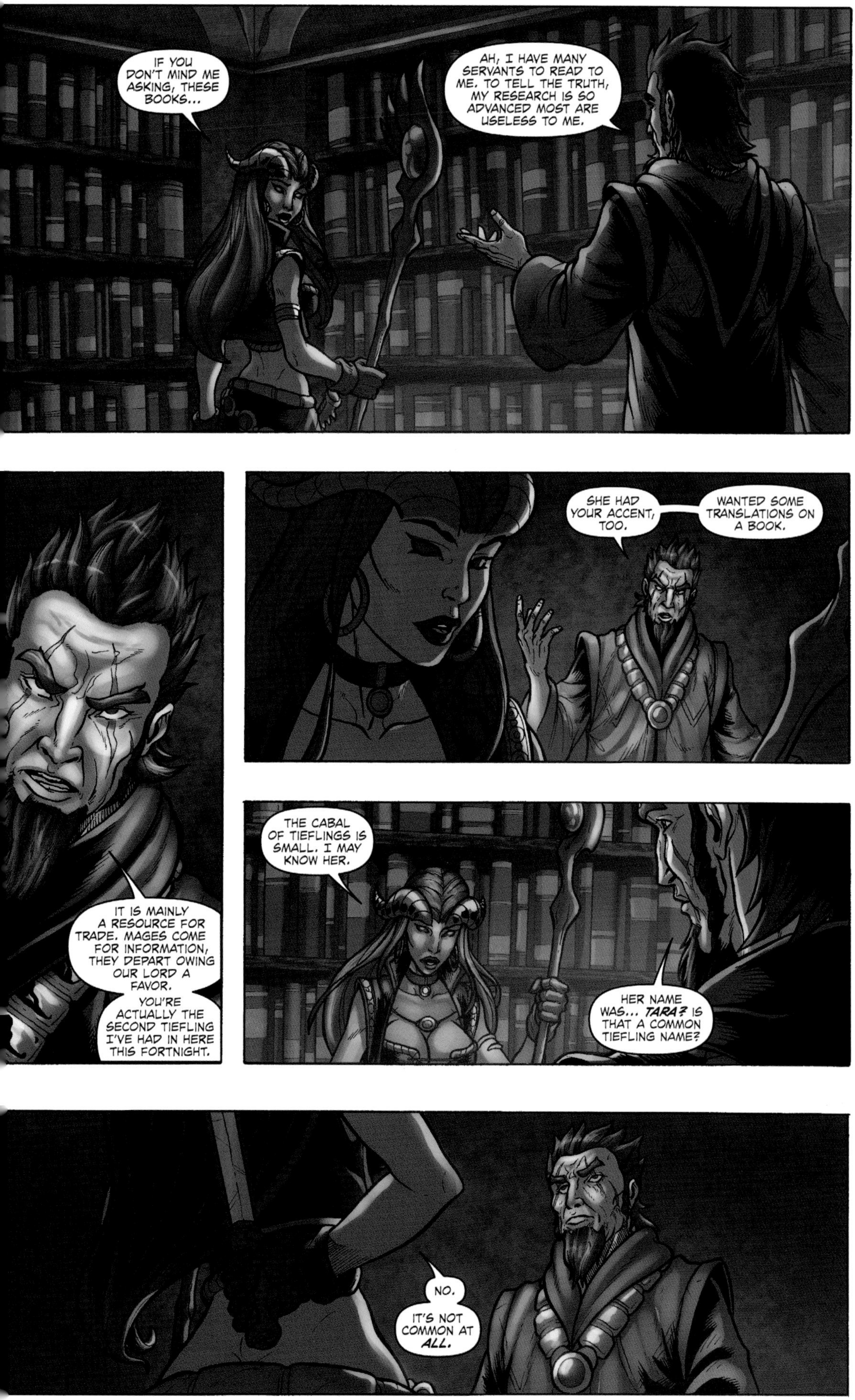
IF YOU DON'T MIND ME ASKING, THESE BOOKS...
AH, I HAVE MANY SERVANTS TO READ TO ME. TO TELL THE TRUTH, MY RESEARCH IS SO ADVANCED MOST ARE USELESS TO ME.
IT IS MAINLY A RESOURCE FOR TRADE. MAGES COME FOR INFORMATION, THEY DEPART OWING OUR LORD A FAVOR.
YOU'RE ACTUALLY THE SECOND TIEFLING I'VE HAD IN HERE THIS FORTNIGHT.
SHE HAD YOUR ACCENT, TOO.
WANTED SOME TRANSLATIONS ON A BOOK.
THE CABAL OF TIEFLINGS IS SMALL. I MAY KNOW HER.
HER NAME WAS... *TARA?* IS THAT A COMMON TIEFLING NAME?
NO.
IT'S NOT COMMON AT *ALL.*

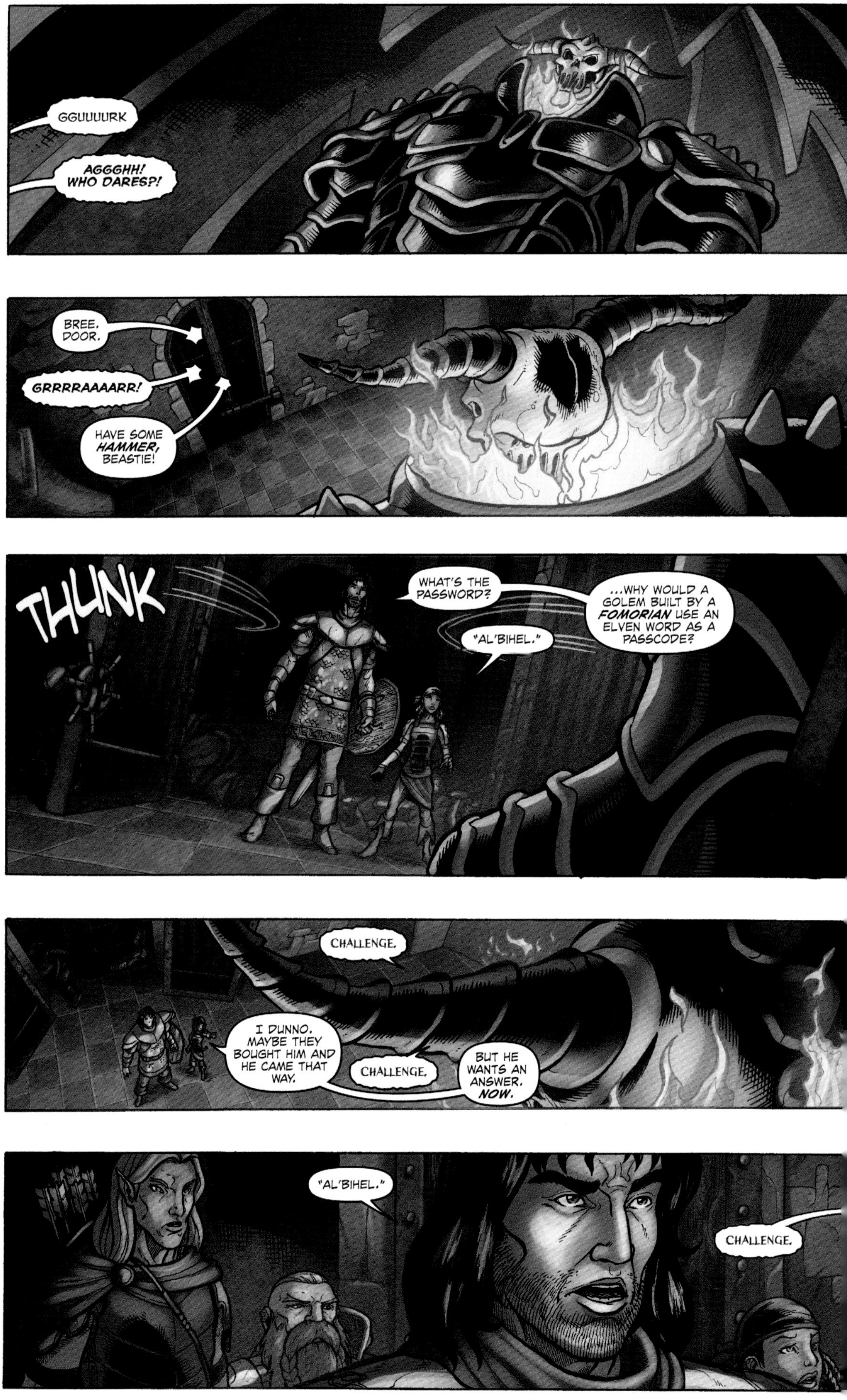
GGUUUURK
AGGGHH! WHO DARES?!
BREE. DOOR.
GRRRRAAAARR!
HAVE SOME HAMMER, BEASTIE!
THUNK
WHAT'S THE PASSWORD?
"AL'BIHEL."
...WHY WOULD A GOLEM BUILT BY A FOMORIAN USE AN ELVEN WORD AS A PASSCODE?
CHALLENGE.
I DUNNO. MAYBE THEY BOUGHT HIM AND HE CAME THAT WAY.
CHALLENGE.
BUT HE WANTS AN ANSWER. NOW.
"AL'BIHEL."
CHALLENGE.

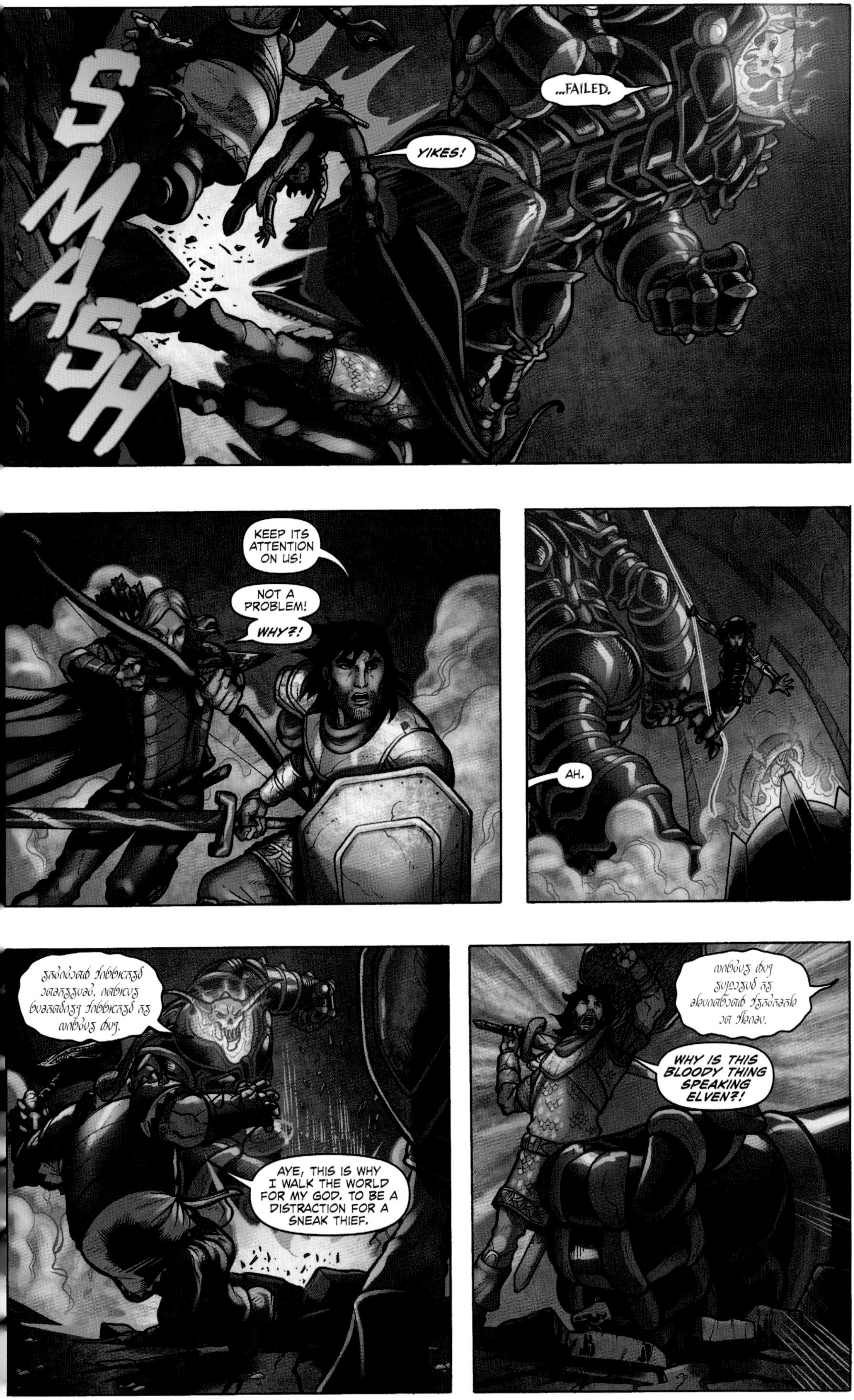
SMASH
...FAILED.
YIKES!
KEEP ITS ATTENTION ON US!
NOT A PROBLEM!
WHY?!
AH.
AYE, THIS IS WHY I WALK THE WORLD FOR MY GOD. TO BE A DISTRACTION FOR A SNEAK THIEF.
WHY IS THIS BLOODY THING SPEAKING ELVEN?!

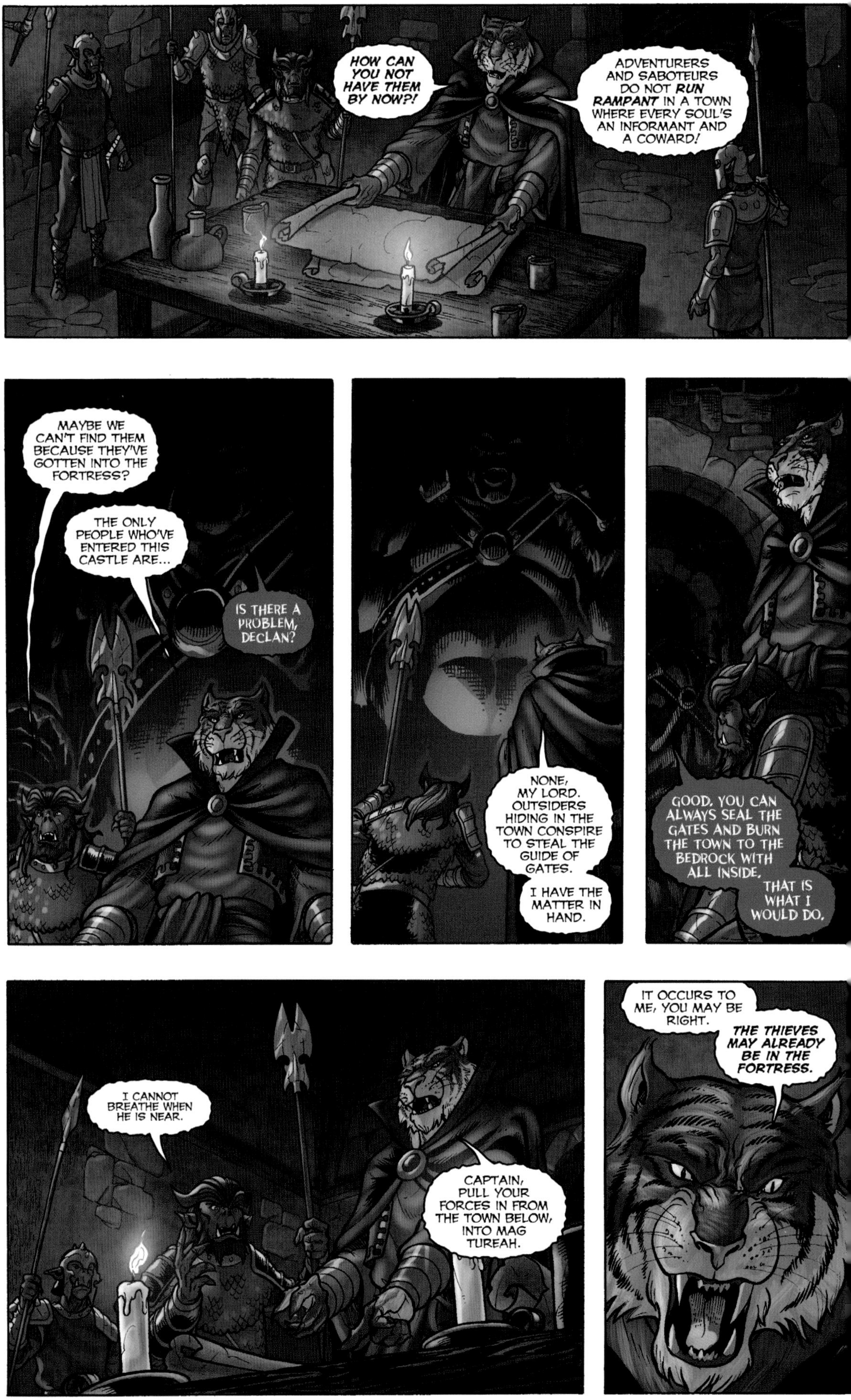
HOW CAN YOU NOT HAVE THEM BY NOW?!
ADVENTURERS AND SABOTEURS DO NOT RUN RAMPANT IN A TOWN WHERE EVERY SOUL'S AN INFORMANT AND A COWARD!
MAYBE WE CAN'T FIND THEM BECAUSE THEY'VE GOTTEN INTO THE FORTRESS?
THE ONLY PEOPLE WHO'VE ENTERED THIS CASTLE ARE...
IS THERE A PROBLEM, DECLAN?
NONE, MY LORD. OUTSIDERS HIDING IN THE TOWN CONSPIRE TO STEAL THE GUIDE OF GATES.
I HAVE THE MATTER IN HAND.
GOOD. YOU CAN ALWAYS SEAL THE GATES AND BURN THE TOWN TO THE BEDROCK WITH ALL INSIDE.
THAT IS WHAT I WOULD DO.
I CANNOT BREATHE WHEN HE IS NEAR.
CAPTAIN, PULL YOUR FORCES IN FROM THE TOWN BELOW, INTO MAG TUREAH.
IT OCCURS TO ME, YOU MAY BE RIGHT.
THE THIEVES MAY ALREADY BE IN THE FORTRESS.

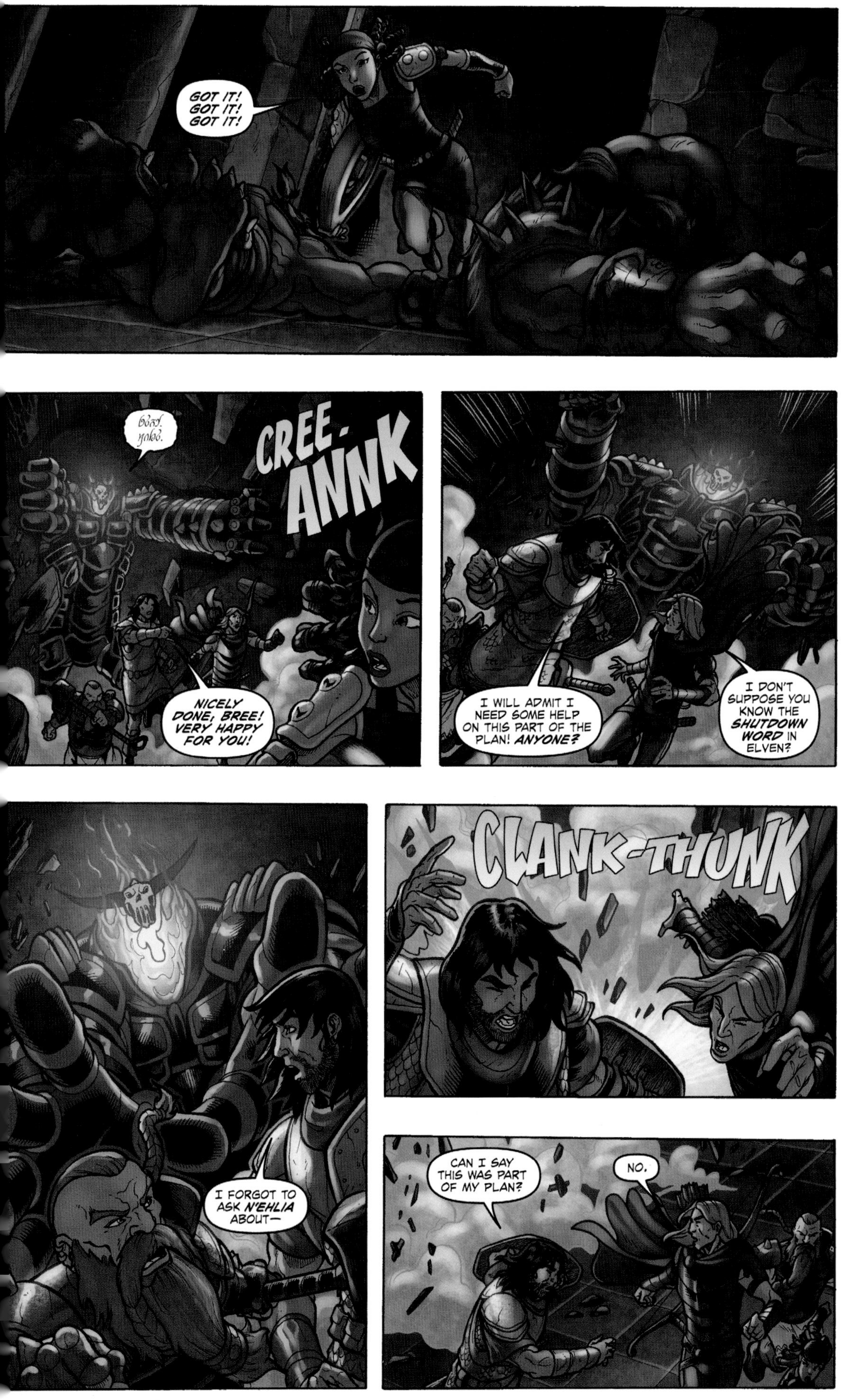
GOT IT! GOT IT! GOT IT!
CREE-ANNK
NICELY DONE, BREE! VERY HAPPY FOR YOU!
I WILL ADMIT I NEED SOME HELP ON THIS PART OF THE PLAN! ANYONE?
I DON'T SUPPOSE YOU KNOW THE SHUTDOWN WORD IN ELVEN?
I FORGOT TO ASK N'EHLIA ABOUT—
CLANK-THUNK
CAN I SAY THIS WAS PART OF MY PLAN?
NO.

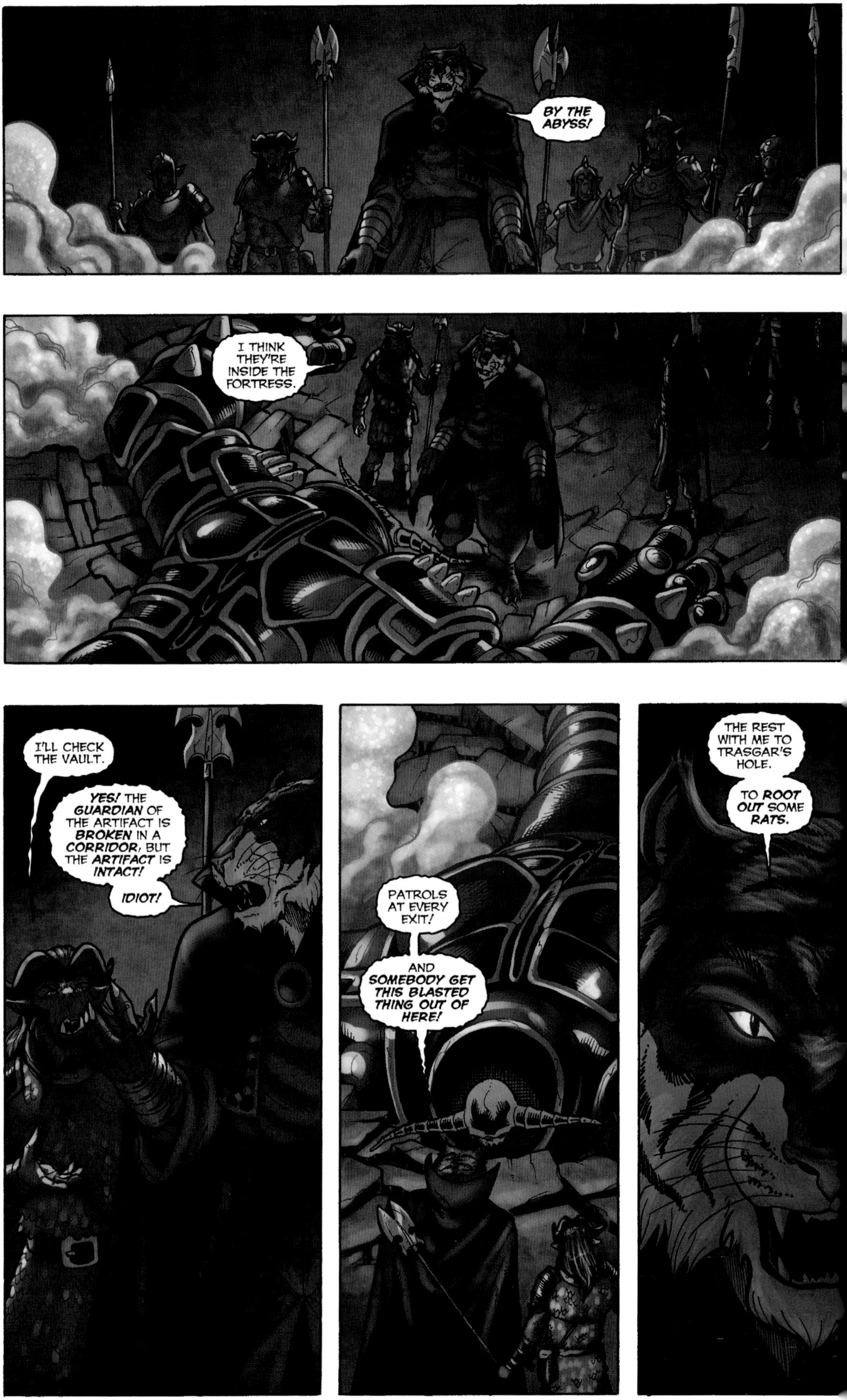

BY THE ABYSS!
I THINK THEY'RE INSIDE THE FORTRESS.
I'LL CHECK THE VAULT.
YES! THE GUARDIAN OF THE ARTIFACT IS BROKEN IN A CORRIDOR, BUT THE ARTIFACT IS INTACT!
IDIOT!
PATROLS AT EVERY EXIT!
AND SOMEBODY GET THIS BLASTED THING OUT OF HERE!
THE REST WITH ME TO TRASGAR'S HOLE.
TO ROOT OUT SOME RATS.

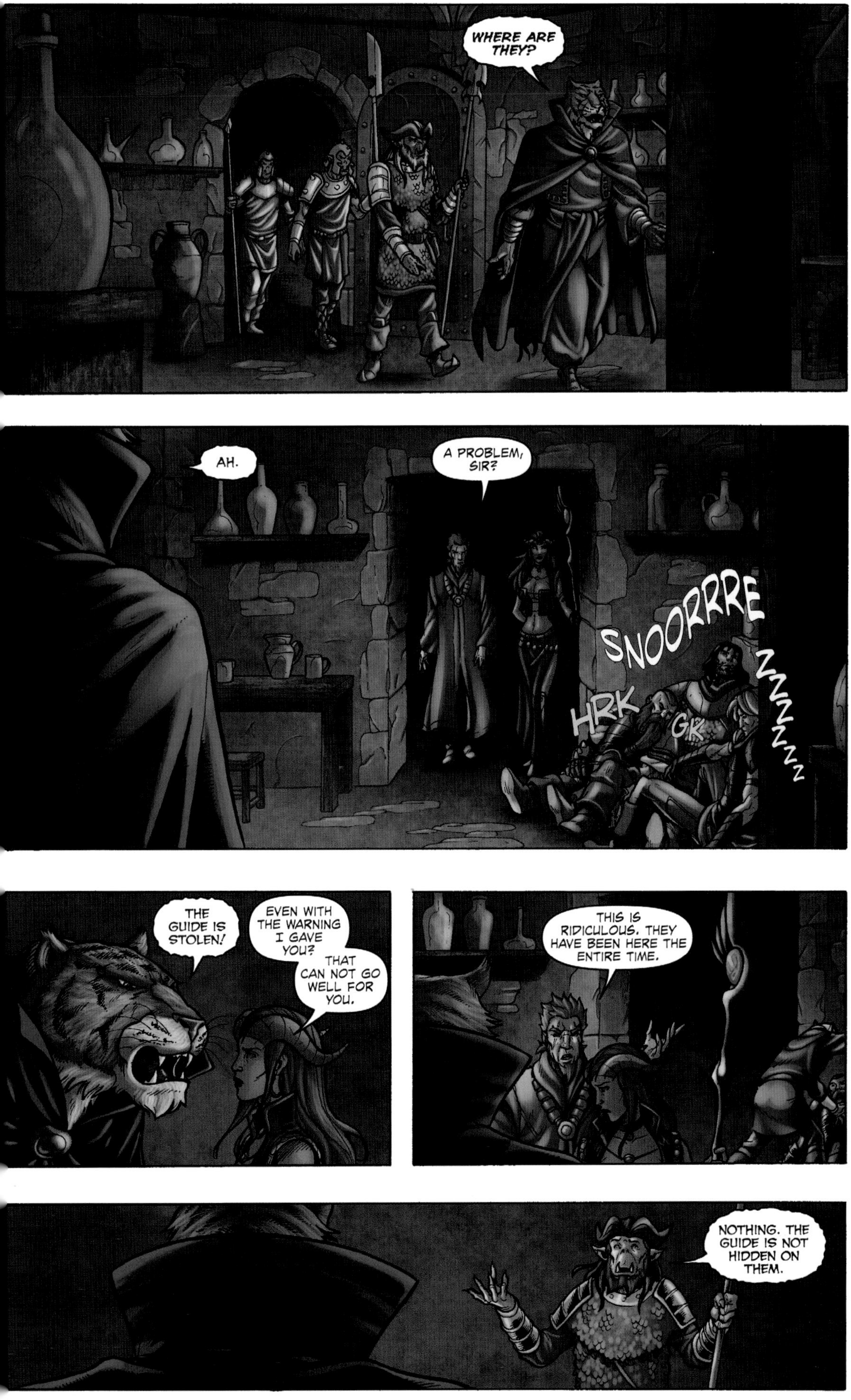
WHERE ARE THEY?
AH.
A PROBLEM, SIR?
SNOORRRE
HRK
GK
ZZZZZZ
THE GUIDE IS STOLEN!
EVEN WITH THE WARNING I GAVE YOU?
THAT CAN NOT GO WELL FOR YOU.
THIS IS RIDICULOUS. THEY HAVE BEEN HERE THE ENTIRE TIME.
NOTHING. THE GUIDE IS NOT HIDDEN ON THEM.

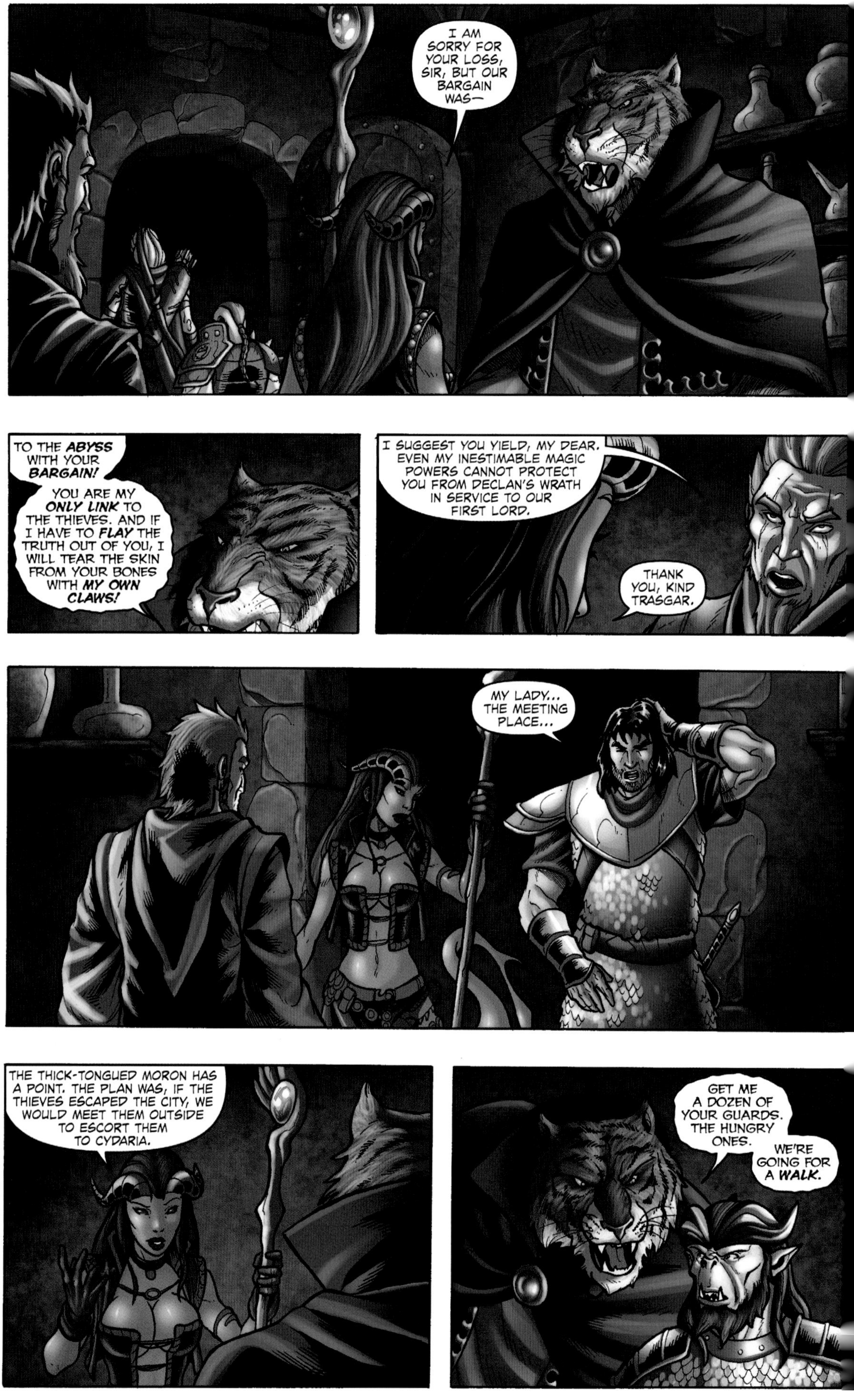
I AM SORRY FOR YOUR LOSS, SIR, BUT OUR BARGAIN WAS—
TO THE ABYSS WITH YOUR BARGAIN!
YOU ARE MY ONLY LINK TO THE THIEVES. AND IF I HAVE TO FLAY THE TRUTH OUT OF YOU, I WILL TEAR THE SKIN FROM YOUR BONES WITH MY OWN CLAWS!
I SUGGEST YOU YIELD, MY DEAR. EVEN MY INESTIMABLE MAGIC POWERS CANNOT PROTECT YOU FROM DECLAN'S WRATH IN SERVICE TO OUR FIRST LORD.
THANK YOU, KIND TRASGAR.
MY LADY... THE MEETING PLACE...
THE THICK-TONGUED MORON HAS A POINT. THE PLAN WAS, IF THE THIEVES ESCAPED THE CITY, WE WOULD MEET THEM OUTSIDE TO ESCORT THEM TO CYDARIA.
GET ME A DOZEN OF YOUR GUARDS. THE HUNGRY ONES.
WE'RE GOING FOR A WALK.

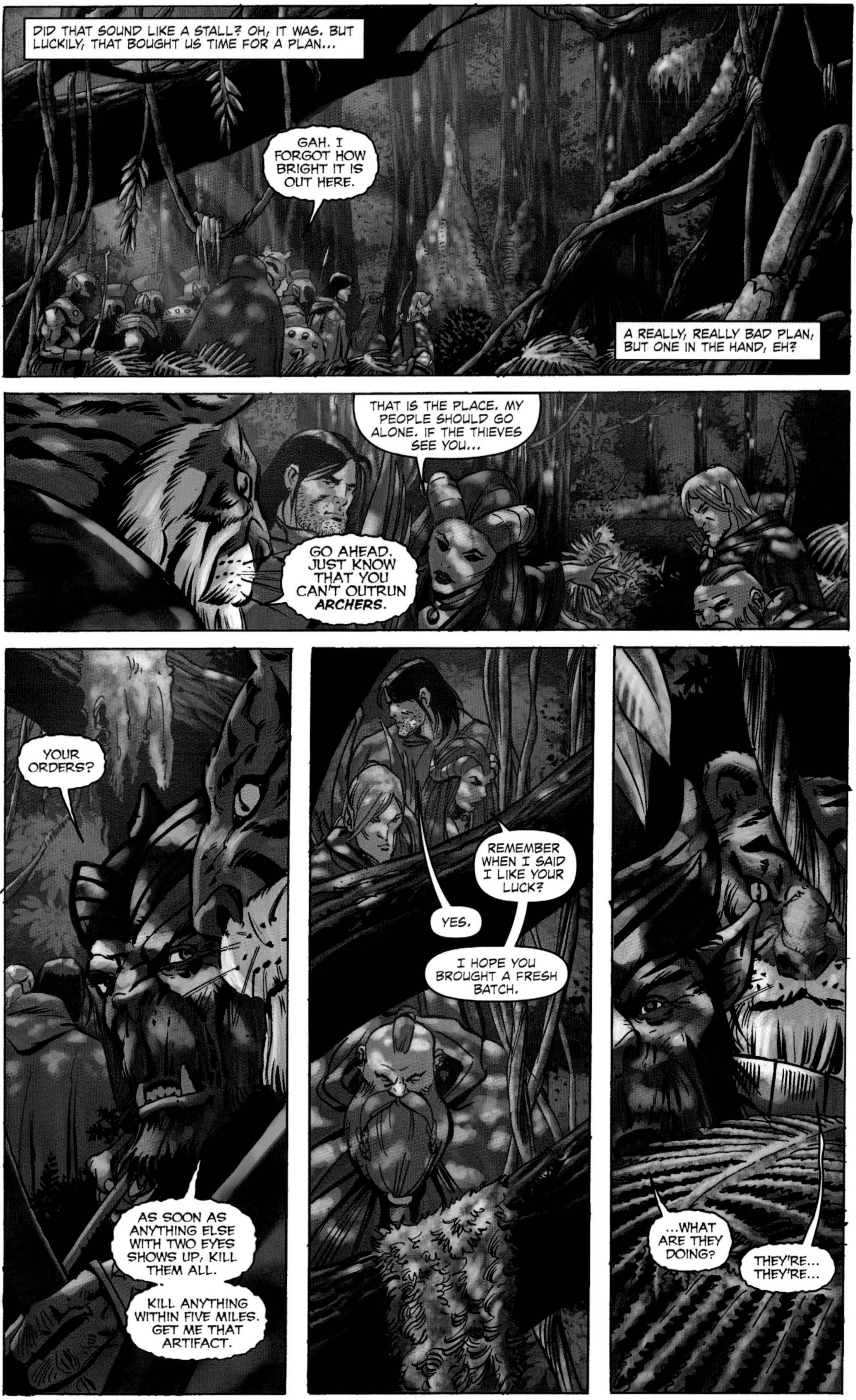
DID THAT SOUND LIKE A STALL? OH, IT WAS. BUT LUCKILY, THAT BOUGHT US TIME FOR A PLAN...
GAH. I FORGOT HOW BRIGHT IT IS OUT HERE.
A REALLY, REALLY BAD PLAN, BUT ONE IN THE HAND, EH?
THAT IS THE PLACE. MY PEOPLE SHOULD GO ALONE. IF THE THIEVES SEE YOU...
GO AHEAD. JUST KNOW THAT YOU CAN'T OUTRUN ARCHERS.
YOUR ORDERS?
AS SOON AS ANYTHING ELSE WITH TWO EYES SHOWS UP, KILL THEM ALL.
KILL ANYTHING WITHIN FIVE MILES. GET ME THAT ARTIFACT.
REMEMBER WHEN I SAID I LIKE YOUR LUCK?
YES.
I HOPE YOU BROUGHT A FRESH BATCH.
...WHAT ARE THEY DOING?
THEY'RE... THEY'RE...

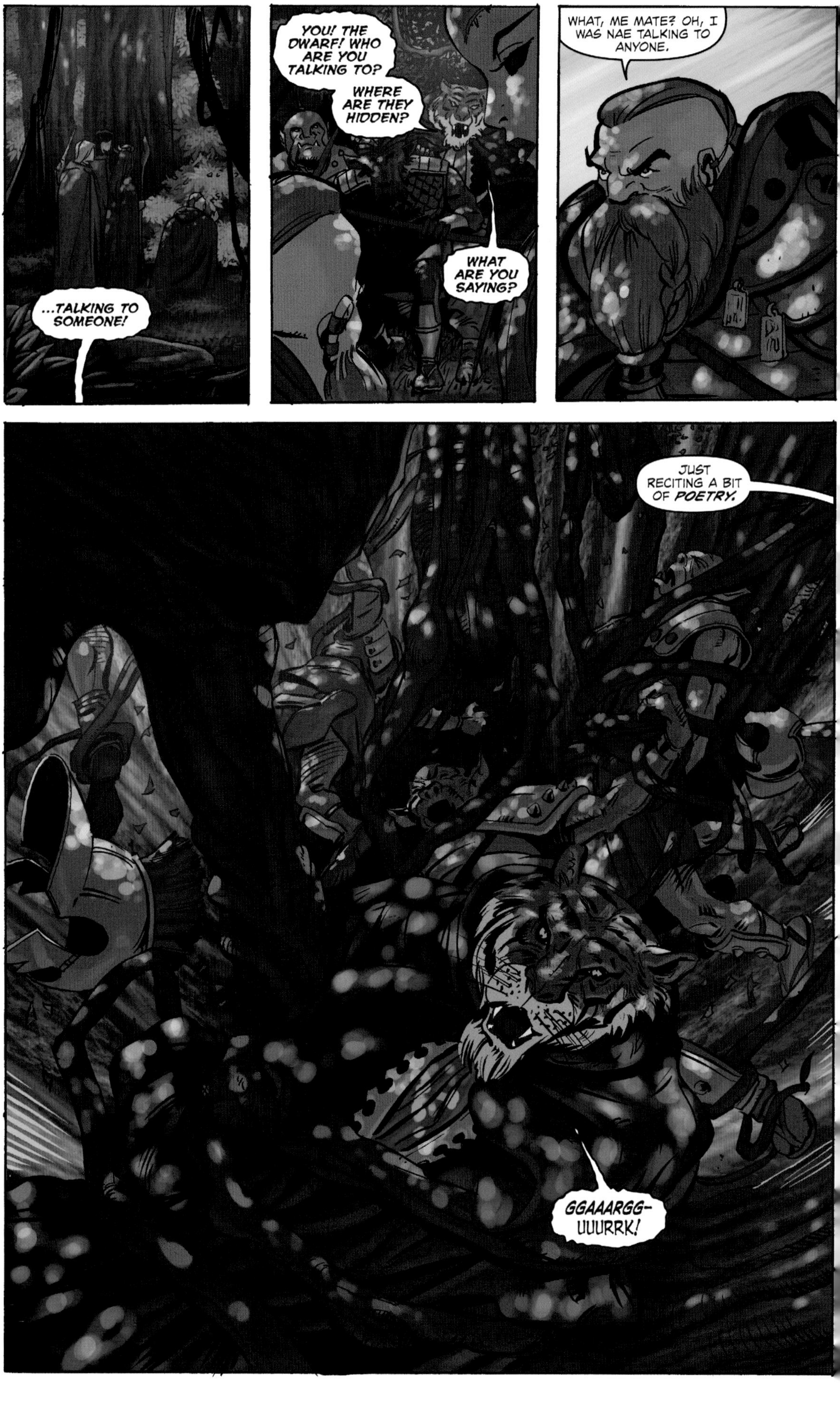
...TALKING TO SOMEONE!
YOU! THE DWARF! WHO ARE YOU TALKING TO?
WHERE ARE THEY HIDDEN?
WHAT ARE YOU SAYING?
WHAT, ME MATE? OH, I WAS NAE TALKING TO ANYONE.
JUST RECITING A BIT OF POETRY.
GGAAARGG-UUURRK!

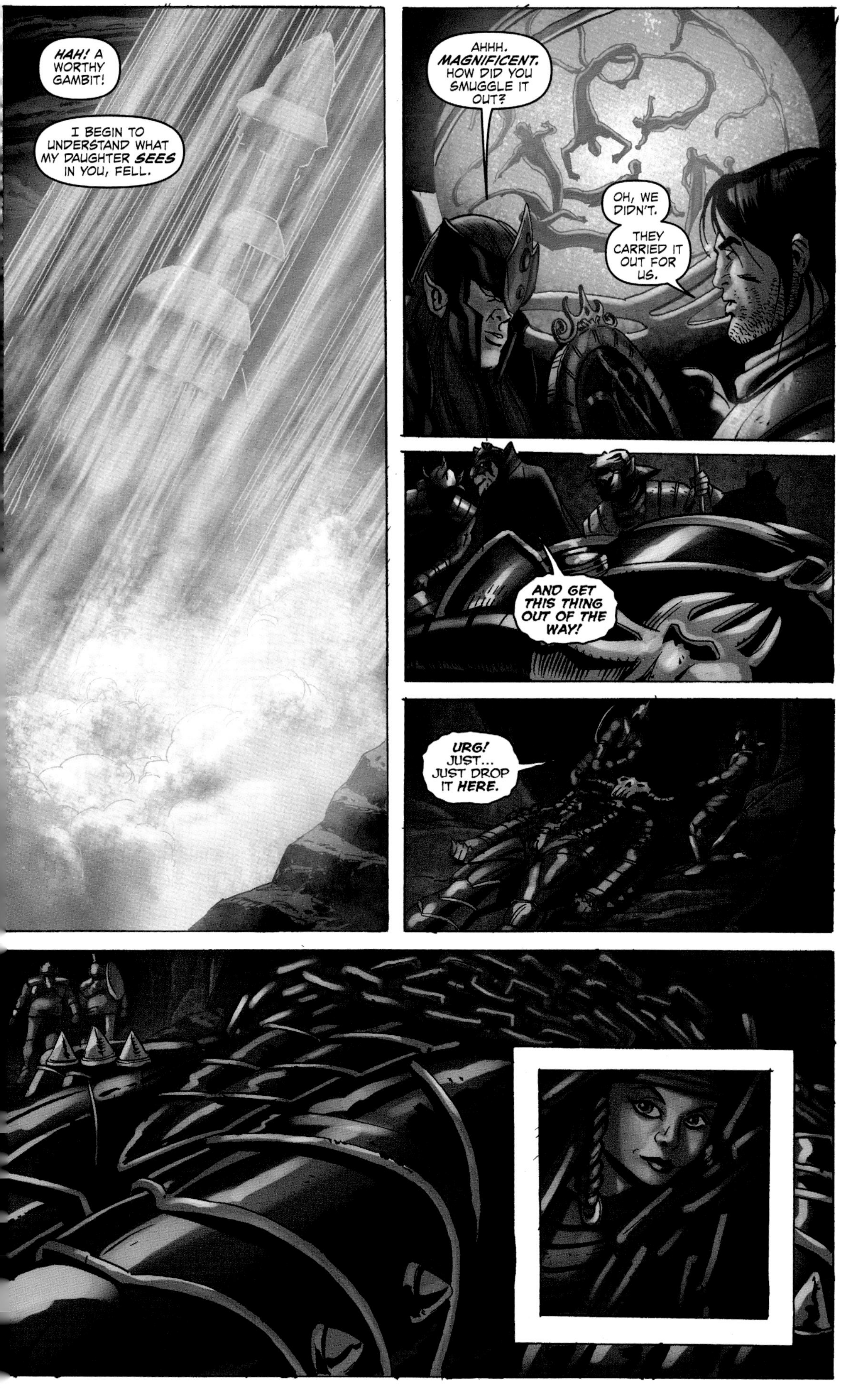
HAH! A WORTHY GAMBIT!
I BEGIN TO UNDERSTAND WHAT MY DAUGHTER SEES IN YOU, FELL.
AHHH. MAGNIFICENT. HOW DID YOU SMUGGLE IT OUT?
OH, WE DIDN'T.
THEY CARRIED IT OUT FOR US.
AND GET THIS THING OUT OF THE WAY!
URG! JUST... JUST DROP IT HERE.

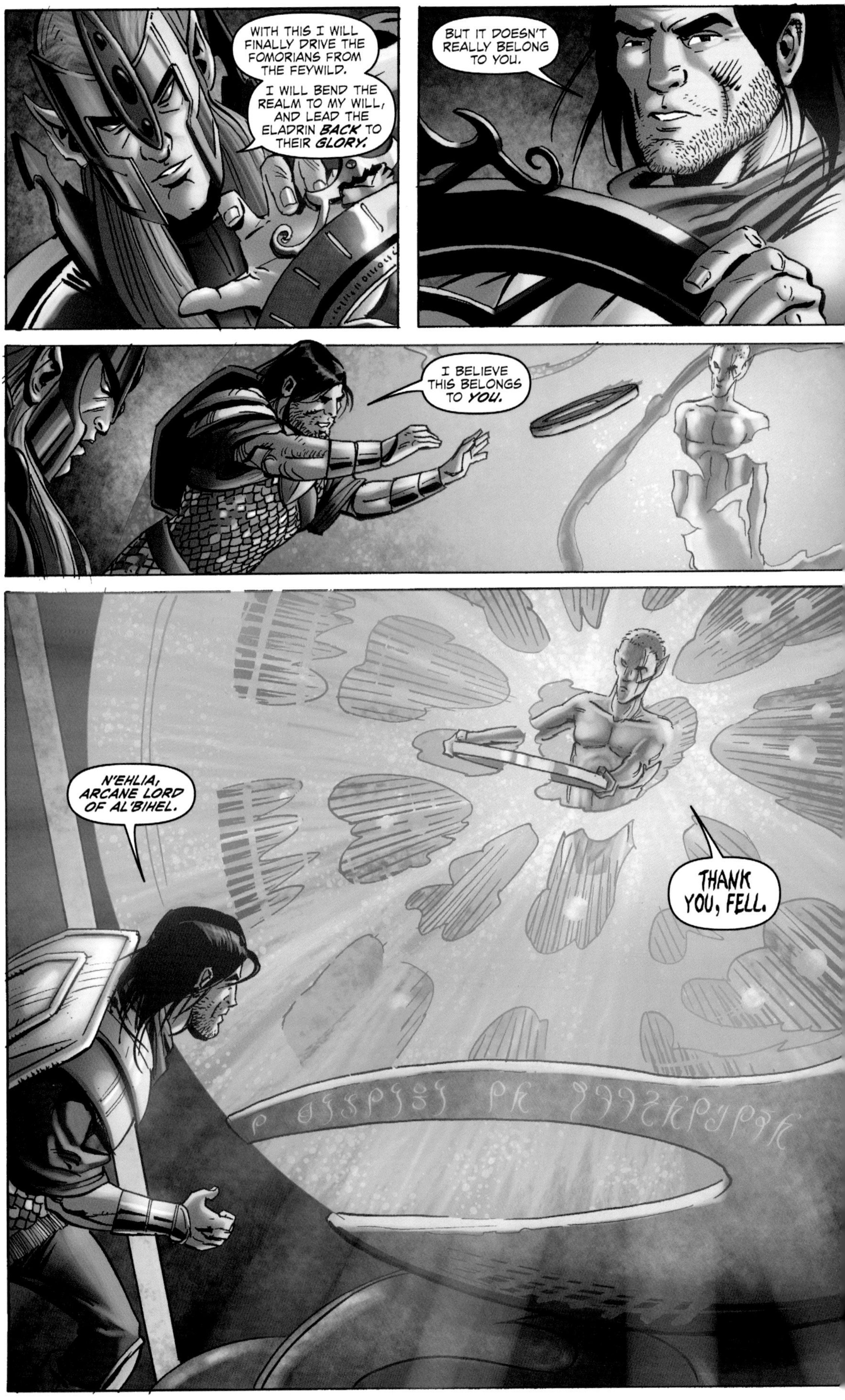
WITH THIS I WILL FINALLY DRIVE THE FOMORIANS FROM THE FEYWILD.
I WILL BEND THE REALM TO MY WILL, AND LEAD THE ELADRIN BACK TO THEIR GLORY.
BUT IT DOESN'T REALLY BELONG TO YOU.
I BELIEVE THIS BELONGS TO YOU.
N'EHLIA, ARCANE LORD OF AL'BIHEL.
THANK YOU, FELL.

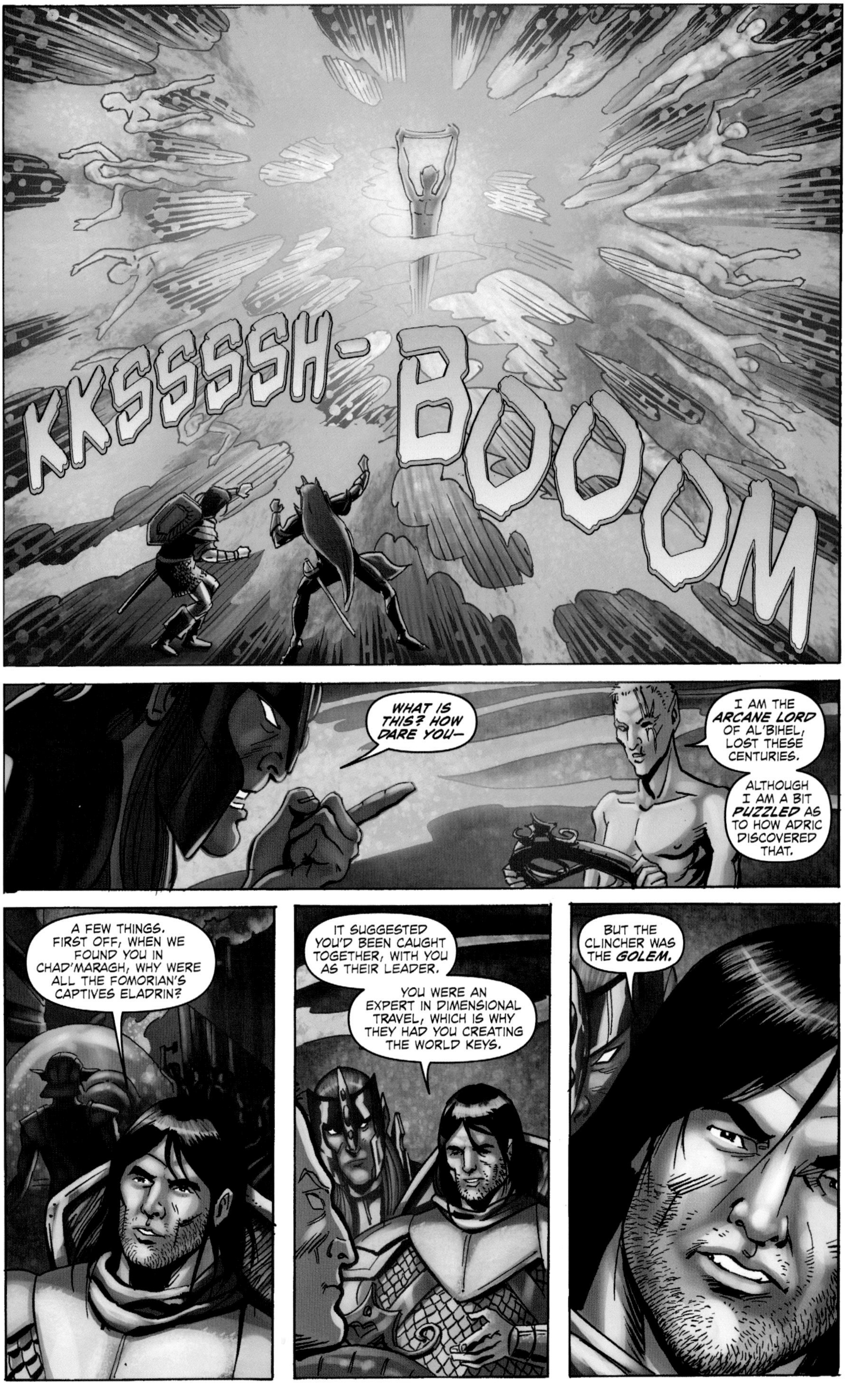
KKSSSSH-BOOOOM
WHAT IS THIS? HOW DARE YOU—
I AM THE ARCANE LORD OF AL'BIHEL, LOST THESE CENTURIES.
ALTHOUGH I AM A BIT PUZZLED AS TO HOW ADRIC DISCOVERED THAT.
A FEW THINGS. FIRST OFF, WHEN WE FOUND YOU IN CHAD'MARAGH, WHY WERE ALL THE FOMORIAN'S CAPTIVES ELADRIN?
IT SUGGESTED YOU'D BEEN CAUGHT TOGETHER, WITH YOU AS THEIR LEADER.
YOU WERE AN EXPERT IN DIMENSIONAL TRAVEL, WHICH IS WHY THEY HAD YOU CREATING THE WORLD KEYS.
BUT THE CLINCHER WAS THE GOLEM.

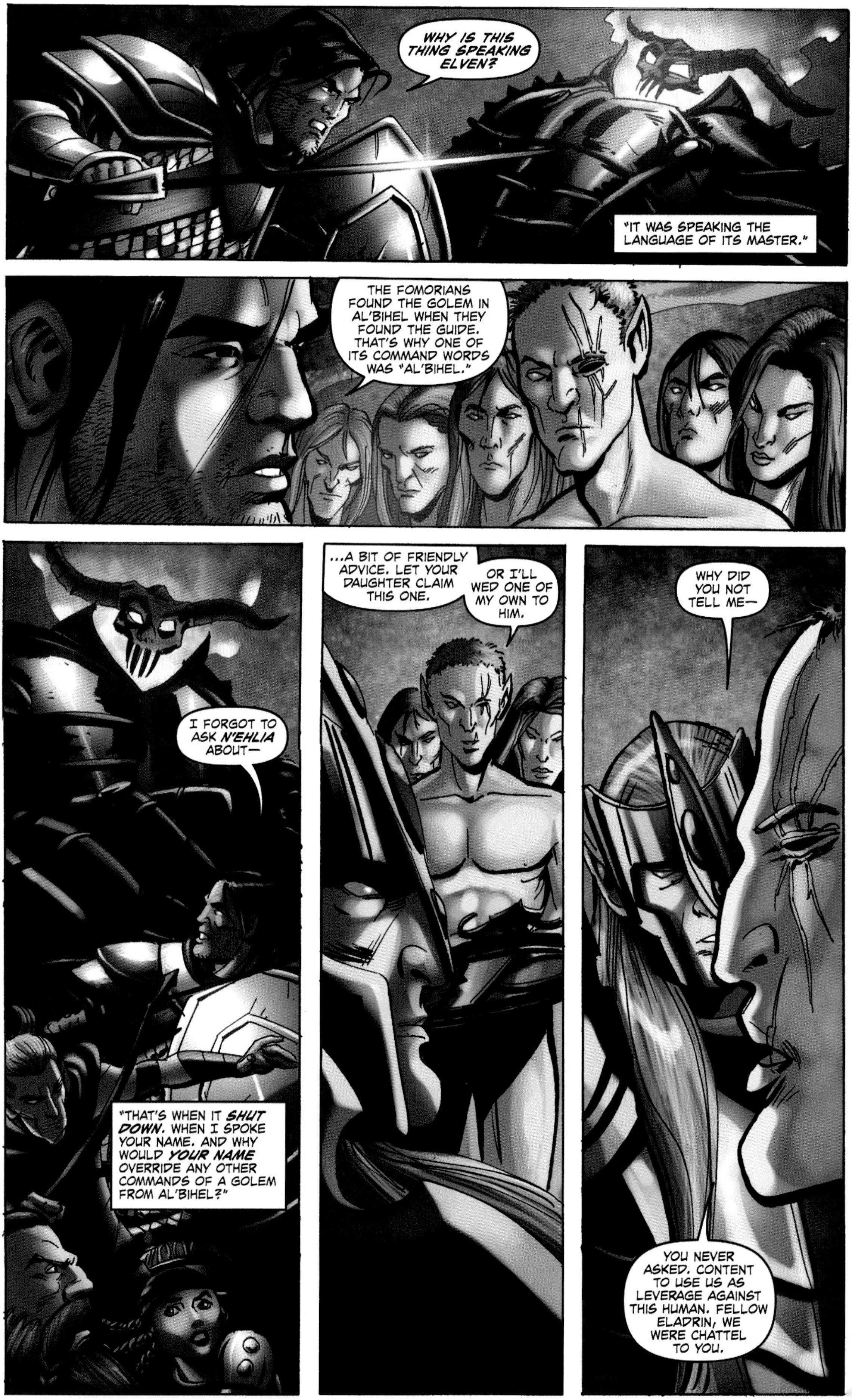
WHY IS THIS THING SPEAKING ELVEN?
"IT WAS SPEAKING THE LANGUAGE OF ITS MASTER."
THE FOMORIANS FOUND THE GOLEM IN AL'BIHEL WHEN THEY FOUND THE GUIDE. THAT'S WHY ONE OF ITS COMMAND WORDS WAS "AL'BIHEL."
I FORGOT TO ASK N'EHLIA ABOUT—
"THAT'S WHEN IT SHUT DOWN. WHEN I SPOKE YOUR NAME. AND WHY WOULD YOUR NAME OVERRIDE ANY OTHER COMMANDS OF A GOLEM FROM AL'BIHEL?"
...A BIT OF FRIENDLY ADVICE. LET YOUR DAUGHTER CLAIM THIS ONE.
OR I'LL WED ONE OF MY OWN TO HIM.
WHY DID YOU NOT TELL ME—
YOU NEVER ASKED. CONTENT TO USE US AS LEVERAGE AGAINST THIS HUMAN. FELLOW ELADRIN, WE WERE CHATTEL TO YOU.

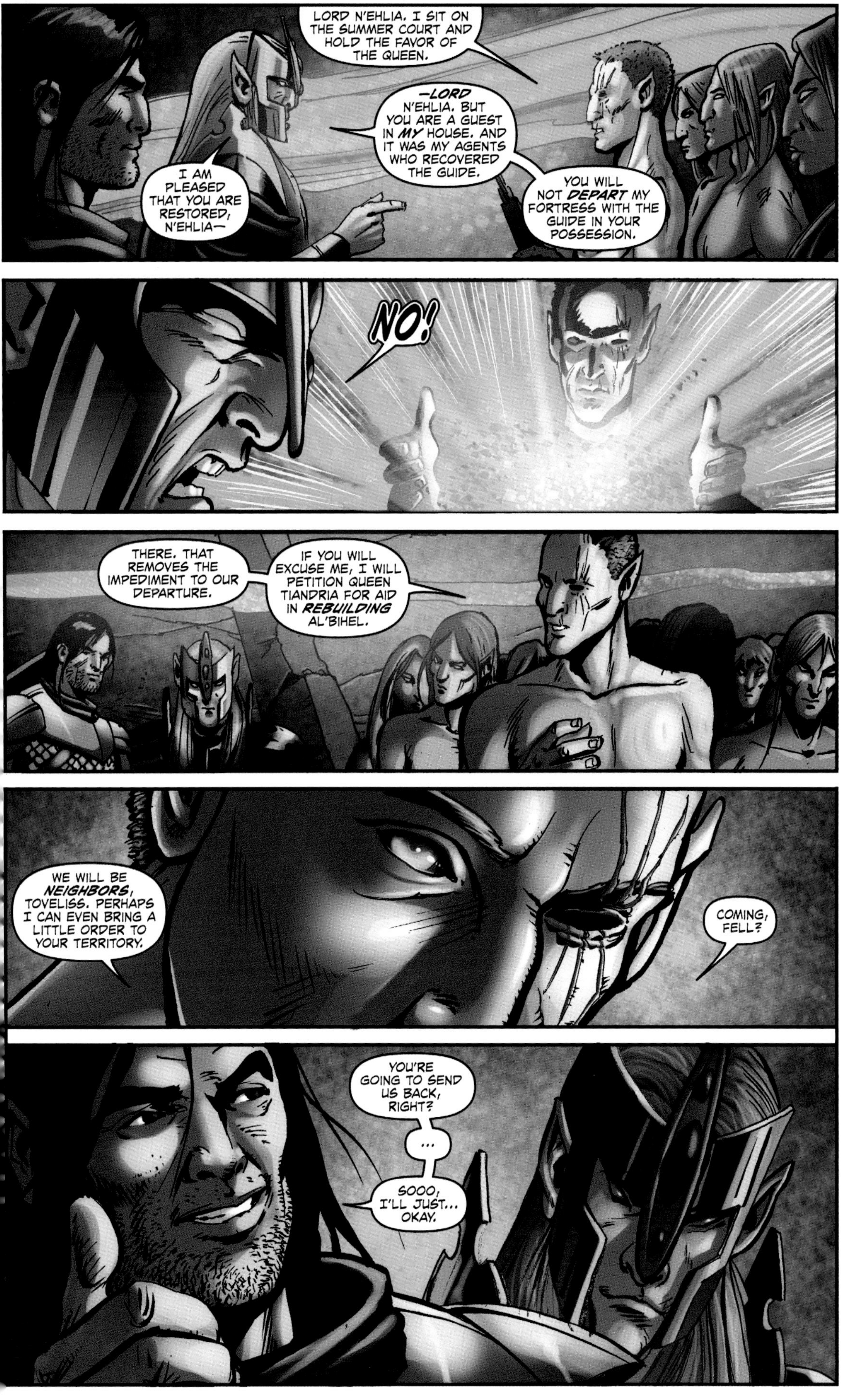
LORD N'EHLIA. I SIT ON THE SUMMER COURT AND HOLD THE FAVOR OF THE QUEEN.
I AM PLEASED THAT YOU ARE RESTORED, N'EHLIA—
—LORD N'EHLIA. BUT YOU ARE A GUEST IN MY HOUSE. AND IT WAS MY AGENTS WHO RECOVERED THE GUIDE.
YOU WILL NOT DEPART MY FORTRESS WITH THE GUIDE IN YOUR POSSESSION.
NO!
THERE. THAT REMOVES THE IMPEDIMENT TO OUR DEPARTURE.
IF YOU WILL EXCUSE ME, I WILL PETITION QUEEN TIANDRIA FOR AID IN REBUILDING AL'BIHEL.
WE WILL BE NEIGHBORS, TOVELISS. PERHAPS I CAN EVEN BRING A LITTLE ORDER TO YOUR TERRITORY.
COMING, FELL?
YOU'RE GOING TO SEND US BACK, RIGHT?
...
SOOO, I'LL JUST... OKAY.

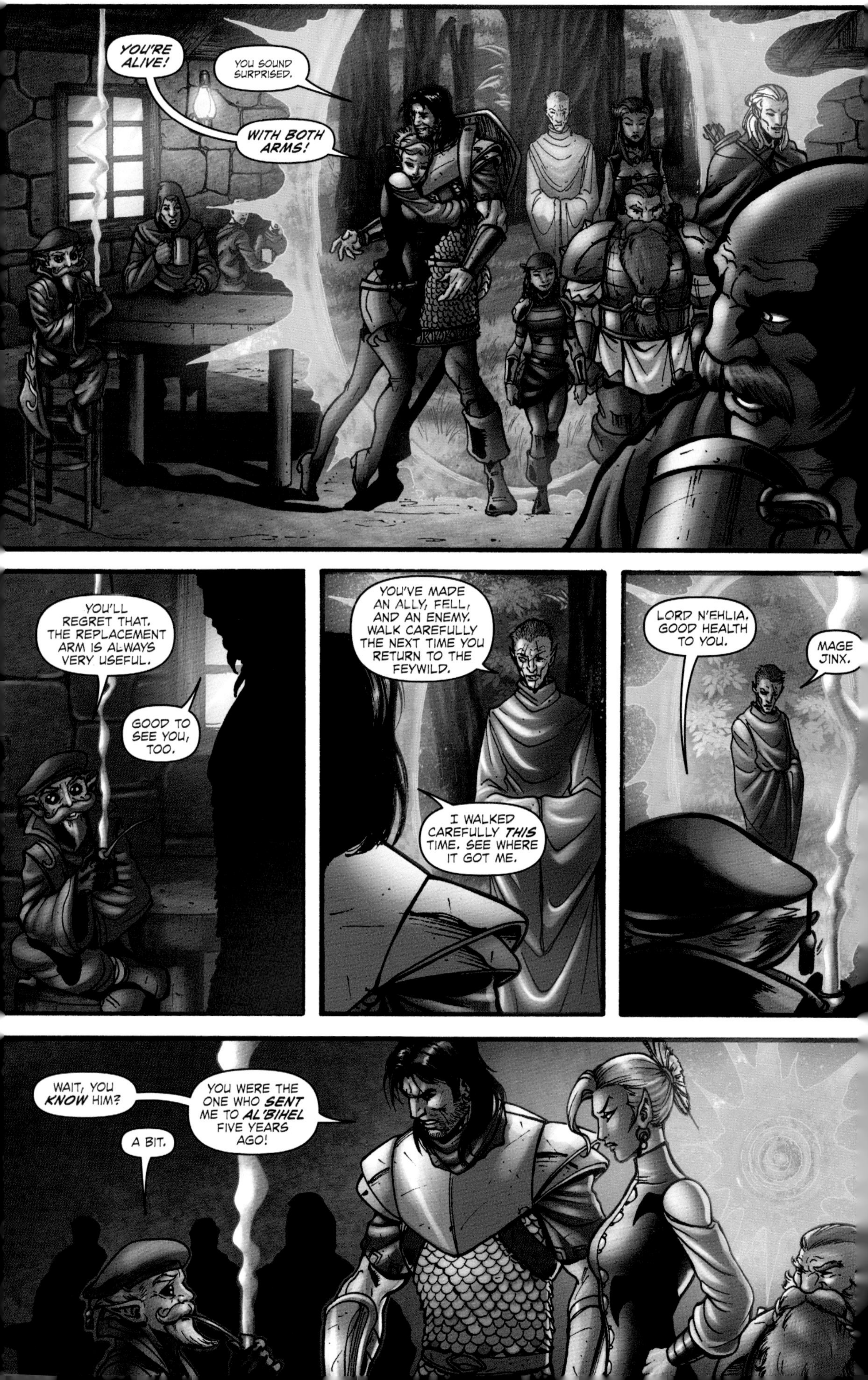
YOU'RE ALIVE!
YOU SOUND SURPRISED.
WITH BOTH ARMS!
YOU'LL REGRET THAT. THE REPLACEMENT ARM IS ALWAYS VERY USEFUL.
GOOD TO SEE YOU, TOO.
YOU'VE MADE AN ALLY, FELL, AND AN ENEMY. WALK CAREFULLY THE NEXT TIME YOU RETURN TO THE FEYWILD.
I WALKED CAREFULLY THIS TIME. SEE WHERE IT GOT ME.
LORD N'EHLIA. GOOD HEALTH TO YOU.
MAGE JINX.
WAIT, YOU KNOW HIM?
A BIT.
YOU WERE THE ONE WHO SENT ME TO AL'BIHEL FIVE YEARS AGO!

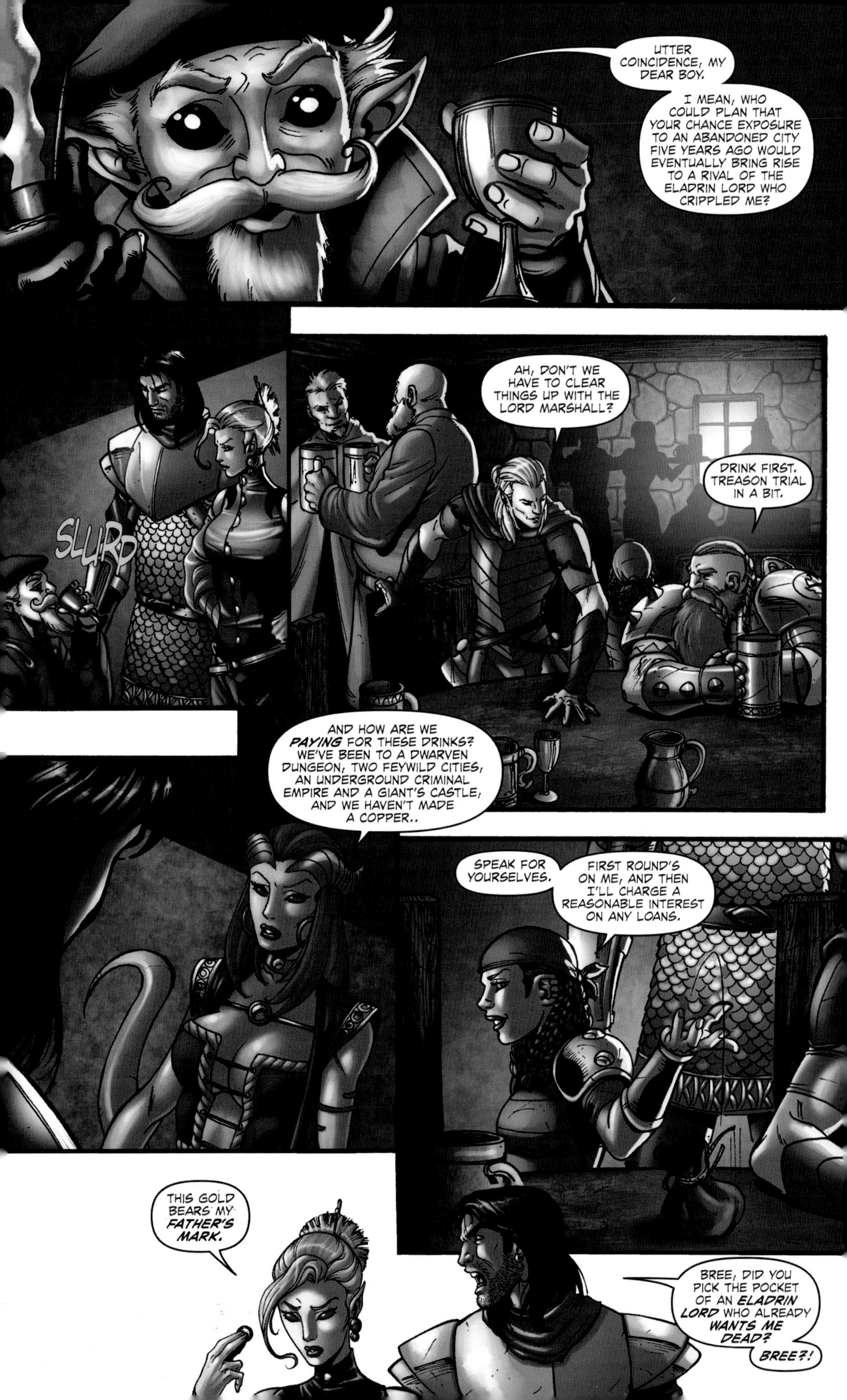
UTTER COINCIDENCE, MY DEAR BOY.
I MEAN, WHO COULD PLAN THAT YOUR CHANCE EXPOSURE TO AN ABANDONED CITY FIVE YEARS AGO WOULD EVENTUALLY BRING RISE TO A RIVAL OF THE ELADRIN LORD WHO CRIPPLED ME?
SLURP
AH, DON'T WE HAVE TO CLEAR THINGS UP WITH THE LORD MARSHALL?
DRINK FIRST. TREASON TRIAL IN A BIT.
AND HOW ARE WE *PAYING* FOR THESE DRINKS? WE'VE BEEN TO A DWARVEN DUNGEON, TWO FEYWILD CITIES, AN UNDERGROUND CRIMINAL EMPIRE AND A GIANT'S CASTLE, AND WE HAVEN'T MADE A COPPER..
SPEAK FOR YOURSELVES.
FIRST ROUND'S ON ME, AND THEN I'LL CHARGE A REASONABLE INTEREST ON ANY LOANS.
THIS GOLD BEARS MY ***FATHER'S MARK.***
BREE, DID YOU PICK THE POCKET OF AN ***ELADRIN LORD*** WHO ALREADY ***WANTS ME DEAD?***
BREE?!

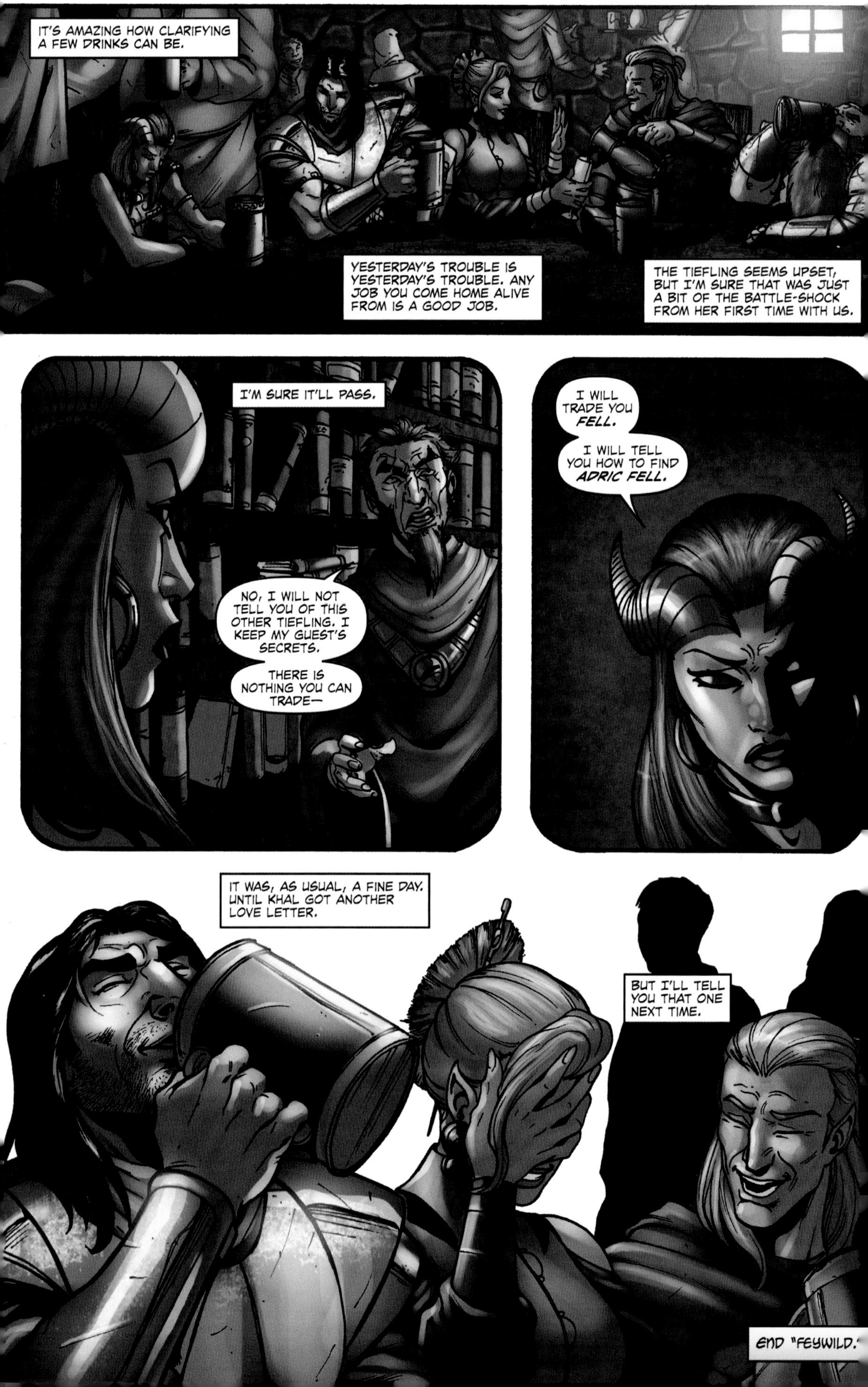
IT'S AMAZING HOW CLARIFYING A FEW DRINKS CAN BE.
YESTERDAY'S TROUBLE IS YESTERDAY'S TROUBLE. ANY JOB YOU COME HOME ALIVE FROM IS A GOOD JOB.
THE TIEFLING SEEMS UPSET, BUT I'M SURE THAT WAS JUST A BIT OF THE BATTLE-SHOCK FROM HER FIRST TIME WITH US.
I'M SURE IT'LL PASS.
NO, I WILL NOT TELL YOU OF THIS OTHER TIEFLING. I KEEP MY GUEST'S SECRETS.
THERE IS NOTHING YOU CAN TRADE—
I WILL TRADE YOU *FELL.*
I WILL TELL YOU HOW TO FIND *ADRIC FELL.*
IT WAS, AS USUAL, A FINE DAY. UNTIL KHAL GOT ANOTHER LOVE LETTER.
BUT I'LL TELL YOU THAT ONE NEXT TIME.
END "FEYWILD."

Art by Tyler Walpole

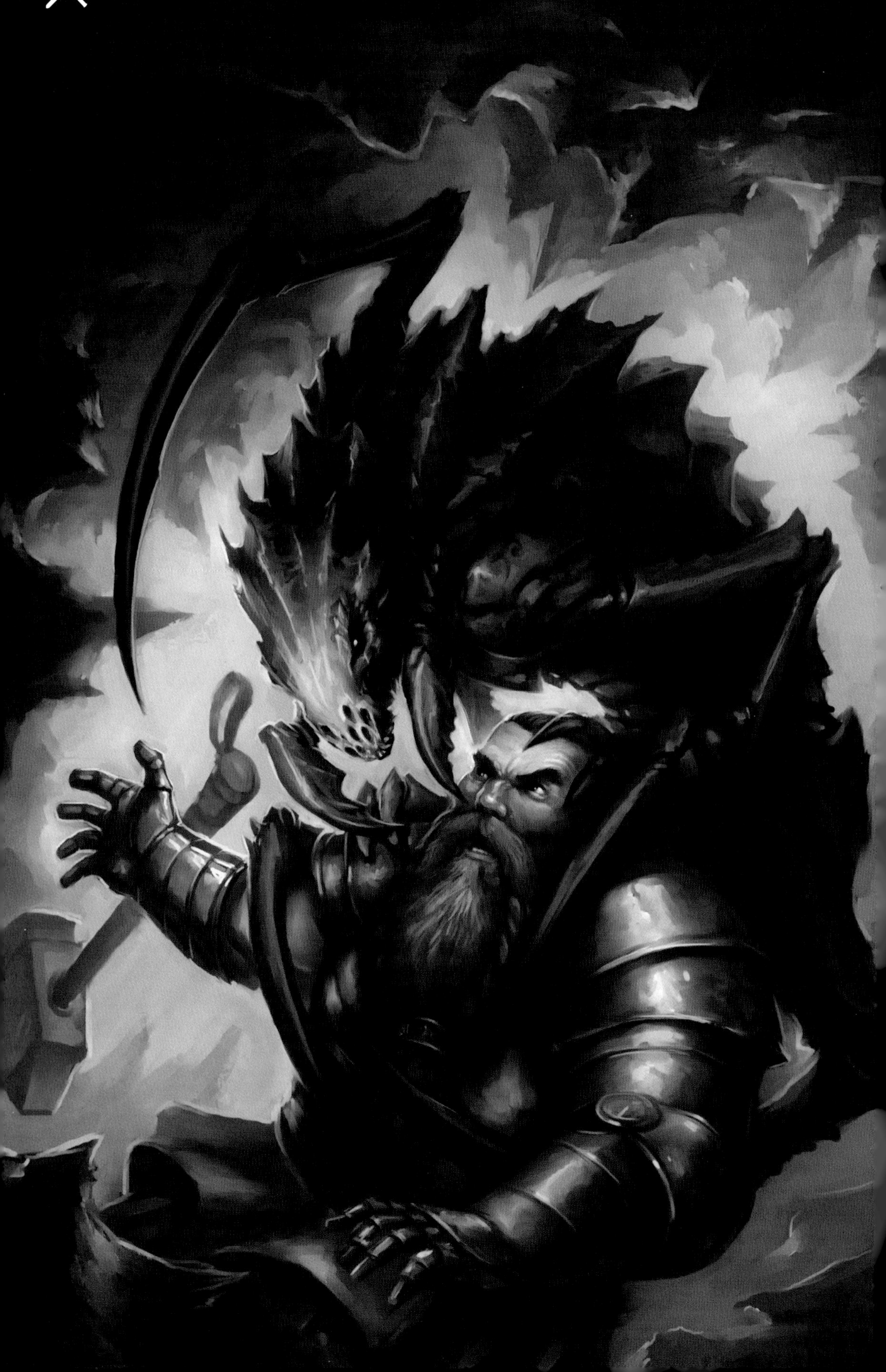

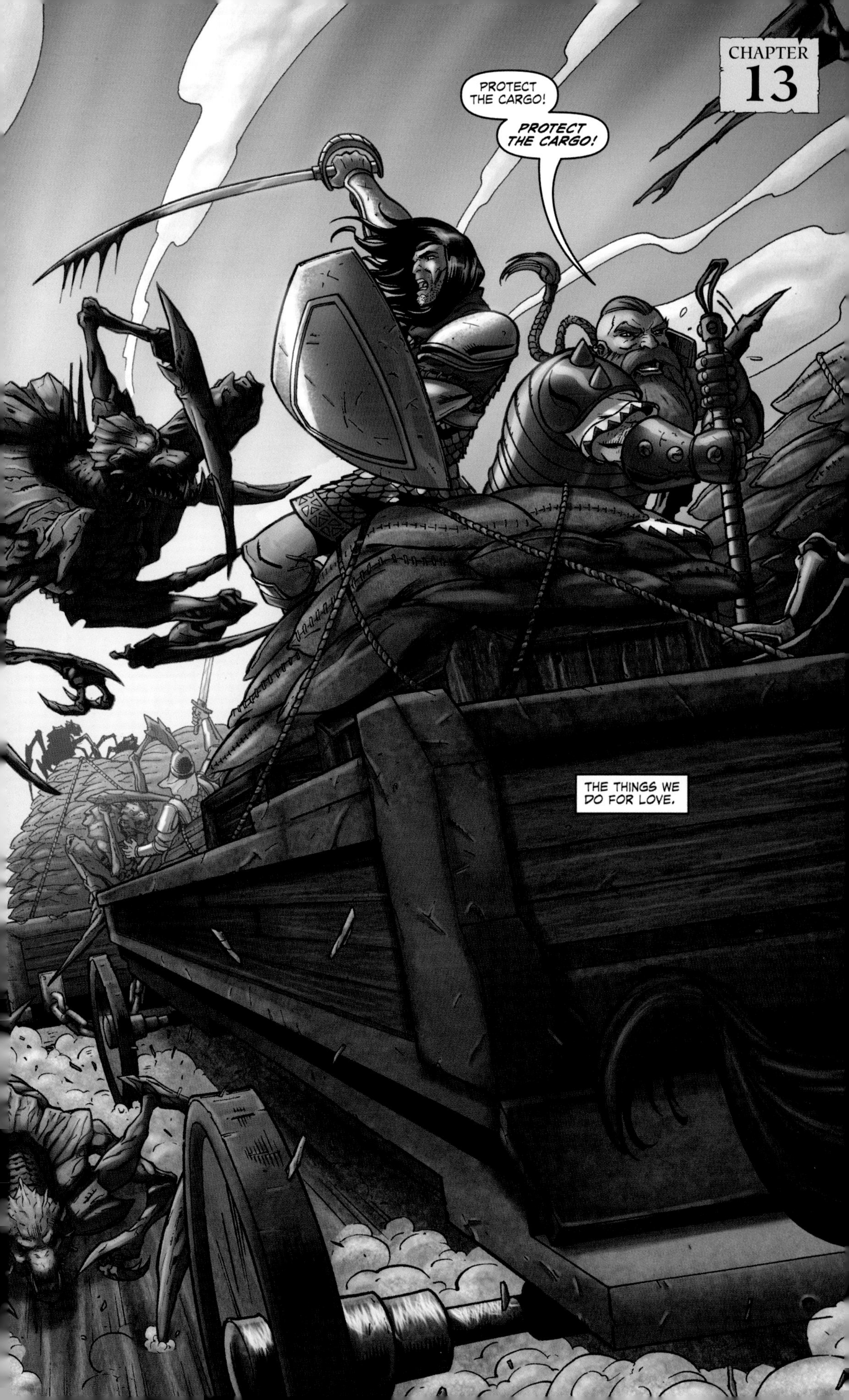
CHAPTER 13
PROTECT THE CARGO!
PROTECT THE CARGO!
THE THINGS WE DO FOR LOVE.

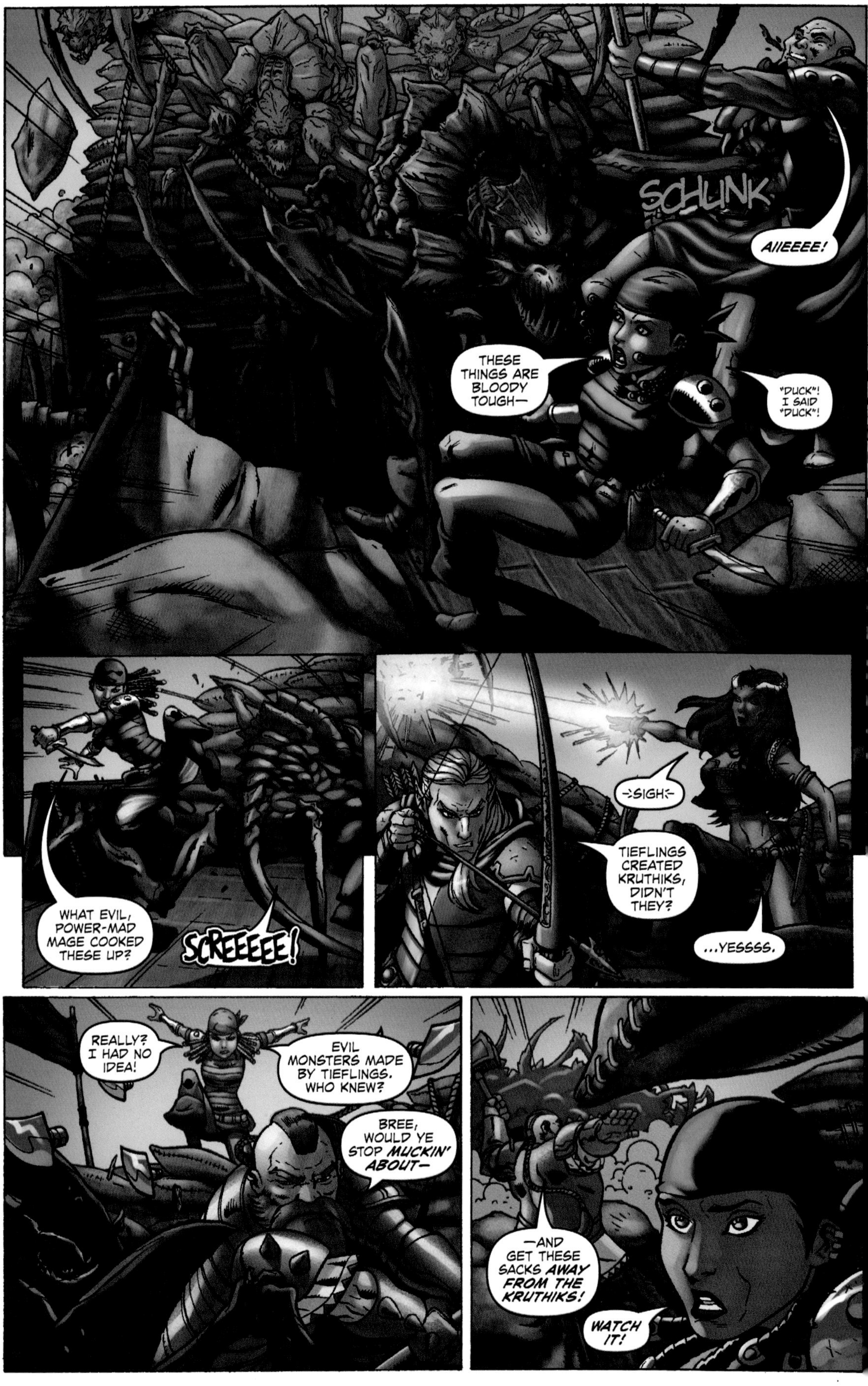
SCHUNK
AIIEEEE!
THESE THINGS ARE BLOODY TOUGH—
"DUCK"! I SAID "DUCK"!
WHAT EVIL, POWER-MAD MAGE COOKED THESE UP?
SCREEEEEE!
-:-SIGH-:-
TIEFLINGS CREATED KRUTHIKS, DIDN'T THEY?
...YESSSS.
REALLY? I HAD NO IDEA!
EVIL MONSTERS MADE BY TIEFLINGS. WHO KNEW?
BREE, WOULD YE STOP *MUCKIN' ABOUT*—
—AND GET THESE SACKS *AWAY FROM THE KRUTHIKS!*
WATCH IT!

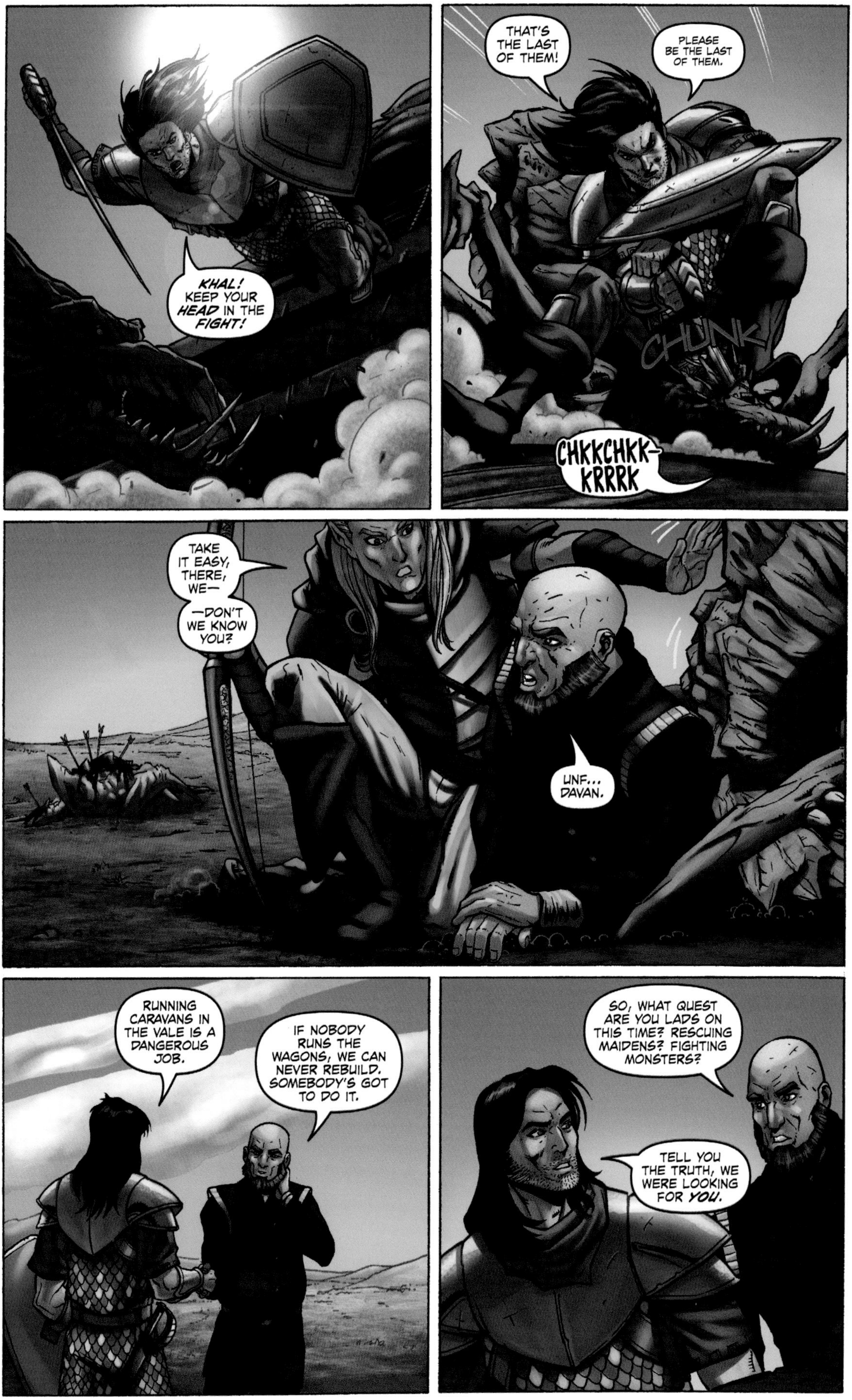
KHAL! KEEP YOUR HEAD IN THE FIGHT!
THAT'S THE LAST OF THEM!
PLEASE BE THE LAST OF THEM.
CHUNK
CHKKCHKK-KRRRK
TAKE IT EASY, THERE, WE—
—DON'T WE KNOW YOU?
UNF... DAVAN.
RUNNING CARAVANS IN THE VALE IS A DANGEROUS JOB.
IF NOBODY RUNS THE WAGONS, WE CAN NEVER REBUILD. SOMEBODY'S GOT TO DO IT.
SO, WHAT QUEST ARE YOU LADS ON THIS TIME? RESCUING MAIDENS? FIGHTING MONSTERS?
TELL YOU THE TRUTH, WE WERE LOOKING FOR YOU.

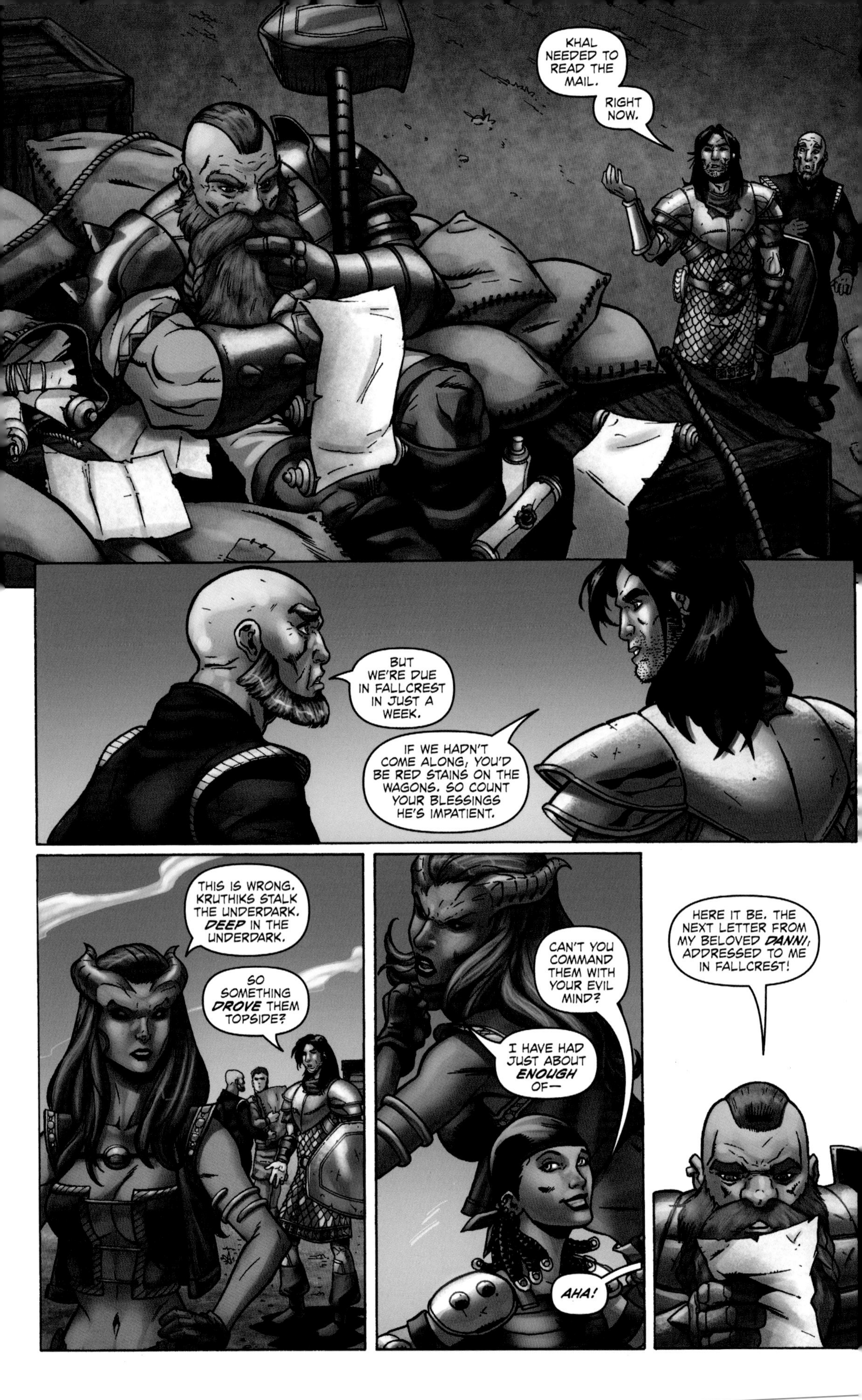
KHAL NEEDED TO READ THE MAIL.
RIGHT NOW.
BUT WE'RE DUE IN FALLCREST IN JUST A WEEK.
IF WE HADN'T COME ALONG, YOU'D BE RED STAINS ON THE WAGONS. SO COUNT YOUR BLESSINGS HE'S IMPATIENT.
THIS IS WRONG. KRUTHIKS STALK THE UNDERDARK. DEEP IN THE UNDERDARK.
SO SOMETHING DROVE THEM TOPSIDE?
CAN'T YOU COMMAND THEM WITH YOUR EVIL MIND?
I HAVE HAD JUST ABOUT ENOUGH OF—
AHA!
HERE IT BE. THE NEXT LETTER FROM MY BELOVED DANNI, ADDRESSED TO ME IN FALLCREST!

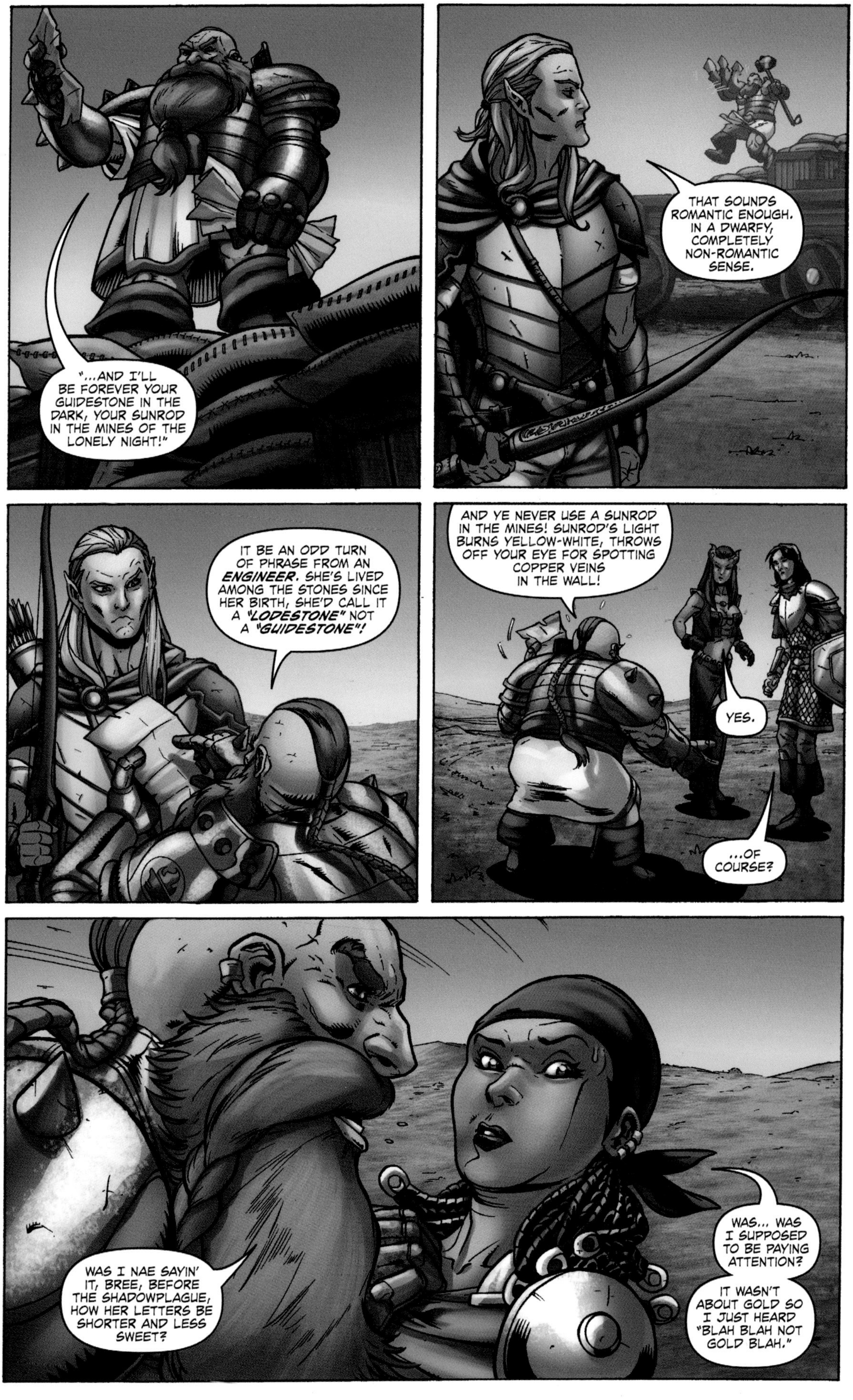
"...AND I'LL BE FOREVER YOUR GUIDESTONE IN THE DARK, YOUR SUNROD IN THE MINES OF THE LONELY NIGHT!"
THAT SOUNDS ROMANTIC ENOUGH. IN A DWARFY, COMPLETELY NON-ROMANTIC SENSE.
IT BE AN ODD TURN OF PHRASE FROM AN *ENGINEER*. SHE'S LIVED AMONG THE STONES SINCE HER BIRTH, SHE'D CALL IT A *"LODESTONE"* NOT A *"GUIDESTONE"*!
AND YE NEVER USE A SUNROD IN THE MINES! SUNROD'S LIGHT BURNS YELLOW-WHITE, THROWS OFF YOUR EYE FOR SPOTTING COPPER VEINS IN THE WALL!
YES.
...OF COURSE?
WAS I NAE SAYIN' IT, BREE, BEFORE THE SHADOWPLAGUE, HOW HER LETTERS BE SHORTER AND LESS SWEET?
WAS... WAS I SUPPOSED TO BE PAYING ATTENTION?
IT WASN'T ABOUT GOLD SO I JUST HEARD "BLAH BLAH NOT GOLD BLAH."

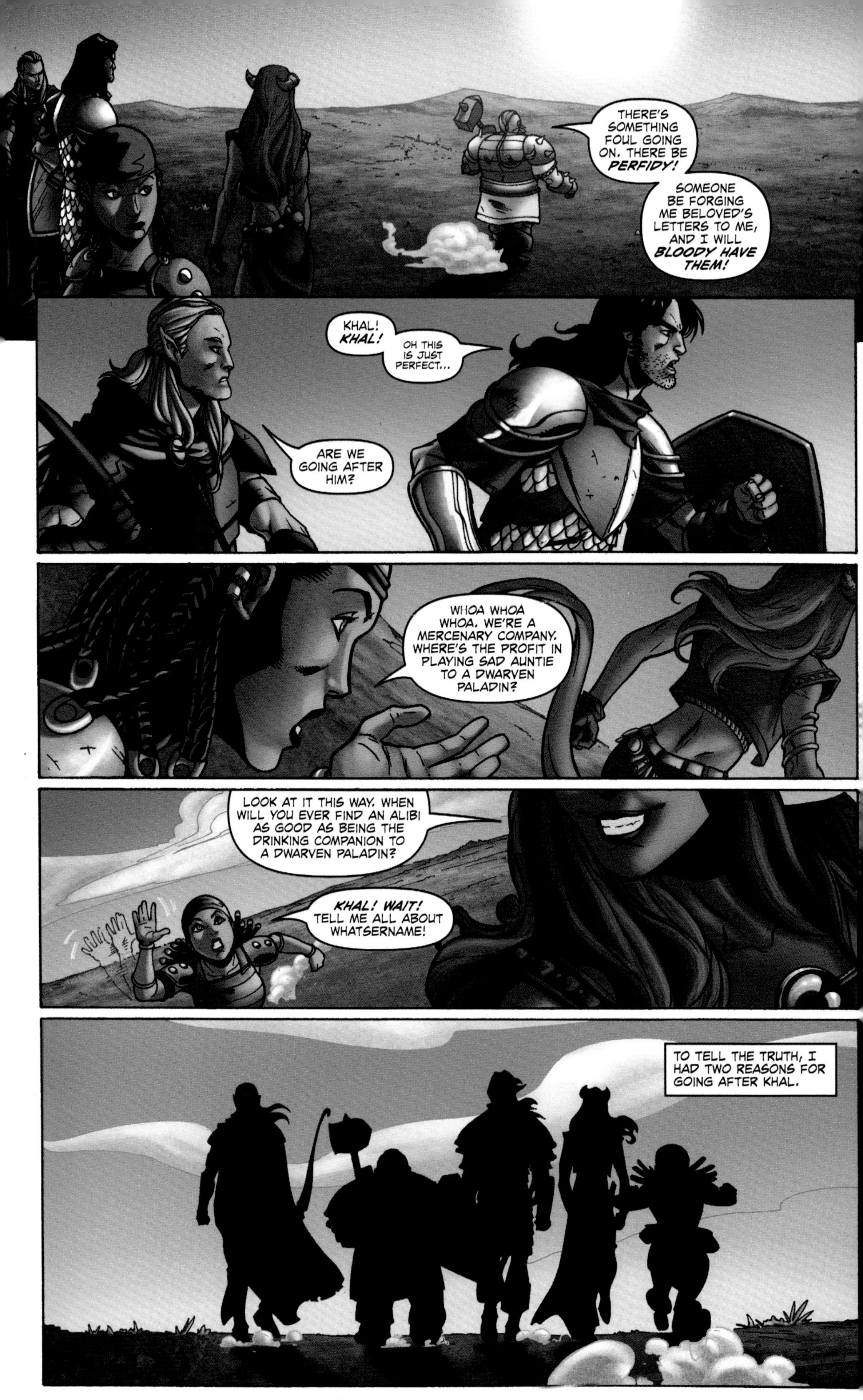
THERE'S SOMETHING FOUL GOING ON. THERE BE PERFIDY!
SOMEONE BE FORGING ME BELOVED'S LETTERS TO ME, AND I WILL BLOODY HAVE THEM!
KHAL! KHAL!
OH THIS IS JUST PERFECT...
ARE WE GOING AFTER HIM?
WHOA WHOA WHOA. WE'RE A MERCENARY COMPANY. WHERE'S THE PROFIT IN PLAYING SAD AUNTIE TO A DWARVEN PALADIN?
LOOK AT IT THIS WAY. WHEN WILL YOU EVER FIND AN ALIBI AS GOOD AS BEING THE DRINKING COMPANION TO A DWARVEN PALADIN?
KHAL! WAIT! TELL ME ALL ABOUT WHATSERNAME!
TO TELL THE TRUTH, I HAD TWO REASONS FOR GOING AFTER KHAL.

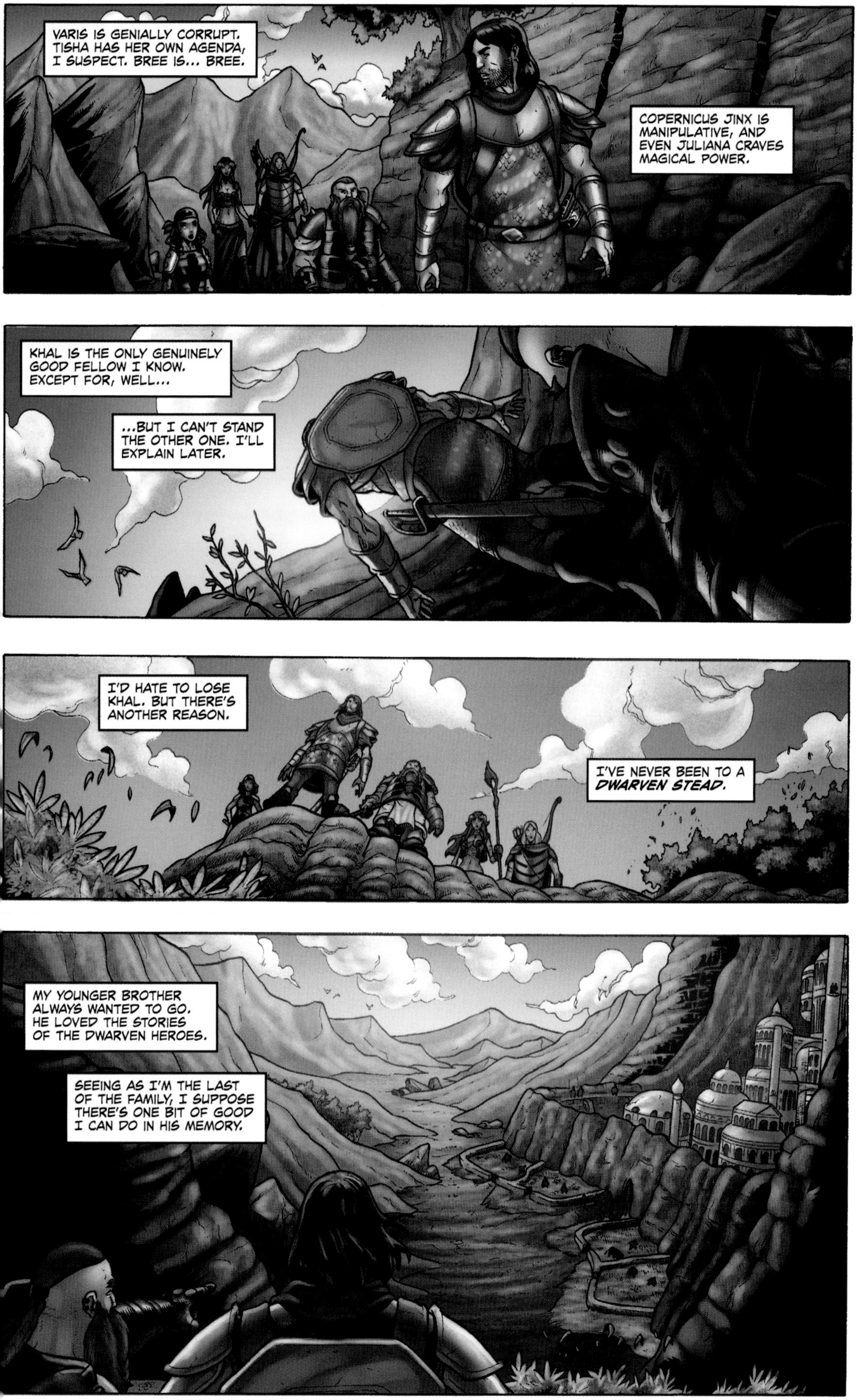
VARIS IS GENIALLY CORRUPT. TISHA HAS HER OWN AGENDA, I SUSPECT. BREE IS... BREE.
COPERNICUS JINX IS MANIPULATIVE, AND EVEN JULIANA CRAVES MAGICAL POWER.
KHAL IS THE ONLY GENUINELY GOOD FELLOW I KNOW. EXCEPT FOR, WELL...
...BUT I CAN'T STAND THE OTHER ONE. I'LL EXPLAIN LATER.
I'D HATE TO LOSE KHAL. BUT THERE'S ANOTHER REASON.
I'VE NEVER BEEN TO A *DWARVEN STEAD.*
MY YOUNGER BROTHER ALWAYS WANTED TO GO. HE LOVED THE STORIES OF THE DWARVEN HEROES.
SEEING AS I'M THE LAST OF THE FAMILY, I SUPPOSE THERE'S ONE BIT OF GOOD I CAN DO IN HIS MEMORY.

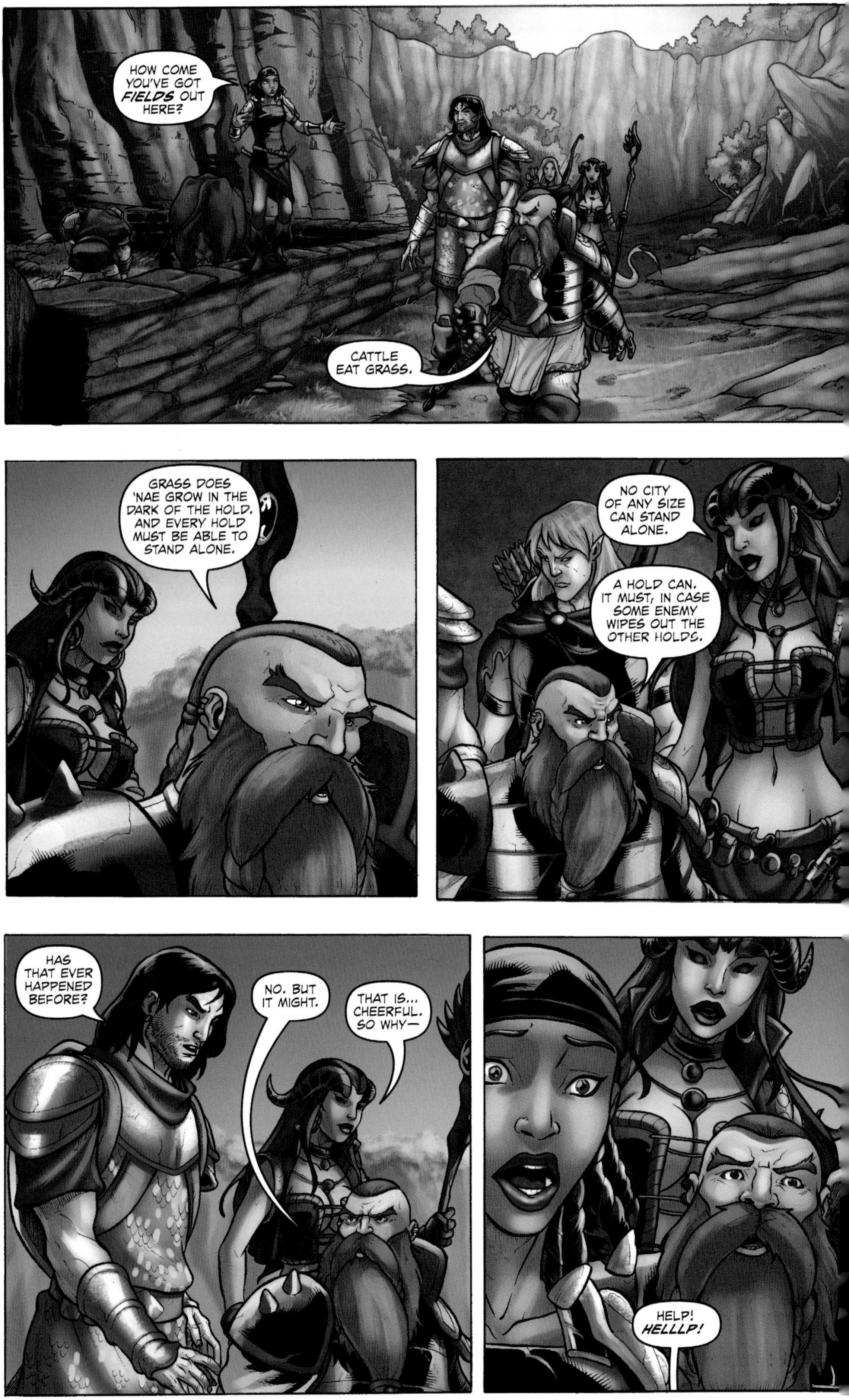
HOW COME YOU'VE GOT *FIELDS* OUT HERE?
CATTLE EAT GRASS.
GRASS DOES 'NAE GROW IN THE DARK OF THE HOLD. AND EVERY HOLD MUST BE ABLE TO STAND ALONE.
NO CITY OF ANY SIZE CAN STAND ALONE.
A HOLD CAN. IT MUST, IN CASE SOME ENEMY WIPES OUT THE OTHER HOLDS.
HAS THAT EVER HAPPENED BEFORE?
NO. BUT IT MIGHT.
THAT IS... CHEERFUL. SO WHY—
HELP! *HELLLP!*

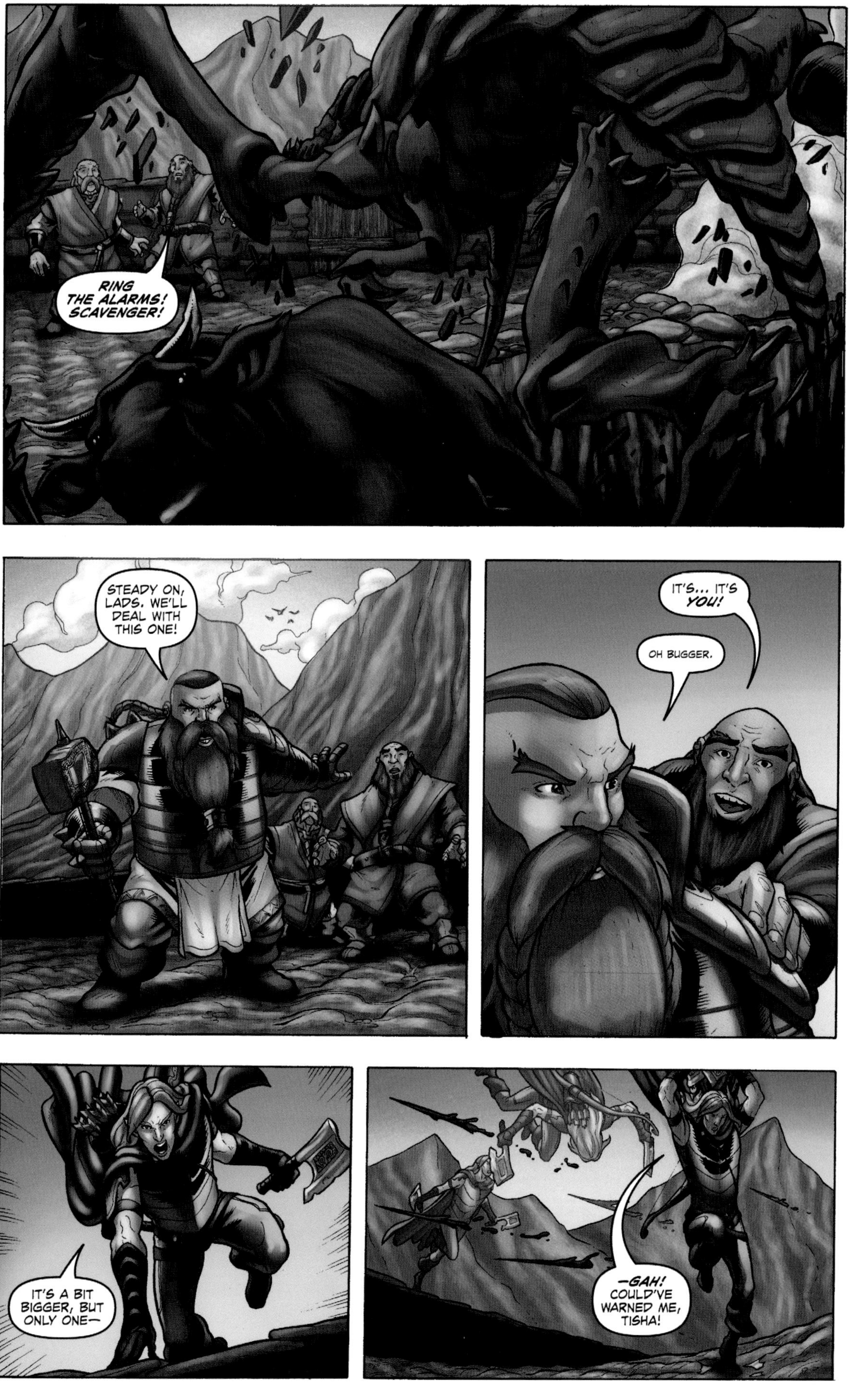
RING THE ALARMS! SCAVENGER!
STEADY ON, LADS. WE'LL DEAL WITH THIS ONE!
IT'S... IT'S YOU!
OH BUGGER.
IT'S A BIT BIGGER, BUT ONLY ONE—
—GAH! COULD'VE WARNED ME, TISHA!

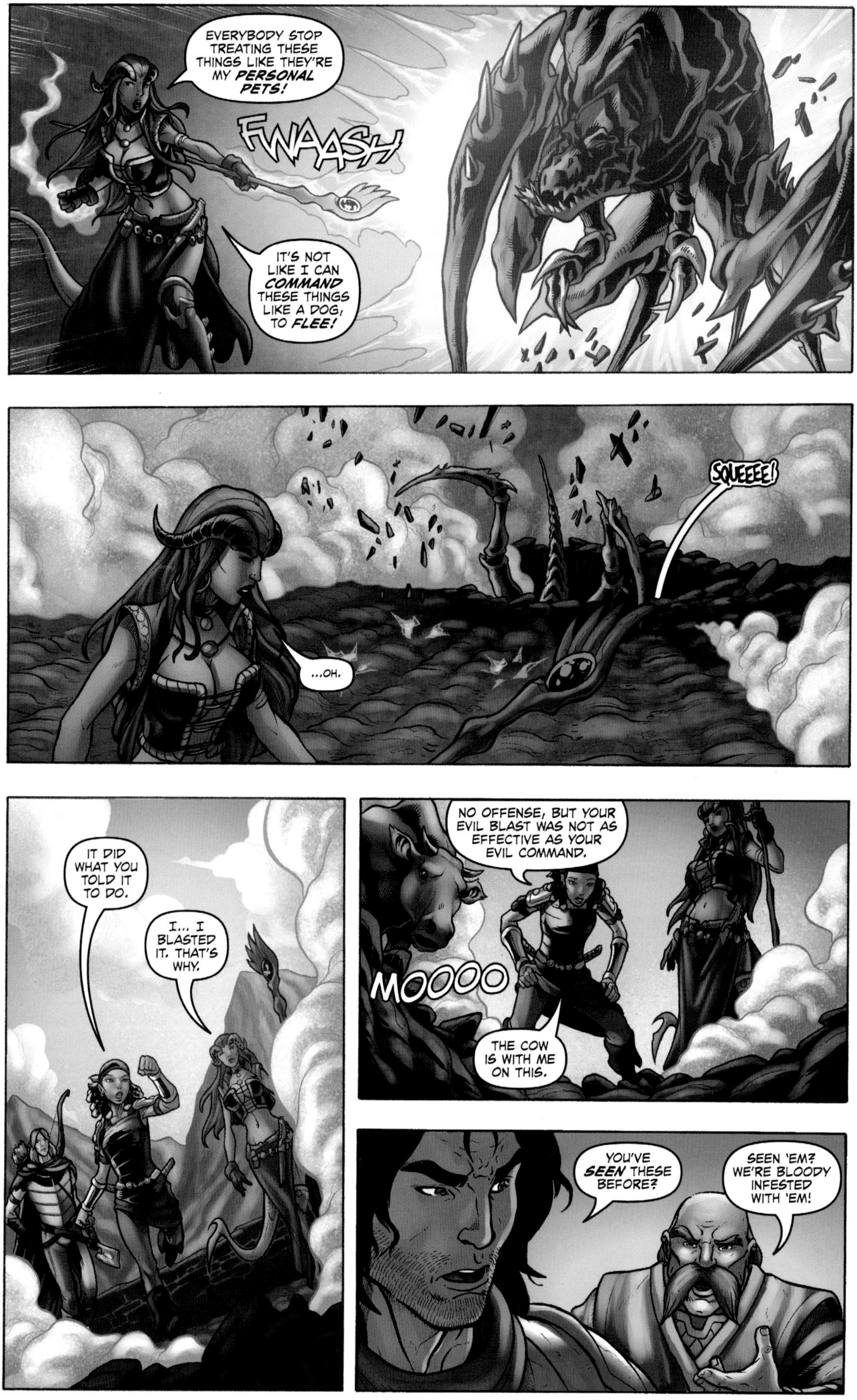
EVERYBODY STOP TREATING THESE THINGS LIKE THEY'RE MY **PERSONAL PETS!**
FWAASH
IT'S NOT LIKE I CAN **COMMAND** THESE THINGS LIKE A DOG, TO **FLEE!**
SQUEEEE!
...OH.
IT DID WHAT YOU TOLD IT TO DO.
I... I BLASTED IT. THAT'S WHY.
NO OFFENSE, BUT YOUR EVIL BLAST WAS NOT AS EFFECTIVE AS YOUR EVIL COMMAND.
MOOOO
THE COW IS WITH ME ON THIS.
YOU'VE **SEEN** THESE BEFORE?
SEEN 'EM? WE'RE BLOODY INFESTED WITH 'EM!

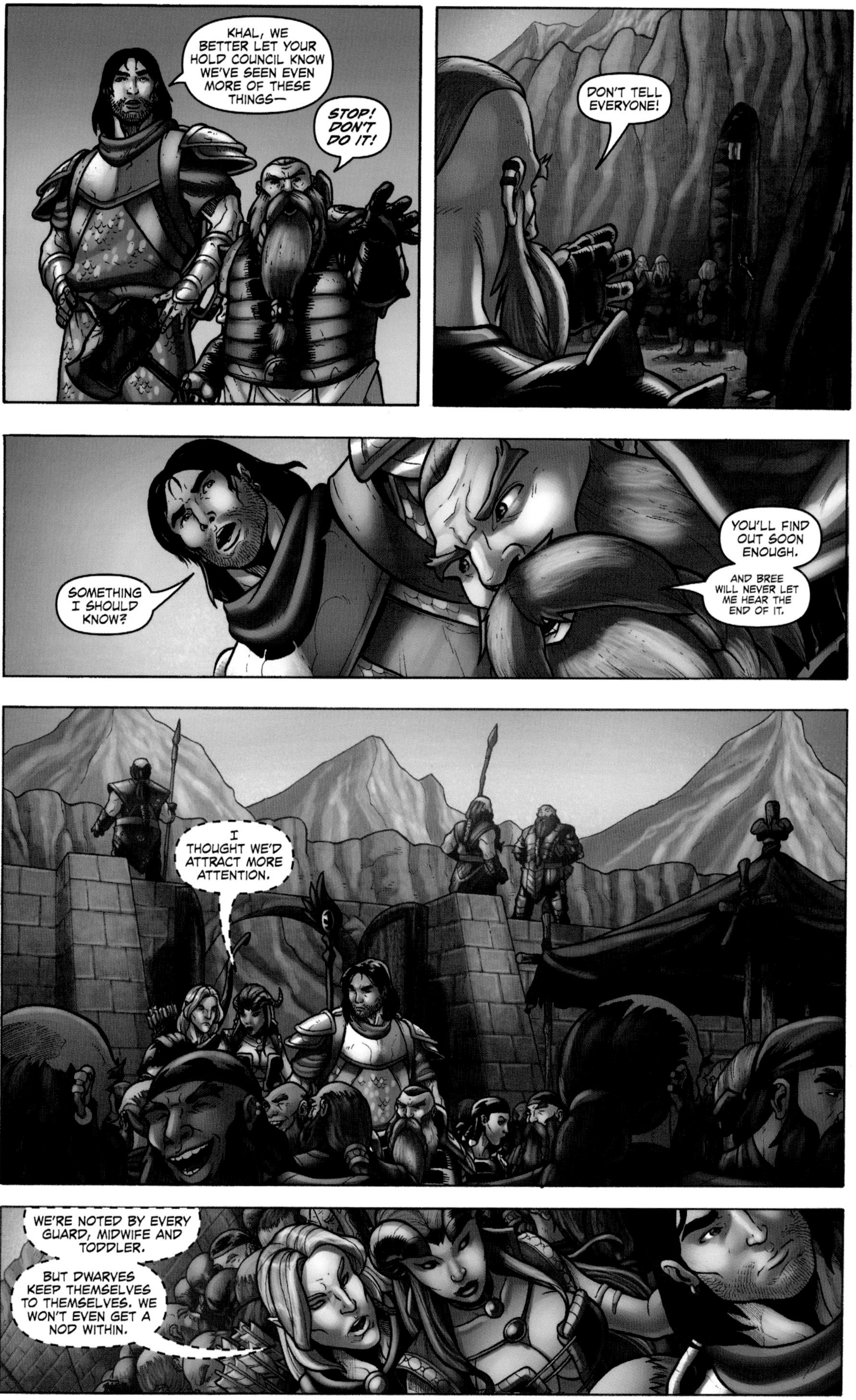

KHAL, WE BETTER LET YOUR HOLD COUNCIL KNOW WE'VE SEEN EVEN MORE OF THESE THINGS—
STOP! DON'T DO IT!
DON'T TELL EVERYONE!
SOMETHING I SHOULD KNOW?
YOU'LL FIND OUT SOON ENOUGH.
AND BREE WILL NEVER LET ME HEAR THE END OF IT.
I THOUGHT WE'D ATTRACT MORE ATTENTION.
WE'RE NOTED BY EVERY GUARD, MIDWIFE AND TODDLER.
BUT DWARVES KEEP THEMSELVES TO THEMSELVES. WE WON'T EVEN GET A NOD WITHIN.

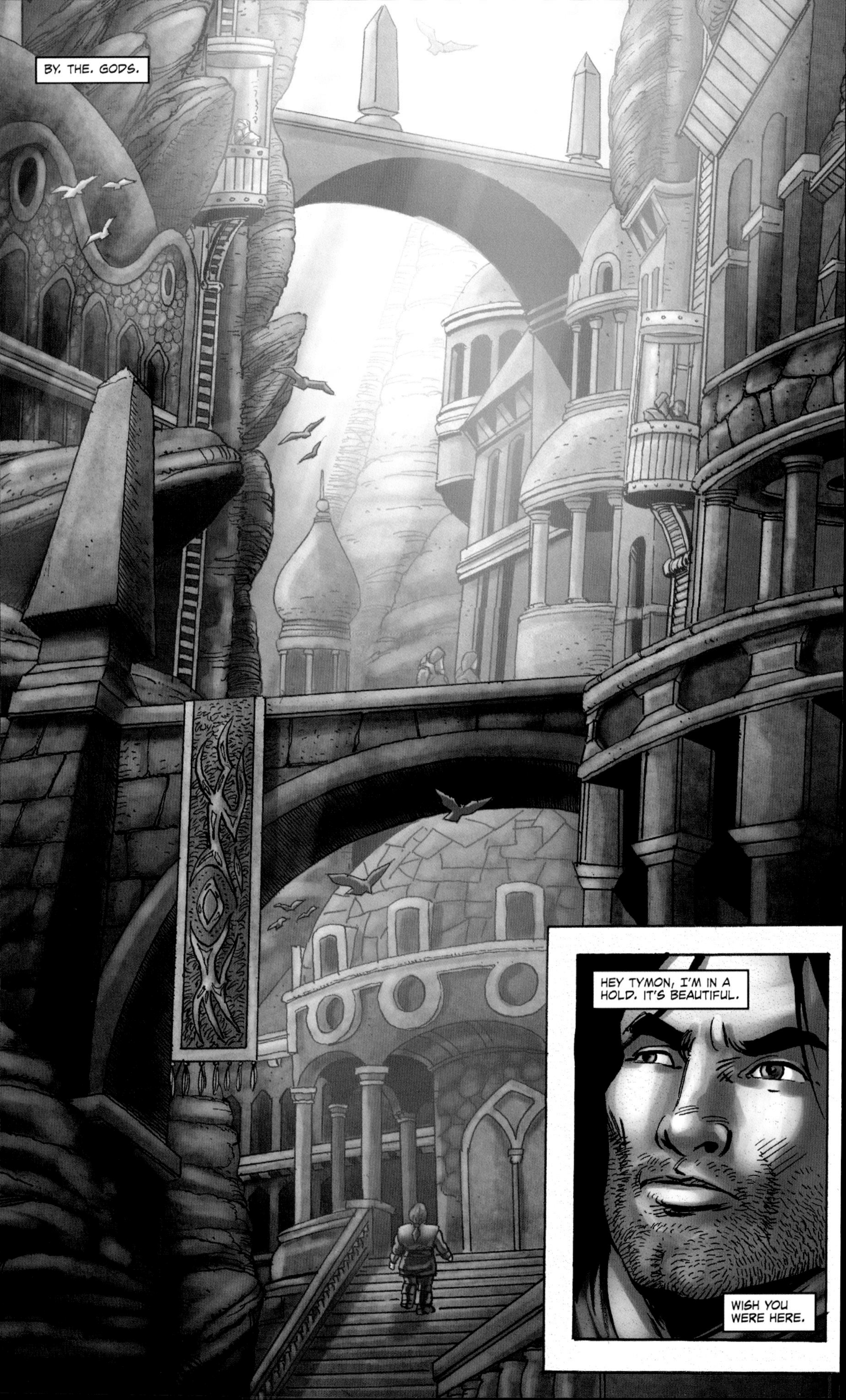
BY. THE. GODS.
HEY TYMON, I'M IN A HOLD. IT'S BEAUTIFUL.
WISH YOU WERE HERE.

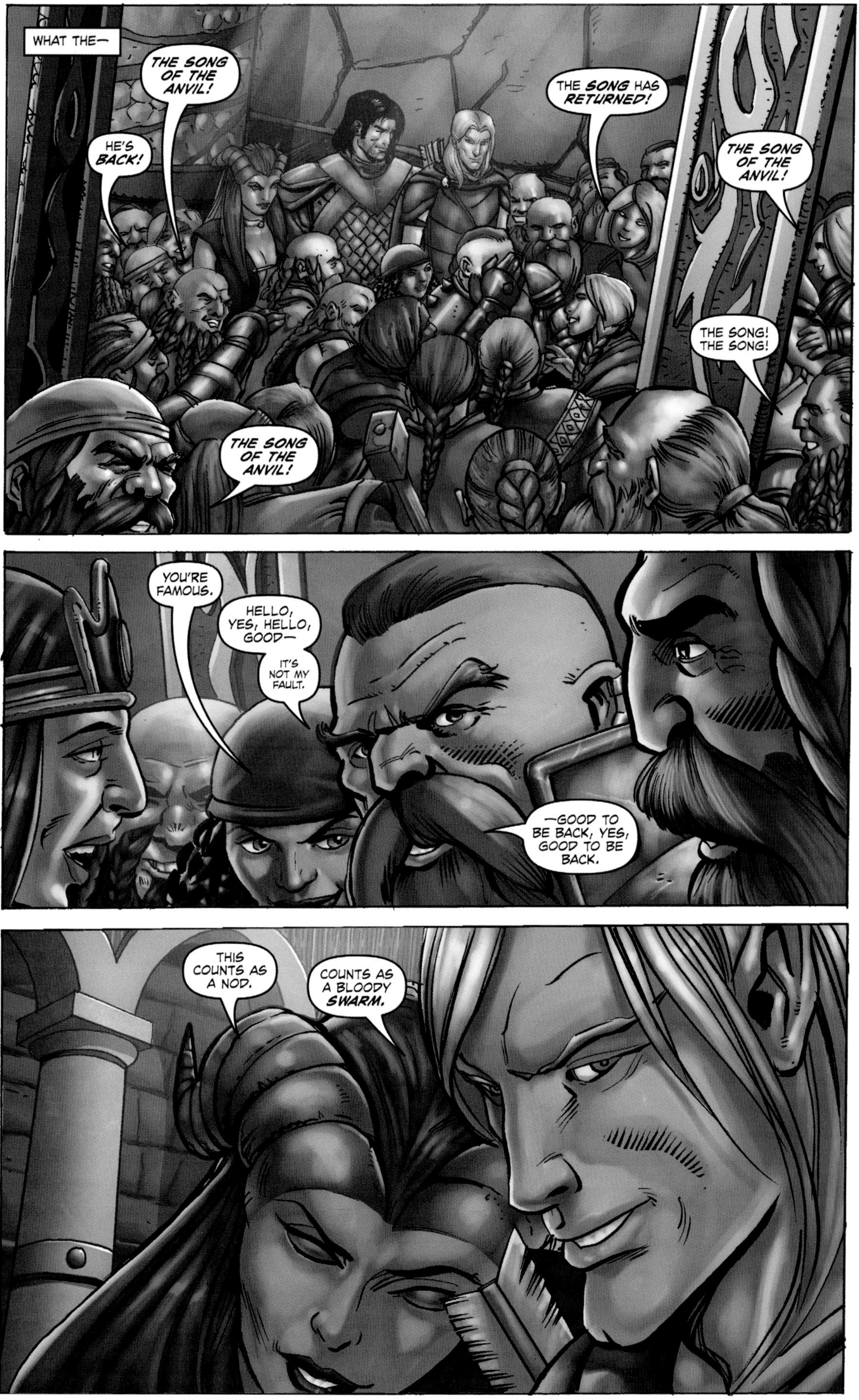
WHAT THE—
THE SONG OF THE ANVIL!
HE'S BACK!
THE SONG HAS RETURNED!
THE SONG OF THE ANVIL!
THE SONG! THE SONG!
THE SONG OF THE ANVIL!
YOU'RE FAMOUS.
HELLO, YES, HELLO, GOOD—
IT'S NOT MY FAULT.
—GOOD TO BE BACK, YES, GOOD TO BE BACK.
THIS COUNTS AS A NOD.
COUNTS AS A BLOODY SWARM.

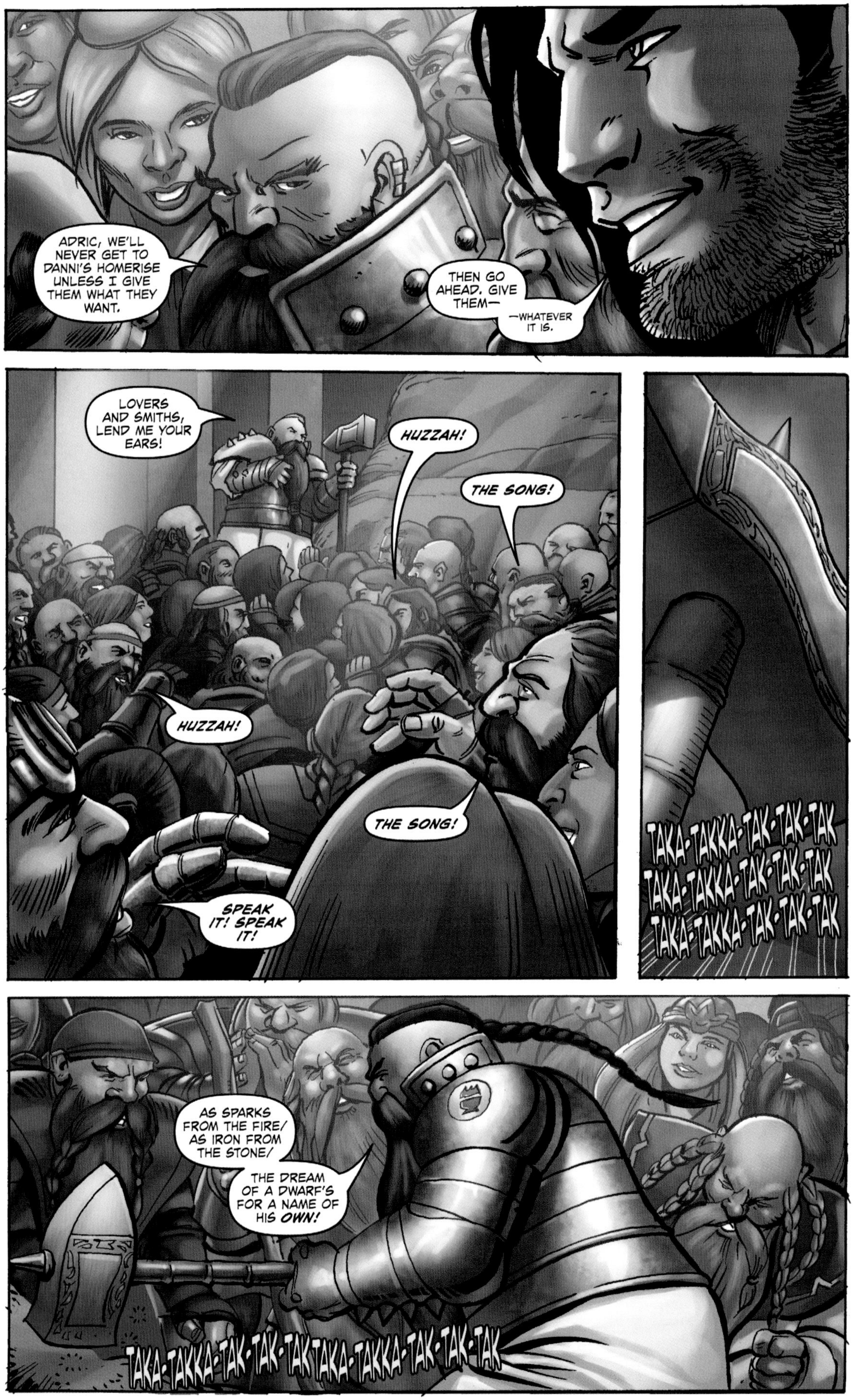
ADRIC, WE'LL NEVER GET TO DANNI'S HOMERISE UNLESS I GIVE THEM WHAT THEY WANT.
THEN GO AHEAD. GIVE THEM—
—WHATEVER IT IS.
LOVERS AND SMITHS, LEND ME YOUR EARS!
HUZZAH!
THE SONG!
HUZZAH!
THE SONG!
SPEAK IT! SPEAK IT!
TAKA-TAKKA-TAK-TAK-TAK
TAKA-TAKKA-TAK-TAK-TAK
TAKA-TAKKA-TAK-TAK-TAK
AS SPARKS FROM THE FIRE/ AS IRON FROM THE STONE/
THE DREAM OF A DWARF'S FOR A NAME OF HIS OWN!
TAKA-TAKKA-TAK-TAK-TAK TAKA-TAKKA-TAK-TAK-TAK

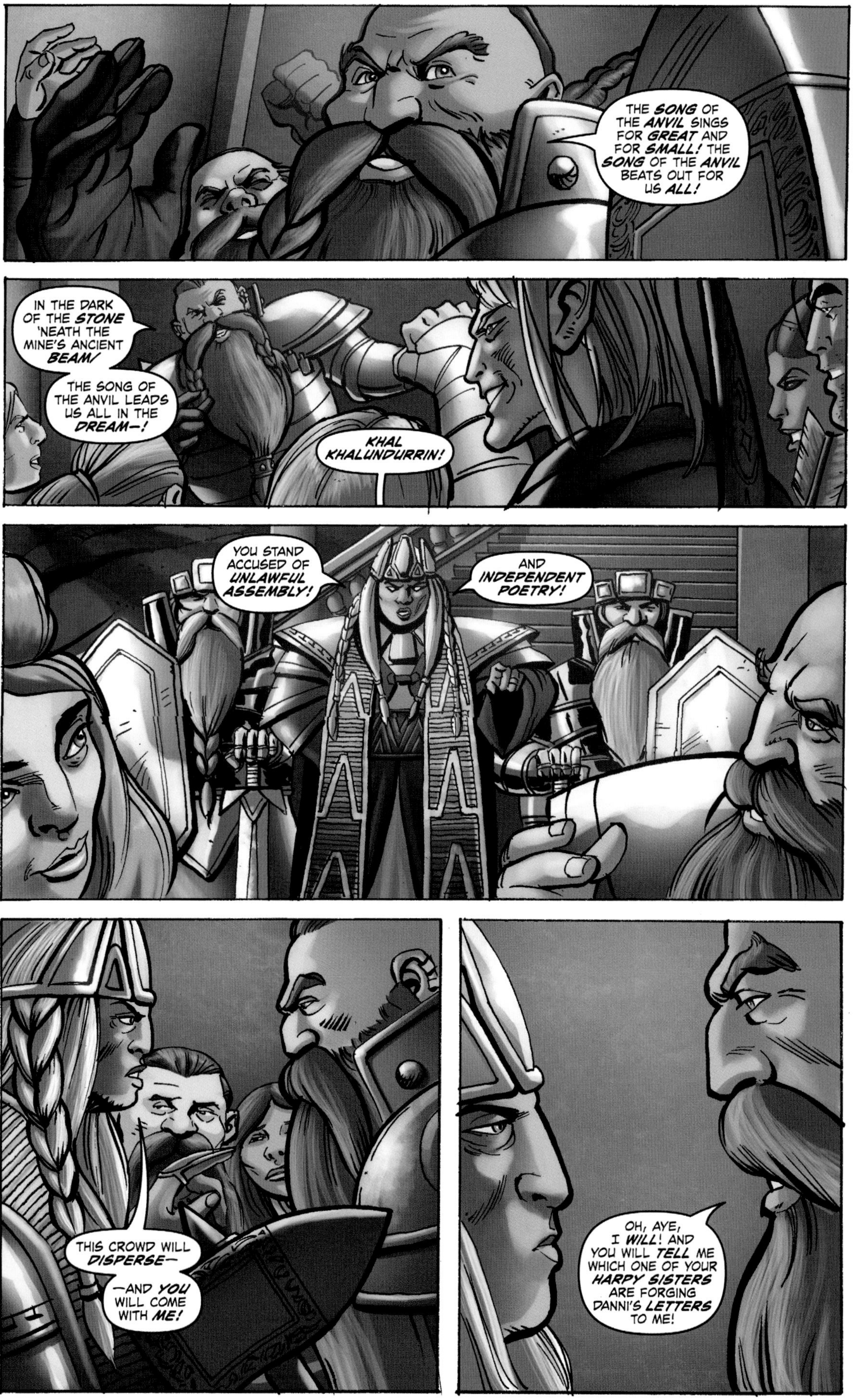
THE SONG OF THE ANVIL SINGS FOR GREAT AND FOR SMALL! THE SONG OF THE ANVIL BEATS OUT FOR US ALL!
IN THE DARK OF THE STONE 'NEATH THE MINE'S ANCIENT BEAM/
THE SONG OF THE ANVIL LEADS US ALL IN THE DREAM—!
KHAL KHALUNDURRIN!
YOU STAND ACCUSED OF UNLAWFUL ASSEMBLY!
AND INDEPENDENT POETRY!
THIS CROWD WILL DISPERSE—
—AND YOU WILL COME WITH ME!
OH, AYE, I WILL! AND YOU WILL TELL ME WHICH ONE OF YOUR HARPY SISTERS ARE FORGING DANNI'S LETTERS TO ME!

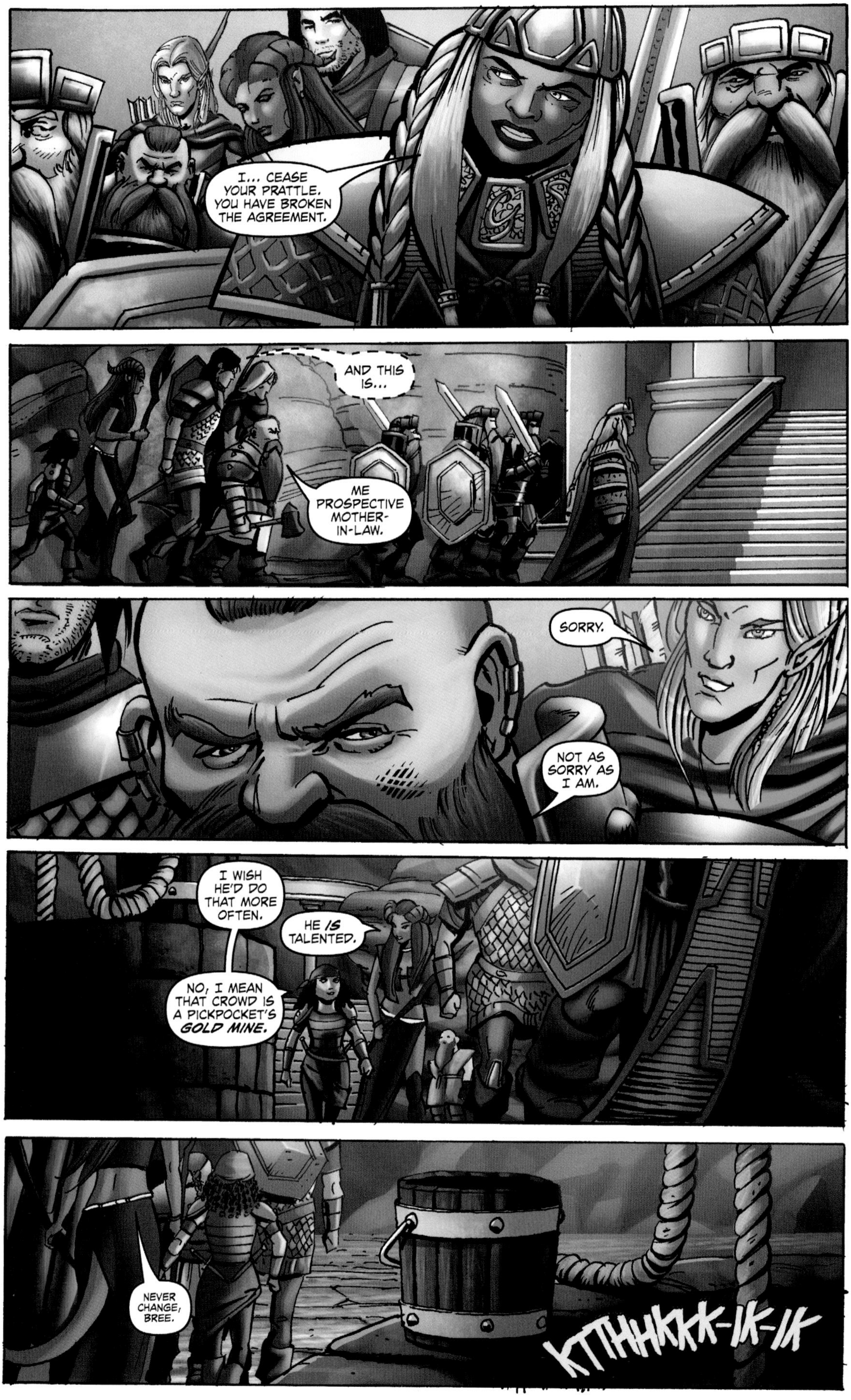
I... CEASE YOUR PRATTLE. YOU HAVE BROKEN THE AGREEMENT.
AND THIS IS...
ME PROSPECTIVE MOTHER-IN-LAW.
SORRY.
NOT AS SORRY AS I AM.
I WISH HE'D DO THAT MORE OFTEN.
HE *IS* TALENTED.
NO, I MEAN THAT CROWD IS A PICKPOCKET'S ***GOLD MINE.***
NEVER CHANGE, BREE.
KTTHHKKK-IK-IK

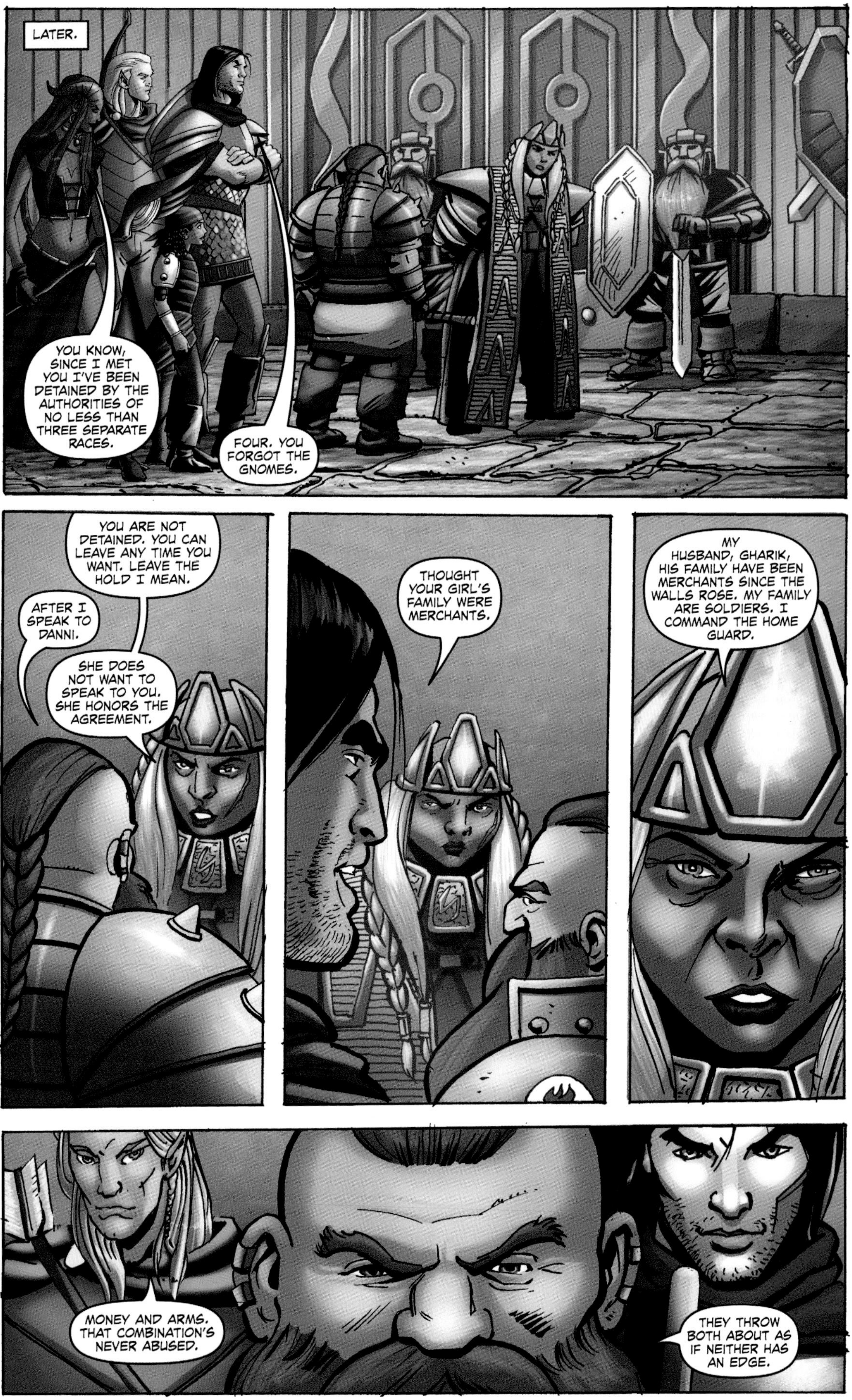
LATER.
YOU KNOW, SINCE I MET YOU I'VE BEEN DETAINED BY THE AUTHORITIES OF NO LESS THAN THREE SEPARATE RACES.
FOUR. YOU FORGOT THE GNOMES.
YOU ARE NOT DETAINED. YOU CAN LEAVE ANY TIME YOU WANT. LEAVE THE HOLD I MEAN.
AFTER I SPEAK TO DANNI.
SHE DOES NOT WANT TO SPEAK TO YOU. SHE HONORS THE AGREEMENT.
THOUGHT YOUR GIRL'S FAMILY WERE MERCHANTS.
MY HUSBAND, GHARIK, HIS FAMILY HAVE BEEN MERCHANTS SINCE THE WALLS ROSE. MY FAMILY ARE SOLDIERS. I COMMAND THE HOME GUARD.
MONEY AND ARMS. THAT COMBINATION'S NEVER ABUSED.
THEY THROW BOTH ABOUT AS IF NEITHER HAS AN EDGE.

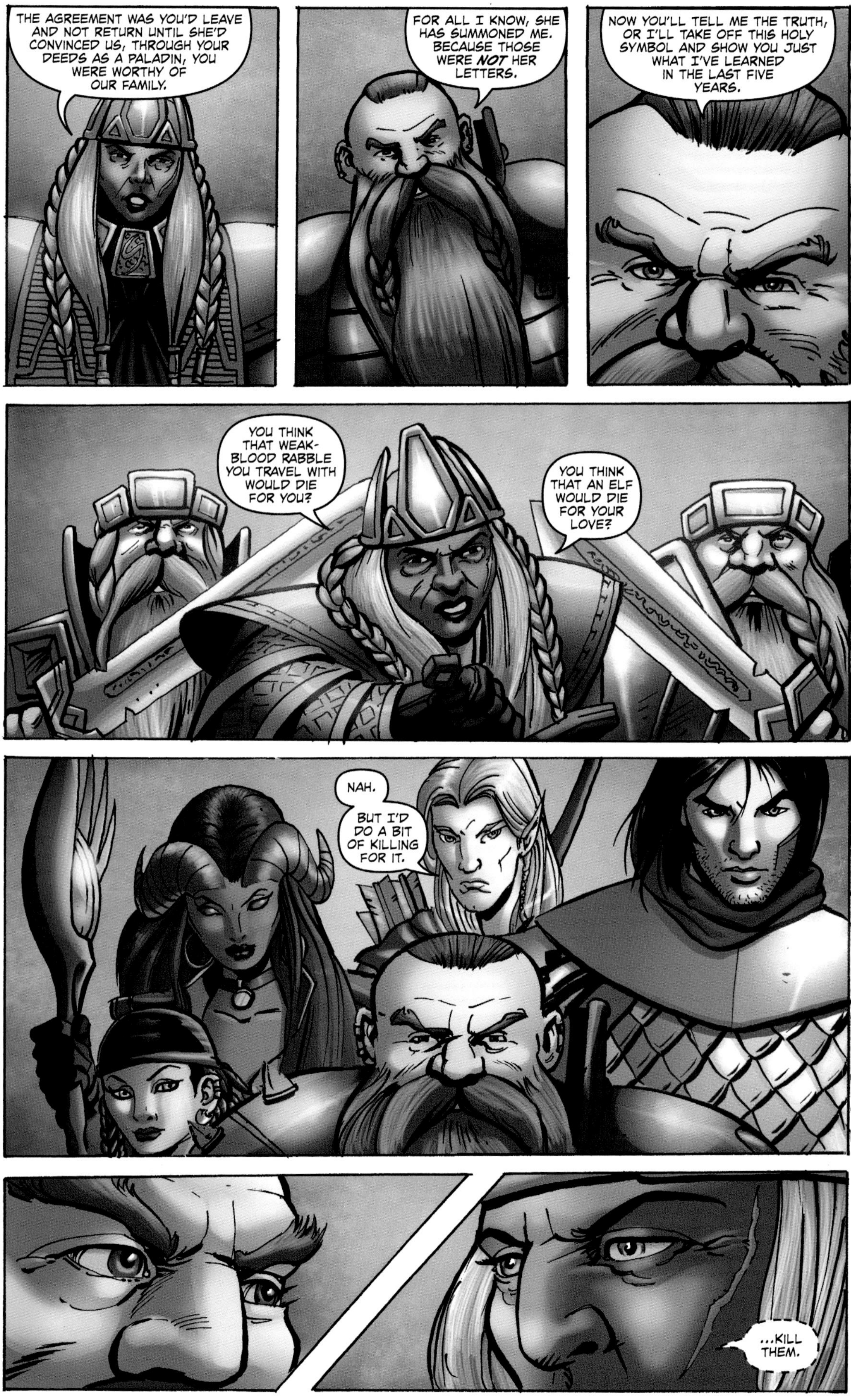
THE AGREEMENT WAS YOU'D LEAVE AND NOT RETURN UNTIL SHE'D CONVINCED US, THROUGH YOUR DEEDS AS A PALADIN, YOU WERE WORTHY OF OUR FAMILY.
FOR ALL I KNOW, SHE HAS SUMMONED ME. BECAUSE THOSE WERE NOT HER LETTERS.
NOW YOU'LL TELL ME THE TRUTH, OR I'LL TAKE OFF THIS HOLY SYMBOL AND SHOW YOU JUST WHAT I'VE LEARNED IN THE LAST FIVE YEARS.
YOU THINK THAT WEAK-BLOOD RABBLE YOU TRAVEL WITH WOULD DIE FOR YOU?
YOU THINK THAT AN ELF WOULD DIE FOR YOUR LOVE?
NAH.
BUT I'D DO A BIT OF KILLING FOR IT.
...KILL THEM.

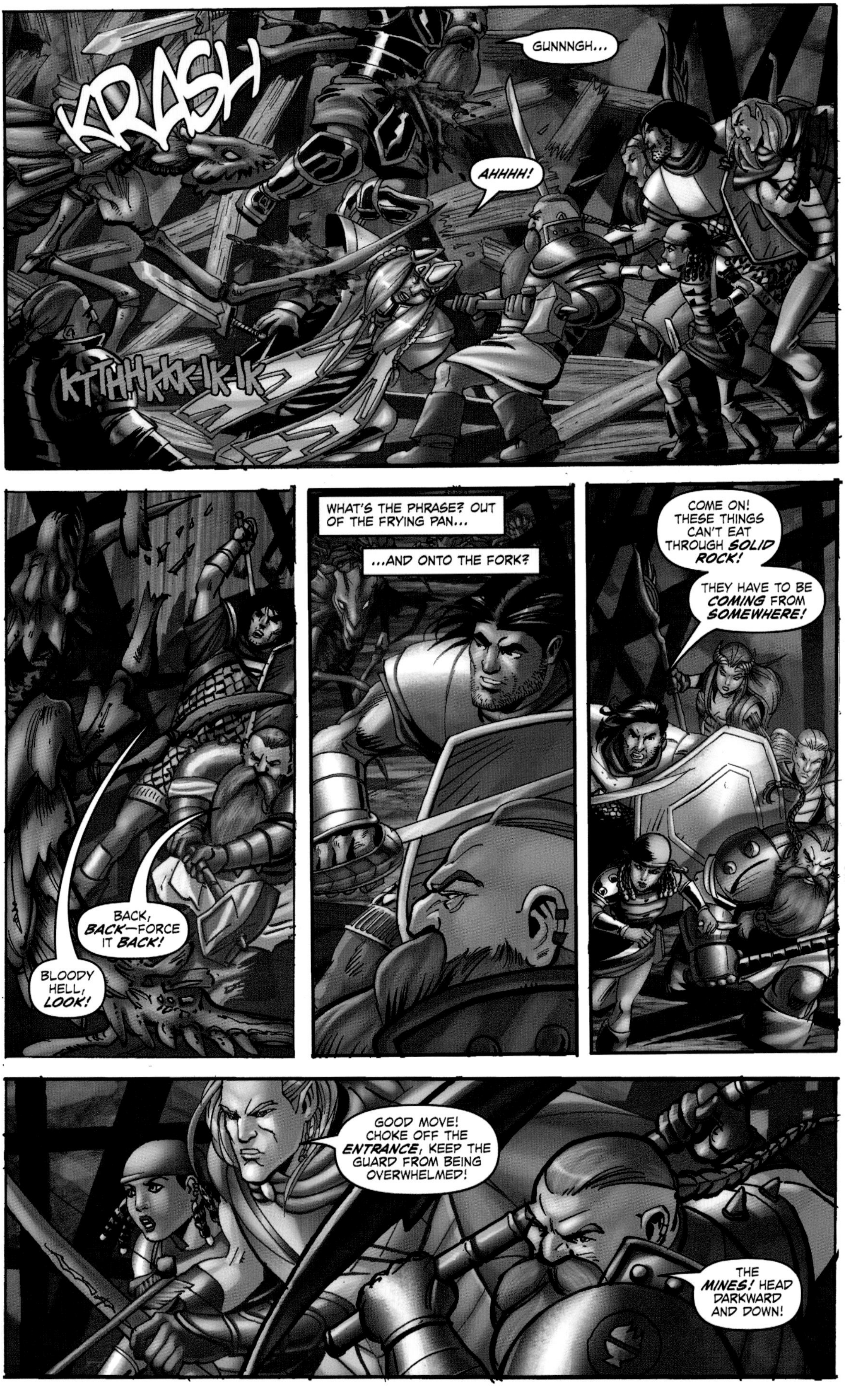
KRASH
GUNNNGH...
AHHHH!
KTTHHKKK IK IK
BACK, BACK—FORCE IT BACK!
BLOODY HELL, LOOK!
WHAT'S THE PHRASE? OUT OF THE FRYING PAN...
...AND ONTO THE FORK?
COME ON! THESE THINGS CAN'T EAT THROUGH SOLID ROCK!
THEY HAVE TO BE COMING FROM SOMEWHERE!
GOOD MOVE! CHOKE OFF THE ENTRANCE, KEEP THE GUARD FROM BEING OVERWHELMED!
THE MINES! HEAD DARKWARD AND DOWN!

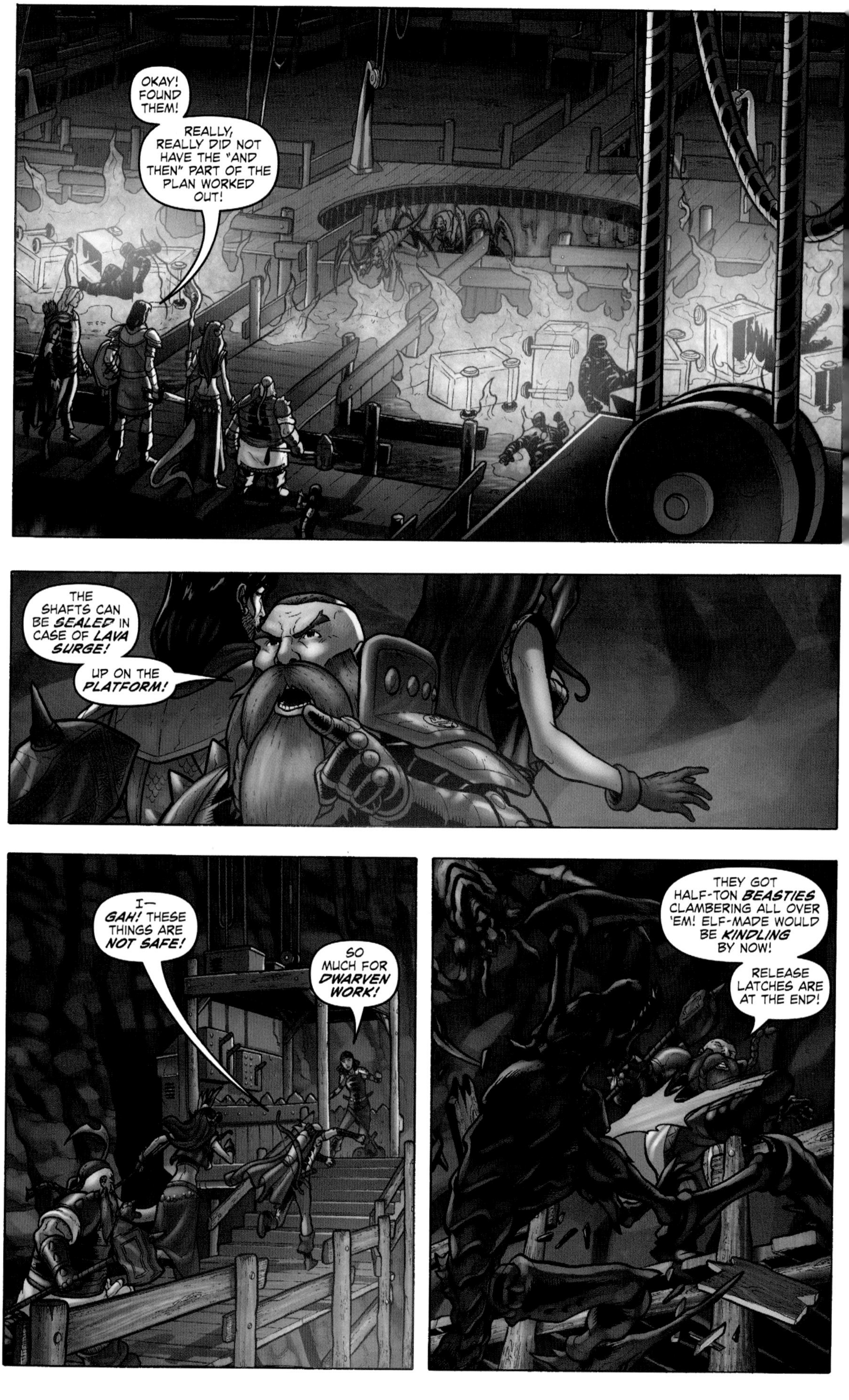
OKAY! FOUND THEM!
REALLY, REALLY DID NOT HAVE THE "AND THEN" PART OF THE PLAN WORKED OUT!
THE SHAFTS CAN BE SEALED IN CASE OF LAVA SURGE!
UP ON THE PLATFORM!
I— GAH! THESE THINGS ARE NOT SAFE!
SO MUCH FOR DWARVEN WORK!
THEY GOT HALF-TON BEASTIES CLAMBERING ALL OVER 'EM! ELF-MADE WOULD BE KINDLING BY NOW!
RELEASE LATCHES ARE AT THE END!

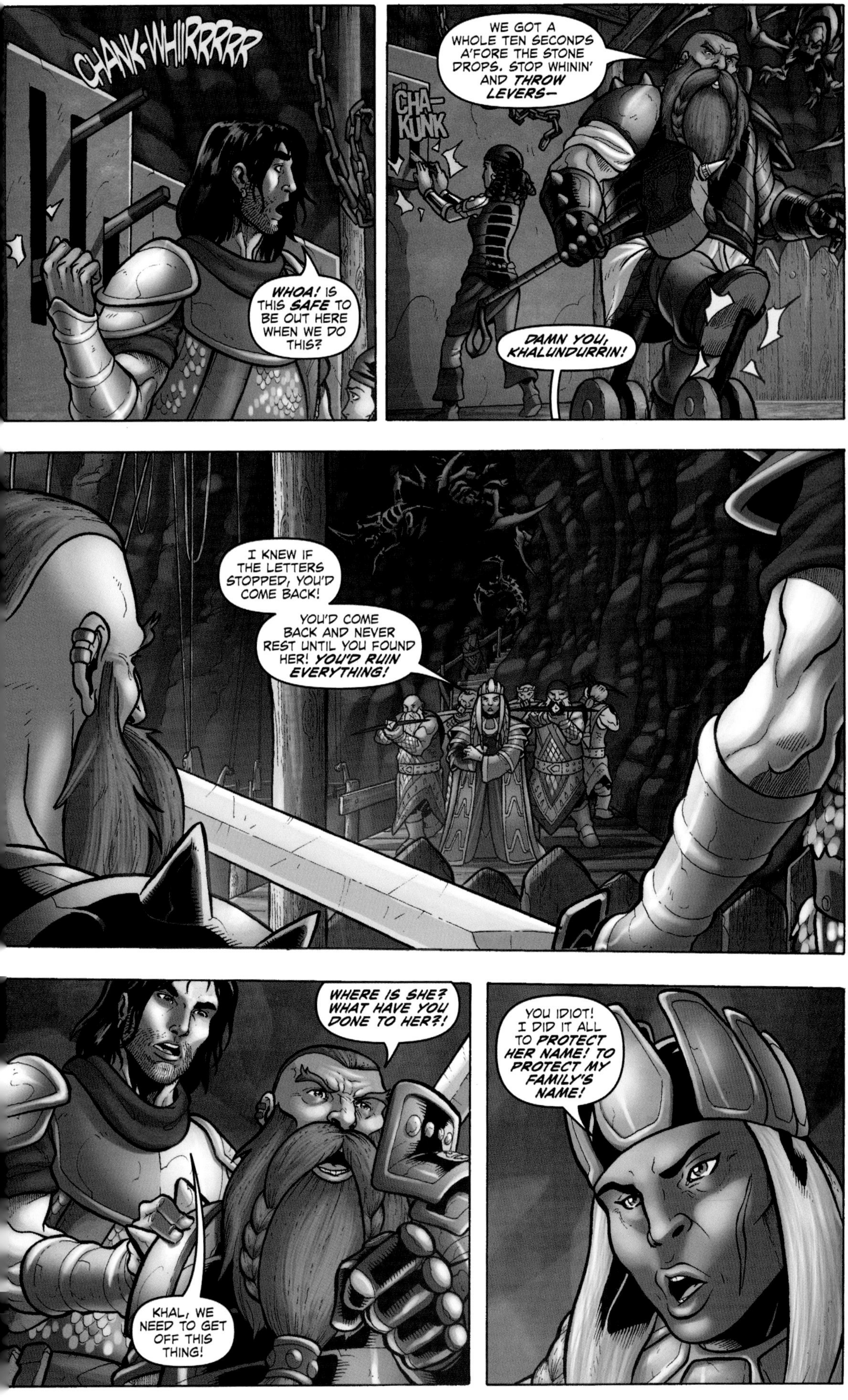
CHANK-WHIIRRRRR
WHOA! IS THIS SAFE TO BE OUT HERE WHEN WE DO THIS?
WE GOT A WHOLE TEN SECONDS A'FORE THE STONE DROPS. STOP WHININ' AND THROW LEVERS—
CHA-KUNK
DAMN YOU, KHALUNDURRIN!
I KNEW IF THE LETTERS STOPPED, YOU'D COME BACK!
YOU'D COME BACK AND NEVER REST UNTIL YOU FOUND HER! YOU'D RUIN EVERYTHING!
WHERE IS SHE? WHAT HAVE YOU DONE TO HER?!
KHAL, WE NEED TO GET OFF THIS THING!
YOU IDIOT! I DID IT ALL TO PROTECT HER NAME! TO PROTECT MY FAMILY'S NAME!

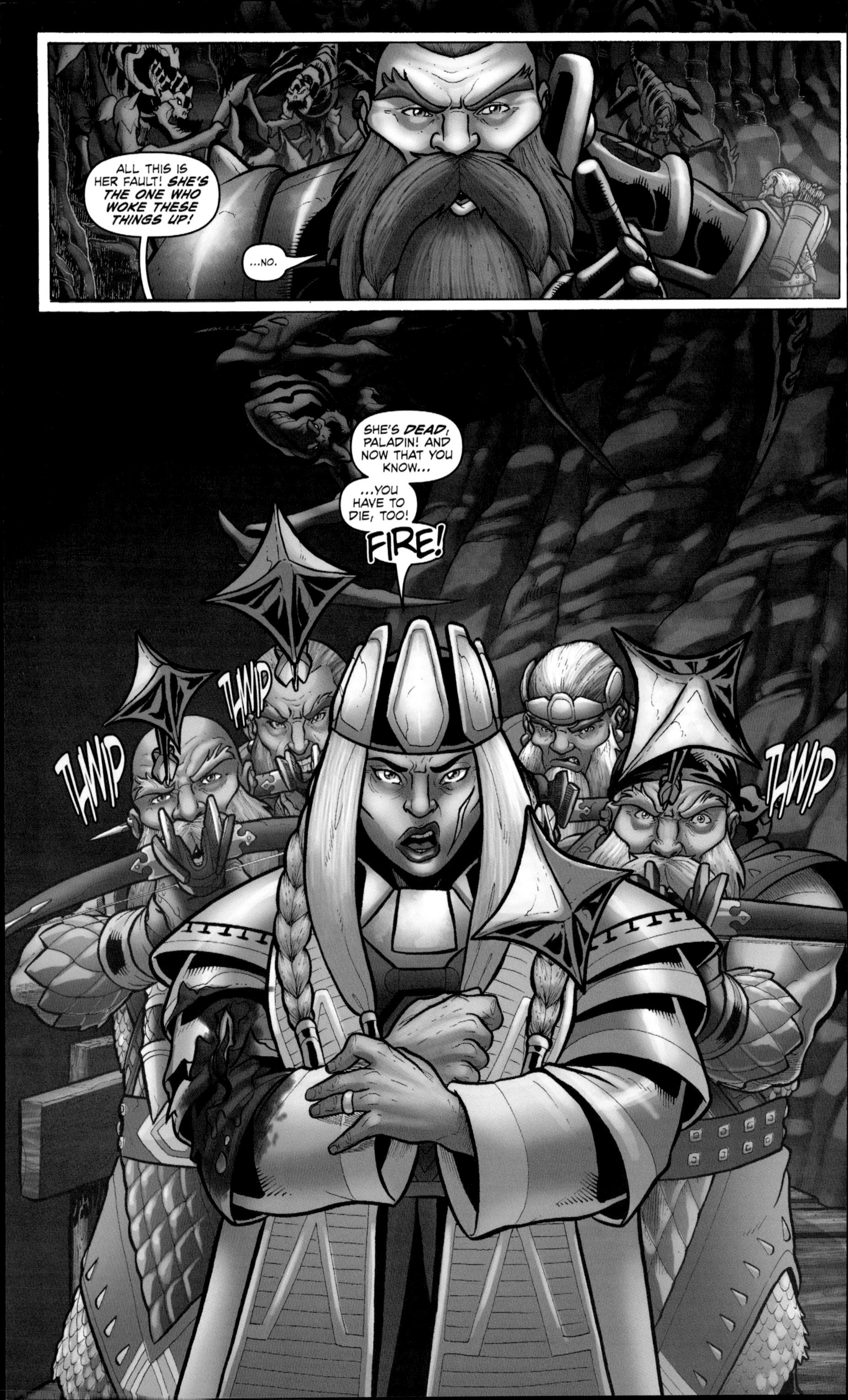
ALL THIS IS HER FAULT! SHE'S THE ONE WHO WOKE THESE THINGS UP!
...NO.
SHE'S DEAD, PALADIN! AND NOW THAT YOU KNOW...
...YOU HAVE TO DIE, TOO!
FIRE!
THWIP
THWIP
THWIP

Art by Tyler Walpole

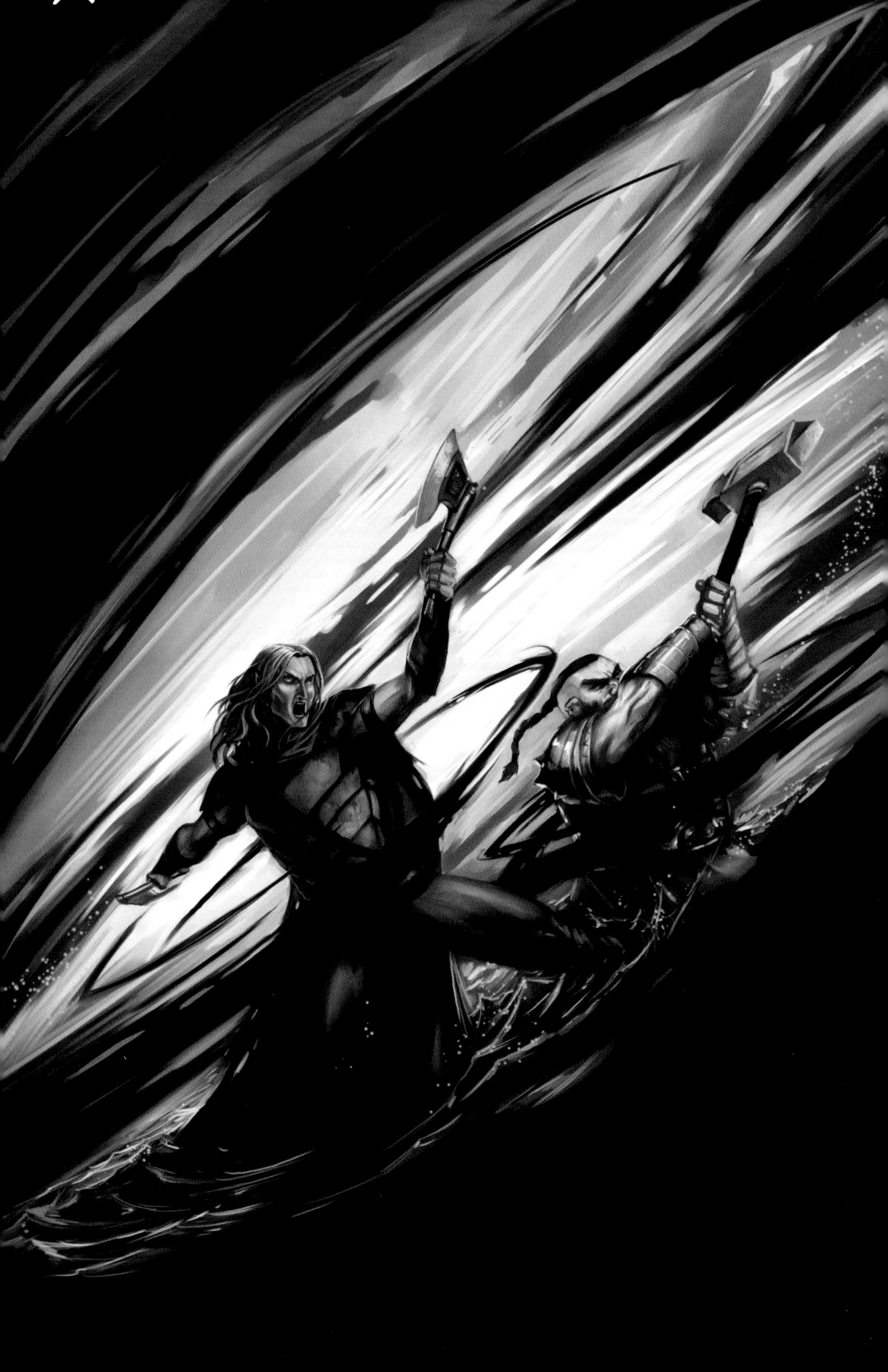

CHAPTER 14

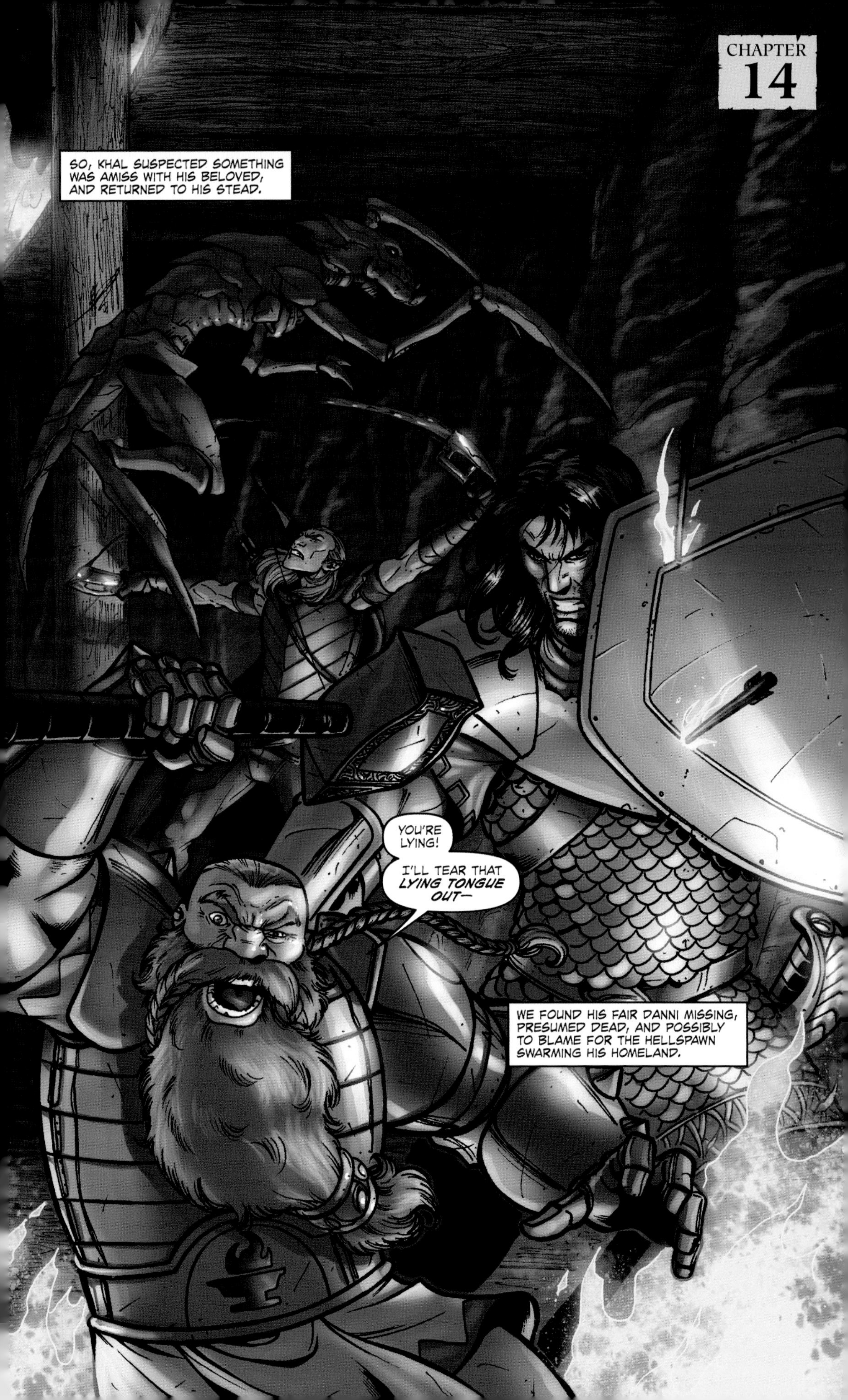
SO, KHAL SUSPECTED SOMETHING WAS AMISS WITH HIS BELOVED, AND RETURNED TO HIS STEAD.
YOU'RE LYING!
I'LL TEAR THAT *LYING TONGUE* OUT—
WE FOUND HIS FAIR DANNI MISSING, PRESUMED DEAD, AND POSSIBLY TO BLAME FOR THE HELLSPAWN SWARMING HIS HOMELAND.

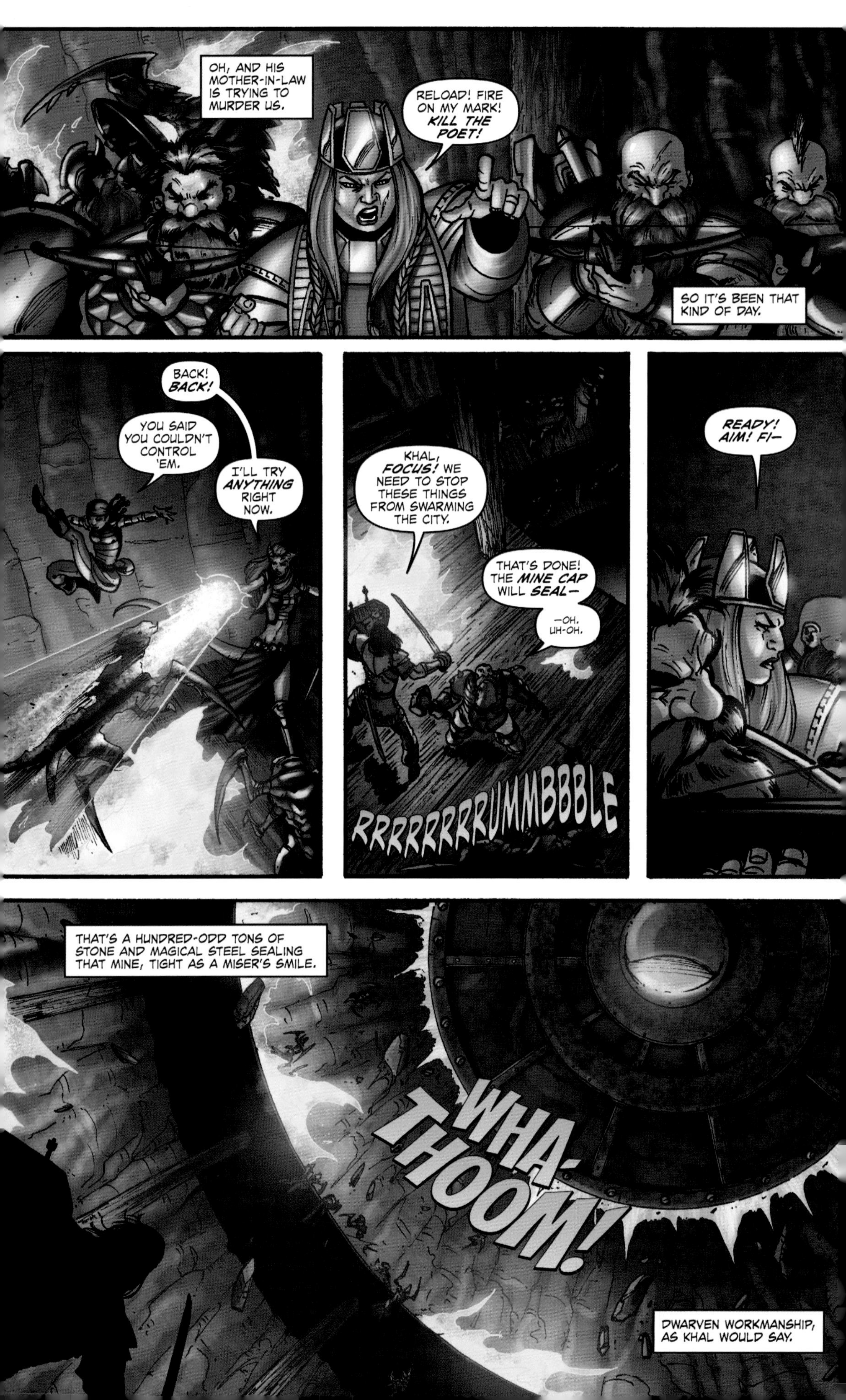
OH, AND HIS MOTHER-IN-LAW IS TRYING TO MURDER US.
RELOAD! FIRE ON MY MARK! KILL THE POET!
SO IT'S BEEN THAT KIND OF DAY.
BACK! BACK!
YOU SAID YOU COULDN'T CONTROL 'EM.
I'LL TRY ANYTHING RIGHT NOW.
KHAL, FOCUS! WE NEED TO STOP THESE THINGS FROM SWARMING THE CITY.
THAT'S DONE! THE MINE CAP WILL SEAL—
—OH. UH-OH.
RRRRRRRRUMMBBBLE
READY! AIM! FI—
THAT'S A HUNDRED-ODD TONS OF STONE AND MAGICAL STEEL SEALING THAT MINE, TIGHT AS A MISER'S SMILE.
WHA-THOOM!
DWARVEN WORKMANSHIP, AS KHAL WOULD SAY.

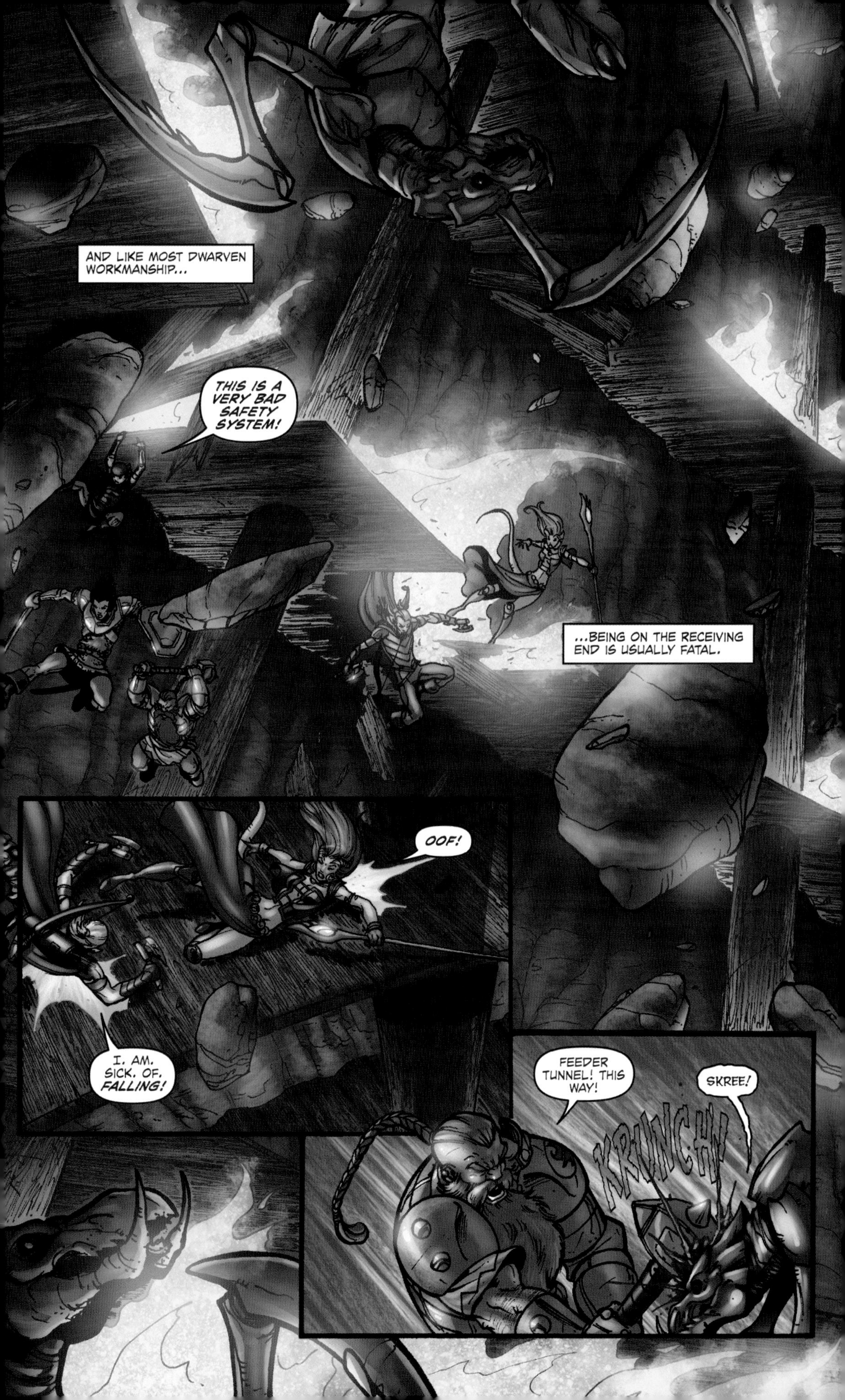
AND LIKE MOST DWARVEN WORKMANSHIP...
THIS IS A VERY BAD SAFETY SYSTEM!
...BEING ON THE RECEIVING END IS USUALLY FATAL.
OOF!
I. AM. SICK. OF. FALLING!
FEEDER TUNNEL! THIS WAY!
SKREE!
KRUNCH!

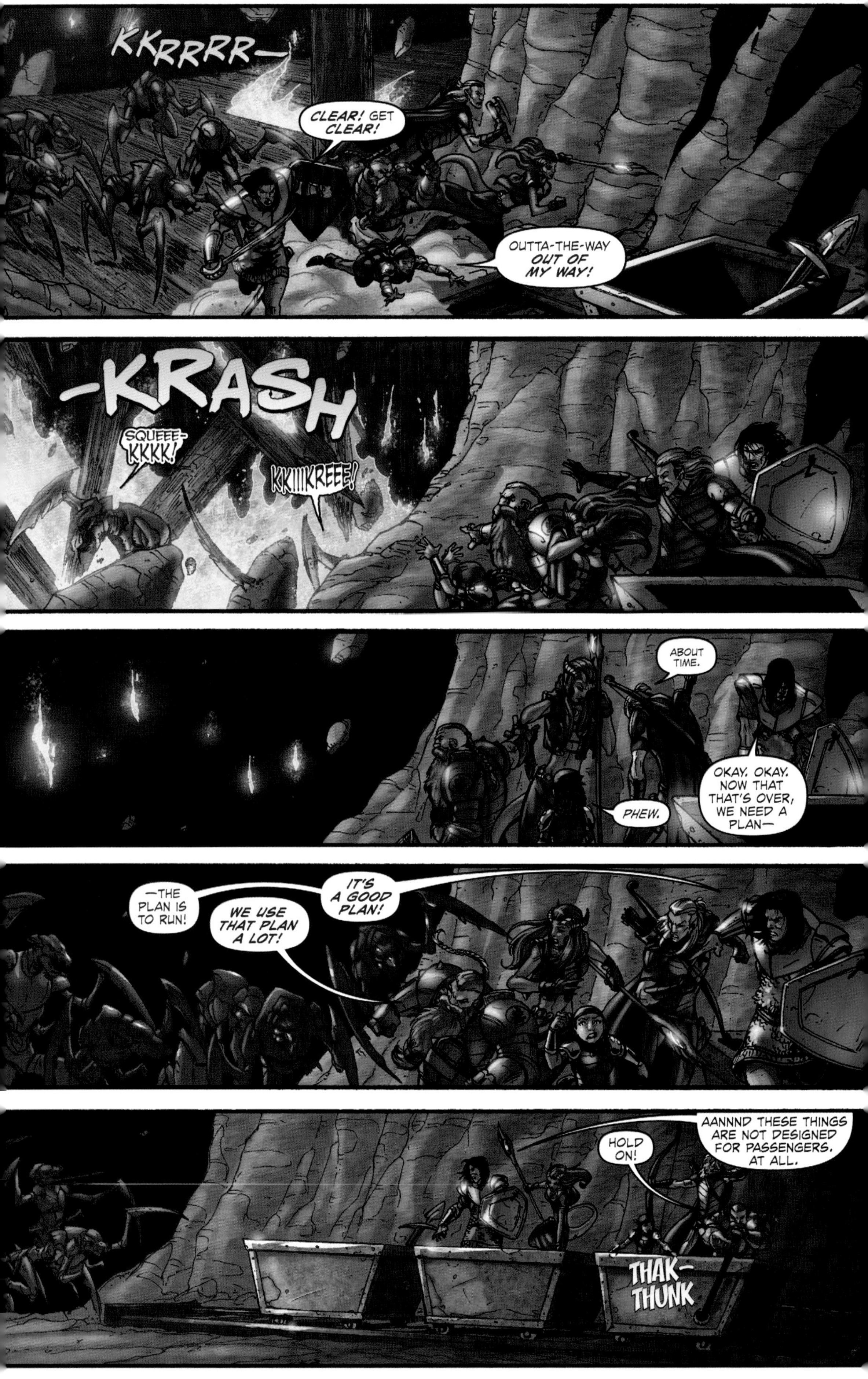
KKRRRR—
CLEAR! GET CLEAR!
OUTTA-THE-WAY OUT OF MY WAY!
-KRASH
SQUEEE-KKKK!
KKIIIKREEE!
ABOUT TIME.
PHEW.
OKAY. OKAY. NOW THAT THAT'S OVER, WE NEED A PLAN—
—THE PLAN IS TO RUN!
IT'S A GOOD PLAN!
WE USE THAT PLAN A LOT!
HOLD ON!
AANNND THESE THINGS ARE NOT DESIGNED FOR PASSENGERS. AT ALL.
THAK-THUNK

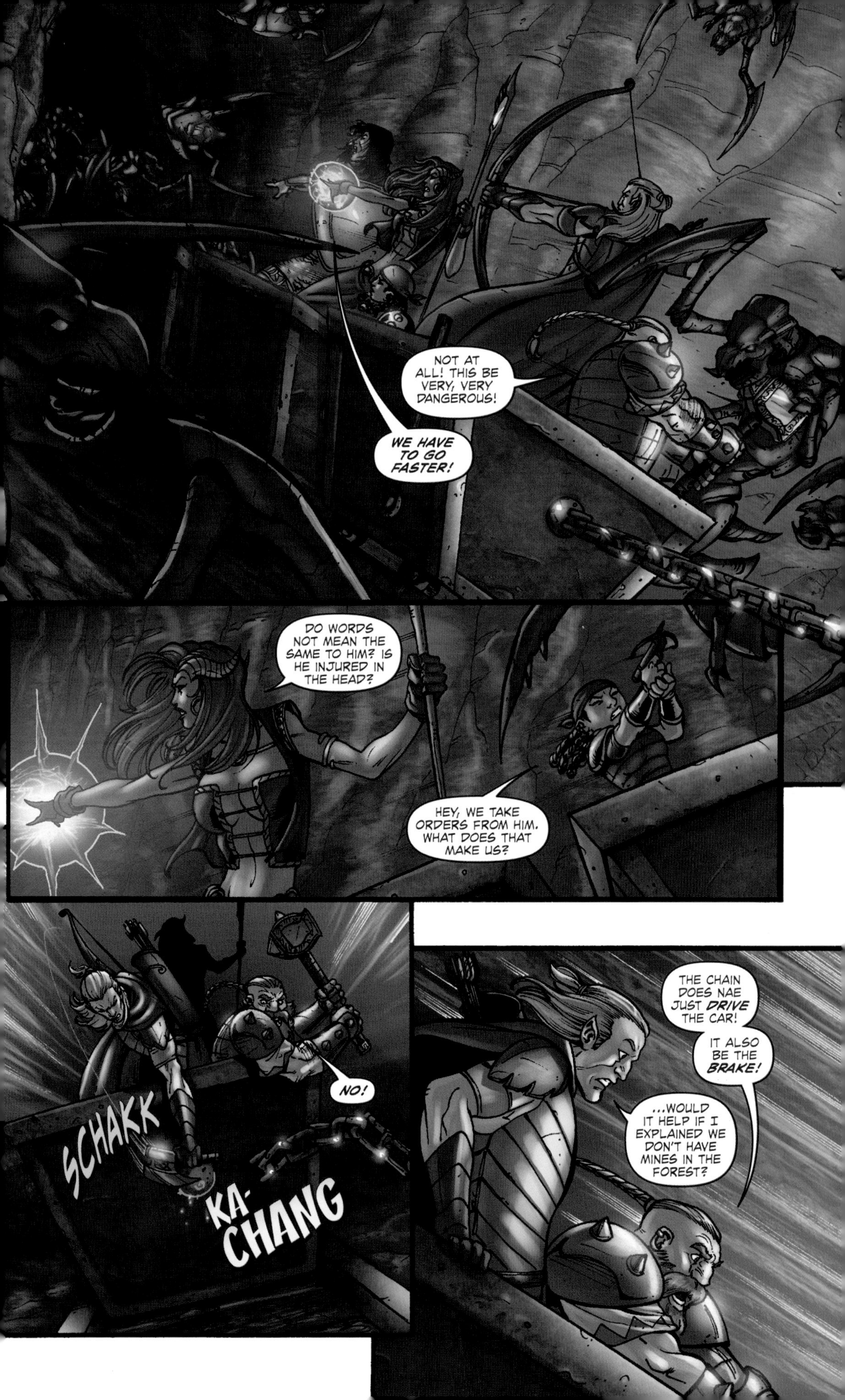
NOT AT ALL! THIS BE VERY, VERY DANGEROUS!
WE HAVE TO GO FASTER!
DO WORDS NOT MEAN THE SAME TO HIM? IS HE INJURED IN THE HEAD?
HEY, WE TAKE ORDERS FROM HIM. WHAT DOES THAT MAKE US?
NO!
SCHAKK
KA-CHANG
THE CHAIN DOES NAE JUST DRIVE THE CAR!
IT ALSO BE THE BRAKE!
...WOULD IT HELP IF I EXPLAINED WE DON'T HAVE MINES IN THE FOREST?

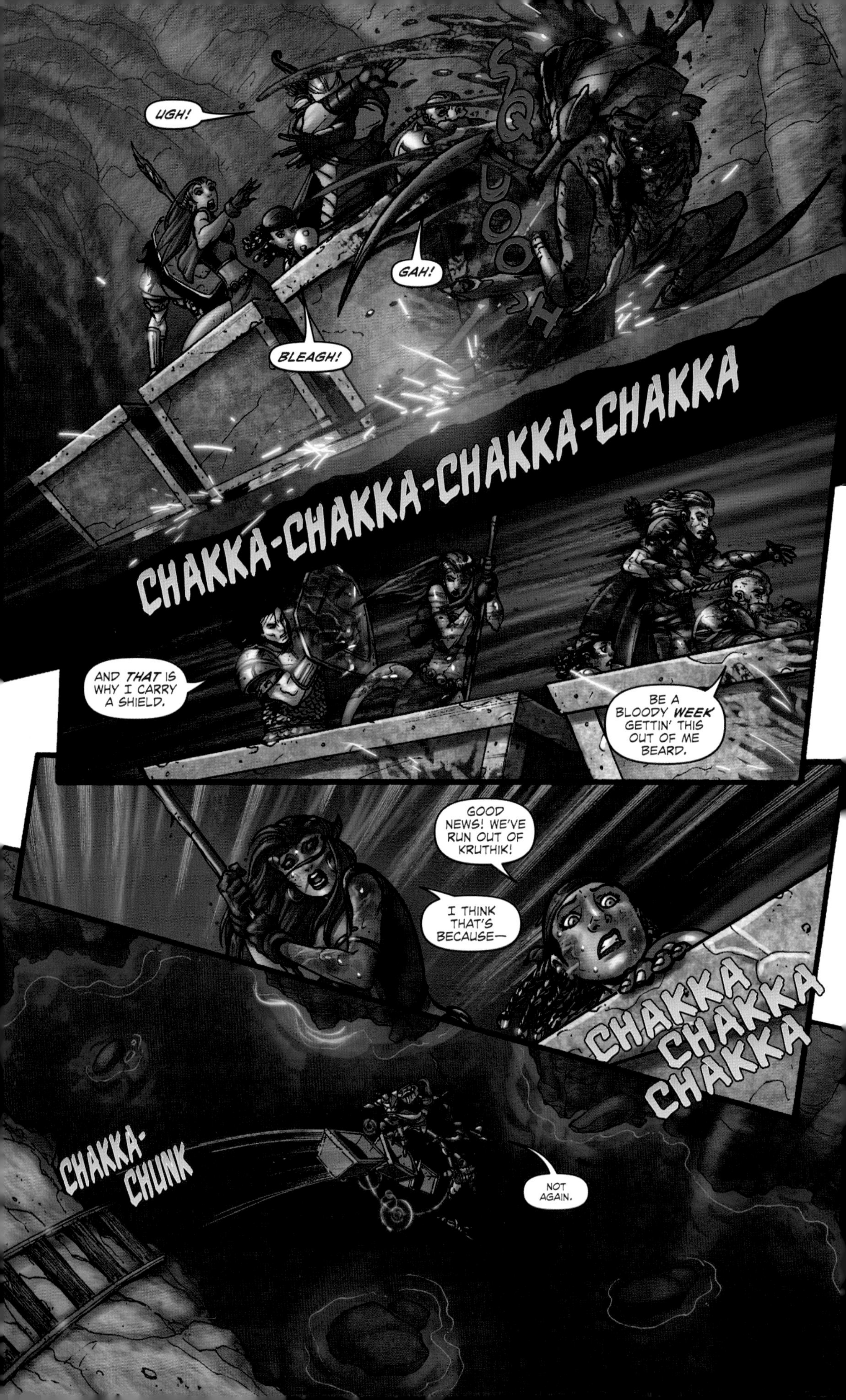
UGH!
SQUOOOSH
GAH!
BLEAGH!
CHAKKA-CHAKKA-CHAKKA-CHAKKA
AND *THAT* IS WHY I CARRY A SHIELD.
BE A BLOODY *WEEK* GETTIN' THIS OUT OF ME BEARD.
GOOD NEWS! WE'VE RUN OUT OF KRUTHIK!
I THINK THAT'S BECAUSE—
CHAKKA CHAKKA CHAKKA
CHAKKA-CHUNK
NOT AGAIN.

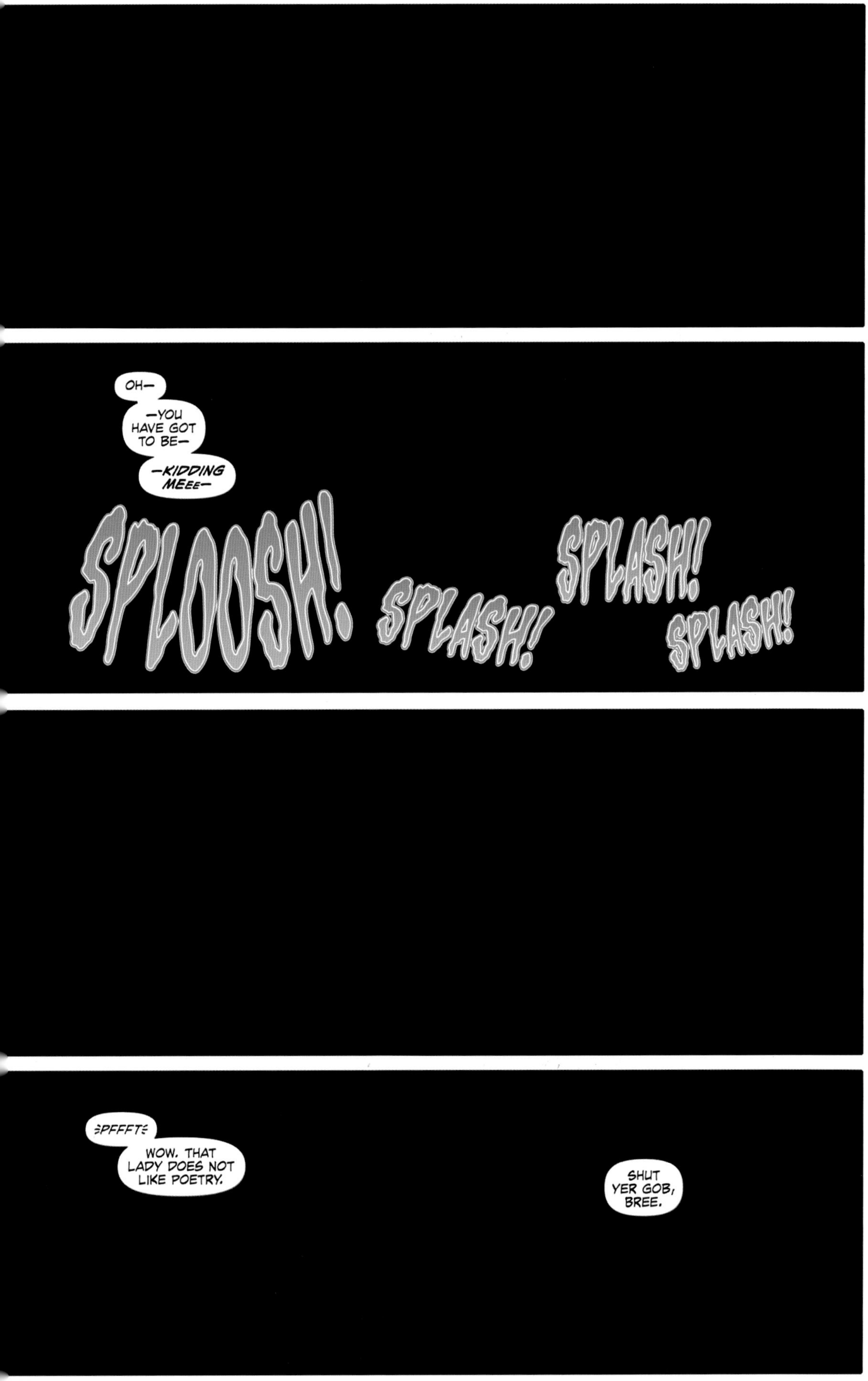
OH—
—YOU HAVE GOT TO BE—
—KIDDING MEEE—
SPLOOSH!
SPLASH!
SPLASH!
SPLASH!
=PFFFT=
WOW. THAT LADY DOES NOT LIKE POETRY.
SHUT YER GOB, BREE.

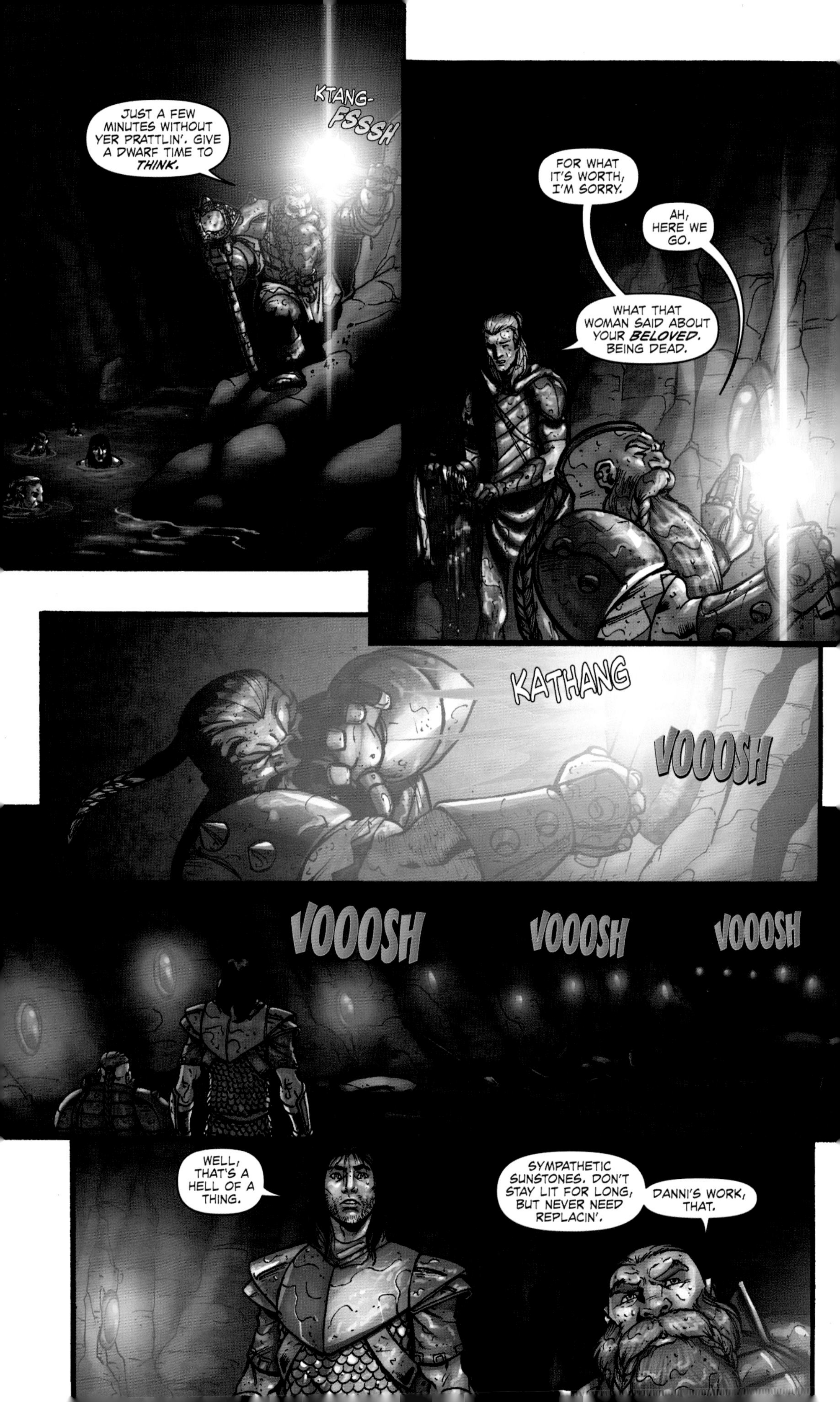
JUST A FEW MINUTES WITHOUT YER PRATTLIN'. GIVE A DWARF TIME TO THINK.
KTANG-FSSSH
FOR WHAT IT'S WORTH, I'M SORRY.
WHAT THAT WOMAN SAID ABOUT YOUR BELOVED. BEING DEAD.
AH, HERE WE GO.
KATHANG
VOOOSH
VOOOSH
VOOOSH
VOOOSH
WELL, THAT'S A HELL OF A THING.
SYMPATHETIC SUNSTONES. DON'T STAY LIT FOR LONG, BUT NEVER NEED REPLACIN'.
DANNI'S WORK, THAT.

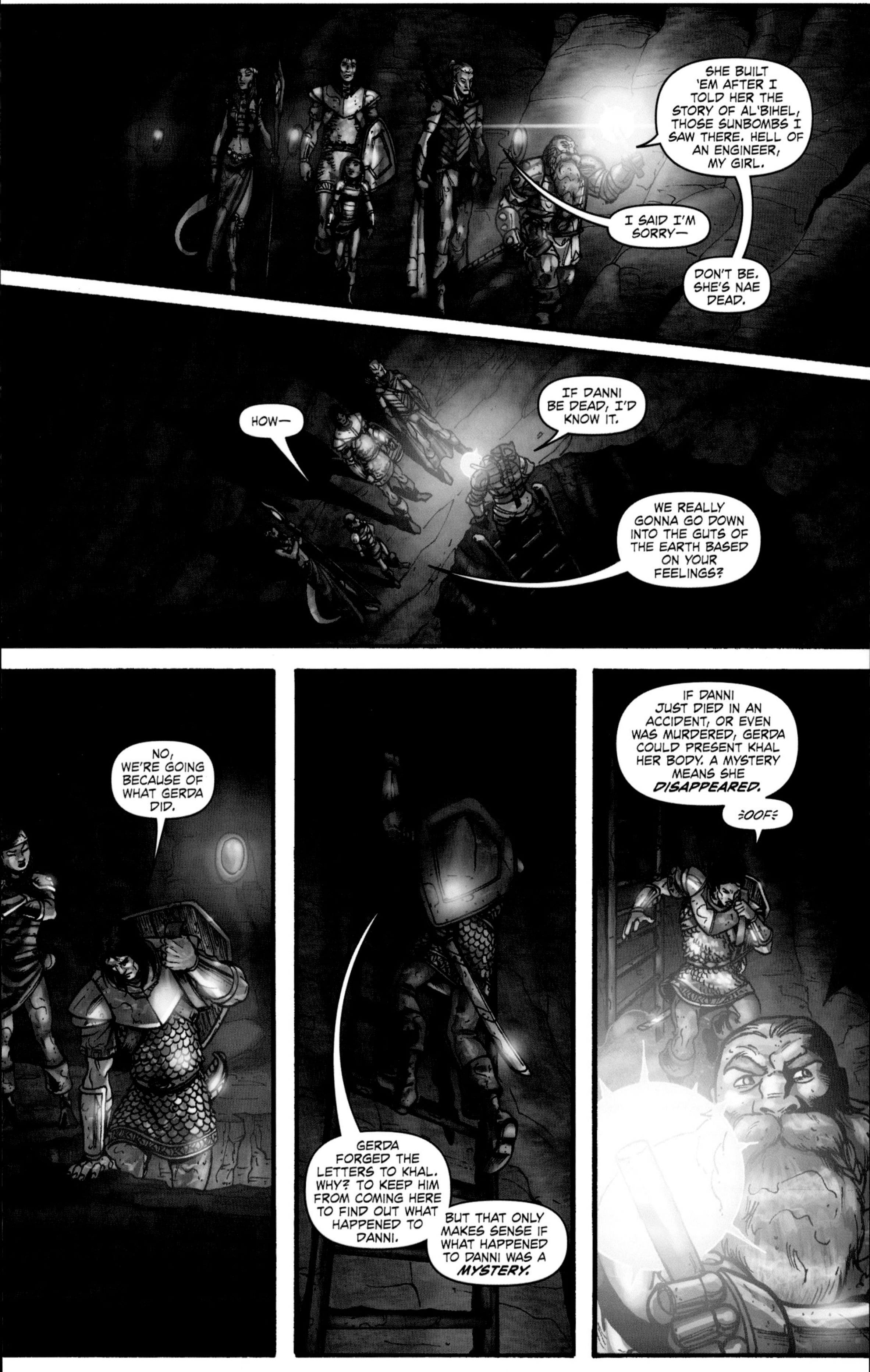
SHE BUILT 'EM AFTER I TOLD HER THE STORY OF AL'BIHEL, THOSE SUNBOMBS I SAW THERE. HELL OF AN ENGINEER, MY GIRL.
I SAID I'M SORRY—
DON'T BE. SHE'S NAE DEAD.
HOW—
IF DANNI BE DEAD, I'D KNOW IT.
WE REALLY GONNA GO DOWN INTO THE GUTS OF THE EARTH BASED ON YOUR FEELINGS?
NO, WE'RE GOING BECAUSE OF WHAT GERDA DID.
GERDA FORGED THE LETTERS TO KHAL. WHY? TO KEEP HIM FROM COMING HERE TO FIND OUT WHAT HAPPENED TO DANNI.
BUT THAT ONLY MAKES SENSE IF WHAT HAPPENED TO DANNI WAS A ***MYSTERY.***
IF DANNI JUST DIED IN AN ACCIDENT, OR EVEN WAS MURDERED, GERDA COULD PRESENT KHAL HER BODY. A MYSTERY MEANS SHE ***DISAPPEARED.***
OOF

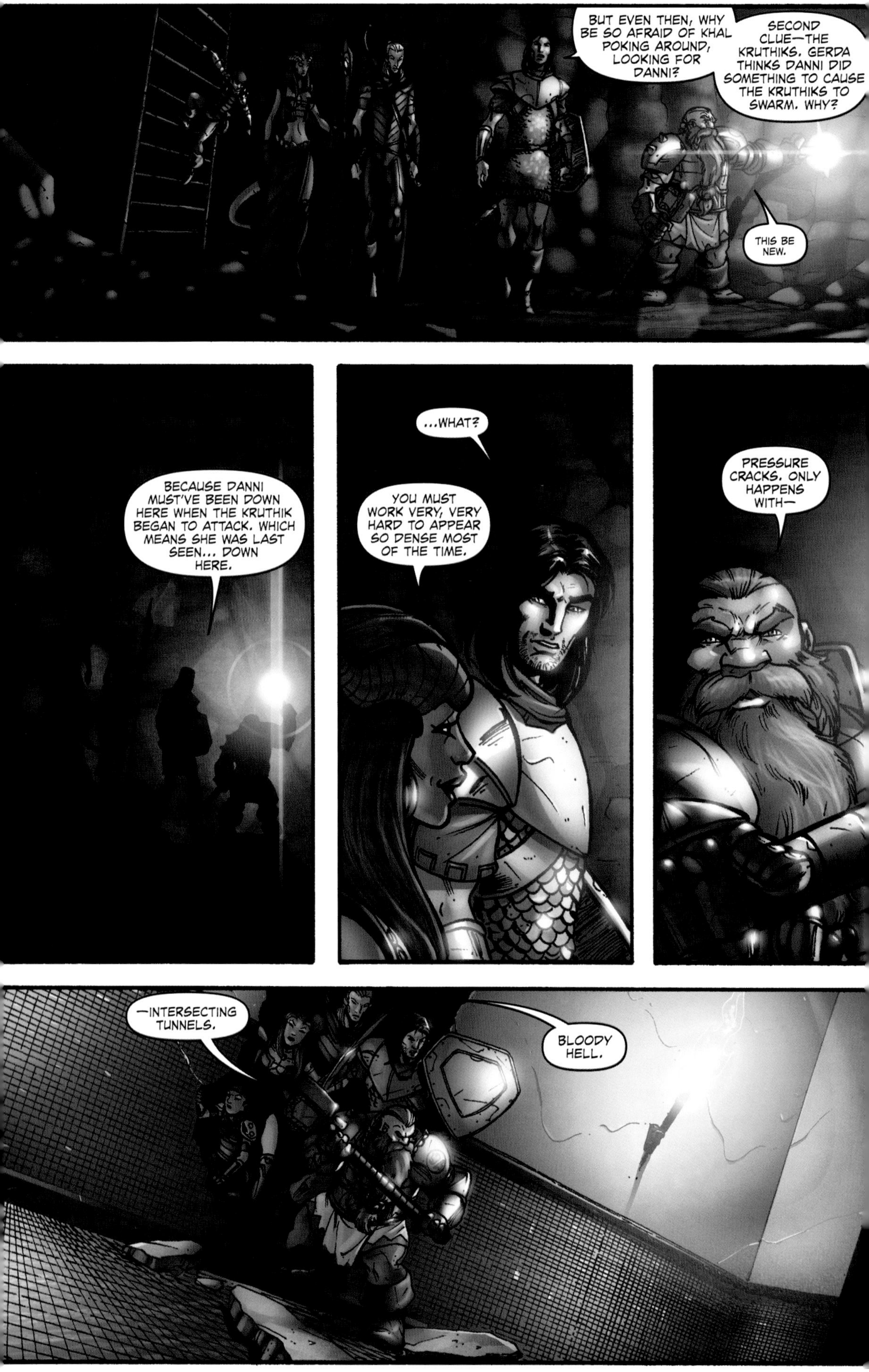
BUT EVEN THEN, WHY BE SO AFRAID OF KHAL POKING AROUND, LOOKING FOR DANNI?
SECOND CLUE—THE KRUTHIKS. GERDA THINKS DANNI DID SOMETHING TO CAUSE THE KRUTHIKS TO SWARM. WHY?
THIS BE NEW.
BECAUSE DANNI MUST'VE BEEN DOWN HERE WHEN THE KRUTHIK BEGAN TO ATTACK. WHICH MEANS SHE WAS LAST SEEN... DOWN HERE.
...WHAT?
YOU MUST WORK VERY, VERY HARD TO APPEAR SO DENSE MOST OF THE TIME.
PRESSURE CRACKS. ONLY HAPPENS WITH—
—INTERSECTING TUNNELS.
BLOODY HELL.

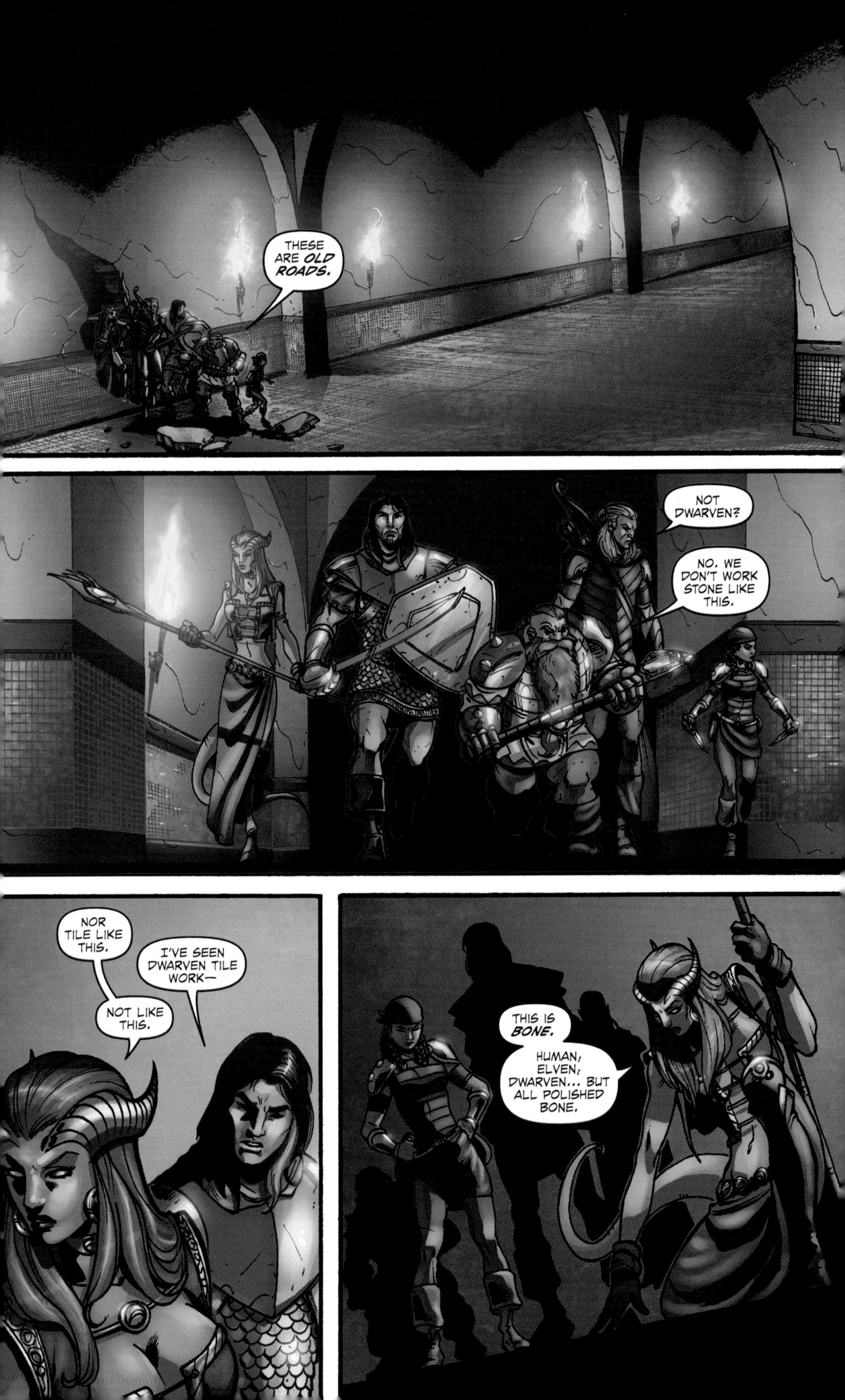

THESE ARE *OLD ROADS.*
NOT DWARVEN?
NO. WE DON'T WORK STONE LIKE THIS.
NOR TILE LIKE THIS.
I'VE SEEN DWARVEN TILE WORK—
NOT LIKE THIS.
THIS IS *BONE.*
HUMAN, ELVEN, DWARVEN... BUT ALL POLISHED BONE.

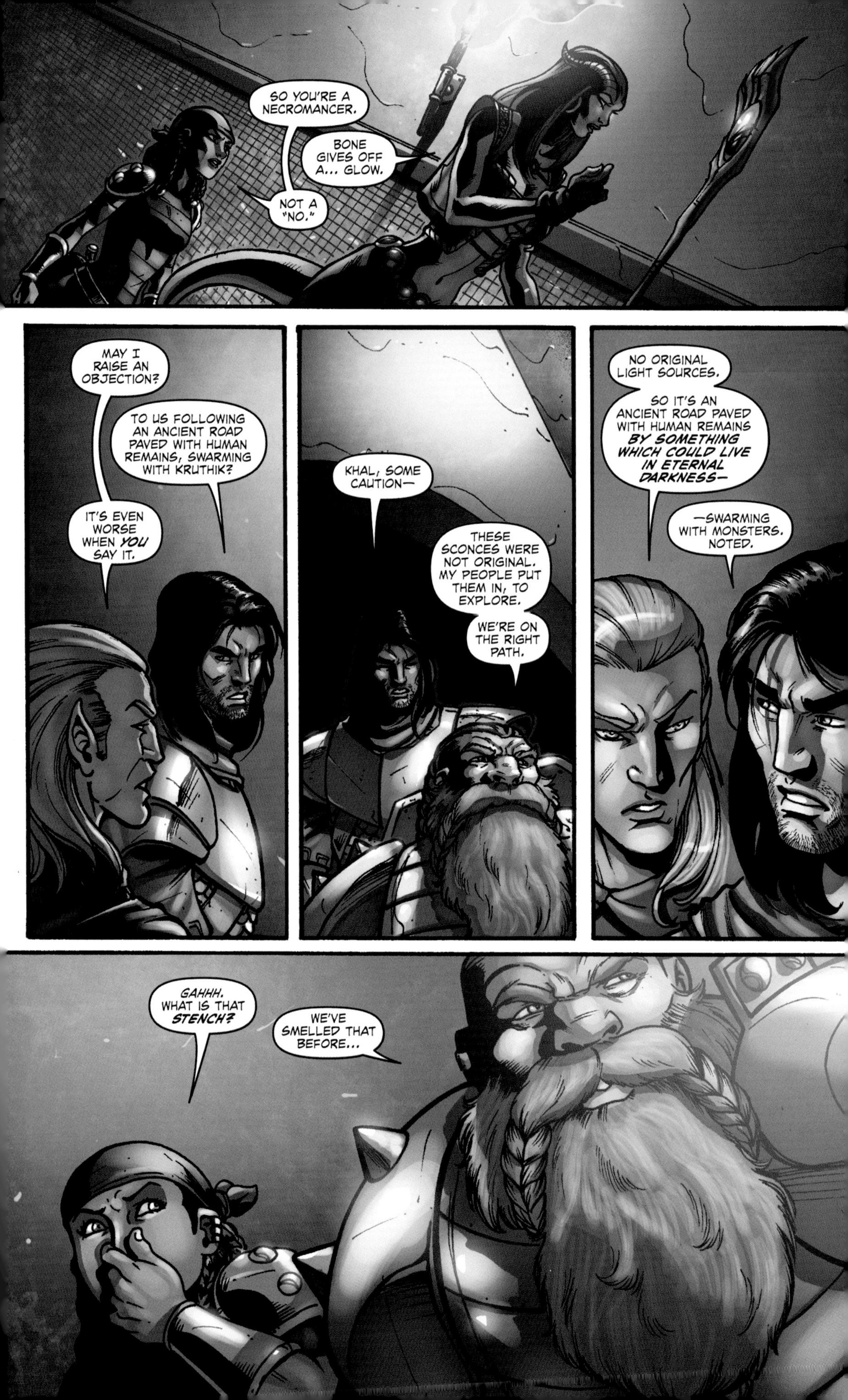
SO YOU'RE A NECROMANCER.
BONE GIVES OFF A... GLOW.
NOT A "NO."
MAY I RAISE AN OBJECTION?
TO US FOLLOWING AN ANCIENT ROAD PAVED WITH HUMAN REMAINS, SWARMING WITH KRUTHIK?
IT'S EVEN WORSE WHEN *YOU* SAY IT.
KHAL, SOME CAUTION—
THESE SCONCES WERE NOT ORIGINAL. MY PEOPLE PUT THEM IN, TO EXPLORE.
WE'RE ON THE RIGHT PATH.
NO ORIGINAL LIGHT SOURCES.
SO IT'S AN ANCIENT ROAD PAVED WITH HUMAN REMAINS ***BY SOMETHING WHICH COULD LIVE IN ETERNAL DARKNESS***—
—SWARMING WITH MONSTERS. NOTED.
GAHHH. WHAT IS THAT ***STENCH?***
WE'VE SMELLED THAT BEFORE...

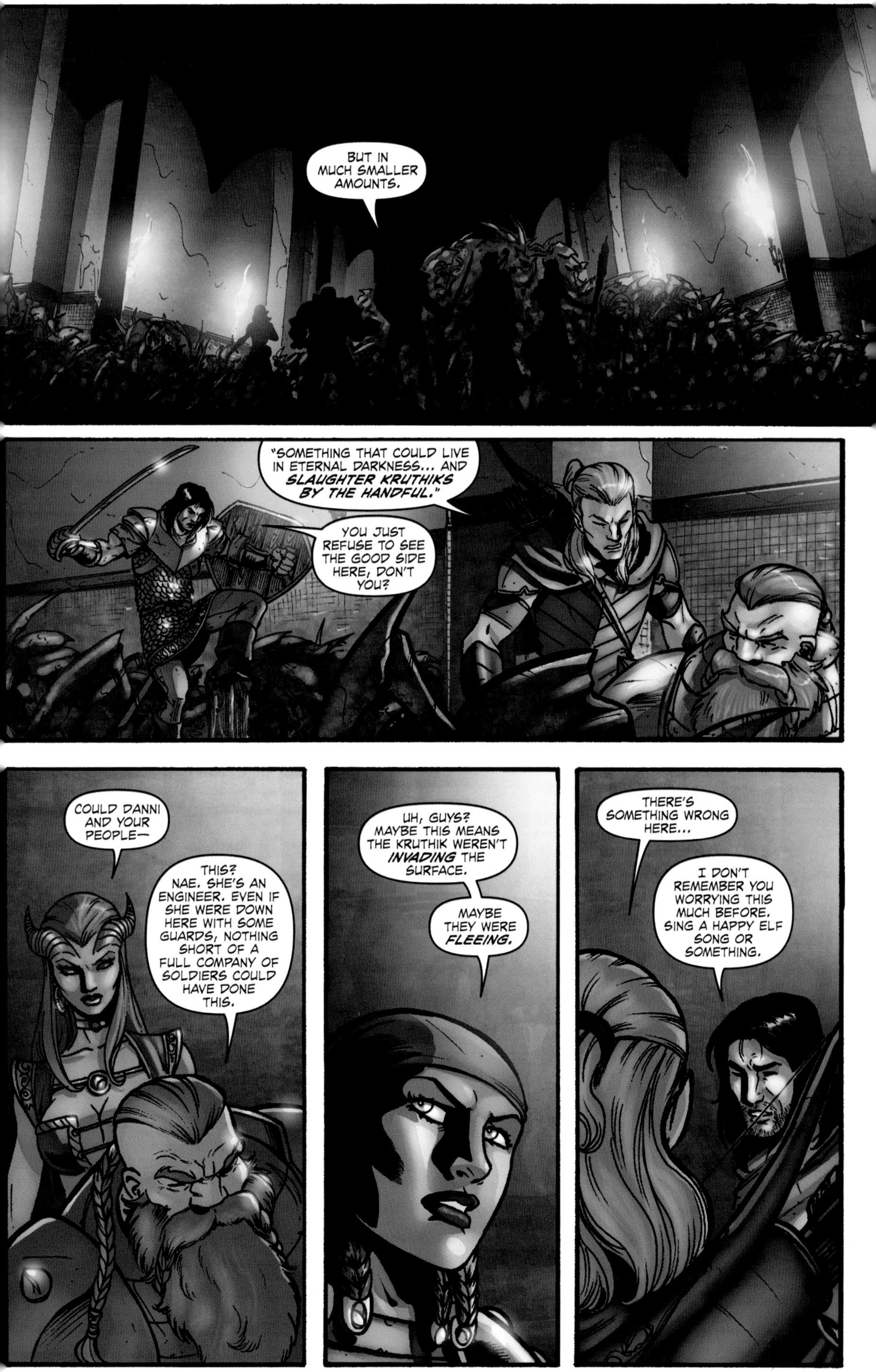
BUT IN MUCH SMALLER AMOUNTS.
"SOMETHING THAT COULD LIVE IN ETERNAL DARKNESS... AND *SLAUGHTER KRUTHIKS BY THE HANDFUL.*"
YOU JUST REFUSE TO SEE THE GOOD SIDE HERE, DON'T YOU?
COULD DANNI AND YOUR PEOPLE—
THIS? NAE. SHE'S AN ENGINEER. EVEN IF SHE WERE DOWN HERE WITH SOME GUARDS, NOTHING SHORT OF A FULL COMPANY OF SOLDIERS COULD HAVE DONE THIS.
UH, GUYS? MAYBE THIS MEANS THE KRUTHIK WEREN'T *INVADING* THE SURFACE.
MAYBE THEY WERE *FLEEING.*
THERE'S SOMETHING WRONG HERE...
I DON'T REMEMBER YOU WORRYING THIS MUCH BEFORE. SING A HAPPY ELF SONG OR SOMETHING.

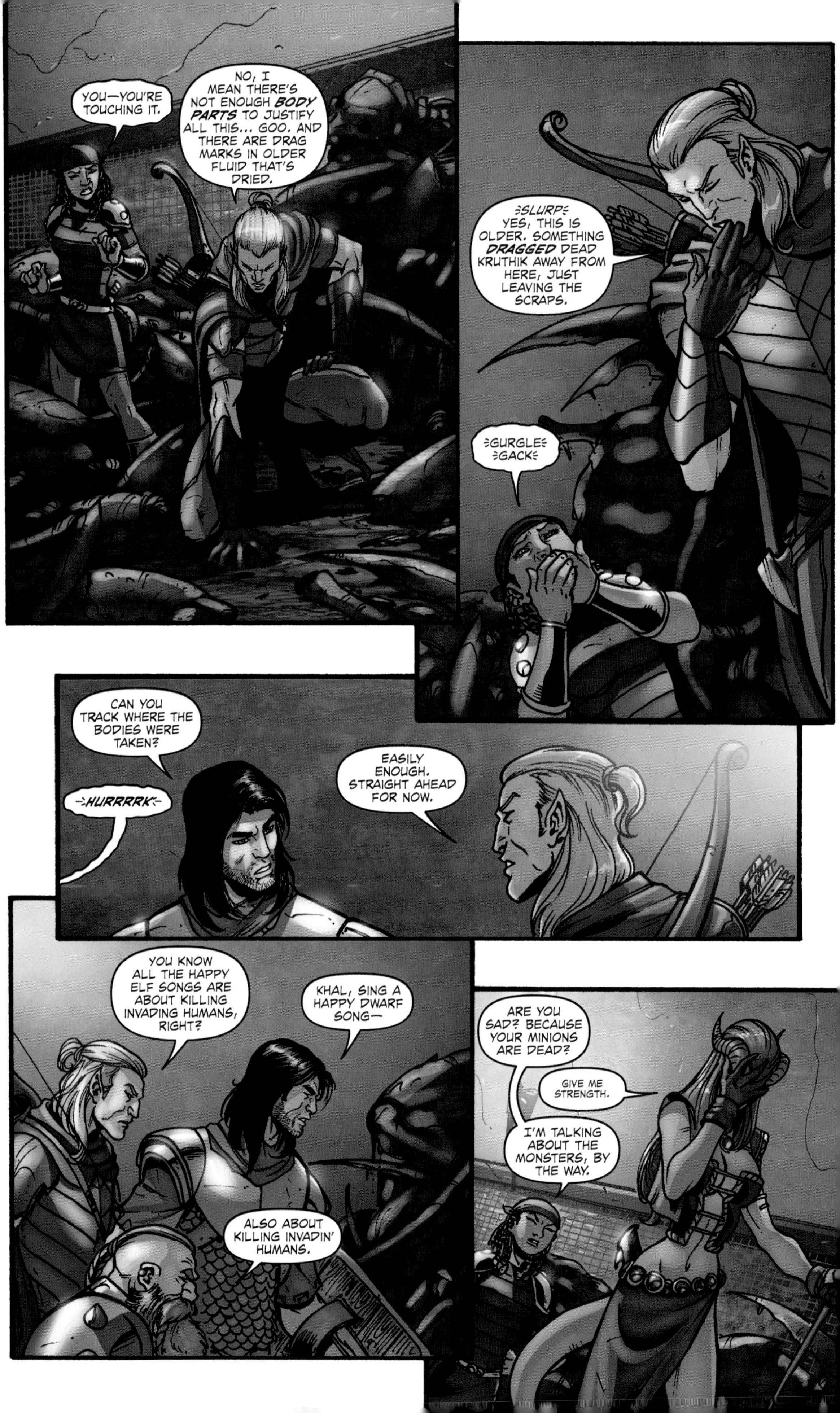
YOU—YOU'RE TOUCHING IT.
NO, I MEAN THERE'S NOT ENOUGH **BODY PARTS** TO JUSTIFY ALL THIS... GOO. AND THERE ARE DRAG MARKS IN OLDER FLUID THAT'S DRIED.
SLURP
YES, THIS IS OLDER. SOMETHING **DRAGGED** DEAD KRUTHIK AWAY FROM HERE, JUST LEAVING THE SCRAPS.
GURGLE
GACK
CAN YOU TRACK WHERE THE BODIES WERE TAKEN?
HURRRRK
EASILY ENOUGH. STRAIGHT AHEAD FOR NOW.
YOU KNOW ALL THE HAPPY ELF SONGS ARE ABOUT KILLING INVADING HUMANS, RIGHT?
KHAL, SING A HAPPY DWARF SONG—
ALSO ABOUT KILLING INVADIN' HUMANS.
ARE YOU SAD? BECAUSE YOUR MINIONS ARE DEAD?
GIVE ME STRENGTH.
I'M TALKING ABOUT THE MONSTERS, BY THE WAY.

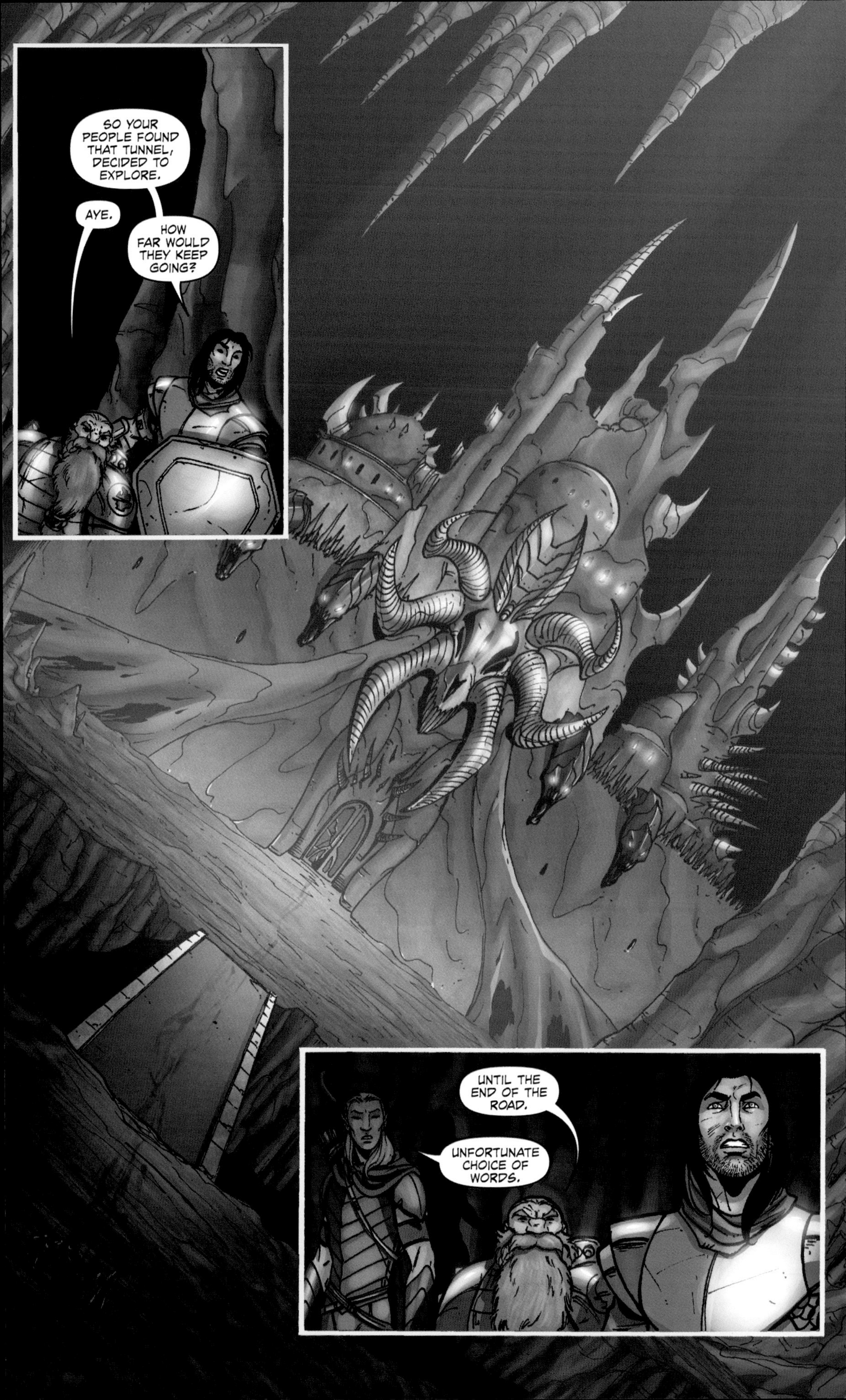

SO YOUR PEOPLE FOUND THAT TUNNEL, DECIDED TO EXPLORE.
AYE.
HOW FAR WOULD THEY KEEP GOING?
UNTIL THE END OF THE ROAD.
UNFORTUNATE CHOICE OF WORDS.

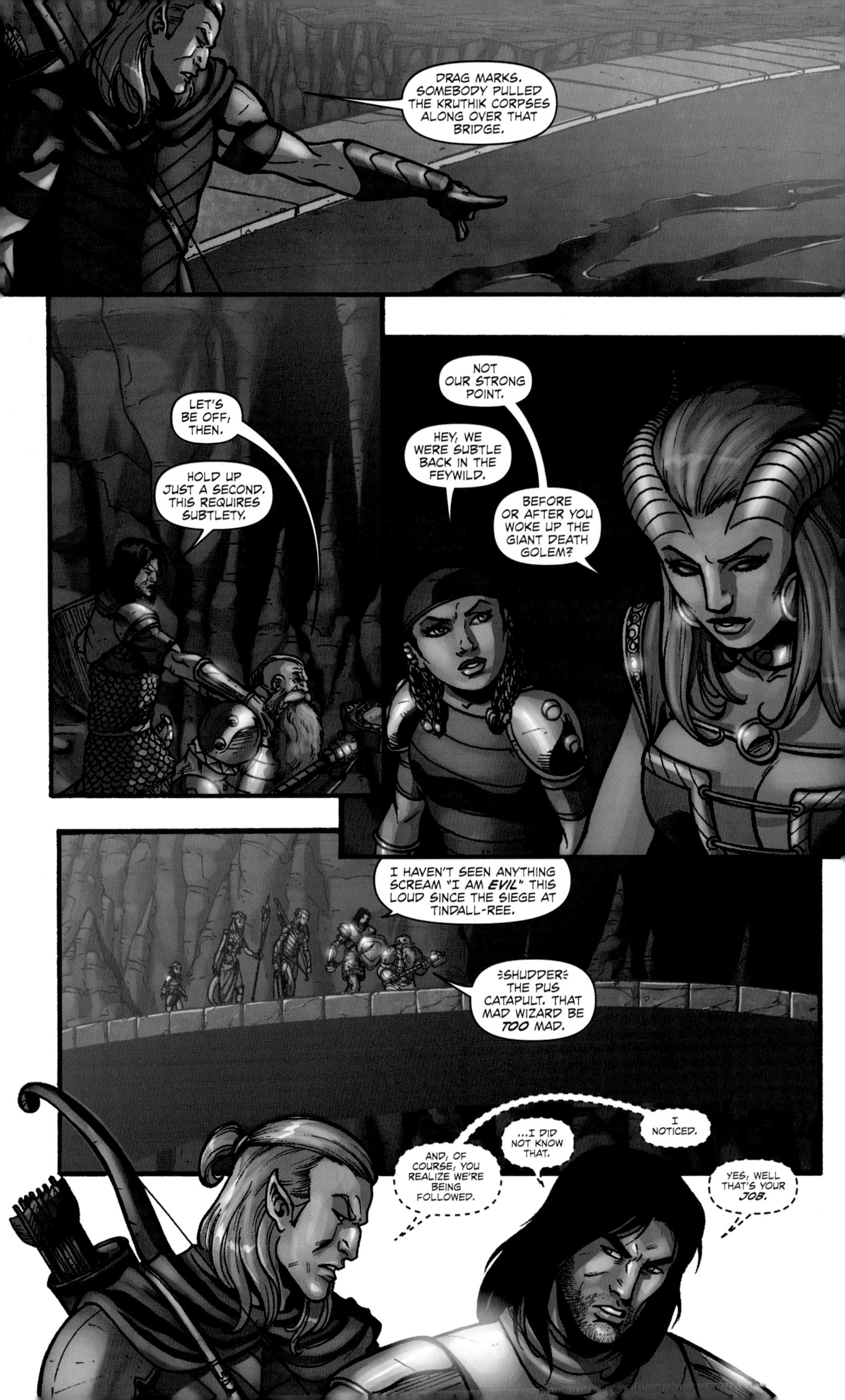
DRAG MARKS. SOMEBODY PULLED THE KRUTHIK CORPSES ALONG OVER THAT BRIDGE.
LET'S BE OFF, THEN.
HOLD UP JUST A SECOND. THIS REQUIRES SUBTLETY.
NOT OUR STRONG POINT.
HEY, WE WERE SUBTLE BACK IN THE FEYWILD.
BEFORE OR AFTER YOU WOKE UP THE GIANT DEATH GOLEM?
I HAVEN'T SEEN ANYTHING SCREAM "I AM *EVIL*" THIS LOUD SINCE THE SIEGE AT TINDALL-REE.
≈SHUDDER≈ THE PUS CATAPULT. THAT MAD WIZARD BE *TOO* MAD.
AND, OF COURSE, YOU REALIZE WE'RE BEING FOLLOWED.
...I DID NOT KNOW THAT.
I NOTICED.
YES, WELL THAT'S YOUR *JOB*.

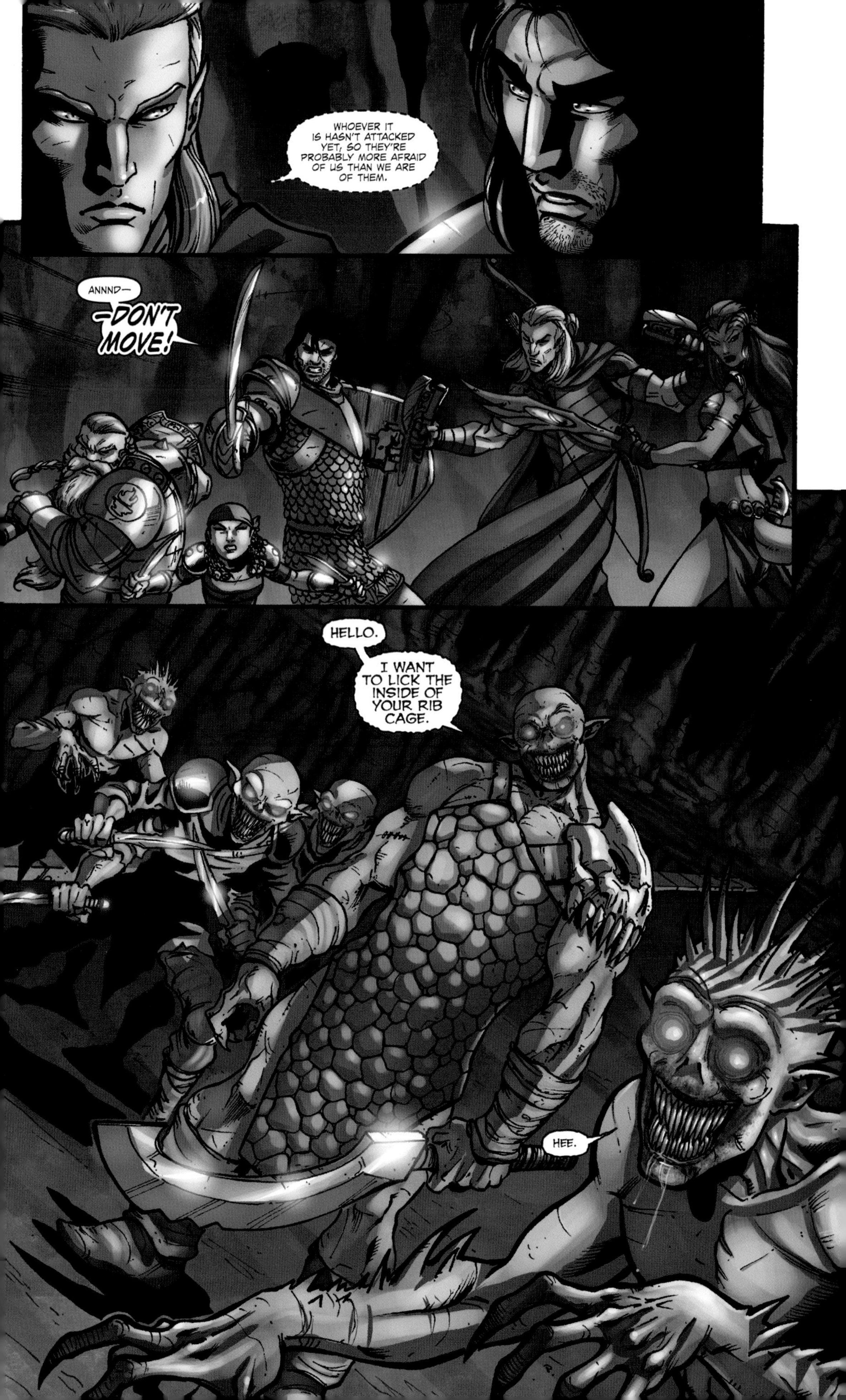
WHOEVER IT IS HASN'T ATTACKED YET, SO THEY'RE PROBABLY MORE AFRAID OF US THAN WE ARE OF THEM.
ANNND—
—DON'T MOVE!
HELLO.
I WANT TO LICK THE INSIDE OF YOUR RIB CAGE.
HEE.

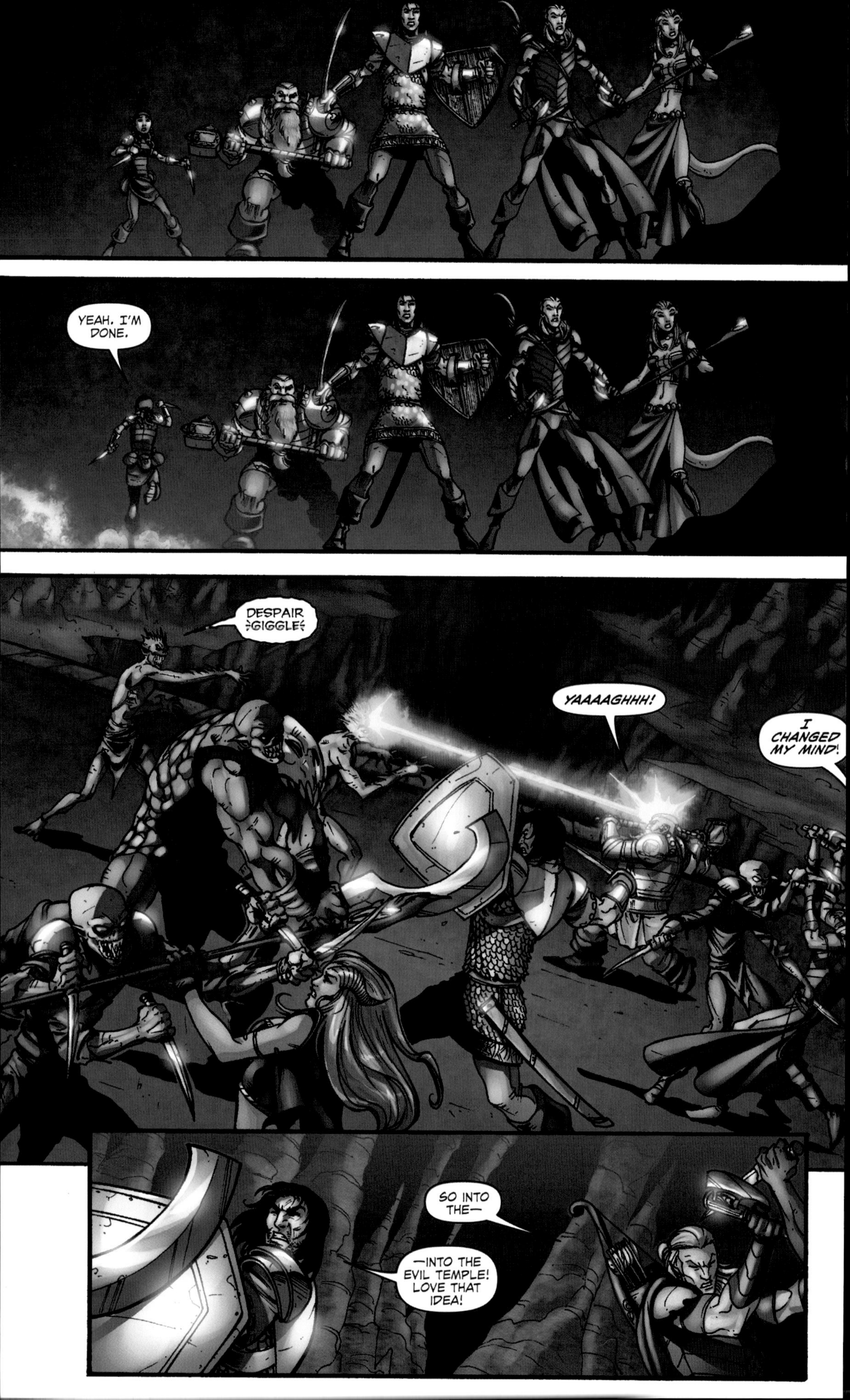
YEAH. I'M DONE.
DESPAIR
GIGGLE
YAAAAGHHH!
I CHANGED MY MIND!
SO INTO THE—
—INTO THE EVIL TEMPLE! LOVE THAT IDEA!

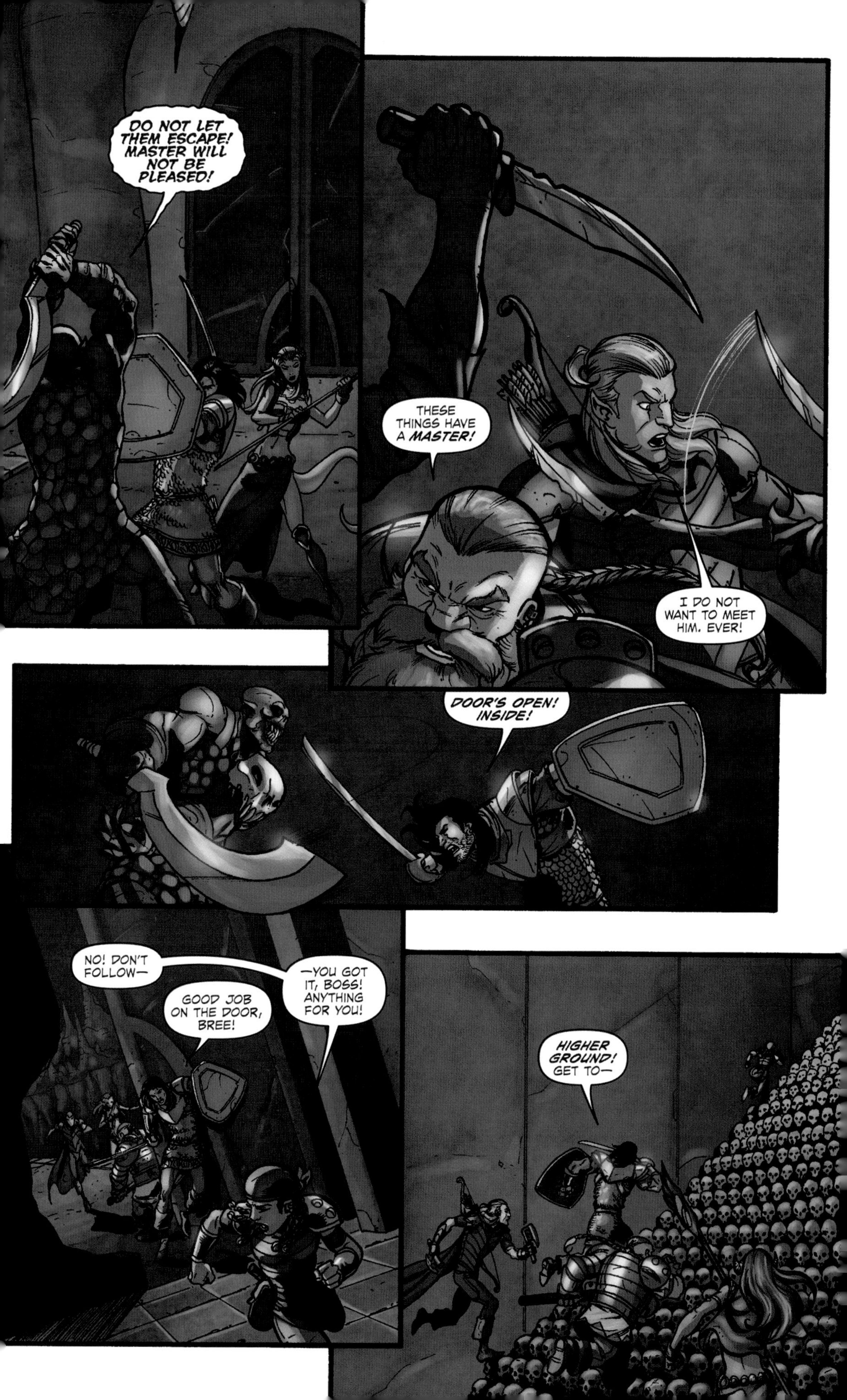
DO NOT LET THEM ESCAPE! MASTER WILL NOT BE PLEASED!
THESE THINGS HAVE A *MASTER!*
I DO NOT WANT TO MEET HIM. EVER!
DOOR'S OPEN! INSIDE!
NO! DON'T FOLLOW—
GOOD JOB ON THE DOOR, BREE!
—YOU GOT IT, BOSS! ANYTHING FOR YOU!
HIGHER GROUND! GET TO—

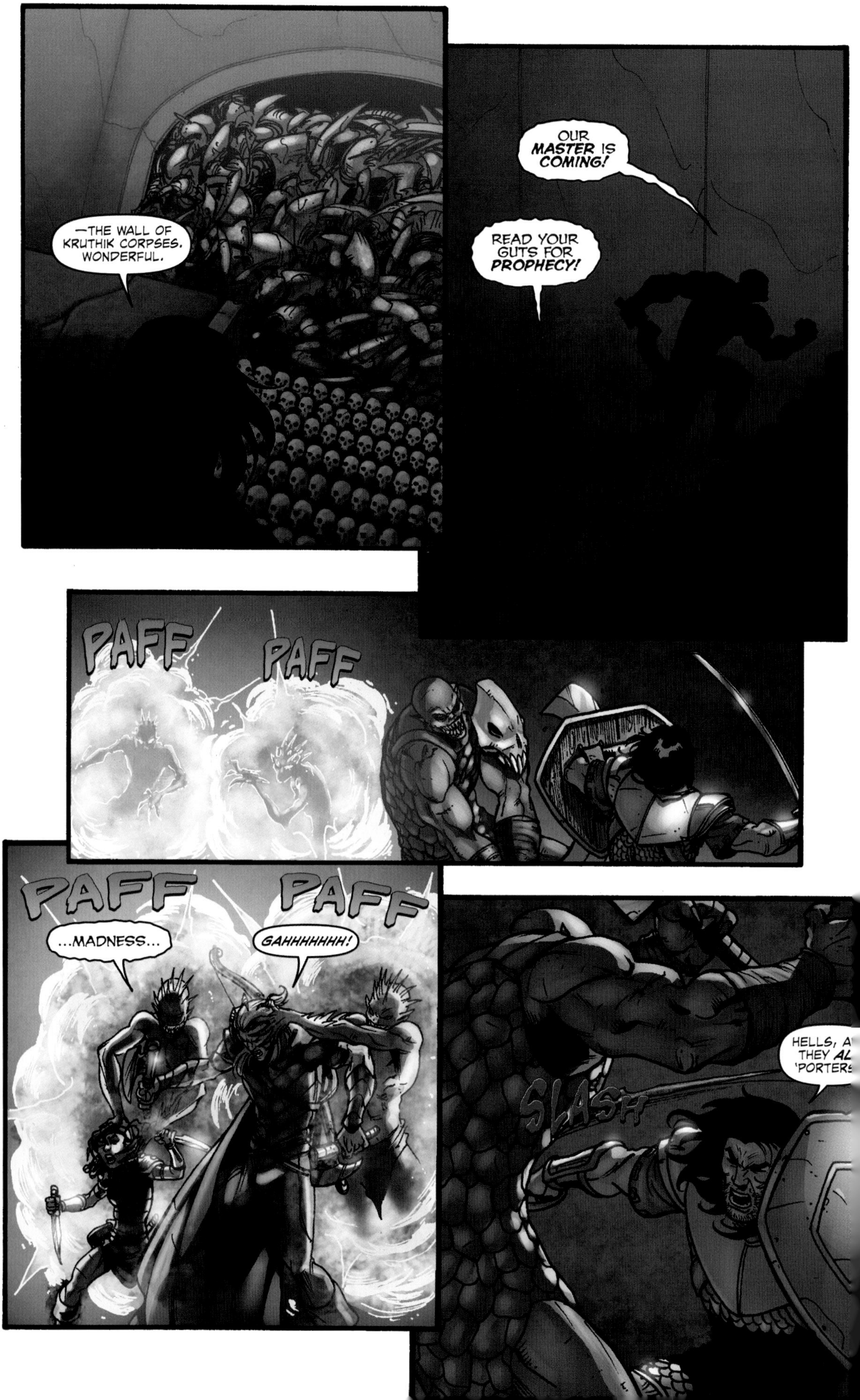
—THE WALL OF KRUTHIK CORPSES. WONDERFUL.
OUR MASTER IS COMING!
READ YOUR GUTS FOR PROPHECY!
PAFF
PAFF
PAFF
PAFF
...MADNESS...
GAHHHHHHH!
SLASH
HELLS, A
THEY AL
'PORTERS

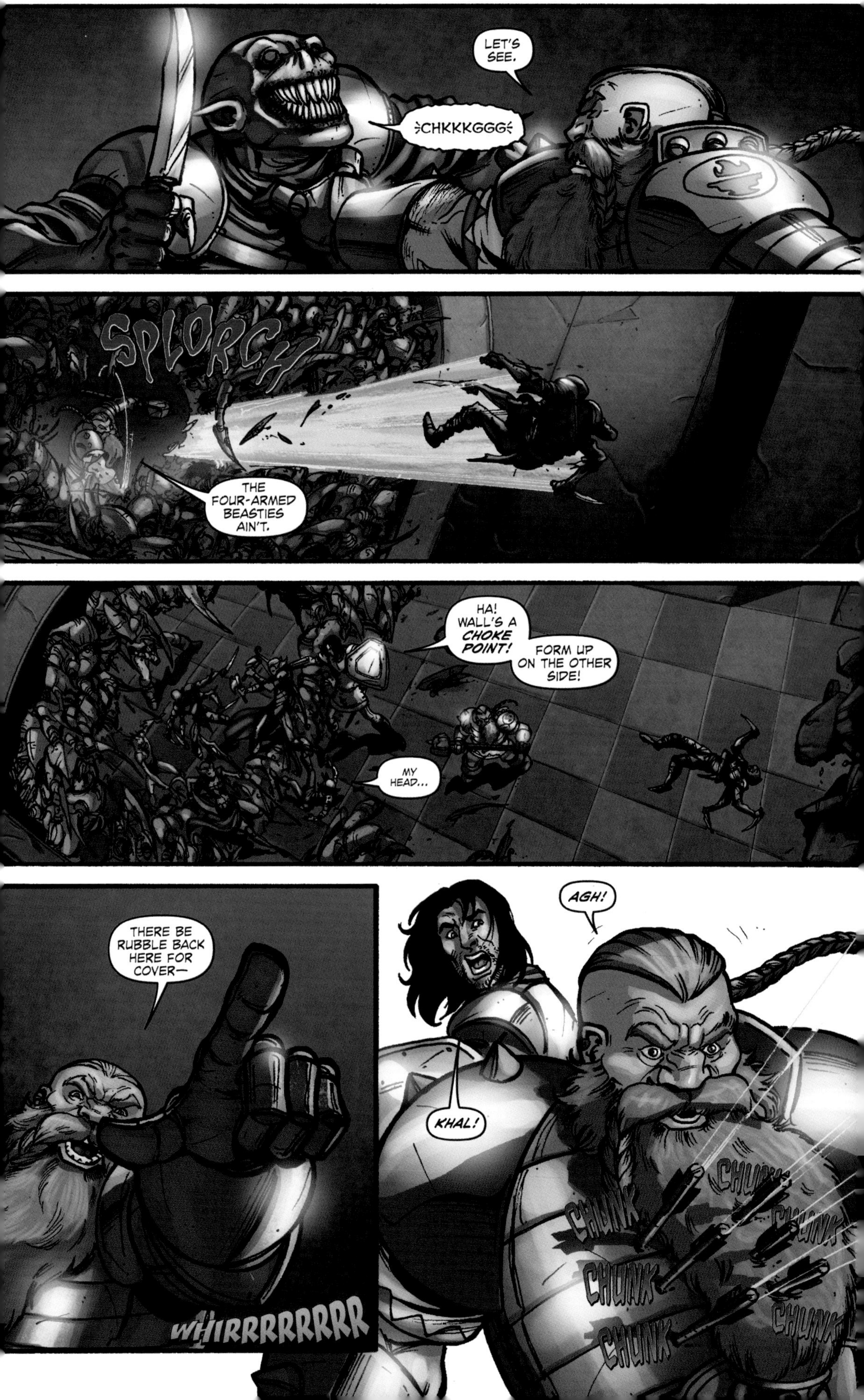
LET'S SEE.
CHKKKGGG
SPLORCH
THE FOUR-ARMED BEASTIES AIN'T.
HA! WALL'S A CHOKE POINT!
FORM UP ON THE OTHER SIDE!
MY HEAD...
THERE BE RUBBLE BACK HERE FOR COVER—
WHIRRRRRRRR
AGH!
KHAL!
CHUNK
CHUNK
CHUNK
CHUNK
CHUNK
CHUNK
CHUNK

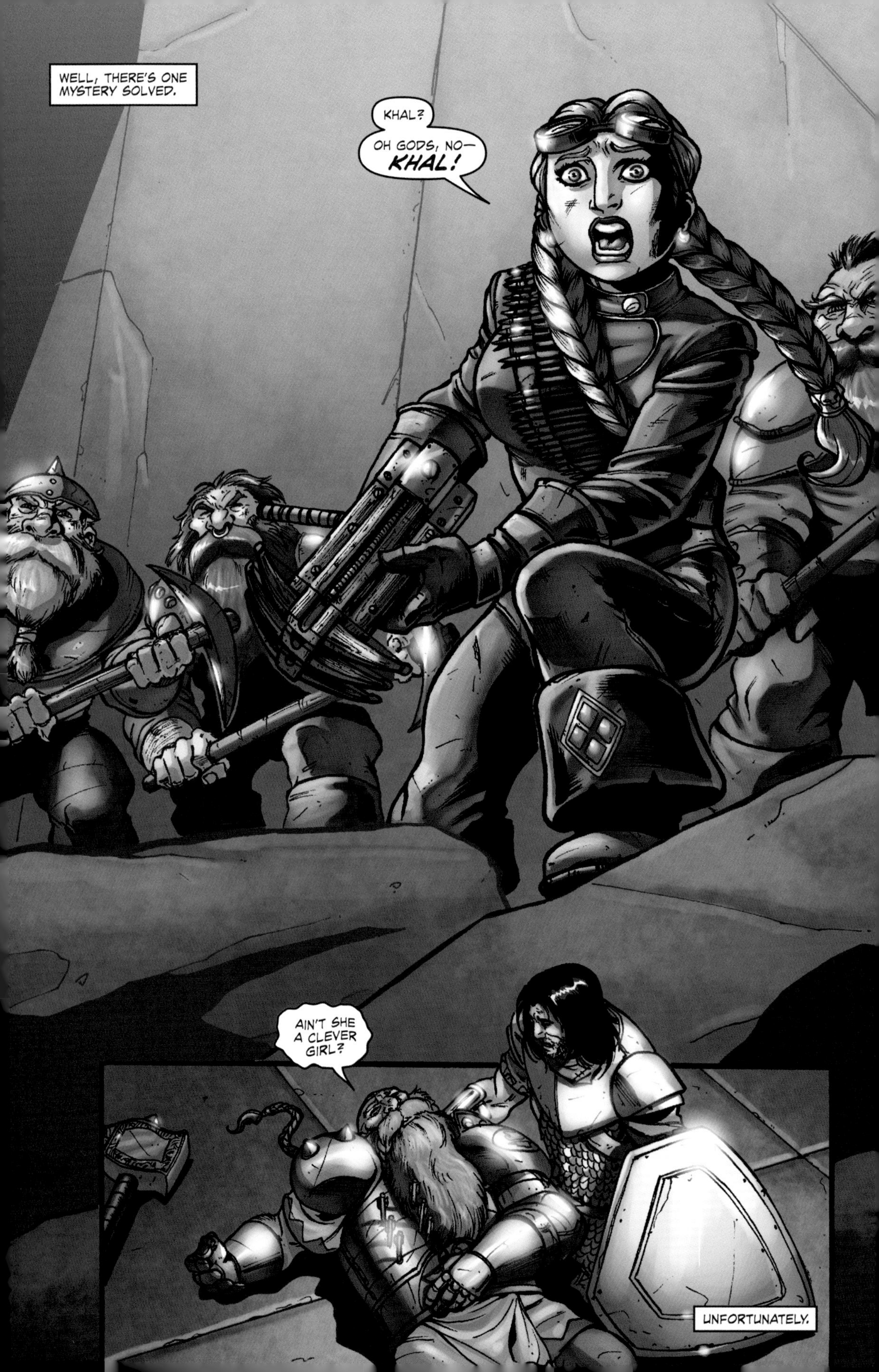
WELL, THERE'S ONE MYSTERY SOLVED.
KHAL?
OH GODS, NO— KHAL!
AIN'T SHE A CLEVER GIRL?
UNFORTUNATELY.

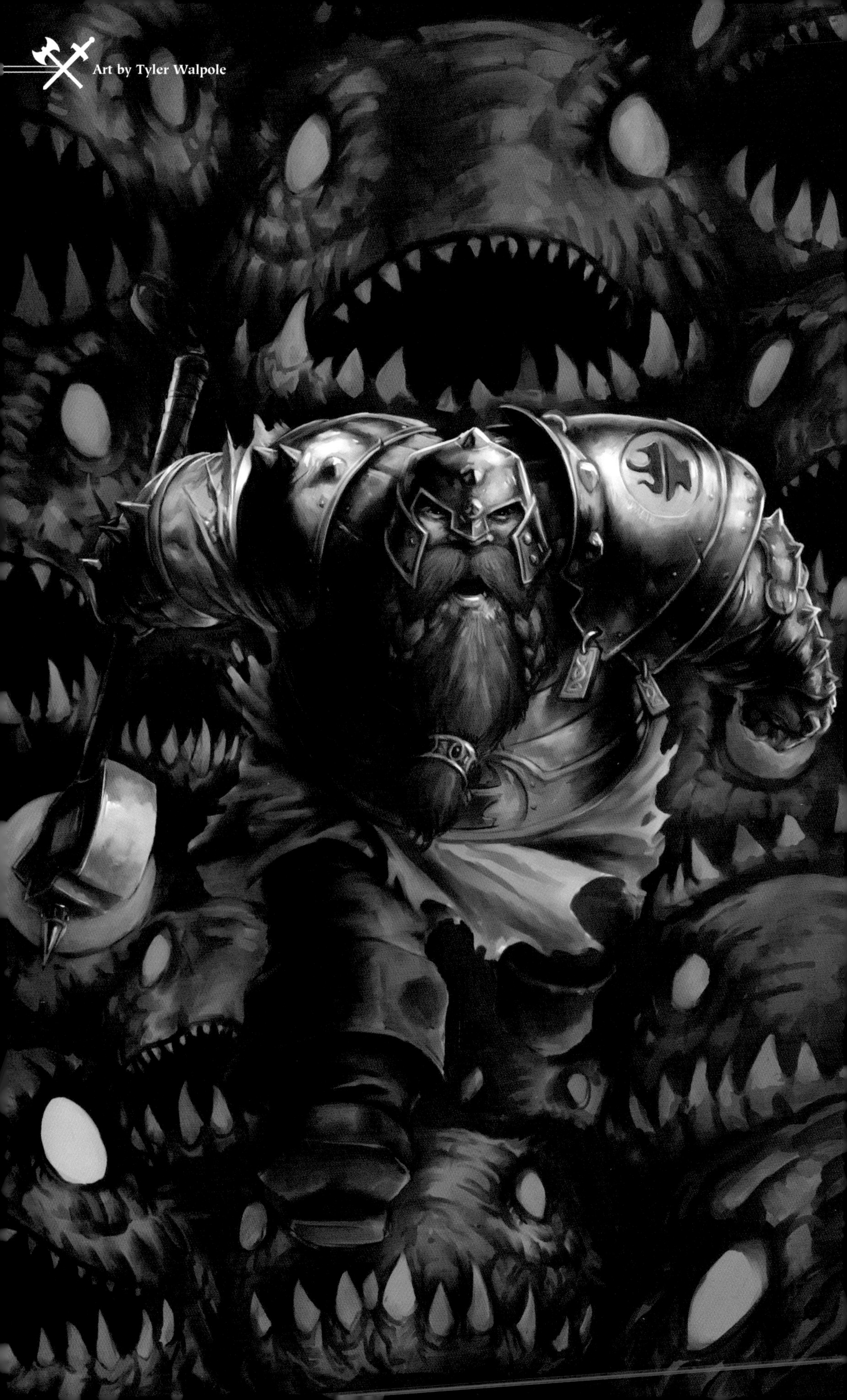

Art by Tyler Walpole

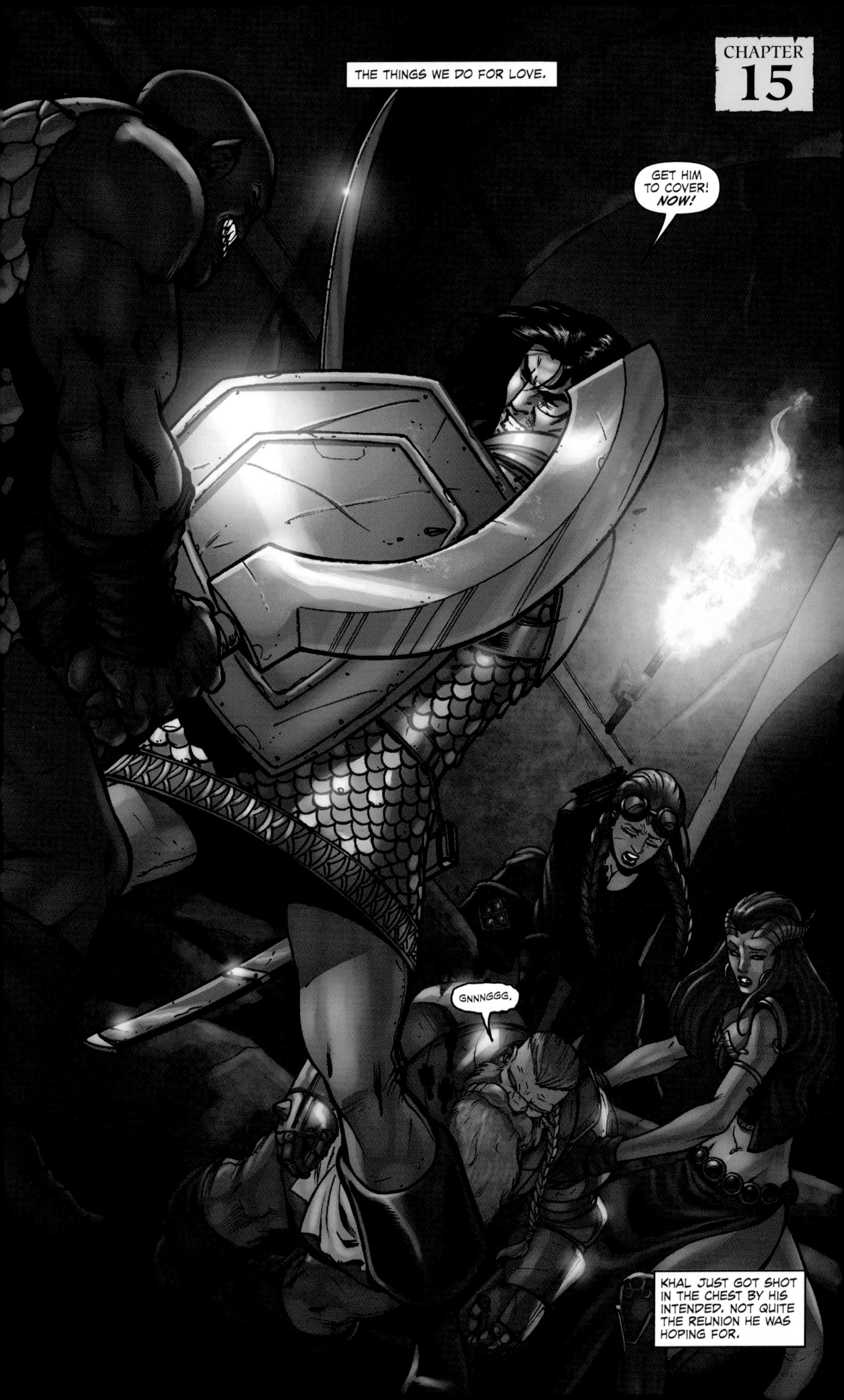
CHAPTER
15
THE THINGS WE DO FOR LOVE.
GET HIM TO COVER! NOW!
GNNNGGG.
KHAL JUST GOT SHOT IN THE CHEST BY HIS INTENDED. NOT QUITE THE REUNION HE WAS HOPING FOR.

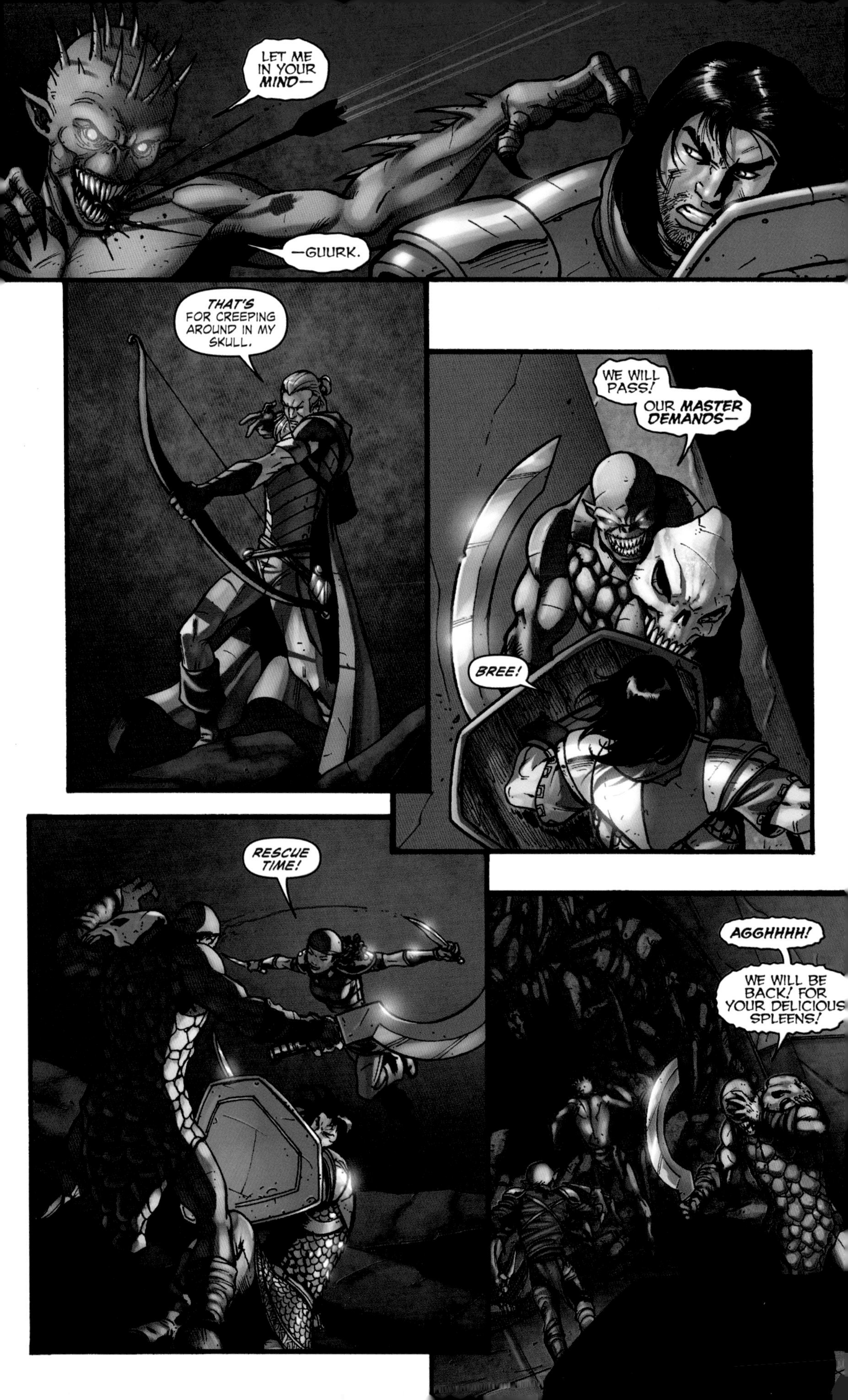
LET ME IN YOUR MIND—
—GUURK.
THAT'S FOR CREEPING AROUND IN MY SKULL.
WE WILL PASS!
OUR MASTER DEMANDS—
BREE!
RESCUE TIME!
AGGHHHH!
WE WILL BE BACK! FOR YOUR DELICIOUS SPLEENS!

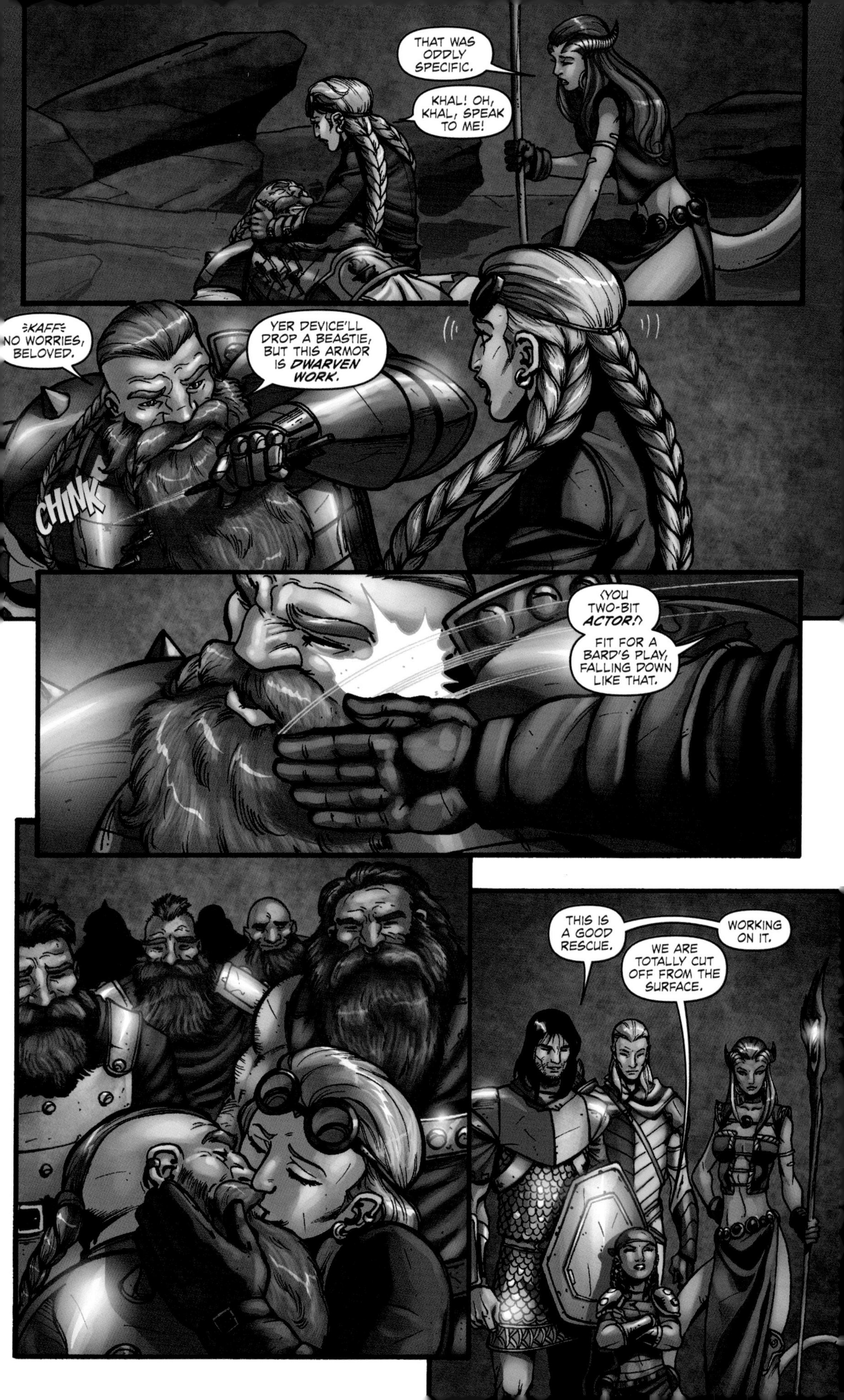
THAT WAS ODDLY SPECIFIC.
KHAL! OH, KHAL, SPEAK TO ME!
≡KAFF≡ NO WORRIES, BELOVED.
YER DEVICE'LL DROP A BEASTIE, BUT THIS ARMOR IS DWARVEN WORK.
CHINK
‹YOU TWO-BIT ACTOR!›
FIT FOR A BARD'S PLAY, FALLING DOWN LIKE THAT.
THIS IS A GOOD RESCUE.
WE ARE TOTALLY CUT OFF FROM THE SURFACE.
WORKING ON IT.

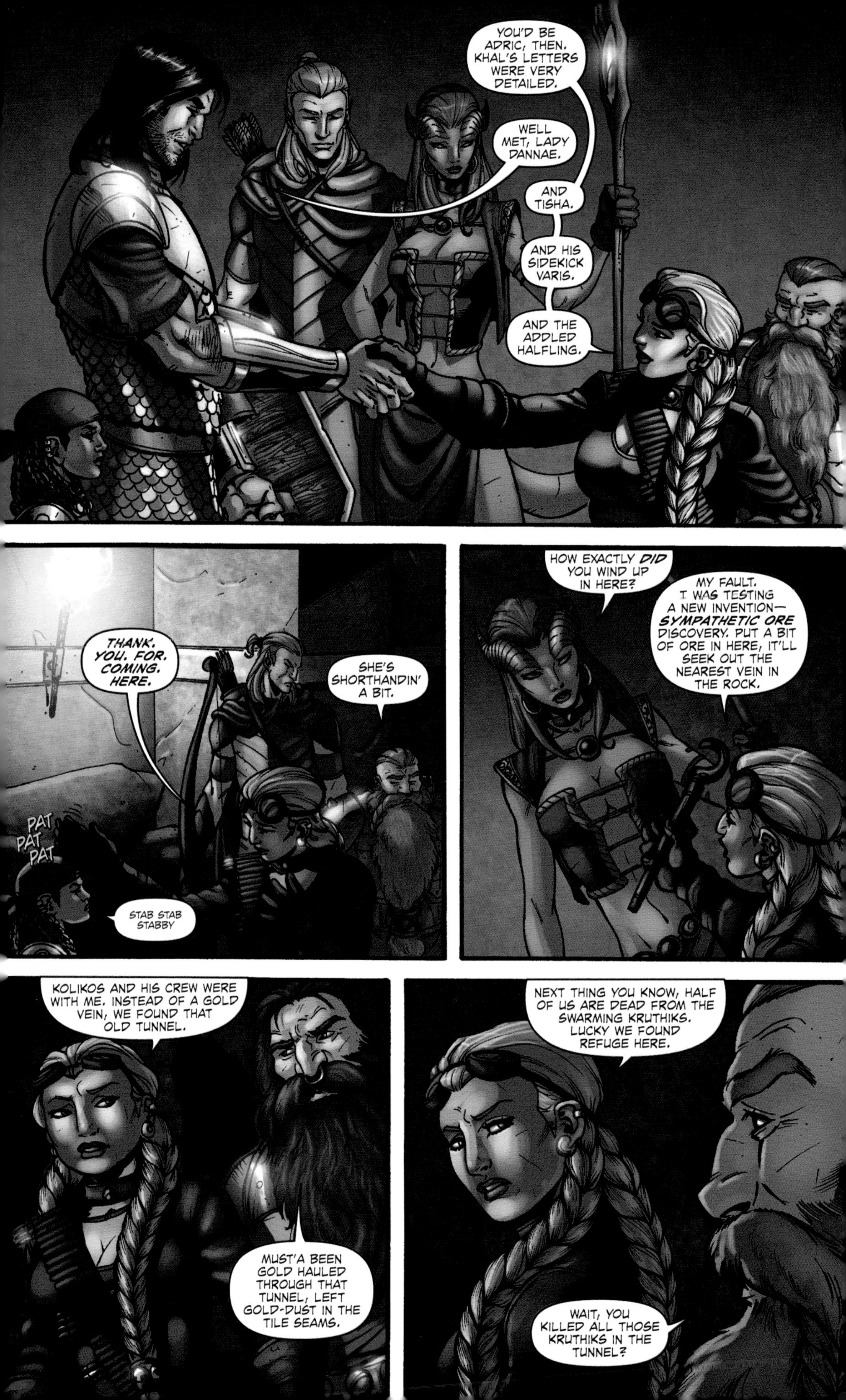

YOU'D BE ADRIC, THEN. KHAL'S LETTERS WERE VERY DETAILED.
WELL MET, LADY DANNAE.
AND TISHA.
AND HIS SIDEKICK VARIS.
AND THE ADDLED HALFLING.
THANK. YOU. FOR. COMING. HERE.
SHE'S SHORTHANDIN' A BIT.
PAT PAT PAT
STAB STAB STABBY
HOW EXACTLY DID YOU WIND UP IN HERE?
MY FAULT. I WAS TESTING A NEW INVENTION— SYMPATHETIC ORE DISCOVERY. PUT A BIT OF ORE IN HERE, IT'LL SEEK OUT THE NEAREST VEIN IN THE ROCK.
KOLIKOS AND HIS CREW WERE WITH ME. INSTEAD OF A GOLD VEIN, WE FOUND THAT OLD TUNNEL.
MUST'A BEEN GOLD HAULED THROUGH THAT TUNNEL, LEFT GOLD-DUST IN THE TILE SEAMS.
NEXT THING YOU KNOW, HALF OF US ARE DEAD FROM THE SWARMING KRUTHIKS. LUCKY WE FOUND REFUGE HERE.
WAIT, YOU KILLED ALL THOSE KRUTHIKS IN THE TUNNEL?

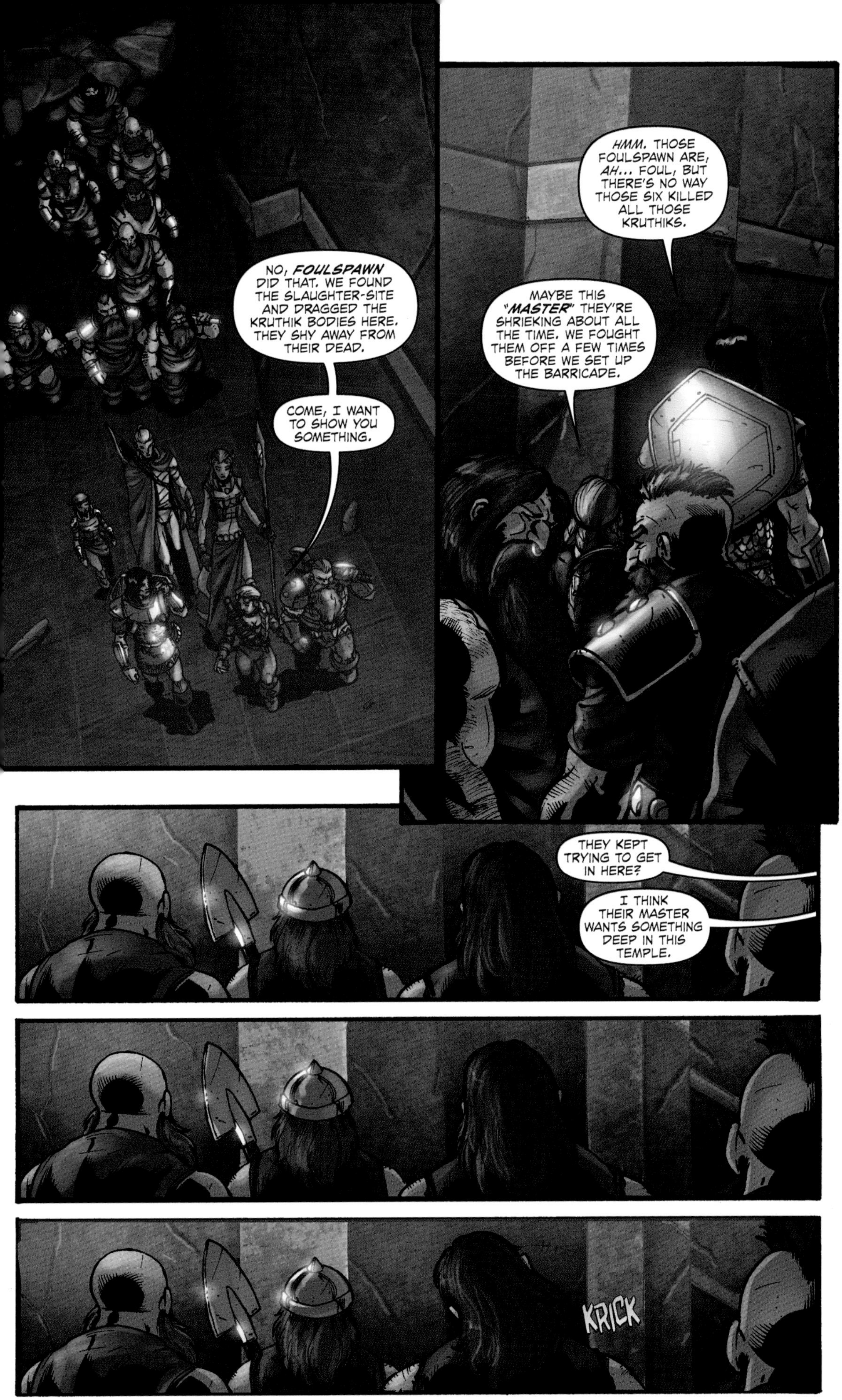

NO, FOULSPAWN DID THAT. WE FOUND THE SLAUGHTER-SITE AND DRAGGED THE KRUTHIK BODIES HERE. THEY SHY AWAY FROM THEIR DEAD.
COME, I WANT TO SHOW YOU SOMETHING.
HMM. THOSE FOULSPAWN ARE, AH... FOUL, BUT THERE'S NO WAY THOSE SIX KILLED ALL THOSE KRUTHIKS.
MAYBE THIS "MASTER" THEY'RE SHRIEKING ABOUT ALL THE TIME. WE FOUGHT THEM OFF A FEW TIMES BEFORE WE SET UP THE BARRICADE.
THEY KEPT TRYING TO GET IN HERE?
I THINK THEIR MASTER WANTS SOMETHING DEEP IN THIS TEMPLE.
KRICK

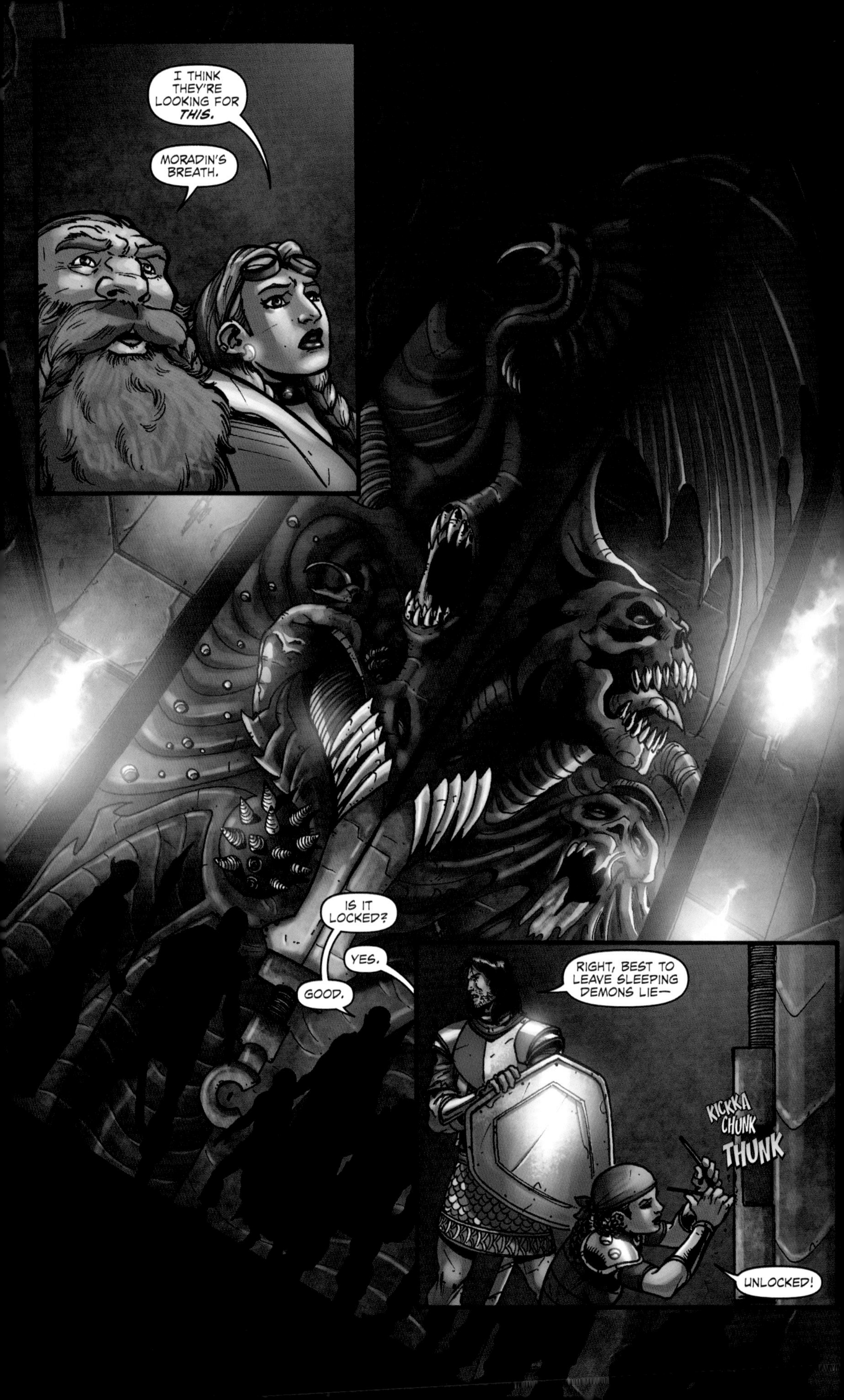
I THINK THEY'RE LOOKING FOR *THIS.*
MORADIN'S BREATH.
IS IT LOCKED?
YES.
GOOD.
RIGHT, BEST TO LEAVE SLEEPING DEMONS LIE—
KICKKA CHUNK
THUNK
UNLOCKED!

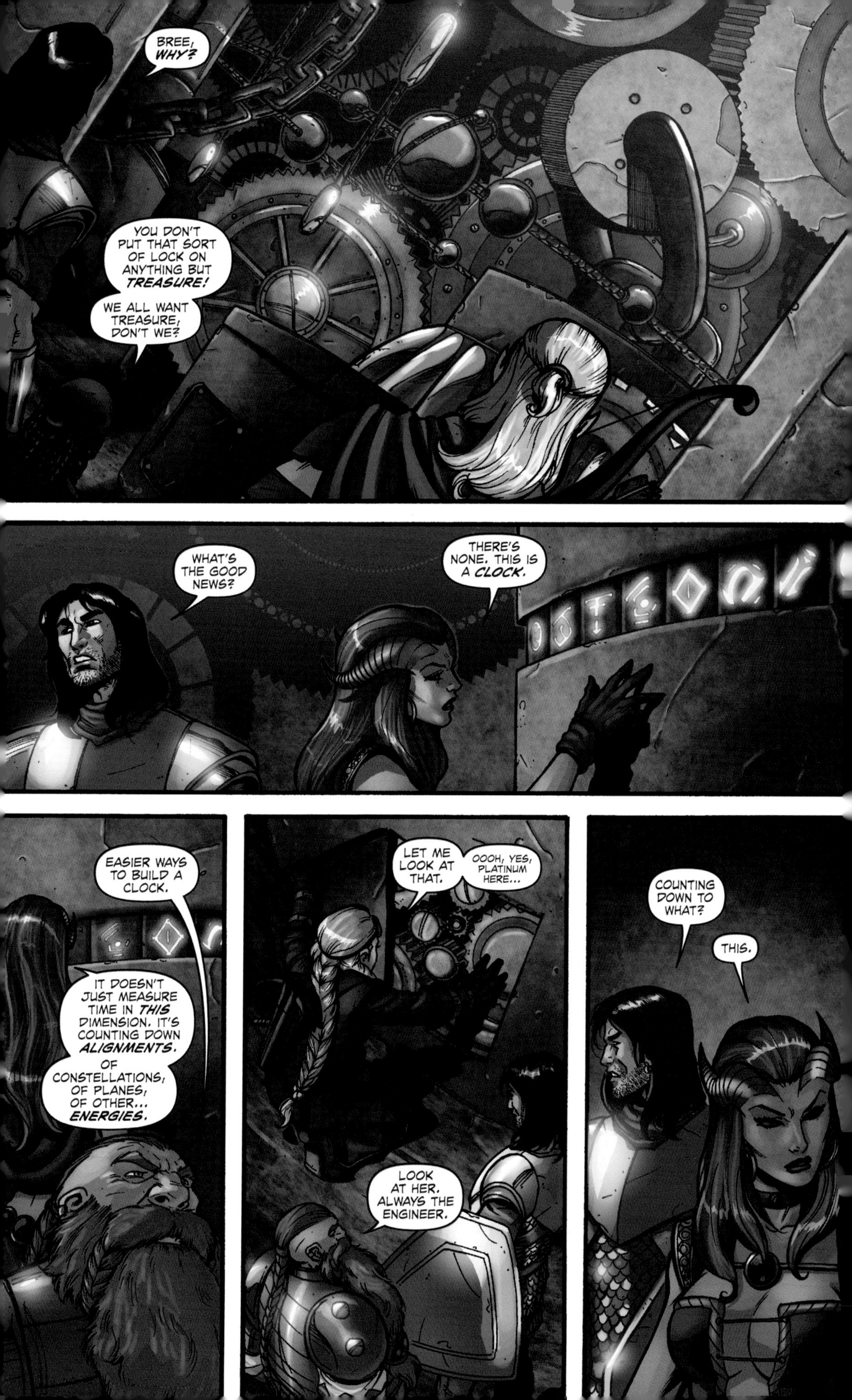
BREE, WHY?
YOU DON'T PUT THAT SORT OF LOCK ON ANYTHING BUT TREASURE!
WE ALL WANT TREASURE, DON'T WE?
WHAT'S THE GOOD NEWS?
THERE'S NONE. THIS IS A CLOCK.
EASIER WAYS TO BUILD A CLOCK.
IT DOESN'T JUST MEASURE TIME IN THIS DIMENSION. IT'S COUNTING DOWN ALIGNMENTS.
OF CONSTELLATIONS, OF PLANES, OF OTHER... ENERGIES.
LET ME LOOK AT THAT.
OOOH, YES, PLATINUM HERE...
LOOK AT HER. ALWAYS THE ENGINEER.
COUNTING DOWN TO WHAT?
THIS.

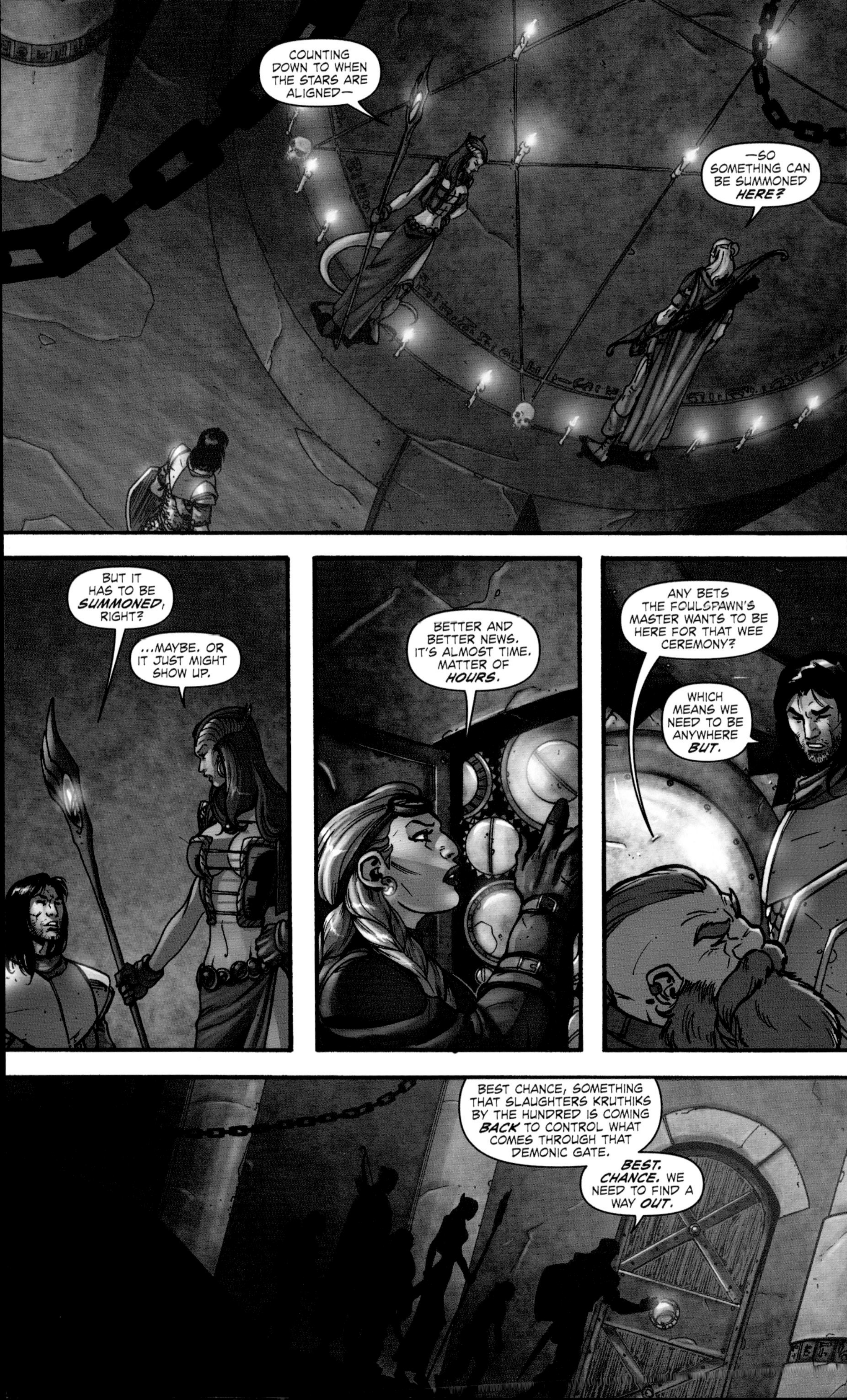
COUNTING DOWN TO WHEN THE STARS ARE ALIGNED—
—SO SOMETHING CAN BE SUMMONED HERE?
BUT IT HAS TO BE SUMMONED, RIGHT?
...MAYBE. OR IT JUST MIGHT SHOW UP.
BETTER AND BETTER NEWS. IT'S ALMOST TIME. MATTER OF HOURS.
ANY BETS THE FOULSPAWN'S MASTER WANTS TO BE HERE FOR THAT WEE CEREMONY?
WHICH MEANS WE NEED TO BE ANYWHERE BUT.
BEST CHANCE, SOMETHING THAT SLAUGHTERS KRUTHIKS BY THE HUNDRED IS COMING BACK TO CONTROL WHAT COMES THROUGH THAT DEMONIC GATE.
BEST. CHANCE. WE NEED TO FIND A WAY OUT.

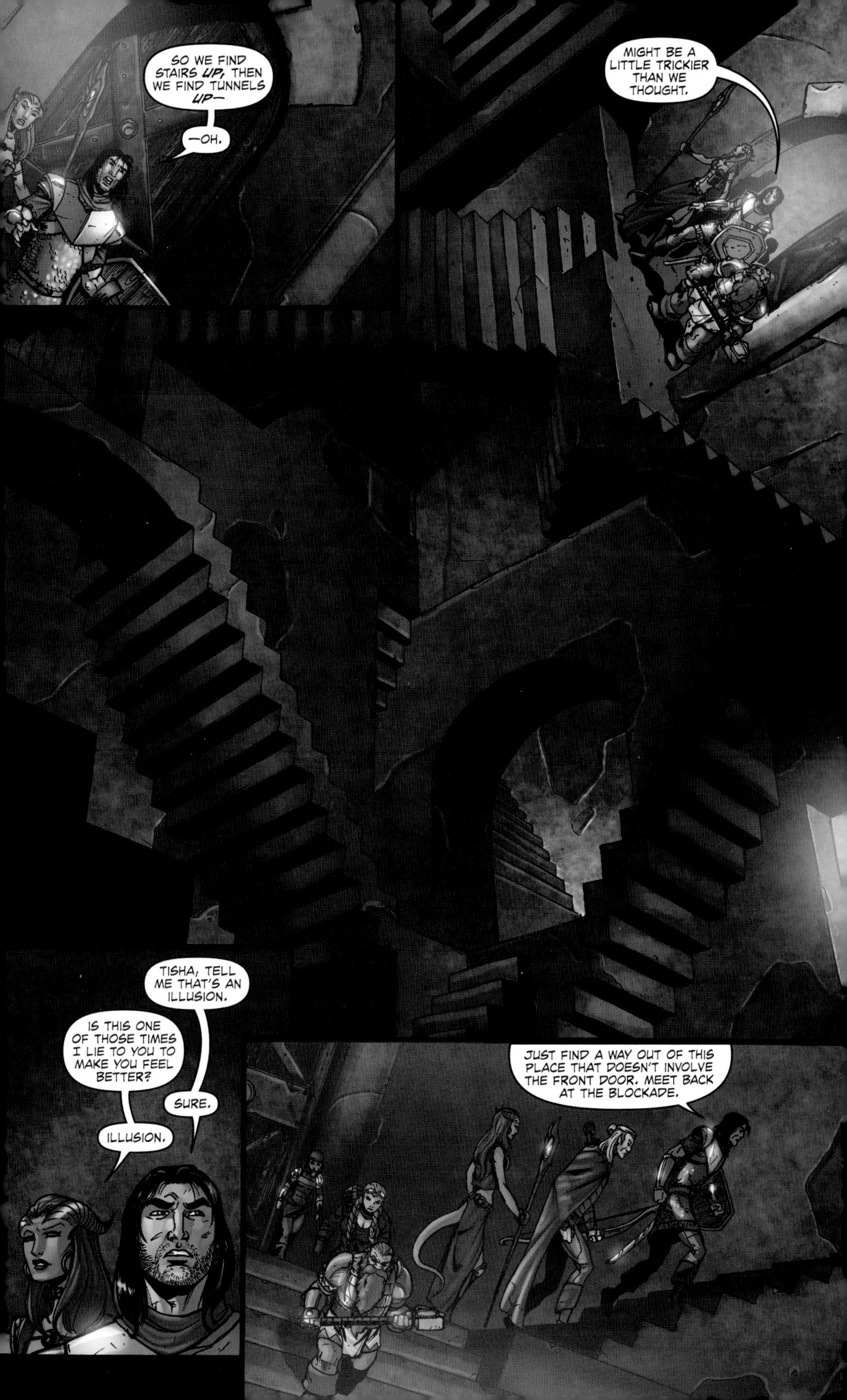
SO WE FIND STAIRS UP, THEN WE FIND TUNNELS UP—
—OH.
MIGHT BE A LITTLE TRICKIER THAN WE THOUGHT.
TISHA, TELL ME THAT'S AN ILLUSION.
IS THIS ONE OF THOSE TIMES I LIE TO YOU TO MAKE YOU FEEL BETTER?
SURE.
ILLUSION.
JUST FIND A WAY OUT OF THIS PLACE THAT DOESN'T INVOLVE THE FRONT DOOR. MEET BACK AT THE BLOCKADE.

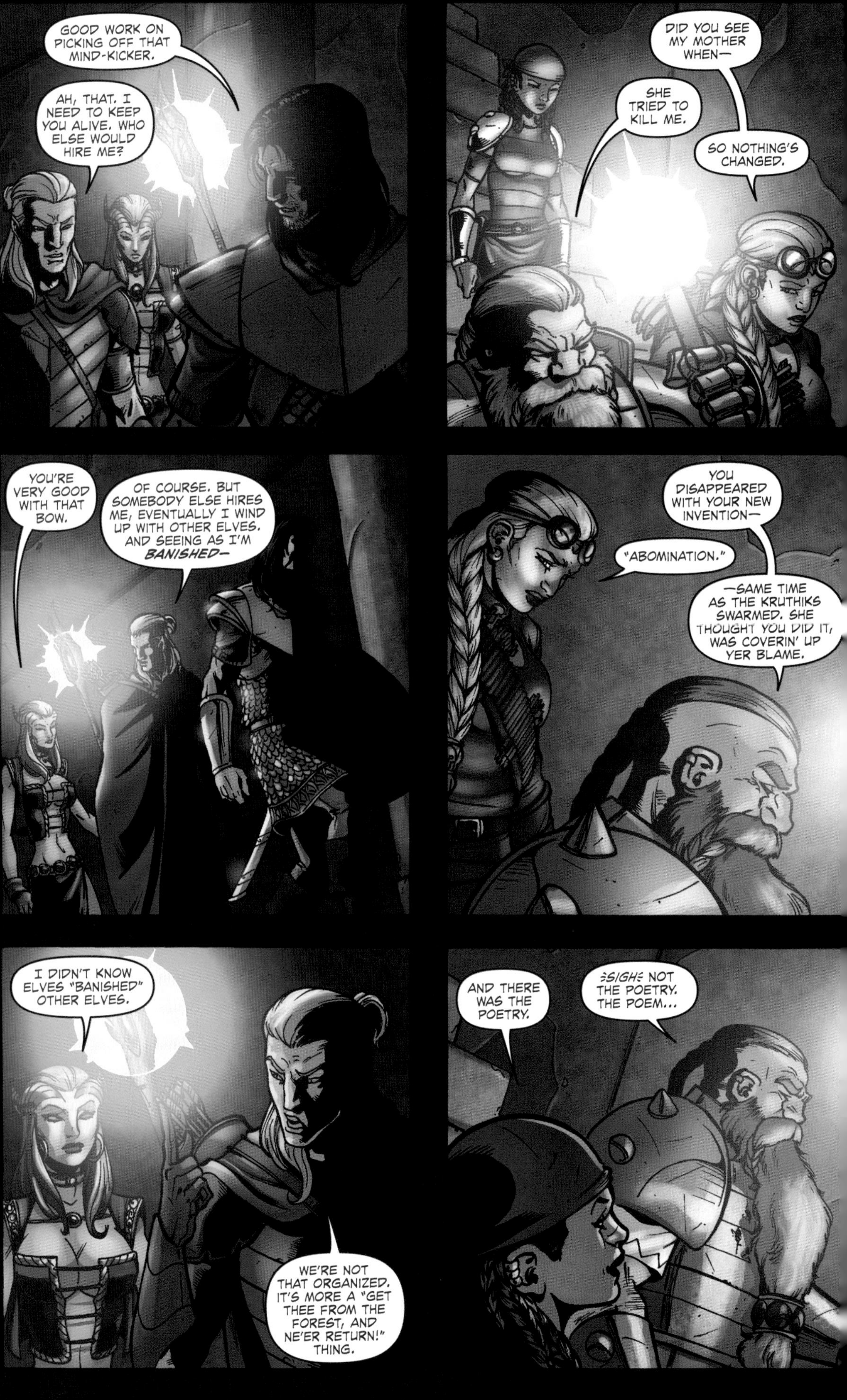
GOOD WORK ON PICKING OFF THAT MIND-KICKER.
AH, THAT. I NEED TO KEEP YOU ALIVE. WHO ELSE WOULD HIRE ME?
DID YOU SEE MY MOTHER WHEN—
SHE TRIED TO KILL ME.
SO NOTHING'S CHANGED.
YOU'RE VERY GOOD WITH THAT BOW.
OF COURSE. BUT SOMEBODY ELSE HIRES ME, EVENTUALLY I WIND UP WITH OTHER ELVES. AND SEEING AS I'M BANISHED—
YOU DISAPPEARED WITH YOUR NEW INVENTION—
"ABOMINATION."
—SAME TIME AS THE KRUTHIKS SWARMED. SHE THOUGHT YOU DID IT, WAS COVERIN' UP YER BLAME.
I DIDN'T KNOW ELVES "BANISHED" OTHER ELVES.
WE'RE NOT THAT ORGANIZED. IT'S MORE A "GET THEE FROM THE FOREST, AND NE'ER RETURN!" THING.
AND THERE WAS THE POETRY.
SIGH NOT THE POETRY. THE POEM...

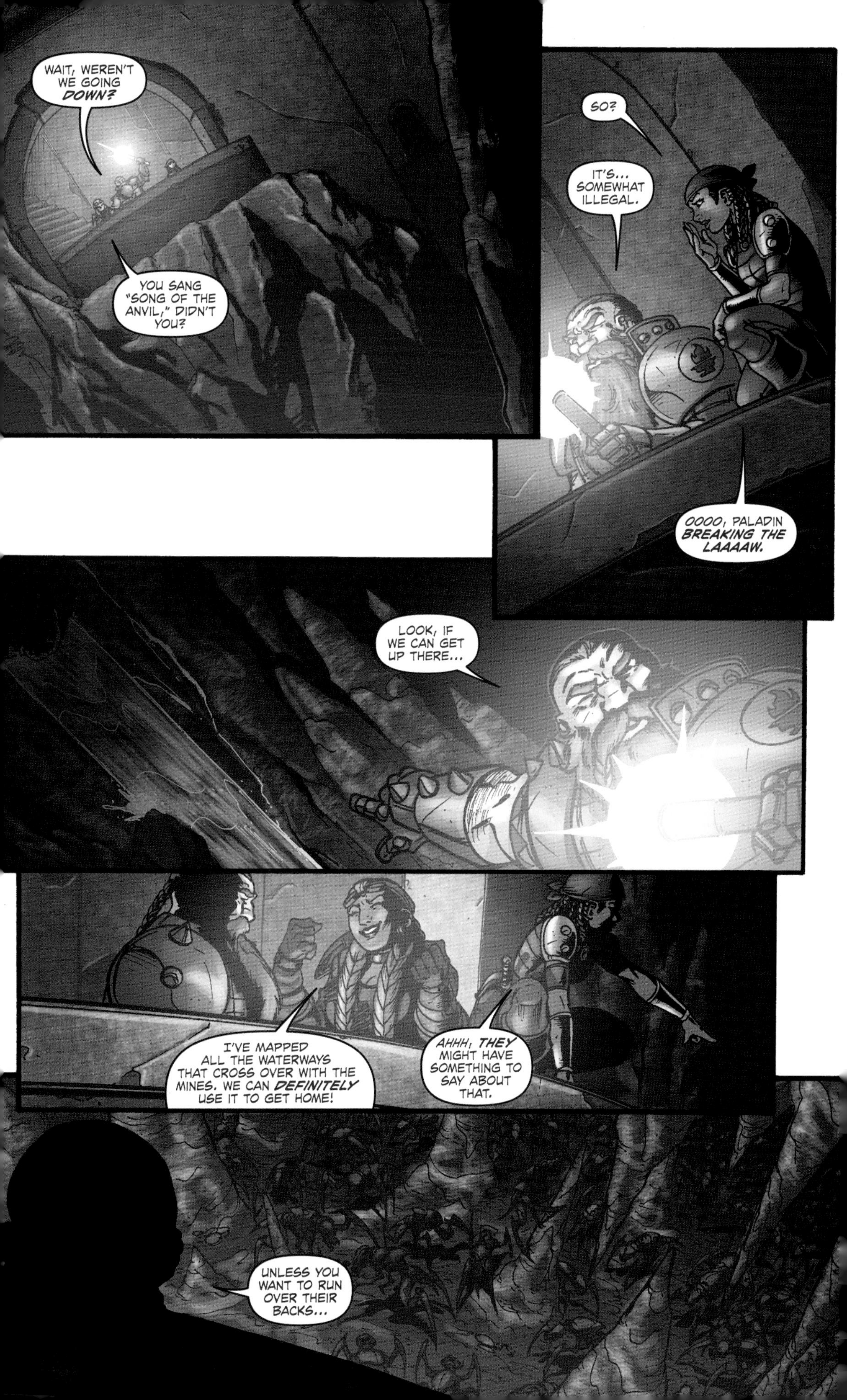
WAIT, WEREN'T WE GOING DOWN?
YOU SANG "SONG OF THE ANVIL," DIDN'T YOU?
SO?
IT'S... SOMEWHAT ILLEGAL.
OOOO, PALADIN BREAKING THE LAAAAW.
LOOK, IF WE CAN GET UP THERE...
I'VE MAPPED ALL THE WATERWAYS THAT CROSS OVER WITH THE MINES. WE CAN DEFINITELY USE IT TO GET HOME!
AHHH, THEY MIGHT HAVE SOMETHING TO SAY ABOUT THAT.
UNLESS YOU WANT TO RUN OVER THEIR BACKS...

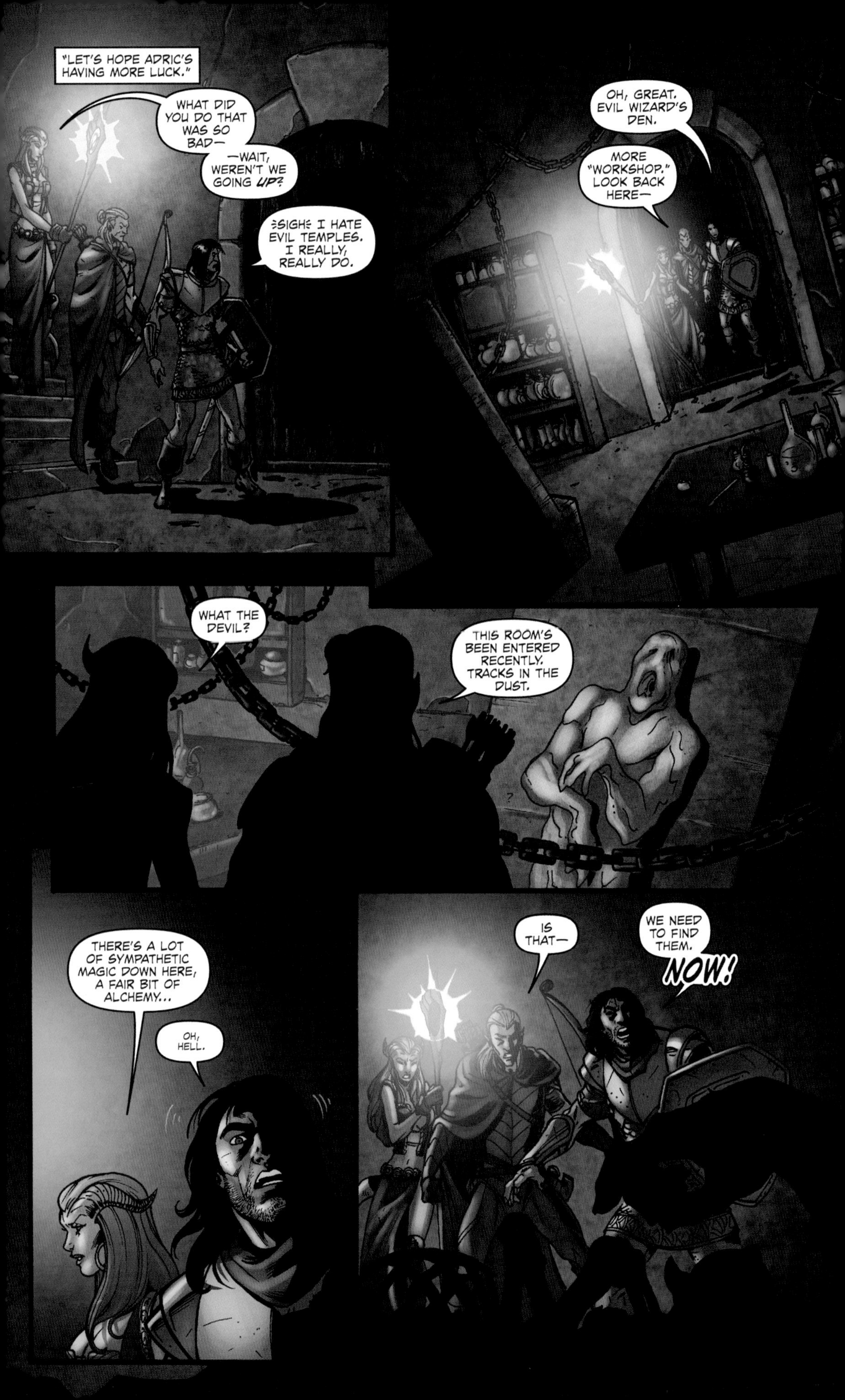
"LET'S HOPE ADRIC'S HAVING MORE LUCK."
WHAT DID YOU DO THAT WAS SO BAD—
—WAIT, WEREN'T WE GOING UP?
=SIGH= I HATE EVIL TEMPLES. I REALLY, REALLY DO.
OH, GREAT. EVIL WIZARD'S DEN.
MORE "WORKSHOP." LOOK BACK HERE—
WHAT THE DEVIL?
THIS ROOM'S BEEN ENTERED RECENTLY. TRACKS IN THE DUST.
THERE'S A LOT OF SYMPATHETIC MAGIC DOWN HERE, A FAIR BIT OF ALCHEMY...
OH, HELL.
IS THAT—
WE NEED TO FIND THEM.
NOW!

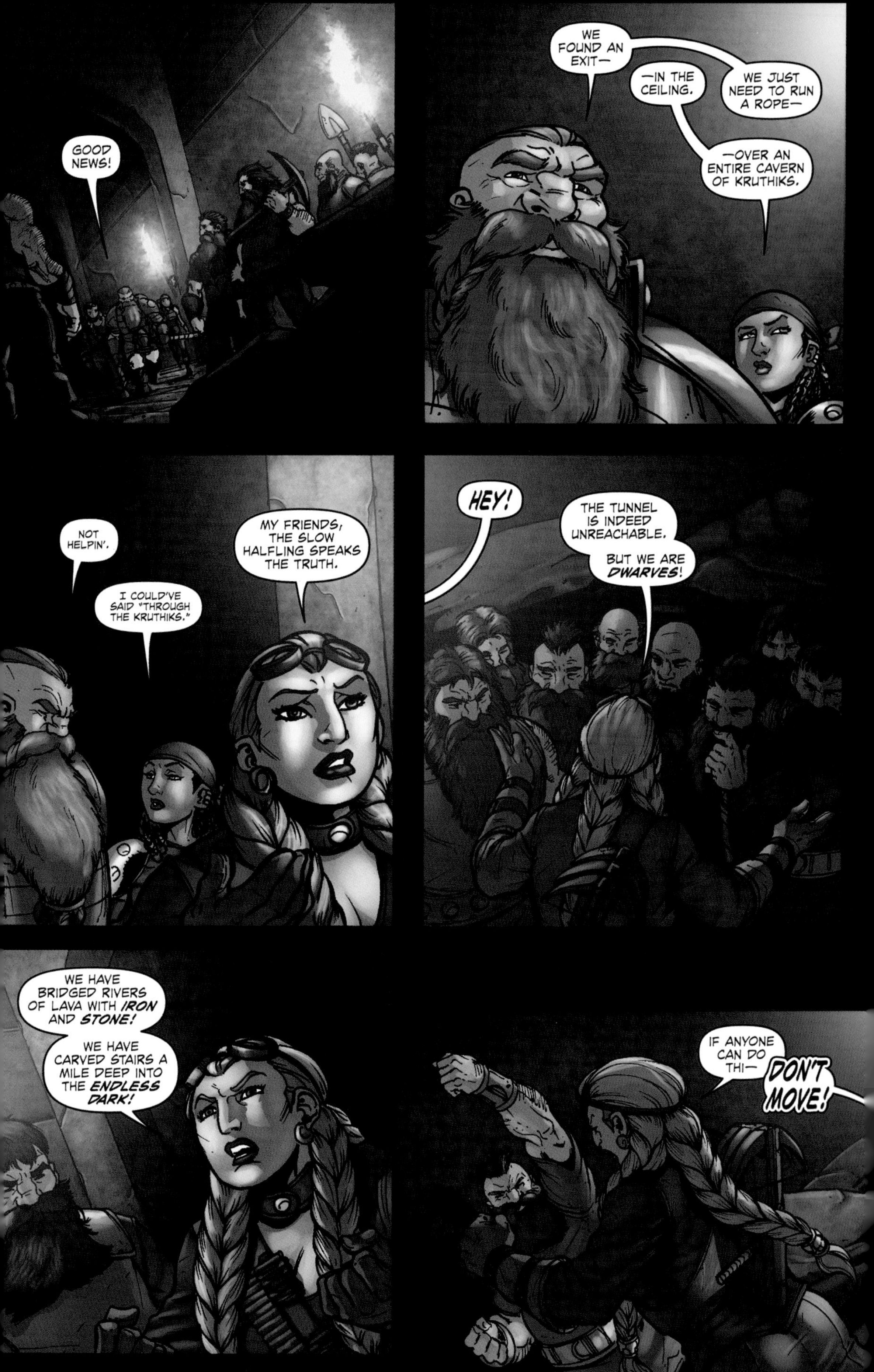
GOOD NEWS!
WE FOUND AN EXIT—
—IN THE CEILING.
WE JUST NEED TO RUN A ROPE—
—OVER AN ENTIRE CAVERN OF KRUTHIKS.
MY FRIENDS, THE SLOW HALFLING SPEAKS THE TRUTH.
NOT HELPIN'.
I COULD'VE SAID "THROUGH THE KRUTHIKS."
HEY!
THE TUNNEL IS INDEED UNREACHABLE.
BUT WE ARE *DWARVES*!
WE HAVE BRIDGED RIVERS OF LAVA WITH *IRON* AND *STONE*!
WE HAVE CARVED STAIRS A MILE DEEP INTO THE *ENDLESS DARK*!
IF ANYONE CAN DO THI—
DON'T MOVE!

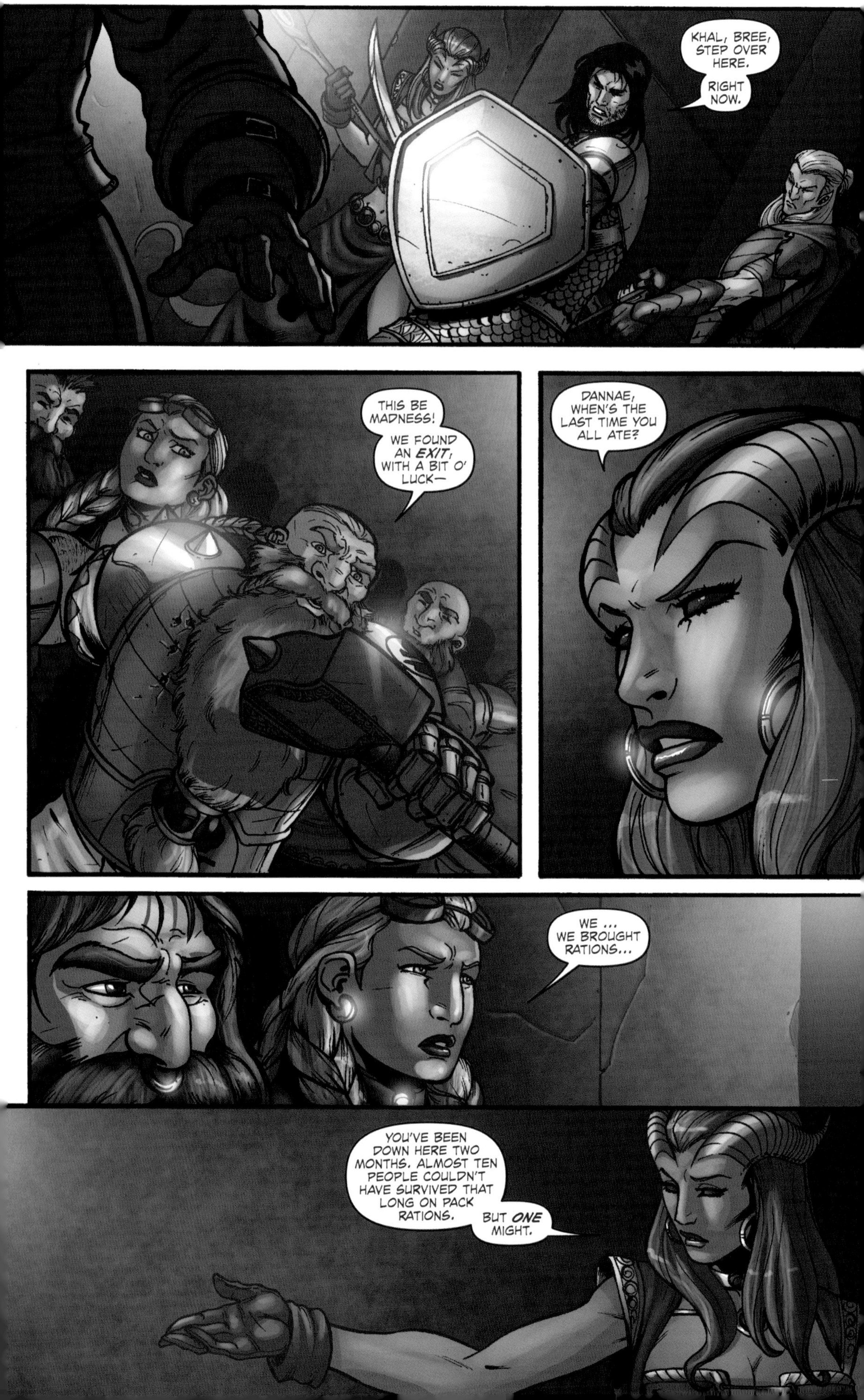

KHAL, BREE, STEP OVER HERE.
RIGHT NOW.
THIS BE MADNESS!
WE FOUND AN *EXIT*; WITH A BIT O' LUCK—
DANNAE, WHEN'S THE LAST TIME YOU ALL ATE?
WE ... WE BROUGHT RATIONS...
YOU'VE BEEN DOWN HERE TWO MONTHS. ALMOST TEN PEOPLE COULDN'T HAVE SURVIVED THAT LONG ON PACK RATIONS.
BUT *ONE* MIGHT.

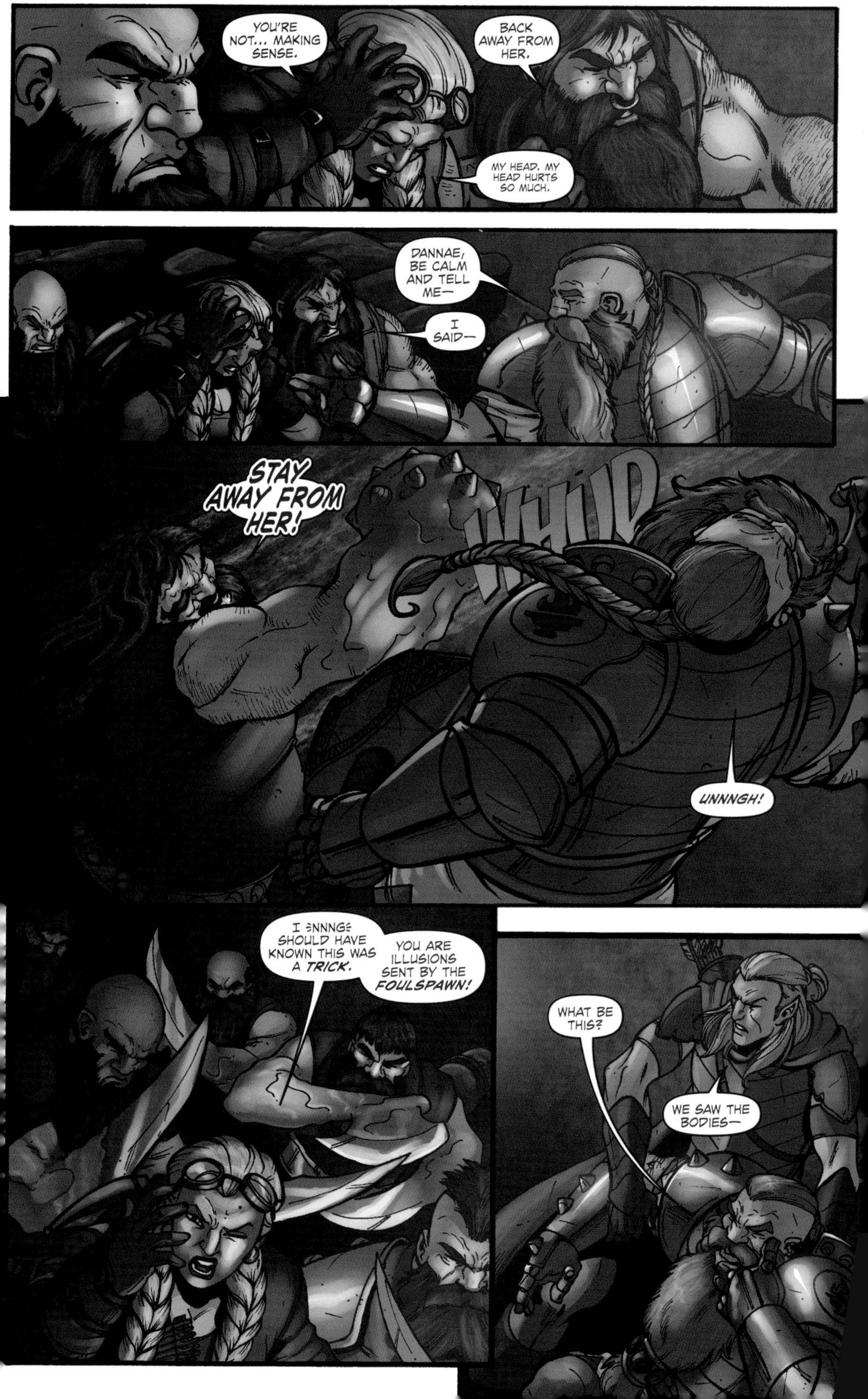
YOU'RE NOT... MAKING SENSE.
BACK AWAY FROM HER.
MY HEAD. MY HEAD HURTS SO MUCH.
DANNAE, BE CALM AND TELL ME—
I SAID—
STAY AWAY FROM HER!
WHUD
UNNNGH!
I =NNNG= SHOULD HAVE KNOWN THIS WAS A TRICK.
YOU ARE ILLUSIONS SENT BY THE FOULSPAWN!
WHAT BE THIS?
WE SAW THE BODIES—

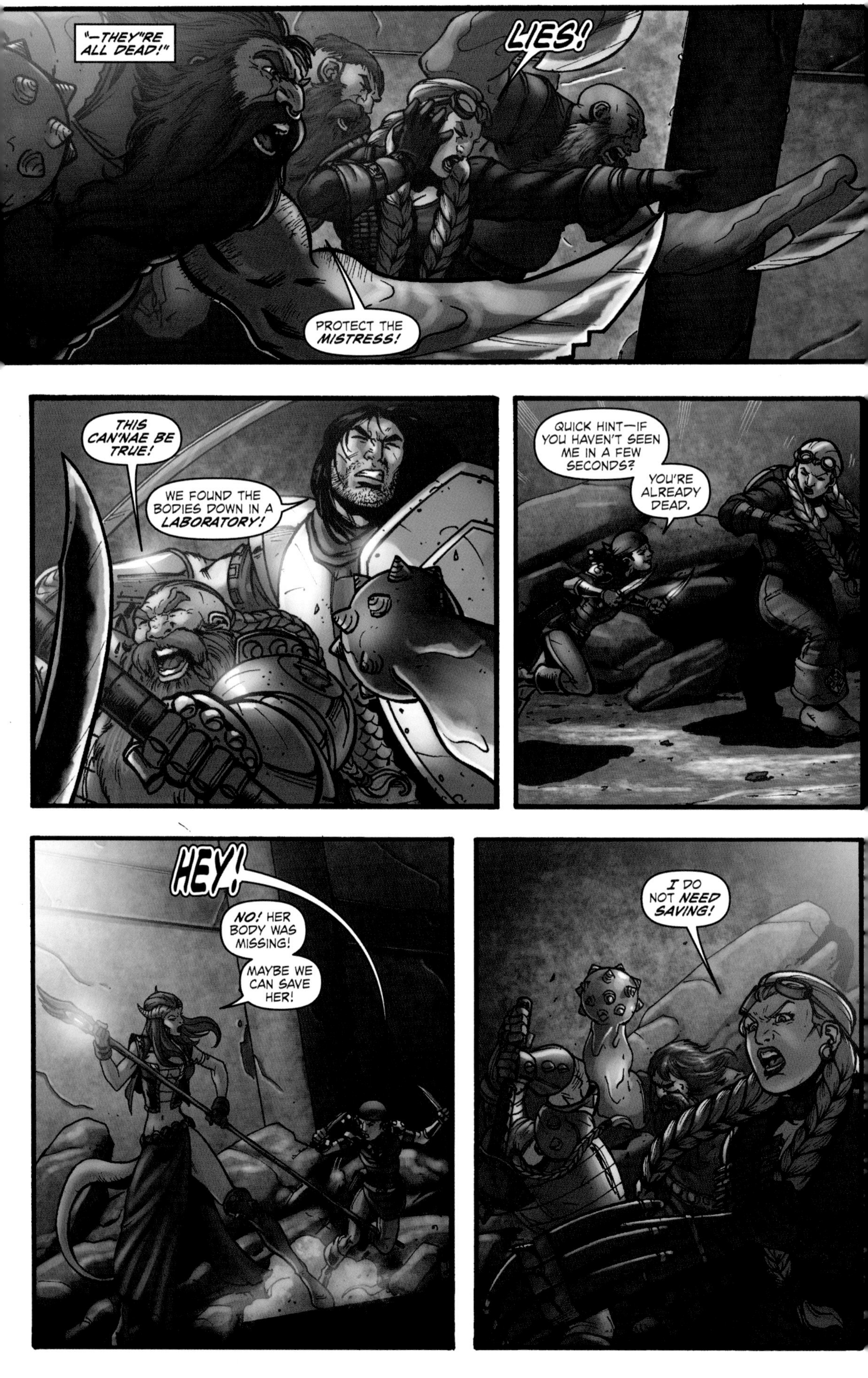
"—THEY"RE ALL DEAD!"
LIES!
PROTECT THE MISTRESS!
THIS CAN'NAE BE TRUE!
WE FOUND THE BODIES DOWN IN A LABORATORY!
QUICK HINT—IF YOU HAVEN'T SEEN ME IN A FEW SECONDS?
YOU'RE ALREADY DEAD.
HEY!
NO! HER BODY WAS MISSING!
MAYBE WE CAN SAVE HER!
I DO NOT NEED SAVING!

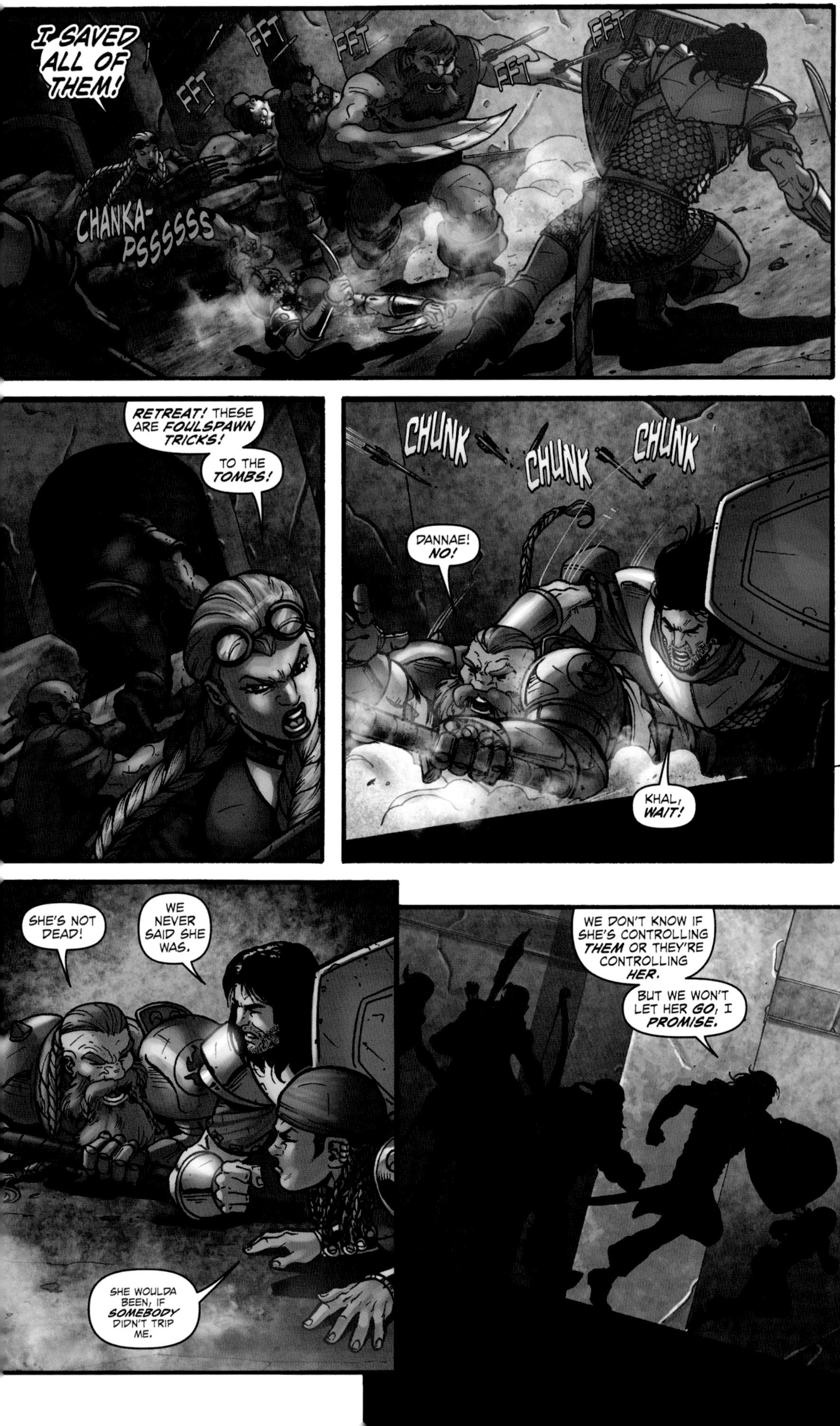
I SAVED ALL OF THEM!
FFT
FFT
FFT
FFT
FFT
CHANKA-PSSSSSS
RETREAT! THESE ARE FOULSPAWN TRICKS!
TO THE TOMBS!
CHUNK
CHUNK
CHUNK
DANNAE! NO!
KHAL, WAIT!
SHE'S NOT DEAD!
WE NEVER SAID SHE WAS.
SHE WOULDA BEEN, IF SOMEBODY DIDN'T TRIP ME.
WE DON'T KNOW IF SHE'S CONTROLLING THEM OR THEY'RE CONTROLLING HER.
BUT WE WON'T LET HER GO, I PROMISE.

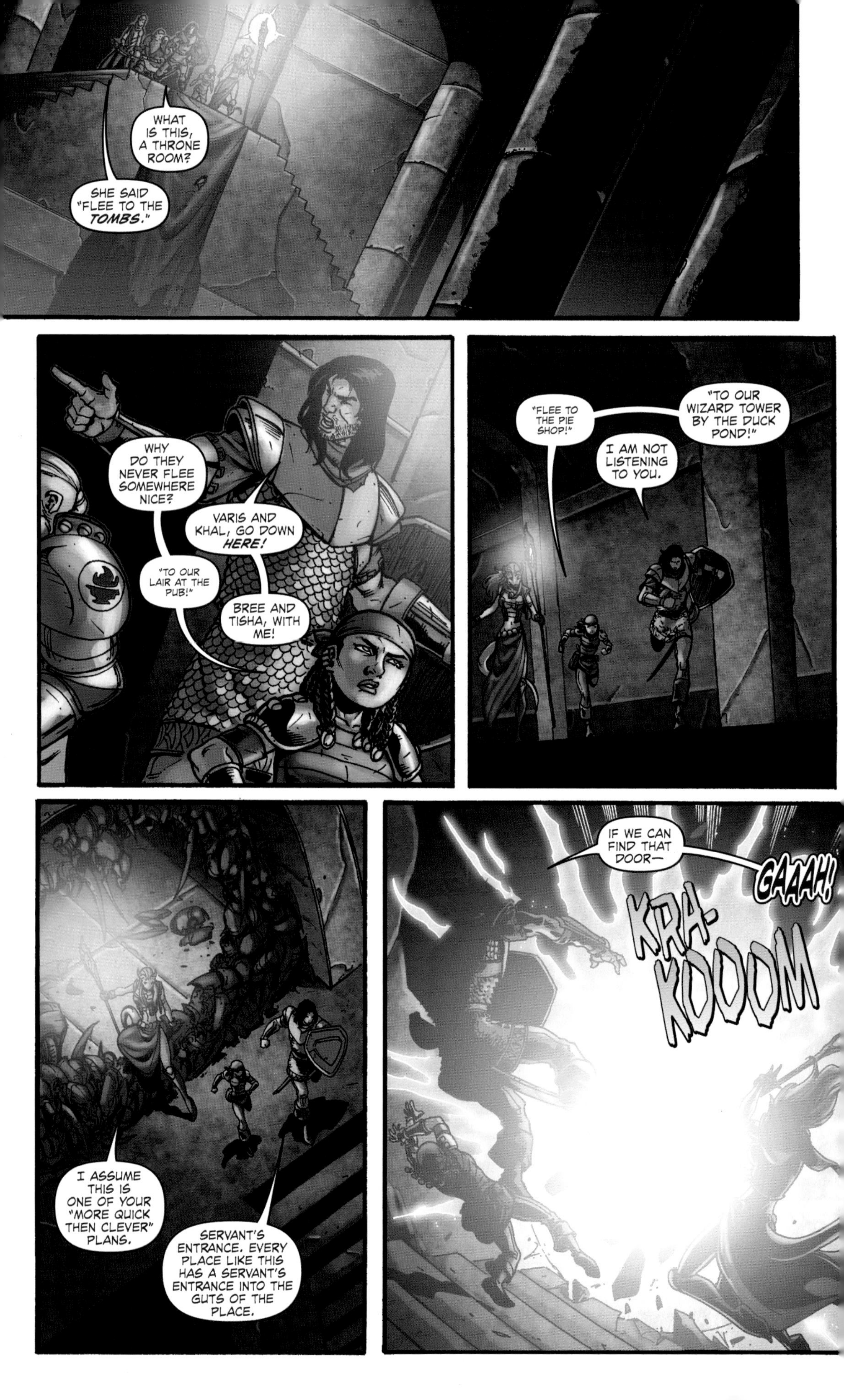
WHAT IS THIS, A THRONE ROOM?
SHE SAID "FLEE TO THE TOMBS."
WHY DO THEY NEVER FLEE SOMEWHERE NICE?
VARIS AND KHAL, GO DOWN HERE!
"TO OUR LAIR AT THE PUB!"
BREE AND TISHA, WITH ME!
"FLEE TO THE PIE SHOP!"
"TO OUR WIZARD TOWER BY THE DUCK POND!"
I AM NOT LISTENING TO YOU.
I ASSUME THIS IS ONE OF YOUR "MORE QUICK THEN CLEVER" PLANS.
SERVANT'S ENTRANCE. EVERY PLACE LIKE THIS HAS A SERVANT'S ENTRANCE INTO THE GUTS OF THE PLACE.
IF WE CAN FIND THAT DOOR—
GAAAH!
KRA-KOOOM

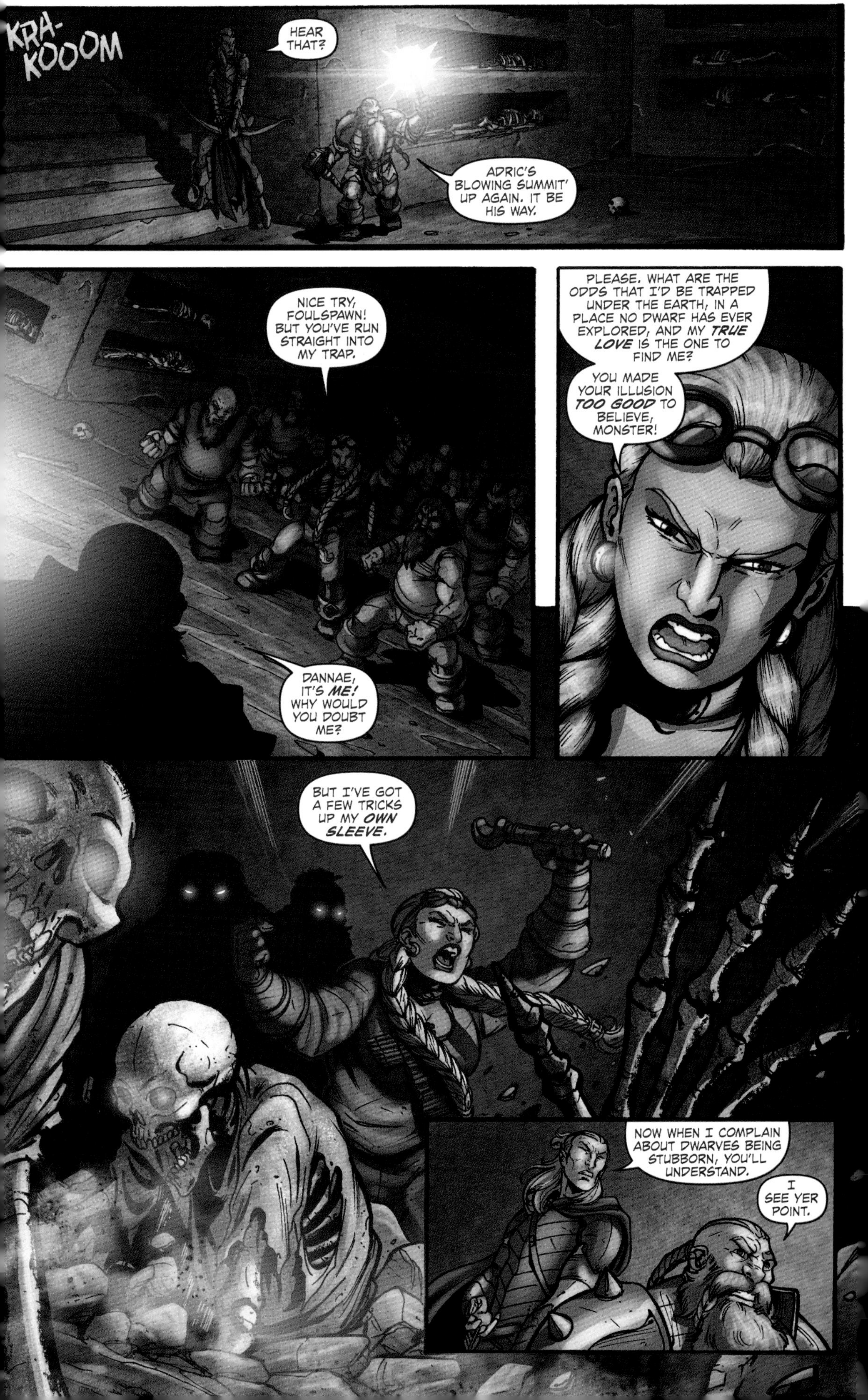
KRA-KOOOM
HEAR THAT?
ADRIC'S BLOWING SUMMIT' UP AGAIN. IT BE HIS WAY.
NICE TRY, FOULSPAWN! BUT YOU'VE RUN STRAIGHT INTO MY TRAP.
DANNAE, IT'S ME! WHY WOULD YOU DOUBT ME?
PLEASE. WHAT ARE THE ODDS THAT I'D BE TRAPPED UNDER THE EARTH, IN A PLACE NO DWARF HAS EVER EXPLORED, AND MY TRUE LOVE IS THE ONE TO FIND ME?
YOU MADE YOUR ILLUSION TOO GOOD TO BELIEVE, MONSTER!
BUT I'VE GOT A FEW TRICKS UP MY OWN SLEEVE.
NOW WHEN I COMPLAIN ABOUT DWARVES BEING STUBBORN, YOU'LL UNDERSTAND.
I SEE YER POINT.

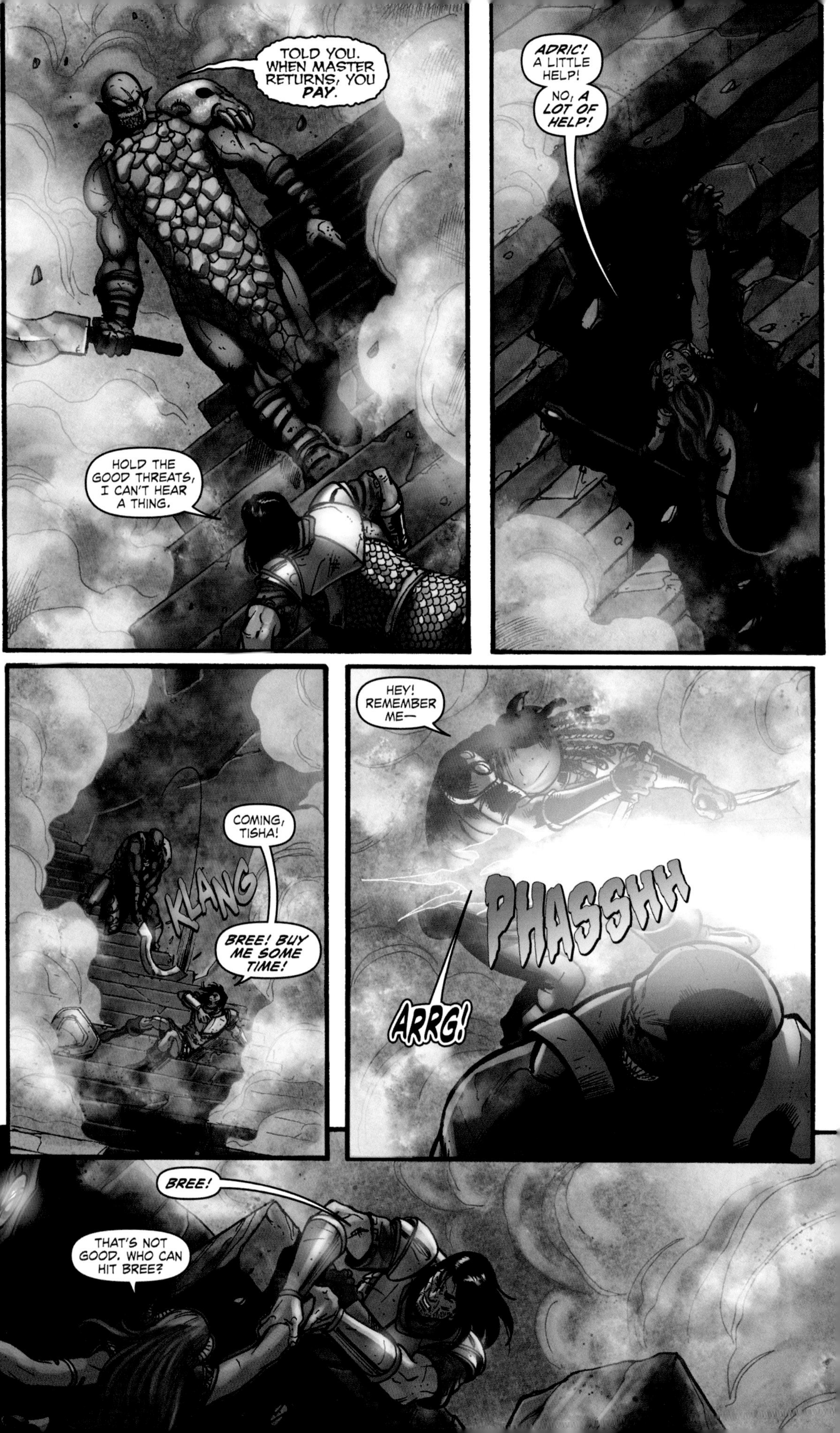
TOLD YOU. WHEN MASTER RETURNS, YOU PAY.
HOLD THE GOOD THREATS, I CAN'T HEAR A THING.
ADRIC! A LITTLE HELP!
NO, A LOT OF HELP!
COMING, TISHA!
KLANG
BREE! BUY ME SOME TIME!
HEY! REMEMBER ME—
PHASSHH
ARRG!
BREE!
THAT'S NOT GOOD. WHO CAN HIT BREE?

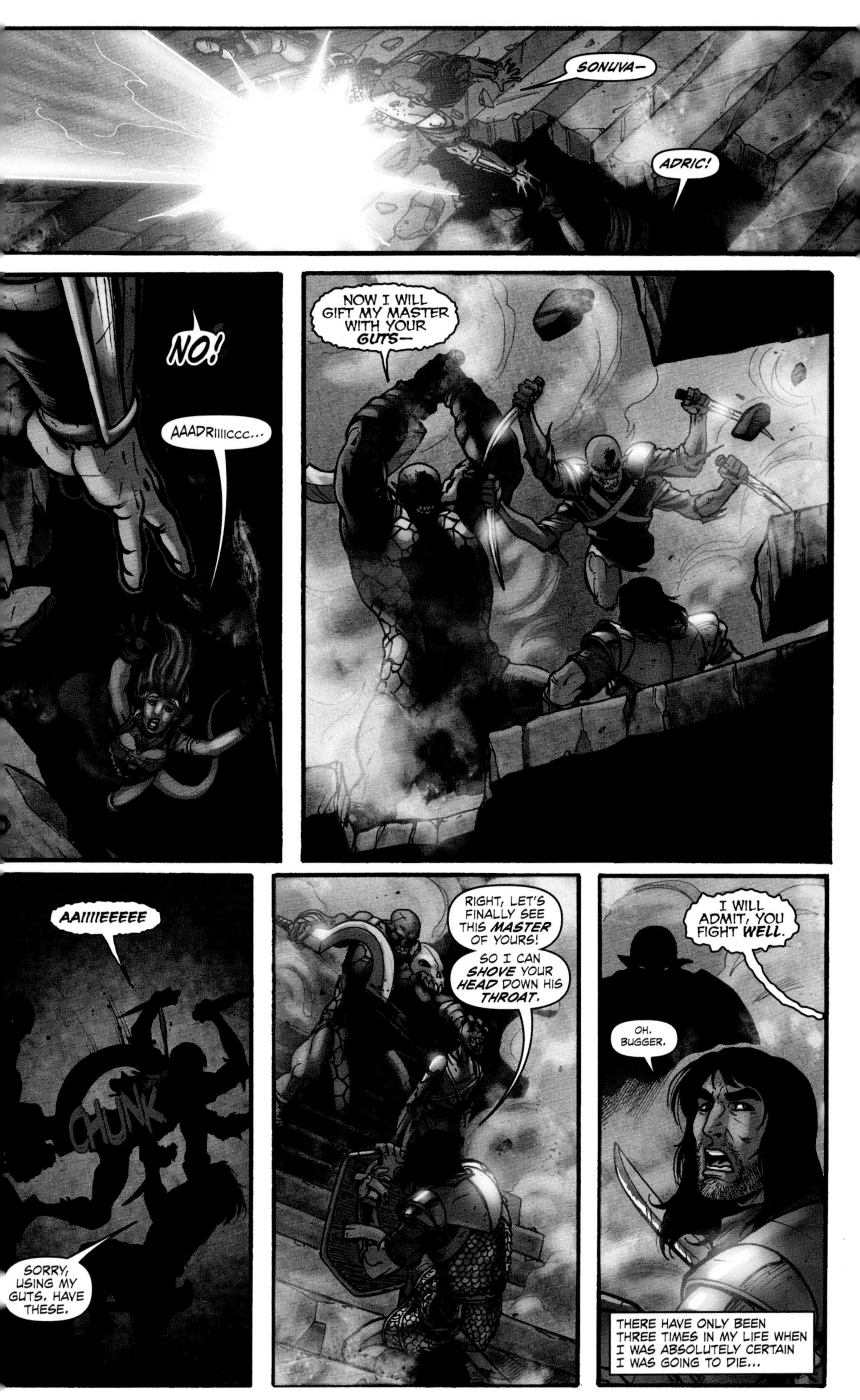
SONUVA—
ADRIC!
NO!
AAADRIIIICCC...
NOW I WILL GIFT MY MASTER WITH YOUR GUTS—
AAIIIIEEEEE
CHUNK
SORRY, USING MY GUTS. HAVE THESE.
RIGHT, LET'S FINALLY SEE THIS MASTER OF YOURS!
SO I CAN SHOVE YOUR HEAD DOWN HIS THROAT.
I WILL ADMIT, YOU FIGHT WELL.
OH. BUGGER.
THERE HAVE ONLY BEEN THREE TIMES IN MY LIFE WHEN I WAS ABSOLUTELY CERTAIN I WAS GOING TO DIE...

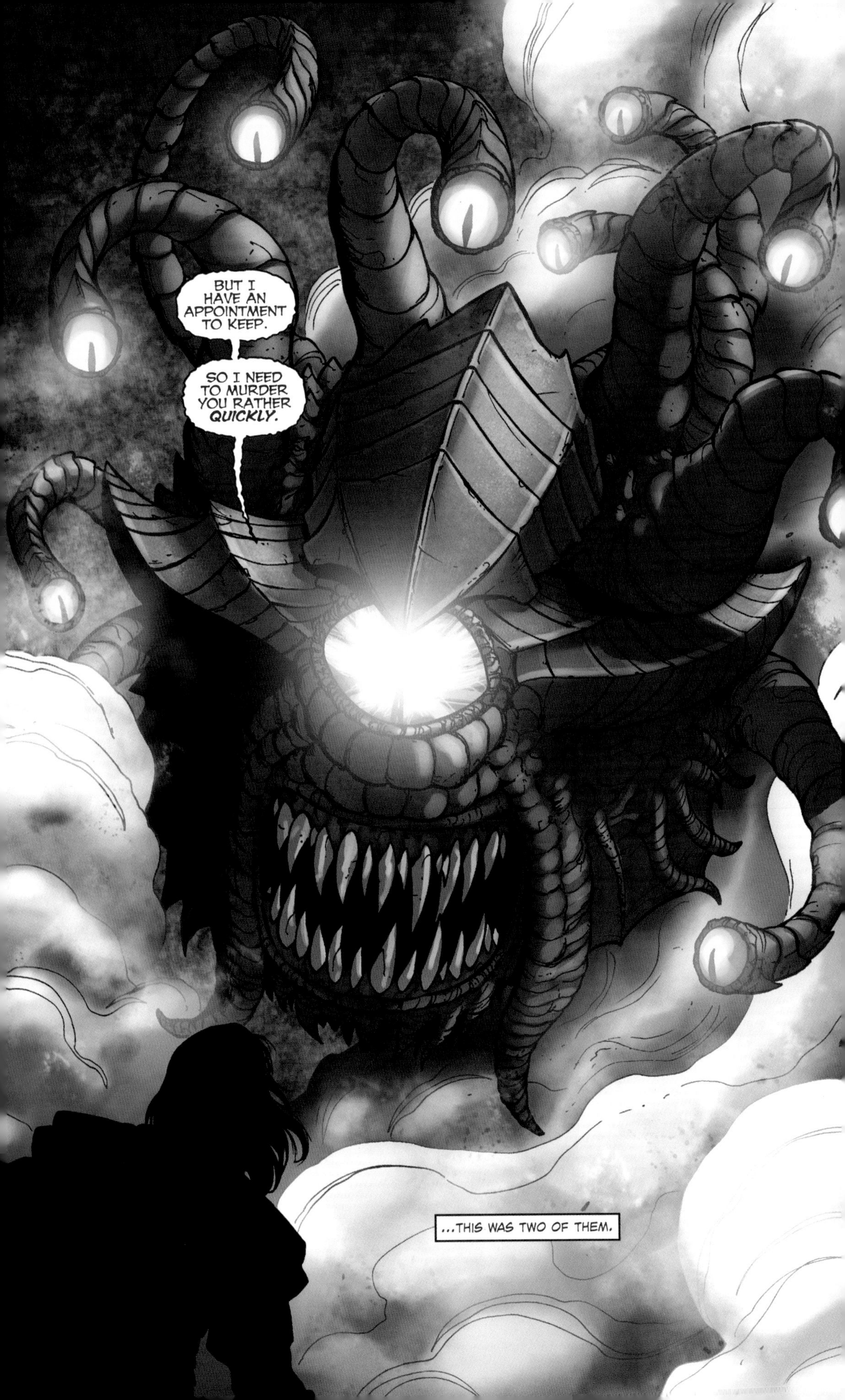
BUT I HAVE AN APPOINTMENT TO KEEP.
SO I NEED TO MURDER YOU RATHER QUICKLY.
...THIS WAS TWO OF THEM.

Art by Tyler Walpole

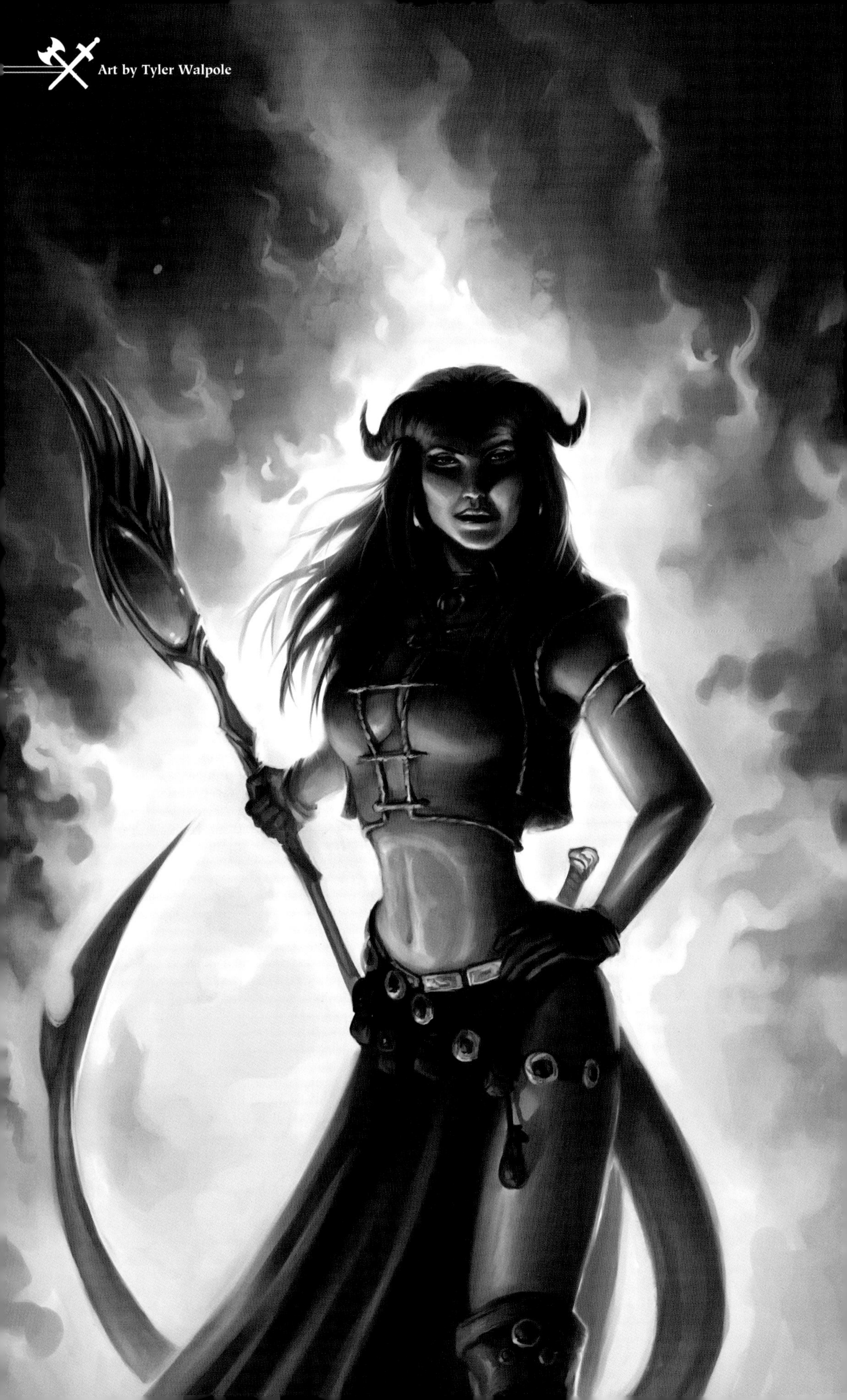

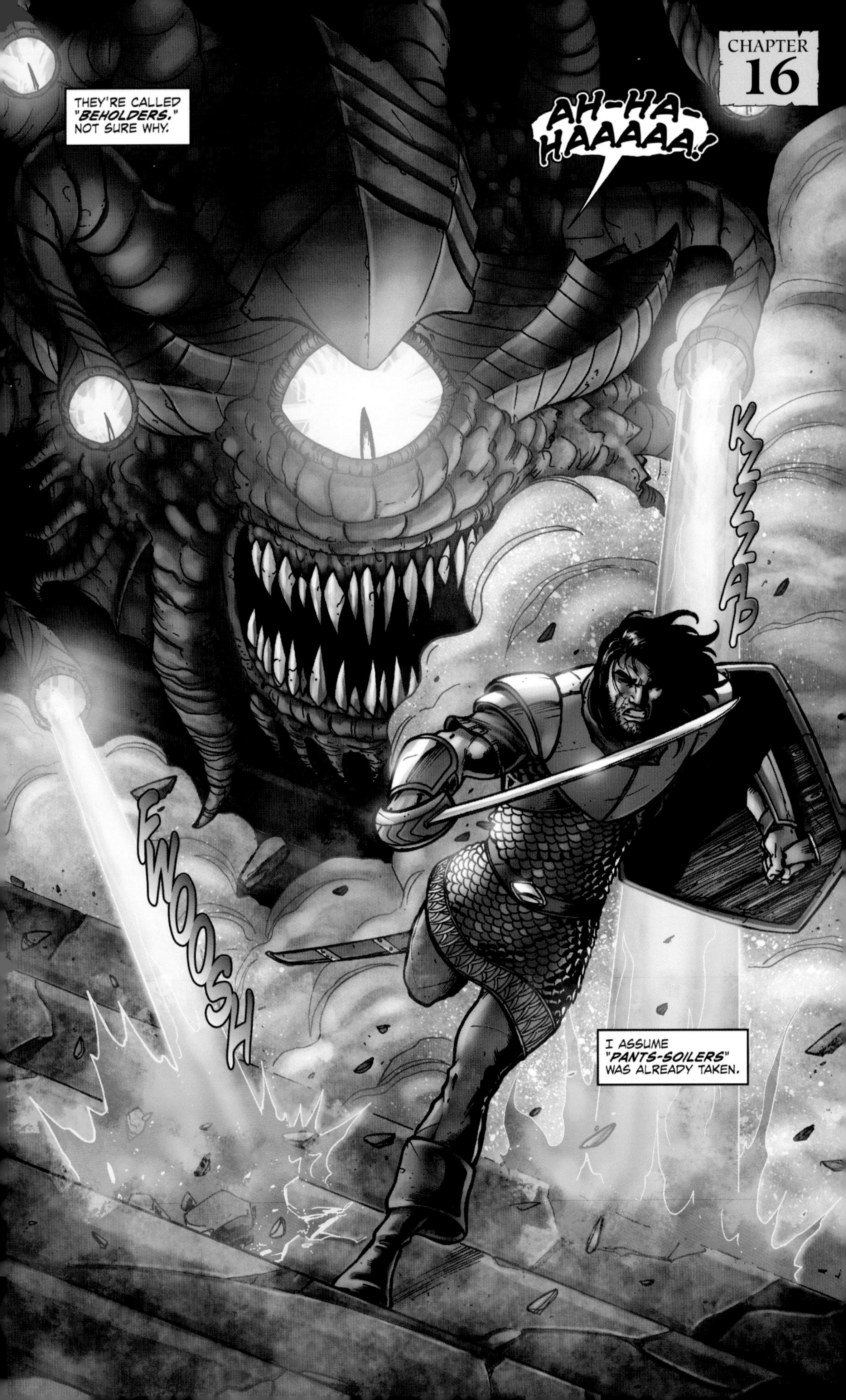
CHAPTER 16
THEY'RE CALLED "BEHOLDERS." NOT SURE WHY.
AH-HA-HAAAAAA!
KZZZAP
FWOOSH
I ASSUME "PANTS-SOILERS" WAS ALREADY TAKEN.

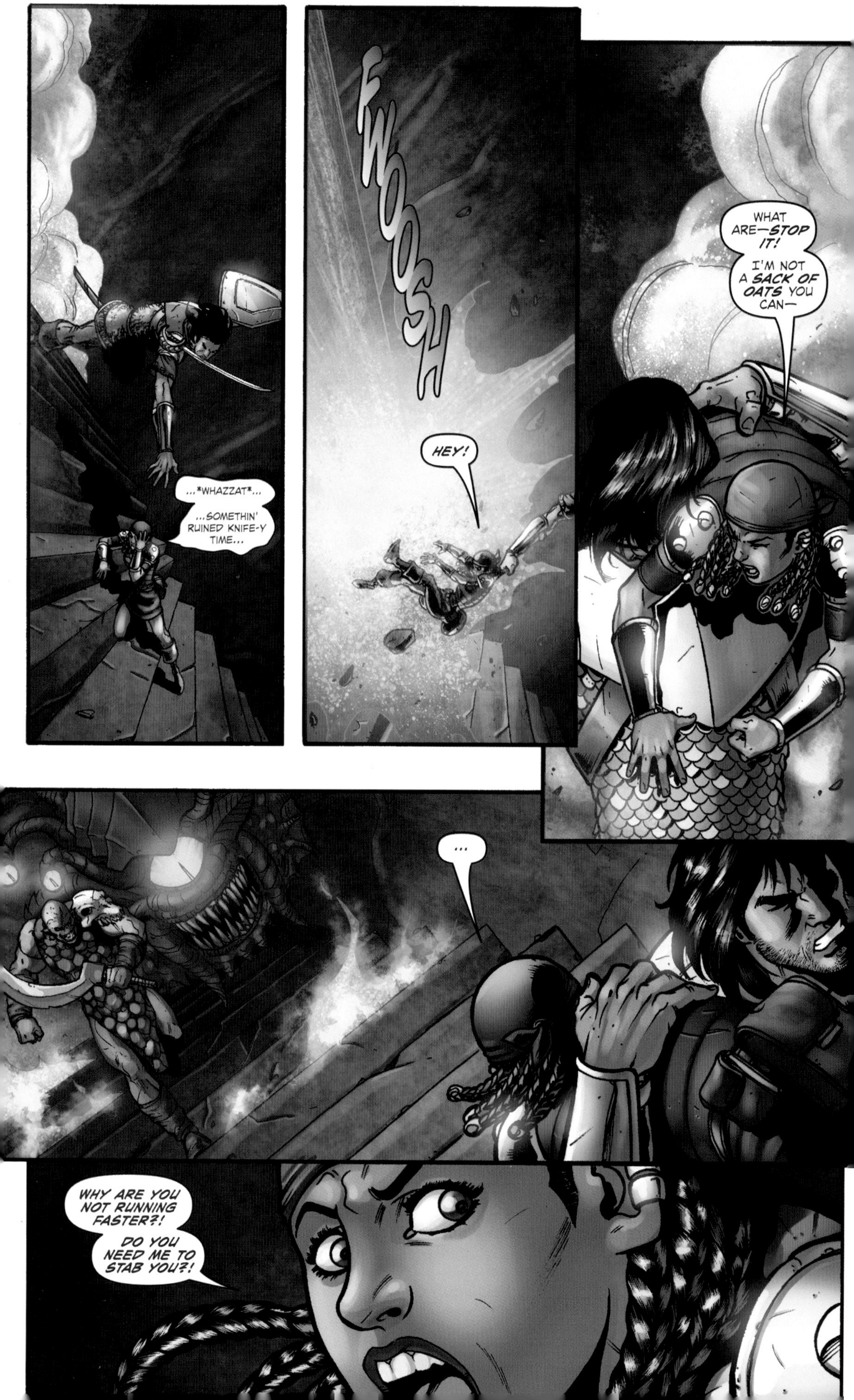
...*WHAZZAT*...
...SOMETHIN' RUINED KNIFE-Y TIME...
FWOOSH
HEY!
WHAT ARE—STOP IT!
I'M NOT A SACK OF OATS YOU CAN—
...
WHY ARE YOU NOT RUNNING FASTER?!
DO YOU NEED ME TO STAB YOU?!

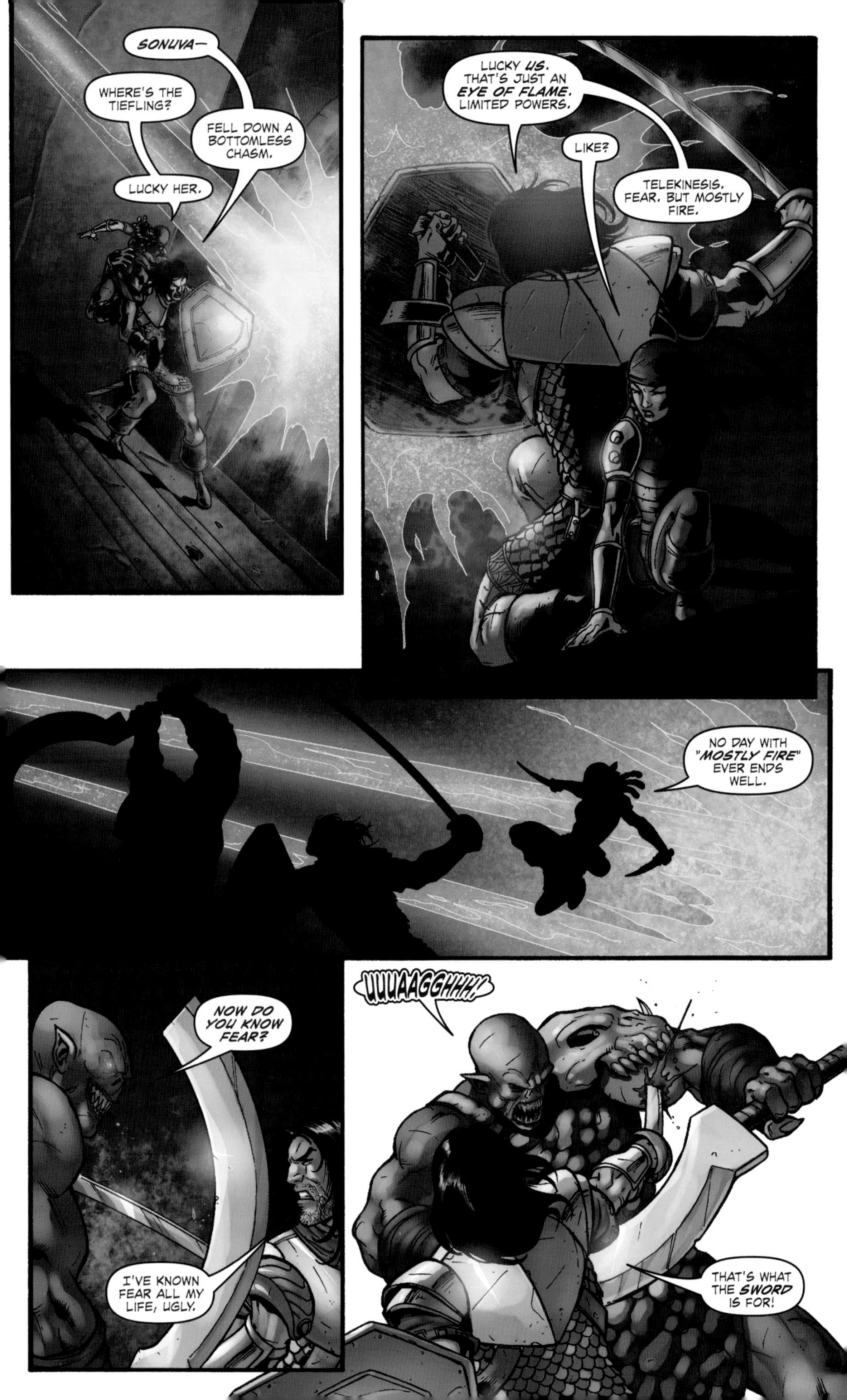
SONUVA—
WHERE'S THE TIEFLING?
FELL DOWN A BOTTOMLESS CHASM.
LUCKY HER.
LUCKY US. THAT'S JUST AN EYE OF FLAME. LIMITED POWERS.
LIKE?
TELEKINESIS. FEAR. BUT MOSTLY FIRE.
NO DAY WITH "MOSTLY FIRE" EVER ENDS WELL.
NOW DO YOU KNOW FEAR?
I'VE KNOWN FEAR ALL MY LIFE, UGLY.
UUUAAGGHHH!
THAT'S WHAT THE SWORD IS FOR!

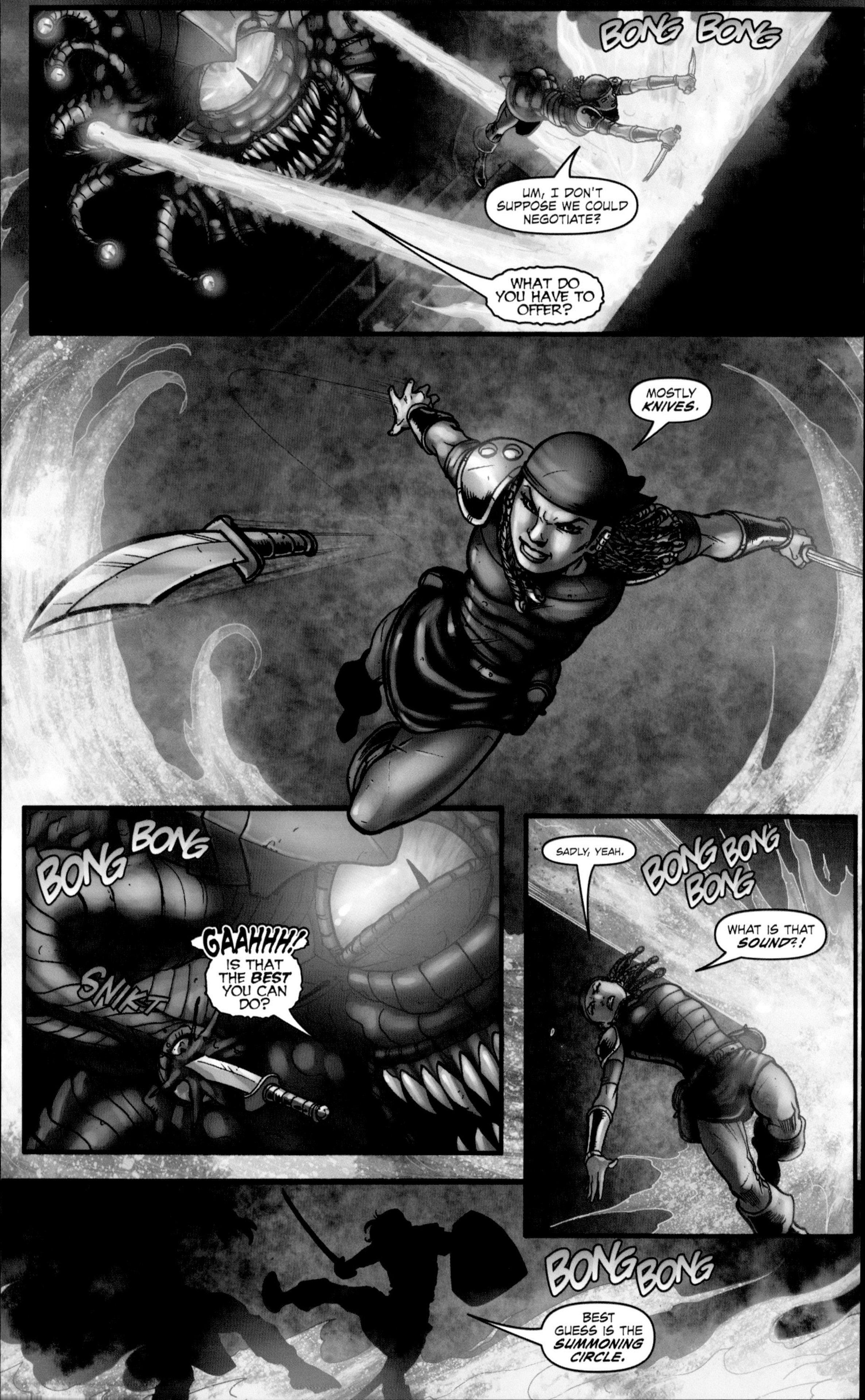
BONG BONG
UM, I DON'T SUPPOSE WE COULD NEGOTIATE?
WHAT DO YOU HAVE TO OFFER?
MOSTLY KNIVES.
BONG BONG
GAAHHH!
IS THAT THE BEST YOU CAN DO?
SNIKT
SADLY, YEAH.
BONG BONG BONG
WHAT IS THAT SOUND?!
BONG BONG
BEST GUESS IS THE SUMMONING CIRCLE.

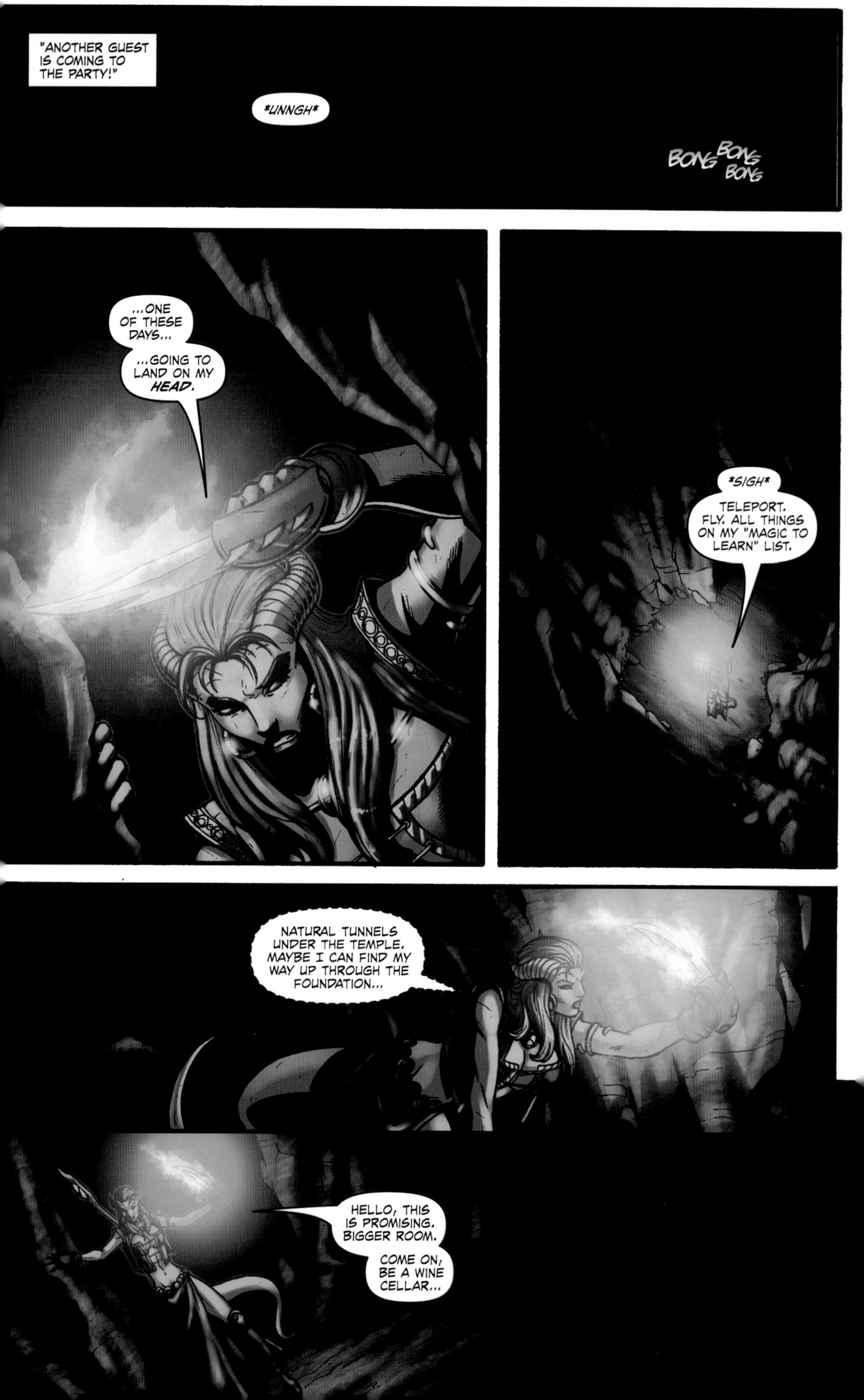
"ANOTHER GUEST IS COMING TO THE PARTY!"
UNNGH
BONG BONG BONG
...ONE OF THESE DAYS...
...GOING TO LAND ON MY *HEAD*.
SIGH
TELEPORT. FLY. ALL THINGS ON MY "MAGIC TO LEARN" LIST.
NATURAL TUNNELS UNDER THE TEMPLE. MAYBE I CAN FIND MY WAY UP THROUGH THE FOUNDATION...
HELLO, THIS IS PROMISING. BIGGER ROOM.
COME ON, BE A WINE CELLAR...

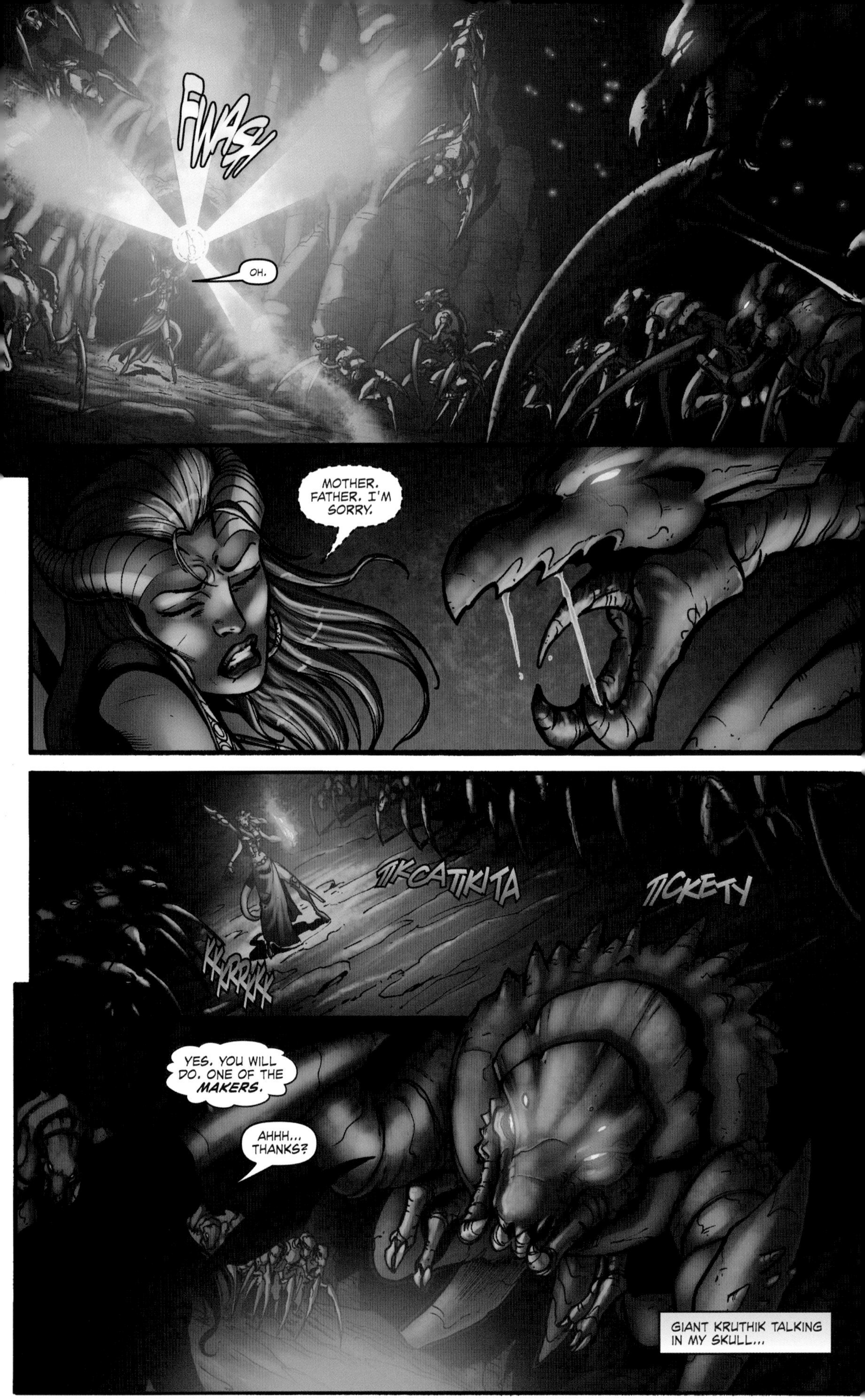
FWASH
OH.
MOTHER. FATHER. I'M SORRY.
TIKCATIKITA
TICKETY
KKRRKK
YES. YOU WILL DO. ONE OF THE *MAKERS*.
AHHH... THANKS?
GIANT KRUTHIK TALKING IN MY SKULL...

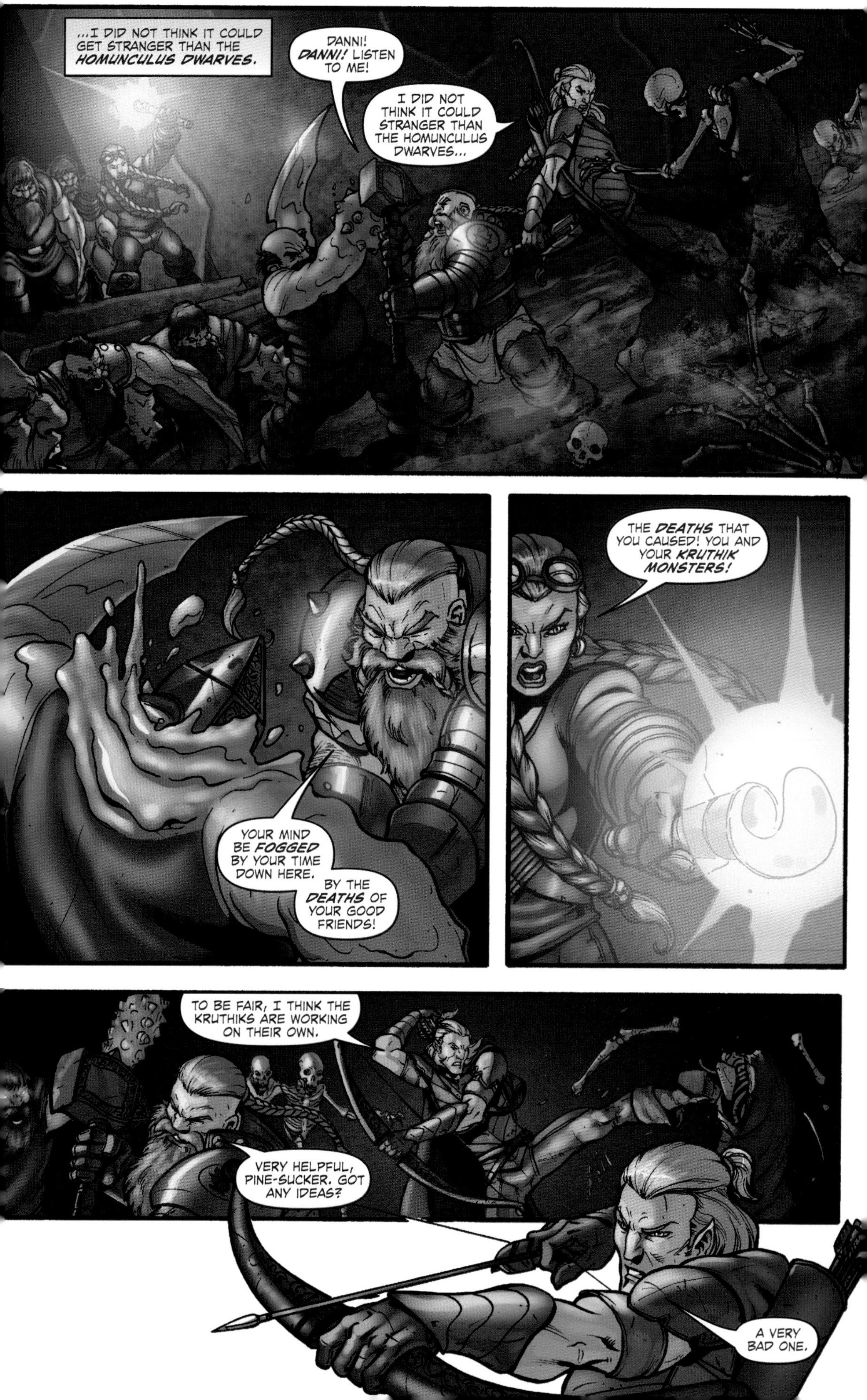
...I DID NOT THINK IT COULD GET STRANGER THAN THE HOMUNCULUS DWARVES.
DANNI! DANNI! LISTEN TO ME!
I DID NOT THINK IT COULD STRANGER THAN THE HOMUNCULUS DWARVES...
YOUR MIND BE FOGGED BY YOUR TIME DOWN HERE.
BY THE DEATHS OF YOUR GOOD FRIENDS!
THE DEATHS THAT YOU CAUSED! YOU AND YOUR KRUTHIK MONSTERS!
TO BE FAIR, I THINK THE KRUTHIKS ARE WORKING ON THEIR OWN.
VERY HELPFUL, PINE-SUCKER. GOT ANY IDEAS?
A VERY BAD ONE.

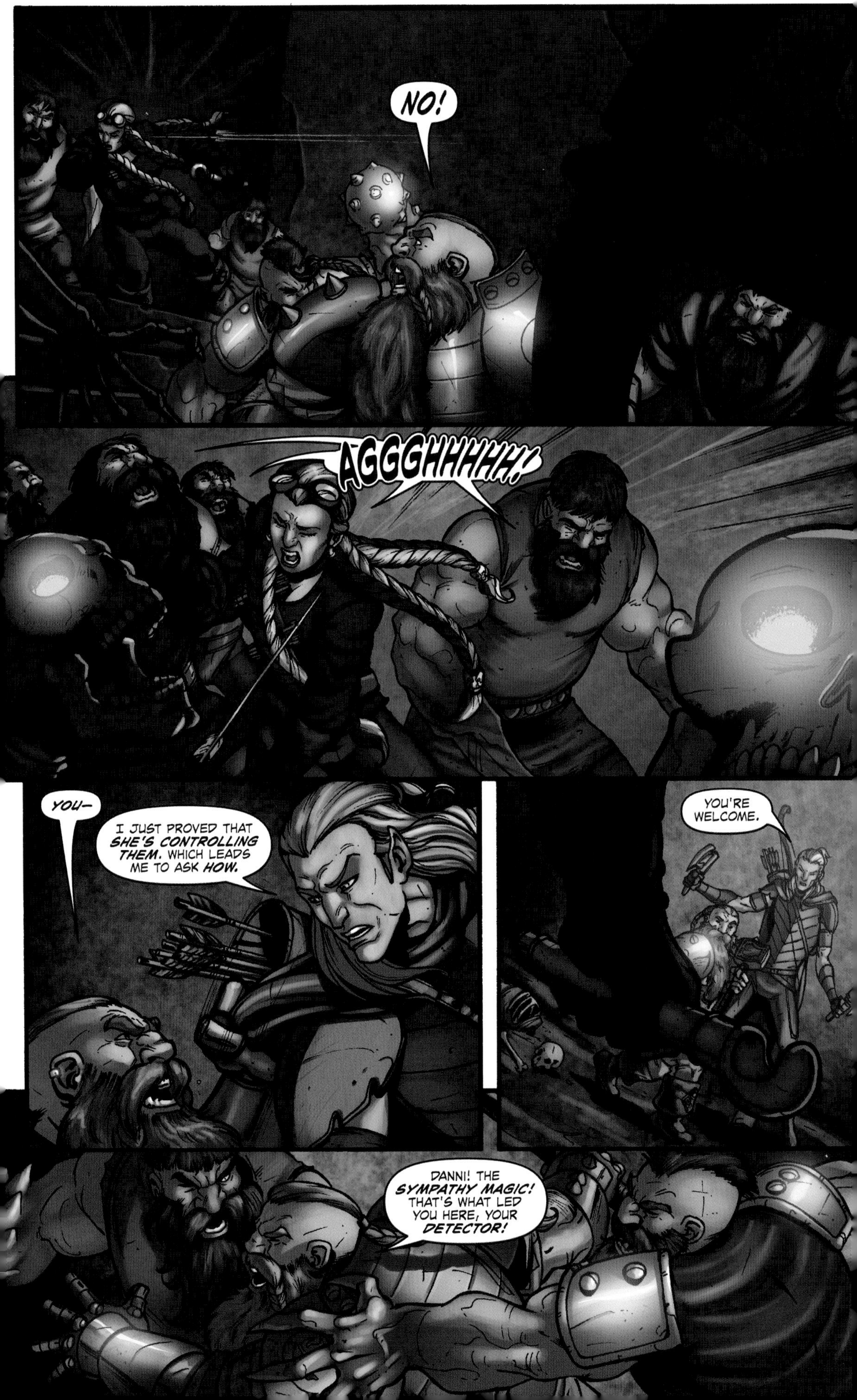
NO!
AGGGHHHHH!
YOU—
I JUST PROVED THAT SHE'S CONTROLLING THEM. WHICH LEADS ME TO ASK HOW.
YOU'RE WELCOME.
DANNI! THE SYMPATHY MAGIC! THAT'S WHAT LED YOU HERE, YOUR DETECTOR!

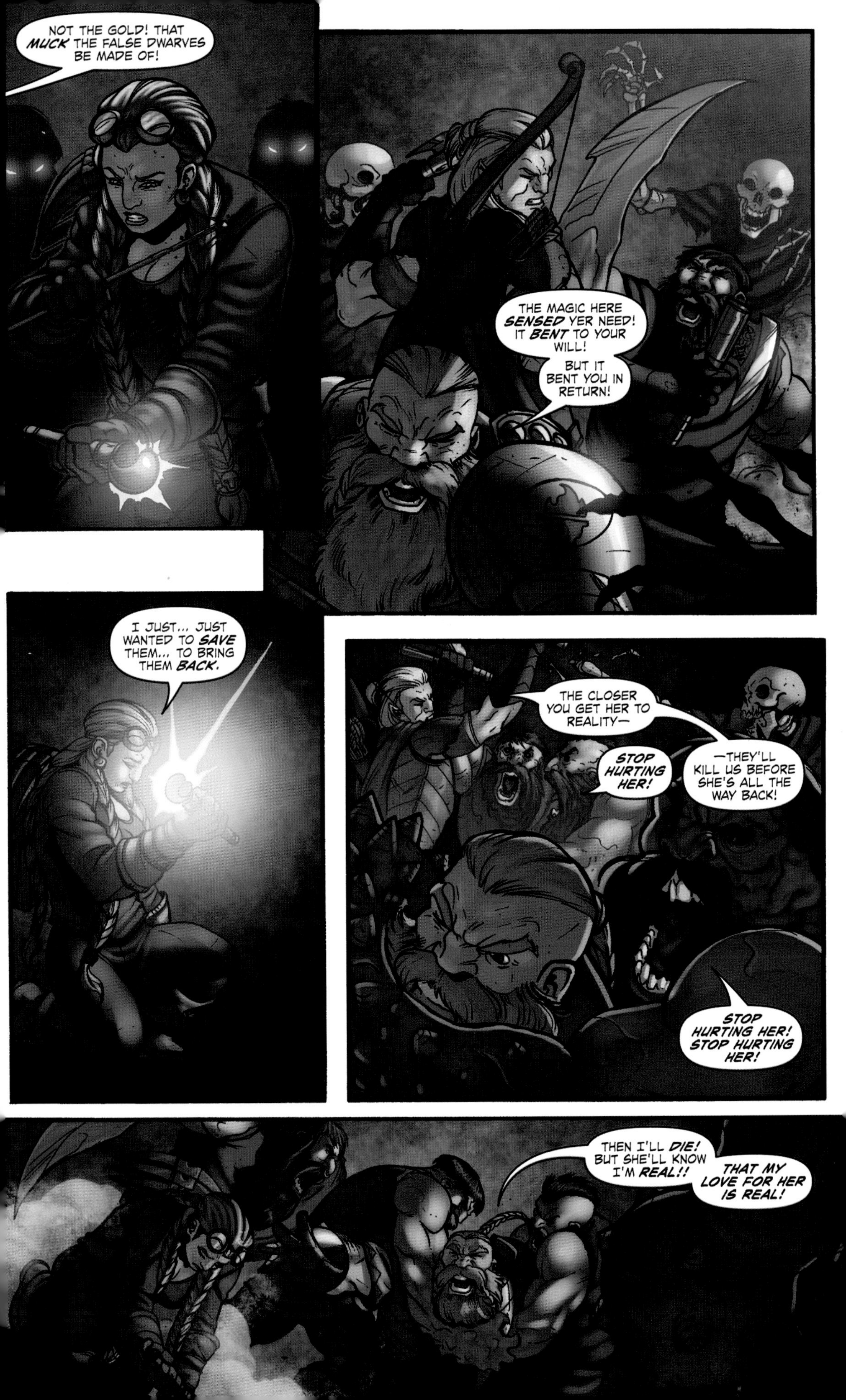
NOT THE GOLD! THAT MUCK THE FALSE DWARVES BE MADE OF!
THE MAGIC HERE SENSED YER NEED! IT BENT TO YOUR WILL!
BUT IT BENT YOU IN RETURN!
I JUST... JUST WANTED TO SAVE THEM... TO BRING THEM BACK.
THE CLOSER YOU GET HER TO REALITY—
STOP HURTING HER!
—THEY'LL KILL US BEFORE SHE'S ALL THE WAY BACK!
STOP HURTING HER! STOP HURTING HER!
THEN I'LL DIE! BUT SHE'LL KNOW I'M REAL!!
THAT MY LOVE FOR HER IS REAL!

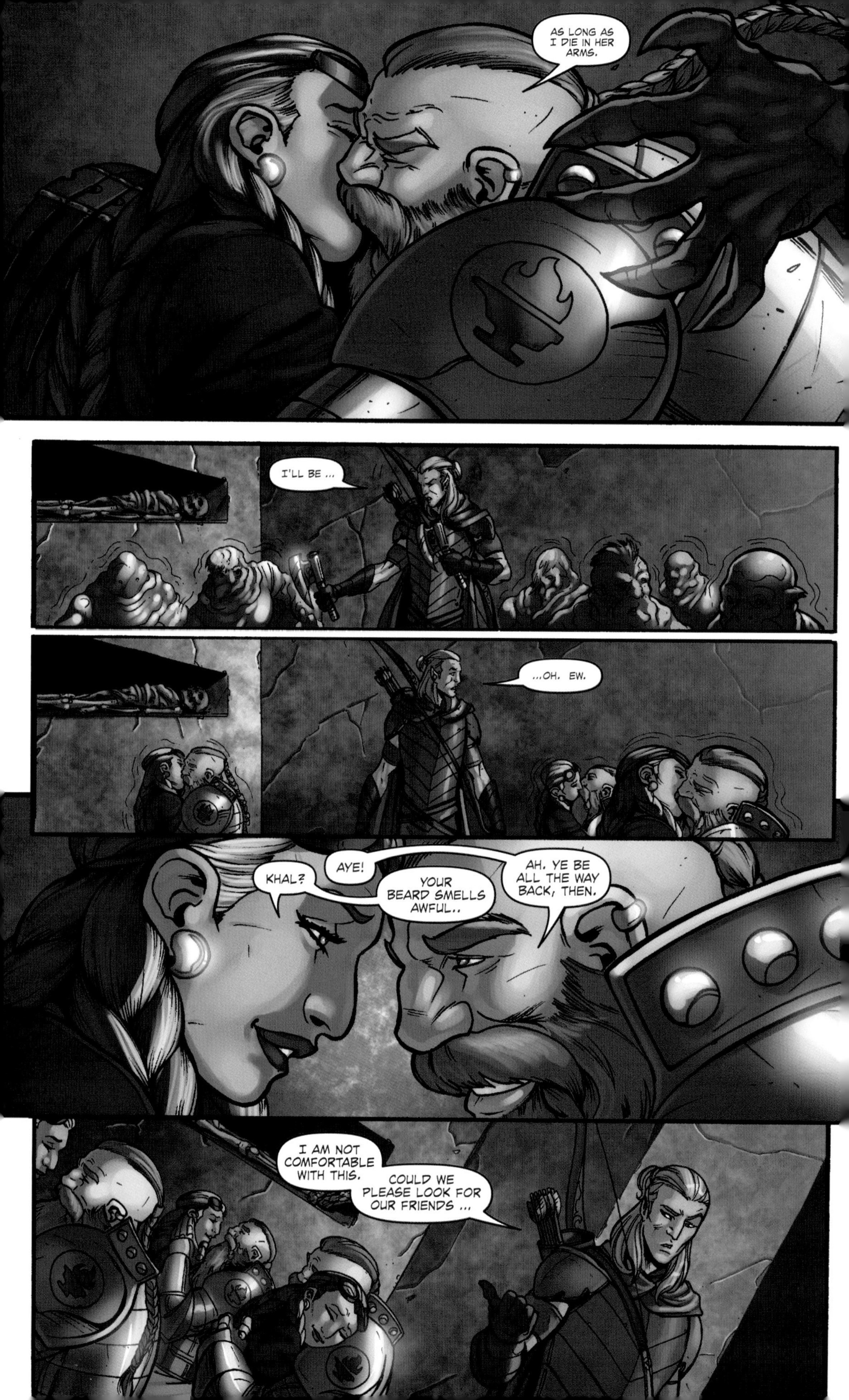
AS LONG AS I DIE IN HER ARMS.
I'LL BE ...
...OH. EW.
KHAL?
AYE!
YOUR BEARD SMELLS AWFUL..
AH. YE BE ALL THE WAY BACK, THEN.
I AM NOT COMFORTABLE WITH THIS.
COULD WE PLEASE LOOK FOR OUR FRIENDS ...

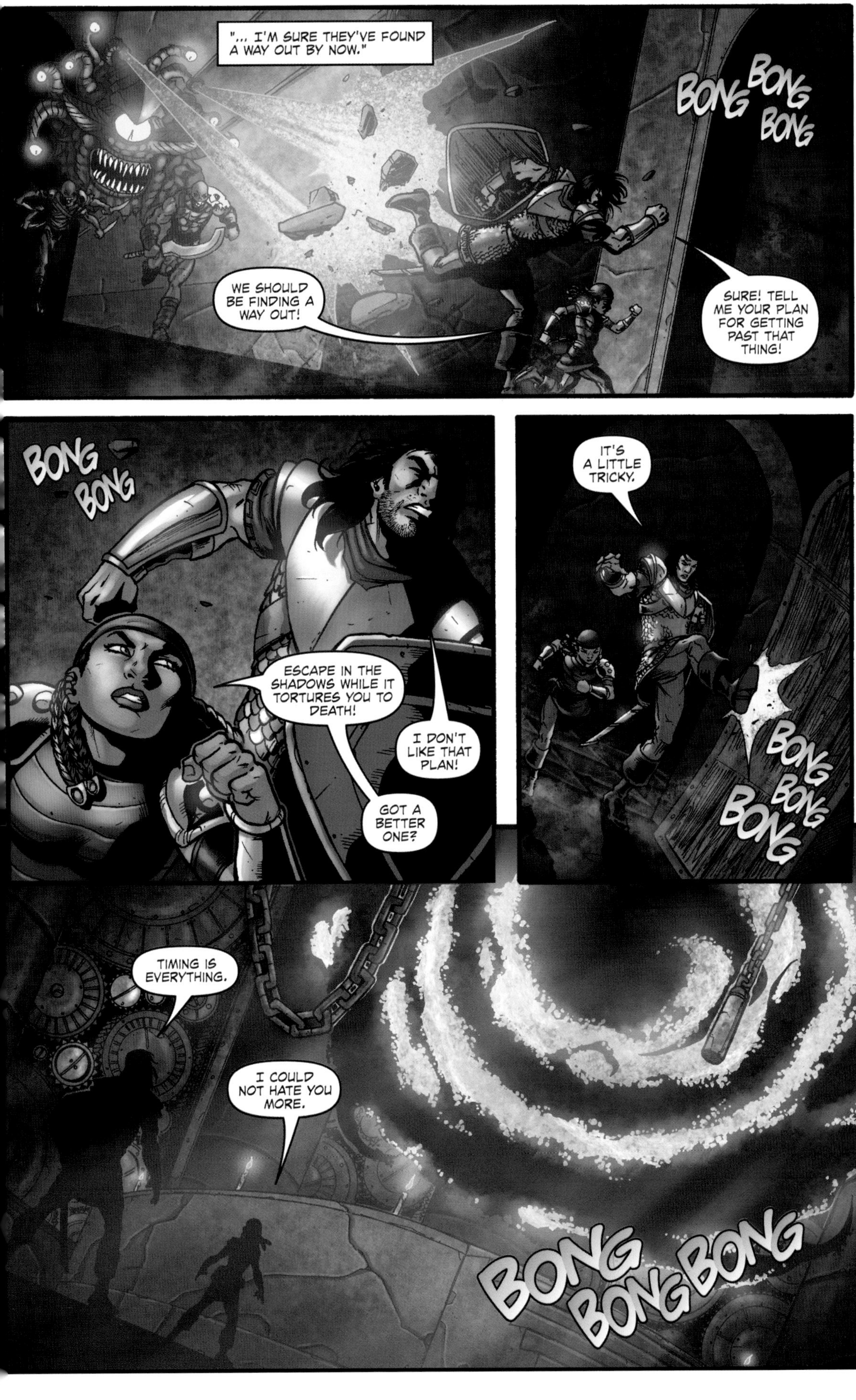
"... I'M SURE THEY'VE FOUND A WAY OUT BY NOW."
BONG BONG BONG
WE SHOULD BE FINDING A WAY OUT!
SURE! TELL ME YOUR PLAN FOR GETTING PAST THAT THING!
BONG BONG
ESCAPE IN THE SHADOWS WHILE IT TORTURES YOU TO DEATH!
I DON'T LIKE THAT PLAN!
GOT A BETTER ONE?
IT'S A LITTLE TRICKY.
BONG BONG BONG
TIMING IS EVERYTHING.
I COULD NOT HATE YOU MORE.
BONG BONG BONG

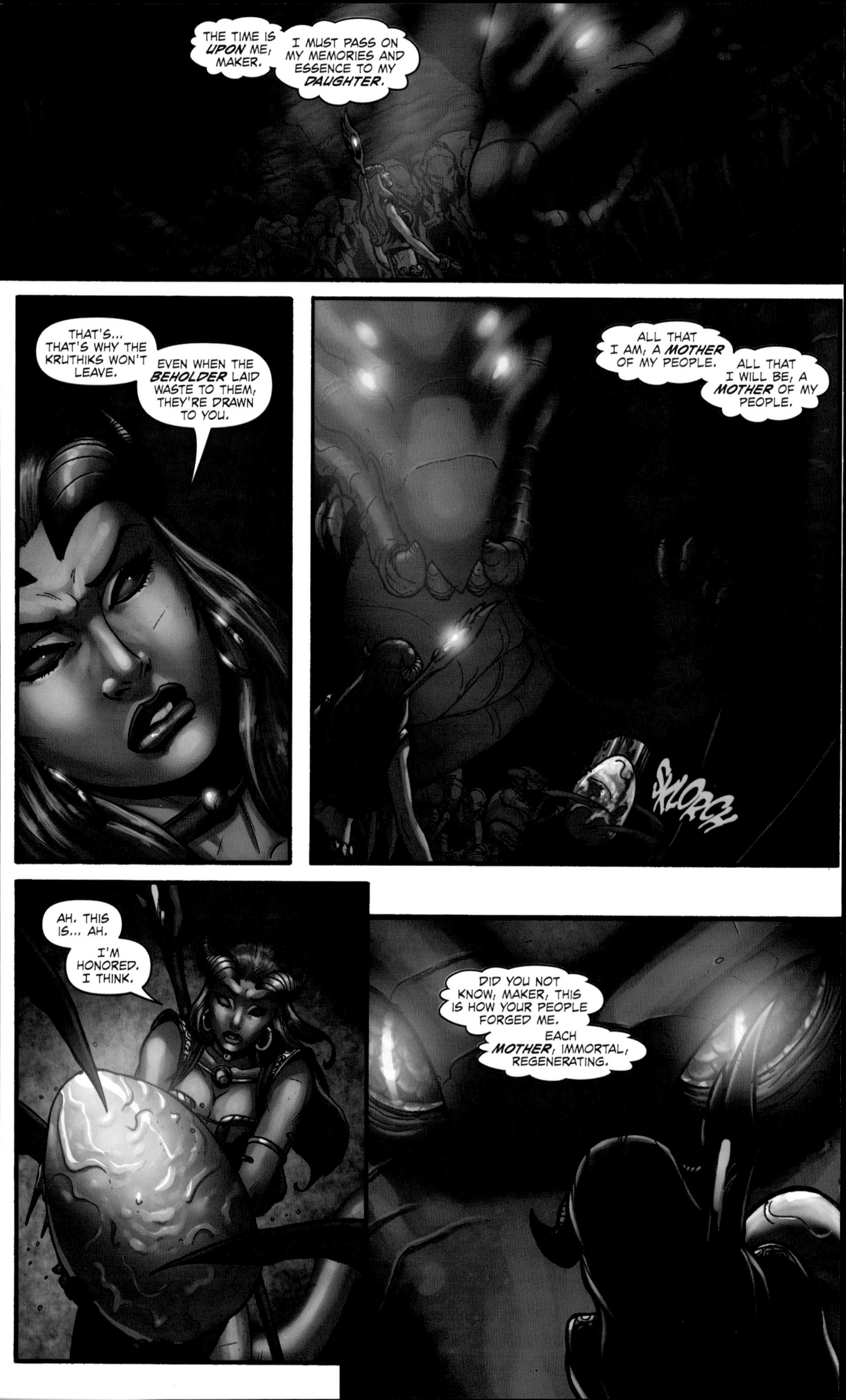

THE TIME IS UPON ME, MAKER.
I MUST PASS ON MY MEMORIES AND ESSENCE TO MY DAUGHTER.
THAT'S... THAT'S WHY THE KRUTHIKS WON'T LEAVE.
EVEN WHEN THE BEHOLDER LAID WASTE TO THEM, THEY'RE DRAWN TO YOU.
ALL THAT I AM, A MOTHER OF MY PEOPLE.
ALL THAT I WILL BE, A MOTHER OF MY PEOPLE.
SKLORCH
AH. THIS IS... AH.
I'M HONORED. I THINK.
DID YOU NOT KNOW, MAKER, THIS IS HOW YOUR PEOPLE FORGED ME.
EACH MOTHER, IMMORTAL, REGENERATING.

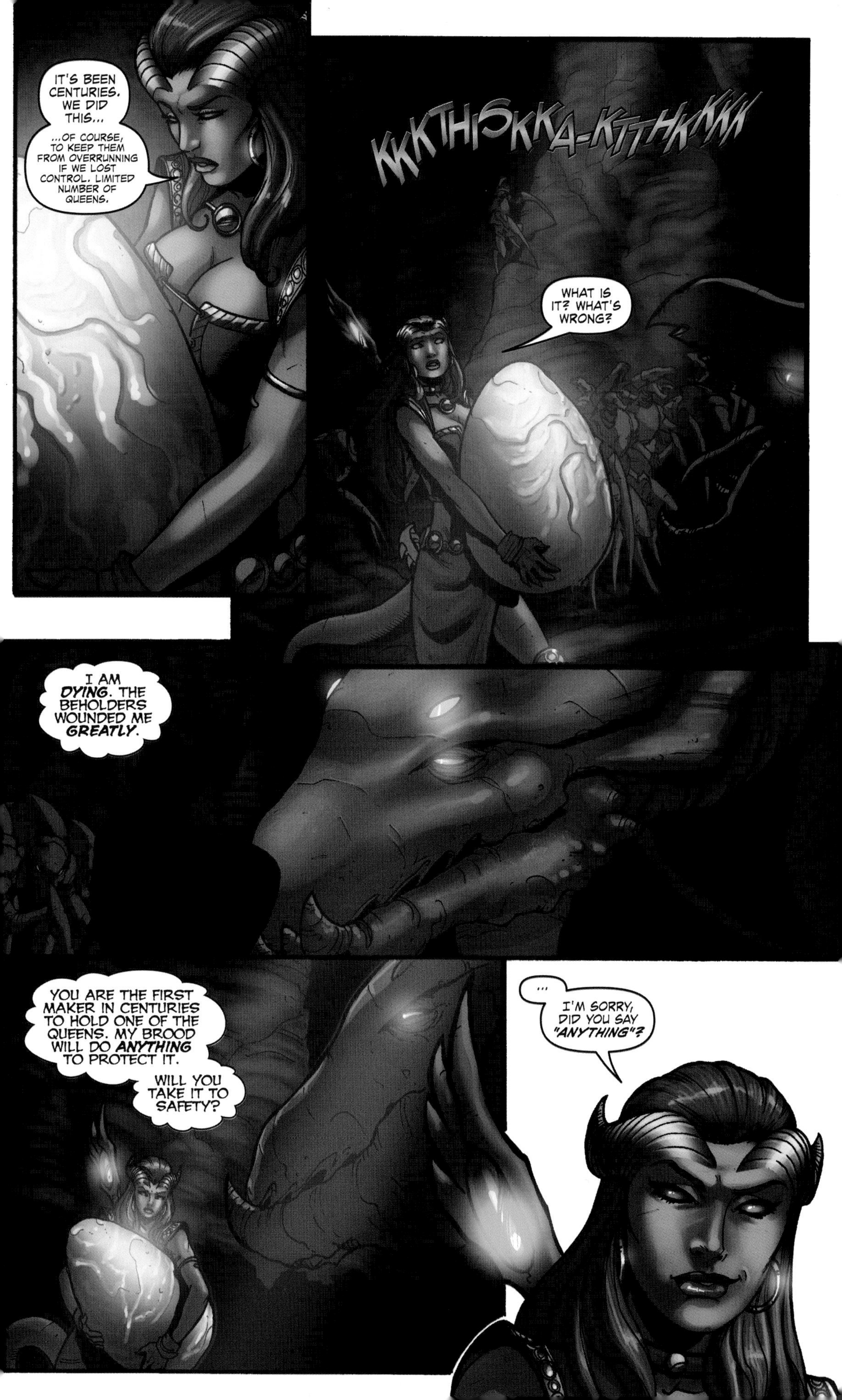

IT'S BEEN CENTURIES. WE DID THIS...
...OF COURSE, TO KEEP THEM FROM OVERRUNNING IF WE LOST CONTROL. LIMITED NUMBER OF QUEENS.
KKKTHISKKA-KITTHKKKK
WHAT IS IT? WHAT'S WRONG?
I AM *DYING*. THE BEHOLDERS WOUNDED ME *GREATLY*.
YOU ARE THE FIRST MAKER IN CENTURIES TO HOLD ONE OF THE QUEENS. MY BROOD WILL DO *ANYTHING* TO PROTECT IT.
WILL YOU TAKE IT TO SAFETY?
...
I'M SORRY, DID YOU SAY *"ANYTHING"*?

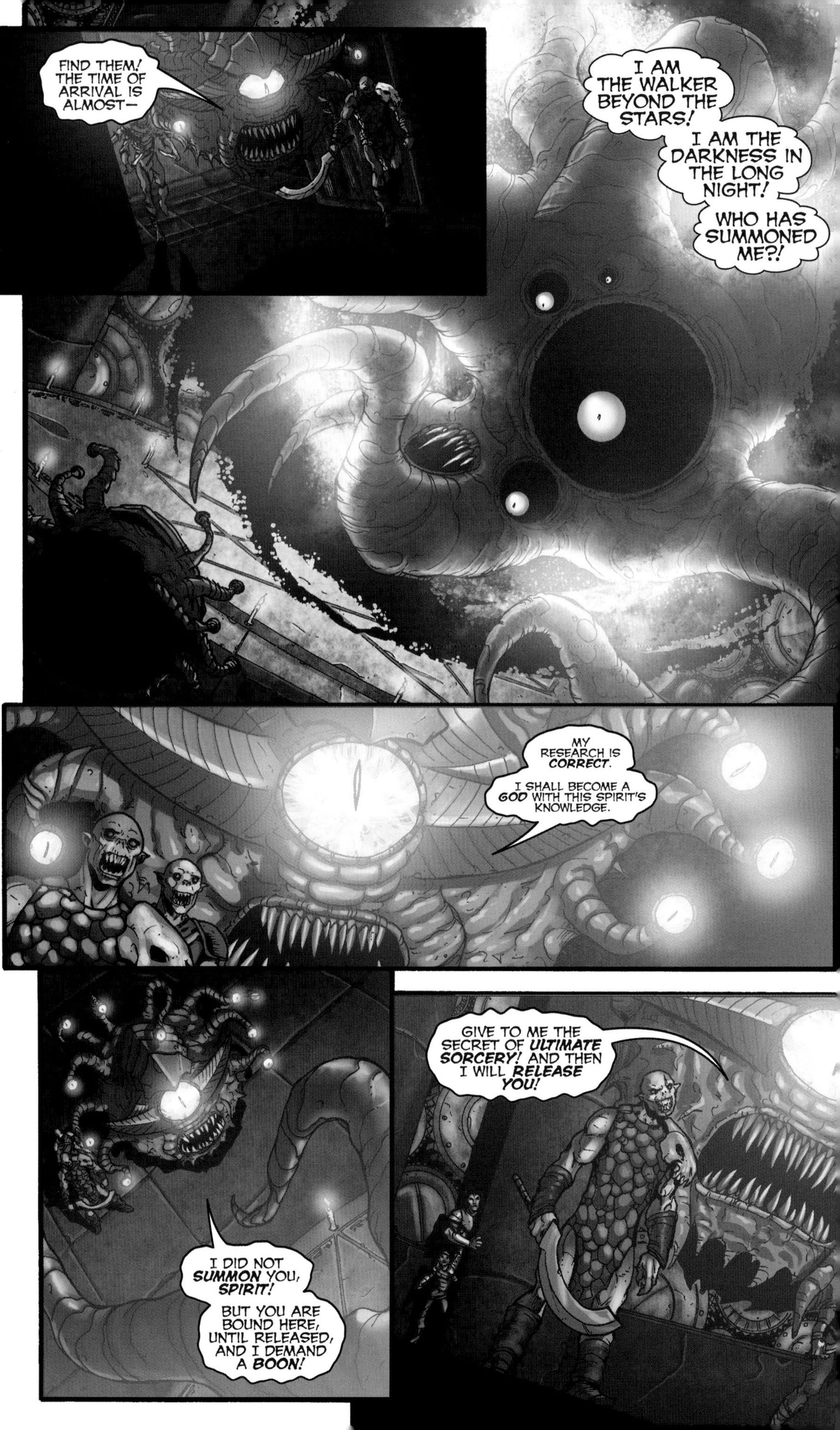
FIND THEM! THE TIME OF ARRIVAL IS ALMOST—
I AM THE WALKER BEYOND THE STARS!
I AM THE DARKNESS IN THE LONG NIGHT!
WHO HAS SUMMONED ME?!
MY RESEARCH IS CORRECT.
I SHALL BECOME A GOD WITH THIS SPIRIT'S KNOWLEDGE.
I DID NOT SUMMON YOU, SPIRIT!
BUT YOU ARE BOUND HERE, UNTIL RELEASED, AND I DEMAND A BOON!
GIVE TO ME THE SECRET OF ULTIMATE SORCERY! AND THEN I WILL RELEASE YOU!

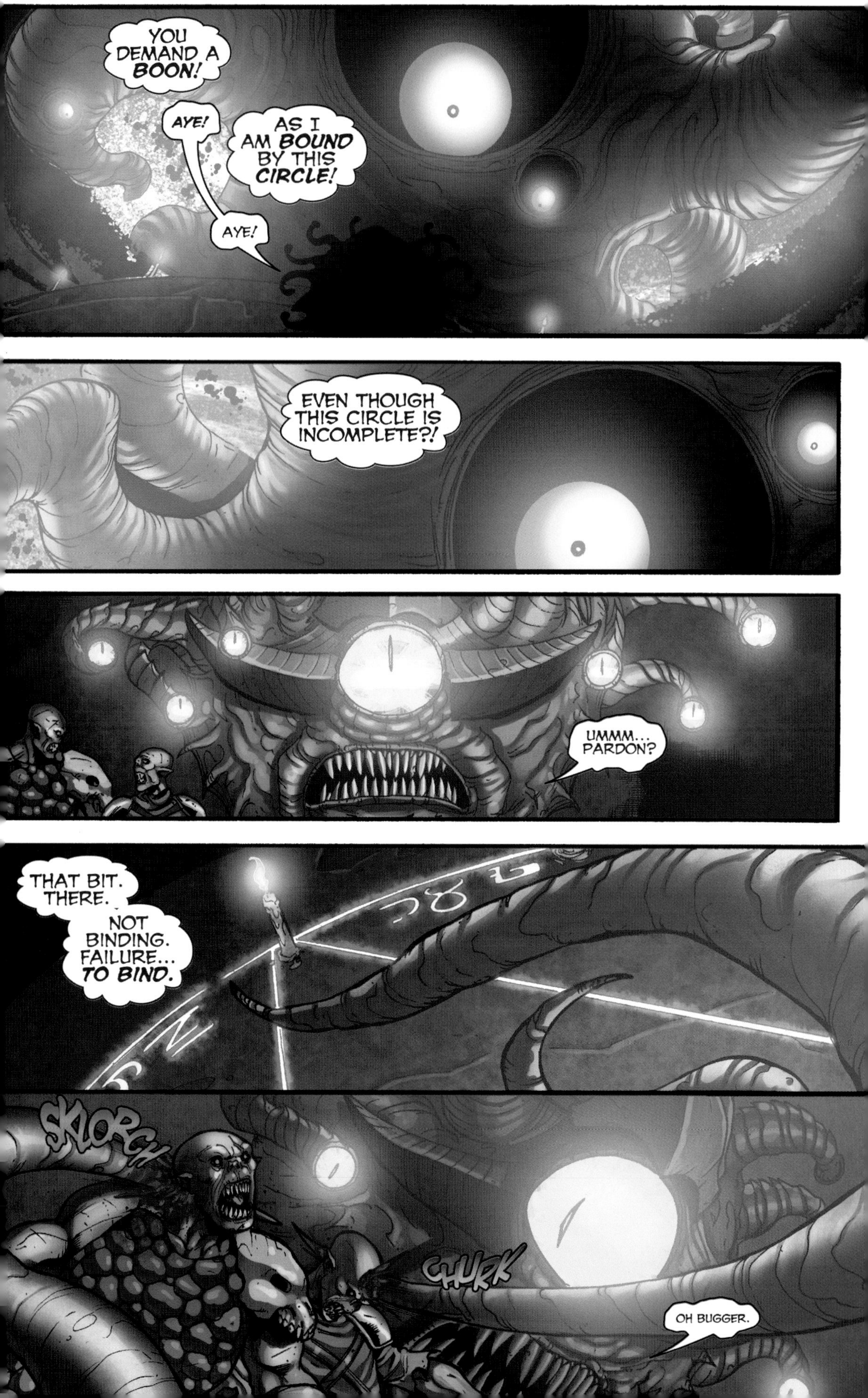
YOU DEMAND A BOON!
AYE!
AS I AM BOUND BY THIS CIRCLE!
AYE!
EVEN THOUGH THIS CIRCLE IS INCOMPLETE?!
UMMM... PARDON?
THAT BIT. THERE.
NOT BINDING. FAILURE... TO BIND.
SKLORCH
CHURK
OH BUGGER.

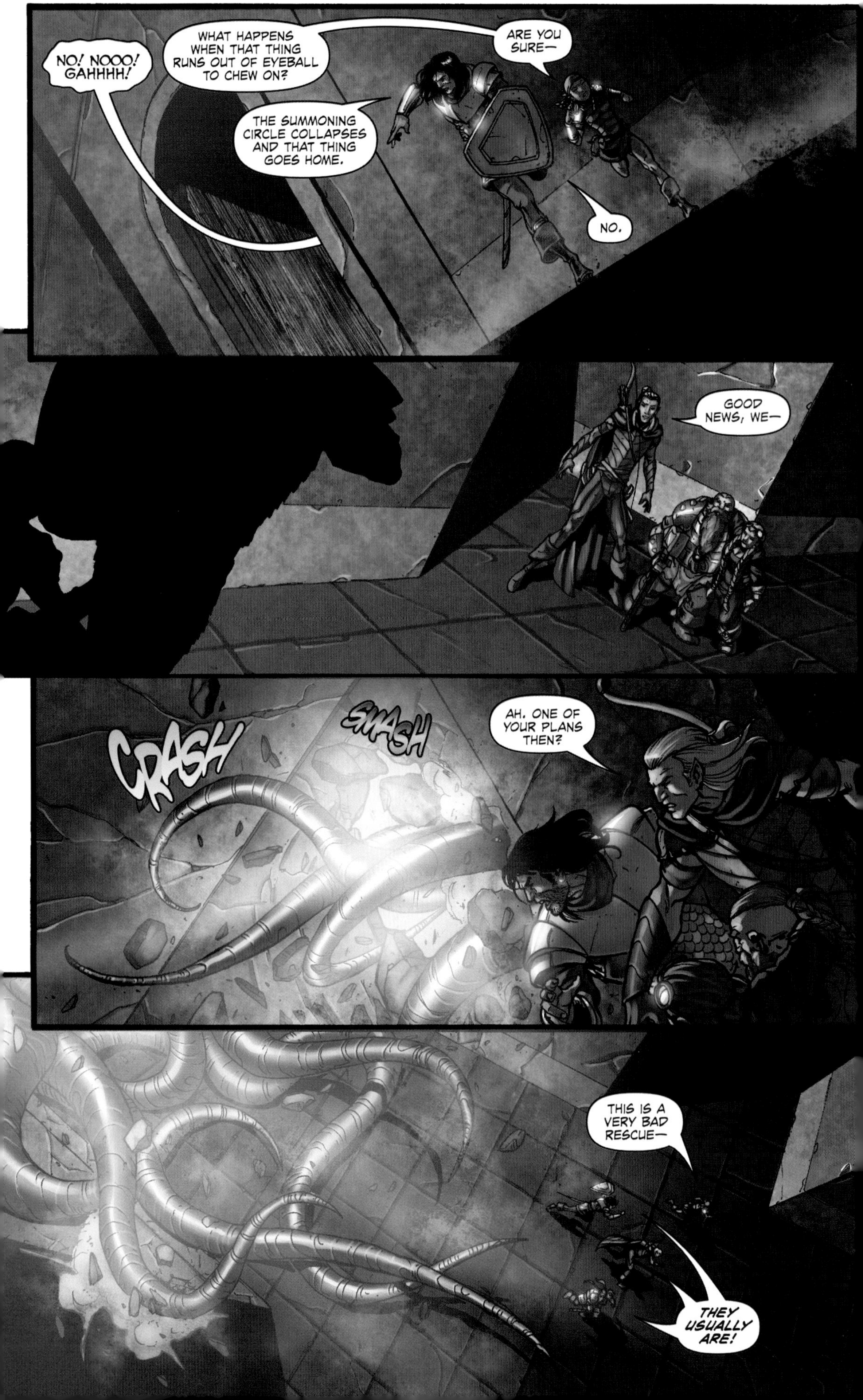
NO! NOOO! GAHHHH!
WHAT HAPPENS WHEN THAT THING RUNS OUT OF EYEBALL TO CHEW ON?
ARE YOU SURE—
THE SUMMONING CIRCLE COLLAPSES AND THAT THING GOES HOME.
NO.
GOOD NEWS, WE—
CRASH
SMASH
AH. ONE OF YOUR PLANS THEN?
THIS IS A VERY BAD RESCUE—
THEY USUALLY ARE!

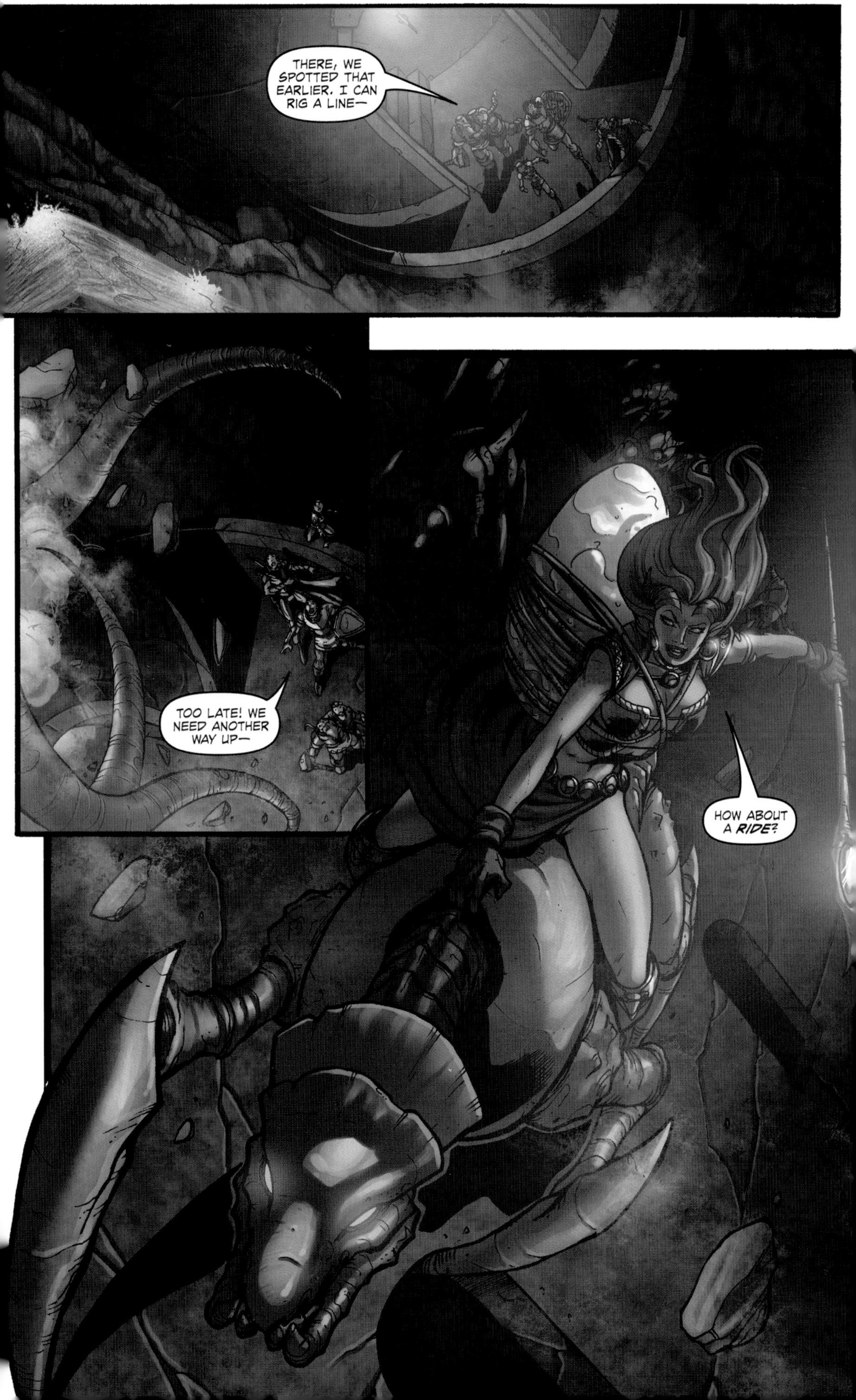
THERE, WE SPOTTED THAT EARLIER. I CAN RIG A LINE—
TOO LATE! WE NEED ANOTHER WAY UP—
HOW ABOUT A *RIDE?*

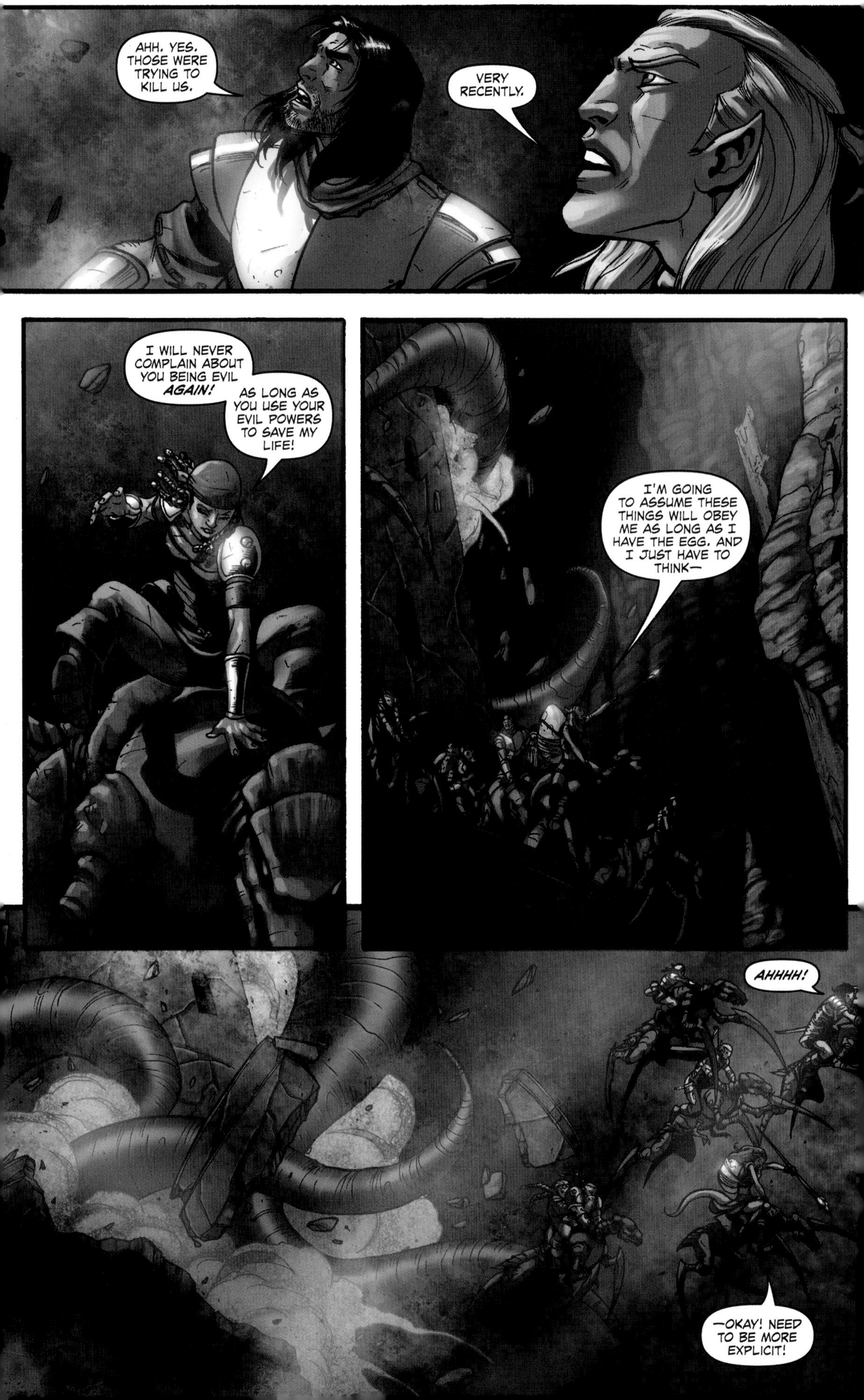
AHH. YES. THOSE WERE TRYING TO KILL US.
VERY RECENTLY.
I WILL NEVER COMPLAIN ABOUT YOU BEING EVIL *AGAIN!*
AS LONG AS YOU USE YOUR EVIL POWERS TO SAVE MY LIFE!
I'M GOING TO ASSUME THESE THINGS WILL OBEY ME AS LONG AS I HAVE THE EGG. AND I JUST HAVE TO THINK—
AHHHH!
—OKAY! NEED TO BE MORE EXPLICIT!

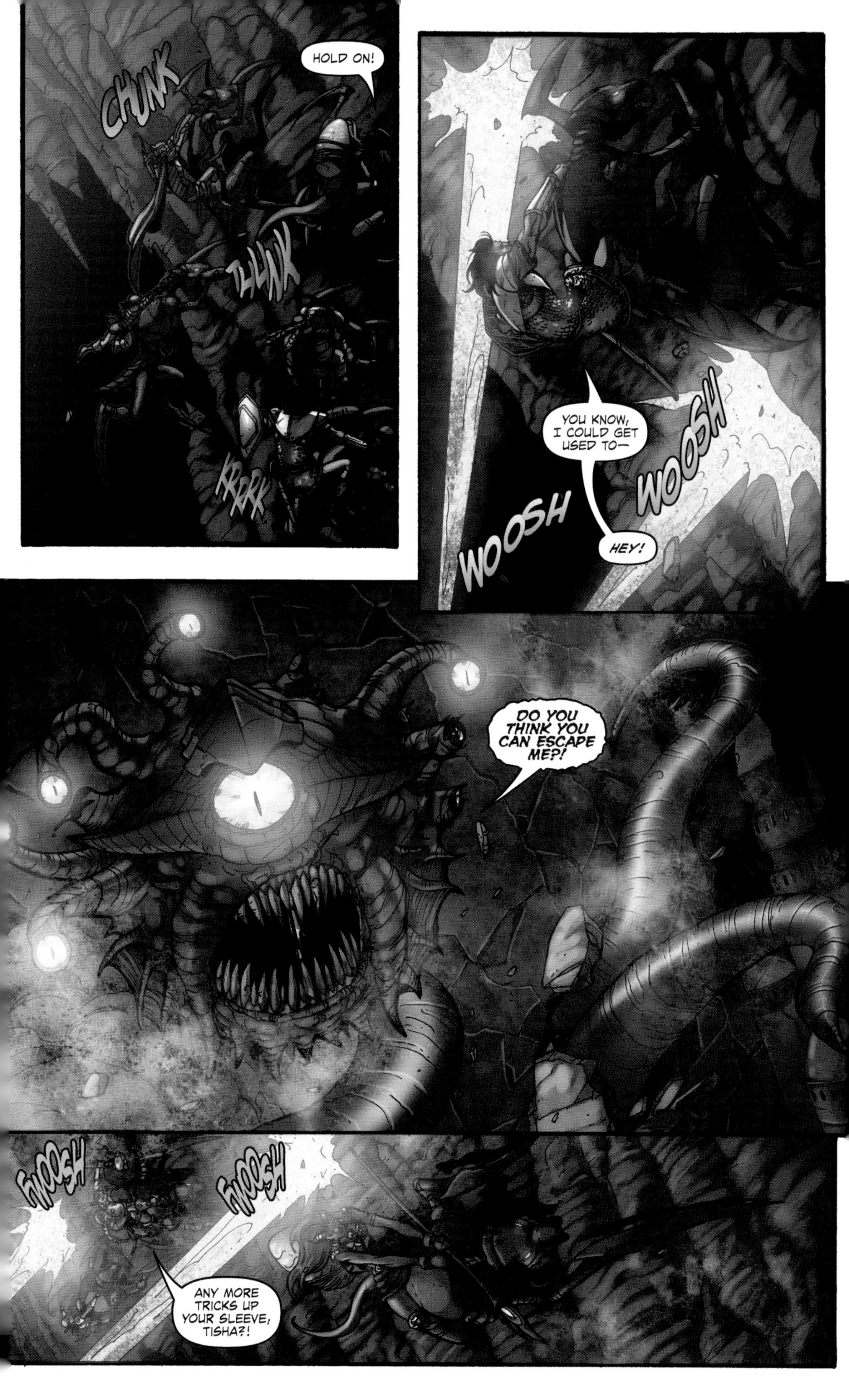
HOLD ON!
CHUNK
THUNK
KRRRK
YOU KNOW, I COULD GET USED TO—
HEY!
WOOSH
WOOSH
DO YOU THINK YOU CAN ESCAPE ME?!
FWOOSH
FWOOSH
ANY MORE TRICKS UP YOUR SLEEVE, TISHA?!

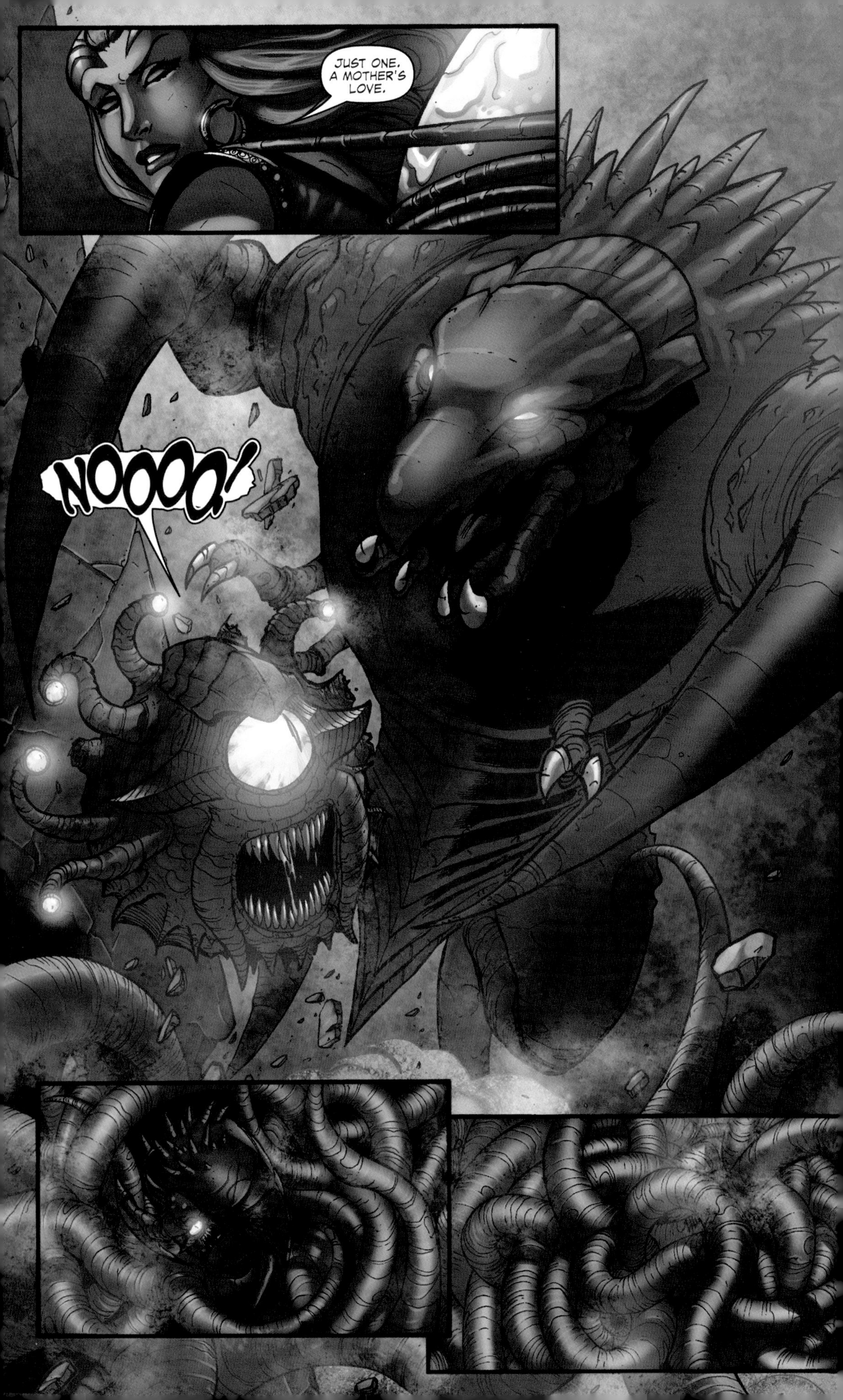
JUST ONE. A MOTHER'S LOVE.
NOOOO!

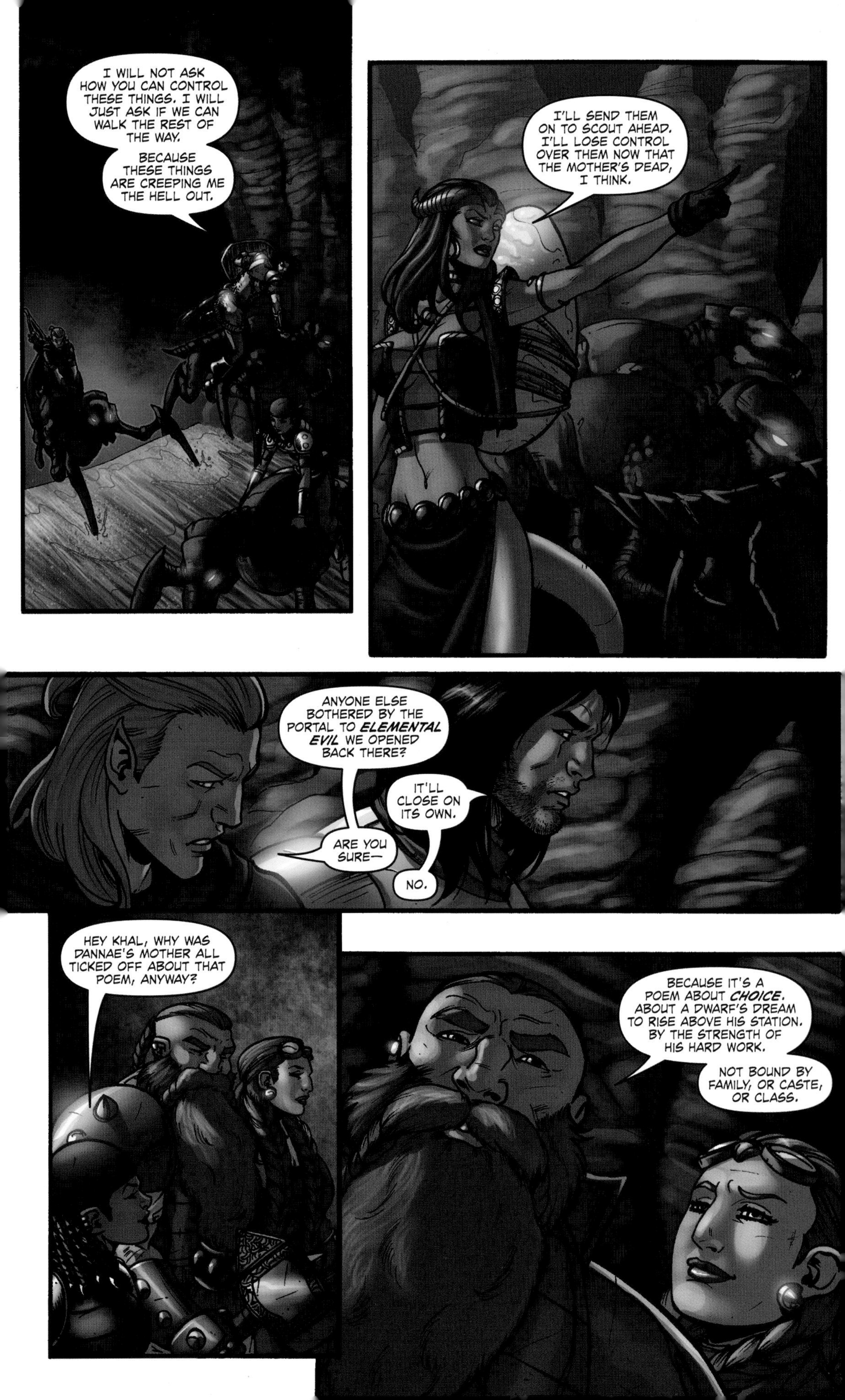
I WILL NOT ASK HOW YOU CAN CONTROL THESE THINGS. I WILL JUST ASK IF WE CAN WALK THE REST OF THE WAY.
BECAUSE THESE THINGS ARE CREEPING ME THE HELL OUT.
I'LL SEND THEM ON TO SCOUT AHEAD. I'LL LOSE CONTROL OVER THEM NOW THAT THE MOTHER'S DEAD, I THINK.
ANYONE ELSE BOTHERED BY THE PORTAL TO ELEMENTAL EVIL WE OPENED BACK THERE?
IT'LL CLOSE ON ITS OWN.
ARE YOU SURE—
NO.
HEY KHAL, WHY WAS DANNAE'S MOTHER ALL TICKED OFF ABOUT THAT POEM, ANYWAY?
BECAUSE IT'S A POEM ABOUT CHOICE. ABOUT A DWARF'S DREAM TO RISE ABOVE HIS STATION. BY THE STRENGTH OF HIS HARD WORK.
NOT BOUND BY FAMILY, OR CASTE, OR CLASS.

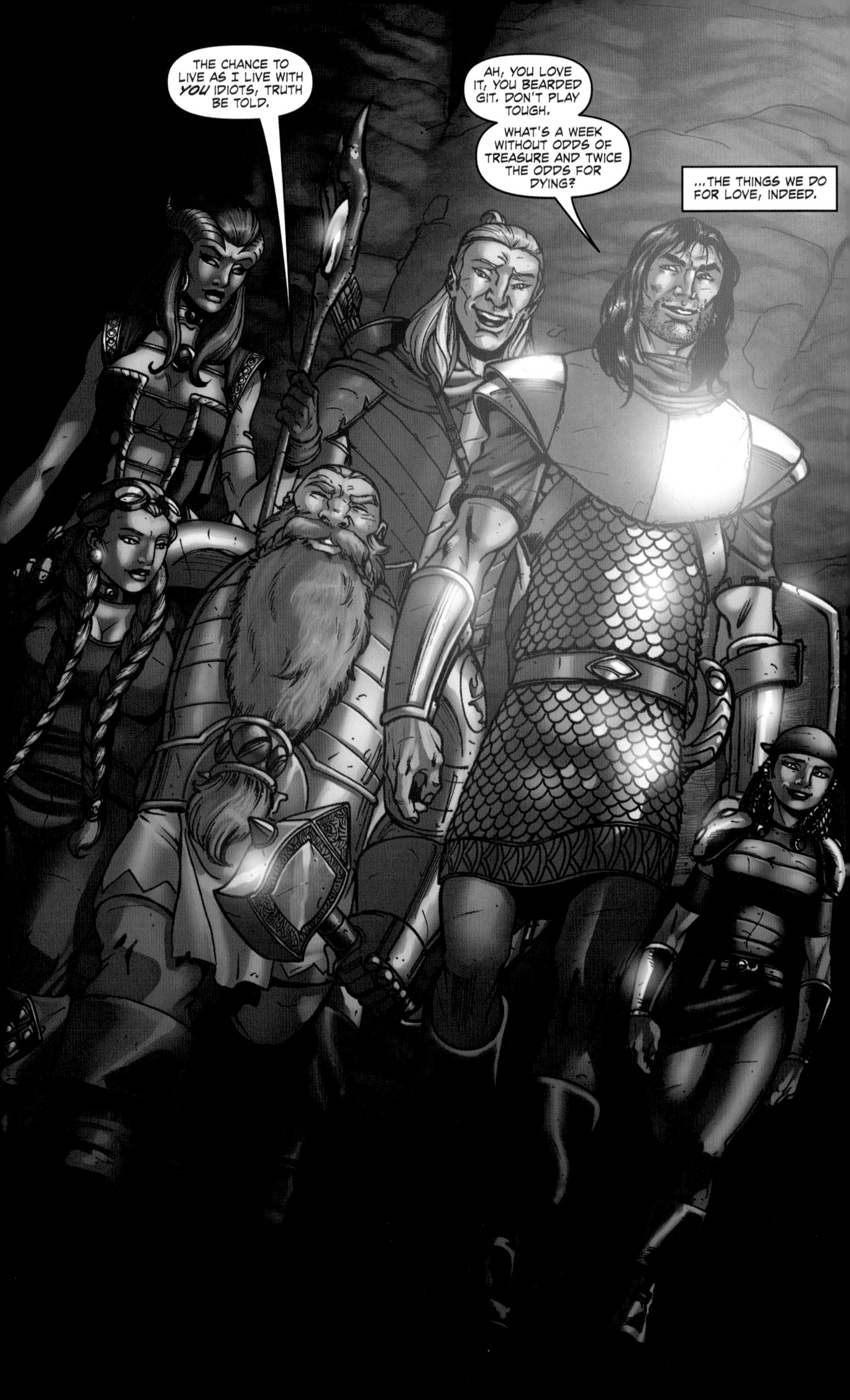
THE CHANCE TO LIVE AS I LIVE WITH *YOU* IDIOTS, TRUTH BE TOLD.
AH, YOU LOVE IT, YOU BEARDED GIT. DON'T PLAY TOUGH.
WHAT'S A WEEK WITHOUT ODDS OF TREASURE AND TWICE THE ODDS FOR DYING?
...THE THINGS WE DO FOR LOVE, INDEED.

Art by Paul Renaud

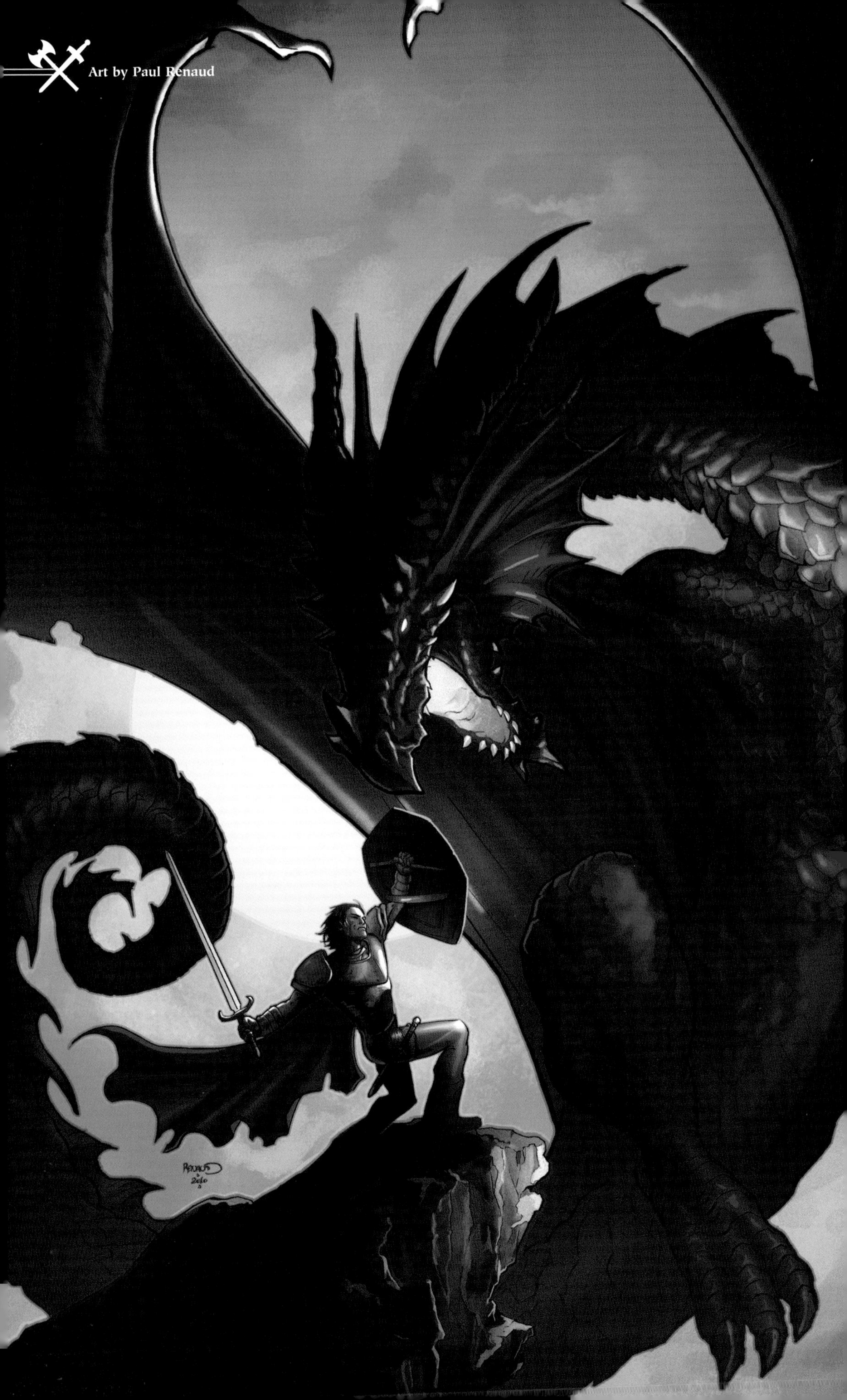

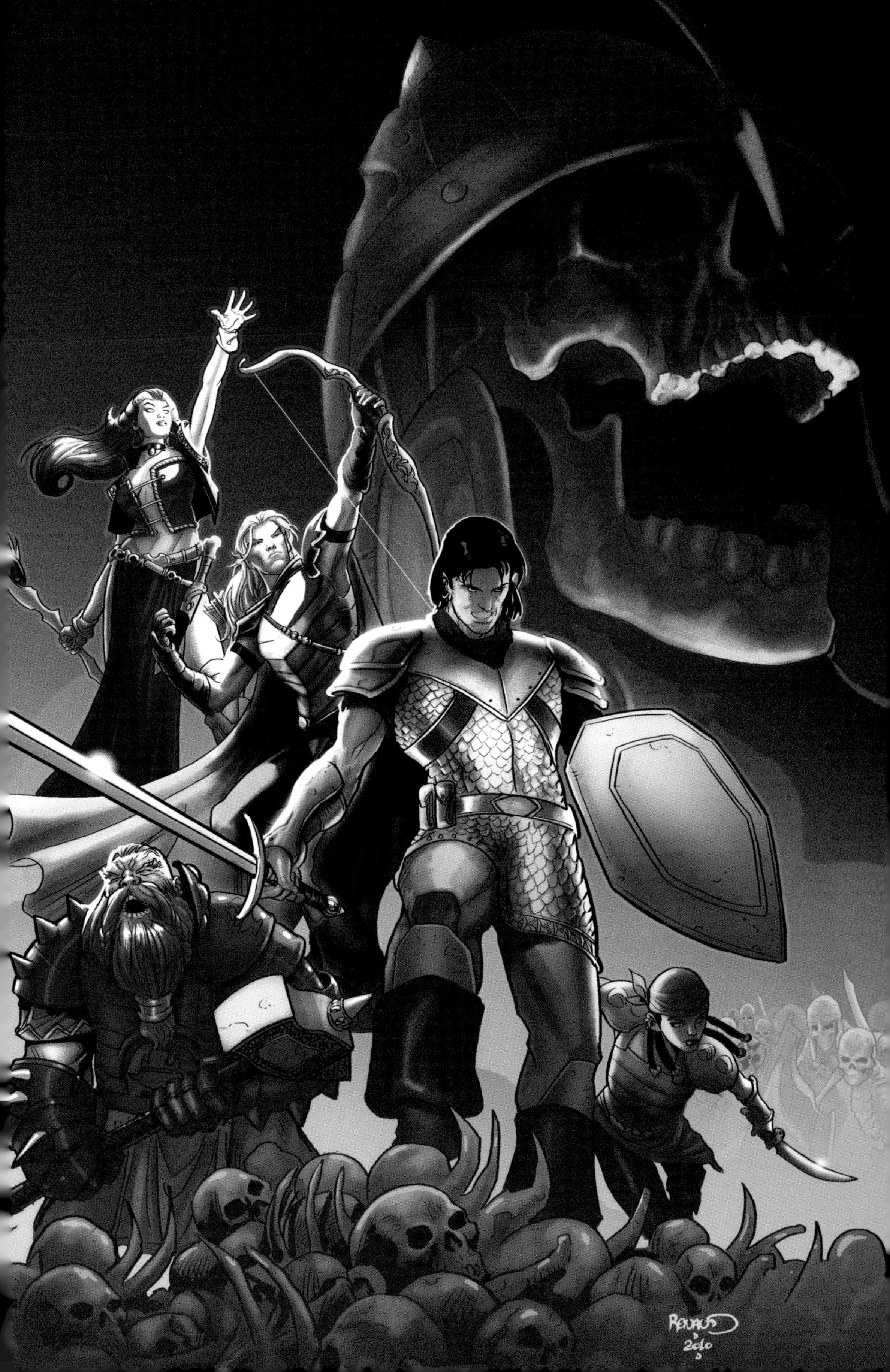

Art by Paul Renaud

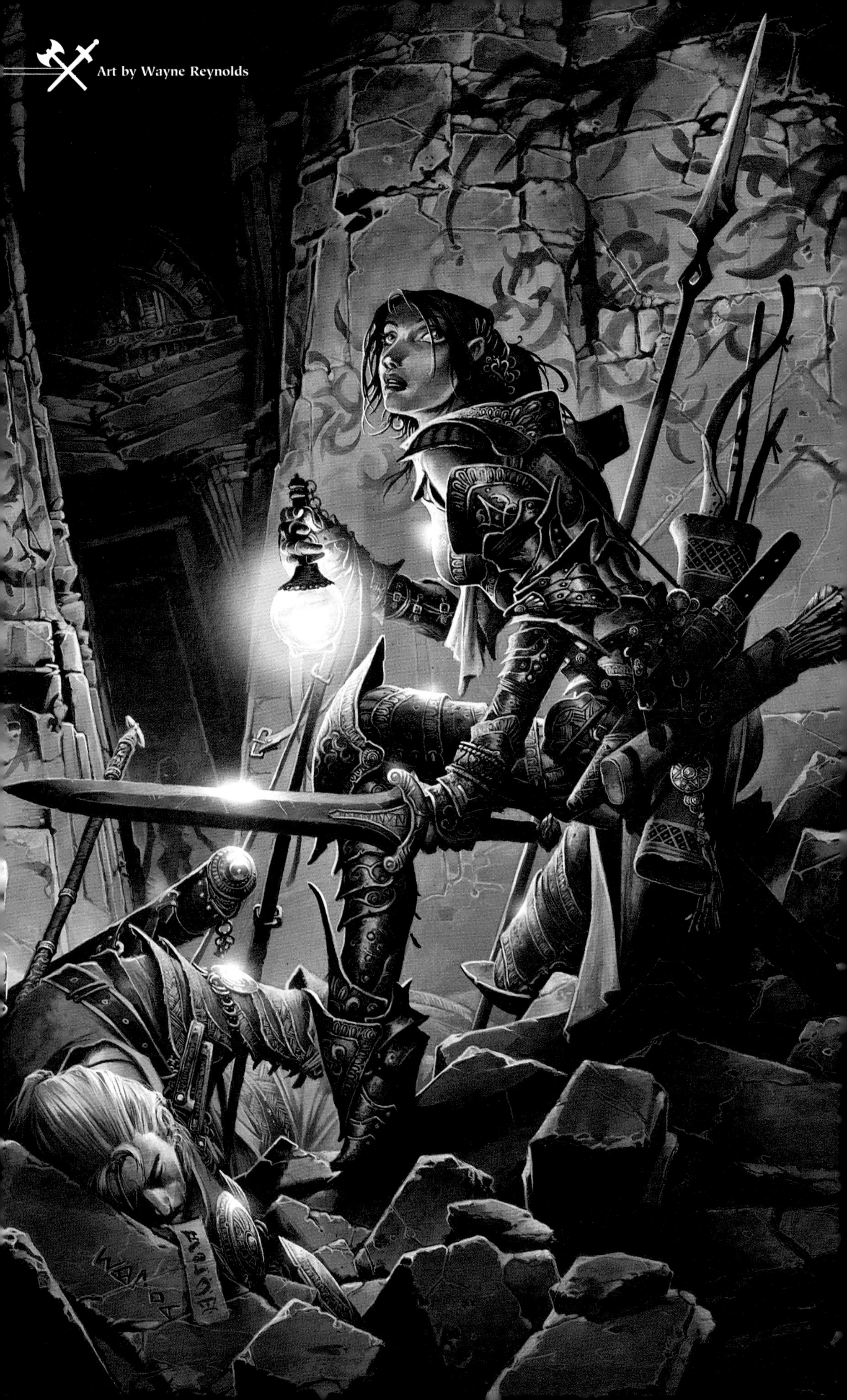

Art by Wayne Reynolds

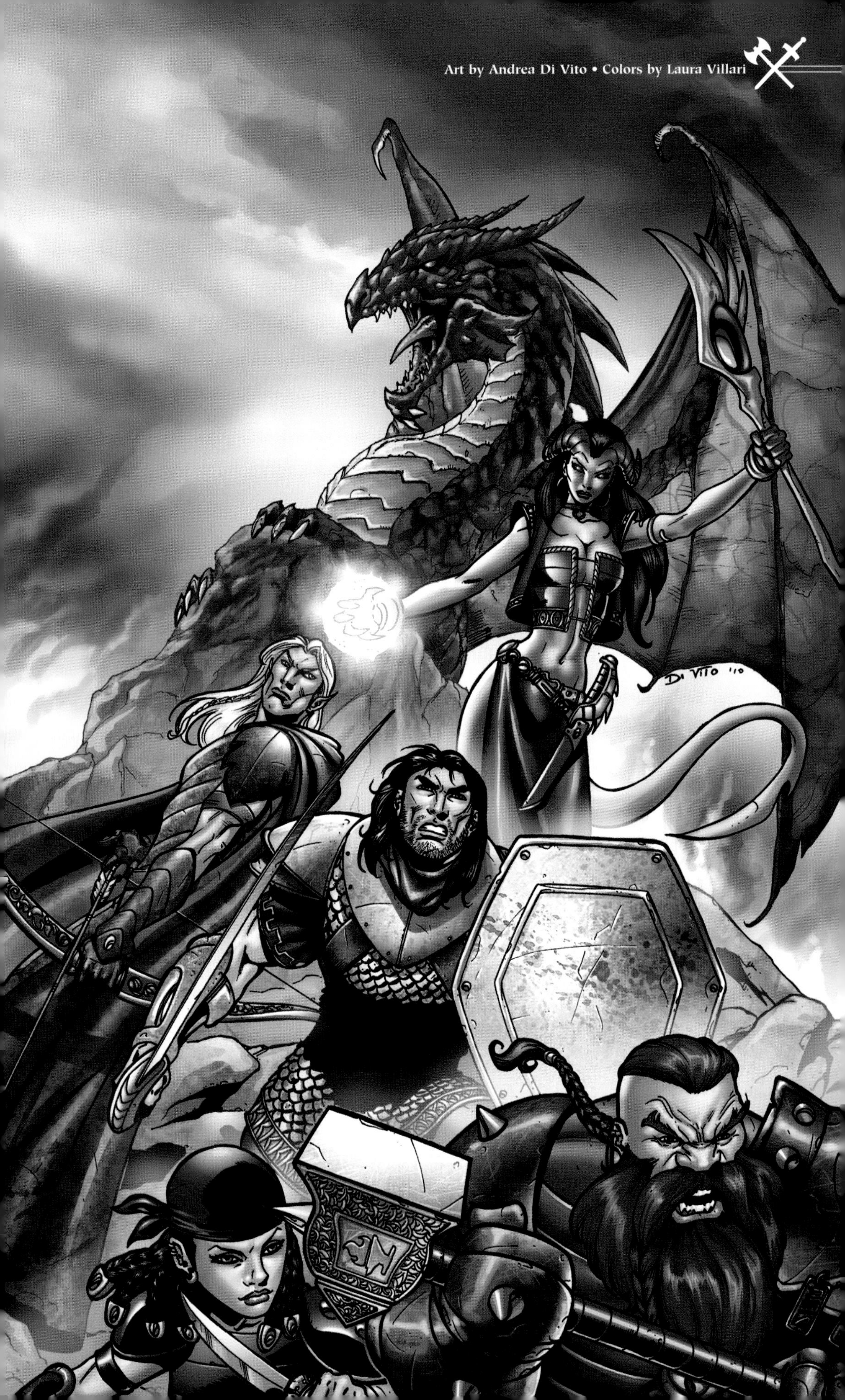
DI VITO '10

Art by Andrea Di Vito • Colors by Laura Villari

Art by Tim Seeley • Colors by Aburtov and Grafikslava

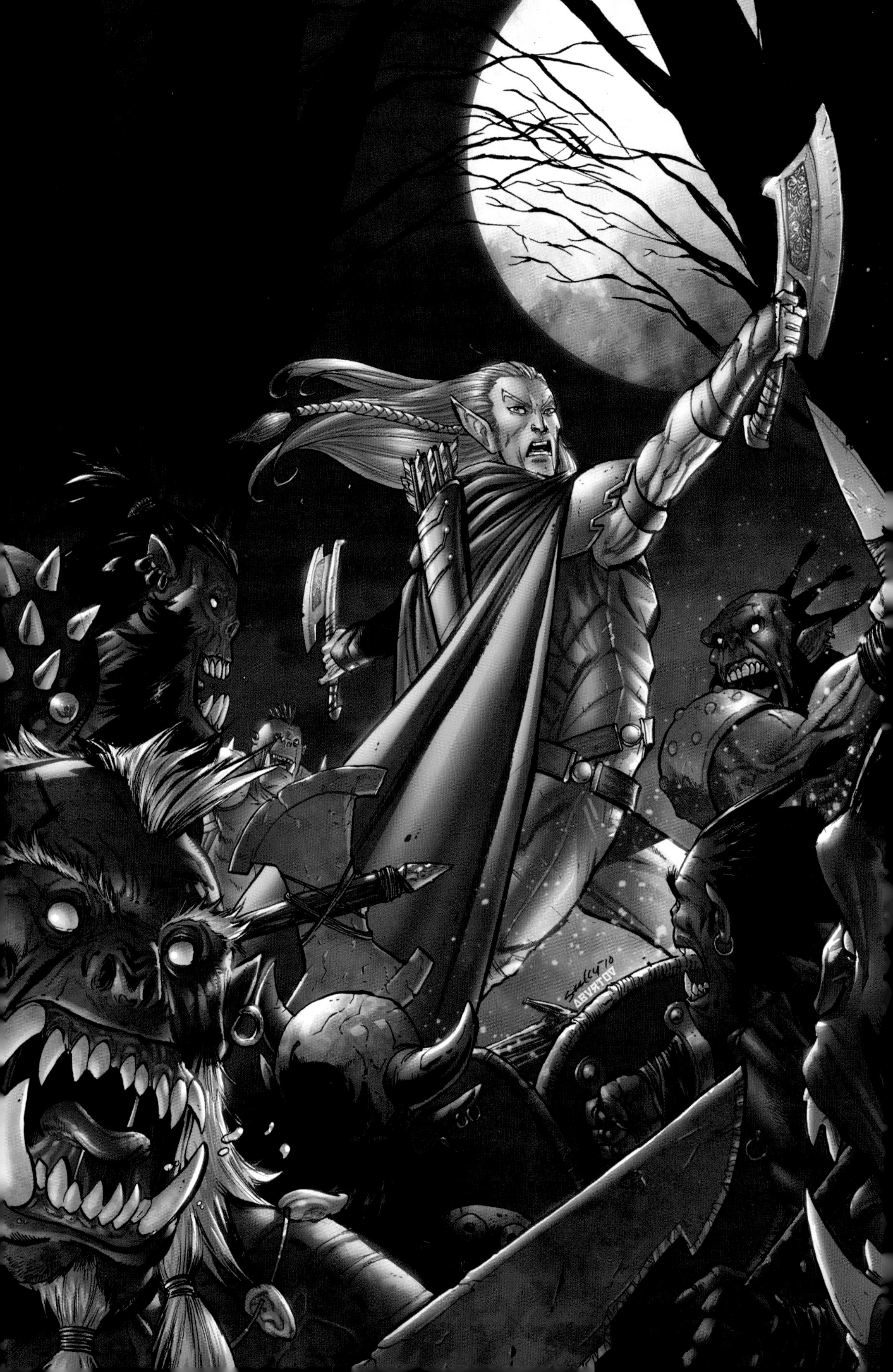

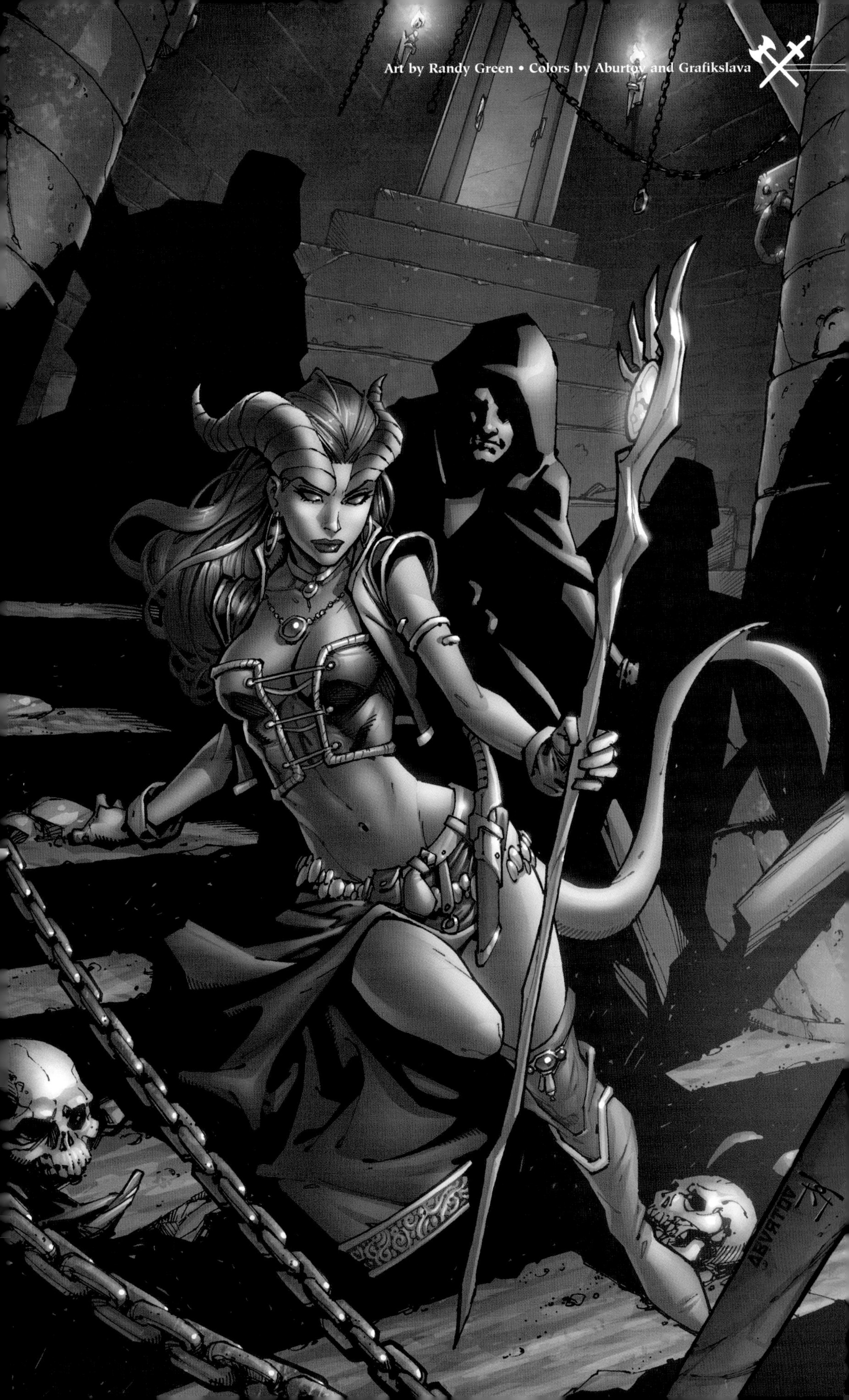

Art by Randy Green • Colors by Aburtov and Grafikslava

Art by Billy Dallas Patton • Colors by Aburtov and Grafikslava

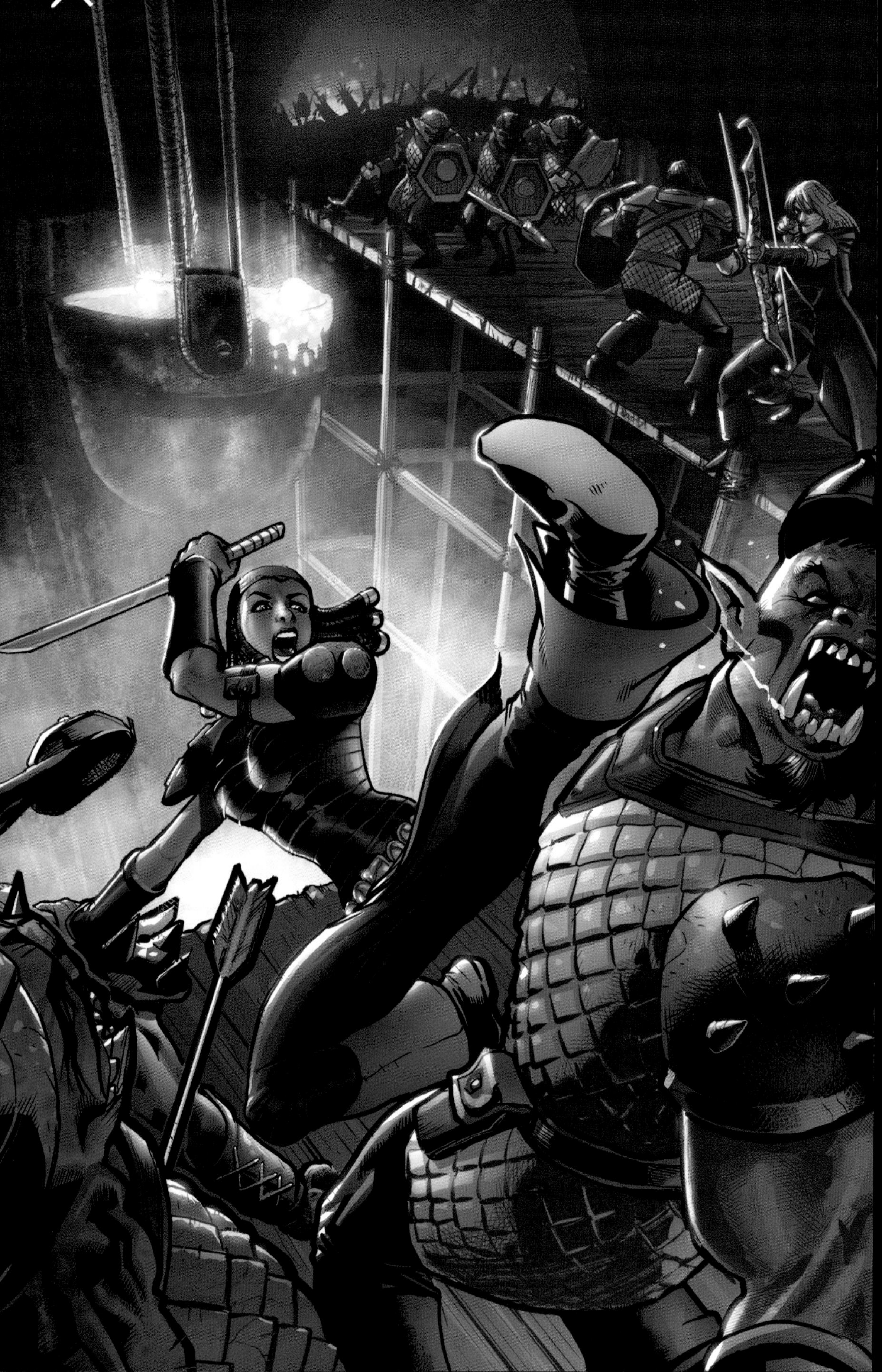

Art by Andrea Di Vito • Colors by Laura Villari

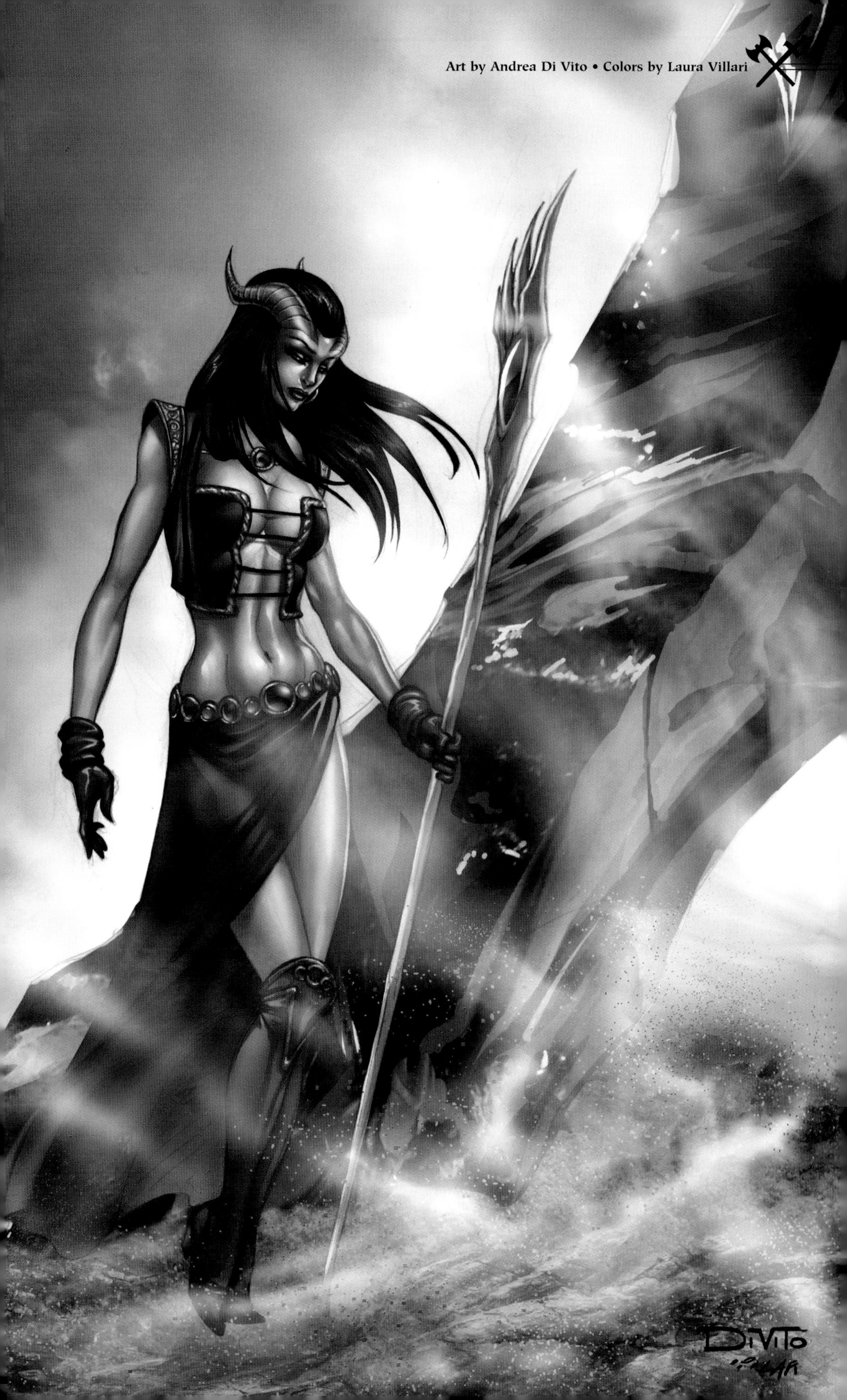
DiVito

Art by Denis Medri • Colors by Paolo Francescutto

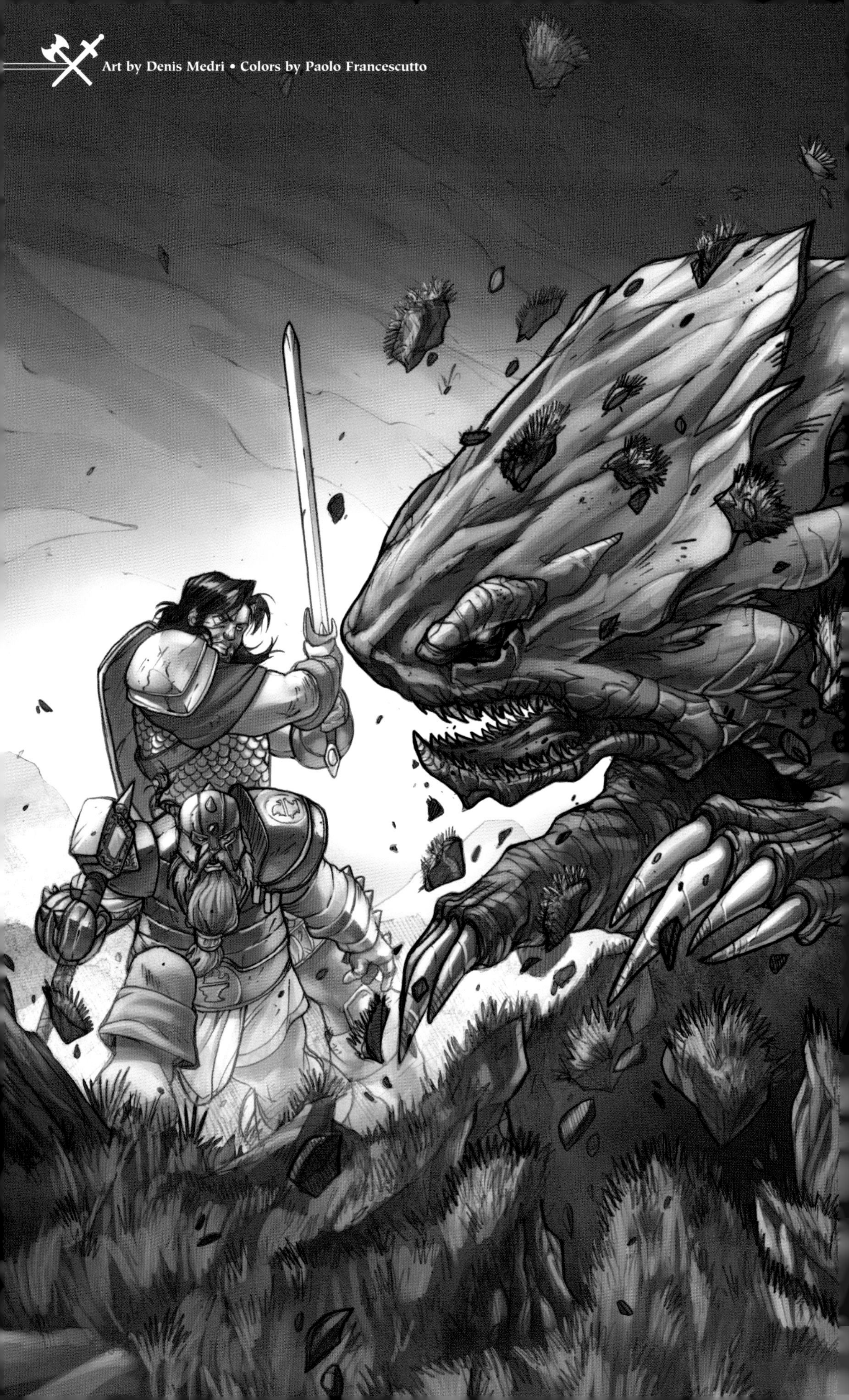

Art by Denis Medri • Colors by Paolo Francescutto

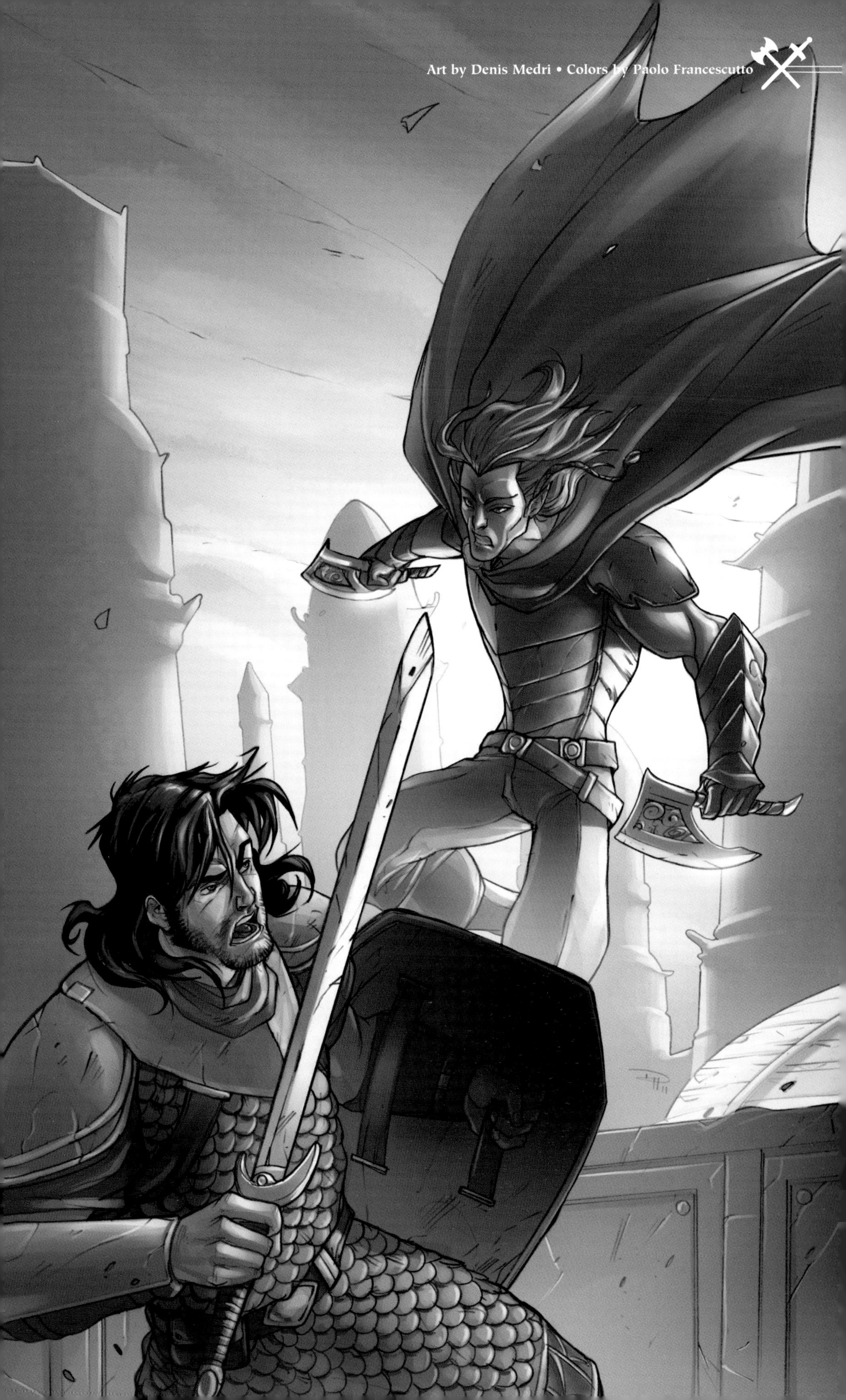

Art by Jorge Lucas

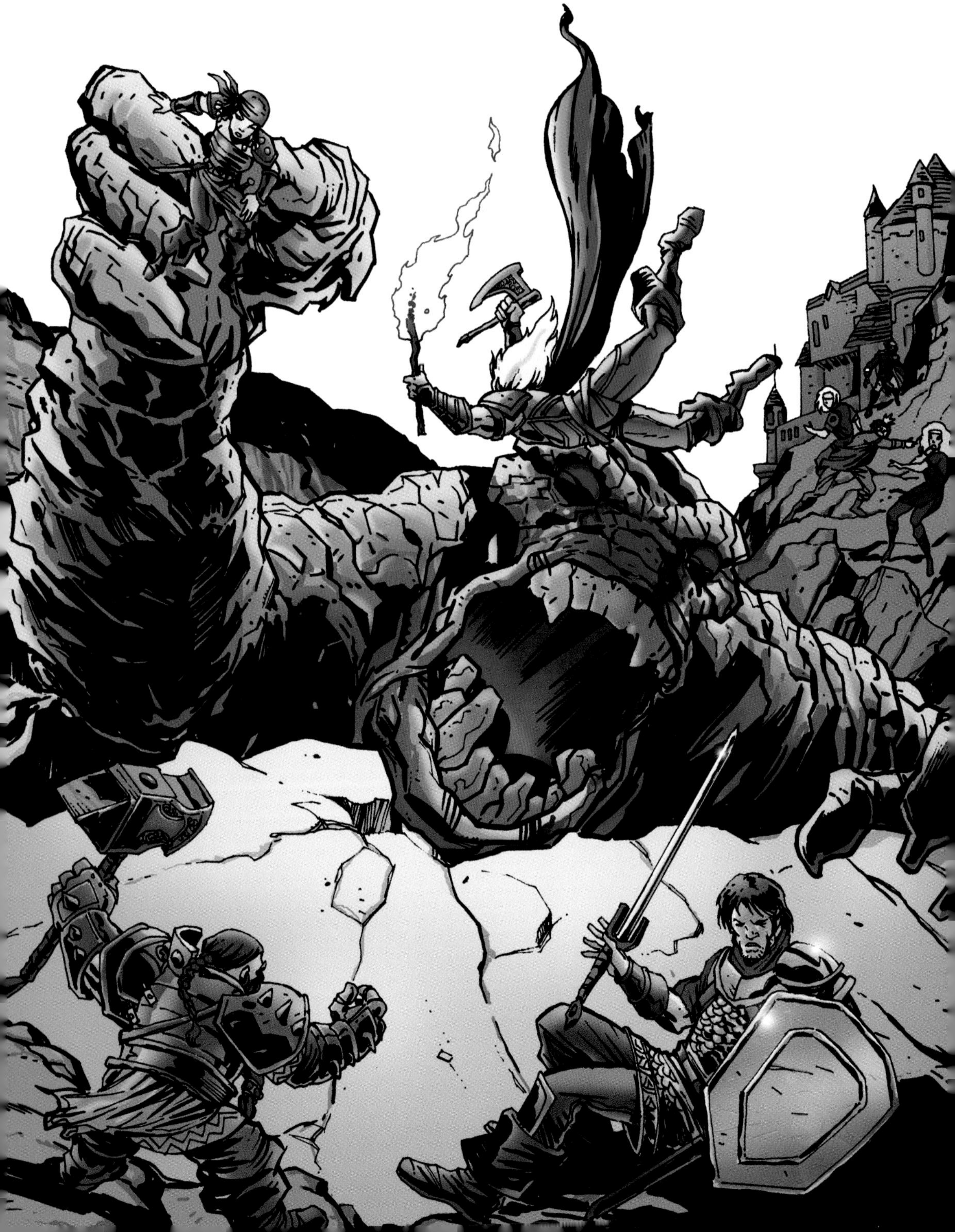

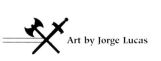

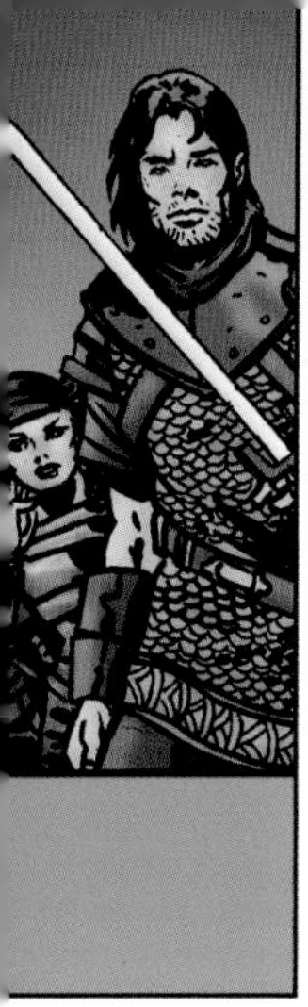

Art by Jorge Lucas

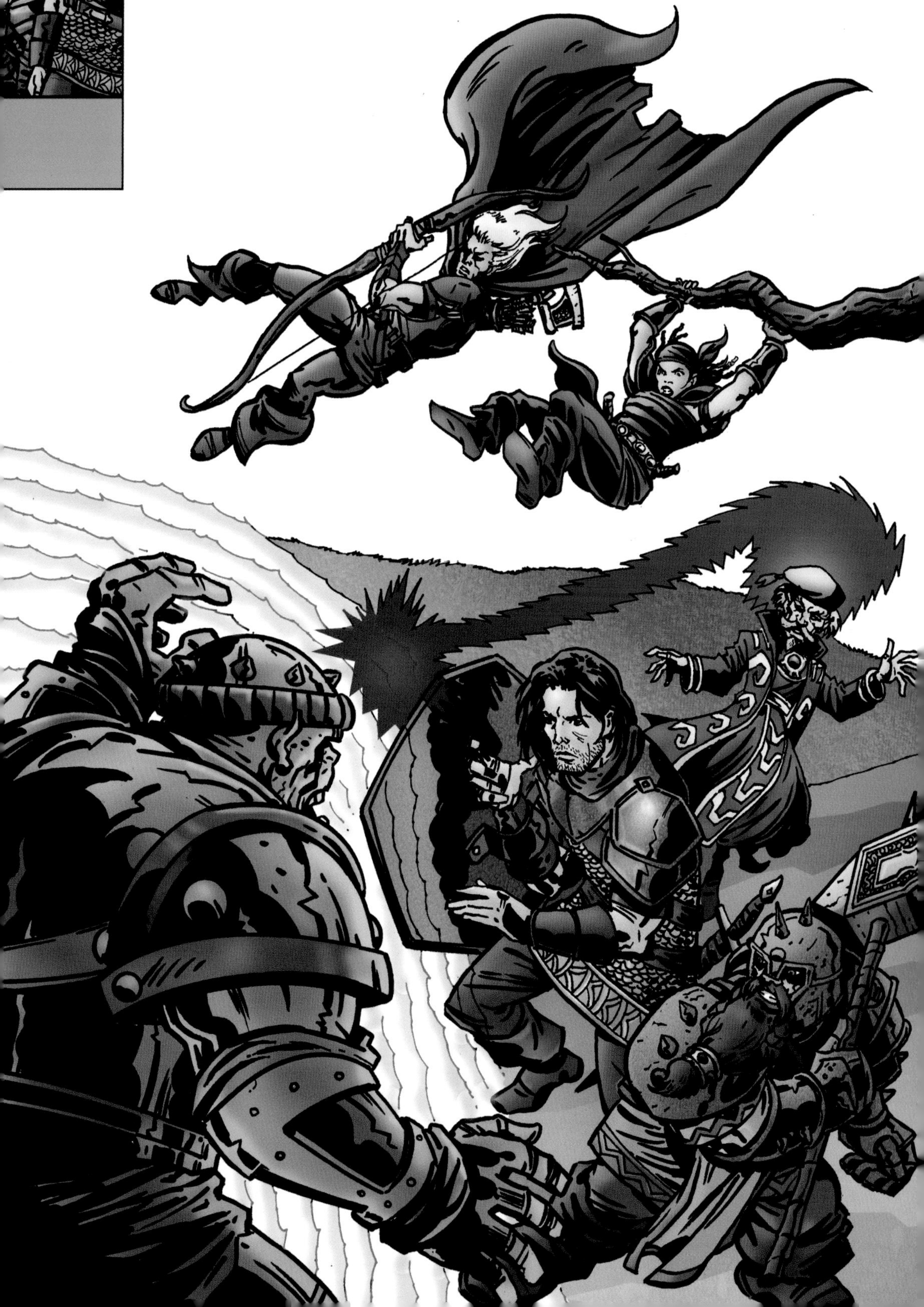

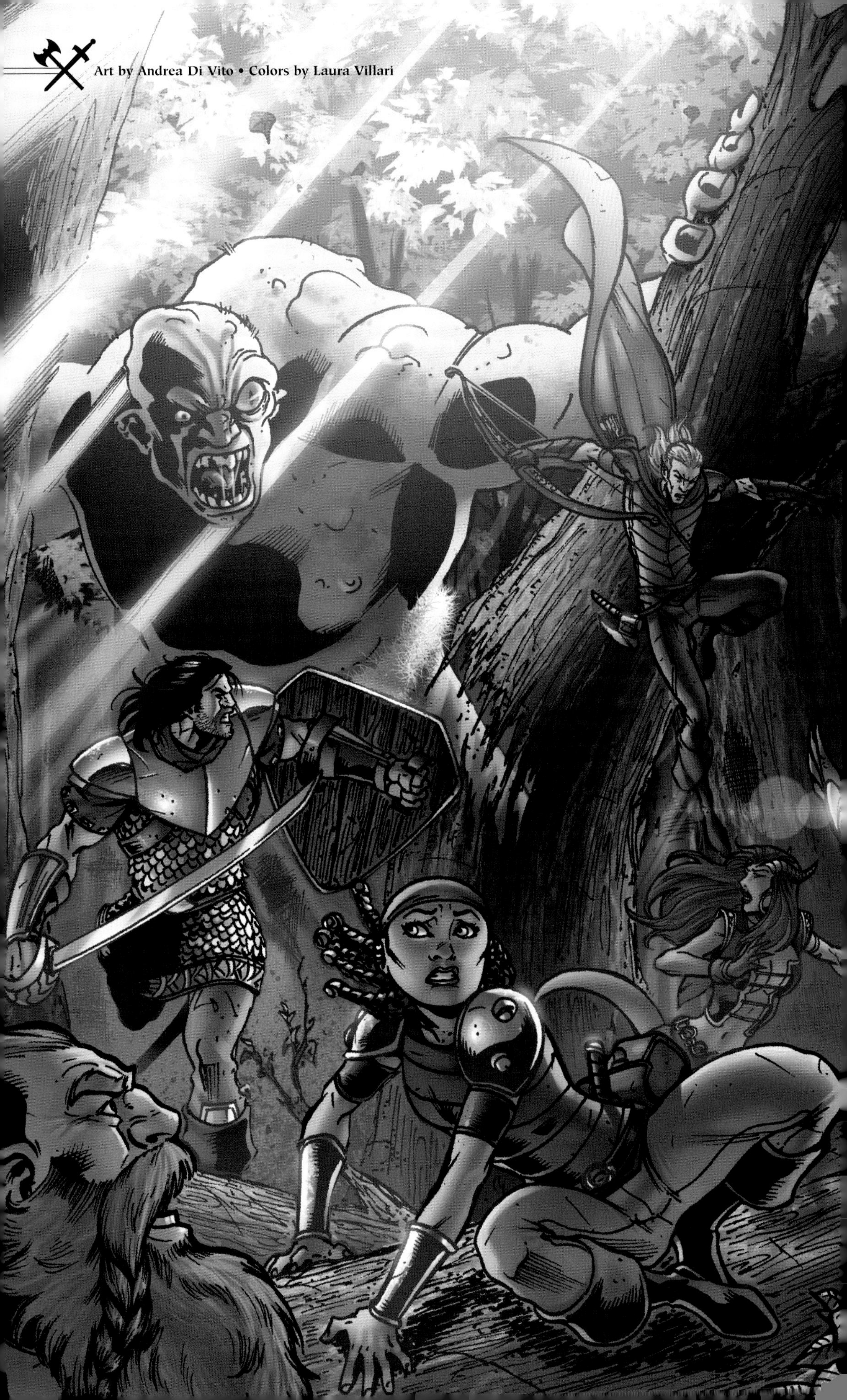

Art by Andrea Di Vito • Colors by Laura Villari

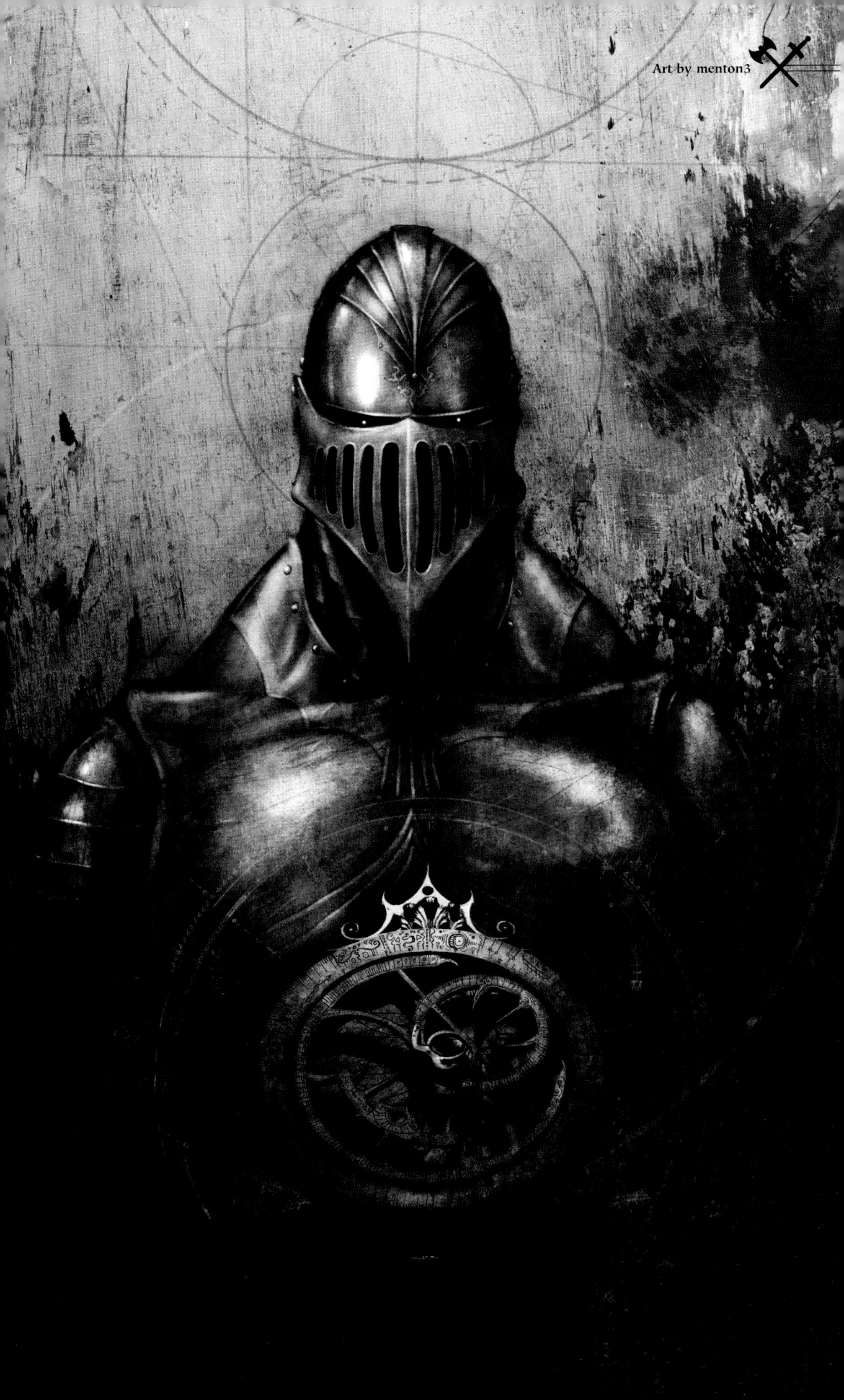

Art by menton3

Art by Steve Ellis

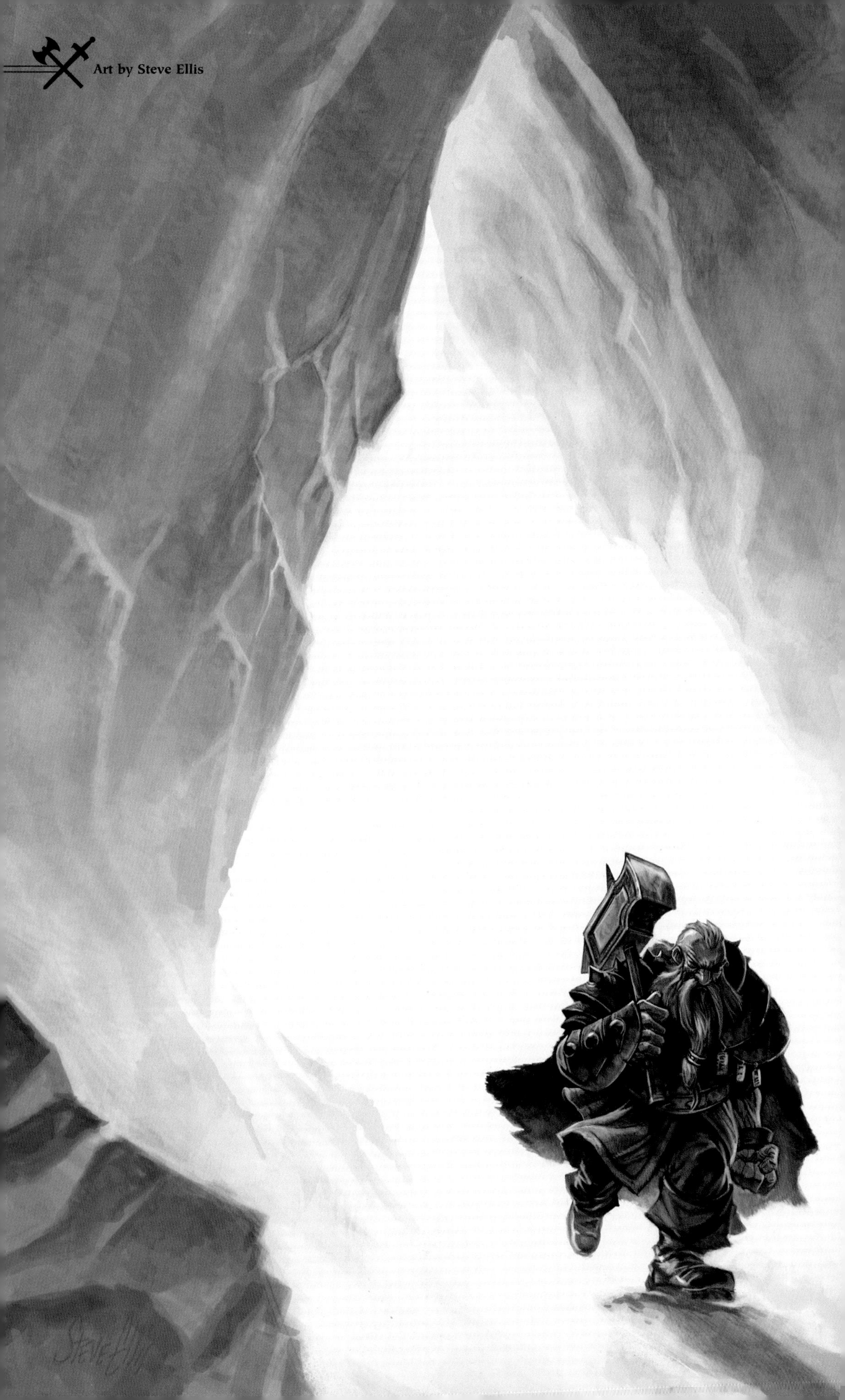

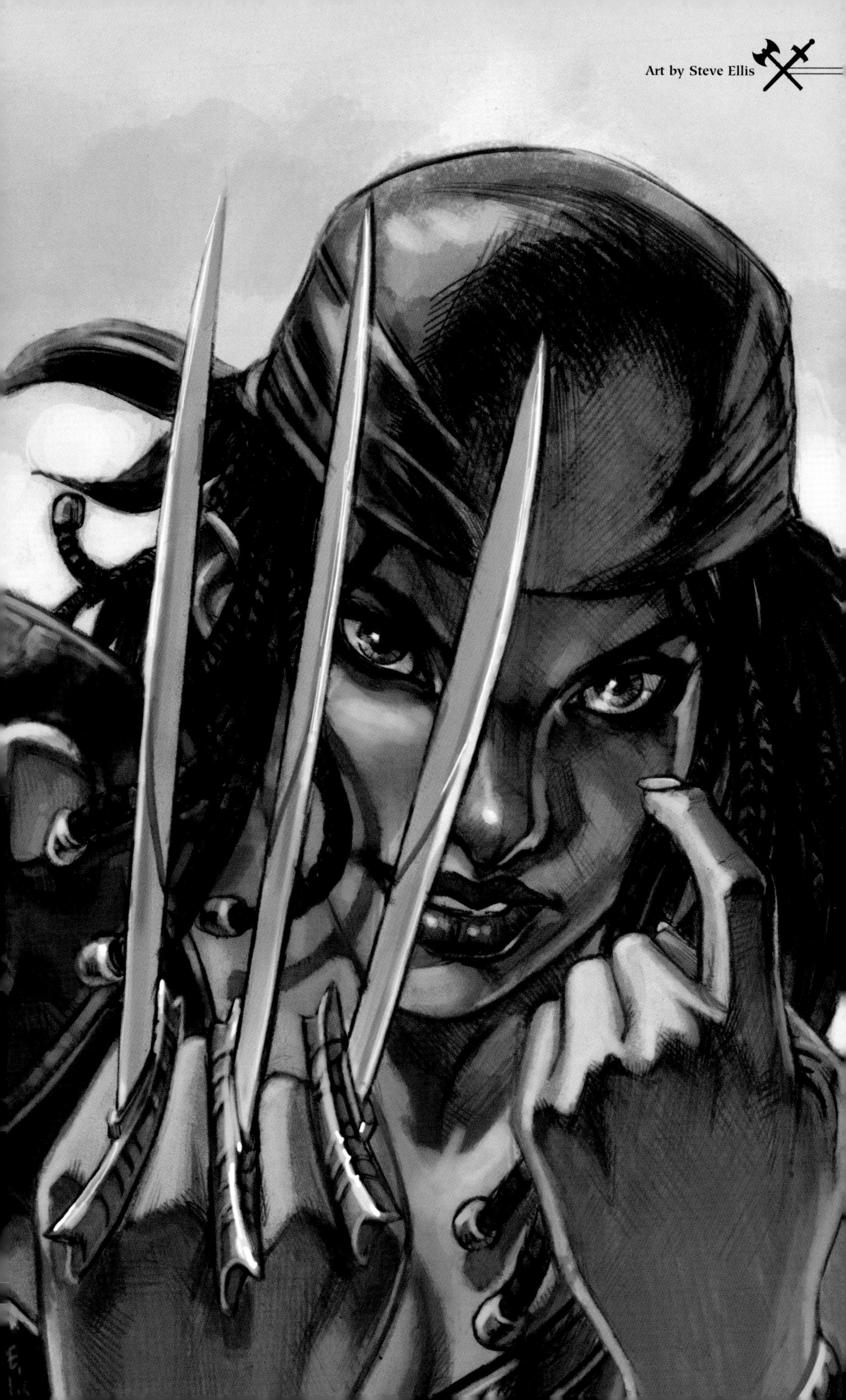

Art by Steve Ellis

Art by Steve Ellis

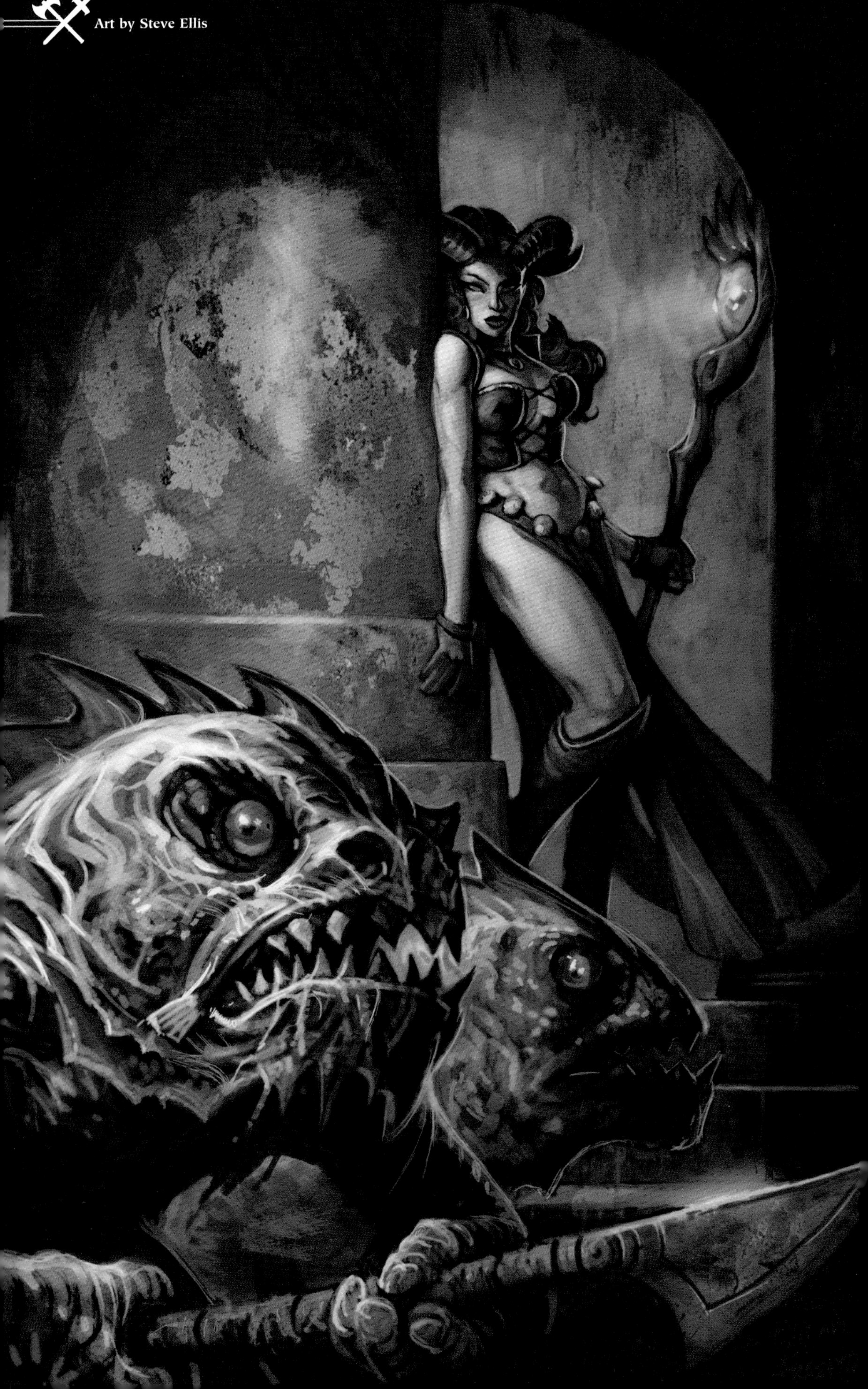

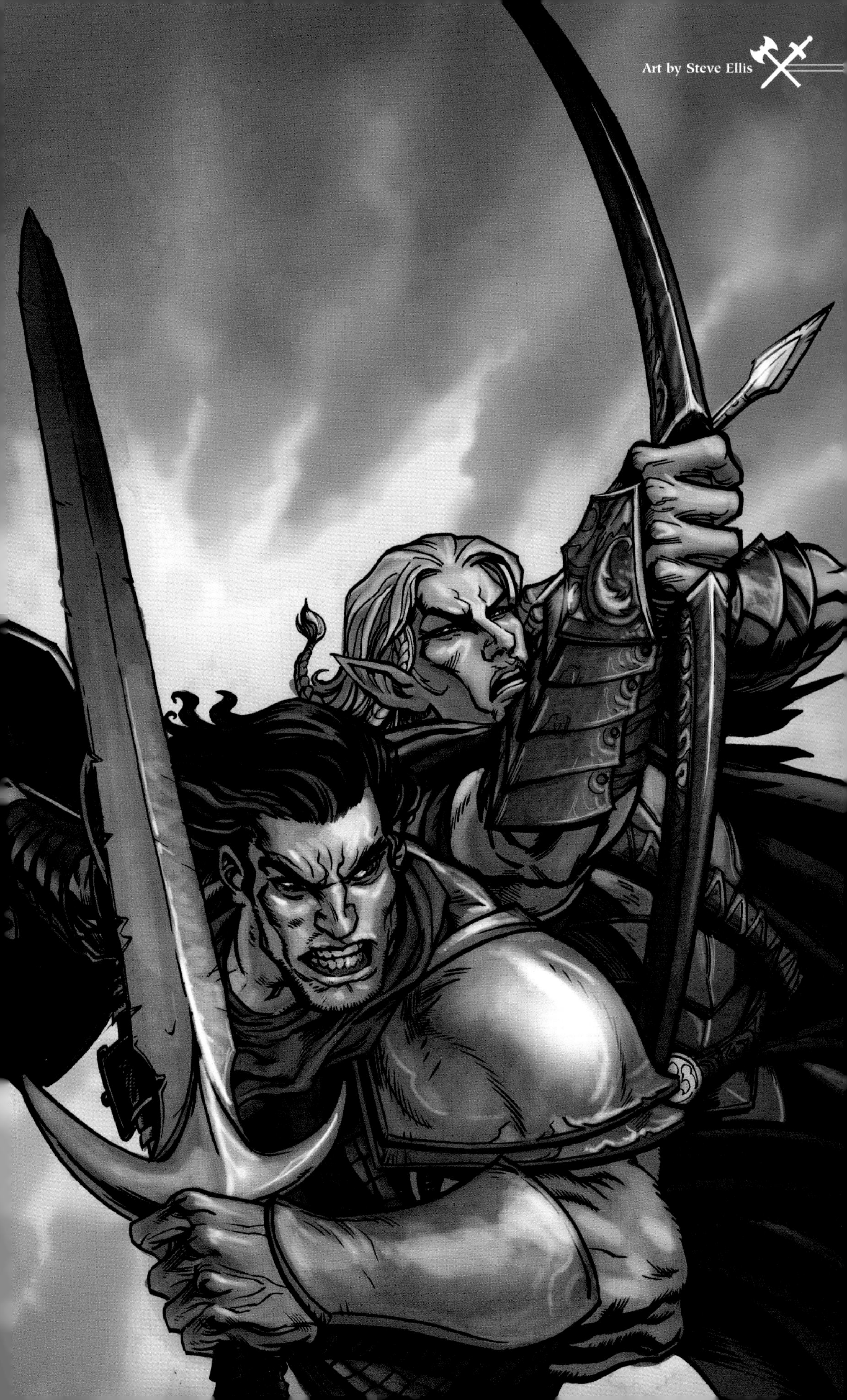
Art by Steve Ellis

SP-1 Featuring ADRIC, KHAL, and other characters!

DUNGEONS & DRAGONS™

Comic & Game Adventure

Bad Day

by John Rogers, Andrea Di Vito, and Bill Slavicsek

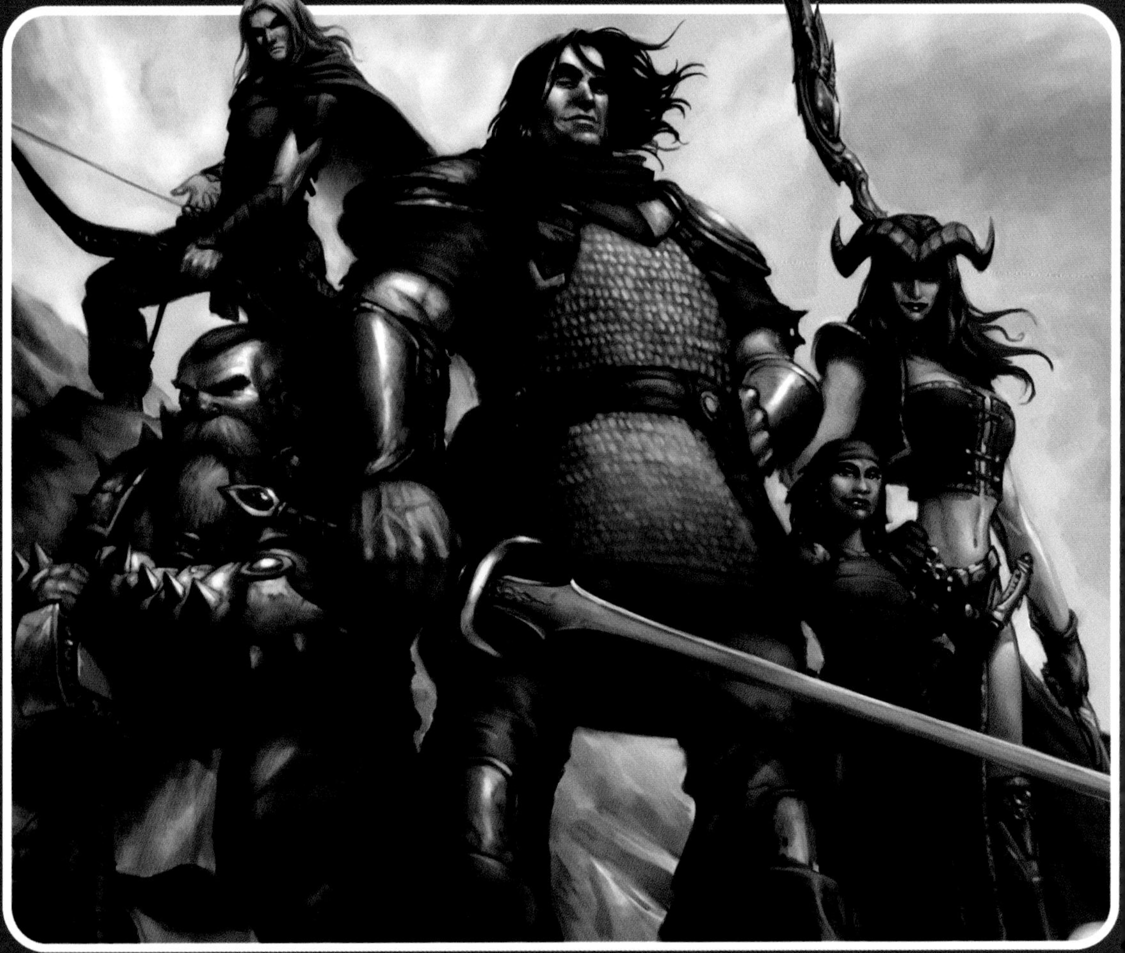

The tavern is alive with drinks shared and talk of adventure. A strange noise emanates from under the floorboards, like giant scurrying rats. Suddenly, zombie-like creatures burst through the floor, sending patrons in all directions. But will you stand and fight?

Licensed By:

IDW · Official Wizards of the Coast Licensed Product · Hasbro

Bad Day
by Bill Slavicsek

Introduction

The new DUNGEONS & DRAGONS comic follows the adventures of Adric and his companions from the town of Fallcrest and into the surrounding countryside of the Nentir Vale and beyond. In Issue #0, they followed gnolls into the Underdark and had to confront a black dragon. And that was just the beginning for the group!

In Issue #1, Adric and his band are having a really Bad Day. It's not just run-of-the-mill bad. It's Epic Bad. We've replicated three of the pivotal scenes in the story in the following three DUNGEONS & DRAGONS roleplaying game encounters. You can use these as the foundation of a longer adventure of your own creation, or you can simply play the three encounters as a short delve that can be used to start off a really bad day for your own band of adventurers.

While Adric and his companions weigh in at the mid to high portion of the heroic tier of play, we've decided to set these encounters at the lower end of the scale, making them perfect for 1st- or 2nd-level adventurers. You can always scale up the encounters if you want to use them to challenge higher-level characters. The *Dungeon Master's Guide* and the *Dungeon Master's Kit* provide guidelines for adjusting the level of encounters.

Adventure Background

These encounters take place in the town of Fallcrest, in the Nentir Vale, as described in the *Dungeon Master's Guide* and the *Dungeon Master's Kit*. You can set it in any town or city in your campaign.

As the adventurers relax between quests at their favorite tavern (in this case, the Staggered Goat), they suddenly get drawn into the middle of strange occurrences that build and build until they're having a really bad day.

Make sure that these encounters take place in a location that the adventurers are familiar with and where they are well known. It doesn't quite work the same if they are anonymous mercenaries just passing through when things start to go bad.

Getting Started

Dungeon Masters need a copy of the DUNGEONS & DRAGONS game rules, which you can find in either the DUNGEONS & DRAGONS *Fantasy Roleplaying Game Starter Set* or the *Dungeon Master's Kit*. Players need a copy of *Heroes of the Fallen Lands* and a character sheet to make characters to use in the adventure.

Once you're ready to begin, check out "Encounter 1: They Came From Beneath the Goat" to get started. And wish your adventurers luck. They're going to need it!

Encounter 1: They Came From Beneath the Goat

Encounter Level 1 (525 XP)

3 zombified townsfolk
9 zombified townsfolk minions

To start the encounter, read:
It's a typical afternoon at the Staggered Goat. The tavern's common room is crowded and noisy, full of leather-clad men and woman of various races, drinking, eating, telling tales, and exchanging secrets in the recessed shadows as far from the Goat's main doors. A barmaid—a lovely half-elf that has served you before—dances toward you with a grin and asks, "What can I get my favorite adventurers this fine afternoon?"

The adventurers are enjoying a much-needed break in the Staggered Goat, a rough-and-tumble tavern in Fallcrest's Lower Quay district. Let the adventurers spend a few moments reminiscing about past exploits, planning upcoming adventures, talking to locals, or even discussing employment opportunities with the other customers before you dive into the heart of the encounter. Here are a couple of roleplaying opportunities you can use while the adventurers are relaxing in the Goat.

Kira the Barmaid

Let the adventurers roleplay chatting with Kira, the half-elf barmaid as she takes their orders. The Goat offers typical tavern fare, including dwarven ale, halfling mead, elven wine, and Nerathi spirits, as well as roasted skewers of meat, chunks of cheese, and loafs of bread.

Kira is friendly and a bit of a flirt, quick with compliments and smiles and lingering touches as she talks, but that only helps make the tips she receives that much more impressive. Hey, even a half-elf barmaid needs to eat and pay the rent!

Cobblegrim

Cobblegrim the dwarf regularly occupies a shadowy booth at the back of the Goat. He's a great source of rumors and he makes a point of knowing who's coming and going in the Lower Quay. For the price of a mug of strong dwarven ale from Hammerfast and a gold piece or two, he's happy to share some of what he knows with anyone who treats him with the deference and respect he feels he deserves.

Cobblegrim has also been known to serve as a broker for local adventurers, hooking up the right team with a wealthy patron whenever the opportunity presents itself. He's a great person to use to send your adventurers off on their next quest for treasure and monster hunting.

Shara Redhair

The tall, striking woman warrior known as Shara leads a group of rival adventurers that includes such notable heroes as Uldane Forden the halfling thief and Albanon the eladrin wizard. She sometimes wanders into the Goat just to see what's going on and to check on the seediest part of the seedier part of town. She can out-drink and out-fight any man or woman in the place, and she often spends an evening or two when she's in town doing just that.

The Bad Day Begins

After you lull the adventurers into a false sense of security with the mundane hustle and bustle of the Staggered Goat, you can then you hit them with the juicy part of this encounter—zombies! Or, more specifically, zombified townsfolk! See "Developments," below, for more information about zombified townsfolk.

When the floor beneath the adventurers breaks open, read:
The floor boards beneath your feet suddenly split apart as something pushes its way up from under the Staggered Goat. Lots of something. Specifically, lots of hands. And arms. And then whole bodies emerge from the newly opened hole. Zombie bodies! The horde of zombies moans as they reach out to grab you.

Tactics

The zombified townsfolk emerge from the hole in the floor to attack the adventurers and anyone else in the tavern. At the beginning of each round, one zombified townsfolk and three minions crawl out of the hole and join the battle. They fight to the death or until the dark energies that have created them run their course.

Development

The townsfolk suffer from a transformation inflicted upon them by energy from the Shadowfell. This energy changes their appearance and befuddles their minds, making them susceptible to the suggestions of the villain behind this foul scheme—the wizard Kurche.

Near the end of the battle, dark energy flows out of the zombified townsfolk and they revert to their natural forms. That's when the dragonborn Captain Gondar and the Fallcrest Guard show up to find that the adventurers have slaughtered innocent citizens.

"In the name of the Lord Warden," Gondar shouts, "hold! You have been caught in the act, and this time you will pay for your crimes!"

The Guard surround the adventurers and take them into custody. It's time to go see the Lord Warden and try to resolve this situation.

Features of the Area

Illumination: Dim light in the tavern.

Crates and Barrels: These are filled with beverages, foodstuffs, and other mundane items. Squares containing crates or barrels are difficult terrain.

Fireplace: A fire burns in the large fireplace. Any creature that enters or starts its turn in the fireplace takes 5 fire damage.

Stairs: The stairs lead to the upper level of the tavern, where a number of small rooms are available for the use of the patrons.

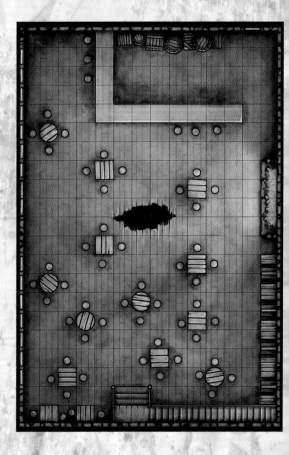

3 Zombified Townsfolk **Level 1 Brute**
Medium natural humanoid   XP 100 each
HP 33; **Bloodied** 16   **Initiative** –1
AC 13, **Fortitude** 14, **Reflex** 11, **Will** 11 **Perception** –1
Speed 4
Traits
Zombie Illusion
    The townsfolk has been infused with dark energy from the
    Shadowfell that makes him or her appear to be a zombie. If
    an adventurer examines a zombified townsfolk closely and
    makes a DC 12 Perception check, he or she notices that the
    zombie isn't rotting or falling apart.
Standard Actions
✦ **Slam ✦ At-Will**
    Attack: Melee 1 (one creature); +6 vs. AC
    Hit: 1d12 + 3 damage, or 1d12 + 8 against a grabbed target.
✦ **Zombie Grasp ✦ At-Will**
    Attack: Melee 1 (one creature); +4 vs. Reflex
    Hit: The zombie grabs the target (escape DC 12) if it does not
    have a creature grabbed.
Str 16 (+3) **Dex** 8 (–1) **Wis** 8 (–1)
Con 13 (+1) **Int** 1 (–5) **Cha** 3 (–4)
Alignment unaligned   **Languages** —

Zombified Townsfolk Minion — Level 5 Minion
Medium natural humanoid   XP 25 each

HP 1; a missed attack never damages a minion. **Initiative** +1
AC 15, **Fortitude** 13, **Reflex** 13, **Will** 11 **Perception** +1
Speed 4

Traits
Zombie Illusion
  The townsfolk has been infused with dark energy from the
  Shadowfell that makes him or her appear to be a zombie. If
  an adventurer examines a zombified townsfolk closely and
  makes a DC 12 Perception check, he or she notices that the
  zombie isn't rotting or falling apart.

Standard Actions
Slam ✦ At-Will
  Attack: Melee 1 (one creature); +7 vs. AC
  Hit: 4 damage.

Str 15 (+2) **Dex** 8 (-1) **Wis** 8 (-1)
Con 12 (+1) **Int** 1 (−5) **Cha** 3 (−4)

Alignment unaligned **Languages** —

Encounter 2: Escape from the Lord Warden's Keep

Encounter Level 4 (875 XP)

Captain Gondar (G)
Lord Warden (W)
6 Fallcrest Guard Pikemen (P)

Assuming the adventurers peacefully accompany
Captain Gondar and the Fallcrest Guard from the
Staggered Goat, they are brought before the Lord
Warden of Fallcrest. The Lord Warden governs the
town from Moonstone Keep, an old castle set atop a
steep-sided hill.

  If the adventurers decide to resist arrest, then
Gondar calls the full weight of the town guard down
upon them. Up to sixty Fallcrest guards can be
roused relatively quickly, and a militia of 350 can be
assembled if necessary. Make it clear that this is a
battle that the adventurers can't win if they attempt
to struggle.

**When the adventurers arrive in the Lord
Warden's hall, read:**
*You are escorted into a large hall within the keep and
brought before the throne of the Lord Warden. He's a
balding, middle-aged man with a keen mind and a dry
wit. Captain Gondar and six Fallcrest Guard surround
you as the dragonborn relates the charges to the Lord
Warden.*

  "Disturbing the peace," Gondar says, "destruction
of property, murder." He points toward the body on
the nearby table, one of the zombies that attacked you
at the Goat. The body appears to be that of a normal
human. Dead, but normal nonetheless.

Roleplaying the Encounter
This encounter starts out as a roleplaying encounter,
wherein Gondar presents the charges against the
adventurers, the Lord Warden asks some questions,
and the adventurers attempt to explain themselves.

  "Let's be frank," the Lord Warden says, "the
town welcomes adventurers and I expect a certain
amount of murder. I encourage it, in fact, as long

as it is properly directed. Outward. At brigands and
monsters. Not at the citizenry."

  The Lord Warden acts reasonably. Gondar does
his best to expose the adventurers for the murderers
he believes them to be. And the Fallcrest Guard look
on with impassive expressions and deadly looking
polearms.

  After everyone has had their say, the door to
the hall swings open and the gnome known as
Copernicus Jinx enters the chamber. "I'm horrified to
hear of this unspeakable tragedy, and I have sensed
a magical disturbance this day. Something dark.
Allow me to get to the heart of the matter."

  Jinx examines the corpse and explains that the
man was infected with shadow. More specifically,
he was infused with the energy of the Shadowfell.
Someone has opened a portal, and dark energies are
flooding through.

Dark Energies
As Jinx finishes his explanation of what he believes
has befallen Fallcrest, Gondar, the Lord Warden,
and the guards are suddenly gripped by terrible
convulsions. Read:

*Dark energies begin to leak from the eyes of the Lord
Warden and the guards, and even the mighty Gondar
seems to be caught in the grip of the shadow magic.
As the convulsions end, the group begins to moan and
turn toward you. That's when Gondar unleashes his
fiery breath weapon at you …*

Tactics
As soon as the Lord Warden and his guards change
into zombies, they attack the adventurers. Even
though the Fallcrest defenders have been zombified,
their training remains as a reflex, and they continue
to employ the weapons and tactics that they are
used to.

Development
After a round of battle, Jinx shouts out, "The portal's
open and more shadow is flooding through. I warded
you against it, and you're welcome, by the way.
Don't kill the guards. They're just possessed. Now
get out of here and find that portal!"

  If the adventurers can move through the doors or
windows, they escape from the keep.

Features of the Area
  Illumination: Bright light from the braziers.
  Gates: The metal gates are down, blocking the
path out of the hall. A DC 19 Strength check is
required to lift a gate.
  Braziers: Fire burns in these large metal bowls.
A brazier can be tipped (DC 12 Strength check)
to cause a close burst 1. Any creature in the burst
takes 5 fire damage and ongoing 5 fire damage (save
ends).
  Doors: The doors lead to lower and higher levels
of the keep.
  Windows: The windows look out upon the keep's
courtyard, 20 feet below.

Captain Gondar (G)   Level 3 Soldier
Medium natural humanoid, dragonborn   XP 150
HP 47; **Bloodied** 23   **Initiative** +4
AC 19, **Fortitude** 16, **Reflex** 15, **Will** 14 **Perception** +2
Speed 5
Standard Actions
⚔ **Longsword** (weapon) ✦ **At-Will**
  Attack: Melee 1 (one creature); +9 vs. AC, or +10 vs. AC while
  the dragonborn is bloodied.
  Hit: 1d8 + 7 damage.
Minor Actions
🔥 **Dragon Breath** (fire) ✦ **Encounter**
  Attack: Close blast 3 (creatures in the blast); +7 vs. Reflex
  Hit: 1d6 + 2 fire damage.
Str 16 (+4) **Dex** 15 (+3) **Wis** 12 (+2)
Con 15 (+3) **Int** 11 (+1) **Cha** 9 (+0)
Alignment unaligned **Languages** Common, Draconic
Equipment scale armor, light shield, longsword

Zombified Lord Warden (W)   Level 2 Controller
Medium natural humanoid, human   XP 125
HP 37; **Bloodied** 18   **Initiative** +2
AC 16, **Fortitude** 12, **Reflex** 12, **Will** 14 **Perception** +1
Speed 4
Traits
☼ **Shroud of Shadow** ✦ **Aura 3**
  Within the aura, bright light is dim light, and dim light is
  darkness. Any enemy that enters the aura or starts its turn
  there takes 5 cold damage.
Zombie Illusion
  The townsfolk has been infused with dark energy from the
  Shadowfell that makes him or her appear to be a zombie. If
  an adventurer examines a zombified townsfolk closely and
  makes a DC 12 Perception check, he or she notices that the
  zombie isn't rotting or falling apart.
Standard Actions
⊕ **Slam** ✦ **At-Will**
  Attack: Melee 1 (one creature); +7 vs. AC
  Hit: 1d8 + 5 damage and the target is slowed (save ends).
Str 12 (+2) **Dex** 17 (+4) **Wis** 11 (+1)
Con 13 (+2) **Int** 10 (+1) **Cha** 12 (+2)
Alignment unaligned   **Languages** —

6 Zombified Pikemen (P)   Level 1 Soldier
Medium natural humanoid, human   XP 100 each
HP 31; **Bloodied** 15 **Initiative** +4
AC 17, **Fortitude** 14, **Reflex** 13, **Will** 11 **Perception** +2
Speed 4
Zombie Illusion
  The townsfolk has been infused with dark energy from the
  Shadowfell that makes him or her appear to be a zombie. If
  an adventurer examines a zombified townsfolk closely and
  makes a DC 12 Perception check, he or she notices that the
  zombie isn't rotting or falling apart.
Standard Actions
⊕ **Halberd** (weapon) ✦ **At-Will**
  Attack: Melee 2 (one creature); +6 vs. AC
  Hit: 1d10 + 2 damage, and the pikeman marks the target until
  the end of the pikeman's next turn.
⚔ **Powerful Strike** (weapon) ✦ **Recharge 5 6**
  Attack: Melee 2 (one creature); +6 vs. AC
  Hit: 2d10 + 2 damage, and the target falls prone.
Triggered Actions
⚔ **Interceding Strike** (weapon) ✦ **At-Will**
  Trigger: An enemy marked by the pikeman makes an attack
  that doesn't include it as a target.
  Attack (Immediate Interrupt): Melee 2 (triggering enemy); +6
  vs. AC
Hit: 1d10 + 2 damage.
Str 16 (+3) **Dex** 14 (+2) **Wis** 11 (+0)
Con 15 (+2) **Int** 10 (+0) **Cha** 12 (+1)
Alignment unaligned   **Languages** —
Equipment chainmail, halberd

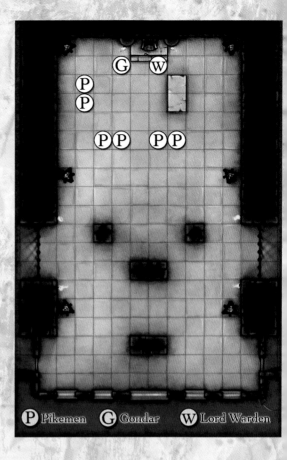

P Pikemen   **G** Gondar   **W** Lord Warden

Encounter 3: Burning Down the Orphanarium

Encounter Level 3 (754 XP)

3 zombified bashers
8 zombified gnashers

Throughout Fallcrest, the dark energies of the
Shadowfell have transformed the townsfolk into
zombies—or at least zombie-like creatures! The
adventurers must navigate through the town,
evading or fighting off zombified townsfolk, as
they search for the mysterious portal that Jinx has
pointed them toward. Along the way, they begin
to notice that the possessed people are all heading
toward the river, and that provides a direction for
the adventurers to follow.

  In addition, a character can make a DC 19 Arcana
check to sense that the dark energy spewing portal
to the Shadowfell is somewhere inside one of the
warehouses along the coast of the river.

  Feel free to run as many scenes between
Moonstone Keep and the docks of the Lower Quay
as you want, but eventually the adventurers reach a
burning warehouse that rises over the river. Read:

*In your search for the portal you notice that all of
the possessed townsfolk are running in the same*

direction—toward the Nentir River. One of the buildings on the riverside is on fire. That's probably not a coincidence. Moreover, the building houses the Orphanarium, where the orphaned children of Fallcrest are cared for. You sense that the portal is within the burning building, where a warehouse full of possessed children are about to be roasted alive.

Time to head into the Orphanarium and save the possessed children!

Inside the Burning Building

When the adventurers enter the Orphanarium, they are greeted by fire and smoke. Don't place any of the zombified townsfolk on the map yet. They appear in their assigned squares after the adventurers get a sense of the situation. Read:

Double doors open into a large open space that reminds you of the lobby of a fine inn—except for the smoke and flames of the fire. To the left, a long desk is unattended, and beyond it a wide staircase climbs to the second floor. Low benches are set against the far walls, and to your right several crates and barrels have been piled neatly so that they reach almost to the ceiling. You can hear cries and moans drifting down from the upper levels of the burning building.

Once the adventurers enter the burning building and begin looking around, the adult zombified bashers (possessed Orphanarium workers) emerge from their hiding places behind the front desk and the piled crates.

After a round of dealing with the fire and the bashers, the zombified gnashers (possessed orphans) leap down from above into the marked squares.

The Fire

The fire has not yet engulfed the building, but it is well on its way. Any creature that enters a burning square or starts its turn there takes 5 fire damage.

A character can attempt to douse a square of fire with a DC 19 Athletics check or a DC 12 Dungeoneering or Nature check. This requires a minor action and the character must be adjacent to the burning square. A character can attempt this up to three times in a round.

Tactics

The zombified bashers emerge from hiding to pound on the intruding adventurers. If possible, a basher attempts to push an adventurer into a burning square every time it hits.

The zombified gnashers leap down from above and try to swarm an adventurer. A gnasher uses its gnashing bite as soon as possible to attempt to clamp its teeth into a target. Note that multiple gnashers will attempt to clamp onto the same target,

thus increasing the ongoing damage that target takes each round. One save stops all ongoing damage.

Development

When only a few of the zombified townsfolk remain, the adventurers hear and feel a great rumble emerging from beneath the Orphanarium. This can happen whenever you want, but a good time for it is when only one basher or two gnashers remain active. Read:

Suddenly the entire building begins to shake as a great noise rumbles up from beneath your feet. The flash of a huge fireball and the sound of a terrible ka-boom follow the terrible rumble, and everything around you begins to collapse and fall!

Next?

If that isn't the start of a really bad day, we don't know what is! Find out what happens next by checking out issue #2 of the DUNGEONS & DRAGONS comic. In the meantime, use this set of encounters as the beginning of your own adventure about shadow portals and possessed townsfolk. The adventure is in your hands …

Features of the Area

Illumination: Bright light from the fire.
Front Desk: The long desk is 4 feet tall.
Fire: Any creature that enters a burning square or starts its turn there takes 5 fire damage.
Stairs: The wide stairs lead up to the Orphanarium's second level.
Crates and Barrels: These are stacked 10 feet high and filled with foodstuffs, clothing, blankets, and other mundane items donated to the Orphanarium. Squares containing crates or barrels are blocking terrain.

3 Zombified Bashers (Z)	Level 3 Brutes
Medium natural humanoid	XP 150 each
HP 54; Bloodied 27	Initiative +0
AC 15, Fortitude 15, Reflex 13, Will 13	Perception +0, Speed 4

Traits
Zombie Illusion
   The townsfolk has been infused with dark energy from the Shadowfell that makes him or her appear to be a zombie. If an adventurer examines a zombified townsfolk closely and makes a DC 12 Perception check, he or she notices that the zombie isn't rotting or falling apart.
Standard Actions
⊕ **Bash ✦ At-Will**
   Attack: Melee 1 (one creature); +8 vs. AC
   Hit: 1d12 + 7 damage, and the target is pushed 1 square.
Str 18 (+5) **Dex** 8 (+0) **Wis** 8 (+0)
Con 14 (+3) **Int** 1 (−4) **Cha** 3 (−3)

Alignment unaligned   **Languages** —

8 Zombified Gnashers   Level 3 Minions
Medium natural humanoid   XP 100 each
HP 1; a missed attack never damages a minion.
Initiative −1
AC 13, **Fortitude** 14, **Reflex** 11, **Will** 11 **Perception** +3
Speed 4
Traits
Zombie Illusion
   The townsfolk has been infused with dark energy from the
   Shadowfell that makes him or her appear to be a zombie. If
   an adventurer examines a zombified townsfolk closely and
   makes a DC 12 Perception check, he or she notices that the
   zombie isn't rotting or falling apart.
Standard Actions
⊕ **Bite ✦ At-Will**
   Attack: Melee 1 (one creature); +8 vs. AC
   Hit: 6 damage, and the gnasher shifts 1 square.
⨪ **Gnashing Bite ✦ Encounter**
   Attack: Melee 1 (one creature); +7 vs. Fortitude
   Hit: 6 damage, and ongoing 3 damage (save ends) as the
   gnasher locks onto the target with its jaws and holds on tight.
   Increase this ongoing damage by 1 for each gnasher that locks
   onto the same target.
Str 15 (+3) **Dex** 8 (+1) **Wis** 8 (+1)
Con 12 (+2) **Int** 1 (−4) **Cha** 3 (−3)

Alignment unaligned   **Languages** —

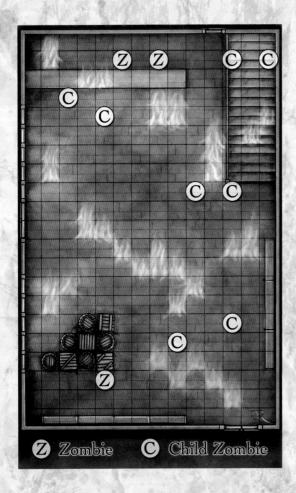

Ⓩ Zombie   Ⓒ Child Zombie

SP-2 Featuring ADRIC, KHAL, and other characters!

DUNGEONS & DRAGONS™

Comic & Game Adventure

Hide in Plain Sight

by John Rogers, Andrea Di Vito, and Christopher Perkins

The orphanarium is engulfed in flames and sinking into the depths of the river. Meanwhile, a dark ritual is being performed in caves beneath the building, possessing the orphans within. Can you save the children and stop the malevolent ceremony?

Licensed By:

Comic and Game Adventure

Hide in Plain Sight

Design by Christopher Perkins
Cartography by Jonathan Roberts

Introduction

The new DUNGEONS & DRAGONS® comic follows the adventures of Adric and his companions. In Issue #1, they defended the town of Fallcrest against a horde of zombies, only to discover (to their horror) that the zombies were actually townsfolk transformed by the dark energies of a Shadowfell portal hidden beneath a burning riverside warehouse.

In this issue, Adric and company rescue several orphans trapped in the burning building and come face-to-face with the villain responsible for opening the Shadowfell portal: a doppelganger wizard named Kurche. Kurche flees and infiltrates a merchant caravan, and that's when things go from bad to worse.

We've replicated three of the pivotal scenes in the story in the following three encounters. You can use these encounters as the continuation of the previous adventure, the foundation of a longer adventure of your own creation, or a short stand-alone adventure.

While Adric and his companions weigh in at the mid-to-high portion of the heroic tier of play, we've decided to set these encounters at the lower end of the scale, making them perfect for 1st- or 2nd-level adventurers. You can always scale up the encounters if you want to challenge higher-level characters. *The Dungeon Master's Guide*® and the *Dungeon Master's Kit*™ provide guidelines for adjusting the level of encounters.

Adventure Background

This adventure picks up where the Issue #1 adventure left off.

The following encounters take place outside the town of Fallcrest, in the Nentir Vale, as described in the *Dungeon Master's Guide* and the *Dungeon Master's Kit*. The setting is generic so that you can place the adventure near any town or city in your campaign.

The first encounter ("Trouble Below") opens with the heroes discovering a hidden cave beneath the burning warehouse. Realizing that his work in Fallcrest is done, Kurche the doppelganger makes a hasty retreat and leaves the heroes to clean up the mess. The second encounter ("Doppelganger Season") is a skill challenge in which the heroes follow Kurche's trail, leading them to a merchant caravan under attack by a ruthless band of orcs ("Gruhn's Gang"). How they fare in the skill challenge determines the difficulty

of the third and final encounter.

Getting Started

Dungeon Masters need a copy of the *Dungeons & Dragons Roleplaying Game* rules, which you can find in either the *Dungeons & Dragons Fantasy Roleplaying Game Starter Set* or the *Dungeon Master's Kit* boxed set. Players need a copy of *Heroes of the Fallen Lands*™ and a character sheet to make characters to use in the adventure.

Once you're ready to begin, jump right into the action with "Encounter 1: Trouble Below."

Encounter 1: Trouble Below

Encounter Level 1 (725 XP)

Kurche, doppelganger wizard (K)
1 explosion (see "Features of the Area")
1 pit trap (see "Features fo the Area")

This encounter begins when the adventurers descend through a hole in the floor of the burning warehouse. The hole opens into an old smugglers' cave hidden underneath the warehouse.

Please read this encounter carefully, as there are a number of features that come into play during the encounter.

You need to keep track of the number of rounds that pass. At the beginning of the second round, burning timbers fall through the hole in the ceiling, dealing damage to anyone underneath and blocking that means of escape. An explosion occurs at the beginning of the fifth round, and the building overhead collapses at the start of the tenth round (see "Features of the Area" for details).

The pit trap remains hidden until triggered or otherwise discovered.

To start the encounter, read:
An evil power has turned many of Fallcrest's citizens into zombie-like horrors, and all signs point to a riverside warehouse south of town. The warehouse, now an orphanage, has caught on fire, and as you evacuate the last of the children from the doomed building, falling timbers punch a hole through the ground floor, revealing a secret cave underneath! From somewhere deep below, you hear maniacal laughter.

There's nothing more that can be seen or heard in the burning warehouse. Due to smoke and other debris, the adventurers must lower themselves down into the hole to investigate further.

It's a 10-foot drop from the warehouse to the floor of the cave below. Characters take 1d10 damage from the fall unless they use a move action to carefully lower themselves or make a trained Acrobatics check to negate the damage.

When the adventurers descend into the cave through the hole in the ceiling, read:

You discover an old smugglers' cave filled with crates and barrels. A circle of stones dominates the middle of the cave, and a pulsating sphere of dark energy hovers in the middle of the circle. A wizard cackles nearby, clearly enamored with the terror he has wrought.

The adventurers begin the encounter in the corner of the cave below the hole in the ceiling.

Tactics

The doppelganger uses *fireball* and follows up with *color spray*. Once per round, it uses *shiv* against an enemy that makes a melee attack against it. It uses its action points to aid its escape.

The doppelganger flees when first bloodied and covers its escape with *fireball*, if necessary. A *fireball* detonated inside the tunnel connecting the smugglers' cave to the river has the side effect of weakening the section of tunnel caught in the burst, creating a zone that lasts until the end of the encounter. Any creature that enters or starts its turn in the zone takes 2 damage from collapsing detritus.

Development

The heroes receive full XP whether they kill the doppelganger or drive it off. Subsequent encounters hinge on the doppelganger escaping with its life. If the adventurers prevent the doppelganger from escaping and it's captured or killed, you can skip the next encounter and save the final encounter for a future occasion. (You never know when you might need an orc ambush!)

Features of the Area

Illumination: Torches provide bright light.

Boat: A small boat with a pole is tethered to the end of the dock that runs alongside the warehouse. The boat can seat up to four Medium creatures and has a speed of 4.

Ceiling: The ceiling is 10 feet high in the cave and feet high in the tunnel.

At the beginning of the second round of combat, burning timbers fall through the hole in the cave ceiling, attacking anyone in the 4 squares directly underneath. The building overhead is collapsing, and the ceiling hole becomes plugged by flaming debris that cannot be cleared.

Free Action
Falling Timbers (fire) ✦ **Encounter**
Attack: 2-square-by-2-square section under the hole in the ceiling (creatures in the area) +4 vs. Reflex
Hit: 1d6 + 6 damage, and the target is restrained and takes ongoing 2 fire damage (save ends both).
Miss: The target is restrained and takes ongoing 2 fire damage (save ends both).

Crates and Barrels: The barrels are filled with

To Fallcrest

Hole Up

S

Ⓚ

Ⓚ Kurche

molasses and oil, while the crates contain foodstuffs and other mundane items. Hidden among the crates and barrels is a random level 1 treasure (see "Treasure" in the Dungeon Master's Guide or the Dungeon Master's Kit). Squares containing crates or barrels are difficult terrain.

Doors: A set of locked wooden doors lead from the cave to a staircase that used to lead up to the warehouse. A fire in the warehouse has filled the staircase with flaming debris that requires 20 standard actions to clear. The doors can be unlocked with the proper key (see "Secret Room" below) or a DC 20 Thievery check. The doors can also be forced open with a DC 18 Strength check.

Explosion: At the beginning of the fifth round of combat, a large explosion rocks the building above. The double doors are blown open by a sudden wave of flames, heat, and debris. Any creature occupying the 2-square-by-3-square area on either side of the doors is attacked. Characters in the pit (see below) have partial cover against the attack.

Free Action
Explosion (fire) ✦ **Encounter**
Attack: Blast 3 originating from the double doors (creatures in the blast) +4 vs. Reflex
Hit: 1d8 + 11 fire damage, and the target falls prone.
Miss: Half damage, and the target does not fall prone.

Pit Trap: This pit trap is disguised to look like a normal section of floor. Creatures adjacent to the pit can detect it with a successful DC 18 Perception check. (Use passive Perception scores unless the creatures are actively searching for traps.) The pit stays open once activated and is 20 feet deep.

Free Action
Pit Trap ✦ Encounter
Trigger: A creature enters the pit's space.
Attack (Free Action): Melee 0 (the triggering creature) +4 vs. Reflex
Hit: 2d10 damage, and the target falls prone at the bottom of the pit.
Miss: The target returns to the last square it occupied.
Effect: The pit is no longer hidden.

Secret Room: Near the pit trap is a small secret room. Characters can detect the secret door with a DC 18 Perception check. (Use passive Perception scores unless a character is actively searching for secret doors.) The room is empty except for a wooden lever set into the far wall. The lever can be used to reset the pit trap or lock the pit's trap doors, thereby allowing creatures to enter the pit's space without triggering the trap.

Hanging on the lever is an iron key on a loop of frayed rope. This key unlocks the doors that lead up to the warehouse (see "Doors" above).

Summoning Stones: In the middle of the cave is a circle of jagged stones. A successful DC 16 Arcana check confirms that the area within the circle is suffused with dark energy seeping in from the Shadowfell. Any creature that enters or starts its turn in the circle takes 5 necrotic damage and is weakened until the end of its current turn. Once the doppelganger flees or is slain, the circle of stones loses its magical traits and is safe to enter.

Tunnel: This partly flooded tunnel connects the old smugglers' cave to the river. The water hinders movement through the tunnel, which is difficult terrain. The mouth of the tunnel is obscured by reeds and requires a DC 14 Perception check to spot from outside.

Wooden Pilings: Six wooden beams support a burning warehouse that partly overhangs the river. The building collapses into the river at the start of the tenth round. Until it collapses, any creature underneath the burning building takes 5 damage at the start of its turn from falling debris. The area between the pilings is treated as difficult terrain because of the wreckage.

Doppelganger Wizard (K)   **Level 2**
Solo Skirmisher
Medium natural humanoid   XP 625
HP 148; **Bloodied** 74   **Initiative** +5
AC 16, **Fortitude** 13, **Reflex** 15, **Will** 14 **Perception** +7
Speed 6
Saving Throws +5; **Action Points** 2
Traits
Focused Mind
    Any dazed or stunned effects on the doppelganger end at the start of its turn.
Shadow Stride
    If the doppelganger moves at least 3 squares from its starting position on its turn, it gains concealment until the start of its next turn.
Standard Actions
⊕ **Sly Dagger** (weapon) ✦ **At-Will**

Attack: Melee 1 (one creature); +5 vs. Reflex
Hit: 1d4 + 8 damage.
Effect: The doppelganger can shift 1 square after the attack.
⊙ **Color Spray** (radiant) ✦ **At-Will**
Attack: Close blast 5 (creatures in the blast); +5 vs. Reflex
Hit: 1d8 + 6 radiant damage, and the target is blinded until the end of the doppelganger's next turn.
⊛ **Fireball** (fire) ✦ **Recharge** when first bloodied
Attack: Area burst 2 within 10 (creatures in the burst); +5 vs. Reflex
Hit: 2d6 + 8 fire damage.
Minor Actions
Change Shape (polymorph) ✦ **At-Will**
Effect: The doppelganger alters its physical form to appear as a Medium humanoid until it uses change shape again or until it drops to 0 hit points (whereupon it assumes its true form). To assume a specific individual's form, the doppelganger must have seen the individual. Other creatures can make a DC 30 Insight check to discern that the form is a disguise.
Triggered Actions
Shiv ✦ At-Will
Trigger: An enemy makes a melee attack against the doppelganger.
Effect (Immediate Interrupt): The doppelganger uses sly dagger against the triggering enemy.
Skills Arcana +9, Bluff +8, Insight +7, Thievery +8
Str 11 (+1) **Dex** 15 (+3) **Wis** 12 (+2)
Con 13 (+2) **Int** 16 (+4) **Cha** 15 (+3)
Alignment Evil   **Languages** Common
Equipment Dagger

Encounter 2: Doppelganger Season

Encounter Level 1 (100 XP)
This skill challenge takes place after the adventurers chase off the doppelganger and escape from the smugglers' cave under the burning riverside warehouse

When the adventurers arrive in the Lord Warden's hall, read:
You escape the smugglers' cave just in time to see the burning warehouse collapse and slide into the river. Rescued orphans begin running back to town, leaving you to track down the villain responsible for this mess

Skill Challenge: Tracking Kurche

After escaping from the cave, the doppelganger headed back toward Fallcrest. Along the way, it stumbled upon a town guard, murdered him, and usurped his identity. Upon seeing a merchant caravan heading out of town, the doppelganger decided to join it, offering its services as a sellsword. These are the facts, but the adventurers must discover what happened if they're to catch the villain.

This skill challenge determines how well the adventurers follow Kurche's trail. There's no question that they'll catch their quarry, but it could take longer than expected, and any delay could have unforeseen consequences!

This skill challenge is unusual in that there are only three checks, and they're made in a specific order. All of the skill checks are made as group checks (see the *Rules Compendium™* for group check rules). In some cases, the heroes have multiple skills to choose from when making the check, but each party member still makes only one check as part of any group check. If at least half of the adventurers succeed on the check, the whole group succeeds. Otherwise, the group gains 1 failure. At the end of the encounter, add up the number of failures to determine what happens.

Primary Skills: Athletics, Diplomacy, Endurance, Insight, Nature, Perception, Streetwise.

Finding the Corpse (DC 12 Perception): If the heroes succeed at the group check, they find the mutilated and stripped corpse of a town guard murdered by the doppelganger.

Fleeing Town (DC 12 Diplomacy, Insight, or Streetwise): If the heroes succeed at the group check, they conclude (based on their own instincts and quick conversations with the local militia) that the doppelganger avoided Fallcrest and hooked up with a merchant caravan that left town recently.

Catching the Caravan (DC 12 Athletics, Endurance, or Nature): If the heroes succeed at the group check, they make good time catching up to the caravan.

0 Failures: If the adventurers succeed at every group check, they earn 100 XP for the skill challenge, and Encounter 3: **Gruhn's Gang** happens as written.

1–3 Failures: Regardless of the number of failures, the adventurers still earn full XP for this skill challenge. For each failure, reduce by 2 the number of caravan defenders in "Encounter 3: Gruhn's Gang."

Encounter 3: Gruhn's Gang

Encounter Level 3 (840 XP)

Gruhn, orc terror (G)
Sheshak, orc slaughter-priest (S)
24 orc maggots (O)
Kurche, doppelganger wizard (K)
Davan, human merchant (D)
12 caravan defenders (C; see also "Skill Challenge Failure" below)

The adventurers track the doppelganger to an old trading post, where a merchant caravan is busy defending itself against a gang of orcs.

The adventurers begin along the bottom edge of the map, so that Gruhn is between them and the trading post.

Kurche the doppelganger is lurking among the caravan defenders in disguise. The doppelganger joined the caravan shortly before it arrived at the trading post. See "Encounter 1: Trouble Below" for the doppelganger's statistics (should they become necessary), and see "Tactics" below for more information about Kurche's role in this encounter.

The XP award for this encounter assumes that some number of orcs either escape or are killed by nonplayer characters.

Skill Challenge Failure

If the adventurers failed one or more of the group checks in "Encounter 2: Doppelganger Season," they arrive late. Reduce the number of caravan defenders by 2 for each failure they gained.

When the adventurers arrive on the scene, read:
Through the trees, you see a roadside clearing in which six horse-drawn wagons encircle a ruined stone building. A small group of merchants and guards duck behind the wagons and crumbled walls, barely holding their own against nearly two dozen orcs. A particularly large and terrifying orc joins the fray. With greatsword in hand, he yells, "That's right, maggots! Paint the ground with their blood!" Standing next to him is a scrawny but crafty-looking orc dressed like a wizard or priest.

In any given round, half of the orc maggots focus their attacks on the caravan defenders instead of the adventurers. If all the caravan defenders including Davan are dead, the orcs attack the heroes *en masse*.

Rather than resolve attacks between orcs and caravan defenders, roll a d6 for each side at the end of every round. Whichever side rolls lower loses one random minion. If the roll is a tie, both sides lose a minion.

Tactics

Gruhn tries to remain adjacent to Sheshak and uses *brunt of the attack* to absorb one attack per round directed at the slaughter-priest. Gruhn isn't a coward, but if half of his orc maggots are slain, he breaks off the attack and orders his force to withdraw.

If Gruhn drops to 0 hit points, Sheshak becomes incensed and fights to the death. Any remaining orc maggots fight until Sheshak drops, at which point they scatter and flee. In battle, Sheshak keeps his distance while using *blood theft* to heal wounded allies.

Roughly one-third of the orc maggots engage in melee combat; the rest take cover and shoot arrows.

The doppelganger tries to blend in with the other caravan defenders. Although it protects itself and other nearby caravan defenders, the doppelganger doesn't go out of its way to draw attention to itself, nor does it take any unnecessary risks (such as attacking a nearby character).

Davan and the caravan defenders take cover and attack orcs that gets too close to them or the horses.

Development

Finding the doppelganger in the chaos of battle
is difficult, to say the least. A character can, as
a standard action, choose to watch one caravan
defender and make a DC 30 Insight check. If the
check succeeds and the defender being watched
is Kurche in disguise, the character successfully
identifies the doppelganger.

If the heroes defeat the orcs, Davan expresses his
gratitude and awards them a random level 2 treasure
(see "Treasure" in the *Dungeon Master's Guide* or
the *Dungeon Master's Kit*). Davan and his fellow
merchants are horrified to learn that their caravan
has been infiltrated by a doppelganger.

Orcs that are captured and interrogated only
seem interested in the goods the merchants are
transporting. They have no other motivation for
attacking the caravan.

What's Next?

Once Gruhn and his orcs are defeated or driven
away, the heroes must return to the task at hand:
confronting the doppelganger that has infiltrated
the merchants' caravan. This confrontation with
the elusive shapeshifter kicks off the adventure
appearing in Issue #3 of this comic series!

Features of the Area

Illumination: Bright light.

Boulders and Deadfalls: Squares occupied by
boulders and fallen trees are difficult terrain. These
low obstacles also provide partial cover to creatures
hidden behind them.

Standing Trees: Creatures cannot enter squares
occupied by tree trunks. However, a creature
adjacent to a tree trunk square can climb the tree
with a DC 10 Athletics check. Creatures up in trees
gain partial concealment.

Stone Hut: The walls of this former trading post
are shattered and range from 3 to 5 feet high. The
crumbling walls provide partial cover to creatures
hidden behind them. Climbing a wall costs an extra
square of movement.

Wagons and Horses: There are three covered
wagons and three open wagons encircling the stone
hut. Two horses pull each covered wagon, while
each open wagon has a single horse tethered to it.
The horses are trained to remain calm in battle, but
if a horse takes damage, it bolts (taking its wagon
and possibly another horse with it). See the *Monster
Manual®* or the *Monster Vault™* for horse statistics.

All of the wagons are loaded with crates and
barrels. A creature can enter a wagon's space either
by climbing onto it or crawling underneath it. Wagon
squares count as difficult terrain. The wagons also
provide partial cover to creatures hidden behind or
underneath them.

Orc Terror (G)   Level 2 Elite Brute (Leader)
Medium natural humanoid   XP 250

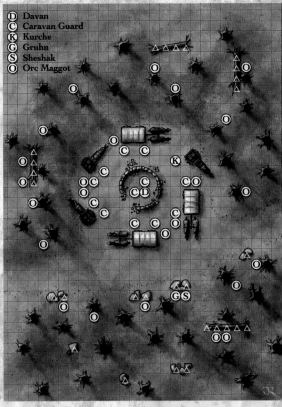

D Davan
C Caravan Guard
K Kurche
G Gruhn
S Sheshak
O Orc Maggot

HP 92; **Bloodied** 46   **Initiative** +3
AC 14, **Fortitude** 15, **Reflex** 13, **Will** 14 **Perception** +7
Speed 6
Saving Throws +2; **Action Points** 1
Standard Actions
⊕ **Greatsword** (weapon) ✦ **At-Will**
    Attack: Melee 1 (one creature); +7 vs. AC
    Hit: 1d10 + 7 damage.
↓ **Double Attack** ✦ **At-Will**
    Effect: The terror makes two melee basic attacks.
Minor Actions
Skin of Terror ✦ **At-Will**
    Effect: The terror chooses an enemy in its line of sight. The
    terror gains resist 5 to attacks made by that enemy until the
    start of the terror's next turn.
Triggered Actions
Brunt of the Attack ✦ **At-Will**
    Trigger: An adjacent ally is hit by an attack.
    Effect (Immediate Interrupt): The terror becomes the target of
    the triggering attack instead.
Skills Athletics +10, Endurance +9, Intimidate +9, Stealth +8
Str 19 (+5) **Dex** 15 (+3) **Wis** 13 (+2)
Con 16 (+4) **Int** 11 (+1) **Cha** 16 (+4)
Alignment Chaotic Evil   **Languages** Common, Giant
Equipment Greatsword

Orc Slaughter-Priest (S) Level 2 Artillery (Leader)
Medium natural humanoid   XP 125
HP 38; **Bloodied** 19   **Initiative** +2
AC 16, **Fortitude** 14, **Reflex** 13, **Will** 14 **Perception** +6
Speed 6
Standard Actions
⊕ **Morningstar** (weapon) ✦ **At-Will**
    Attack: Melee 1 (one creature); +7 vs. AC
    Hit: 1d10 + 5 damage.
⊗ **Blood Theft** ✦ **At-Will**
    Attack: Ranged 20 (one creature); +5 vs. Fortitude
    Hit: 2d6 damage, and one ally within 5 squares of the
    slaughter-priest gains 3 temporary hit points.
☀ **Wrath of Gruumsh** ✦ **At-Will Recharge** 4 5 6

Attack: Area burst 1 within 10 (enemies in the burst); +5 vs. Fortitude

Hit: The target gains vulnerable 5 to all damage until the end of the slaughter-priest's next turn.

Skills Athletics +9, Endurance +8, Religion +6, Stealth +7

Str 12 (+2) **Dex** 12 (+2) **Wis** 11 (+1)

Con 14 (+3) **Int** 10 (+1) **Cha** 14 (+3)

Alignment Chaotic Evil   **Languages** Common, Giant

Equipment Morningstar

Orc Maggots (O)   **Level 2 Minion Soldier**

Medium natural humanoid   XP 31 each

HP 1; a missed attack never damages a minion   **Initiative** +4

AC 18, **Fortitude** 16, **Reflex** 14, **Will** 13 **Perception** +6

Speed 6

Standard Actions

⊕ **Battleaxe** (weapon) ✦ **At-Will**

Attack: Melee 1 (one creature); +7 vs. AC

Hit: 5 damage.

Effect: The target is marked until the end of the maggot's next turn.

⊗ **Longbow** (weapon) ✦ **At-Will**

Attack: Ranged 20 (one creature); +7 vs. AC

Hit: 5 damage.

Effect: The target is marked until the end of the maggot's next turn.

Skills Athletics +9, Endurance +8, Stealth +7

Str 16 (+4) **Dex** 12 (+2) **Wis** 10 (+1)

Con 15 (+3) **Int** 8 (+0) **Cha** 9 (+0)

Alignment Chaotic Evil   **Languages** Common, Giant

Equipment Battleaxe, longbow with 12 arrows

Human Merchant (D)   **Level 1 Skirmisher**

Medium natural humanoid   XP –

HP 27; **Bloodied** 13   **Initiative** +4

AC 15, **Fortitude** 13, **Reflex** 14, **Will** 13 **Perception** +0

Speed 6

Saving Throws +2; **Action Points** 1

Standard Actions

⊕ **Longsword** (weapon) ✦ **At-Will**

Effect: The merchant can shift 1 square before or after attacking.

Attack: Melee 1 (one creature); +6 vs. AC

Hit: 1d8 + 5 damage.

Skills Diplomacy +6, Streetwise +6

Str 12 (+1) **Dex** 14 (+2) **Wis** 11 (+0)

Con 11 (+0) **Int** 10 (+0) **Cha** 12 (+1)

Alignment Unaligned   **Languages** Common, Dwarven

Equipment Longsword

---

12 Caravan Defenders (C)   **Level 1**   **Minion Soldier**

Medium natural humanoid   XP –

HP 1; a missed attack never damages a minion. **Initiative** +4

AC 17, **Fortitude** 15, **Reflex** 13, **Will** 12 **Perception** +6

Speed 6

Saving Throws +2; **Action Points** 1

Standard Actions

⊕ **Longsword** (weapon) ✦ **At-Will**

Attack: Melee 1 (one creature); +6 vs. AC

Hit: 4 damage.

Effect: The target is marked until the end of the caravan defender's next turn.

Str 15 (+4) **Dex** 12 (+2) **Wis** 9 (+1)

Con 11 (+3) **Int** 10 (+0) **Cha** 10 (+0)

Alignment Unaligned   **Languages** Common

Equipment Longsword, Chainmail

SP-11 Featuring ADRIC, KHAL, and other characters!

DUNGEONS & DRAGONS™

Comic & Game Adventure

It Goes Horribly Right

by John Rogers, Andrea Di Vito, and Logan Bonner

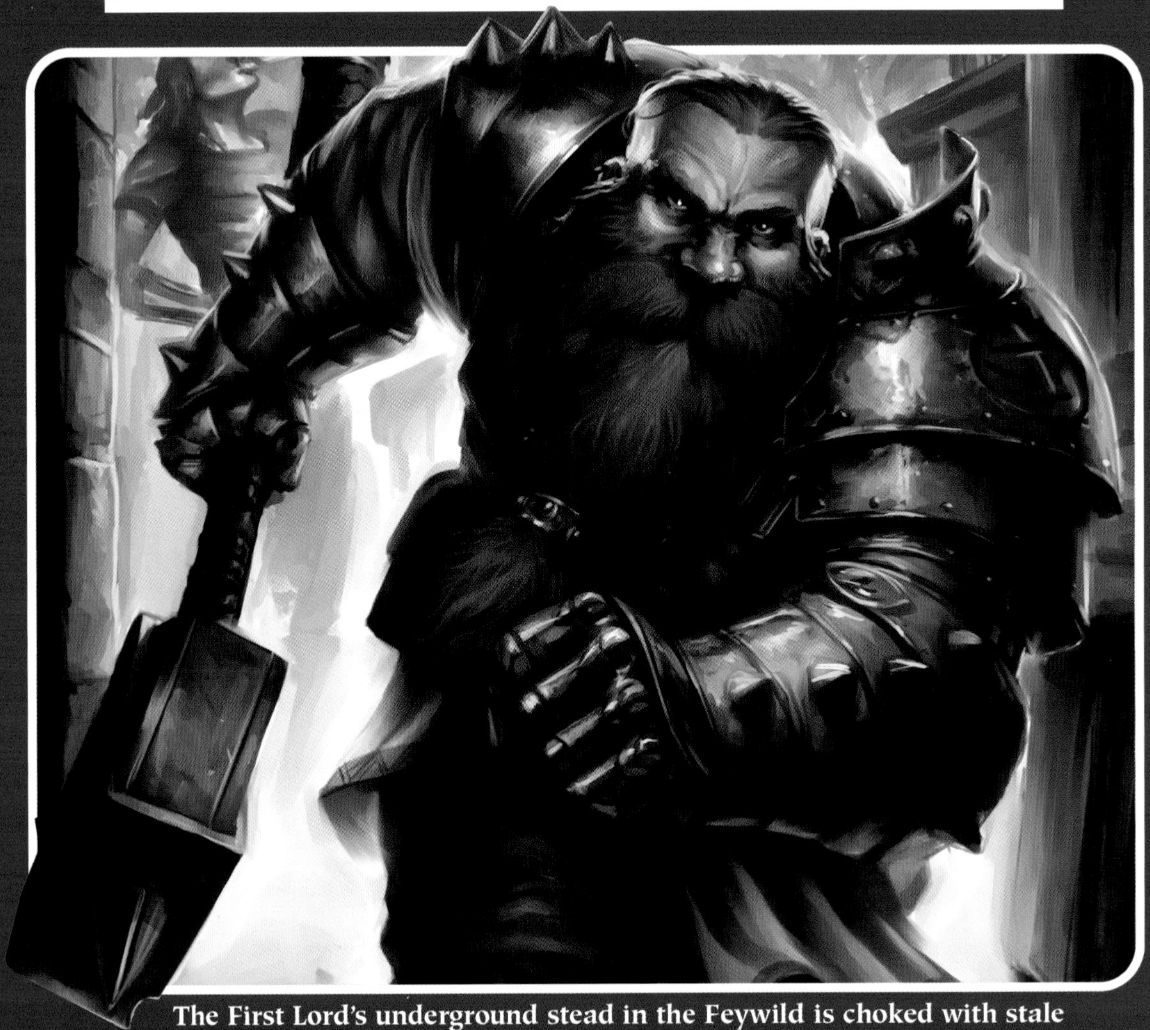

The First Lord's underground stead in the Feywild is choked with stale air and the stench of slaves. A bargain has been struck with a powerful Rakshasa, bringing you one step closer to an artifact that could send you home. But an old acquaintance recognizes you and is about to blow your cover. Will you continue the bluff or stand and fight?

Licensed By:

IDW · Official Wizards of the Coast Licensed Product · Hasbro

Comic and Game Adventure

It Goes Horribly Right

By Logan Bonner
Cartography by Jonathan Roberts

Introduction

Fell's Five grabbed the Guide of Gates and got out alive in DUNGEONS & DRAGONS #11. Now your adventurers can dupe Declan, skirt the spear trap, grapple with the guardian golem, and retrieve the relic in your home D&D campaign!

These encounters are best for characters of level 5–7.

Adventure Background

The fomorians. Malformed, insane, megalomaniacal giants. Nasty customers. They corrupt the underworld of the Feywild, and sometimes their rot creeps up to the surface.

The eladrin do what they can to stop the giants' advances into the world above, but Toveliss E'Teall, Lord of Cydaria, has bigger plans. He wants to recover the Guide of Gates, an artifact tied to planar travel, and use it to create portals into the fomorian caverns. The eladrin could negate the giants' advantage by taking the fight right to them. Toveliss might even be able to banish the misshapen creatures out of the Feywild entirely.

The Guide sits inside a vault in what was once Al'bihel, the City of Stairs. This majestic city fell long ago, abandoned by the eladrin who built it. Toveliss seeks out the adventurers to travel there and retrieve it for him. It could be they need a favor from him (such as a return trip back to the natural world), or that respect for the dead keeps the eladrin away from the city.

Toveliss warns the adventurers that the powerful fomorian Thrumbolg, the First Lord, has strongholds near the old city, and that they should be wary. Unfortunately, the eladrin doesn't realize that Thrumbolg seized Al'bihel itself, filling it with hobgoblin

forces and putting his seneschal Declan in charge of everyday operations.

Getting the Guide will require outsmarting the masters of the evil city. Are your adventurers up to the job?

Using N'ehlia

We find out in this issue that N'ehlia was the arcane lord of Al'bihel all along! It's an interesting puzzle, and a great twist, but requires more setup than this adventure has space to cover. If you can, bring N'ehlia's people into the story before the adventurers meet Toveliss, and plant some major clues about him—the same sort Adric figured out!

Quests

Look for ways to put your adventurers in debt to Toveliss, get them on Thrumbolg's bad side, or secure something else they care about inside the vault along with the Guide.

QUEST: RETRIEVE THE GUIDE OF GATES
6th-Level Major Quest (1,250 XP)

If the adventurers manage to break into the vault and snag the Guide of Gates—and manage to get back out—they complete this quest. Whether or not they need to return it to Toveliss is up to you.

Getting Started

The Dungeon Master needs a copy of the DUNGEONS & DRAGONS game rules, which you can find in either the DUNGEONS & DRAGONS *Fantasy Roleplaying Game Starter Set* or the *Dungeon Master's Kit*. Players need a copy of *Heroes of the Fallen Lands* or *Heroes of the Forgotten Kingdoms* and a character sheet to make characters to use in the adventure.

Once you're ready to begin, flip to Encounter 1 and give your players a glimpse of what terrible things the future might bring!

Encounter 1: In the First Lord's Realm

It should be clear to the players that their characters can't simply fight their way into the city. The following skill challenge covers some ways to gain entry. Reward clever thinking, and have characters say what they want to do rather than just rattle off skills they want to use. After all, Tisha didn't just say "I roll a Bluff check." She came up with a story about other thieves and backed it up with bravado that impressed Declan!

Skill Challenge: Get Inside

The adventurers need to bypass the guard posts to enter the city. They also need to find the vault once they get inside.

Level: 6 (XP 250).

Complexity: 1 (requires 4 successes before 3 failures).

Success: The adventurers are inside the city and are able to sneak away or explore freely, depending on how well they convinced Declan to trust them.

Failure: The adventurers are inside the city, but under arrest or stuck in a torture room they'll need to escape from.

First, read or paraphrase:
The journey from Cydaria to Al'bihel doesn't seem long, but time passes strangely in the Feywild. Apart from some minor animal attacks and a tense journey through a dryad's grove, the trip is largely uneventful.

The great towers of Al'bihel stand cracked and ruined. Between their sheer sides stand the gates into the city, each guarded by a group of hobgoblins or bugbears. None of these guards looks particularly smart. It seems the First Lord didn't expect intruders to dare enter his realm.

Inside the city gates, all sorts of humanoids roam back and forth, doing whatever business Thrumbolg demands be done. The streets bustle with activity, and it would be difficult for outsiders to pass by unnoticed.

Stage 1: Front Gates

After one or two successes, the adventurers can get past the gates.

Talk to the Guards: A clever story, or even a not-so-clever one, can fool the guards (Bluff DC 15). They can be negotiated with (Diplomacy 23), and money makes things run smoothly (automatic success for a bribe of 300 gp or more). If the adventurers mention something the guards haven't heard about, they might be taken to Declan to sort it all out. They'll have to tell him their story and hope it still holds up (DC 15 in the same skill already used).

Sneak In: Staying out of notice is tough in the busy streets (Stealth DC 23). Characters who look monstrous (like minotaurs or even shifters) might be able to pass more easily. Eladrin and elves have no chance.

Tunnel Under: Fomorian tunnels run below the city. Adventurers who realize this can travel through them to get inside (Dungeoneering 15). A secondary Nature check doesn't give a success, but lets a character find out about the tunnels.

Scale the Walls: The eladrin-crafted towers are practically impossible to climb for characters of this level.

Stage 2: Getting to the Vault

If the adventurers meet with Declan, he introduces them to Trasgar. It's easy to tell that they can trick the blind mage if they get Declan out of the way. If the PCs made it in without meeting Declan, they need to find the vault.

Get Declan out of the Way: The adventurers might create a distraction (Bluff DC 15, but many other skills could apply) to get Declan to leave them in Trasgar's care while he takes care of other matters. If the adventurers are clever, they might be able to watch Declan like Bree did, and figure out clues for bypassing the vault's defenses.

Locate the Vault: The Guide can be found in many ways: sensed magically (Arcana DC 15), found after asking around (Streetwise DC 15, though word might get around), or recalled from the lore about Al'bihel (History DC 15).

Encounter 2: The Vault

Encounter Level 9 (2,150 XP)*

*That includes the golem. They probably won't kill the golem. If they correctly guess or research the passcode for the golem, they receive half XP for defeating it (600 XP).

1 vault golem (G)
4 bugbear thugs (B)
1 spear trap hallway

This encounter really contains several stages that can be completed in a hurry or done sporadically.

First comes the trapped hallway, where only the white squares are safe. Second come the bugbear guards (who might take on adventurers while they're still on the tiles). Then the vault door needs to be opened, and that's a little tricky. Now that the vault's open, the adventurers need to dodge the golem or deactivate it. Beyond the golem, the adventurers can finally find the Guide of Gates—the grand prize.

Cheating

Fell's Five made short work of the challenges in the hallway and vault, mostly thanks to Bree's scouting. In other words, they cheated. You might set up a chance for your adventurers to spy on Declan or find some diagrams in Trasgar's study that show how the vault lock works.

Have the adventurers place their miniatures on the bottom edge of the map.

When the adventurers enter the hallway, read or paraphrase:
A long hallway tiled in white and brown stone, stretches out ahead of you. At the end of the hall, four bugbears stand guard. They look nervous, and they seem to be moving very carefully. Their attention isn't totally focused on their job.

The bugbears stand in front of a pair of massive wooden doors with a giant metal disk-shaped lock. The mess of levers on the lock probably needs to be switched into a certain configuration, and it certainly looks complicated.

If the adventurers stay at the end of the hall and don't make too much noise, they have a bit of time before the bugbears notice them. Since the bugbears are distracted, their passive Perception is only 11.

Tactics

The bugbears take great care to avoid stepping on the trapped tiles. They won't go past the center point of the hallway unless they're being torn up by ranged attacks. In combat, they try to flank for combat advantage. A bugbear might even bull rush an adventurer onto a brown tile to trigger the spear trap.

Vault Lock

The doors to the vault can be opened by correctly positioning a series of levers. This requires two consecutive successful DC 15 Thievery checks. Each check takes a standard action. If a character succeeds once and fails with the next check, he or she can use a minor action to reset the lock to last correct position.

If the lock is successfully opened, the doors swing wide to reveal the golem.

Golem

Before the adventure, decide on the golem's passcodes. By default, it has three: two rotating passcodes that allow the speaker to pass, and one master key that shuts down the golem. The "Golem Passcodes" sidebar gives suggestions for ways you might make the passcode fit your campaign.

The golem is a simple creature, built only to guard the vault. Either the person who enters says the passcode and is trustworthy, or says the wrong passcode and must be *KILLED.*

When the adventurers get into the vault and first see the golem, read or paraphrase:
The massive doors swing inward to reveal a stone vault. Inside stands a giant-sized golem. Its body is made of fine metal plates, and its head is a flaming skull with long horns.

Behind it, a golden sextant-like object floats above an ornate pedestal. It gives off ripples of arcane power, and it feels like the very fabric of the Feywild pulses in its presence.

The golem peers down, then speaks one word in a gravely voice: "Challenge." It seems to be asking for a passcode of some kind. The golem waits about 1 round before issuing its challenge again. Attacking the golem or trying to get past it to reach the

Guide of Gates causes it to begin fighting immediately.

If an adventurer recites the correct passcode, read:
The golem says, "Challenge accepted. Do not kill." It then stands aside, allowing full access to the Guide of Gates.

If an adventurer recites the wrong passcode or waits too long, read:
The golem pulls back its massive fist and intones, "Challenge failed." The flames around its head flare, and it strikes!

Now the golem rolls initiative and fights the adventurers. Its words can appear in another language, like they did in the comic, or in Common, depending on how you alter the golem to fit your campaign.

While the golem fights, it gives a second chance to recite the password. If a character understands the golem's language, read:
The golem says, "Rotating password incorrect, answer secondary password or master key."

The master key shuts down the golem entirely rather than just making it step aside. It's the last resort!

Golem Passcodes

The golem in the vault with the Guide of Gates requires a passcode to bypass. It's entirely likely your group won't know the passcode and will just need to fight or run, but you have some options to drop passcode hints.

In the comic, all of the passcodes we heard were eladrin words. Adventurers who do research into the history of Al'bihel might figure out the passcodes. You can use N'ehlia's name even if you didn't incorporate him into the backstory. He can just be the last arcane lord of Al'bihel.

You can instead adapt the passcodes to use something else from your campaign. You can add decorations to the golem that match ones the adventurers saw earlier, then have the passcodes fit another civilization they've encountered.

Remember, nobody says you have to know for sure what the passcodes are! If one of your players makes a guess that

seems pretty plausible, roll with it. They'll always talk about the time they figured out the golem's password with a wild guess.

Features of the Area

Illumination: Bright light.

Tiles: The goblins have already started up their campfire. Any creature that enters or ends its turn in the campfire takes 5 fire damage.

Vault Doors: Opening the lock is detailed in the "Vault Lock" section. The doors are sturdy wood (AC 3, Fortitude 15, 150 hit points). Breaking them down requires a DC 20 Strength check.

Guide of Gates: The Guide itself rests on a pedestal in the vault.

Spear Trap Hallway

Only the white squares in the hallway are safe. Stepping on a square of brown stone triggers the spear trap in the ceiling above.

Spear Trap Hallway	Level 6 Trap
Object	XP 250

Detect Perception DC 24 **Initiative** —
HP 15 per spear, 40 per trigger plate
AC 17, Fortitude 14, Reflex 14, Will —
Immune necrotic, poison, psychic, forced movement, all conditions, ongoing damage

TRIGGERED ACTIONS

⚔ **Attack** ✦ **At-Will**
Trigger: A creature enters one of the brown trigger squares or starts its turn there.
Attack (Opportunity Action): Melee 1 (triggering creature); +11 vs. AC
Hit: 2d6 + 7 damage.

COUNTERMEASURES

•**Disable:** Thievery DC 23. *Success:* A single trigger square and its associated spear no longer function.

4 Bugbear Thugs (B)	Level 4 Brute
Medium natural humanoid	XP 175 each

HP 65; **Bloodied** 32 **Initiative** +7
AC 16, **Fortitude** 15, **Reflex** 15, **Will** 11
Perception +8
Speed 6 Low-light vision

TRAITS

Bushwhack
The bugbear gains a +4 bonus to attack rolls against a creature that has no allies adjacent to it.

STANDARD ACTIONS

⊕ **Morningstar** (weapon) ✦ **At-Will**
Attack: Melee 1 (one creature); +9 vs. AC

Hit: 2d8 + 6 damage, or 3d8 + 6 if the bugbear has combat advantage against the target.

Handaxe (weapon) ✦ **At-Will**

Attack: Ranged 10 (one creature); +9 vs. AC

Hit: 1d6 + 6 damage.

Skills Stealth +12

Str 20 (+7) **Dex** 20 (+7) **Wis** 13 (+3)

Con 15 (+4) **Int** 8 (+1) **Cha** 10 (+2)

Alignment evil **Languages** Common, Goblin

Equipment leather armor, morningstar, 2 handaxes

1 Vault Golem (G) Level 11 Elite Brute

Large natural animate (construct)

XP 1,200

HP 276; **Bloodied** 138 **Initiative** +11

AC 23, **Fortitude** 25, **Reflex** 23, **Will** 21

Perception +9

Speed 6 (cannot shift) Darkvision

Immune disease, poison

Saving Throws +2; **Action Points** 1

TRAITS

Interfering Bolts

When the golem takes lightning damage, it is slowed until the end of its next turn.

STANDARD ACTIONS

Slam (keywords) ✦ **At-Will**

Attack: Melee 2 (one creature); +16 vs. AC

Hit: 2d10 + 13 damage.

Double Slam ✦ **At-Will**

Effect: The golem uses *slam* twice, each time against a different target.

Golem Rampage ✦ **Recharge** ⚄ ⚅

Effect: The golem moves up to its speed +2. During this movement, the golem can move through enemies' spaces, and when the golem first enters any creature's space, it uses *slam* against that creature.

TRIGGERED ACTIONS

Thundering Stomp ✦ **At-Will**

Trigger: The golem starts its turn with two or more enemies adjacent to it.

Attack (Free Action): Close burst 1 (creatures in the burst); +14 vs. Fortitude

Hit: 1d10 + 5 damage, and the target falls prone.

Str 22 (+11) **Dex** 18 (+9) **Wis** 14 (+7)

Con 18 (+9) **Int** 3 (+1) **Cha** 3 (+1)

Alignment unaligned **Languages** Common, Elven

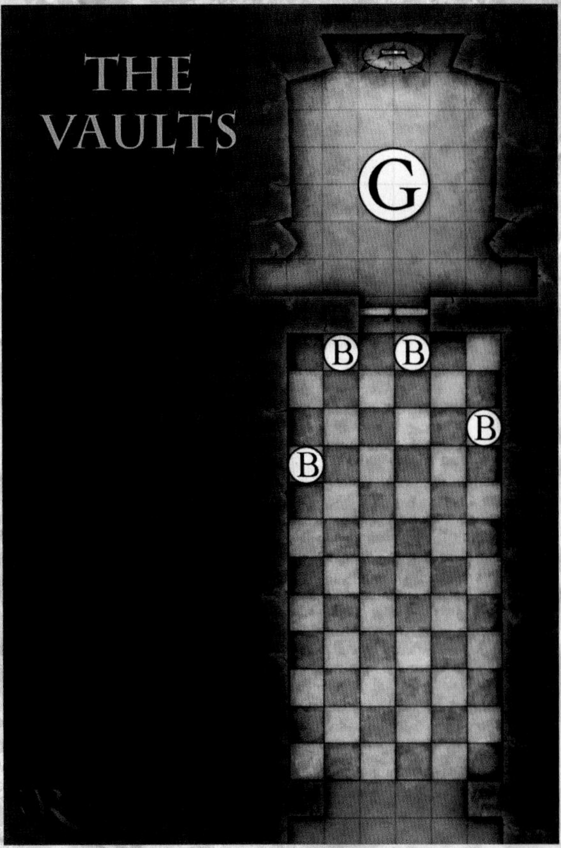
THE VAULTS
G
B
B
B
B

Encounter 3: Not Out of the Woods Yet

Encounter Level 8 (1,850 XP)

Declan the Seneschal (D)
9 hobgoblin battle guards (H)
1 dryad witch (W)

As the adventurers exit the city, hopefully with the Guide of Gates in hand, Declan and his troops follow in hot pursuit. This scenario assumes the adventurers are on the run, but many different plot developments could lead to a situation with the adventurers outside between Declan's forces and an angry dryad.

If the adventurers make it out without Declan in pursuit, add more dryads and fight only them. *Monster Vault* contains more versions of dryads you can use to fill out the encounter.

Have the players place their miniatures just barely in the grass, north of the chasm.

Read:

Declan rushes out of one of the towers, hobgoblin troops swarming around him. He shouts, "They have the Guide! Bring me their heads, preferably in pieces!"

Whenever a creature reaches the southern part of the map just past the chasm, read:

The trees rustle, and a female form steps out, wreathed in leaves. The dryad stares at you and the hobgoblins. "You intrude in my grove! What can you offer to save your lives?"

Roll for initiative.

The Dryad's Allegiance

The dryad isn't on either side: She hates everyone equally. Adventurers could convince her to attack only Declan's forces. The dryad asks for an offering, but it needs to be a thing of beauty or something related to the woods. Even just explaining that the hobgoblins are the ones who maintain this foul city in the middle of the forest could be enough. Anyone who attacks the dryad is in for serious retribution.

Tactics

Hobgoblins advance in waves rather than rushing in. Don't have them all attack the adventurers at once.

Declan will help solve the "too many hobgoblins" problem by blowing them up with *death bloom*. The rakshasa likes to stand safely behind his hobgoblins and shout orders

The dryad attacks both sides equally, going after whoever seems like the easiest target at the time. See the sidebar.

Conclusion

The adventurers escape with the Guide of Gates. Assuming they go back to meet Toveliss in Cydaria, he makes good on any promises he gave them. He might even have some future work for them once he finishes unlocking the secrets of the Guide and sending forces into the fomorian realms.

Features of the Area

Illumination: Bright light.

Trees: Creatures can stand in the smaller clusters of trees. A creature in the same square as a tree has partial cover.

Chasm: The pit in the middle of the map is 20 feet (4 squares) deep. A creature that falls in takes 2d10 falling damage. Climbing back up requires a DC 15 Athletics check.

Fallen Tree and Giant Roots: The large fallen tree serves as a bridge over the chasm, as do the massive roots coming from the southeast corner of the map. Moving onto one of these costs 1 extra square of movement.

Declan the Seneschal   Level 8 Artillery
Medium natural humanoid, rakshasa
XP 350

HP 66; **Bloodied** 33   **Initiative** +7
AC 22, **Fortitude** 19, **Reflex** 22, **Will** 21
Perception +6
Speed 6   Low-light vision

STANDARD ACTIONS

⊕ **Claw** ✦ **At-Will**
Attack: Melee 1 (one creature); +13 vs. AC
Hit: 2d6 + 4 damage, and ongoing 5 damage (save ends).

⊗ **Acid Bolt** (acid) ✦ **At-Will**
Attack: Ranged 10 (one creature); +13 vs. Reflex
Hit: 2d6 + 8 acid damage, and each creature adjacent to the target takes 5 acid damage.

❊ **Death Bloom** (necrotic) ✦ **At-Will**
Requirement: One of Declan's allies must be in origin square of the burst.
Effect: The ally in the origin square dies.
Attack: Area burst 1 within 10 (enemies in the burst); +13 vs. Fortitude
Hit: 1d6 + 4 necrotic damage, and ongoing 10 necrotic damage (save ends).
Miss: Half damage.

MINOR ACTIONS

Deceptive Veil (illusion) ✦ **At-Will**
Effect: The rakshasa disguises itself to appear as a Medium humanoid until it uses deceptive veil again or until it drops to 0 hit points. Other creatures can make a DC 29 Insight check to discern that the form is an illusion.

TRIGGERED ACTIONS

Illusory Escape (illusion) ✦ **Recharge** when first bloodied
Trigger: An enemy makes a ranged attack against Declan.
Effect (Immediate Reaction): Declan becomes invisible, and an illusion of him appears in his square. The transition is indiscernible to observers, and the illusion lasts until the start of Declan's next turn or until a creature attacks the illusion. After the illusion appears, Declan shifts up to his speed.

Str 15 (+6)   **Dex** 16 (+7)   **Wis** 15 (+6)
Con 12 (+5)   **Int** 20 (+9)   **Cha** 18 (+8)
Alignment evil   **Languages** Common, Elven

10 Hobgoblin Battle Guards (H)
Level 3 Soldier

Medium natural humanoid   XP 150 each
HP 49; **Bloodied** 24   **Initiative** +5
AC 19, **Fortitude** 17, **Reflex** 15, **Will** 15
Perception +8
Speed 6   Low-light vision

STANDARD ACTIONS
⊕ **Flail** (weapon) ✦ At-Will
  Attack: Melee 1 (one creature); +8 vs.
    AC
  Hit: 1d10 + 5 damage, and the hobgoblin
    marks the target until the start of the
    hobgoblin's next turn.

MOVE ACTIONS
Phalanx Movement ✦ At-Will
  Effect: Close burst 1 (allies in the burst).
    The hobgoblin and each target can shift
    1 square as a free action. The target
    must shift to a square adjacent to the
    hobgoblin.

TRIGGERED ACTIONS
Share Shield ✦ At-Will
  Trigger: An adjacent ally is hit by an
    attack against AC or Reflex.
  Effect (Immediate Interrupt): The ally
    gains a +2 bonus to AC and Reflex
    against the triggering attack

Str 19 (+5)   **Dex** 14 (+3)   **Wis** 15 (+3)
Con 17 (+4)   **Int** 10 (+1)   **Cha** 10 (+1)
Alignment evil   **Languages** Common,
Goblin
Equipment chainmail, heavy shield, flail

1 Dryad Witch (W)   Level 8 Controller

Medium fey humanoid (plant)   XP 350
HP 84; **Bloodied** 42   **Initiative** +7
AC 22, **Fortitude** 18, **Reflex** 20, **Will** 22
Perception +14
Speed 8 (forest walk)

STANDARD ACTIONS
⊕ **Thorny Vine** ✦ At-Will
  Attack: Melee 2 (one creature); +13 vs.
    AC
  Hit: 2d8 + 7 damage.
  Effect: The dryad can slide the target 1
    square.
🏹 **Beguiling Verdure** (charm) ✦ At-Will
  Attack: Ranged 5 (one dazed creature);
    +11 vs. Will
  Hit: The dryad slides the target up to the
    target's speed, and the target must then
    make a basic attack as a free action
    against a creature of the dryad's choice.
↞ **Soporific Fragrance** (charm) ✦
  Recharge ⚁ ⚂ ⚃
  Attack: Close blast 3 (enemies in the
    blast); +11 vs. Will
  Hit: The target is dazed (save ends).

MOVE ACTIONS
Treestride (teleportation) ✦ At-Will
  Requirement: The dryad must be adjacent
    to a tree or a Large plant.

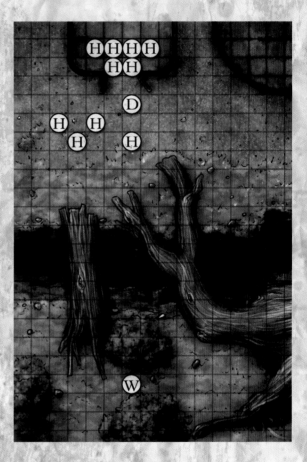

  Effect: The dryad teleports up to 8
    squares to a square adjacent to a tree
    or a Large plant.

MINOR ACTIONS
Deceptive Veil (illusion) ✦ At-Will
  Effect: The dryad disguises itself to
    appear as a Medium humanoid (usually
    a beautiful elf or eladrin) until it uses
    deceptive veil again or until it drops to 0
    hit points. Other creatures can make a
    DC 29 Insight check to discern that the
    form is an illusion.

Str 11 (+4)   **Dex** 17 (+7)   **Wis** 20 (+9)
Con 12 (+5)   **Int** 12 (+5)   **Cha** 16 (+7)
Alignment unaligned **Languages** Elven

DUNGEONS & DRAGONS®

ADRIC FELL
CHARACTER NAME

Class: Knight (Fighter)   Level: 7
Race: Human   Gender: Male
Alignment: Good
Languages: Common, Dwarven

ABILITIES AND SKILLS

18 Strength   +4   +7
Strength measures your physical power.

Athletics   ☒ Trained   MISC   +12

15 Constitution   +2   +5
Constitution represents health, stamina, and vital force.

Endurance   ☒ Trained   MISC   +10

12 Dexterity   +1   +4
Dexterity measures coordination, agility, and balance.

Acrobatics   ☐ Trained   MISC   +4
Stealth   ☐ Trained   MISC   +4
Thievery   ☐ Trained   MISC   +4

10 Intelligence   +0   +3
Intelligence describes how well you learn and reason.

Arcana   ☐ Trained   MISC   +3
History   ☐ Trained   MISC   +3
Religion   ☐ Trained   MISC   +3

10 Wisdom   +0   +3
Wisdom measures common sense, self-discipline, and empathy.

Dungeoneering   ☐ Trained   MISC   +3
Heal   ☐ Trained   MISC   +3
Insight   ☐ Trained   MISC   +3
Nature   ☐ Trained   MISC   +3
Perception   ☐ Trained   MISC   +3

14 Charisma   +2   +5
Charisma measures force of personality and leadership.

Bluff   ☐ Trained   MISC   +5
Diplomacy   ☒ Trained   MISC   +10
Intimidate   ☒ Trained   MISC   +10
Streetwise   ☐ Trained   MISC   +5

COMBAT STATISTICS

+7 Initiative
Roll initiative to determine the turn order in combat.

6 Speed
Your speed is the number of squares you can move with a move action.

DEFENSES

26 Armor Class (AC)   CALCULATIONS
AC measures how hard it is to physically land an attack on you.

21 Fortitude   CALCULATIONS
Fortitude measures your toughness and resilience.

19 Reflex   CALCULATIONS
Reflex measures your ability to deflect or dodge attacks.

17 Will   CALCULATIONS
Will measures your strength of will and self-discipline.

+11 Attack Bonus   +2 vicious saber   1d8+9

Attack Bonus   WEAPON   POWER   DAMAGE
When you attack, roll a d20 and add your attack bonus. Compare the result to the monster's defense to see if you hit. If you do hit, roll damage.

65 Hit Points   Bloodied   32
Your hit points measure the damage you can take before falling unconscious. Your bloodied value is half of your hit points (rounded down).

Healing Surge Value   20
Surges Per Day   11
When you spend a healing surge, you regain hit points equal to your healing surge value, which is one-quarter of your hit points (rounded down).

CURRENT HIT POINTS

Temporary Hit Points   Surges Remaining

ACTIONS IN COMBAT

On your turn in combat, you can take three actions:
✦ A standard action, which is usually an attack
✦ A move action, which involves movement
✦ A minor action, which is simple and quick
You can give up an action to take another action from lower on the list, so you can take a move or a minor action instead of a standard action or a minor action instead of a move action.

POWERS AND FEATS

Heroic Effort (encounter; racial trait)

Battle Guardian (at-will)

Defend the Line (at-will; stance)

Defender Aura (at-will)

Measured Cut (at-will; stance)

Poised Assault (at-will; stance)

Battle Leader (encounter)

Dauntless Endurance (encounter)

Power Strike (2/encounter)

Weapon Specialization: Bladed Step

Heavy Armor Agility (feat)

Heavy Blade Expertise (feat)

Improved Defenses (feat)

Shield Finesse (feat)

Swift Recovery (feat)

Weapon Focus: Heavy Blades (feat)

EQUIPMENT AND MAGIC ITEMS

+2 vicious saber (scimitar)

+2 chainmail

+2 light shield

Adventurer's kit

    Backpack

    Bedroll

    Flint and steel

    Belt pouch

    Trail rations (10 days)

    50-foot rope

    Sunrods (2)

    Waterskin

Gauntlets of blood (level 4 magic item)

    +2 damage against bloodied targets

Belt of vigor (level 2 magic item)

WEALTH

1,800 gp

CHARACTER SKETCH

CHARACTER NOTES

Use this space however you like: to record what happens on your adventures, track quests, describe your background and goals, note the names of the other characters in your party, or draw a picture of your character.

EXPERIENCE POINTS (XP)
11,500

XP for next level: 13,000

DUNGEONS & DRAGONS®

BREE THREE-HANDS (CHARACTER NAME)

Class: Rogue (Thief) Level: 7

Race: Halfling Gender: Female

Alignment: Unaligned

Languages: Common, Giant

ABILITIES AND SKILLS

Score	Ability / Skill	Trained	Modifier / Misc.	Check
15	**Strength**		+2	+5
	Strength measures your physical power.			
	Athletics	☒ Trained		+10
10	**Constitution**		+0	+3
	Constitution represents health, stamina, and vital force.			
	Endurance	☐ Trained		+3
21	**Dexterity**		+5	+8
	Dexterity measures coordination, agility, and balance.			
	Acrobatics	☒ Trained		+15
	Stealth	☒ Trained		+13
	Thievery	☒ Trained		+15
10	**Intelligence**		+0	+3
	Intelligence describes how well you learn and reason.			
	Arcana	☐ Trained		+3
	History	☐ Trained		+3
	Religion	☐ Trained		+3
8	**Wisdom**		-1	+2
	Wisdom measures common sense, self-discipline, and empathy.			
	Dungeoneering	☐ Trained		+2
	Heal	☐ Trained		+2
	Insight	☐ Trained		+2
	Nature	☐ Trained		+2
	Perception	☒ Trained		+7
13	**Charisma**		+1	+4
	Charisma measures force of personality and leadership.			
	Bluff	☒ Trained		+9
	Diplomacy	☐ Trained		+4
	Intimidate	☐ Trained		+4
	Streetwise	☒ Trained		+9

COMBAT STATISTICS

+8 Initiative — *Roll initiative to determine the turn order in combat.*

6 Speed — *Your speed is the number of squares you can move with a move action.*

DEFENSES

Score	Defense	Calculations
22	**Armor Class (AC)** — *AC measures how hard it is to physically land an attack on you.*	
17	**Fortitude** — *Fortitude measures your toughness and resilience.*	
22	**Reflex** — *Reflex measures your ability to deflect or dodge attacks.*	
16	**Will** — *Will measures your strength of will and self-discipline.*	

Bonus		Power	Damage
+15	**Attack Bonus**	melee basic	1d6 + 9
+12	**Attack Bonus**	melee ranged	1d4+ 7

When you attack, roll a d20 and add your attack bonus. Compare the result to the monster's defense to see if you hit. If you do hit, roll damage.

52 Hit Points Bloodied 26

Your hit points measure the damage you can take before falling unconscious. Your bloodied value is half of your hit points (rounded down).

Healing Surge Value: 13

Surges Per Day: 6

When you spend a healing surge, you regain hit points equal to your healing surge value, which is one-quarter of your hit points (rounded down).

CURRENT HIT POINTS

Temporary Hit Points *Surges Remaining*

ACTIONS IN COMBAT

On your turn in combat, you can take three actions:

- *A standard action, which is usually an attack*
- *A move action, which involves movement*
- *A minor action, which is simple and quick*

You can give up an action to take another action from lower on the list, so you can take a move or a minor action instead of a standard action or a minor action instead of a move action.

POWERS AND FEATS

Fleeting Ghost (at-will)

Tactical Trick (at-will)

Thug's Trick (at-will)

Tumbling Trick (at-will)

Unbalancing Trick (at-will)

Frigid Darkness (encounter)

Backstab (encounter)

Cunning Escape (encounter)

Hidden Blade (encounter)

Second Chance (encounter)

Dark One's Own Luck (daily)

Halfling Traits: bold, nimble reaction

Aggressive Advantage (feat)

Cunning Stalker (feat)

Master at Arms (feat)

Terrain Advantage (feat)

EQUIPMENT AND MAGIC ITEMS

+2 luckblade short sword

+2 short sword

+2 veteran's leather armor

+2 amulet of protection

Throwing daggers

Adventurer's kit

    Backpack

    Bedroll

    Flint and steel

    Belt pouch

    Trail rations (10 days)

    50-foot rope

    Sunrods (2)

    Waterskin

WEALTH

1,800 gp

CHARACTER SKETCH

CHARACTER NOTES

Nicknamed "Three-Hands" because she always seems to get an extra share of the treasure, Bree drinks too much, cheats at cards . . . she's pure thief. A cutpurse. A smuggler. Name a crime, she's tried it once. Bree appears to live a carefree life in pursuit of next week's gambling money. Despite her best intentions, she's always getting wrapped up in the affairs of the halfling families traveling through Fallcrest. Although Adric needs her to pick locks and support his more outrageous plans, sometime soon they're going to have a chat.

Use this space however you like: to record what happens on your adventures, track quests, describe your background and goals, note the names of the other characters in your party, or draw a picture of your character.

EXPERIENCE POINTS (XP)
11,500

XP for next level: 13,000

DUNGEONS & DRAGONS®

KHAL KHALUNDURRIN

Class: Cavalier (Paladin) Level: 7
Race: Dwarf Gender: Male
Alignment: Good
Languages: Common, Dwarven

ABILITIES AND SKILLS

19 Strength +4 | +7
Strength measures your physical power.

Athletics ☒ Trained | | +12

16 Constitution +3 | +6
Constitution represents health, stamina, and vital force.

Endurance ☒ Trained | +2 | +13

10 Dexterity +0 | +3
Dexterity measures coordination, agility, and balance.

Acrobatics ☐ Trained | | +3
Stealth ☐ Trained | | +3
Thievery ☐ Trained | | +3

10 Intelligence +0 | +3
Intelligence describes how well you learn and reason.

Arcana ☐ Trained | | +3
History ☐ Trained | | +3
Religion ☐ Trained | | +3

11 Wisdom +1 | +4
Wisdom measures common sense, self-discipline, and empathy.

Dungeoneering ☐ Trained | +2 | +6
Heal ☒ Trained | | +9
Insight ☐ Trained | | +4
Nature ☐ Trained | | +4
Perception ☐ Trained | | +4

15 Charisma +2 | +5
Charisma measures force of personality and leadership.

Bluff ☐ Trained | | +5
Diplomacy ☒ Trained | | +10
Intimidate ☐ Trained | | +5
Streetwise ☐ Trained | | +5

COMBAT STATISTICS

+7 Initiative
Roll initiative to determine the turn order in combat.

5 Speed
Your speed is the number of squares you can move with a move action.

DEFENSES

24 Armor Class (AC) CALCULATIONS
AC measures how hard it is to physically land an attack on you.

22 Fortitude CALCULATIONS
Fortitude measures your toughness and resilience.

18 Reflex CALCULATIONS
Reflex measures your ability to deflect or dodge attacks.

20 Will CALCULATIONS
Will measures your strength of will and self-discipline.

+11 Attack Bonus | +2 warhammer | 1d10+7

Attack Bonus | WEAPON / POWER | DAMAGE
When you attack, roll a d20 and add your attack bonus. Compare the result to the monster's defense to see if you hit. If you do hit, roll damage.

67 Hit Points Bloodied 33
Your hit points measure the damage you can take before falling unconscious. Your bloodied value is half of your hit points (rounded down).

Healing Surge Value | 18
Surges Per Day | 13

When you spend a healing surge, you regain hit points equal to your healing surge value, which is one-quarter of your hit points (rounded down).

CURRENT HIT POINTS

Temporary Hit Points Surges Remaining

ACTIONS IN COMBAT

On your turn in combat, you can take three actions:
✦ A standard action, which is usually an attack
✦ A move action, which involves movement
✦ A minor action, which is simple and quick
You can give up an action to take another action from lower on the list, so you can take a move or a minor action instead of a standard action or a minor action instead of a move action.

POWERS AND FEATS

Defender Aura (at-will)

Righteous Radiance (at-will)

Valiant Strike (at-will)

Vengeful Strike (at-will)

Holy Smite (2/encounter)

Improved Righteous Shield (encounter)

Fiery Smite (daily)

Restore Vitality (daily)

Wrath of the Gods (daily)

Dwarf Traits:

   Cast-Iron Stomach, Dwarven Resilience,

   Encumbered Speed, Stand Your Ground

Armor Finesse (feat)

Disciple of Stone (feat)

Improved Defenses (feat)

Weapon Focus: Hammers (feat)

EQUIPMENT AND MAGIC ITEMS

+2 defensive warhammer

+2 delver's plate armor

+2 holy symbol of Moradin

+3 amulet of protection

Adventurer's kit

   Backpack

   Bedroll

   Flint and steel

   Belt pouch

   Trail rations (10 days)

   50-foot rope

   Sunrods (2)

   Waterskin

Climber's kit

WEALTH

2,000 gp plus hidden wealth

CHARACTER SKETCH

Use this space to draw a picture of your character, your character's symbol, or some other identifying mark.

CHARACTER NOTES

Khal is a paladin of Moradin, a cavalier of valor. He's on the road to love. In order to wed the blue-eyed girl of his dreams, Khal must rise to a social rank acceptable to her family. Unfortunately, her merchant clan has little use or love for such a stalwart Dwarf of the Gods. So Khal's ministering to other traveling dwarves, hunting for religious artifacts to rise in his order, and collecting enough gold to meet his intended's dowry. He tends to get distracted in battle if some interesting bit of ancient detritus catches his eye. Khal is also renowned in his homestead as an accomplished dwarven poet.

Use this space however you like: to record what happens on your adventures, track quests, describe your background and goals, note the names of the other characters in your party, or draw a picture of your character.

EXPERIENCE POINTS (XP)
11,500

XP for next level: 13,000

DUNGEONS & DRAGONS®

TISHA SWORNHEART
CHARACTER NAME

Class: Warlock (Star Pact) Level: 7

Race: Tiefling   Gender: Female

Alignment: Unaligned

Languages: Common, Deep Speech

ABILITIES AND SKILLS

11	**Strength**	MODIFIER +0	+3
Strength measures your physical power.

| Athletics | ☐ Trained | MISC | +3 |

| 15 | **Constitution** | MODIFIER +2 | +5 |
Constitution represents health, stamina, and vital force.

| Endurance | ☐ Trained | MISC | +5 |

| 10 | **Dexterity** | MODIFIER +0 | +3 |
Dexterity measures coordination, agility, and balance.

Acrobatics	☐ Trained	MISC	+3
Stealth	☐ Trained	MISC	+5
Thievery	☒ Trained	MISC	+8

| 16 | **Intelligence** | MODIFIER +3 | +6 |
Intelligence describes how well you learn and reason.

Arcana	☐ Trained	MISC	+6
History	☐ Trained	MISC	+6
Religion	☐ Trained	MISC	+6

| 10 | **Wisdom** | MODIFIER +0 | +3 |
Wisdom measures common sense, self-discipline, and empathy.

Dungeoneering	☐ Trained	MISC	+3
Heal	☐ Trained	MISC	+3
Insight	☒ Trained	MISC	+8
Nature	☐ Trained	MISC	+3
Perception	☐ Trained	MISC	+3

| 19 | **Charisma** | MODIFIER +4 | +7 |
Charisma measures force of personality and leadership.

Bluff	☒ Trained	MISC	+14
Diplomacy	☐ Trained	MISC	+7
Intimidate	☐ Trained	MISC	+7
Streetwise	☒ Trained	MISC	+12

COMBAT STATISTICS

+7	**Initiative**		6	**Speed**

Roll initiative to determine the turn order in combat.

Your speed is the number of squares you can move with a move action.

DEFENSES

20	**Armor Class (AC)**	CALCULATIONS
AC measures how hard it is to physically land an attack on you.

| 18 | **Fortitude** | CALCULATIONS |
Fortitude measures your toughness and resilience.

| 20 | **Reflex** | CALCULATIONS |
Reflex measures your ability to deflect or dodge attacks.

| 21 | **Will** | CALCULATIONS |
Will measures your strength of will and self-discipline.

| +3 | **Attack Bonus** | melee basic | 1d4 |
| +9 | **Attack Bonus** | eldritch blast | 1d10 + 6 |

When you attack, roll a d20 and add your attack bonus. Compare the result to the monster's defense to see if you hit. If you do hit, roll damage.

57	**Hit Points**	Bloodied	28

Your hit points measure the damage you can take before falling unconscious. Your bloodied value is half of your hit points (rounded down).

| Healing Surge Value | 14 |
| Surges Per Day | 8 |

When you spend a healing surge, you regain hit points equal to your healing surge value, which is one-quarter of your hit points (rounded down).

CURRENT HIT POINTS

Temporary Hit Points   Surges Remaining

ACTIONS IN COMBAT

On your turn in combat, you can take three actions:
✦ A standard action, which is usually an attack
✦ A move action, which involves movement
✦ A minor action, which is simple and quick
You can give up an action to take another action from lower on the list, so you can take a move or a minor action instead of a standard action or a minor action instead of a move action.

POWERS AND FEATS

Dire Radiance (at-will)

Fate of the Void (at-will)

Warlock's Curse (at-will)

Beguiling Tongue (encounter)

Far Realm Phantasm (encounter)

Frigid Darkness (encounter)

Infernal Wrath (encounter)

Witchfire (encounter)

Curse of the Bloody Fangs (daily)

Curse of the Dark Dream (daily)

Dark One's Own Luck (daily)

Tiefling Traits: bloodhunt, resist 8 fire

Improved Defenses (feat)

Improved Initiative (feat)

Killing Curse (feat)

Warlock's Sight (feat)

EQUIPMENT AND MAGIC ITEMS

+2 hexer's rod (implement)

+2 irrefutable leather armor

+2 amulet of protection

Adventurer's kit

   Backpack

   Bedroll

   Flint and steel

   Belt pouch

   Trail rations (10 days)

   50-foot rope

   Sunrods (2)

   Waterskin

WEALTH

1,800 gp

CHARACTER SKETCH

CHARACTER NOTES

Tisha is manipulative, tricky, sexy, and painfully aware of how tieflings are perceived. Half the time she's willing to seduce someone to get what she needs, half the time she'll lecture puzzled villagers about prejudice. She's on the road to finding her missing sister, who was last seen in Fallcrest. The siblings have unresolved issues that Tisha won't discuss with anyone. Along the way, she looks for opportunities to increase her power. As a warlock, she has forged a pact with the stars, and it remains to be seen whether this pact will come back to bite her.

Use this space however you like: to record what happens on your adventures, track quests, describe your background and goals, note the names of the other characters in your party, or draw a picture of your character.

EXPERIENCE POINTS (XP)
11,500

XP for next level: 13,000

DUNGEONS & DRAGONS®

VARIS
CHARACTER NAME

Class: Scout (Ranger) Level: 7
Race: Elf Gender: Male
Alignment: Good
Languages: Common, Elven

ABILITIES AND SKILLS

Score	Ability / Skill	Trained	Modifier / Misc.	Check
11	**Strength**		+0	+3
	Strength measures your physical power.			
	Athletics	☐ Trained		+3
15	**Constitution**		+2	+5
	Constitution represents health, stamina, and vital force.			
	Endurance	☐ Trained		+5
19	**Dexterity**		+4	+7
	Dexterity measures coordination, agility, and balance.			
	Acrobatics	☒ Trained		+12
	Stealth	☒ Trained		+12
	Thievery	☐ Trained		+7
10	**Intelligence**		+0	+3
	Intelligence describes how well you learn and reason.			
	Arcana	☐ Trained		+3
	History	☐ Trained		+3
	Religion	☐ Trained		+3
16	**Wisdom**		+3	+6
	Wisdom measures common sense, self-discipline, and empathy.			
	Dungeoneering	☐ Trained		+6
	Heal	☒ Trained		+11
	Insight	☐ Trained		+6
	Nature	☒ Trained	+2	+13
	Perception	☒ Trained	+2	+13
10	**Charisma**		+0	+3
	Charisma measures force of personality and leadership.			
	Bluff	☐ Trained		+3
	Diplomacy	☐ Trained		+3
	Intimidate	☐ Trained		+3
	Streetwise	☐ Trained		+3

COMBAT STATISTICS

+7 Initiative
Roll initiative to determine the turn order in combat.

7 Speed
Your speed is the number of squares you can move with a move action.

DEFENSES

23 Armor Class (AC) CALCULATIONS
AC measures how hard it is to physically land an attack on you.

17 Fortitude CALCULATIONS
Fortitude measures your toughness and resilience.

21 Reflex CALCULATIONS
Reflex measures your ability to deflect or dodge attacks.

18 Will CALCULATIONS
Will measures your strength of will and self-discipline.

Attack Bonus		Power	Damage
+12	Attack Bonus	+2 handaxe	1d6 + 10
+9	Attack Bonus	longbow	1d10 + 4

When you attack, roll a d20 and add your attack bonus. Compare the result to the monster's defense to see if you hit. If you do hit, roll damage.

57 Hit Points Bloodied 28
Your hit points measure the damage you can take before falling unconscious. Your bloodied value is half of your hit points (rounded down).

Healing Surge Value 14
Surges Per Day 9

When you spend a healing surge, you regain hit points equal to your healing surge value, which is one-quarter of your hit points (rounded down).

CURRENT HIT POINTS

Temporary Hit Points *Surges Remaining*

ACTIONS IN COMBAT

On your turn in combat, you can take three actions:
- *A standard action, which is usually an attack*
- *A move action, which involves movement*
- *A minor action, which is simple and quick*

You can give up an action to take another action from lower on the list, so you can take a move or a minor action instead of a standard action or a minor action instead of a move action.

POWERS AND FEATS

Aspect of the Charging Ram (at-will)

Aspect of the Cunning Fox (at-will)

Aspect of the Soaring Hawk (at-will)

Dual Weapon Attack (at-will)

Elven Accuracy (encounter)

Power Strike (2/encounter)

Reactive Shift (encounter)

Oak Skin (daily)

Step of Morning Mist (daily)

Wilderness Knacks: Ambush Expertise,
    Watchful Rest, Wilderness Tracker

Elf Traits: Group Awareness, Wild Step

Axe Expertise (feat)

Cunning Stalker (feat)

Two-Weapon Defense (feat)

Two-Weapon Fighting (feat)

EQUIPMENT AND MAGIC ITEMS

+2 handaxe (main hand weapon)

+2 handaxe (off-hand weapon)

+2 hero's hide armor

+2 cloak of resistance

Longbow

Quiver of arrows

Adventurer's kit

   Backpack

   Bedroll

   Flint and steel

   Belt pouch

   Trail rations (10 days)

   50-foot rope

   Sunrods (2)

   Waterskin

Assorted knickknacks

WEALTH

500 gp

CHARACTER SKETCH

CHARACTER NOTES

Varis hates the forest. Oh, don't get us wrong. Varis is a very good ranger. He can track by moonlight, smell humans from a mile off, hear the whisper of arrowflight during a thunderstorm . . . he just really, really likes pubs and songs and buildings and cats. He's convinced that urban structures are natural outgrowths of nature, with just as much wonder and variety as the forests they're built near. He adventures to see new towns. Varis fights with a matched set of axes that cut through flesh and bone as well as trees. Like all elves, Varis has low-light vision.

Use this space however you like: to record what happens on your adventures, track quests, describe your background and goals, note the names of the other characters in your party, or draw a picture of your character.

EXPERIENCE POINTS (XP)
11,500

XP for next level: 13,000

DUNGEONS & DRAGONS®

COPERNICUS JINX
CHARACTER NAME

Class: Wizard   Level: 13

Race: Gnome   Gender: Male

Alignment: Unaligned

Languages: Common, Elven

ABILITIES AND SKILLS

12 Strength — MODIFIER +1 — +7
Strength measures your physical power.

Athletics — ☐ Trained — MISC — +7

15 Constitution — MODIFIER +2 — +8
Constitution represents health, stamina, and vital force.

Endurance — ☐ Trained — MISC — +10

11 Dexterity — MODIFIER +0 — +6
Dexterity measures coordination, agility, and balance.

Acrobatics — ☐ Trained — MISC — +6

Stealth — ☐ Trained — MISC — +10

Thievery — ☐ Trained — MISC — +6

21 Intelligence — MODIFIER +5 — +11
Intelligence describes how well you learn and reason.

Arcana — ☒ Trained — MISC — +18

History — ☒ Trained — MISC — +16

Religion — ☐ Trained — MISC — +11

15 Wisdom — MODIFIER +2 — +8
Wisdom measures common sense, self-discipline, and empathy.

Dungeoneering — ☐ Trained — MISC — +8

Heal — ☐ Trained — MISC — +8

Insight — ☒ Trained — MISC — +13

Nature — ☐ Trained — MISC — +10

Perception — ☐ Trained — MISC — +8

15 Charisma — MODIFIER +2 — +8
Charisma measures force of personality and leadership.

Bluff — ☐ Trained — MISC — +10

Diplomacy — ☒ Trained — MISC — +13

Intimidate — ☐ Trained — MISC — +10

Streetwise — ☐ Trained — MISC — +8

COMBAT STATISTICS

+6 Initiative
Roll initiative to determine the turn order in combat.

5 Speed
Your speed is the number of squares you can move with a move action.

DEFENSES

24 Armor Class (AC) — CALCULATIONS
AC measures how hard it is to physically land an attack on you.

21 Fortitude — CALCULATIONS
Fortitude measures your toughness and resilience.

27 Reflex — CALCULATIONS
Reflex measures your ability to deflect or dodge attacks.

23 Will — CALCULATIONS
Will measures your strength of will and self-discipline.

+12 Attack Bonus — melee basic — ATTACK — 1d4 + 1

auto Attack Bonus — magic missile — DAMAGE — 11

When you attack, roll a d20 and add your attack bonus. Compare the result to the monster's defense to see if you hit. If you do hit, roll damage.

73 Hit Points — Bloodied — 36
Your hit points measure the damage you can take before falling unconscious. Your bloodied value is half of your hit points (rounded down).

Healing Surge Value — 18

Surges Per Day — 8

When you spend a healing surge, you regain hit points equal to your healing surge value, which is one-quarter of your hit points (rounded down).

CURRENT HIT POINTS

Temporary Hit Points   *Surges Remaining*

ACTIONS IN COMBAT

On your turn in combat, you can take three actions:
✦ *A standard action, which is usually an attack*
✦ *A move action, which involves movement*
✦ *A minor action, which is simple and quick*
You can give up an action to take another action from lower on the list, so you can take a move or a minor action instead of a standard action or a minor action instead of a move action.

POWERS AND FEATS

At-Will Powers:

Arc Lightning, Burning Hands, Light, Mage Hand,

Magic Missile, Phantasmal Assault,

Prestidigitation

Encounter Powers:

Burning Hands, Enigmatic Spellcasting,

Fade Away, Ghost Sound, Hold Monster,

Illusory Obstacles, Kelgore's Undeniable Fire,

Lightning Bolt, Maze of Mirrors, Phantom Foes,

Shield, Shock Sphere, Twisting Lightning

Daily Powers:

Blur, Dimension Door, Expeditious Retreat,

Fireball, Fountain of Flame, Ice Storm,

Invisibility, Kelgore's Well of Power, Mass

Resistance, Phantom Chasm, Symphony of the

Dark Court, Tasha's Forcible Conscription

EQUIPMENT AND MAGIC ITEMS

+3 magic wand

+3 elven cloak

+3 cloth armor of cleansing

Flask of alchemist's fire

Flask of alchemist's frost

Spellbook

Class/Other Features:

Enigmatic Action, Evocation Action, Expert Mage,

Evocation Apprentice, Evocation Expert,

Illusion Apprentice, Illusion Expert,

Reactive Stealth, Trickster's Cunning

Feats:

Alchemist, Burn Everything, Gnome Phantasmist,

Magic of the Mists, Resilient Focus, Ritual Caster,

Superior Reflexes, War Wizardry

WEALTH

3,300 gp

CHARACTER SKETCH

DiVito '11

CHARACTER NOTES

Copernicus, a gnome wizard, is Adric's old wartime commander and, quite possibly, an insane alchemist whose entire right arm has been replaced with an eladrin crystalline prosthetic. Adric owes him a favor he can never quite repay. Copernicus lays somewhere between patron and annoying uncle.

Use this space however you like: to record what happens on your adventures, track quests, describe your background and goals, note the names of the other characters in your party, or draw a picture of your character.

EXPERIENCE POINTS (XP)
39,000

XP for next level: 47,000

DUNGEONS & DRAGONS®

JULIANA D'MESSINA
CHARACTER NAME

Class: Wizard Level: 7
Race: Eladrin Gender: Female
Alignment: Good
Languages: Common, Elven

ABILITIES AND SKILLS

Score	Ability / Skill	Trained	Modifier / Misc.	Check
11	**Strength**		+0	+3
	Strength measures your physical power.			
	Athletics	☐ Trained		+3
13	**Constitution**		+1	+4
	Constitution represents health, stamina, and vital force.			
	Endurance	☐ Trained		+6
11	**Dexterity**		+0	+3
	Dexterity measures coordination, agility, and balance.			
	Acrobatics	☐ Trained		+3
	Stealth	☐ Trained		+3
	Thievery	☒ Trained		+9
19	**Intelligence**		+4	+7
	Intelligence describes how well you learn and reason.			
	Arcana	☒ Trained		+15
	History	☒ Trained		+15
	Religion	☐ Trained		+7
13	**Wisdom**		+1	+4
	Wisdom measures common sense, self-discipline, and empathy.			
	Dungeoneering	☐ Trained		+4
	Heal	☐ Trained		+4
	Insight	☒ Trained		+10
	Nature	☒ Trained		+10
	Perception	☐ Trained		+4
16	**Charisma**		+3	+6
	Charisma measures force of personality and leadership.			
	Bluff	☐ Trained		+6
	Diplomacy	☐ Trained		+6
	Intimidate	☐ Trained		+8
	Streetwise	☐ Trained		+6

COMBAT STATISTICS

+7 Initiative — *Roll initiative to determine the turn order in combat.*

6 Speed — *Your speed is the number of squares you can move with a move action.*

DEFENSES

Score	Defense	Calculations
19	**Armor Class (AC)**	
	AC measures how hard it is to physically land an attack on you.	
16	**Fortitude**	
	Fortitude measures your toughness and resilience.	
19	**Reflex**	
	Reflex measures your ability to deflect or dodge attacks.	
21	**Will**	
	Will measures your strength of will and self-discipline.	

Bonus		Power	Damage
+8	**Attack Bonus**	+2 dagger	1d4 + 2
auto	**Attack Bonus**	magic missile	8

When you attack, roll a d20 and add your attack bonus. Compare the result to the monster's defense to see if you hit. If you do hit, roll damage.

52 Hit Points Bloodied 26

Your hit points measure the damage you can take before falling unconscious. Your bloodied value is half of your hit points (rounded down).

Healing Surge Value: 13
Surges Per Day: 7

When you spend a healing surge, you regain hit points equal to your healing surge value, which is one-quarter of your hit points (rounded down).

CURRENT HIT POINTS

Temporary Hit Points *Surges Remaining*

ACTIONS IN COMBAT

On your turn in combat, you can take three actions:
- ✦ *A standard action, which is usually an attack*
- ✦ *A move action, which involves movement*
- ✦ *A minor action, which is simple and quick*

You can give up an action to take another action from lower on the list, so you can take a move or a minor action instead of a standard action or a minor action instead of a move action.

POWERS AND FEATS

At-Will Powers:

Arc Lightning, Freezing Burst, Ghost Sound,

Mage Hand, Magic Missile, Prestidigitation

Encounter Powers:

Blissful Ignorance, Charm of Misplaced Wrath,

Charm of the Defender, Dispel Magic, Fey Step,

Illusory Obstacles, Lightning Bolt, Shield,

Shock Sphere

Daily Powers:

Dimension Door, Expeditious Retreat, Fireball,

Fountain of Flame, Phantom Chasm, Visions of

Avarice

Feats:

Disciple of Lore, Expert Mage, Improved

Initiative, Toughness, Wand Expertise

CHARACTER SKETCH

Use this space to draw a picture of your character, your character's symbol, or some other identifying mark.

CHARACTER NOTES

Adric and this eladrin wizard have a flirty, bickering relationship. Half the time she gets in over her head and needs a sword to get her out. The other half of the time, she's bailing Adric out of whatever insane scheme he's stumbled into. Juliana has a difficult relationship with her family. They want her back in the Feywild; she wants to muck about with the humans and unravel mysteries. When Adric needs serious magical knowledge — or someone who knows what fork to use at a banquet — he'll often cajole Juliana into joining him.

EQUIPMENT AND MAGIC ITEMS

+2 magic wand (doubles as hairpin)

+2 luckblade dagger

+2 veteran's cloth armor

+2 amulet of protection

Spellbook

Adventurer's kit

Backpack, bedroll, flint and steel, belt pouch,

trail rations (10 days), 50-foot rope, sunrods (2),

waterskin

Other Features:

+5 to saving throws against charm

Fey origin

Use this space however you like: to record what happens on your adventures, track quests, describe your background and goals, note the names of the other characters in your party, or draw a picture of your character.

WEALTH

3,300 gp

EXPERIENCE POINTS (XP)

11,500

XP for next level: 13,000

Glossary

Kruthik: Kruthiks burrow through the earth, riddling the Underdark with tunnels. They hunt in packs and nest in sprawling subterranean warrens. Kruthiks dig tunnels that remain intact behind them. They communicate with one another through a series of hisses and chitters.

Kruthik Hatchling		Level 2 Minion
Small natural beast (reptile)		XP 31

Initiative +4 — **Senses** Perception +1; low-light vision, tremorsense 10

Gnashing Horde aura 1; an enemy that ends its turn in the aura takes 2 damage.

HP 1; a missed attack never damages a minion.

AC 15; **Fortitude** 13, **Reflex** 15, **Will** 12

Speed 8, burrow 2 (tunneling), climb 8

⊕ **Claw** (standard; at-will)
+5 vs. AC; 4 damage.

Alignment Unaligned   **Languages** –

Str 13 (+2)	**Dex** 16 (+4)	**Wis** 10 (+1)
Con 13 (+2)	**Int** 4 (-2)	**Cha** 6 (-1)

Kruthik Young		Level 2 Brute
Small natural beast (reptile)		XP 125

Initiative +4 — **Senses** Perception +1; low-light vision, tremorsense 10

Gnashing Horde aura 1; an enemy that ends its turn in the aura takes 2 damage.

HP 43; **Bloodied** 21

AC 15; **Fortitude** 13, **Reflex** 14, **Will** 11

Speed 8, burrow 2, climb 8

⊕ **Claw** (standard; at-will)
+5 vs. AC; 1d8 + 2 damage.

Alignment Unaligned   **Languages** –

Str 15 (+3)	**Dex** 16 (+4)	**Wis** 10 (+1)
Con 13 (+2)	**Int** 4 (-2)	**Cha** 6 (-1)

Kruthik Adult		Level 4 Brute
Medium natural beast (reptile)		XP 175

Initiative +6 — **Senses** Perception +4; low-light vision, tremorsense 10

Gnashing Horde aura 1; an enemy that ends its turn in the aura takes 2 damage.

HP 67; **Bloodied** 33

AC 17; **Fortitude** 14, **Reflex** 15, **Will** 13

Speed 6, burrow 3 (tunneling), climb 6

⊕ **Claw** (standard; at-will)
+8 vs. AC; 1d10 + 3 damage.

⌁ **Toxic Spikes** (standard; recharge ⚄ ⚅) ✦ **Poison**
The kruthik makes 2 attacks against two different targets: ranged 5; +7 vs. AC; 1d8 + 4 damage, and the target takes ongoing 5 poison damage and is slowed (save ends both).

Alignment Unaligned   **Languages** –

Str 17 (+5)	**Dex** 18 (+6)	**Wis** 12 (+4)
Con 17 (+5)	**Int** 4 (-1)	**Cha** 8 (+1)

Bulette: The creature that attacked the caravan in this issue is a bulette. Heavily armed predators that burrow through the earth, bulettes hunt for morsels to slake their appetite and once satisfied, retreat underground.

Bulette	Level 9 Elite Skirmisher
Large natural beast	XP 800

Initiative +7   **Senses** Perception +5; darkvision, tremorsense 20
HP 204; **Bloodied** 102; see also *second wind*
AC 27; **Fortitude** 26, **Reflex** 21, **Will** 21
Saving Throws +2
Speed 6, burrow 6; see also *earth furrow*
Action Points 1
⊕ **Bite** (standard; at-will)
    Before it bites, the bulette can make a standing long jump (as a free action) without provoking opportunity attacks; +14 vs. AC; 2d6 + 7 damage, or 4d6 + 7 damage against a prone target.
↩ **Rising Burst** (standard; at-will)
    Close burst 2; the bulette sprays rock and dirt into the air when it rises out of the ground; +13 vs. AC; 1d6 + 7 damage.
↯ **Earth Furrow** (move; at-will)
    The bulette moves up to its burrow speed just below the surface of the ground, avoiding opportunity attacks as it passes underneath other creatures' squares. As it burrows beneath the space of a Medium or smaller creature on the ground, the bulette makes an attack against the creature: +8 vs. Fortitude; on a hit, the target is knocked prone.
Ground Eruption
    The squares into which a bulette surfaces and the squares it leaves when it burrows underground become difficult terrain.
Second Wind (standard; encounter) ✦ **Healing**
    The bulette spends a healing surge and regains 51 hit points. It gains a +2 bonus to all defenses until the start of its next turn.
Alignment Unaligned   **Languages** –
Skills Athletics +16, Endurance +15
Str 24 (+11)   **Dex** 13 (+5)   **Wis** 12 (+5)
Con 22 (+10)   **Int** 2 (+0)   **Cha** 8 (+3)

Drow: The drow are a cursed people, a deviant and evil race firmly in the grasp of Lolth, a dark goddess. Exiled from the Feywild for rising up against their eladrin kin, the drow nurse ancient grudges. They wallow in lies and cruelty, plotting vengeance against their ancestral enemies. Few drow escape their treacherous communities, instead finding an early death on the end of a poisoned blade or strapped to an altar of Lolth.

Dryad: Dryads are wild, mysterious creatures found deep in secluded woodlands. Fierce protectors of the forest, they brook no insolence from interlopers. See below for this creature's stat block.

Dryad	Level 9 Skirmisher
Medium fey humanoid (plant)	XP 400

Initiative +9   **Senses** Perception +12
HP 92; **Bloodied** 46
AC 23; **Fortitude** 22, **Reflex** 21, **Will** 21
Speed 8 (forest walk)
⊕ **Claws** (standard; at-will)
    +14 vs. AC; 1d8 + 4 damage, or 1d8 + 9 damage if the target is the only enemy adjacent to the dryad.
Deceptive Veil (minor; at-will) ✦ **Illusion**
    The dryad can disguise itself to appear as any Medium humanoid, usually a beautiful elf or eladrin. A successful Insight check (opposed by the dryad's Bluff check) pierces the disguise.
Treestride (move; at-will) ✦ **Teleportation**
    The dryad can teleport 8 squares if it begins and ends adjacent to a tree, a treant, or a plant of Large size or bigger.
Alignment Unaligned   **Languages** Elven
Skills Bluff +10, Insight +12, Stealth +12
Str 19 (+8)   **Dex** 17 (+7)   **Wis** 17 (+7)
Con 12 (+5)   **Int** 10 (+4)   **Cha** 13 (+5)

Quickling: Quicklings are swift, wicked fey that kill other creatures for food, treasure, or sport. They like to set ambushes and outwit enemies, and they frequently ally with other creatures that share their desires. If their escapades enrage an adversary too strong to overcome, quicklings have no problem fleeing in a chorus of nerve-grating laughter, leaving their so-called allies to fend for themselves.

Quickling Runner	Level 9 Skirmisher
Small fey humanoid	XP 400

Initiative +13   **Senses** Perception +7; low-light vision
HP 96; **Bloodied** 48
AC 24 (28 against opportunity attacks); **Fortitude** 20, **Reflex** 24, **Will** 20
Speed 12, climb 6; see also *fey shift* and *quick cuts*
⊕ **Short Sword** (standard; at-will) ✦ **Weapon**
    +14 vs. AC; 1d6 + 7 damage.
↯ **Quick Cuts** (standard; at-will) ✦ **Weapon**
    The quickling moves its speed. At any two points during its move, the quickling makes a melee basic attack at a -2 penalty. The quickling cannot use this power while immobilized or slowed.
Fey Shift (standard; encounter)
    The quickling runner shifts 10 squares.
Maintain Mobility (minor; recharge ⚁ ⚂ ⚃)
    An immobilized quickling runner is no longer immobilized.
Alignment Evil   **Languages** Elven
Skills Acrobatics +21, Bluff +9, Stealth +16
Str 9 (+3)   **Dex** 24 (+11)   **Wis** 17 (+7)
Con 16 (+7)   **Int** 14 (+6)   **Cha** 10 (+4)
Equipment short sword

Rakshasa: Despite their bestial features, rakshasas are clever, malicious, and sophisticated. Although rakshasas come in many varieties, they all share some common traits, namely their feline heads, backward claws, and taste for luxury. Rakshasas often conceal their true appearance, using illusion magic to adopt whatever disguises serve them best. Rakshasas prefer to mislead would-be adversaries instead of fighting them, but if combat becomes necessary, rakshasas are fierce and ruthless.

Rakshasa Noble	Level 19 Controller
Medium natural humanoid	XP 2,400

Initiative +14   **Senses** Perception +19; low-light vision
HP 178; **Bloodied** 89
AC 33; **Fortitude** 31, **Reflex** 33, **Will** 34; see also *phantom image*
Speed 7
⊕ **Claw** (standard; at-will)
+22 vs. AC; 1d6 + 3 damage, and the target is blinded until the end of the rakshasa noble's next turn.
↗ **Mind Twist** (standard; at-will) ✦ **Psychic**
Ranged 20; +22 vs. Will; 3d6 + 7 psychic damage, and the target is dazed (save ends).
↗ **Phantom Lure** (standard; at-will) ✦ **Charm**
Ranged 10; +22 vs. Will; the target slides 5 squares.
↗ **Frightful Phantom** (standard; recharge ⚄ ⚅) ✦ **Fear**
Ranged 5; +22 vs. Will; 4d8 + 7 psychic damage, the target is pushed 5 squares, and the target is stunned (save ends).
Deceptive Veil (minor; at-will) ✦ **Illusion**
The rakshasa noble can disguise itself to appear as any Medium humanoid. A successful Insight check (opposed by the rakshasa's Bluff check) pierces the disguise.
Phantom Image (minor; recharge ⚄ ⚅) ✦ **Illusion**
Until the end of the rakshasa noble's next turn, any creature that attacks the rakshasa's AC or Reflex defense must roll twice and use the lower attack roll result. If either result is a critical hit, use that result instead.
Alignment Evil   **Languages** Common
Skills Arcana +20, Athletics +17, Bluff +21, Diplomacy +21, History +20, Insight +19, Intimidate +21
| **Str** 16 (+12) | **Dex** 20 (+14) | **Wis** 20 (+14) |
| **Con** 18 (+13) | **Int** 22 (+15) | **Cha** 24 (+16) |

Iron Golem: Created to guard their masters and their masters' secrets, golems have no sense of self and follow orders without question. Infused with potent toxins, iron golems thunder toward foes and bash them into mush.

Iron Golem	Level 20 Elite Soldier
Large natural animate (construct)	XP 5,600

Initiative +14   **Senses** Perception +10; darkvision
Noxious Fumes (Poison) aura 2; while the iron golem is bloodied, each creature that enters the aura or starts its turn there takes 5 poison damage.
HP 386; **Bloodied** 193; see also *toxic death*
AC 36; **Fortitude** 36, **Reflex** 30, **Will** 28
Immune disease, poison, sleep
Saving Throws +2
Speed 6 (cannot shift)
Action Points 1
⊕ **Iron Blade** (standard; at-will)
Reach 2; +27 vs. AC; 2d10 + 3 damage, and the target is marked (save ends).
↓ **Cleave** (standard; at-will)
The iron golem makes two *iron blade* attacks, each against a different target.
↓ **Dazing Fist** (immediate interrupt, when a creature marked by the iron golem and within its reach moves or shifts; at-will)
Reach 2; targets the triggering creature; +25 vs. Fortitude; the target is dazed (save ends).
⬅ **Breath Weapon** (standard; recharge ⚄ ⚅) ✦ **Poison**
Close blast 3; +25 vs. Fortitude; 3d8 + 9 poison damage, and ongoing 5 poison damage (save ends).
⬅ **Toxic Death** (when first bloodied and again when the iron golem drops to 0 hit points) ✦ **Poison**
Close burst 3; +25 vs. Fortitude; 2d8 + 6 poison damage, and ongoing 10 poison damage (save ends).
Alignment Unaligned   **Languages** –
| **Str** 27 (+18) | **Dex** 15 (+12) | **Wis** 11 (+10) |
| **Con** 25 (+17) | **Int** 3 (+6) | **Cha** 3 (+6) |
Equipment longsword